Marvin Kaye, award-winning author and
anthologist, has compiled several collections of
fantasy fiction, and has written many acclaimed
fantasy novels including *The Incredible Umbrella,
The Amorous Umbrella, The Masters of Solitude* and
Winterwind. Kaye is an associate professor of
creative writing at New York University and the
artistic director of the Open Book theatre company
in New York.

My special thanks to Saralee Kaye for handling all the paperwork and telephone negotiations pertinent to acquiring stories in this anthology.

The counsel and aid of Ellen Asher is deeply appreciated, and there ought to be a special medal stamped for the untiring efforts and sunny disposition of my editor, Mary Sherwin, not to mention the assault on her nerves associated with reading some of the terrors herein.

Many thanks to Dick Baldwin for suggesting the part title, "Acts of God and Other Horrors," and to innumerable other people who gave advice, suggestions and aid in tracking down copyright owners. Special thanks to Parke Godwin, Pat LoBrutto, Charles Grant, Bob Weinberg, Adele Leone, Richard Monaco, John Silbersack, Karen Haas and too many others to include, but deepest gratitude is extended to all who guided us in this selection.

Every effort has been made to identify and obtain the permission of the copyright owners, but many fine fantasy tales are by authors very difficult to track down. If any unintentional use of copyrighted material has occurred herein, please get in touch care of the publisher and we will do our best to rectify the situation.

Masterpieces of Terror and the Supernatural

A Treasury of Spellbinding Tales Old & New

Selected by
Marvin Kaye

·

With
Saralee Kaye

WARNER BOOKS

A *Warner* Book

First published in Great Britain by
Macdonald and Co (Publishers) Ltd in 1991
This edition published by Warner in 1992

A CIP catalogue record for this book
is available from the British Library.

ISBN 0 7515 0030 5

Printed in England by Clays Ltd, St Ives plc

Warner Books
A Division of
Little, Brown and Company (UK) Limited
165 Great Dover Street
London SE1 4YA

ACKNOWLEDGMENTS

"The Professor's Teddy Bear" copyright © 1948 by *Weird Tales*. Copyright © 1953 by Theodore Sturgeon. Reprinted by permission of Kirby McCauley Ltd.

"Bubnoff and the Devil," English adaptation copyright © 1975 by Marvin Kaye. First appeared in *Fiends and Creatures* (Popular Library, 1975).

"The Erl-King," English adaptation copyright © 1985 by Marvin Kaye.

"The Quest for *Blank Claveringi*" originally appeared in 1967 in slightly altered form in *The Saturday Evening Post* as "The Snails," and was published by Doubleday in 1970 in the Patricia Highsmith short-story collection *The Snail-Watcher and Other Stories*. Copyright © 1967 and 1970 by Patricia Highsmith.

"A Malady of Magicks" copyright © 1978 by Craig Shaw Gardner.

"Lan Lung" copyright © 1980 by Simulation Publications, Inc. Used by permission of the author.

"The Dragon over Hackensack" copyright © 1985 by Richard L. Wexelblat. Permission granted by the author.

"The Faceless Thing" copyright © 1963 by Health Knowledge, Inc. Reprinted by permission of the author.

"When the Clock Strikes" from *Weird Tales*, copyright © 1980 by Lin Carter; copyright © 1983 by Tanith Lee.

"Eumenides in the Fourth Floor Lavatory" copyright © 1979. First appeared in *Chrysalis IV*, edited by Roy Torgeson.

"The Black Wedding" reprinted by permission of Farrar, Straus & Giroux Inc. "The Black Wedding" from *The Spinoza of Market Street* by Isaac Bashevis Singer. Copyright © 1958, 1960, 1961 by Isaac Bashevis Singer.

"Sardonicus" copyright © 1960 by Ray Russell. First appeared in *Playboy*.

"Graveyard Shift" reprinted by permission of Don Congdon Associates, Inc. Copyright © 1947, renewed 1975 by Richard Matheson.

"Flies" copyright © 1953 by Fantasy House, Inc.; copyright © 1969 by Isaac Asimov.

Contents

LOVERS AND OTHER MONSTERS

ACTS OF GOD AND OTHER HORRORS

INTRODUCTION

In Search of Masterpieces

I've discovered a curious fact about myself and a few other anthologists who also write fiction. We are naturally pleased when someone expresses a favorable opinion of one of our novels or short stories, but we are even more flattered by praise for the anthologies we edit. At first glance, this may seem puzzling. Shouldn't one's own literary effusions be dearer than mere gatherings of other writers' work?

The answer is no. Every anthology puts the editor's taste squarely on the line. Everything he chooses, everything he leaves out, is a testament to and indictment of his education, sensitivity, sophistication and I suppose even his IQ. One may conceal the darkest personal secrets in the labyrinth of character and plot that comprises a novel, but those who assay to edit a collection of any size and scope run the risk of exposing themselves in public. It is, therefore, perhaps excusable if an anthologist attempts to justify his intentions before streaking naked through Parnassus.

When I edited *Ghosts: A Treasury of Chilling Tales Old and New* (Doubleday, 1981), I attempted to gather together sufficient materials in one volume to effectively define the folklore of ghosthood. In so doing, I offered several stories perhaps less artfully written but necessary because of some essential bit of ghost-myth embodied in the plot. This method, however, is inappropriate in the present collection since the title clearly states that the contents consists of "masterpieces".

Let me, however, beg the issue. What *is* a masterpiece? A tale that time has not buried, that still speaks to us long after its author is dead? That is assuredly the best test, but how may it be applied to contemporary fiction? If you peruse the table of contents, you will note the names of quite a few living writers—Robert Bloch,

Stanley Ellin, Ed Hoch, Richard Matheson, to name a few. Clearly, the criterion of time cannot be applied in their cases. Then what act of hubris permits me to call their stories masterpieces?

Frankly, I don't know. I may very well be wrong about the enduring potential of some of the tales in the pages to come. The word "masterpieces" is employed with some trepidation, on the same theory that if I ever owned a ship I'd call it the *Pansy* or the *Pitifully Insignificant* because Poseidon seems to have it in for sea vessels with grandiose names like the *Titanic*.

Nevertheless, I am meekly prepared to defend my choices on the ground of personal memorability. Any story that gave my jaded spine a chill seemed to present proper credentials for membership in the club. As a further test, I allowed some time to lapse before making up my mind on certain tales. Aickman's "The Hospice," for instance. I deleted it from my ghost anthology in 1981 because I found it puzzlingly obscure. Maybe, but I've been mulling it over ever since. A story that hangs around that long in the subconscious must have something potent to recommend it.

As in my other anthologies, I have limited each author to a single entry and have tried to avoid any tale too often anthologized. In a few cases, I waived this point when conscience would not permit me to omit a key work, but most of what follows should serve, I hope, as a complement rather than a repeat of other collections on the market or in secondhand bookshops.

Some of the stories you will find herein are gentle excursions into the occult, and one or two items are provided for comic relief, but let the reader be warned . . . most of this collection is devoted to varying degrees of terror, horror and what the French call the *conte cruelle*. The publisher offers no guarantees against nightmares, and the cautious customer will do well to nibble sparingly at the mushrooms lest they turn out to be toadstools.

In Quest of Terror

In spite of their common confusion in the media, the terms "horror" and "terror" are not interchangeable. Boris Karloff once delineated between them by dismissing horror as mere insistence on the gory and otherwise repugnant—the numbingly banal atrocities seen on the Six O'Clock News (and in Hollywood's dreary splatter films). Terror, according to Karloff, is rooted in cosmic fear of the unknown. It is the more dreadful experience by far, but its very profundity makes it more difficult to achieve artistically. That is surely why most of our contemporary horror writers are *nothing more* than horror writers. The liberal use of ghastly murders and decaying corpses is the stuff of pornography. The psychology of terror, like true erotica, demands far more technique to comprehend and employ.

In his cornerstone essay, *Supernatural Horror in Literature*, H. P. Lovecraft makes much the same point, though he switches the terms. But the distinction remains, and Lovecraft devotes a good deal of space recommending tales and novels that sound the note of cosmic fear. It is this dark music which I have sought to bring you in *Masterpieces of Terror and the Supernatural*. Sometimes it sounds too softly for every listener to hear (see "Oshidori" by Lafcadio Hearn or Stephen Crane's "The Upturned Face"), while in other instances such as Isaac Bashevis Singer's "The Black Wedding," you'd have to be tone-deaf to miss it. Even such horrific exercises as Richard Matheson's "Graveyard Shift" were not chosen for their inescapable bloodiness, but rather for their icy insights into human nature at its inexplicable worst.

For a more extended discussion of terror, as well as miscellaneous notes on a few of the stories in this book, see the "Afterword." A modest bibliography of other recommended reading is also included for those of you who crave still more punishment.

MARVIN KAYE
Manhattan, August 1984.

FIENDS AND CREATURES

In the following tales, agents of Hell hobnob with various kinds of beasties. You will meet a distinguished vampire, giant snails, a tiny but thoroughly nasty demon, some dragons and no less illustrious a clan than Satan himself, his granddaughter and his grandmother (even His Nibs doesn't know why he never had a mother).

The promise and threat of power looms over these stories. The diabolical representatives quest for human lives, blood, souls. Some of them—the Erl-King, for instance—simply take what they're after; others, such as Stevenson's Bottle Imp, make offers we ought to refuse. Then there are the monsters—Highsmith's *claveringi*, Hoch's thing in the ooze—embodiments of unbridled brute force with no moral law to satisfy but their own appetites.

Nietzsche stated that the will to power leads the spiritually superior being to perform acts of great benevolence, but the evil brood awaiting you in this section are obviously untutored in philosophy.

Our first story is distinguished by a guest appearance by none other than Count Dracula himself. (See the "Afterword" for details). BRAM STOKER, born in Dublin in 1847, left behind a number of uncollected fantasy tales, so his widow gathered some of them into volume form in 1914 and added the following excised episode from her husband's most popular literary work. "Dracula's Guest" surely must have been the opening chapter of the book, and its narrator is Jonathan Harker, en route to Transylvania to sell the Count some property in England. (Indeed, the novel itself opens with the words "Left Munich at 8:35 P.M., on 1st May . . .") Some canny publisher ought to restore it in some future edition of the great vampire novel; it makes an excellent prologue to the horrors to come.

Dracula's Guest

BY BRAM STOKER

When we started for our drive the sun was shining brightly on Munich, and the air was full of the joyousness of early summer. Just as we were about to depart, Herr Delbrück (the maître d'hôtel of the Quatre Saisons, where I was staying) came down, bareheaded, to the carriage and, after wishing me a pleasant drive, said to the coachman, still holding his hand on the handle of the carriage door:

"Remember you are back by nightfall. The sky looks bright but there is a shiver in the north wind that says there may be a sudden storm. But I am sure you will not be late." Here he smiled, and added, "for you know what night it is."

Johann answered with an emphatic, "Ja, mein Herr," and, touching his hat, drove off quickly. When we had cleared the town, I said, after signalling to him to stop:

"Tell me, Johann, what is to-night?"

He crossed himself, as he answered laconically: "Walpurgis nacht." Then he took out his watch, a great, old-fashioned German silver thing as big as a turnip, and looked at it, with his eyebrows gathered together and a little impatient shrug of his shoulders. I realized that this was his way of respectfully protesting against the unnecessary delay, and sank back in the carriage, merely motioning him to proceed. He started off rapidly, as if to make up for lost time. Every now and then the horses seemed to throw up their heads and sniffed the air suspiciously. On such occasions I often looked round in alarm. The road was pretty bleak, for we were traversing a sort of high, wind-swept plateau. As we drove, I saw a road that looked but little used, and which seemed to dip through a little, winding valley. It looked so inviting that, even at the risk of offending him, I called Johann to stop—and when he had pulled up, I told him I would like to drive down that road. He made all sorts of excuses, and frequently crossed himself as he spoke. This somewhat piqued my curiosity, so I asked him various questions. He answered fencingly, and repeatedly looked at his watch in protest. Finally I said:

"Well, Johann, I want to go down this road. I shall not ask you to come unless you like; but tell me why you do not like to go, that is all I ask." For answer he seemed to throw himself off the box, so quickly did he reach the ground. Then he stretched out his hands appealingly to me, and implored me not to go. There was just enough of English mixed with the German for me to understand the drift of his talk. He seemed always just about to tell me something—the very idea of which evidently frightened him; but each time he pulled himself up, saying, as he crossed himself: "Walpurgis nacht!"

I tried to argue with him, but it was difficult to argue with a man when I did not know his language. The advantage certainly rested with him, for although he began to speak in English, of a very crude and broken kind, he always got excited and broke into his native tongue—and every time he did so, he looked at his watch. Then the horses became restless and sniffed the air. At this he grew very pale, and, looking around in a frightened way, he suddenly jumped forward, took them by the bridles and led them on some twenty feet. I followed, and asked why he had done this. For answer he crossed himself, pointed to the spot we had left and drew his carriage in the direction of the other road, indicating a cross, and said, first in German, then in English: "Buried him—him what killed themselves."

I remembered the old custom of burying suicides at cross-roads: "Ah! I see, a suicide. How interesting!" But for the life of me I could not make out why the horses were frightened.

Whilst we were talking, we heard a sort of sound between a yelp

and a bark. It was far away; but the horses got very restless, and
it took Johann all his time to quiet them. He was pale, and said:
"It sounds like a wolf—but yet there are no wolves here now."

"No?" I said, questioning him; "is it long since the wolves were
so near the city?"

"Long, long," he answered, "in the spring and summer; but with
the snow the wolves have been here not so long."

Whilst he was petting the horses and trying to quiet them, dark
clouds drifted rapidly across the sky. The sunshine passed away,
and a breath of cold wind seemed to drift past us. It was only a
breath, however, and more in the nature of a warning than a fact,
for the sun came out brightly again. Johann looked under his lifted
hand at the horizon and said:

"The storm of snow, he comes before long time." Then he
looked at his watch again, and, straightaway holding his reins
firmly—for the horses were still pawing the ground restlessly and
shaking their heads—he climbed to his box as though the time had
come for proceeding on our journey.

I felt a little obstinate and did not at once get into the carriage.

"Tell me," I said, "about this place where the road leads," and
I pointed down.

Again he crossed himself and mumbled a prayer, before he
answered: "It is unholy."

"What is unholy?" I enquired.

"The village."

"Then there is a village?"

"No, no. No one lives there hundreds of years." My curiosity
was piqued: "But you said there was a village."

"There was."

"Where is it now?"

Whereupon he burst out into a long story in German and
English, so mixed up that I could not quite understand exactly
what he said, but roughly I gathered that long ago, hundreds of
years, men had died there and been buried in their graves; and
sounds were heard under the clay, and when the graves were
opened, men and women were found rosy with life, and their
mouths red with blood. And so, in haste to save their lives (aye,
and their souls!—and here he crossed himself) those who were left
fled away to other places, where the living lived, and the dead
were dead and not—not something. He was evidently afraid to
speak the last words. As he proceeded with his narration, he grew

more and more excited. It seemed as if his imagination had got hold of him, and he ended in a perfect paroxysm of fear—white-faced, perspiring, trembling and looking round him, as if expecting that some dreadful presence would manifest itself there in the bright sunshine on the open plain. Finally, in an agony of desperation, he cried:

"Walpurgis nacht!" and pointed to the carriage for me to get in. All my English blood rose at this, and, standing back, I said:

"You are afraid, Johann—you are afraid. Go home; I shall return alone; the walk will do me good." The carriage door was open. I took from the seat my oak walking-stick—which I always carry on my holiday excursions—and closed the door, pointing back to Munich, and said, "Go home, Johann—Walpurgis nacht doesn't concern Englishmen."

The horses were now more restive than ever, and Johann was trying to hold them in, while excitedly imploring me not to do anything so foolish. I pitied the poor fellow, he was so deeply in earnest; but all the same I could not help laughing. His English was quite gone now. In his anxiety he had forgotten that his only means of making me understand was to talk my language, so he jabbered away in his native German. It began to be a little tedious. After giving the direction, "Home!" I turned to go down the cross-road into the valley.

With a despairing gesture, Johann turned his horses towards Munich. I leaned on my stick and looked after him. He went slowly along the road for a while: then there came over the crest of the hill a man tall and thin. I could see so much in the distance. When he drew near the horses, they began to jump and kick about, then to scream with terror. Johann could not hold them in; they bolted down the road, running away madly. I watched them out of sight, then looked for the stranger, but I found that he, too, was gone.

With a light heart I turned down the side road through the deepening valley to which Johann had objected. There was not the slightest reason, that I could see, for his objection; and I daresay I tramped for a couple of hours without thinking of time or distance, and certainly without seeing a person or a house. So far as the place was concerned, it was desolation itself. But I did not notice this particularly till, on turning a bend in the road, I came upon a scattered fringe of wood; then I recognized that I had been impressed unconsciously by the desolation of the region through which I had passed.

I sat down to rest myself, and began to look around. It struck me that it was considerably colder than it had been at the commencement of my walk—a sort of sighing sound seemed to be around me, with, now and then, high overhead, a sort of muffled roar. Looking upwards I noticed that great thick clouds were drifting rapidly across the sky from north to south at a great height. There were signs of coming storm in some lofty stratum of the air. I was a little chilly, and, thinking that it was the sitting still after the exercise of walking, I resumed my journey.

The ground I passed over was now much more picturesque. There were no striking objects that the eye might single out; but in all there was a charm of beauty. I took little heed of time and it was only when the deepening twilight forced itself upon me that I began to think of how I should find my way home. The brightness of the day had gone. The air was cold, and the drifting of clouds high overhead was more marked. They were accompanied by a sort of far-away rushing sound, through which seemed to come at intervals that mysterious cry which the driver had said came from a wolf. For a while I hesitated. I had said I would see the deserted village, so on I went, and presently came on a wide stretch of open country, shut in by hills all around. Their sides were covered with trees which spread down to the plain, dotting, in clumps, the gentler slopes and hollows which showed here and there. I followed with my eye the winding of the road, and saw that it curved close to one of the densest of these clumps and was lost behind it.

As I looked there came a cold shiver in the air, and the snow began to fall. I thought of the miles and miles of bleak country I had passed, and then hurried on to seek the shelter of the wood in front. Darker and darker grew the sky, and faster and heavier fell the snow, till the earth before and around me was a glistening white carpet the further edge of which was lost in misty vagueness. The road was here but crude, and when on the level its boundaries were not so marked, as when it passed through the cuttings; and in a little while I found that I must have strayed from it, for I missed underfoot the hard surface, and my feet sank deeper in the grass and moss. Then the wind grew stronger and blew with ever increasing force, till I was fain to run before it. The air became icy-cold, and in spite of my exercise I began to suffer. The snow was now falling so thickly and whirling around me in such rapid eddies that I could hardly keep my eyes open. Every now and then the heavens were torn asunder by vivid lightning, and in the flashes I could see ahead of me a great mass of trees, chiefly yew and cypress all heavily coated with snow.

I was soon amongst the shelter of the trees, and there, in comparative silence, I could hear the rush of the wind high overhead. Presently the blackness of the storm had become merged in the darkness of the night. By-and-by the storm seemed to be passing away: it now only came in fierce puffs or blasts. At such moments the weird sound of the wolf appeared to be echoed by many similar sounds around me.

Now and again, through the black mass of drifting cloud, came a straggling ray of moonlight, which lit up the expanse, and showed me that I was at the edge of a dense mass of cypress and yew trees. As the snow had ceased to fall, I walked out from the shelter and began to investigate more closely. It appeared to me that, amongst so many old foundations as I had passed, there might be still standing a house in which, though in ruins, I could find some sort of shelter for a while. As I skirted the edge of the copse, I found that a low wall encircled it, and following this I presently found an opening. Here the cypresses formed an alley leading up to a square mass of some kind of building. Just as I caught sight of this, however, the drifting clouds obscured the moon, and I passed up the path in darkness. The wind must have grown colder, for I felt myself shiver as I walked; but there was hope of shelter, and I groped my way blindly on.

I stopped, for there was a sudden stillness. The storm had passed; and, perhaps in sympathy with nature's silence, my heart seemed to cease to beat. But this was only momentarily; for suddenly the moonlight broke through the clouds, showing me that I was in a graveyard, and that the square object before me was a great massive tomb of marble, as white as the snow that lay on and all around it. With the moonlight there came a fierce sigh of the storm, which appeared to resume its course with a long, low howl, as of many dogs or wolves. I was awed and shocked, and felt the cold perceptibly grow upon me till it seemed to grip me by the heart. Then, while the flood of moonlight still fell on the marble tomb, the storm gave further evidence of renewing, as though it was returning on its track. Impelled by some sort of fascination, I approached the sepulchre to see what it was, and why such a thing stood alone in such a place. I walked around it, and read, over the Doric door, in German—

COUNTESS DOLINGEN OF GRATZ
IN STYRIA
SOUGHT AND FOUND DEATH.
1801.

On the top of the tomb, seemingly driven through the solid marble—for the structure was composed of a few vast blocks of stone—was a great iron spike or stake. On going to the back I saw, graven in great Russian letters:

"The dead travel fast."

There was something so weird and uncanny about the whole thing that it gave me a turn and made me feel quite faint. I began to wish, for the first time, that I had taken Johann's advice. Here a thought struck me, which came under almost mysterious circumstances and with a terrible shock. This was Walpurgis Night!

Walpurgis Night, when, according to the belief of millions of people, the devil was abroad—when the graves were opened and the dead came forth and walked. When all evil things of earth and air and water held revel. This very place the driver had specially shunned. This was the depopulated village of centuries ago. This was where the suicide lay; and this was the place where I was alone—unmanned, shivering with cold in a shroud of snow with a wild storm gathering again upon me! It took all my philosophy, all the religion I had been taught, all my courage, not to collapse in a paroxysm of fright.

And now a perfect tornado burst upon me. The ground shook as though thousands of horses thundered across it; and this time the storm bore on its icy wings, not snow, but great hailstones which drove with such violence that they might have come from the thongs of Balearic slingers—hailstones that beat down leaf and branch and made the shelter of the cypresses of no more avail than though their stems were standing-corn. At the first I had rushed to the nearest tree; but I was soon fain to leave it and seek the only spot that seemed to afford refuge, the deep Doric doorway of the marble tomb. There, crouching against the massive bronze-door, I gained a certain amount of protection from the beating of the hail-stones, for now they only drove against me as they ricochetted from the ground and the side of the marble.

As I leaned against the door, it moved slightly and opened inwards. The shelter of even a tomb was welcome in that pitiless tempest, and I was about to enter it when there came a flash of forked-lightning that lit up the whole expanse of the heavens. In the instant, as I am a living man, I saw, as my eyes were turned into the darkness of the tomb, a beautiful woman, with rounded cheeks and red lips, seemingly sleeping on a bier. As the thunder broke overhead, I was grasped as by the hand of a giant and hurled out into the storm. The whole thing was so sudden that, before I could realize the shock, moral as well as physical, I found the hailstones beating me down. At the same time I had a strange, dominating feeling that I was not alone. I looked towards the tomb. Just then there came another blinding flash, which seemed to strike the iron stake that surmounted the tomb and to pour through to the earth, blasting and crumbling the marble, as in a burst of flame. The dead woman rose for a moment of agony, while she was lapped in the flame, and her bitter scream of pain was drowned in the thundercrash. The last thing I heard was this mingling of dreadful sound, as again I was seized in the giant-grasp and dragged away, while the hailstones beat on me, and the air around seemed reverberant with the howling of wolves. The last sight that I remembered was a vague, white, moving mass, as if all the graves around me had sent out the phantoms of their sheeted-dead, and they were closing in on me through the white cloudiness of the driving hail.

Gradually there came a sort of vague beginning of consciousness; then a sense of weariness that was dreadful. For a time I remembered nothing; but slowly my senses returned. My feet seemed positively racked with pain, yet I could not move them. They seemed to be numbed. There was an icy feeling at the back of my neck and all down my spine, and my ears, like my feet, were dead, yet in torment; but there was in my breast a sense of warmth which was, by comparison, delicious. It was as a nightmare—a physical nightmare, if one may use such an expression; for some heavy weight on my chest made it difficult for me to breathe.

This period of semi-lethargy seemed to remain a long time, and as it faded away I must have slept or swooned. Then came a sort of loathing, like the first stage of sea-sickness, and a wild desire to be free from something—I knew not what. A vast stillness enveloped me, as though all the world were asleep or dead—only broken by the low panting as of some animal close to me. I felt a warm rasping at my throat, then came a consciousness of the awful truth, which chilled me to the heart and sent the blood surging up through my brain. Some great animal was lying on me and now licking my throat. I feared to stir, for some instinct of prudence bade me lie still; but the brute seemed to realize that there was now some change in me, for it raised its head. Through my eyelashes I saw above me the two great flaming eyes of a gigantic wolf. Its sharp white teeth gleamed in the gaping red mouth, and I could feel its hot breath fierce and acrid upon me.

For another spell of time I remembered no more. Then I became conscious of a low growl, followed by a yelp, renewed again and again. Then, seemingly very far away, I heard a "Holloa! holloa!" as of many voices calling in unison. Cautiously I raised my head and looked in the direction whence the sound came; but the cemetery blocked my view. The wolf still continued to yelp in a strange way, and a red glare began to move round the grove of cypresses, as though following the sound. As the voices drew closer, the wolf yelped faster and louder. I feared to make either sound or motion. Nearer came the red glow, over the white pall which stretched into the darkness around me. Then all at once from beyond the trees there came at a trot a troop of horsemen bearing torches. The wolf rose from my breast and made for the cemetery. I saw one of the horsemen (soliders by their caps and their long military cloaks) raise his carbine and take aim. A companion knocked up his arm, and I heard the ball whizz over my head. He had evidently taken my body for that of the wolf. Another sighted the animal as it slunk away, and a shot followed. Then, at a gallop, the troop rode forward—some towards me, others following the wolf as it disappeared amongst the snow-clad cypresses.

As they drew nearer I tried to move, but was powerless, although I could see and hear all that went on around me. Two or three of the soldiers jumped from their horses and knelt beside me. One of them raised my head, and placed his hand over my heart.

"Good news, comrades!" he cried. "His heart still beats!"

Then some brandy was poured down my throat; it put vigour into me, and I was able to open my eyes fully and look around. Lights and shadows were moving among the trees, and I heard men call to one another. They drew together, uttering frightened exclamations; and the lights flashed as the others came pouring out of the cemetery pell-mell, like men possessed. When the further ones came close to us, those who were around me asked them eagerly:

"Well, have you found him?"

The reply rang out hurriedly:

"No! no! Come away quick—quick! This is no place to stay, and on this of all nights!"

"What was it?" was the question, asked in all manner of keys. The answer came variously and all indefinitely as though the men were moved by some common impulse to speak, yet were restrained by some common fear from giving their thoughts.

"It—it—indeed!" gibbered one, whose wits had plainly given out for the moment.

"A wolf—and yet not a wolf!" another put in shudderingly.

"No use trying for him without the sacred bullet," a third remarked in a more ordinary manner.

"Serve us right for coming out on this night! Truly we have earned our thousand marks!" were the ejaculations of a fourth.

"There was blood on the broken marble," another said after a pause—"the lightning never brought that there. And for him—is he safe? Look at his throat! See, comrades, the wolf has been lying on him and keeping his blood warm."

The officer looked at my throat and replied:

"He is all right; the skin is not pierced. What does it all mean? We should never have found him but for the yelping of the wolf."

"What became of it?" asked the man who was holding up my head, and who seemed the least panic-stricken of the party, for his hands were steady and without tremor. On his sleeve was the chevron of a petty officer.

"It went to its home," answered the man, whose long face was pallid, and who actually shook with terror as he glanced around him fearfully. "There are graves enough there in which it may lie. Come, comrades—come quickly! Let us leave this cursed spot."

The officer raised me to a sitting posture, as he uttered a word of command; then several men placed me upon a horse. He sprang to the saddle behind me, took me in his arms, gave the word to advance; and, turning our faces away from the cypresses, we rode away in swift, military order.

As yet my tongue refused its office, and I was perforce silent.

I must have fallen asleep; for the next thing I remembered was finding myself standing up, supported by a solider on each side of me. It was almost broad daylight, and to the north a red streak of sunlight was reflected, like a path of blood, over the waste of snow. The officer was telling the men to say nothing of what they had seen, except that they found an English stranger, guarded by a large dog.

"Dog! that was no dog," cut in the man who had exhibited such fear. "I think I know a wolf when I see one."

The young officer answered calmly: "I said a dog."

"Dog!" reiterated the other ironically. It was evident that his courage was rising with the sun; and, pointing to me, he said, "Look at his throat. Is that the work of a dog, master?"

Instinctively I raised my hand to my throat, and as I touched it I cried out in pain. The men crowded round to look, some stooping down from their saddles; and again there came the calm voice of the young officer:

"A dog, as I said. If aught else were said we should only be laughed at."

I was then mounted behind a trooper, and we rode on into the surburbs of Munich. Here we came across a stray carriage, into which I was lifted, and it was driven off to the Quatre Saisons— the young officer accompanying me, whilst a trooper followed with his horse, and the others rode off to their barracks.

When we arrived, Herr Delbrück rushed so quickly down the steps to meet me, that it was apparent he had been watching within. Taking me by both hands he solicitously led me in. The officer saluted me and was turning to withdraw, when I recognized his purpose, and insisted that he should come to my rooms. Over a glass of wine I warmly thanked him and his brave comrades for saving me. He replied simply that he was more than glad, and that Herr Delbrück had at the first taken steps to make all the searching party pleased; at which ambiguous utterance the maître d'hotel smiled, while the officer pleaded duty and withdrew.

"But Herr Delbrück," I enquired, "how and why was it that the soliders searched for me?"

He shrugged his shoulders, as if in depreciation of his own deed, as he replied:

"I was so fortunate as to obtain leave from the commander of the regiment in which I served, to ask for volunteers."

"But how did you know I was lost?" I asked.

"The driver came hither with the remains of his carriage, which had been upset when the horses ran away."

"But surely you would not send a search-party of soldiers merely on this account?"

"Oh, no!" he answered; "but even before the coachman arrived, I had this telegram from the Boyar whose guest you are," and he took from his pocket a telegram which he handed to me, and I read:

BISTRITZ.

"Be careful of my guest—his safety is most precious to me. Should aught happen to him, or if he be missed, spare nothing to find him and ensure his safety. He is English and therefore adventurous. There are often dangers from snow and wolves and night. Lose not a moment if you suspect harm to him. I answer your zeal with my fortune.—Dracula."

As I held the telegram in my hand, the room seemed to whirl around me; and, if the attentive maître d'hotel had not caught me, I think I should have fallen. There was something so strange in all this, something so weird and impossible to imagine, that there grew on me a sense of my being in some way the sport of opposite forces—the mere vague idea of which seemed in a way to paralyse me. I was certainly under some form of mysterious protection. From a distant country had come, in the very nick of time, a message that took me out of the danger of the snow-sleep and the jaws of the wolf.

THEODORE STURGEON *is the award-winning author of the science-fiction* classic More Than Human, *and has written hordes of short stories, many of them quite terrifying, as well as an undeservedly forgotten novel of psychotic vampirism,* Some Of Your Blood. *The ensuing story has one of the weirdest lead paragraphs you'll ever encounter, and you may wonder what it's all about, but be patient: the mysteries eventually will be cleared up, and you may wish they hadn't been.*

The Professor's Teddy Bear

BY THEODORE STURGEON

"Sleep," said the monster. It spoke with its ear, with little lips writhing deep within the folds of flesh, because its mouth was full of blood.

"I don't want to sleep now. I'm having a dream," said Jeremy. "When I sleep, all my dreams go away. Or they're just pretend dreams. I'm having a real dream now."

"What are you dreaming now?" asked the monster.

"I am dreaming that I'm grown up—"

"Seven feet tall and very fat," said the monster.

"You're silly," said Jeremy. "I will be five feet, six and three-eighth inches tall. I will be bald on top and will wear eyeglasses like little thick ashtrays. I will give lectures to young things about human destiny and the metempsychosis of Plato."

"What's a metempsychosis?" asked the monster hungrily.

Jeremy was four and could afford to be patient. "A metempsychosis is a thing that happens when a person moves from one house to another."

"Like when your daddy moved here from Monroe Street?"

"Sort of. But not that kind of a house, with shingles and sewers and things. *This* kind of a house," he said, and smote his little chest.

"Oh," said the monster. It moved up and crouched on Jeremy's throat, looking more like a teddy bear than ever. "Now?" it begged. It was not very heavy.

"Not now," said Jeremy petulantly. "It'll make me sleep. I want to watch my dream some more. There's a girl who's not listening to my lecture. She's thinking about her hair."

"What about her hair?" asked the monster.

"It's brown," said Jeremy. "It's shiny, too. She wishes it were golden."

"Why?"

"Somebody named Bert likes golden hair."

"Go ahead and make it golden then."

"I can't! What would the other young ones say?"

"Does that matter?"

"Maybe not. Could I make her hair golden?"

"Who is she?" countered the monster.

"She is a girl who will be born here in about twenty years," said Jeremy. The monster snuggled closer to his neck.

"If she is to be born here, then of course you can change her hair. Hurry and do it and go to sleep."

Jeremy laughed delightedly.

"What happened?" asked the monster.

"I changed it," said Jeremy. "The girl behind her squeaked like the mouse with its leg caught. Then she jumped up. It's a big lecture-room, you know, built up and away from the speaker-place. It has steep aisles. Her foot slipped on the hard step."

He burst into joyous laughter.

"Now what?"

"She broke her neck. She's dead."

The monster sniggered. "That's a very funny dream. Now change the other girl's hair back again. Nobody else saw it, except you?"

"Nobody else saw," said Jeremy. "There! It's changed back again. She never even knew she had golden hair for a little while."

"That's fine. Does that end the dream?"

"I s'pose it does," said Jeremy regretfully. "It ends the lecture, anyhow. The young people are all crowding around the girl with the broken neck. The young men all have sweat under their noses. The girls are all trying to put their fists into their mouths. You can go ahead."

The monster made a happy sound and pressed its mouth hard against Jeremy's neck. Jeremy closed his eyes.

The door opened. "Jeremy, darling," said Mummy. She had a

tired, soft face and smiling eyes. "I heard you laugh."

Jeremy opened his eyes slowly. His lashes were so long that when they swung up, there seemed to be a tiny wind, as if they were dark weather fans. He smiled, and three of his teeth peeped out and smiled too. "I told Fuzzy a story, Mummy," he said sleepily, "and he liked it."

"You darling," she murmured. She came to him and tucked the covers around his chin. He put up his hand and kept the monster tight against his neck.

"Is Fuzzy sleeping?" asked Mummy, her voice crooning with whimsy.

"No," said Jeremy. "He's hungering himself."

"How does he do that?"

"When I eat, the—the hungry goes away. Fuzzy's different."

She looked at him, loving him so much that she did not—could not think. "You're a strange child," she whispered, "and you have the pinkest cheeks in the whole wide world."

"Sure I have," he said.

"What a funny little laugh!" she said, paling.

"That wasn't me. That was Fuzzy. He thinks you're funny."

Mummy stood over the crib, looking down at him. It seemed to be the frown that looked at him, while the eyes looked past. Finally she wet her lips and patted his head. "Good night, baby."

"Good night, Mummy." He closed his eyes. Mummy tiptoed out. The monster kept right on doing it.

It was nap-time the next day, and for the hundredth time Mummy had kissed him and said, "You're so *good* about your nap, Jeremy!" Well, he was. He always went straight up to bed at nap-time, as he did at bedtime. Mummy didn't know why, of course. Perhaps Jeremy did not know. Fuzzy knew.

Jeremy opened the toy-chest and took Fuzzy out. "You're hungry, I bet," he said.

"Yes. Let's hurry."

Jeremy climbed into the crib and hugged the teddy bear close. "I keep thinking about that girl," he said.

"What girl?"

"The one whose hair I changed."

"Maybe because it's the first time you've changed a person."

"It is not! What about the man who fell into the subway hole?"

"You moved the hat. The one that blew off. You moved it under his feet so that he stepped on the brim with one foot and caught his toe in the crown, and tumbled in."

"Well, what about the little girl I threw in front of the truck?"

"You didn't touch her," said the monster equably. "She was on roller skates. You broke something in one wheel so it couldn't turn. So she fell right in front of the truck."

Jeremy thought carefully. "Why didn't I ever touch a person before?"

"I don't know," said Fuzzy. "It has something to do with being born in this house, I think."

"I guess maybe," said Jeremy doubtfully.

"I'm hungry," said the monster, settling itself on Jeremy's stomach as he turned on his back.

"Oh, all right," Jeremy said. "The next lecture?"

"Yes," said Fuzzy eagerly. "Dream bright, now. The big things that you say, lecturing. Those are what I want. Never mind the people there. Never mind you, lecturing. The things you say."

The strange blood flowed as Jeremy relaxed. He looked up to the ceiling, found the hairline crack that he always stared at while he dreamed real, and began to talk.

"There I am. There's the—the room, yes, and the—yes, it's all there, again. There's the girl. The one who has the brown, shiny hair. The seat behind her is empty. This must be after that other girl broke her neck."

"Never mind that," said the monster impatiently. "What do you say?"

"I—" Jeremy was quiet. Finally Fuzzy nudged him. "Oh. It's all about yesterday's unfortunate occurrence, but, like the show of legend, our studies must go on."

"Go on with it then," panted the monster.

"All right, all right," said Jeremy impatiently. "Here it is. We come now to the Gymnosophists, whose ascetic school has had no recorded equal in its extremism. Those strange gentry regarded clothing and even food as detrimental to purity of thought. The Greeks also called them *Hylobioi*, a term our more erudite students will notice as analogous to the Sanskrit *Vana-Prasthas*. It is evident that they were a profound influence on Diogenes Laërtius, the Elisian founder of pure skepticism . . ."

And so he droned on and on. Fuzzy crouched on his body, its soft ears making small masticating motions; and sometimes when stimulated by some particularly choice nugget of esoterica, the ears drooled.

At the end of nearly an hour, Jeremy's soft voice trailed off, and he was quiet. Fuzzy shifted in irritation. "What is it?"

"That girl," said Jeremy. "I keep looking back to that girl while I'm talking."

"Well, stop doing it. I'm not finished."

"There isn't any more, Fuzzy. I keep looking and looking back to that girl until I can't lecture any more. Now I'm saying all that about the pages in the book and the assignment. The lecture is over."

Fuzzy's mouth was almost full of blood. From its ears, it sighed. "That wasn't any too much. But if that's all, then it's all. You can sleep now if you want to."

"I want to watch for a while."

The monster puffed out its cheeks. The pressure inside was not great. "Go on, then." It scrabbled off Jeremy's body and curled up in a sulky huddle.

The strange blood moved steadily through Jeremy's brain. With his eyes wide and fixed, he watched himself as he would be, a slight, balding professor of philosophy.

He sat in the hall, watching the students tumbling up the steep aisles, wondering at the strange compulsion he had to look at that girl, Miss—Miss—what was it?

Oh. "Miss Patchell!"

He started, astonished at himself. He had certainly not meant to call out her name. He clasped his hands tightly, regaining the dry stiffness which was his closest approach to dignity.

The girl came slowly down the aisle steps, her wide-set eyes wondering. There were books tucked under her arm, and her hair shone. "Yes, Professor?"

"I—" He stopped and cleared his throat. "I know it's the last class today, and you are no doubt meeting someone. I shan't keep you very long . . . and if I do," he added, and was again astonished at himself, "you can see Bert tomorrow."

"Bert? Oh!" She colored prettily. "I didn't know you knew about—how *could* you know?"

He shrugged. "Miss Patchell," he said. "You'll forgive an old—ah—middle-aged man's rambling, I hope. There is something about you that—that—"

"Yes?" Caution, and an iota of fright were in her eyes. She glanced up and back at the now empty hall.

Abruptly he pounded the table. "I will *not* let this go on for another instant without finding out about it. Miss Patchell, you are becoming afraid of me, and you are wrong."

"I th-think I'd better . . ." she said timidly, and began backing off.

"*Sit down!*" he thundered. It was the very first time in his entire life that he had thundered at anyone, and her shock was not one whit greater than his. She shrank back and into a front-row seat, looking a good deal smaller than she actually was, except about the eyes, which were much larger.

The professor shook his head in vexation. He rose, stepped down off the dais, and crossed to her, sitting in the next seat.

"Now be quiet and listen to me." The shadow of a smile twitched his lips and he said, "I really don't know what I am going to say. Listen, and be patient. It couldn't be more important."

He sat a while, thinking, chasing vague pictures around in his mind. He heard, or was conscious of, the rapid but slowing beat of her frightened heart.

"Miss Patchell," he said, turning to her, his voice gentle, "I have not at any time looked into your records. Until—ah—yesterday, you were simply another face in the class, another source of quiz papers to be graded. I have not consulted the registrar's files for information about you. And, to my almost certain knowledge, this is the first time I have spoken with you."

"That's right, sir," she said quietly.

"Very good, then." He wet his lips. "You are twenty-three years old. The house in which you were born was a two-story affair, quite old, with a leaded bay window at the turn of the stairs. The small bedroom, or nursery, was directly over the kitchen. You could hear the clatter of dishes below you when the house was quiet. The address was 191 Bucyrus Road."

"How—oh yes! How did you know?"

He shook his head, and then put it between his hands. "I don't know. I don't know. I lived in that house, too, as a child. I don't know how I knew that you did. There are things in here—" He rapped his head, shook it again. "I thought perhaps you could help."

*   *   *

She looked at him. He was a small man, brilliant, tired, getting old swiftly. She put a hand on his arm. "I wish I could," she said warmly. "I do wish I could."

"Thank you, child."

"Maybe if you told me more—"

"Perhaps. Some of it is—ugly. All of it is cloudy, long ago, barely remembered. And yet—"

"Please go on."

"I remember," he half whispered, "things that happened long ago that way, and recent things I remember—twice. One memory is sharp and clear, and one is old and misty. And I remember, in the same misty way, what is happening now and—and what *will* happen!"

"I don't understand."

"That girl. That Miss Symes. She—died here yesterday."

"She was sitting right behind me," said Miss Patchell.

"I know it! I knew what was going to happen to her. I knew it mistily, like an old memory. That's what I mean. I don't know what I could have done to stop it. I don't think I could have done anything. And yet, down deep I have the feeling that it's my fault—that she slipped and fell because of something I did."

"Oh, no!"

He touched her arm in mute gratitude for the sympathy in her tone, and grimaced miserably. "It's happened before," he said. "Time and time and time again. As a boy, as a youth, I was plagued with accidents. I led a quiet life. I was not very strong and books were always more my line than baseball. And yet I witnessed a dozen or more violent, useless deaths—automobile accidents, drownings, falls, and one or two—" his voice shook— "which I won't mention. And there were countless minor ones— broken bones, maimings, stabbings . . . and every time, in some way, it was my fault, like the one yesterday . . . and I—I—"

"Don't," she whispered. "Please don't. You were nowhere near Elaine Symes when she fell."

"I was nowhere near any of them! That never mattered. It never took away the burden of guilt. Miss Patchell—"

"Catherine."

"Catherine. Thank you so much! There are people called by insurance actuaries, 'accident prone.' Most of these are involved in accidents through their own negligence, or through some psychological quirk which causes them to defy the world, or to demand attention, by getting hurt. But some are simply present at accidents, without being involved at all—catalysts of death, if you'll pardon a flamboyant phrase. I am, apparently, one of these."

"Then—how could you feel guilty?"

"It was—" He broke off suddenly, and looked at her. She had a gentle face, and her eyes were filled with compassion. He shrugged. "I've said so much," he said. "More would sound no more fantastic, and do me no more damage."

"There'll be no damage from anything you tell me," she said, with a sparkle of decisiveness.

He smiled his thanks this time, sobered, and said, "These horrors—the maimings, the deaths—they were *funny*, once, long ago. I must have been a child, a baby. Something taught me, then, that the agony and death of others was to be promoted and enjoyed. I remember, I—almost remember when that stopped. There was a—a toy, a—a—"

Jeremy blinked. He had been staring at the fine crack in the ceiling for so long that his eyes hurt.

"What are you doing?" asked the monster.

"Dreaming real," said Jeremy. "I am grown up and sitting in the big empty lecture place, talking to the girl with the brown hair that shines. Her name's Catherine."

"What are you talking about?"

"Oh, all the funny dreams. Only—"

"Well?"

"They're not so funny."

The monster scurried over to him and pounced on his chest. "Time to sleep now. And I want to—"

"No," said Jeremy. He put his hands over his throat. "I have enough now. Wait until I see some more of this real-dream."

"What do you want to see?"

"Oh, I don't know. There's something , . ."

"Let's have some fun," said the monster. "This is the girl you can change, isn't it?"

"Yes."

"Go ahead. Give her an elephant's trunk. Make her grow a beard. Stop her nostrils up. Go on. You can do anything." Jeremy grinned briefly, and then said, "I don't want to."

"Oh, go on. Just see how funny . . ."

*   *   *

"A toy," said the professor. "But more than a toy. It could talk, I think. If I could only remember more clearly!"

"Don't try so hard. Maybe it will come," she said. She took his hand impulsively. "Go ahead."

"It was—something—" the professor said haltingly, "—something soft and not too large. I don't recall . . ."

"Was it smooth?"

"No. Hairy—fuzzy. *Fuzzy!* I'm beginning to get it. Wait, now . . . A thing like a teddy bear. It talked. It—why, of course! It was alive!"

"A pet, then. Not a toy."

"Oh, no," said the professor, and shuddered. "It was a toy, all right. My mother thought it was, anyway. It made me—dream real."

"You mean, like Peter Ibbetson?"

"No, no. Not like that." He leaned back, rolled his eyes up. "I used to see myself as I would be later, when I was grown. And before. Oh. Oh—I think it was then—Yes! It must have been then that I began to see all those terrible accidents. It was! It was!"

"Steady," said Catherine. "Tell me quietly."

He relaxed. "Fuzzy. The demon—the monster. I know what it did, the devil. Somehow it made me see myself as I grew. It made me repeat what I had learned. And it—it changed the knowledge into blood, the way a plant changes sunlight and water into cellulose!"

"I don't understand," she said again.

"You don't? How could you? How can I? I know that that's what it did, though. It made me—why, I was spouting my lectures here to the beast when I was four years old! The words of them, the sense of them, came from me *now* to me *then*. And I gave it to the monster, and it ate the knowledge and spiced it with the things it made me do in my real-dreams. It made me trip a man up on a hat, of all absurd things, and fall into a subway excavation. And when I was in my teens, I was right by the excavation to see it happen. And that's the way with all of them! All the horrible accidents I have witnessed, I have half-remembered before they happened. There's no stopping any of them. What am I going to do?"

There were tears in her eyes. "What about me?" she whispered—more, probably to get his mind away from his despair than for any other reason.

"You. There's something about you, if only I could remember. Something about what happened to that—that toy, that beast. You were in the same environment as I, as that devil. Somehow, you are vulnerable to it and—Catherine, Catherine, I think that something was done to you that—"

He broke off. His eyes widened in horror. The girl sat beside him, helping him, pitying him, and her expression did not change. But—everything else about her did.

Her face shrank, shrivelled. Her eyes lengthened. Her ears grew long, grew until they were like donkey's ears, like rabbit's ears, like horrible, long hairy spider's legs. Her teeth lengthened into tusks. Her arms shrivelled into jointed straws, and her body thickened.

It smelled like rotten meat.

There were filthy claws scattering out of her polished open-toed shoes. There were bright sores. There were—other things. And all the while she—*it*—held his hand and looked at him with pity and friendliness.

The professor—

Jeremy sat up and flung the monster away. "It isn't funny!" he screamed. "It isn't funny, it isn't, it—*isn't!*"

The monster sat up and looked at him with its soft, bland, teddy-bear expression. "Be quiet," it said. "Let's make her all squashy now, like soft-soap. And hornets in her stomach. And we can put her—"

Jeremy clapped his hands over his ears and screwed his eyes shut. The monster talked on. Jeremy burst into tears, leapt from the crib and, hurling the monster to the floor, kicked it. It grunted. "That's funny!" screamed the child. "Ha ha!" he cried, as he planted both feet in its yielding stomach. He picked up the twitching mass and hurled it across the room. It struck the nursery clock. Clock and monster struck the floor together in a flurry of glass, metal, and blood. Jeremy stamped it all into a jagged, pulpy mass, blood from his feet mixing with blood from the monster, the same strange blood which the monster had pumped into his neck . . .

Mummy all but fainted when she ran in and saw him. She screamed, but he laughed, screaming. The doctor gave him sedatives until he slept, and cured his feet. He was never very strong after that. They saved him, to live his life and to see his real-dreams; funny dreams, and to die finally in a lecture room, with his eyes distended in horror while horror froze his heart, and a terrified young woman ran crying, crying for help.

Like the composer Tchaikovsky, IVAN TURGENEV *(1818–83) was greatly influenced in his art by Western models. Turgenev's years in Paris infused an urbanity and polish into his masterwork,* Fathers and Sons, *as well as other tales and vignettes of Russian life that he created in* Sketches of a Sportsman, Virgin Soil, *etc. In the following tongue-in-cheek adventure, we are afforded a generous dollop of Turgenev's dryly understated sense of the ridiculous, without, however, sacrificing character credibility. Bubnoff himself is a familiar sort of chap, and we can only assume that his diabolical hosts derive from the (second class) lieutenant's thoroughly Slavic view of things infernal.*

Bubnoff and the Devil

BY IVAN TURGENEV

Twilight was falling. The old women who owned the three houses lining the half-mile country road closed up the shutters for the night; the chickens were already asleep in their sheds.

But Lieutenant (second class) Ivan Andreivich Bubnoff did not mind the solitude. He strolled briskly down the quiet roadway, his hands in his pockets, and imagined what it would be like if he were Napoleon.

His reverie was disturbed by the approach of a short man, who appeared out of the gathering dusk. The stranger affected outlandish garments, and Bubnoff concluded that it must be Telyushkin, a wealthy local who was reputed to dress in the manner of the Turks. But Bubnoff had never set eyes on Telyushkin, and when the stranger spoke, the soldier immediately realized his assumption was incorrect.

"Good evening," the other said casually. "I would like to introduce myself. I am the Devil."

"Uh-oh," thought Bubnoff. "One of us is drunk. Either way, I'm getting out of here."

But the grinning stranger gestured and the lieutenant suddenly found he could not move.

"Neither of us is drunk, my good Ivan Andreivich Bubnoff. I

actually am the Devil."

"One of us is crazy," thought Ivan. "Either way, I'd better get going—"

But the other grasped the officer by his coat collar and spoke again. "Now tell me, Bubnoff," he said in a loud voice, "what do you think it would be like if you were Napoleon?"

When Bubnoff heard the tenor of his recent thoughts so accurately echoed, he was somewhat reassured. "After all," he said to himself, "perhaps this is the Devil."

"I will convince you that I am," the other replied. "Look at those thistles. What would you like me to do with them? Perhaps you would care to see them dance like Cossacks?"

With a bored gesture of his hand, the short man caused the thistles to perform a really first-rate Cossack dance. Bubnoff was impressed, but the Devil did not stop there. To further prove his identity, he swallowed his hooves and brought them out through his throat. He merrily juggled his eyeballs, then removed his nose and made a present of it to Ivan Andreivich, who put it in his jacket pocket.

"*Now*, Ivan Andreivich Bubnoff, *who am I?*"

"You are the Devil, right enough!" the other exclaimed. "But what do you want of me?"

"Nothing in particular. I was just a trifle bored, to tell the truth, and thought I might join you for a little walk and perhaps a talk. Do you mind?"

"Not in the least!" said Bubnoff, and the two tramped along the road like two old comrades.

"This is what I would call an absolutely unique experience," the lieutenant said to himself. "Perhaps I am drunk after all." He grabbed the bristles of his mustache and yanked at them to see if he would wake. His neck began to creak.

"I shouldn't do that, if I were you," said the Devil. "You might pull too hard and yank your head from the shoulders—like this!" With that, he grabbed a handful of Bubnoff's hair and tugged his head straight off his neck. It would have surprised the soldier, if he'd had time to think about it, but a headless officer cannot command such a function by the very nature of the experience. The Devil played ball with Ivan Andreivich's head, then replaced it on the soldier's neck. As soon as he did, Bubnoff contrived to make an appropriate remark which he thought wittily suited to the occasion. The Devil winked and the two laughed like childhood friends.

After a time, they came to a forest and the soldier began to grow uneasy. "Look here," he asked anxiously, "you aren't planning to lead me to some ravine where I will fall and die and be munched by buzzards, are you? I should not much care for that, you know!"

"My, my, what a notion!" exclaimed the Devil. "What do you take me for? I should never do such a thing to my good friend, Ivan Andreivich!"

As he spoke, the Devil approached the bole of a gigantic oak tree, withered and twisted like some malignant creature of the night. He rested there, and Bubnoff heard an eerie croaking from somewhere above. Looking up, he saw the flutter of wings and an ancient raven settled into the branches of the oak.

Bubnoff was not a bird fancier, so what he thought was a raven was actually a crow. But, in truth, the crow was really one of the many changing shapes of the Devil's Grandma. (He did not have a mother, only a grandmother—why, nobody knew, not even the Devil.)

"I am now going to introduce you to my Grandma," the Devil told the soldier, who began to protest.

"But I am not properly attired!"

"Never fear, she does not stand on such ceremony. But," the Devil cautioned, "I must ask you to please refrain from crossing yourself, or we will have to part company. Now will you kindly bite my tail off? Just the very end will do, you know."

As he made his peculiar request, the Devil flicked his tail so that the soft spade-tip hovered just a few inches in front of Bubnoff's lips.

"What a disgusting idea!" cried the soldier. "I shall do no such thing!"

"And why not?"

"Well," Bubnoff sputtered, floundering for a reason, "because it would hurt you, I suppose."

"Bah! What an idea! It would give me the greatest pleasure!" He pushed the appendage into Ivan Andreivich's mouth, but the officer yanked it out again.

"I say," he pleaded, "is it absolutely essential that I do this?"

The Devil nodded solemnly. Bubnoff, with a sigh, grasped the tail and raised it to his lips, then paused.

"I suppose," he said, "your tail will taste positively awful!"

"I beg your pardon!" the other said, his feelings a trifle ruffled.

"My tail will taste exactly like whatever food you wish to taste. Go ahead, imagine any culinary delight whatever—that is what my tail's flavor will resemble."

"Very well," Ivan said, after a moment's thought, "I am partial to pickles and syrup." He bit the tail . . .

The Devil did not lie. His tail tasted like pickles and syrup (with just a trace of brimstone).

By the time Bubnoff had swallowed the tail-tip, the universe whirled about his ears and he found himself inside a small, reasonably neat room. An old harridan with a huge nose was sitting in a rocking chair cracking walnuts. The Devil waved his arm in her direction.

"Grandma, allow me to present Lieutenant (second class) Ivan Andreivich Bubnoff. Ivan Andreivich . . . my Grandma."

The introductions completed, the Devil indicated a chair for the officer and left him alone with his Grandma so he could go try on a new pair of horns.

Bubnoff sat there in awkward silence. Not only did he not know what to say to the old crone, but his knowledge of protocol did not extend to the proper form of address for so venerable a personage as the grandmother of the Devil. At length, he began to utter a polite inanity, but the old woman immediately stopped him.

"There's no need for empty words," she cackled in a strange voice. As she did, each syllable seemed to fly through the air at him in a concentric spiral. Bubnoff's awkwardness disappeared, but the crone simply sat there, cracking walnuts, looking at him as if she expected him to speak. He shrugged and kept his peace, until at last, wearied by the silence, the Devil's Grandma jumped up from her rocker, grasped Bubnoff by the hands and began to dance with great speed about the room.

"Come, love, come dance with me, little Bubnoff," she sang as they cavorted.

Ivan Andreivich's head began to spin and at length he called out to the Devil to come rescue him.

The Devil dashed in, his new horns upon his head. Catching his ancestor under the arms, he respectfully led her to her seat. Then he asked the lieutenant to forgive the old woman's whims.

"Now, Ivan Andreivich," he added, "because I wish to be a good host to you, I am going to let you meet my lovely little granddaughter. Her tail is barely sprouted, for she is quite young, but I trust in your honor and know you will not play upon her lack of experience. Bibbidibobbidibu! Please come in!"

The Devil's granddaughter entered from another room, curtsied before the soldier, and shyly clung to her great-great-grandmother.

Bubnoff bowed to her. "What did you say her name was?" he asked.

"Bibbidibobbidibu," the Devil replied.

"That doesn't sound like a Russian name," observed the soldier.

"We are from other parts," the Devil answered.

Bubnoff approached the Devil's granddaughter and bent over to kiss her hand, noting the slight curvature of the nails as he did. It made her fingers look like claws. As he pressed his lips to her dainty hand, he felt a tingling in them like sparks of lightning.

"Will you come with me to the garden for a walk?" she asked him in a low voice.

"Nothing could make me happier," Ivan Andreivich replied, although it was evident by the way the crone eyed the Devil that she was not much in favor of the proposed stroll. But the Devil did not object, so Bubnoff and Bibbidibobbidibu left the room in one another's company.

Though the Devil's garden looked like any other garden, Bubnoff noted uneasily that the vegetation therein was apparently in some kind of pain since every flower, bush and shrub emitted groans of anguish.

The Devil's granddaughter walkcd by the lieutenant's side for some time in silence. Then she looked up at Bubnoff, emitted a deep sigh and told him that she was in love.

"With whom?" he asked politely.

"With you, Ivan Andreivich," she answered, her tongue flicking lightly over her lips.

"Pray contain yourself," he told her, remembering that his honor was at stake.

"But how may I? For I love you, and I want you to reciprocate my ardor," she said cajolingly. "I will make a garland of roses for you, redder than the blush of my cheeks. I will give you nuts to eat and the juice of many ferns to drink, and we will be glad, my Bubnoff, for I love you!"

He stared at her, moved, and nearly spoke his love to her, but as he looked into her eyes, it seemed they shone like some predator cat; her nostrils flared and the tongue flicked again over her lips, which parted to reveal the whitest and sharpest of teeth . . .

"I am sorry," he said firmly, "but I cannot say I love you, my child. Let us go back to your home."

"But where is it?" she mocked.

Bubnoff took a step, faltered, and flailed his arms about to keep balance. He was on the pinnacle of a high column, standing on one leg only; the other kicked in the empty air. The column was slippery with some kind of sticky fluid and thousands of tiny demons clambered with great difficulty towards the top, falling back, climbing again, chattering and laughing as they tried to attain the grand prize of the slippery race—Bubnoff himself.

High in the air above his head floated Bibbidibobbidibu, tittering evilly at his plight.

"Help!" called the lieutenant. "Devil, this is unkind of you!" He found it hard to call out for fear of disturbing his precarious balance.

"Bubnoff Child! Where have you gone?" the Devil's voice suddenly called.

As soon as the voice rang out, the soldier found himself back in the garden, with Bibbidibobbidibu by his side.

"For shame, my little one!" the Devil chided the girl. "Ivan Andreivich is an honored guest. You have treated him ill. Come, my friend, let us leave this silly urchin!"

"Silly urchin!" she snapped. "Indeed! Why, I am not so young as all that. Already my horns are beginning to sprout." She lowered her head, parted her hair and showed two tiny, delicate horns to Bubnoff.

The officer, who had always been the most earthbound of mortals, suddenly leapt in the air, pirouetted twice and bent down to kiss the tips of Bibbidibobbidibu's horns. As he did, the horn swelled and punched him smartly on the chin.

Later that evening, the family sat around the table with their guest. Bubnoff sat to the right of the old crone who occupied the head of the table. The Devil faced him, and Bibbidibobbidibu's chair was at the foot of the table.

"I wonder," thought Bubnoff, "what we are going to have for dinner."

Just then, a huge covered platter entered the room, bowed and hopped up on the table by itself.

Turning to her grandson, the old woman said, "I do believe we had better marry Lieutenant (second class) Bubnoff to our little Bibbidibobbidibu."

"Positively," nodded the Devil.

"What a notion," thought the soldier. "I cannot marry the Devil's granddaughter. Just think if there were children! What rank in society would they occupy? If I had a son by her, could he become a soldier? This is dreadful! I should never have nibbled on the Devil's tail!"

"Now understand," said the Devil, "while I wish this marriage to take place, I would not for a moment consider it without the consent of both principals. I have too much love for my granddaughter to coerce her to wed one she does not fancy. Likewise, I have the highest esteem for my companion Ivan Andreivich. We shall put the matter to the question directly. My child—tell me truly—do you love my friend Bubnoff here?"

"Oh, she certainly does," cackled the Devil's Grandma. "Look at the way she is licking her lips!"

It was true. Bibbidibobbidibu once more let her crimson tongue-tip flick hungrily over the sharp teeth in her dainty little mouth . . .

"She will eat me alive!" Bubnoff suddenly shouted in fear.

"*Bon appetit!*" the Devil murmured.

"What?" Ivan Andreivich shouted again. "I am an officer and an honored guest! One does not eat a guest!"

"But of course we do!" the Devil argued. "It is absolutely necessary for us to do it—and extremely enjoyable, besides!"

"You shall *not* enjoy me at my expense!" the soldier angrily proclaimed, making flamboyant gestures with his arms. "I am getting out of here. I was a damned fool to eat the tip of your tail!"

He tried to get up, but he could not budge. His chair had turned into a gigantic tarantula that grasped him with diabolic strength.

The Devil, the old woman and Bibbidibobbidibu all laughed at Bubnoff's plight. The crone's cackle was like the bleat of a goat, and the girl gurgled with sensual delight as the soldier squirmed helplessly.

"Let me out!" Bubnoff protested. "Avaunt, fiends, in the Holy name—"

"Stop him! He will cross himself!" the Devil roared.

Bibbidibobbidibu jumped up and, smiling in her predatory manner, bit off Bubnoff's arm at the shoulder. The giant tureen opened and the screaming soldier was dumped inside and spiced with pepper and brimstone, oil and vinegar and the scarlet juice of cranberries. Weird music sounded in the air around the grisly supper scene as the three fiends ate the lieutenant and picked his bones clean. Bibbidibobbidibu was awarded the prize of the soldier's heart, which she devoured with gusto, while the Devil almost gagged on a trouser-button.

In the morning, Lieutenant (second class) Ivan Andreivich Bubnoff woke face down in the middle of the lonely country road. He bounded up, terrified, sure that he was not there, but really in pieces in the viscera of the three demons. It took the better part of the day for him to calm down and realize he was still alive.

Bubnoff, though he lived to a ripe old age and eventually became a lieutenant first class, never forgot his evening with the Devil. Many times he would assure his fellow officers that if he were Napoleon, he would round up every single demon and murder them all on the spot!

—English adaptation by Marvin Kaye

Born in Fort Worth in 1921, patricia highsmith *now resides in Europe, where she divides her time between writing, painting and sculpture, with some piano-playing on the side. Author of the critically acclaimed suspense novels* Strangers On a Train, The Glass Cell, The Talented Mr. Ripley, *and others, Ms. Highsmith has written a remarkable series of horror stories, many of them concerned with the mistreated animal kingdom. It's difficult to work up any sympathy, though, for the monsters in "The Quest for* Blank Claveringi," *which, like the author's earlier story,* "The Snail Watcher," *does for escargot what Hitchcock's* The Birds *did for our feathered friends.*

The Quest for Blank Claveringi

BY PATRICIA HIGHSMITH

Avery Clavering, a professor of zoology at a California university, heard of the giant snails of Kuwa in a footnote of a book on molluscs. His sabbatical had been coming up in three months when he read the few lines:

It is said by Matusas Islands natives that snails even larger than this exist on the uninhabited island of Kuwa, twenty-five miles distant from the Matusas. The Matusans claim that these snails have a shell diameter of twenty feet and that they are man-eating. Dr. Wm J. Stead, now living in the Matusas, visited Kuwa in 1949 without finding any snails at all, but the legend persists.

The item aroused Professor Clavering's interest, because he very much wanted to discover some animal, bird, reptile or even mollusc to which he could give his name. *Something-or-other Claveringi.* The professor was forty-eight. His time, perhaps, was not growing short, but he had achieved no particular renown. The discovery of a new species would win him immortality in his field.

The Matusas, the professor saw on a map, were three small

islands arranged like the points of an isosceles triangle not far from Hawaii. He wrote a letter to Dr. Stead and received the following reply, written on an abominable typewriter, so many words pale, he could scarcely read it:

April 8th, 19—

Dear Professor Clavering:

I have long heard of the giant snails of Kuwa, but before you make a trip of such length, I must tell you that the natives here assure me a group of them went about twenty years ago to Kuwa to exterminate these so-called man-eating snails which they imagined could swim the ocean between Kuwa and the Matusas and do some damage to the latter island. They claim to have killed off the whole community of them except for one old fellow they could not kill. This is typical of native stories— there's always one that got away. I haven't much doubt the snails were not bigger than three feet across and that they were not **** (here a word was illegible, due both to the pale ribbon and a squashed insect). You say you read of my effort in 1949 to find the giant snails. What the footnote did not say is that I have made several trips since to find them. I retired to the Matusas, in fact, for that purpose. I now believe the snails to be mere folklore, a figment of the natives' imagination. If I were you, I would not waste time or money on an expedition.

Yours sincerely,
Wm. J. Stead, M.D.

Professor Clavering had the money and the time. He detected a sourness in Dr. Stead's letter. Maybe Dr. Stead had just had bad luck. By post, Professor Clavering hired a thirty-foot sail-boat with an auxiliary motor from Hawaii. He wanted to make the trip alone from the Matusas. *Blank Claveringi.* Regardless of the size, the snail was apt to be different from any known snail, because of its isolation—if it existed. He planned to go one month ahead of his wife and to join her and their twenty-year-old daughter Wanda in Hawaii for a more orthodox holiday after he had visited Kuwa. A month would give him plenty of time to find the snail, even if there were only one, to take photographs, and make notes.

It was late June when Professor Clavering, equipped with water tanks, tinned beef, soup and milk, biscuits, writing materials, camera, knife, hatchet and a Winchester .22 which he hardly knew how to use, set forth from one of the Matusas bound for Kuwa. Dr. Stead, who had been his host for a few days, saw him off. Dr.

Stead was seventy-five, he said, but he looked older, due perhaps to the ravages of drink and the apparently aimless life he led now. He had not looked for the giant snail in two years, he said.

"I've given the last third of my life to looking for this snail, you might say," Dr. Stead added. "But that's man's fate, I suppose, the pursuit of the non-existent. Well—good luck to you, Professor Clavering!" He waved his old American straw hat as the *Samantha* left the dock under motor power.

Professor Clavering had made out to Stead that if he did find snails, he would come back at once, get some natives to accompany him, and return to Kuwa with materials to make crates for the snails. Stead had expressed doubt whether he could persuade any natives to accompany him, if the snail or snails were really large. But then, Dr. Stead had been negative about everything pertaining to Professor Clavering's quest. Professor Clavering was glad to get away from him.

After about an hour, Professor Clavering cut the motor and tentatively hoisted some sail. The wind was favourable, but he knew little about sails, and he paid close attention to his compass. At last, Kuwa came into view, a tan hump on a sea of blue. He was quite close before he saw any greenery, and this was only the tops of some trees. Already, he was looking for anything resembling a giant snail, and regretting he had not brought binoculars, but the island was only three miles long and one mile broad. He decided to aim for a small beach. He dropped anchor, two of them, in water so clear he could see the sand under it. He stood for a few minutes on the deck.

The only life he saw was a few birds in the tops of trees, brightly coloured, crested birds, making cries he had never heard before. There was no low-lying vegetation whatsoever, none of the grass and reeds that might have been expected on an island such as this—much like the Matusas in the soil colour—and this augured well of the presence of snails that might have devoured everything green within their reach. It was only a quarter to two. Professor Clavering ate part of a papaya, two boiled eggs, and brewed coffee on his alcohol burner, as he had had nothing to eat since 6 A.M. Then, with his hunting knife and hatchet in the belt of his khaki shorts, and his camera around his neck, he lowered himself into the water. The *Samantha* carried no rowboat.

He sank up to his neck, but he could walk on the bottom. He held the camera high. He emerged panting, as he was some twenty

pounds overweight. Professor Clavering was to regret every one
of those pounds before the day was over, but as he got his breath
and looked around him, and felt himself drying off in the warm
sunlight, he was happy. He wiped his hatchet and knife with dry
sand, then walked inland, alert for the rounded form of a snail's
shell, moving or stationary, anywhere. But as snails were more or
less nocturnal, he thought any snails might well be sleeping in
some cave or crevice with no idea of emerging until nightfall.

He decided to cross the island first, then follow the coast to right
or left and circle the island. He had not gone a quarter of a mile,
when his heart gave a leap. Ten yards before him, he saw three
bent saplings with their top leaves chewed off. The young trees
were four inches in diameter at their base. It would have taken a
considerable weight to bend them down, something like a hundred
pounds. The professor looked on the trees and the ground for the
glaze left by snails, but found none. But rain could have washed
it away. A snail whose shell was three feet in diameter would not
weigh enough to bend such a tree, so Professor Clavering now
hoped for something bigger. He pushed on.

He arrived at the other side of the island. The sea had eaten a
notch into the shore, forming a mostly dry gully of a hundred
yards' length and a depth of thirty feet. The land here was sandy
but moist, and there was, he saw, a little vegetation in the form
of patchy grass. But here, the lower branches of all the trees had
been divested of their leaves, and so long ago that the branches
had dried and fallen off. All this bespoke the presence of land
snails. Professor Clavering stooped and looked down into the
gulley. He saw, just over the edge of his side of the crevice, the
pink-tan curve of something that was neither rock nor sand. If it
was a snail, it was monstrous. Involuntarily, he took a step
backward, scattering pebbles down the gulley.

The professor ran round the gulley to have a better look. It was
a snail, and its shell was about fifteen feet high. He had a view of
its left side, the side without the spiral. It resembled a peach-
coloured sail filled with wind, and the sunlight made nacreous,
silvery patches gleam and twinkle as the great thing stirred. The
little rain of pebbles had aroused it, the professor realized. If the
shell was fifteen or eighteen feet in diameter, he reckoned that
the snail's body or foot would be something like six yards long
when extended. Rooted to the spot, the professor stood, thrilled
as much by the (as yet) empty phrase *Blank Claveringi* which

throbbed in his head as by the fact he was looking upon something no man had seen before, or at least no scientist. The crate would have to be bigger than he had thought, but the *Samantha* would be capable of taking it on her forward deck.

The snail was backing to pull its head from the narrow part of the gulley. The moist body, the color of tea with milk, came into view with the slowness of an enormous snake awakening from slumber. All was silent, except for pebbles dropping from the snail's underside as it lifted its head, except for the professor's constrained breathing. The snail's head, facing inland, rose higher and higher, and its antennae, with which it saw, began to extend. Professor Clavering realized he had disturbed it from its diurnal sleep, and a brief terror caused him to retreat again, sending more pebbles down the slope.

The snail heard this, and slowly turned its enormous head toward him.

The professor felt paralysed. A gigantic face regarded him, a face with drooping, scalloped cheeks or lips, with antennae six feet long now, the eyes on the ends of them scrutinizing him at his own level and scarcely ten feet away, with the disdain of a Herculean lorgnette, with the unknown potency of a pair of oversized telescopes. The snail reared so high, it had to arch its antennae to keep him in view. Six yards long? It would be more like eight or ten yards. The snail turned itself to move toward him.

Still, the professor did not budge. He knew about snails' teeth, the twenty-odd thousand pairs of them even in a small garden snail, set in comblike structures, the upper front teeth visible, moving up and down constantly just under transparent flesh. A snail of this size, with proportionate teeth, could chew through a tree as quickly as a woodman's axe, the professor thought. The snail was advancing up the bank with monumental confidence. He had to stand still for a few seconds simply to admire it. *His* snail! The professor opened his camera and took a picture, just as the snail was hauling its shell over the edge of the quarry.

'You are magnificent!' Professor Clavering said in a soft and awestruck voice. Then he took a few steps backward.

It was pleasant to think he could skip nimbly about, comparatively speaking, observing the snail from all angles, while the snail could only creep toward him at what seemed the rate of one yard in ten seconds. The professor thought to watch the snail for an hour or so, then go back to the *Samantha* and write some notes.

He would sleep aboard the boat, take some more photographs tomorrow morning, then start under engine power back to the Matusas. He trotted for twenty yards, then turned to watch the snail approach.

The snail travelled with its head lifted three feet above the ground, keeping the professor in the focus of its eyes. It was moving faster. Professor Clavering retreated sooner than he intended, and before he could get another picture.

Now Professor Clavering looked around for a mate of the snail. He was rather glad not to see another snail, but he cautioned himself not to rule out the possibility of a mate. It wouldn't be pleasant to be cornered by two snails, yet the idea excited him. Impossible to think of a situation in which he could not escape from two slow, lumbering creatures like the—the what? *Amygdalus Persica* (his mind stuck on peaches, because of the beautiful colour of the shell) *Carnivora* (perhaps) *Claveringi*. That could be improved upon, the professor thought as he walked backward, watching.

A little grove of trees gave him an idea. If he stood in the grove, the snail could not reach him, and he would also have a close view. The professor took a stand amid twelve or fifteen trees, all about twenty feet high. The snail did not slacken its speed, but began to circle the grove, still watching the professor. Finding no opening big enough between two trees, the snail raised its head higher, fifteen feet high, and began to creep up on the trees. Branches cracked, and one tree snapped.

Professor Clavering ducked and retreated. He had a glimpse of a great belly gliding unhurt over a jagged tree trunk, of a circular mouth two feet across, open and showing the still wider upper band of teeth like shark's teeth, munching automatically up and down. The snail cruised gently down over the tree tops, some of which sprang back into position as the snail's weight left them.

Click! went the professor's camera.

What a sight that had been! Something like a slow hurdle. He imagined entertaining friends with an account of it, substantiated by the photograph, once he got back to California. Old Professor McIlroy of the biology department had laughed at him for spending seven thousand dollars on an effort he predicted would be futile!

Professor Clavering was tiring, so he cut directly for the *Samantha*. He noticed that the snail veered also in a direction that would intercept him, if they kept on at their steady though different speeds, and the professor chuckled and trotted for a bit. The snail also picked up speed, and the professor remembered the wide, upward rippling of the snail's body as it had hurdled the trees. It would be interesting to see how fast the snail could go on a straight course. Such a test would have to wait for America.

He reached the water and saw his beach a few yards away to his right, but no ship was there. He'd made a mistake, he thought, and his beach was on the other side of the island. Then he caught sight of the *Samantha* half a mile out on the ocean, drifting away.

"*Damn!*" Professor Clavering said aloud. He'd done something wrong with the anchors. Did he dare try to swim to it? The distance frightened him, and it was growing wider every moment.

A rattle of pebbles behind him made him turn. The snail was hardly twenty feet away.

The professor trotted down toward the beach. There was bound to be some slit on the coast, a cave however small, where he could be out of reach of the snail. He wanted to rest for a while. What really annoyed him now was the prospect of a chilly night without blankets or food. The Matusas natives had been right: there was nothing to eat on Kuwa.

Professor Clavering stopped dead, his shoes sliding on sand and pebbles. Before him, not fifty feet away on the beach, was another snail as big as the one following him, and somewhat lighter in colour. Its tail was in the sea, and its muzzle dripped water as it reared itself to get a look at him.

It was this snail, the professor realized, that had chewed through the hemp ropes and let the boat go free. Was there something about new hemp ropes that appealed to snails? This question he put out of his mind for the nonce. He had a snail before and behind him. The professor trotted on along the shore. The only crevice of shelter he was sure existed was the gulley on the other side of the island. He forced himself to walk at a moderate pace for a while, to breathe normally, then he sat down and treated himself to a rest.

The first snail was the first to appear, and as it had lost sight of him, it lifted its head and looked slowly to right and left, though without slackening its progress. The professor sat motionless, bare head lowered, hoping the snail would not see him. But he was not that lucky. The snail saw him and altered course to a straight line for him. Behind it came the second snail—its wife? its husband?—

the professor could not tell and there was no way of telling.

Professor Clavering had to leave his resting place. The weight of his hatchet reminded him that he at least had a weapon. A good scare, he thought, a minor wound might discourage them. He knew they were hungry, that their teeth could tear his flesh more easily than they tore trees, and that alive or dead, he would be eaten by these snails if he permitted it to happen. He drew his hatchet and faced them, conscious that he cut a not very formidable figure with his slight paunch, his pale, skinny legs, his height of five feet seven, about a third the snails' height, but his brows above his glasses were set with a determination to defend his life.

The first snail reared when it was ten feet away. The professor advanced and swung the hatchet at the projecting mantle on the snail's left side. He had not dared get close enough, his aim was inches short, and the weight of the hatchet pulled the professor off balance. He staggered and fell under the raised muzzle, and had just time to roll himself from under the descending mouth before it touched the ground where he had been. Angry now, he circled the snail and swung a blow at the nacreous shell, which turned the blade. The hatchet took an inch-deep chip, but nothing more. The professor swung again, higher this time and in the centre of the shell's posterior, trying for the lung valve beneath, but the valve was still higher, he knew, ten feet from the ground, and once more his hatchet took only a chip. The snail began to turn itself to face him.

The professor then confronted the second snail, rushed at it and swung the hatchet, cutting it in the cheek. The hatchet sank up to its wooden handle, and he had to tug to get it out, and then had to run a few yards, as the snail put on speed and reared its head for a biting attack. Glancing back, the professor saw that no liquid (he had not, of course, expected blood) came from the cut in the snail's cheek, and in fact he couldn't see the cut. And the blow had certainly been no discouragement to the snail's advance.

Professor Clavering began to walk at a sensible pace straight for the snails' lair on the other side of the island. By the time he scrambled down the side of the gulley, he was winded and his legs hurt. But he saw to his relief that the gulley narrowed to a sharp V. Wedged in that, he would be safe. Professor Clavering started into the V, which had an overhanging top rather like a cave, when he saw that what he had taken for some rounded rocks were moving—at least some of them were. They were baby snails! They were larger than good-sized beach balls. And the professor saw, from the way a couple of them were devouring grass blades, that they were hungry.

A snail's head appeared high on his left. The giant parent snail began to descend the gulley. A crepitation, a pair of antennae against the sky on his right, heralded the arrival of the second snail. He had nowhere to turn except the sea, which was not a bad idea, he thought, as these were land snails. The professor waded out and turned left, walking waist-deep in water. It was slow going, and a snail was coming after him. He got closer to the land and ran in thigh-deep water.

The first snail, the darker one, entered the water boldly and crept along in a depth of several inches, showing signs of being willing to go into deeper water when it got abreast of Professor Clavering. The professor hoped the other snail, maybe the mother, had stayed with the young. But it hadn't. It was following along the land, and accelerating. The professor plunged wildly for the shore where he would be able to move faster.

Now, thank goodness, he saw rocks. Great igneous masses of rocks covered a sloping hill down to the sea. There was bound to be a niche, some place there where he could take shelter. The sun was sinking into the ocean, it would be dark soon, and there was no moon, he knew. The professor was thirsty. When he reached the rocks, he flung himself like a corpse into a trough made by four or five scratchy boulders, which caused him to lie in a curve. The rocks rose two feet above his body, and the trough was hardly a foot wide. A snail couldn't, he reasoned, stick its head down here and bite him.

The peachy curves of the snails' shells appeared, and one, the second, drew closer.

"I'll strike it with my hatchet if it comes!" the professor swore to himself. "I'll cut its face to ribbons with my knife!" He was now reconciled to killing both adults, because he could take back a pair of the young ones, and in fact more easily because they were smaller.

The snail seemed to sniff like a dog, though inaudibly as its muzzle hovered over the professor's hiding place. Then with majestic calm it came down on the rocks between which the professor lay. Its slimy foot covered the aperture and within seconds had blocked out almost all the light.

Professor Clavering drew his hunting knife in anger and panic, and plunged it several times into the snail's soft flesh. The snail seemed not even to wince. A few seconds later, it stopped moving, though the professor knew that it was not only not dead, as the stabs hadn't touched any vital organs, but that it had fastened itself over his trench in the firmest possible way. No slit of light showed. The professor was only grateful that the irregularity of the rocks must afford a supply of air. Now he pressed frantically with his palms against the snail's body, and felt his hands slip and scrape against rock. The firmness of the snail, his inability to budge it, made him feel slightly sick for a moment.

An hour passed. The professor almost slept, but the experience was more like a prolonged hallucination. He dreamed, or feared, that he was being chewed by twenty thousands pairs of teeth into a heap of mince, which the two giant snails shared with their offspring. To add to his misery, he was cold and hungry. The snail's body gave no warmth, and was even cool.

Some hours later, the professor awoke and saw stars above him. The snail had departed. It was pitch dark. He stood up cautiously, trying not to make a sound, and stepped out of the crevice. He was free! On a sandy stretch of beach a few yards away, Professor Clavering lay down, pressed against a vertical face of rock. Here he slept the remaining hours until dawn.

He awakened just in time, and perhaps not the dawn but a sixth sense had awakened him. The first snail was coming toward him and was only ten feet away. The professor got up on trembling legs, and trotted inland, up a slope. An idea came to him: if he could push a boulder of, say, five hundred pounds—possible with a lever—on to an adult snail in the gulley, and smash the spot below which its lung lay, then he could kill it. Otherwise, he could think of no other means at his disposal that could inflict a fatal injury. His gun might, but the gun was on the *Samantha*. He had already estimated that it might be a week, or never, that help would come from the Matusas. The *Samantha* would not necessarily float back to the Matusas, would not necessarily be seen by any other ship for days, and even if it was seen, would it be apparent she was drifting? And if so, would the spotters make a beeline for the Matusas to report it? Not necessarily. The professor bent quickly and licked some dew from a leaf. The snails were twenty yards behind him now.

The trouble is, I'm becoming exhausted, he said to himself.

He was even more tired at noon. Only one snail pursued him, but the professor imagined the other resting or eating a tree top, in order to be fresh later. The professor could trot a hundred yards, find a spot to rest in, but he dared not shut his eyes for long, lest he sleep. And he was definitely weak from lack of food.

So the day passed. His idea of dropping a rock down the gulley was thwarted by two factors: the second snail was guarding the gulley now, at the top of its V, and there was no such rock as he needed within a hundred yards.

When dusk came, the professor could not find the hill where the igneous rocks were. Both snails had him in their sight now. His watch said a quarter to seven. Professor Clavering took a deep breath and faced the fact that he must make an attempt to kill one or both snails before dark. Almost without thinking, or planning— he was too spent for that—he chopped down a slender tree and hacked off its branches. The leaves of these branches were devoured by the two snails five minutes after the branches had fallen to the ground. The professor dragged his tree several yards inland, and sharpened one end of it with the hatchet. It was too heavy a weapon for one hand to wield, but in two hands, it made a kind of battering ram, or giant spear.

At once, Professor Clavering turned and attacked, running with the spear pointed slightly upward. He aimed for the first snail's mouth, but struck too low, and the tree end penetrated about four inches into the snail's chest—or the area below its face. No vital organ here, except the long, straight oesophagus, which in these giant snails would be set deeper than four inches. He had nothing for his trouble but lacerated hands. His spear hung for a few seconds in the snail's flesh, then fell out on to the ground. The professor retreated, pulling his hatchet from his belt. The second snail, coming up abreast of the other, paused to chew off a few inches of the tree stump, then joined its mate in giving attention to Professor Clavering. There was something contemptuous, something absolutely assured, about the snails' slow progress toward him, as if they were thinking, "Escape us a hundred, a thousand times, we shall finally reach you and devour every trace of you."

The professor advanced once more, circled the snail he had just hit with the tree spear, and swung his hatchet at the rear of its shell. Desperately, he attacked the same spot with five or six direct hits, for now he had a plan. His hacking operation had to be halted, because the second snail was coming up behind him. Its snout and an antenna even brushed the professor's legs moistly and staggered him, before he could step out of its way. Two more hatchet blows the professor got in, and then he stopped, because his right arm hurt. He had by no means gone through the shell, but he had no strength for more effort with the hatchet. He went back for his spear. His target was a small one, but he ran toward it with desperate purpose.

The blow landed. It even broke through.

The professor's hands were further torn, but he was oblivious of them. His success made him as joyous as if he had killed both his enemies, as if a rescue ship with food, water, and a bed were even then sailing into Kuwa's beach.

The snail was twisting and rearing up with pain.

Professor Clavering ran forward, lifted the drooping spear and pushed it with all his might farther into the snail, pointing it upward to go as close as possible to the lung. Whether the snail died soon or not, it was *hors de combat*, the professor saw. And he himself experienced something like physical collapse an instant after seeing the snail's condition. He was quite incapable of taking on the other snail in the same manner, and the other snail was coming after him. The professor tried to walk in a straight line away from both snails, but he weaved with fatigue and faintness. He looked behind him. The unhurt snail was thirty feet away. The wounded snail faced him, but was motionless, half in and half out of its shell, suffering in silence some agony of asphyxiation. Professor Clavering walked on.

Quite by accident, just as it was growing dark, he came upon his field of rocks. Among them he took shelter for the second time. The snail's snout probed the trench in which he lay, but he could not quite reach him. Would it not be better to remain in the trench tomorrow, to hope for rain for water? He fell asleep before he could come to any decision.

Again, when the professor awakened at dawn, the snail had departed. His hands throbbed. Their palms were encrusted with dried blood and sand. He thought it wise to go to the sea and wash them in salt water.

The giant snail lay between him and the sea, and at his approach, the snail very slowly began to creep toward him. Professor Clavering made a wobbling detour and continued on his way toward the water. He dipped his hands and moved them rapidly back and forth, at last lifted water to his face, longed to wet his dry mouth, warned himself that he should not, and yielded anyway, spitting out the water almost at once. Land snails hated salt and could be killed by salt crystals. The professor angrily flung handfuls of water at the snail's face. The snail only lifted its head higher, out of the professor's range. Its form was slender now, and it had, oddly, the grace of a horned gazelle, of some animal of the deer family. The snail lowered its snout, and the professor trudged away, but not quickly enough: the snail came down on his shoulder and the suctorial mouth clamped.

The professor screamed. *My God*, he thought, as a piece of his shirt, a piece of flesh and possibly bone was torn from his left shoulder, *why was I such an ass as to linger?* The snail's weight pushed him under, but it was shallow here, and he struggled to his feet and walked toward the land. Blood streamed hotly down his side. He could not bear to look at his shoulder to see what had happened, and would not have been surprised if his left arm had dropped off in the next instant. The professor walked on aimlessly in shallow water near the land. He was still going faster than the snail.

Then he lifted his eyes to the empty horizon, and saw a dark spot in the water in the mid-distance. He stopped, wondering if it were real or a trick of his eyes: but now he made out the double body of a catamaran, and he thought he saw Dr. Stead's straw hat. They had come from the Matusas!

"Hello!" the professor was shocked at the hoarseness, the feebleness of his voice. Not a chance that he had been heard.

But with hope now, the professor's strength increased. He headed for a little beach—not his beach, a smaller one—and when he got there he stood in its centre, his good arm raised, and shouted, "Dr. *Stead!* This way!—On the beach!" He could definitely see Dr. Stead's hat and four dark heads.

There was no answering shout. Professor Clavering could not tell if they had heard him or not. And the accursed snail was only thirty feet away now! He'd lost his hatchet, he realized. And the camera that had been under water with him was now ruined, and so were the two pictures in it. No matter. He would live.

"*Here!*" he shouted, again lifting his arm.

The natives heard this. Suddenly all heads in the catamaran turned to him.

Dr. Stead pointed to him and gesticulated, and dimly Professor

Clavering heard the good doctor urging the boatman to make for the shore. He saw Dr. Stead half stand up in the catamaran.

The natives gave a whoop—at first Professor Clavering thought it a whoop of joy, or of recognition, but almost at once a wild swing of the sail, a splash of a couple of oars, told him that the natives were trying to change their course.

Pebbles crackled. The snail was near. And this of course was what the natives had seen—the giant snail.

"*Please—Here!*" the professor screamed. He plunged again into the water. "*Please!*"

Dr. Stead was trying, that the professor could see. But the natives were rowing, paddling with hands even, and their sail was carrying them obliquely away.

The snail made a splash as it entered the sea. To drown or to be eaten alive? The professor wondered. He was waist-deep when he stumbled, waist-deep but head under when the snail crashed down upon him, and he realized as the thousands of pairs of teeth began to gnaw at his back, that his fate was both to drown and to be chewed to death.

The activity and rhythms of riding dominate several poems and songs of the supernatural, one of the most famous of which is "The Erl-King" by JOHANN WOLFGANG VON GOETHE *(1749—1843), author of the great German poem-drama, Faust. "The Erl-King," subject of at least one art song, probably inspired "The Demon of the Gibbet" by Fitz-James O'Brien, but also note Bürger's "Lenore" (both included in this volume).*

The Erl-King

BY JOHANN WOLFGANG VON GOETHE

Who spurs his steed so late this night?
A man whose son is sick with fright.
He hugs his child to keep him warm
But can't outride the fearful storm.

"Why do you shiver, son, and cry?"
"Because the Erl-King's drawing nigh—
I see his shroud. I hear him moan."
"'Tis but the fog—we ride alone."

*"O little child, come ride with me.
We'll greet my mother merrily.
She'll pick you flowers, and present bring,
And dress you like a little king."*

"O, father, help! Do you not know
The Erl-King's voice that whispers low?"
"O, rest my son. O, peace, my child—
'Tis but the wind that blows so wild."

*"O, little child, let's ride away.
With you my daughters wish to play.
They'll give you gifts that you may keep.
They'll dance. They'll sing so you may sleep."*

"O, father, help! O, can't you see
The Erl-King's daughters beckon me?"
"My son, forget these idle fears—
You see the willow weep its tears."

*"O, little child, I love you so.
That I will never let you go."*
"O, father, help, or I'll take flight!
The Erl-King's clutch is cold and tight!"

The shivering rider hugs his son,
Then spurs his steed into a run
That brings them home. The father cries,
For in his arms his baby dies.

English adaptation by Marvin Kaye

The legend of the imp in a bottle is said to be traceable to the folklore of remote German villages from the eighteenth and nineteenth centuries. Richard John Smith, actor and stage manager, turned the myth into a stage play, The Bottle Imp, *produced in 1828, but he based his theatre piece on a literary reworking of the same theme published in 1826 (date approximate) and variously attributed to La Motte Fouqué and Johann Karl August Musäus.* ROBERT LOUIS STEVENSON, *renowned author of* Treasure Island, Doctor Jekyll and Mr. Hyde *and* The Body Snatcher, *saw the Smith stage play and decided to create his own idiosyncratic version of the plot. He set his story in his beloved South Seas, and here it is.*

The Bottle Imp

BY ROBERT LOUIS STEVENSON

There was a man of the island of Hawaii, whom I shall call Keawe; for the truth is, he still lives, and his name must be kept secret; but the place of his birth was not far from Honaunau, where the bones of Keawe the Great lie hidden in a cave. The man was poor, brave, and active; he could read and write like a schoolmaster; he was a first-rate mariner besides, sailed for some time in the island steamers, and steered a whaleboat on the Kamakua coast. At length it came in Keawe's mind to have a sight of the great world and foreign cities, and he shipped on a vessel bound to San Francisco.

This is a fine town, with a fine harbour, and rich people uncountable; and, in particular there is one hill which is covered with palaces. Upon this hill Keawe was one day taking a walk, with his pocket full of money, viewing the great houses upon either hand with pleasure. "What fine houses there are!" he was thinking, "and how happy must these people be who dwell in them, and take no care for the morrow!" The thought was in his mind when he came abreast of a house that was smaller than some others, but all finished and beautiful like a toy; the steps of that house shone like silver, and the borders of the garden bloomed like garlands, and the windows were bright like diamonds; and Keawe stopped and wondered at the excellence of all he saw. So stopping, he was aware of a man that looked forth upon him through a window, so clear that Keawe could see him as you see a fish in a pool upon the reef. The man was elderly, with a bald head and a black beard; and his face was heavy with sorrow, and he bitterly sighed. And the truth of it is, that as Keawe looked in upon the man, and the man looked out upon Keawe, each envied the other.

All of a sudden the man smiled and nodded, and beckoned Keawe to enter, and met him at the door of the house.

"This is a fine house of mine," said the man, and bitterly sighed. "Would you not care to view the chambers?"

So he led Keawe all over it, from the cellar to the roof, and there was nothing there that was not perfect of its kind, and Keawe was astonished.

"Truly," said Keawe, "this is a beautiful house; if I lived in the like of it, I should be laughing all day long. How comes it, then, that you should be sighing?"

"There is no reason," said the man, "why you should not have a house in all points similar to this, and finer, if you wish. You have some money, I suppose?"

"I have fifty dollars," said Keawe; "but a house like this will cost more than fifty dollars."

The man made a computation. "I am sorry you have no more," said he, "for it may raise you trouble in the future; but it shall be yours at fifty dollars."

"The house?" asked Keawe.

"No, not the house," replied the man; "but the bottle. For I must tell you, although I appear to you so rich and fortunate, all my fortune, and this house itself and its garden, came out of a bottle not much bigger than a pint. This is it."

And he opened a lockfast place, and took out a round-bellied bottle with a long neck; the glass of it was white like milk, with changing rainbow colours in the grain. Withinsides something obscurely moved, like a shadow and a fire.

"This is the bottle," said the man; and, when Keawe laughed, "You do not believe me?" he added. "Try, then, for yourself. See if you can break it."

So Keawe took the bottle up and dashed it on the floor till he was weary; but it jumped on the floor like a child's ball, and was not injured.

"This is a strange thing," said Keawe. "For by the touch of it, as well as by the look, the bottle should be of glass."

"Of glass it is," replied the man, sighing more heavily than ever; "but the glass of it was tempered in the flames of hell. An imp lives in it, and that is the shadow we behold there moving; or, so I suppose. If any man buy this bottle the imp is at his command; all that he desires—love, fame, money, houses like this house, ay, or a city like this city—all are his at the word uttered. Napoleon had this bottle, and by it he grew to be the king of the world; but he sold it at the last and fell. Captain Cook had this bottle, and by it he found his way to so many islands; but he too sold it, and was slain upon Hawaii. For, once it is sold, the power goes and the protection; and unless a man remain content with what he has, ill will befall him."

"And yet you talk of selling it yourself?" Keawe said.

"I have all I wish, and I am growing elderly," replied the man. "There is one thing the imp cannot do—he cannot prolong life; and it would not be fair to conceal from you there is a drawback to the bottle; for if a man dies before he sells it, he must burn in hell for ever."

"To be sure, that is a drawback and no mistake," cried Keawe. "I would not meddle with the thing. I can do without a house, thank God; but there is one thing I could not be doing with one particle, and that is to be damned."

"Dear me, you must not run away with things," returned the man. "All you have to do is to use the power of the imp in moderation, and then sell it to someone else, as I do to you, and finish your life in comfort."

"Well, I observe two things," said Keawe. "All the time you keep sighing like a maid in love—that is one; and for the other, you sell this bottle very cheap."

"I have told you already why I sigh," said the man. "It is because I fear my health is breaking up; and, as you said yourself, to die and go to the devil is a pity for anyone. As for why I sell so cheap, I must explain to you there is a peculiarity about the bottle. Long ago, when the devil brought it first upon earth, it was extremely expensive, and was sold first of all to Prester John for many millions of dollars; but it cannot be sold at all, unless sold at a loss. If you sell it for as much as you paid for it, back it comes to you again like a homing pigeon. It follows that the price has kept falling in these centuries, and the bottle is now remarkably cheap. I bought it myself from one of my great neighbours on this hill, and the price I paid was only ninety dollars. I could sell for as high as eighty-nine dollars and ninety-nine cents, but not a penny dearer, or back the thing must come to me. Now, about this there are two bothers. First, when you offer a bottle so singular for eighty-odd dollars, people suppose you to be jesting. And second—but there is no hurry about that—and I need not go into it. Only remember it must be coined money that you sell it for."

"How am I to know that this is all true?" asked Keawe.

"Some of it you can try at once," replied the man. "Give me your fifty dollars, take the bottle, and wish your fifty dollars back into your pocket. If that does not happen, I pledge you my honour I will cry off the bargain and restore your money."

"You are not deceiving me?" said Keawe.

The man bound himself with a great oath.

"Well, I will risk that much," said Keawe, "for that can do no harm," and he paid over his money to the man, and the man handed him the bottle.

"Imp of the bottle," said Keawe, "I want my fifty dollars back." And sure enough, he had scarce said the word before his pocket was as heavy as ever.

"To be sure this is a wonderful bottle," said Keawe.

"And now good-morning to you, my fine fellow, and the devil go with you for me," said the man.

"Hold on," said Keawe, "I don't want any more of this fun. Here, take your bottle back."

"You have bought it for less than I paid for it," replied the man, rubbing his hands. "It is yours now; and, for my part, I am only concerned to see the back of you." And with that he rang for his Chinese servant, and had Keawe shown out of the house.

Now, when Keawe was in the street, with the bottle under his arm, he began to think. "If all is true about this bottle, I may have made a losing bargain," thinks he. "But perhaps the man was only fooling me." The first thing he did was to count his money; the sum was exact—forty-nine dollars American money, and one Chili piece. "That looks like the truth," said Keawe. "Now I will try another part."

The streets in that part of the city were as clean as a ship's decks, and though it was noon, there were no passengers. Keawe set the bottle in the gutter and walked away. Twice he looked back, and there was the milky, round-bellied bottle where he left it. A third time he looked back and turned a corner; but he had scarce done so, when something knocked upon his elbow, and behold! it was the long neck sticking up; and as for the round belly, it was jammed into the pocket of his pilot-coat.

"And that looks like the truth," said Keawe.

The next thing he did was to buy a corkscrew in a shop, and go apart in a secret place in the fields. And there he tried to draw the cork, but as often as he put the screw in, out it came again, and the cork was as whole as ever.

"This is some new sort of cork," said Keawe, and all at once he began to shake and sweat, for he was afraid of that bottle.

On his way back to the port-side he saw a shop where a man sold shells and clubs from the wild islands, old heathen deities, old coined money, pictures from China and Japan, and all manner of things that sailors bring in their sea-chest. And here he had an idea. So he went in and offered the bottle for a hundred dollars. The man of the shop laughed at him at first, and offered him five; but, indeed, it was a curious bottle, such glass was never blown in any human glass-works, so prettily the colours shone under the milky way, and so strangely the shadow hovered in the midst; so, after he had disputed a while after the manner of his kind, the shopman gave Keawe sixty silver dollars for the thing and set it on a shelf in the midst of his window.

"Now," said Keawe, "I have sold that for sixty which I bought for fifty—or, to say truth, a little less, because one of my dollars was from Chili. Now I shall know the truth upon another point."

So he went back on board his ship, and when he opened his chest, there was the bottle, which had come more quickly than himself. Now Keawe had a mate on board whose name was Lopaka.

"What ails you," said Lopaka, "that you stare in your chest?"

They were alone in the ship's forecastle, and Keawe bound him to secrecy, and told all.

"This is a very strange affair," said Lopaka; "and I fear you will be in trouble about this bottle. But there is one point very clear—that you are sure of the trouble, and you had better have the profit in the bargain. Make up your mind what you want with it; give the order, and it is done as you desire, I will buy the bottle myself; for I have an idea of my own to get a schooner, and go trading through the islands."

"That is not my idea," said Keawe; "but to have a beautiful house and garden on the Kona Coast, where I was born, the sun shining in at the door, flowers in the garden, glass in the windows, pictures on the walls, and toys and fine carpets on the tables, for all the world like the house I was in this day—only a storey higher, and with balconies all about like the King's palace; and to live there without care and make merry with my friends and relatives."

"Well," said Lopaka, "let us carry it back with us to Hawaii; and if all comes true as you suppose, I will buy the bottle, as I said, and ask a schooner."

Upon that they were agreed, and it was not long before the ship returned to Honolulu, carrying Keawe and Lopaka, and the bottle. They were scarce come ashore when they met a friend upon the beach, who began at once to condole with Keawe.

"I do not know what I am to be condoled about," said Keawe.

"Is it possible you have not heard," said the friend, "your uncle—that good old man—is dead, and your cousin—that beautiful boy—was drowned at sea?"

Keawe was filled with sorrow, and, beginning to weep and to lament, he forgot about the bottle. But Lopaka was thinking to himself, and presently, when Keawe's grief was a little abated, "I have been thinking," said Lopaka, "had not your uncle lands in Hawaii, in the district of Kaü?"

"No," said Keawe, "not in Kaü: they are on the mountain side— a little be-south Kookena."

"These lands will now be yours?" asked Lopaka.

"And so they will," says Keawe, and began again to lament for his relatives.

"No," said Lopaka, "do not lament at present. I have a thought in my mind. How if this should be the doing of the bottle? For here is the place ready for your house."

"If this be so," cried Keawe, "it is a very ill way to serve me by killing my relatives. But it may be, indeed; for it was in just such a station that I saw the house with my mind's eye."

"The house, however, is not yet built," said Lopaka.

"No, nor like to be!" said Keawe; "for though my uncle has some coffee and ava and bananas, it will not be more than will keep me in comfort; and the rest of that land is the black lava."

"Let us go to the lawyer," said Lopaka; "I have still this idea in my mind."

Now, when they came to the lawyer's it appeared Keawe's uncle had grown monstrous rich in the last days, and there was a fund of money.

"And here is the money for the house!" cried Lopaka.

"If you are thinking of a new house," said the lawyer, "here is the card of a new architect of whom they tell me great things."

"Better and better!" cried Lopaka. "Here is all made plain for us. Let us continue to obey orders."

So they went to the architect, and he had drawings of houses on his table.

"You want something out of the way," said the architect. "How do you like this?" and he handed a drawing to Keawe.

Now, when Keawe set eyes on the drawing, he cried out aloud, for it was the picture of his thought exactly drawn.

"I am in for this house," thought he. "Little as I like the way it comes to me, I am in for it now, and I may as well take the good along with the evil."

So he told the architect all that he wished, and how he would have that house furnished, and about the pictures on the wall and the knick-knacks on the tables; and he asked the man plainly for how much he would undertake the whole affair.

The architect put many questions, and took his pen and made a computation; and when he had done he named the very sum that Keawe had inherited.

Lopaka and Keawe looked at one another and nodded.

"It is quite clear," thought Keawe, "that I am to have this house, whether or no. It comes from the devil, and I fear I will get little good by that; and of one thing I am sure, I will make no more wishes as long as I have this bottle. But with the house I am saddled, and I may as well take the good along with the evil."

So he made his terms with the architect, and they signed a paper; and Keawe and Lopaka took ship again and sailed to Australia; for it was concluded between them they should not interfere at all, but leave the architect and the bottle imp to build and to adorn the house at their own pleasure.

The voyage was a good voyage, only all the time Keawe was holding in his breath, for he had sworn he would utter no more wishes, and take no more favours, from the devil. The time was up when they got back. The architect told them that the house was ready, and Keawe and Lopaka took a passage in the *Hall*, and went down Kona way to view the house, and see if all had been done fitly according to the thought that was in Keawe's mind.

Now, the house stood on the mountain side, visible to ships. Above, the forest ran up into the clouds of rain; below, the black lava fell in cliffs, where the kings of old lay buried. A garden bloomed about the house with every hue of flowers; and there was an orchard of papaya on the one hand and an orchard of bread-fruit on the other, and right in front, towards the sea, a ship's mast had been rigged up and bore a flag. As for the house, it was three stories high, with great chambers and broad balconies on each. The windows were of glass, so excellent that it was as clear as water and as bright as day. All manner of furniture adorned the chambers. Pictures hung upon the wall in golden frames—pictures of ships, and men fighting, and of the most beautiful women, and of singular places; nowhere in the world are there pictures of so bright a colour as those Keawe found hanging in his house. As for the knick-knacks, they were extraordinarily fine: chiming clocks and musical boxes, little men with nodding heads, books filled with pictures, weapons of price from all quarters of the world, and the most elegant puzzles to entertain the leisure of a solitary man. And as no one would care to live in such chambers, only to walk through and view them, the balconies were made so broad that a whole town might have lived upon them in delight, and Keawe knew not which to prefer, whether the back porch, where you get the land breeze and looked upon the orchards and the flowers, or the front balcony, where you could drink the wind of the sea, and look down the steep wall of the mountain and see the *Hall* going by once a week or so between Hookena and the hills of Pele, or the schooners plying up the coast for wood and ava and bananas.

When they had viewed all, Keawe and Lopaka sat on the porch.

"Well," asked Lopaka, "is it all as you designed?"

"Words cannot utter it," said Keawe. "It is better than I dreamed, and I am sick with satisfaction."

"There is but one thing to consider," said Lopaka, "all this may be quite natural, and the bottle imp have nothing whatever to say to it. If I were to buy the bottle, and got no schooner after all, I should have put my hand in the fire for nothing. I gave you my word, I know; but yet I think you would not grudge me one more proof."

"I have sworn I would take no more favours," said Keawe. "I have gone already deep enough."

"This is no favour I am thinking of," replied Lopaka. "It is only to see the imp himself. There is nothing to be gained by that, and so nothing to be ashamed of, and yet, if I once saw him, I should be sure of the whole matter. So indulge me so far, and let me see the imp; and, after that, here is the money in my hand, and I will buy it."

"There is only one thing I am afraid of," said Keawe. "The imp may be very ugly to view, and if you once set eyes upon him you might be very undesirous of the bottle."

"I am a man of my word," said Lopaka. "And here is the money betwixt us."

"Very well," replied Keawe, "I have a curiosity myself. So come, let us have one look at you, Mr. Imp."

Now as soon as that was said, the imp looked out of the bottle, and in again, swift as a lizard; and there sat Keawe and Lopaka turned to stone. The night had quite come, before either found a thought to say or voice to say it with; and then Lopaka pushed the money over and took the bottle.

"I am a man of my word," said he, "and had need to be so, or I would not touch this bottle with my foot. Well, I shall get my schooner and a dollar or two for my pocket; and then I will be rid of this devil as fast as I can. For, to tell you the plain truth, the look of him has cast me down."

"Lopaka," said Keawe, "do not you think any worse of me than you can help; I know it is night, and the roads bad, and the pass by the tombs an ill place to go by so late, but I declare since I have seen that little face, I cannot eat or sleep or pray till it is gone from me. I will give you a lantern, and a basket to put the bottle in, and any picture or fine thing in all my house that takes your fancy; and be gone at once, and go sleep at Hookena with Nahinu."

"Keawe," said Lopaka, "many a man would take this ill; above all, when I am doing you a turn so friendly, as to keep my word and buy the bottle; and for that matter, the night and the dark, and the way by the tombs, must be all tenfold more dangerous to a man with such a sin upon his conscience and such a bottle under his arm. But for my part, I am so extremely terrified myself, I have not the heart to blame you. Here I go, then; and I pray God you may be happy in your house, and I fortunate with my schooner, and both get to heaven in the end in spite of the devil and his bottle."

So Lopaka went down the mountain; and Keawe stood in his front balcony, and listened to the clink of the horses' shoes, and watched the lantern go shining down the path, and along the cliff of caves where the old dead are buried; and all the time he trembled and clasped his hands, and prayed for his friend, and gave glory to God that he himself was escaped out of that trouble.

But the next day came very brightly, and that new house of his was so delightful to behold that he forgot his terrors. One day followed another, and Keawe dwelt there in perpetual joy. He had his place on the back porch; it was there he ate and lived, and read the stories in the Honolulu newspapers; but when any one came by they would go in and view the chambers and the pictures. And the fame of the house went far and wide; it was called *Ka-Hale Nui*—the Great House—in all Kona; and sometimes the Bright House, for Keawe kept a Chinaman, who was all day dusting and furbishing; and the glass, and the gilt, and the fine stuffs, and the pictures, shone as bright as the morning. As for Keawe himself, he could not walk in the chambers without singing, his heart was so enlarged; and when ships sailed by upon the sea, he would fly his colours on the mast.

So time went by, until one day Keawe went upon a visit as far as Kailua to certain of his friends. There he was well feasted; and left as soon as he could the next morning, and rode hard, for he was impatient to behold his beautiful house; and, besides, the night then coming on was the night in which the dead of old days go abroad in the sides of Kona; and having already meddled with the devil, he was the more chary of meeting with the dead. A little beyond Honaunau, looking far ahead, he was aware of a woman bathing in the edges of the sea; and she seemed a well-grown girl, but he thought no more of it. Then he saw her white shift flutter as she put it on, and then her red holoku; and by the time he came abreast of her she was done with her toilet, and had come up from the sea, and stood by the track-side in her red holoku, and she was all freshened with the bath, and her eyes shone and were kind. Now Keawe no sooner beheld her than he drew rein.

"I thought I knew every one in this country," said he. "How comes it that I do not know you?"

"I am Kokua, daughter of Kiano," said the girl, "and I have just returned from Oahu. Who are you?"

"I will tell you who I am in a little," said Keawe, dismounting from his horse, "but not now. For I have a thought in my mind, and if you knew who I was, you might have heard of me, and would not give me a true answer. But tell me, first of all, one thing: are you married?"

At this Kokua laughed out loud. "It is you who ask questions," she said. "Are you married yourself?"

"Indeed, Kokua, I am not," replied Keawe, "and never thought to be until this hour. But here is the plain truth. I have met you here at the roadside, and I saw your eyes, which are like the stars, and my heart went to you as swift as a bird. And so now, if you want none of me, say so, and I will go on to my own place; but if you think me no worse than any other young man, say so, too, and I will turn aside to your father's for the night, and to-morrow I will talk with the good man."

Kokua said never a word, but she looked at the sea and laughed.

"Kokua," said Keawe, "if you say nothing, I will take that for the good answer; so let us be stepping to your father's door."

She went on ahead of him, still without speech; only sometimes she glanced back and glanced away again, and she kept the strings of her hat in her mouth.

Now, when they had come to the door, Kiano came out on his veranda, and cried out and welcomed Keawe by name. At that the girl looked over, for the fame of the great house had come to her ears; and, to be sure, it was a great temptation. All that evening they were very merry together; and the girl was as bold as brass under the eyes of her parents, and made a mark of Keawe, for she had a quick wit. The next day he had a word with Kiano, and found the girl alone.

"Kokua," said he, "you made a mark of me all the evening; and it is still time to bid me go. I would not tell you who I was, because I have so fine a house, and I feared you would think too much of that house and too little of the man that loves you. Now you know all, and if you wish to have seen the last of me, say so at once."

"No," said Kokua, but this time she did not laugh, nor did Keawe ask for more.

This was the wooing of Keawe; things had gone quickly, but so an arrow goes, and the ball of a rifle swifter still, and yet both may strike the target. Things had gone fast, but they had gone far also, and the thought of Keawe rang in the maiden's head; she heard his voice in the breach of the surf upon the lava, and for this young man that she had seen but twice she would have left father and mother and her native islands. As for Keawe himself, his horse flew up the path of the mountain under the cliff of tombs, and the sound of the hoofs, and the sound of Keawe singing to himself for pleasure, echoed in the caverns of the dead. He came to the Bright House, and still he was singing. He sat and ate in the broad balcony, and the Chinaman wondered at his master, to hear how he sang between the mouthfuls. The sun went down into the sea, and the night came; and Keawe walked the balconies by lamplight, high on the mountains, and the voice of his singing startled men on ships.

"Here am I now upon my high place," he said to himself. "Life may be no better; this is the mountain top; and all shelves about me towards the worse. For the first time I will light up the chambers, and bathe in my fine bath with the hot water and the cold, and sleep above in the bed of my bridal chamber."

So the Chinaman had word, and he must rise from sleep and light the furnaces; and as he walked below, beside the boilers, he heard his master singing and rejoicing above him in the lighted chambers. When the water began to be hot the Chinaman cried to his master: and Keawe went into the bathroom; and the Chinaman heard him sing as he filled the marble basin; and heard him sing, and the singing broken, as he undressed; until of a sudden, the song ceased. The Chinaman listened, and listened; he called up the house to Keawe to ask if all were well, and Keawe answered him "Yes," and bade him go to bed; but there was no more singing in the Bright House; and all night long the Chinaman heard his master's feet go round and round the balconies without repose.

Now, the truth of it was this: as Keawe undressed for his bath, he spied upon his flesh a patch like a patch of lichen on a rock, and it was then that he stopped singing. For he knew the likeness of that patch, and knew that he was fallen in the Chinese Evil.[1]

Now, it is a sad thing for any man to fall into this sickness. And it would be a sad thing for anyone to leave a house so beautiful and so commodious, and depart from all his friends to the north coast of Molokai, between the mighty cliff and the sea-breakers. But what was that to the case of the man Keawe, he who had met his love but yesterday and won her but that morning, and now saw all his hopes break, in a moment, like a piece of glass?

A while he sat upon the edge of the bath, then sprang, with a cry, and ran outside; and to and fro, to and fro, along the balcony, like one despairing.

"Very willingly could I leave Hawaii, the home of my fathers,"

[1]Leprosy.

Keawe was thinking. "Very lightly could I leave my house, the high-placed, the many-windowed, here upon the mountains. Very bravely could I go to Molokai, to Kalaupapa by the cliffs, to live with the smitten and to sleep there, far from my fathers. But what wrong have I done, what sin lies upon my soul, that I should have encountered Kokua coming cool from the seawater in the evening? Kokua, the soul ensnarer! Kokua, the light of my life! Her may I never wed, her may I look upon no longer, her may I no more handle with my loving hand; and it is for this, it is for you, O Kokua! that I pour my lamentations!"

Now you are to observe what sort of a man Keawe was, for he might have dwelt there in the Bright House for years, and no one been the wiser of his sickness; but he reckoned nothing of that, if he must lose Kokua. And again he might have wed Kokua even as he was; and so many would have done, because they have the souls of pigs; but Keawe loved the maid manfully, and he would do her no hurt and bring her in no danger.

A little beyond the midst of the night, there came in his mind the recollection of that bottle. He went round to the back porch, and called to memory the day when the devil had looked forth; and at the thought ice ran in his veins.

"A dreadful thing is in the bottle," thought Keawe, "and dreadful is the imp, and it is a dreadful thing to risk the flames of hell. But what other hope have I to cure my sickness or to wed Kokua? What!" he thought, "would I beard the devil once, only to get me a house, and not face him again to win Kokua?"

Thereupon he called to mind it was the next day the *Hall* went by on her return to Honolulu. "There must I go first," he thought, "and see Lopaka. For the best hope that I have now is to find that same bottle I was so pleased to be rid of."

Never a wink could he sleep; the food stuck in his throat; but he sent a letter to Kiano, and about the time when the steamer would be coming, rode down beside the cliff of the tombs. It rained; his horse went heavily; he looked up at the black mouths of the caves, and he envied the dead that slept there and were done with trouble; and called to mind how he had galloped by the day before, and was astonished. So he came down to Hookena, and there was all the country gathered for the steamer as usual. In the shed before the store they sat and jested and passed the news; but there was no matter of speech in Keawe's bosom, and he sat in their midst and looked without on the rain falling on the houses, and the surf beating among the rocks, and the sighs arose in his throat.

"Keawe of the Bright House is out of spirits," said one to another. Indeed, and so he was, and little wonder.

Then the *Hall* came, and the whale-boat carried him on board. The after-part of the ship was full of Haoles[2]— who had been to visit the volcano, as their custom is; and the midst was crowded with Kanakas, and the forepart with wild bulls from Hilo and horses from Kaü; but Keawe sat apart from all in his sorrow, and watched for the house of Kiano. There it sat low upon the shore in the black rocks, and shaded by the cocoa-palms, and there by the door was a red holoku, no greater than a fly, and going to and fro with a fly's busyness. "Ah, queen of my heart," he cried, "I'll venture my dear soul to win you!"

Soon after, darkness fell and the cabins were lit up, and the Haoles sat and played at the cards and drank whisky as their custom is; but Keawe walked the deck all night; and all the next day, as they steamed under the lee of Maui or of Molokai, he was still pacing to and fro like a wild animal in a menagerie.

Towards evening they passed Diamond Head, and came to the pier of Honolulu. Keawe stepped out among the crowd and began to ask for Lopaka. It seemed he had become the owner of a schooner—none better in the islands—and was gone upon an adventure as far as Pola-Pola or Kahiki; so there was no help to be looked for from Lopaka. Keawe called to mind a friend of his, a lawyer in the town (I must not tell his name), and inquired of him. They said he was grown suddenly rich, and had a fine new house upon Waikiki shore; and this put a thought in Keawe's head, and he called a hack and drove to the lawyer's house.

The house was all brand new, and the trees in the garden no greater than walking-sticks, and the lawyer, when he came, had the air of a man well pleased.

"What can I do to serve you?" said the lawyer.

"You are a friend of Lopaka's," replied Keawe, "and Lopaka purchased from me a certain piece of goods that I thought you might enable me to trace."

The lawyer's face became very dark. "I do not profess to misunderstand you, Mr. Keawe," said he, "though this is an ugly business to be stirring in. You may be sure I know nothing, but yet I have a guess, and if you would apply in a certain quarter I

[2]Whites

think you might have news."

And he named the name of a man, which, again, I had better not repeat. So it was for days, and Keawe went from one to another, finding everywhere new clothes and carriages, and fine new houses, and men everywhere in great contentment, although, to be sure, when he hinted at his business their faces would cloud over.

"No doubt I am upon the track," thought Keawe. "These new clothes and carriages are all the gifts of the little imp, and these glad faces are the faces of men who have taken their profit and got rid of the accursed thing in safety. When I see pale cheeks and hear sighing, I shall know that I am near the bottle."

So it befell at last he was recommended to a Haole in Beritania Street. When he came to the door, about the hour of the evening meal, there were the usual marks of the new house, and the young garden, and the electric light shining in the windows; but when the owner came, a shock of hope and fear ran through Keawe; for here was a young man, white as a corpse, and black about the eyes, the hair shedding from his head, and such a look in his countenance as a man may have when he is waiting for the gallows.

"Here it is, to be sure," thought Keawe, and so with this man he noways veiled his errand. "I am come to buy the bottle," said he.

At the word, the young Haole of Beritania Street reeled against the wall.

"The bottle!" he gasped. "To buy the bottle!" Then he seemed to choke, and seizing Keawe by the arm, carried him into a room and poured out wine in two glasses.

"Here is my respects," said Keawe, who had been much about with Haoles in his time. "Yes," he added, "I am come to buy the bottle. What is the price by now?"

At that word the young man let his glass slip through his fingers, and looked upon Keawe like a ghost.

"The price," says he; "the price! You do not know the price?"

"It is for that I am asking you," returned Keawe. "But why are you so much concerned? Is there anything wrong about the price?"

"It has dropped a great deal in value since your time, Mr. Keawe," said the young man, stammering.

"Well, well, I shall have the less to pay for it," said Keawe. "How much did it cost you?"

The young man was as white as a sheet.

"Two cents," said he.

"What!" cried Keawe, "two cents? Why, then, you can only sell it for one. And he who buys it—" The words died upon Keawe's tongue; he who bought it could never sell it again, the bottle and the bottle imp must abide with him until he died, and when he died must carry him to the red end of hell.

The young man of Beritania Street fell upon his knees. "For God's sake, buy it!" he cried. "You can have all my fortune in the bargain. I was mad when I bought it at that price. I had embezzled money at my store; I was lost else; I must have gone to jail."

"Poor creature," said Keawe, "you would risk your soul upon so desperate an adventure, and to avoid the proper punishment of your own disgrace; and you think I could hesitate with love in front of me. Give me the bottle, and the change which I make sure you have all ready. Here is a five-cent piece."

It was as Keawe supposed; the young man had the change ready in a drawer; the bottle changed hands, and Keawe's fingers were no sooner clasped upon the stalk than he had breathed his wish to be a clean man. And sure enough, when he got home to his room, and stripped himself before a glass, his flesh was whole like an infant's. And here was the strange thing: he had no sooner seen this miracle than his mind was changed within him, and he cared naught for the Chinese Evil, and little enough for Kokua; and had but the one thought, that here he was bound to the bottle imp for time and for eternity, and had no better hope but to be a cinder for ever in the flames of hell. Away ahead of him he saw them blaze with his mind's eye, and his soul shrank, and darkness fell upon the light.

When Keawe came to himself a little, he was aware it was the night when the band played at the hotel. Thither he went, because he feared to be alone; and there, among happy faces, walked to and fro, and heard the tunes go up and down, and saw Berger beat the measure, and all the while he heard the flames crackle and saw the red fire burning in the bottomless pit. Of a sudden the band played *Hiki-ao-ao*; that was a song that he had sung with Kokua, and at the strain courage returned to him.

"It is done now," he thought, "and once more let me take the good along with the evil."

So it befell that he returned to Hawaii by the first steamer, and as soon as it could be managed he was wedded to Kokua, and carried her up the mountain side to the Bright House.

Now it was so with these two, that when they were together Keawe's heart was stilled; but as soon as he was alone he fell into a brooding horror, and heard the flames crackle, and saw the red fire burn in the bottomless pit. The girl, indeed, had come to him wholly; her heart leaped in her side at sight of him, her hand clung to his; and she was so fashioned, from the hair upon her head to the nails upon her toes, that none could see her without joy. She was pleasant in her nature. She had the good word always. Full of song she was, and went to and fro in the Bright House, the brightest thing in its three stories, carolling like the birds. And Keawe beheld and heard her with delight, and then must shrink upon one side, and weep and groan to think upon the price that he had paid for her; and then he must dry his eyes, and wash his face, and go and sit with her on the broad balconies, joining in her songs, and, with a sick spirit, answering her smiles.

There came a day when her feet began to be heavy and her songs more rare; and now it was not Keawe only that would weep apart, but each would sunder from the other and sit in opposite balconies with the whole width of the Bright House betwixt. Keawe was so sunk in his despair, he scarce observed the change, and was only glad he had more hours to sit alone and brood upon his destiny, and was not so frequently condemned to pull a smiling face on a sick heart. But one day, coming softly through the house, he heard the sound of a child sobbing, and there was Kokua rolling her face upon the balcony floor, and weeping like the lost.

"You do well to weep in this house, Kokua," he said. "And yet I would give the head off my body that you (at least) might have been happy."

"Happy!" she cried. "Keawe, when you lived alone in your Bright House you were the word of the island for a happy man; laughter and song were in your mouth, and your face was as bright as the sunrise. Then you wedded poor Kokua; and the good God knows what is amiss in her—but from that day you have not smiled. Oh!" she cried, "what ails me? I thought I was pretty, and I knew I loved him. What ails me, that I throw this cloud upon my husband?"

"Poor Kokua," said Keawe. He sat down by her side, and sought to take her hand; but that she plucked away. "Poor Kokua," he said again. "My poor child—my pretty. And I had thought all this while to spare you! Well, you shall know all. Then, at least, you will pity poor Keawe; then you will understand how much he loved you in the past—that he dared hell for your possession—and how much he loves you still (the poor condemned one), that he can yet call up a smile when he beholds you."

With that he told her all, even from the beginning.

"You have done this for me?" she cried. "Ah, well, then what do I care!" and she clasped and wept upon him.

"Ah, child!" said Keawe, "and yet, when I consider of the fire of hell, I care a good deal!"

"Never tell me," said she, "no man can be lost because he loved Kokua, and no other fault. I tell you, Keawe, I shall save you with these hands, or perish in your comany. What! you loved me and gave your soul, and you think I will not die to save you in return?"

"Ah, my dear, you might die a hundred times: and what difference would that make?" he cried, "except to leave me lonely till the time comes for my damnation?"

"You know nothing," said she. "I was educated in a school in Honolulu; I am no common girl. And I tell you I shall save my lover. What is this you say about a cent? But all the world is not American. In England they have a piece they call a farthing, which is about half a cent. Ah! sorrow!" she cried, "that makes it scarcely better, for the buyer must be lost, and we shall find none so brave as my Keawe! But, then, there is France; they have a small coin there which they call a centime, and these go five to the cent, or thereabout. We could not do better. Come, Keawe, let us go to the French islands; let us go to Tahiti as fast as ships can bear us. There we have four centimes, three centimes, two centimes, one centime; four possible sales to come and go on; and two of us to push the bargain. Come, my Keawe! kiss me, and banish care. Kokua will defend you."

"Gift of God!" he cried. "I cannot think that God will punish me for desiring aught so good. Be it as you will then, take me where you please: I put my life and my salvation in your hands."

Early the next day Kokua went about her preparations. She took Keawe's chest that he went with sailoring; and first she put the bottle in a corner, and then packed it with the richest of their clothes and the bravest of the knickknacks in the house. "For," said she, "we must seem to be rich folks, or who would believe in the bottle?" All the time of her preparation she was as gay as a bird; only when she looked upon Keawe the tears would spring in her eye, and she must run and kiss him. As for Keawe, a weight was off his soul; now that he had his secret shared, and some hope in front of him, he seemed like a new man, his feet went lightly on the earth, and his breath was good to him again. Yet was terror still at his elbow; and ever and again, as the wind blows out a taper, hope died in him, and he saw the flames toss and the red fire burn in hell.

It was given out in the country they were gone pleasuring in the States, which was thought a strange thing, and yet not so strange as the truth, if any could have guessed it. So they went to Honolulu in the *Hall*, and thence in the *Umatilla* to San Francisco with a crowd of Haoles, and at San Francisco took their passage by the mail brigantine, the *Tropic Bird*, for Papeete, the chief place of the French in the south islands. Thither they came, after a pleasant voyage, on a fair day of the Trade Wind, and saw the reef with the surf breaking and Motuiti with its palms, and the schooner riding withinside and the white houses of the town low down along the shore among green trees, and overhead the mountains and the clouds of Tahiti, the wise island.

It was judged the most wise to hire a house, which they did accordingly, opposite the British Consul's, to make a great parade of money, and themselves conspicuous with carriages and horses. This it was very easy to do, so long as they had the bottle in their possession; for Kokua was more bold than Keawe, and, whenever she had a mind, called on the imp for twenty or a hundred dollars. At this rate they soon grew to be remarked in the town; and the strangers from Hawaii, their riding and their driving, the fine holokus, and the rich lace of Kokua, became the matter of much talk.

They got on well after the first with the Tahiti language, which is indeed like to the Hawaiian, with a change of certain letters; and as soon as they had any freedom of speech, began to push the bottle. You are to consider it was not an easy subject to introduce; it was not easy to persuade people you are in earnest, when you offer to sell them for four centimes the spring of health and riches inexhaustible. It was necessary besides to explain the dangers of the bottle; and either people disbelieved the whole thing and laughed, or they thought the more of the darker part, became overcast with gravity, and drew away from Keawe and Kokua, as from persons who had dealings with the devil. So far from gaining ground, these two began to find they were avoided in the town; the children ran away from them screaming, a thing intolerable to Kokua; Catholics crossed themselves as they went by; and all persons began with one accord to disengage themselves from their advances.

Depression fell upon their spirits. They would sit at night in their new house, after a day's weariness, and not exchange one word, or the silence would be broken by Kokua bursting suddenly into sobs. Sometimes they would pray together; sometimes they would have the bottle out upon the floor, and sit all evening watching how the shadow hovered in the midst. At such times they would be afraid to go to rest. It was long ere slumber came to them, and, if either dozed off, it would be to wake and find the other silently weeping in the dark, or, perhaps, to wake alone, the other having fled from the house and the neighbourhood of that bottle, to pace under the bananas in the little garden, or to wander on the beach by moonlight.

One night it was so when Kokua awoke. Keawe was gone. She felt in the bed and his place was cold. Then fear fell upon her, and she sat up in bed. A little moonshine filtered through the shutters. The room was bright, and she could spy the bottle on the floor. Outside it blew high, the great trees of the avenue cried aloud, and the fallen leaves rattled in the veranda. In the midst of this Kokua was aware of another sound; whether of a beast or of a man she could scarce tell, but it was as sad as death, and cut her to the soul. Softly she arose, set the door ajar, and looked forth into the moonlit yard. There, under the bananas, lay Keawe, his mouth in the dust, and as he lay he moaned.

It was Kokua's first thought to run forward and console him; her second potently witheld her. Keawe had borne himself before his wife like a brave man; it became her little in the hour of weakness to intrude upon his shame. With the thought she drew back into the house.

"Heaven," she thought, "how careless have I been—how weak! It is he, not I, that stands in this eternal peril; it was he, not I, that took the curse upon his soul. It is for my sake, and for the love of a creature of so little worth and such poor help, that he now beholds so close to him the flames of hell—ay, and smells the smoke of it, lying without there in the wind and moonlight. Am I so dull of spirit that never till now I have surmised my duty, or have I seen it before and turned aside? But now, at least, I take up my soul in both the hands of my affection; now I say farewell to the white steps of heaven and the waiting faces of my friends. A love for a love, and let mine be equalled with Keawe's! A soul for a soul, and be it mine to perish!"

She was a deft woman with her hands, and was soon apparelled. She took in her hands the charge—the precious centimes they kept ever at their side; for this coin is little used, and they had made provision at a government office. When she was forth in the avenue clouds came on the wind, and the moon was blackened. The town slept, and she knew not whither to turn till she heard one coughing in the shadow of the trees.

"Old man," said Kokua, "what do you here abroad in the cold night?"

The old man could scarce express himself for coughing, but she made out that he was old and poor, and a stranger in the island.

"Will you do me a service?" said Kokua. "As one stranger to another, and as an old man to a young woman, will you help a daughter of Hawaii?"

"Ah," said the old man. "So you are the witch from the Eight Islands, and even my old soul you seek to entangle. But I have heard of you, and defy your wickedness."

"Sit down here," said Kokua, "and let me tell you a tale." And she told him the story of Keawe from the beginning to the end.

"And now," said she, "I am his wife, whom he bought with his soul's welfare. And what should I do? If I went to him myself and offered to buy it, he will refuse. But if you go, he will sell it eagerly; I will await you here; you will buy it for four centimes, and I will buy it again for three. And the Lord strengthen a poor girl!"

"If you meant falsely," said the old man, "I think God would strike you dead."

"He would!" cried Kokua. "Be sure He would. I could not be so treacherous; God would not suffer it."

"Give me the four centimes and await me here," said the old man.

Now, when Kokua stood alone in the street, her spirit died. The wind roared in the trees, and it seemed to her the rushing of the flames of hell; the shadows towered in the light of the street lamp, and they seemed to her the snatching hands of evil ones. If she had had the strength, she must have run away, and if she had had the breath, she must have screamed aloud; but, in truth, she could do neither, and stood and trembled in the avenue, like an affrighted child.

Then she saw the old man returning, and he had the bottle in his hand.

"I have done your bidding," said he. "I left your husband weeping like a child; to-night he will sleep easy." And he held the bottle forth.

"Before you give it me," Kokua panted, "take the good with the evil—ask to be delivered from your cough."

"I am an old man," replied the other, "and too near the gate of the grave to take a favour from the devil. But what is this? Why do you not take the bottle? Do you hesitate?"

"Not hesitate!" cried Kokua. "I am only weak. Give me a moment. It is my hand resists, my flesh shrinks back from the accursed thing. One moment only!"

The old man looked upon Kokua kindly. "Poor child!" said he, "you fear: your soul misgives you. Well, let me keep it. I am old, and can never more be happy in this world, and as for the next—"

"Give it me!" gasped Kokua. "There is your money. Do you think I am so base as that? Give me the bottle."

"God bless you, child," said the old man.

Kokua concealed the bottle under her holoku, said farewell to the old man, and walked off along the avenue, she cared not whither. For all roads were now the same to her, and led equally to hell. Sometimes she walked, and sometimes ran; sometimes she screamed out loud in the night, and sometimes lay by the wayside in the dust and wept. All that she had heard of hell came back to her; she saw the flames blaze, and she smelled the smoke, and her flesh withered on the coals.

Near day she came to her mind again, and returned to the house. It was even as the old man said—Keawe slumbered like a child. Kokua stood and gazed upon his face.

"Now, my husband," said she, "it is your turn to sleep. When you wake it will be your turn to sing and laugh. But for poor Kokua, alas! that meant no evil—for poor Kokua no more sleep, no more singing, no more delight, whether in earth or heaven."

With that she lay down in the bed by his side, and her misery was so extreme that she fell in a deep slumber instantly.

Late in the morning her husband woke her and gave her the good news. It seemed he was silly with delight, for he paid no heed to her distress, ill though she dissembled it. The words stuck in her mouth, it mattered not; Keawe did the speaking. She ate not a bite, but who was to observe it? For Keawe cleared the dish. Kokua saw and heard him, like some strange thing in a dream; there were times when she forgot or doubted, and put her hands to her brow; to know herself doomed and hear her husband babble seemed so monstrous.

All the while Keawe was eating and talking, and planning the time of their return, and thanking her for saving him and fondling her, and calling her the true helper after all. He laughed at the old man that was fool enough to buy that bottle.

"A worthy man he seemed," Keawe said. "But no one can judge by appearances. For why did the old reprobate require the bottle?"

"My husband," said Kokua humbly, "his purpose may have been good."

Keawe laughed like an angry man.

"Fiddle-de-dee!" cried Keawe. "An old rogue, I tell you; and an old ass to boot. For the bottle was hard enough to sell at four centimes; and at three it will be quite impossible. The margin is not broad enough, the thing begins to smell of scorching—brrr!" said he, and shuddered. "It is true I bought it myself at a cent, when I knew not there were smaller coins. I was a fool for my pains; there will never be found another, and whoever has that bottle now will carry it to the pit."

"O my husband!" said Kokua. "Is it not a terrible thing to save oneself by the eternal ruin of another? It seems to me I could not laugh. I would be humbled. I would be filled with melancholy. I would pray for the poor holder."

Then Keawe, because he felt the truth of what she said, grew the more angry. "Heighty-teighty!" cried he. "You may be filled with melancholy if you please. It is not the mind of a good wife. If you thought at all of me, you would sit shamed."

Thereupon he went out, and Kokua was alone.

What chance had she to sell that bottle at two centimes? None, she perceived. And if she had any, here was her husband hurrying her away to a country where there was nothing lower than a cent. And here—on the morrow of her sacrifice—was her husband leaving her and blaming her.

She would not even try to profit by what time she had, but sat in the house, and now had the bottle out and viewed it with unutterable fear, and now, with loathing, hid it out of sight.

By-and-by Keawe came back, and would have her take a drive.

"My husband, I am ill," she said. "I am out of heart. Excuse me, I can take no pleasure."

Then was Keawe more wroth than ever. With her, because he

thought she was brooding over the case of the old man; and with himself, because he thought she was right and was ashamed to be so happy.

"This is your truth," cried he, "and this your affection! Your husband is just saved from eternal ruin, which he encountered for the love of you—and you can take no pleasure! Kokua, you have a disloyal heart."

He went forth again furious, and wandered in the town all day. He met friends, and drank with them; they hired a carriage and drove into the country, and there drank again. All the time Keawe was ill at ease, because he was taking this pastime while his wife was sad, and because he knew in his heart that she was more right than he; and the knowledge made him drink the deeper.

Now there was an old brutal Haole drinking with him, one that had been a boatswain of a whaler—a runaway, a digger in gold mines, a convict in prisons. He had a low mind and a foul mouth; he loved to drink and to see others drunken; and he pressed the glass upon Keawe. Soon there was no more money in the company.

"Here, you!" says the boatswain, "you are rich, you have been always saying. You have a bottle or some foolishness."

"Yes," says Keawe, "I am rich; I will go back and get some money from my wife, who keeps it."

"That's a bad idea, mate," said the boatswain. "Never you trust a petticoat with dollars. They're all as false as water; you keep an eye on her."

Now this word stuck in Keawe's mind; for he was muddled with what he had been drinking.

"I should not wonder but she was false, indeed," thought he. "Why else should she be so cast down at my release? But I will show her I am not the man to be fooled. I will catch her in the act."

Accordingly, when they were back in town, Keawe bade the boatswain wait for him at the corner by the old calaboose, and went forward up the avenue alone to the door of his house. The night had come again; there was a light within, but never a sound; and Keawe crept about the corner, opened the back door softly, and looked in.

There was Kokua on the floor, the lamp at her side; before her was a milk-white bottle, with a round belly and a long neck; and as she viewed it, Kokua wrung her hands.

A long time Keawe stood and looked in the doorway. At first

he was struck stupid; and then fear fell upon him that the bargain had been made amiss, and the bottle had come back to him as it came at San Francisco; and at that his knees were loosened, and the fumes of the wine departed from his head like mists off a river in the morning. And then he had another thought; and it was a strange one, that made his cheeks to burn.

"I must make sure of this," thought he.

So he closed the door, and went softly round the corner again, and then came noisily in, as though he were but now returned. And, lo! by the time he opened the front door no bottle was to be seen; and Kokua sat in a chair and started up like one awakened out of sleep.

"I have been drinking all day and making merry," said Keawe. "I have been with good companions, and now I only came back for money, and return to drink and carouse with them again."

Both his face and voice were as stern as judgment, but Kokua was too troubled to observe.

"You do well to use your own, my husband," said she, and her words trembled.

"Oh, I do well in all things," said Keawe, and he went straight to the chest and took out money. But he looked besides in the corner where they kept the bottle, and there was no bottle there.

At that the chest heaved upon the floor like a sea-billow, and the house spun about him like a wreath of smoke, for he saw she was lost now, and there was no escape. "It is what I feared," he thought. "It is she who has bought it."

And then he came to himself a little and rose up; but the sweat streamed on his face as thick as the rain and as cold as the well-water.

"Kokua," said he, "I said to you to-day what ill became me. Now I return to house with my jolly companions," and at that he laughed a little quietly. "I will take more pleasure in the cup if you forgive me."

She clasped his knees in a moment, she kissed his knees with flowing tears.

"Oh," she cried, "I ask but a kind word!"

"Let us never one think hardly of the other," said Keawe, and was gone out of the house.

Now, the money that Keawe had taken was only some of that store of centime pieces they had laid in at their arrival. It was very sure he had no mind to be drinking. His wife had given her soul for him, now he must give his for hers; no other thought was in the world with him.

At the corner, by the old calaboose, there was the boatswain waiting.

"My wife has the bottle," said Keawe, "and, unless you help me to recover it, there can be no more money and no more liquor tonight."

"You do not mean to say you are serious about that bottle?" cried the boatswain.

"There is the lamp," said Keawe. "Do I look as if I was jesting?"

"That is so," said the boatswain. "You look as serious as a ghost."

"Well, then," said Keawe, "here are two centimes; you just go to my wife in the house, and offer her these for the bottle, which (if I am not much mistaken) she will give you instantly. Bring it to me here, and I will buy it back from you for one; for that is the law with this bottle, that it still must be sold for a less sum. But whatever you do, never breathe a word to her that you have come from me."

"Mate, I wonder are you making a fool of me?" asked the boatswain.

"It will do you no harm if I am," returned Keawe.

"That is so, mate," said the boatswain.

"And if you doubt me," added Keawe, "you can try. As soon as you are clear of the house, wish to have your pocket full of money, or a bottle of the best rum, or what you please, and you will see the virtue of the thing."

"Very well, Keawe," says the boatswain. "I will try; but if you are having your fun out of me, I will take my fun out of you with a belaying-pin."

So the whaler-man went off up the avenue; and Keawe stood and waited. It was near the same spot where Kokua had waited the night before; but Keawe was more resolved, and never faltered in his purpose; only his soul was bitter with despair.

It seemed a long time he had to wait before he heard a voice singing in the darkness of the avenue. He knew the voice to be the boatswain's; but it was strange how drunken it appeared upon a sudden.

Next the man himself came stumbling into the light of the lamp. He had the devil's bottle buttoned in his coat; another bottle was in his hand; and even as he came in view he raised it to his mouth and drank.

"You have it," said Keawe. "I see that."

"Hands off!" cried the boatswain, jumping back. "Take a step near me, and I'll smash your mouth. You thought you could make a catspaw of me, did you?"

"What do you mean?" cried Keawe.

"Mean?" cried the boatswain. "This is a pretty good bottle, this is; that's what I mean. How I got it for two centimes I can't make out; but I am sure you shan't have it for one."

"You mean you won't sell?" gasped Keawe.

"No, sir," cried the boatswain. "But I'll give you a drink of the rum, if you like."

"I tell you," said Keawe, "the man who has that bottle goes to hell."

"I reckon I'm going anyway," returned the sailor; "and this bottle's the best thing to go with I've struck yet. No, sir!" he cried again, "this is my bottle now, and you can go and fish for another."

"Can this be true?" Keawe cried. "For your own sake, I beseech you, sell it me!"

"I don't value any of your talk," replied the boatswain. "You thought I was a flat, now you see I'm not; and there's an end. If you won't have a swallow of the rum, I'll have one myself. Here's your health, and goodnight to you!"

So off he went down the avenue towards town, and there goes the bottle out of the story.

But Keawe ran to Kokua light as the wind; and great was their joy that night; and great, since then, has been the peace of all their days in the Bright House.

Humor and fantasy ought to be natural companions, but true wit is as sadly lacking in the genre as it is in contemporary "serious" fiction. One happy exception is the Ebenezum series of CRAIG SHAW GARDNER, *a personable young New England bookdealer who moonlights as a deliciously mad fantasist. The sorcerer Ebenezum and his "Archie Goodwin" amanuensis, the apprentice Wunt, have a knack for getting into scrapes with ghosts, demons, dragons, witches and other terrifying critters. Fortunately, Ebenezum is a magician of great power. Unfortunately, he is allergic to magic; it makes him sneeze, which louses up his most potent spells. For those of you who know the Ebenezum tales and wonder how he first acquired his occupational hazard, read on. "A Malady of Magicks" is the first of the series, and it tells you. It won Craig the honor of appearing in the DAW anthology, Year's Best Fantasy Stories (1978), edited by Lin Carter.*

A Malady of Magicks

BY CRAIG SHAW GARDNER

(I)

"A good magician always watches his feet. It also does no harm to be constantly aware of the nearest exit."
> —from *The Teachings of Ebenezum* Vol. 3.

May I state now, once and for all, that I did not see the bucket.

My master, the wizard Ebenezum, was expounding at great length to a potential client concerning his abilities to sniff out sorcery wherever it might occur. He was also carefully avoiding any mention of the affliction that allowed him to do this so well.

I was crossing the room with a full load of firewood. The last of it, I might add, which we could ill afford to burn, save that, in those days and that place, the best way to attract a client was to pretend that you didn't need one. Thus the roaring fire on a day only moderately cool. And Ebenezum, who filled the room with grand gestures while speaking smoothly from beneath his great gray beard. Like any magician worth his runes, he could easily talk a customer into enchantment before any magicks were expended. Such an expert was he in fact, that I got caught up in the conversation and did not watch my feet.

Curse that bucket anyways! Down I went, spilling firewood across the table between the wizard and his client, neatly breaking his spell.

Ebenezum turned on me with eyes full of cosmic anger, another trick he was all too good at.

"See!" the client shrieked in a high voice. "I am cursed! It follows me wherever I go!" He hugged short arms around his pudgy body.

The wizard turned back to him, anger replaced by a smile so warm it would melt the ice on Midwinter Eve. "You don't know my apprentice," he said softly. "Cursed, no. Clumsy, yes."

Pudgy's hands came back to the table, "B-but . . ."

"The only curse here is when I signed a seven-year contract for his services." The magician smiled broadly. "I assure you, no magic is involved."

"If you say so." The client managed to smile. I picked myself off the bench and smiled back. Just joy and happiness all around.

"I feel I can trust you," the client continued. "Will you look at my barn?"

"Certainly." The magician managed to cough gently without losing his smile.

The client, who had obviously dealt with artists long enough to know what such coughs meant, reached within the blue silk sash that circled his ample waist and pulled out a small purse. It thunked most satisfyingly when he dropped it on the table.

The client shrugged. "My crops have been good . . ." He frowned. "Till late."

"They shall be good again. When shall we—"

"As soon as possible. Perhaps tomorrow, at dawn?"

The wizard's face did not betray the slightest agony at the mention of so early an hour, a fact which conclusively proved our dire straits.

"Dawn then, good Samus," he said. They bowed, and the gentleman farmer took his leave.

"Put out that fire," were the wizard's first words to me. He scratched his neck below the beard. "Interesting. Your fall shortened our negotiations considerably—yet favorably. Mayhaps there is a way we can even get your clumsiness to work for you. We'll make a wizard of you yet!" He clapped me on the shoulder. "I have to check my scrolls. Clean up in here. We start work all too early on the morrow."

(II)

"Illusions can be created in multitudinous forms, and vary in effectiveness to the degree your customer wishes to be fooled."
—*The Teaching of Ebenezum*, Vol. 12

"If my calculations be right," Ebenezum said with a tug at his beard, "the farm should be over the next rise."

I silently thanked all the gods, few though they were, who looked kindly on sorcerers' assistants. Ebenezum had loaded such a variety of magical paraphernalia into the pack on my back that I was near to doubled over with the weight. Only my stout oak staff kept my head from reaching my feet, and even that sturdy wood seemed to bend considerably every time I leaned against it.

Ebenezum studied my discomfort for a moment, then raised his hand in the way he does when on the verge of a great pronouncement.

"Remember, Wunt," he said. "The total sorcerer must develop both mind *and* body." He waved me to follow him with an ease of motion made possible by the fact that he carried nothing at all.

We reached the top of the hill. There was the farm, laid out before us in the full colors of dawn. The light hurt my eyes.

"Come, come, good Wunt!" Ebenezum called as he started down the hill. "Granted that the hour is ungodly. Still, this is a small job at best, finished before the end of morning." He tugged his beard again. "What could it be? Some crops trampled, a few animals loose from their pens? A minor elemental, at worst!"

The beard-fingers came free to wave in the air. "There is, of course, the matter of the dead sow. In my opinion, however, that turn of events was as much the sow's fault as the elemental's. In all, an easy day's work!"

Despite my back, I must admit that it cheered me to see Ebenezum once again embarking on a professional errand. A few mystic passes, a quick spell, and the sprite would be on its way.

Even Ebenezum should be able to manage that before his malady overtook him. And that meant money in the coffers, not to mention an opportunity to reconfirm a reputation.

There were certain malicious types in the local mystical community who claimed that Ebenezum's wizardry was done. Just jealous of his great power, they were. Certainly, the outcome of Ebenezum's recent battle with that major demon of the third Netherhell had had its unfortunate side. The demon had, of course, been removed. Quite possibly destroyed. But the highly charged struggle had had its effect on the wizard as well. He had emerged from his trance to discover that he had developed an aversion to all things sorcerous. In fact, any great concentration of magicks would cause Ebenezum to go into an uncontrollable fit of sneezing.

A misfortune of this type might have totally defeated a lesser mage, but not Ebenezum. He had immediately set to discovering strategies in which he might use his malady to advantage.

All thoughts of magicians and misfortunes fled from my morning-dulled head, however, when I saw the girl.

I was to discover, when we were at last introduced, that she was farmer Samus' daughter, Alea. But what need had I for names? The vision of her alone was enough to keep me for the rest of my waking moments. Her skin was the color of young peaches plucked fresh from the tree and highlighted by the colors of dawn. Her hair took the color of sunlight breaking through the clouds after a spring rain. The rest of her? How could I possibly describe the rest of her?

"Wunt!" Ebenezum called over his shoulder. "Are you coming, or have you decided to grow roots?"

I hoisted my pack more firmly on my shoulders and hurried after him, never taking my eyes from the girl. Perhaps I might talk to her. And then, of course, there were touching, and kissing, and other activities of a similar nature.

"Ho!" Ebenezum called. I dragged my eyes away from perfection to discover he wasn't calling me at all. Rather, he was hailing a small knot of men involved in animated discourse slightly up the road.

The group turned to look at us. There were four of them. From their drab garb, I guessed three of them to be farmers. Probably hired hands or sharecroppers for the richer Samus. Two of these were virtually identical in appearance. Short and broad, their shoulder width close to their height, they both wore caps, earth colored like the rest of their garments, pulled close to their eyes. One of them picked at his teeth with a dirty fingernail. The other absently twirled a finger about in his ear. Beside this, they were mirror images.

The third hand was thinner, taller and younger than the other two; close to my age and height. Of course, he did not carry himself with one-tenth my stature, but what can you expect of farmers? Besides this, his eyes were much too small, brown bugs darting about his face. Altogether not a fit companion for the young lady in the nearby field.

Now that I had suitably disposed of the first three, I turned my attention to the last member of the group. He was dressed differently, even flamboyantly, his coat a riot of red and blue, his pantaloons a yellow-green. And the conical black cap that rose at an angle above his head of curly red hair carried a seal. The seal of the magician's guild. I turned to Ebenezum.

He waved an arm clad in the much more respectable royal blue, inlaid with threads of gold, in the other's direction. "A merchant mage," he said, his voice heavy with distaste. "Sometimes you just can't avoid them."

The gaudily clad pretender to the sorcerous arts bowed low as we approached. "Greetings, fellow practitioners!" he called behind a smile that cut across the lower third of his face. "I am Glauer, master magician."

Although the merchant stood a good two inches taller than my master, Ebenezum still managed to stare down at him. "Ebenezum," he said, his tone quiet and clear in its authority, "and Wuntvor, his apprentice."

"Ebenezum," Glauer whispered, and his eyes shifted away for a minute, stunned by the presence of so great a mage. But his gaze snapped back just as quickly, his eyes filled with a cunning that brought new meaning to his merchant smile. Glauer had heard the rumors.

"I have been talking to these good citizens," the merchant continued; his voice, if possible, even bolder and more brash than before. "They tell me that their employer is having a bit of trouble with the spirits. 'Tis probably far too small a matter for one of your eminence, but I thought I might offer my humble assistance."

"Magician Glauer," Ebenezum intoned in a voice so powerful that it caused the farmhands to take a few steps back from the merchant. "These are my people. They are my trust. No task is too large, nor too small, where the people of this village are concerned!"

Glauer stepped closer, his voice and expression both subdued. "I meant no disrespect, sir. We in the profession must do everything we can to help one another. I have heard of your recent misfortunes, and would like to offer my not insubstantial services. Very discreetly, of course. And for the merest portion of the fee you will receive from the grateful farmer. Come now!" He touched my master's deep blue sleeve. "Surely you could use my services?"

"Services?" Ebenezum shook away the other man's hand, his voice full of wizardly rage. "I can think of nothing of yours we can use. We have no need at the moment for pots and pans!"

He turned toward the others. "Now, can someone tell us where we might find Master Samus?"

The thin hand pointed. "He'll be in the main house, beyond the barn there."

Ebenezum nodded and strode briskly toward the main house, leaving me hard pressed to keep up. Behind us I could hear the twin laughter of teeth and the ear, and I imagined the merchant still scowled in our direction. The other man seemed not to have reacted one way or the other to the incident. Rather, the last time I glimpsed him, he had stared thoughtfully off toward the horizon.

We rounded the barn enclosure and spied the great stone house, closer to a mansion than a cottage, with a bit of a fortress thrown in for good measure. The place looked as if it had been built to withstand any discretion of man or nature. It occurred to me that there was only one power that the formidable structure was not proof against: magic.

Shutters banged open on an upper story, and Samus' balding head appeared between two elaborately carved gargoyles. "Good! Good!" he cried. "I'll be down immediately!"

"You must be the magicians," a voice said behind us. A voice, which at the very least combined the sweetest notes ever sung by nightbirds with the fluid music of a forest stream. I turned to see the young woman of the field. The pack I had been removing from my back slipped and threatened to fall. Whether it was my quick move or the moisture that had suddenly appeared on my palms where I gripped the straps, I do not know, but what was apparent was the imminent breakage of many arcane and irreplaceable pieces of sorcerous equipment on the stone steps on which we stood. I tried to juggle the load back to balance, but it was beyond me. The pack fell. If not for the quick moves of Ebenezum, who worked with the speed known only to magicians and others familiar with sleight-of-hand, the box would have met stone and sure destruction.

I turned and smiled at the girl. Her look of alarm over recent events turned to a smile in return. Behind me Ebenezum said something that I did not quite catch, save that the tone was rather harsh in the presence of one as perfect as the loveliness approaching.

"Rather a close call," she said softly. Her lips made each word a beautiful experience.

I waved aside her concerns. "'Tis nothing. Are we not magicians? A wave of our hands, and the box would fall up!" A good choice of words, that. Her eyes grew wide with wonder.

I became aware of other voices. One was that of Samus. "This is Alea, my only daughter." "Most pleased," said my master, and I lost the blue of her eyes for a minute as she acknowledged the mage. Fortunately, they returned to me almost immediately, and my world was whole again.

Someone was calling my name. Repeatedly.

"Wunt!" It was Ebenezum. I nodded vaguely in his direction. "Master Samus is taking me on an inspection of his lands, so that I might see the affected areas for myself. If you could manage it, I would like you to set up our equipment just inside the barn."

"The barn?" I said, unable to take my eyes away from Alea. "Very good."

"Yes, the barn! This very minute!"

That broke the spell for a second. I glanced at my master (avoiding the eyes) and grabbed my pack and staff.

"Would you like me to show you the way?" Alea said. Her hand brushed against mine, cool and light.

I smiled and nodded and we walked the twenty paces to the livestock enclosure.

A graceful finger pointed to one of the pens. "That's where the hog was killed. We found him dead one dawn, wedged between two fence slats." I nodded, savoring every word. Each of her inflections was like a minstrel song.

We walked in silence for a minute. "How do you find farm life?" I asked, mostly to hear her voice again.

The corners of Alea's mouth turned down, bringing a charming wistfulness to her face. "Most times, dull," she said. "Life is slow out here; full of chores and the same old faces. It is not one tenth so interesting, I am sure, as your exciting life in the village."

I shrugged. "I suppose so. Still, you have the open air and the friendship of the others working on the farm, don't you?"

"Ah, Wuntvor, there are some things that the air cannot give you. As to the others, all Father ever thinks of is money. Two of our hands, Frinak and Franik, they're brothers, you know, they're nice, but—frankly—they're rather simple. And as to the other hand . . ." She sighed.

"The other hand?" I prompted, hoping that my interest in the matter was not too obvious.

"Tollar? He's sweet, I guess, in a way. A little coarse, of course. He's very taken with me, you know. He even asked for my hand in marriage. Of course, that would never do. As father is continually reminding me, Tollar is far below my station."

She touched my elbow. "If we turn here, we can enter the back door of the barn." She led me around a corner of the weathered wooden structure. She held my arm firmly now. "There's a hay loft that I think you'll be particularly interested in."

I was looking at her, and so did not see the foot until it struck me on the forehead. I stumbled against her but managed to keep from falling. She hugged me suddenly and strong, an action I found delightfully surprising until I saw the reason for it. The foot that hit me belonged to Tollar, the third hand, or at least what was left of him. His body hung from the rafters, strangely dark and bloated.

"Perhaps," I whispered, "we should go out and find my master."

Alea agreed that was a very good idea. Neither of us particularly cared to pass beneath the corpse again, so we decided to walk as quickly as possible through the barn's all-too-dark interior. Holding each other as tightly as movement would allow, we began our flight through the shadowed recesses to the small square of light at the other end.

Then came the banging in the loft, so loud that we would have heard it even if we hadn't lost the power to speak (and possibly to breathe). We ran.

Out into the sunlight. Both of us, shouting at the top of our voices. Out to the approaching Samus and Ebenezum, both clearly astonished at our behavior.

"Is there something wrong?" Ebenezum inquired.

"Magic!" Alea said.

Ebenezum pulled at his beard. "If so, it will be the first I've seen today. Come. Show us this sorcery."

We led them back to the barn. As we walked, I told the wizard about the strangely altered farm hand.

"But you say there's been no sorcery?" I asked.

"Nary a twitch." Ebenezum rubbed his nose.

"But Farmer Samus—"

The mage cut me off with a wave of his palm. "There is more here than is apparent to the eye."

We turned the corner of the barn. The doorway was empty. The body was gone.

"Obviously," Ebenezum added.

"What are you trying to do, daughter?" Samus exploded.

"But Tollar!" Alea said. "And the noise—"

Ebenezum raised his hand for silence. There were still noises inside the barn.

"What does this mean?" Samus asked.

The mage's hand went even farther up in the air. He sneezed.

Two figures could be seen in silhouette as they escaped through the far door of the barn.

"Sorcery!" Ebenezum cried.

"Those two, running?" the farmer asked.

"No, closer! Much closer." The wizard's sleeve flew to his nose. He lowered it after a moment. "That's better. Near this door. A recent spell, but minor at best." He turned to me. "Describe what happened again."

I retold the story carefully, point by point; the foot, Alea and then me seeing the body with the odd distortions.

Alea began to sob. "Poor Tollar. What did he do to deserve this? He might have been beneath my station, but he was sweet."

I put my hand on her shoulder to comfort her. Samus glared at me rather pointedly. I took my hand away.

Samus looked at my master. "But what about the body?"

Ebenezum sniffed, "Oh, I expect we'll see it again, sooner or later."

Alea's tears broke out anew.

"I believe the best course would be to explore our surroundings," Ebenezum continued, already walking out of the barn, "and interview everyone we meet."

Especially anyone traveling in pairs, I silently added. I retrieved my staff. I might have need of it.

We met the two other hands at the edge of the pens. They were herding a small flock of sheep into one of the enclosures.

"Franik!"

One hand looked up. "Yes, Master Samus?"

"Have you seen anyone pass here?"

The hand's broad brow wrinkled. He took his finger from his ear to scratch at his receding hairline. "Anyone? Since when, master?"

"Any strangers, then?"

"Strangers?"

"Two of them!" Samus was getting a bit red in the face.

"Let's see. Not that I can recall. Wait a minute. Frinak?"

"Yes, brother?"

"Did you see anyone?"

"Any strangers? Not that I can recall. Leastways, not today. As I remember, someone new passed by a week ago Tuesday. Would that be any help? Don't get many new faces around here."

This was getting us nowhere. There was obviously only one pair of men unaccounted for anywhere around the farm. I decided to take a more direct approach.

I stepped forward, pointing my staff at the two villains.

"What were you two doing in the barn?"

That startled them. "In the barn?" one of them said (I think it was Franik). "We do all sorts of things in the barn."

"That's true. We bail hay."

"Feed the stock."

"'Course we shovel manure." They both made a face—the same one. "That job always takes too long. Be surprised how much manure just one horse or cow can come up with. Some of them not even full grown, either."

"No!" I said, frantic to end this line of conversation. "Not what do you do when you're in the barn. *When* were you in the barn?"

"Oh, all sorts of times. Days, nights. Can't tell, exactly."

I rapped my staff on the poached earth. "No! When were you in there *last*?" My brow was getting moist from the mental exertion. Were they going to thwart me in front of my master? In front of Alea?

Even worse, could they really be innocent?

My questioning was cut short by a clatter on the road. I looked past the hands. Whatever made the noise was hidden by a copse of trees.

"Aha!" Ebenezum cried. "I thought he'd show himself eventually! Quick, Wunt! Through those trees!" I followed him at a good trot into the woods.

The trees soon thinned to bushes, and the shrubbery bordered a road. A wagon was leaving a hiding place of overgrown greenery, making for the mud path that passed for a country highway.

"Quick, Wunt! They mustn't get away!"

I sprinted ahead as the wagon turned onto the lane. It was brightly painted in red and yellow, drawn by a single horse whose harness was decorated with multicolored plumes. Large letters on the side proclaimed "The Great Glauer, Magician-at-Large."

I put on extra speed and darted in front of the horse. "Stop!" I cried and raised my staff. "If you value your safety!"

The staff almost dropped from my hands. There, on the wagon seat, was Glauer, reins in hand. But next to him sat the unexpected. Tollar. Alive.

Well, we had faced worse things than reanimated corpses. Or so I told myself at that moment. I reaffirmed my grip on the staff, ready to thwack anyone who made a move against me.

"Oh, Fesnard Encundum!" Glauer said in a peeved tone. He made a series of three mystic passes.

A spell of entanglement! I tried to fight it off, but the magic was already at work in my system. My arms wrapped around my body, reaching with intertwined fingers for the legs which in turn sought my chin. Soon, I would be caught in a hopeless knot!

Ebenezum stepped in front of the carriage. "Stop, knave!" he cried. "You'll not find me so easy to deal with!"

Was there going to be a magician's duel? I watched helplessly from my prison of arms and legs.

"Wait!" It was Tollar speaking. "Everything can be explained!"

Ebenezum stopped himself mid-gesture and wiped his nose, his hands ready to conjure should there be any treachery.

"This is my fault entirely," Tollar said. "It's all for Alea. I couldn't live without her. Oh, she's friendly enough, I'll grant that. But she wouldn't marry me. Her father insists that I am beneath her station!"

He hit the wooden seat beside him with his fist. "Beneath her station! I couldn't bear it! I decided to take matters into my own hands. I'd arrange for certain small disasters to occur. When

Samus was convinced that he was cursed, I would bring Glauer in. And circumstances would present themselves so that Gluaer could remove the curse only with my help. I would be a hero. Perhaps enough of a hero to marry Alea.

"The plan was a good one. Samus is notoriously tight. Even with a curse, I figured he would not pay for a magician with a stature greater than Glauer's!" The last remark warranted a vitriolic look from the merchant.

"But," Tollar continued, "as fortune would have it, Samus heard that Ebenezum's rates had declined. To get a sorcerer of his reputation for little more than Glauer was a bargain even Samus couldn't pass. It was hopeless—unless we moved quickly and put our plan into effect before Ebenezum could interfere.

"The barn was the best place; in the midst of the farm, yet our actions would be hidden. What better place to come up with a quick supernatural explanation, not to mention a magical cure?

"And all would have gone well, if you hadn't stumbled on me before we were ready."

Tollar's bloated body returned to my mind's eye. "But you—"

"Simple hallucination spell," Ebenezum muttered.

"Well, I had to think fast!" Glauer barked. "You can't expect a masterpiece every time!"

"Master—" Ebenezum growled, but stopped to let Tollar finish his tale.

"Once you'd spotted us, the game was over. I decided we should leave as quietly as possible. However, we failed even there."

"Little wonder," Ebenezum said, glaring at the other magician.

"That does it!" Glauer screamed. "I'll not suffer humiliation at the hands of a mage who has lived off his reputation for the past twenty years!"

"What?" Ebenezum quickly returned his hands to gesture position.

"I have resources far beyond your imagination, mage!" Glauer shouted. "My plan was brilliant, dazzling in scope!" He pulled a large bottle, mottled blue and green, from behind the seat of the cart. "Would you expect a minor magician to control such as this?"

Ebenezum's hands dropped to his sides. "Netherhells, man! You know not what you hold!"

Glauer smiled at that. "Quite the contrary. I know its power, and its risk."

Tollar and I looked from one magician to the other. Tollar said it first: "What is it?"

Glauer held it aloft, the better for all to see. "Bottled demon."

"Put it down, man!" Ebenezum urged. "If it gets loose it might devour us all."

Glauer's smile got broader still. "What? The great magician is afraid? What will people say, when Glauer defeats a demon the great Ebenezum was afraid to face?"

With that, he pulled the cork from the bottle.

And a demon materialized in our midst. Short, squat, the color of dirty brick. He appeared to be a bit muscle-bound, although it just may have been that he had four arms where most of us have two.

"Good afternoon," the creature said in a voice of cultured gravel. "Dinner time."

"He must be contained!" Ebenezum cried, clutching his nose.

"Contained?" Glauer waved the bottle. "I thought that was part of the enchantment. The fellow who sold me this bottle assured me . . ."

"Tasty, tasty morsels," the demon said, allowing its head to circle completely around and survey each of us in turn. It stopped when it saw me. "Entangled. How nice. A quick bite."

It stepped toward me.

Glauer continued to make a series of gestures toward the creature, none of which seemed to have any effect at all. Tollar mentioned something about it being high time he sought his fortune in the west and sprinted into the fields. Ebenezum waved his hand toward me just before he sneezed. I was free! I grabbed my staff and jumped to my feet.

"Come now, lad," the demon said. "Let's not be difficult. Just one swallow. You'll like it in my stomach. They tell me it's quite colorful." It took another step forward.

I hit the top of its head as hard as I could with my staff.

"Upstart!" The creature's eyes filled with demonic anger. "It would have been so easy. A simple swallow! Now, I'll be forced to chew!"

It lunged for me. My feet, seeking to get as far and fast as possible, tripped. I fell. The creature's claws swept the air above me. I manged to rap its head with my staff again. The demon screamed in a rage beyond the human as Ebenezum shook his head briskly and managed a quick breath. He mumbled a few quick words before the sneezing started again. The demon was pulled away from me by invisible forces.

"Magicians!" The demon spun to face the other two; Ebenezum caught in a sneezing fit, Glauer lost in his ineffectual gestures.

"You!" It pointed at Glauer, who, after all, was the only one currently involved in anything vaguely sorcerous. "I'll teach you to come between me and my dinner!"

"Stop, demon!" Glauer shrieked. He waved interlocked fingers at the creature as he stamped his right foot in a peculiar rhythm. It appeared to do as little good as anything he had done before.

The demon's tail flicked with irritation. "Must we be so tiresome?" It surveyed the merchant mage, a forked tongue passing over crooked fangs. "Yes, you'll do quite nicely."

"Hold!" Glauer said, changing his gestures. "I am not the great magician here!"

"Really?" the demon said as it strolled toward its snack. "And who is? Perhaps," it gestured toward Ebenezum, "that pitiful human lost in a sneezing fit?"

Glauer gave up his gestures altogether. The demon was upon him. "Wait!" he cried. His voice was getting higher by the word. "My resources are virtually without limit. Perhaps I have something to offer you."

"Most assuredly." The demon reached for him. "'Tis called a full stomach."

"But . . ."

"Alas, magician. We all have our bad days." It swallowed Glauer with rather more noise than was necessary.

The creature wiped its fangs with the back of a clawed hand, then turned to face Ebenezum and me. "Who's next?"

Ebenezum took a deep breath. A dozen words flew from his mouth, his hands dancing around them.

The demon began to fade. It looked down at its disappearing form. "Oh, drat!" it said. "And me without a decent meal in eight hundred years! Ah, well." It waved in our direction. "Perhaps we shall meet again, my tasty tidbits. Ta ta—for now."

Its words hung in the now empty air, only a faint sulphur smell left behind. Ebenezum had a final sneezing fit, then was able to breathe again.

Alea ran toward us out of the woods, followed by Samus walking at a more leisurely pace. She rushed straight to me, saying how worried she had been and how brave I was. After so arduous a day, I decided that I could stand there for a moment and absorb the praise.

"What happened?" Samus asked as he approached Ebenezum.
The wizard shrugged his sleeves out to a more respectful
position before looking the gentleman farmer in the eye. "Alas,"
he said. "Poor Glauer. He let the bottle get the better of him."

(III)

"There is nothing so rewarding as a day's work well done, save perhaps
for a full stomach with a warm fire, a purse full of gold, or a three day
vacation in the pleasure gardens of Vushta."

— *The Teachings of Ebenezum*, Vol. 23

Ebenezum had gone into the great house with Samus to explain
what had happened on the farm, as well as to demand a larger fee
(It *had* been a demon, after all!). So it was that I found myself
alone with Alea again. I must admit, had it not been for her
presence, I would have long since quit this dismal countryside.

I walked with her in silence around the farm, caught in her
fragile web of beauty. She took my hand at last and led me to the
door of the barn, the place where we had first come together —
unpleasant though the initial circumstances might have been.
Now, with all sorcery fled, the enclosure was a different place,
filled with quiet dark and the soft smell of hay. I looked into Alea's
face, the lines even more graceful in shadow.

"Alea," I said, my voice stuck in my throat, "do you think
that — the two of us . . ."

She laughed; the wind through a mountain stream. "Dear
Wuntvor! I'm afraid that's impossible. Father would never allow
it. You are far beneath my station."

My world fell away from me. Agony stabbed my chest. My eyes
searched the straw-strewn floor for answers.

Alea pulled my hand. I blindly followed. She spoke brightly. I
forced myself to make sense of the words.

" — and I want to show you the hay loft. It's very comfortable.
And very private."

She turned to me, her eyes catching mine. "Father conducts my
formal affairs. He pays no attention to my recreation."

She smiled a tiny smile and led me to a ladder in the hay strewn
dark.

I began to see some advantages to the farming life.

M. LUCIE CHIN *is a promising young fantasy writer who specializes in tales with Oriental settings. Her Chinese ghost story, "Ku Mei Li," was one of the highpoints of* Elsewhere, Volume I, *an Ace anthology series edited by Terri Windling and Mark Alan Arnold. "Lan Lung" first appeared in the premier issue of* Ares *magazine in an abridged version entitled "Dragon . . .Ghost" which, nevertheless, was selected as one of the year's best fantasy stories (DAW series, #7). At the author's request, the complete and retitled tale appears below.*

Lan Lung

BY M. LUCIE CHIN

Hsu Yuen Pao was a Taoist monk; an eccentric wanderer, an educated man, a poet and a magician. To me he was mentor, protector, companion and friend. He was sometimes called by the peasants we encountered The Man Who Walks With Ghosts.

I am the ghost.

Or so I have been told. So often in fact that after all the time I have been here that alone might be enough, but there is more. I remember dying. That is I remember the event; the time, the place, the circumstances, the stupidity . . . but not the moment itself. Sometimes I think I am still falling; it was a long way from the top of the Wall, and all my life since that asinine mistake is just a dream, one long last thought between living and dying. But only sometimes. It is hard to believe when the night is cold enough to freeze dragon fire. It is hard to believe when drought turns rivers to muddy washes and rice fields to waste lands and a poor traveler must become a thief to eat. At such times it is easier to believe I have always been here, following Hsu Yuen Pao across the land, that the first thirty years of my life as I recall them are the dream.

But in the end that too is utterly unbelievable. I know too much of another place and time. In my childhood mankind reached for the stars. The Sons of Han have yet to reach across the sea.

I do not know the date by any measure of time I was ever

taught. I can not translate the Lunar calendar into the Julian of my memory. It is ancient China; the women have not yet begun to bind their feet and no man in this land has ever seen a European. That is what I know of now. What of then?

I was born in Boston, Massachusetts, on the 12th of June 2010, a fourth generation American of Chinese descent. My name was Daniel Wing and the extent of my ethnic education was limited to the salutations exchanged on Chinese New Year and the names of my favorite edibles. Barefoot on the road I stand five feet nine-and-a-half inches and at the time of the accident atop the Great Wall of China I was as much a tourist as any of the obvious caucasians who made up my group, following the polite guide who filled our heads with images of the past.

It was early April atop the Wall. Somewhere on the way down, as I exchanged one reality for another, it became warm and balmy late spring and I became gwai . . . the ghost. Towering above that diminutive ancient population, dressed strangely, babbling incomprehensibly, understanding nothing and no one I was a perfect candidate for ghosthood; a nonperson, inhuman. Gwai. It is the only word the Chinese have for those who are not of the Sons of Han, the True People, the Chinese themselves. It expresses, more than a lack of life, a lack of *reality*. It suits perfectly, these days, my own concept of myself.

It is said that a ghost grows faint when touched by the breath of a living man. To spit upon him robs him of his powers to change form and vanish. I was spit upon often in the days before Hsu Yuen Pao found me. He was a wise man. He understood about ghosts far better than the peasants who harried and chased me from their villages and fields. I did not trust him particularly but he was quiet and patient and fed me and talked for me until I learned enough to speak for myself.

He was a small man, even among his own people, and he wore his garments oddly and in a most casual manner. He was young in appearance, though generally travel worn, but his obsidian eyes seemed old as time, deep as wells, seeming to hold yet conceal the knowledge of great age. Villagers sometimes whispered that he had found the secret of eternal life, the personal immortality the ancient Taoist monks sought relentlessly. His hair was very black and carefully braided into the longest queue I have ever seen, which he wore looped through his sash in the back for convenience. There hung about his person and around his neck an array of bags, pouches and containers of many types and sizes, and across his back was slung a long, narrow sheath. It was curved, seemingly to better fit the line of his body, and nearly a yard long, black and slim enough to house only the most needle thin of blades. A most unusual and impractical weapon, I felt, but surely one of great value, for the hilt was the purest and clearest of pale pink crystal and in gossamer script of gold upon the scabbard were the two chapters yü and yu; one the ideograph for abundance, the other the symbol for fish.

He was afraid of nothing. Brave, in my opinion, to the edge of foolishness, mischievous as a child when the mood struck him, and we were frequently in trouble of one sort or another.

There was not a dialect we encountered which he did not speak with fluency and command, and he wrote poems I have never gained the skill to appreciate. I loved them, though I could not read them.

In the quiet of night or as we walked the endless land, migrating more or less with the seasons, he would tell me of ghosts and he would tell me of dragons.

"The face of the earth is covered with the endless, invisible trails of the dragon Lung Mei. To build a house or bury the dead upon such a spot is a great fortune."

He often said he felt that he and I had met upon such a spot.

In the second summer of my new existence we made a leisurely journey toward the western mountains. At the convergence of certain mountain streams there is a cataract called the Dragon Gate. The great carp of the rivers migrate yearly to this spot to make the valiant but usually futile attempt to leap the falls. Those fish who succeed and gain the higher waters are immediately rewarded and transformed into dragons. They then climb to the highest peaks, mount the passing clouds and are born off into the heavens.

The Dragon Gate and the slopes around it are also the site of rare dragon bones of the finest quality and Hsu Yuen Pao had made this journey often to collect them for geomancy and medical uses. Among the bags and pouches he wore were several in which he carried such things in small shards or ground into powders. I had seen him use them on occasion in the villages we passed through, sometimes to good effect, sometimes not. I think that if there is *any*thing to be said for the power of belief to heal, those bones have worked miracles.

I had my suspicions about them, not that I could positively identify them. That was the point. They could have been anything. They were not abundant except at the foot of the falls (where the implications to me were obvious) but Yuen Pao picked through such as we found with selective care.

In the evenings as we sorted our small horde, setting some to dry by the fire and grinding the more fragile ones into fine powders, he would instruct me as best he could, considering the still simple state of my vocabulary.

"Small bones marked with wide lines are female," he said. "Rough bones with narrow lines are male. The variegated colors are most esteemed while yellow and white are of medium value and black are inferior. The light yellow, flesh-colored, white and black are efficacious in curing diseases of the internal organs having their respective colors. If bones are impure or gathered by women they should not be used.

"Dragons occasionally change their bones, regularly shed their skins and horns. The lofty peaks of mountains, cloud shrouded or misty, contain the bones of great and venerable dragons which attract moisture and passing clouds.

"Remember, Little Brother, Lung is the god of all waters and the lord of all scaled creatures. When Lung is small all fish are small. When he is of great size and well pleased with himself there is abundance in all the land."

He was patronizing and often condescending. But he was also totally fascinating; no less so for believing himself everything he told me. And I learned. Sifting through the convoluted speech patterns the Chinese love, the multiple meanings and implications, carefully sorting fact from myth and tradition, anecdote from parable, I slowly built a body of knowledge I could rely on . . . in one way or another. My preconceptions and skeptical nature frequently got in the way, however, and my memories of another place and time. The first severe blow to these notions came at the end of a month on the slopes around the falls.

There had been a great display of heat lightning far off on the eastern plain during the night and I had been amused by Yuen Pao's suggestions that it was an omen of some sort, by the seriousness with which he sat up much of the night watching the patterns of light and the scanty film of clouds hovering above the mountaintops looking for interpretations. He found none, though.

We spent the morning descending to lower slopes through forests of hardwood and conifers and rhododendrons. Farther north and west the giant panda roamed these mountain ranges. Below on the plain, bamboo and catalpa and a great diversity of flora had not yet been obliterated by the demands of cultivation. It had been a lush world we passed through on our way up to the Dragon Gate. On our way down we became increasingly aware that the character of the vegetation had changed. It had lost its robust verdancy.

In the afternoon we passed a village nestled where three mountain streams converged. In spite of this the crops which had earlier promised abundant yields were now only mediocre and that at the cost of great labor to irrigate. At the next village we spent the night.

Their situation was much the same but there was word that the central flatlands were suffering badly. What had been scanty rain upon the mountains slopes and valley in the past month had not reached the plains at all. Even here there was fear that the harvest would be disastrously poor—if, indeed, the crop would be harvestable before the monsoon. Every morning the women and girls offered sweet rice steamed with sausages and nuts, bound in leaves, to the rain god, tossing them into the streams by the dozens. Beside the fields and in the bamboo groves braces of swallows hung from poles with long banners of red paper inscribed with respectful prayers.

Hsu Yuen Pao looked about, nodding sagely as we walked, and did not bother to explain. But I got the gist of things pretty well by that time. The Chinese system of education by osmosis was quite workable . . . if it was the only thing you had to *do* with your life, which in my case was literally true.

He marked our course southeast as we continued toward the plain. It was his contention that we must reach the coastal lands before the monsoon season. For transients such as we, the semitropical climate of the southern coast was a necessity of life. That had not occurred to me the year before. Then I had simply followed. The journey would take weeks on foot and in a rarely used corner of my mind I wondered how long it would have taken by car.

Things were not yet so bad in the lowlands as we had expected to find on that first day down and at noon we stopped in a bamboo grove, still delicately lovely in the motionless air. No breeze

rattled the stalks or stroked the leaves but there is something
inherently cooling about bamboo groves, especially the fresh
yellow/green shoots which we collected to boil with a little rice for
our meal. I took the pack which I had become accustomed to
carrying from my back and went about collecting the youngest
shoots. When I returned with my pockets full I found Yuen Pao
standing across the grove looking at me so oddly it stopped me in
my tracks.

"Brother Gwai," he said somberly. "The night of the lightning
was indeed an omen. But it was not for me to understand."

I have never been an endlessly patient man. Occasionally the
obliqueness of his technique exasperated me.

"Brother Pao," I said. "I do not understand. I am not a prophet.
I know nothing of dreams or omens. I am ignorant. Please speak
more plainly." I had learned to talk humbly in this land.

"Lan Lung," he said in a low tone.

The lazy deaf one? I was perplexed. Colloquialisms are
confusing in any language. Particularly so in Chinese. But lung is
also the word for dragon. Being unable to hear, the dragon came
to be known by the word for its only handicapp. Lan Lung, then,
was also a lazy dragon. I had heard the term as an epithet hurled
at street beggars. It made utterly no sense in a bamboo grove. I
did not understand and said so.

Yuen Pao instructed me to stay exactly where I was till he
returned, then he seemed literally to vanish. I sat down and waited
for nearly an hour. When he returned there was a brace of
swallows in his hand and the odd look was still on his face.

I went to my pack as he told me, folded back the flap, stepped
aside and waited. Yuen Pao approached the pack cautiously,
slowly swinging the dead birds by their feet, wings trussed with
red cord.

At first I watched Yuen Pao. Then I watched what he watched.
There was the smallest ripple of movement within my bag. Hsu
Yuen Pao said one word.

The creature that emerged was tiny, palm-sized. It seemed, as
the young of many reptiles may, exquisitely perfect in miniature.

"*This*," I said, my smile broad with delight, "is a *dragon?*"

"Do not deceive yourself, Little Brother, Lan Lung is dragon
enough for any man."

Gesturing for me to move farther aside, he offered the swallows
before him and backed slowly away. Within the shadow of the

pack tiny eyes flashed incandescently orange, bobbed up and down, and were extinguished by daylight as it crept from cover.

It was not as tiny as I had at first thought, though still small and precious. A large handful then, perhaps a foot long head to tail. It had a vaguely bovine head with a long, broad nostriled snout. Scalloped plates of scale, white rimmed in blue, green and orange, lay flat against the head, three rows deep behind the eyes and below the jaw. Its muzzle bristled with catlike lavender whiskers and upon its crown were short, blunt, double-branching horns.

Eying the birds greedily the little lizard arched his sinuous, serpentine body and rose upon his haunches stroking the air with four clawed paws. The sleek body was covered with lacelike scales, white edged in pale blue, and the curved claws were deep cobalt. There were flat plates of scale similar to those about his head at each shoulder and hip. It had no wings nor was the spine serrated, but there played about the body a vague bright aura.

As the dragon's muscles bunched and he sank down upon his haunches, tail braced, he opened his mouth, but instead of a hiss there was a sound like the chiming of small brass bells. Hsu Yuen Pao swung the birds in a gentle arc, tossing them several feet into the grove. The dragon sprang, covering incredible distance in a single leap, as though gravity had no meaning for him. And as he moved he seemed to grow. He was cat-sized when he landed upon the swallows and began to devour them quickly.

With the dragon thus occupied, Yuen Pao, moving carefully, collected our few belongings and steered me with deliberate lack of hurry from the grove.

We shortly came upon a road and followed it for a couple of hours in silence before stopping to prepare the bamboo shoots still in my pockets. Yuen Pao was deeply contemplative but for the first time in my admittedly limited experience he also seemed burdened by a weight of uncertainty. As we ate he told me a story.

Lung is the greatest of all creatures living in the world besides man himself. But as there are lazy men, so too are there lazy dragons. They do not like to exert themselves in the task of directing rain clouds about the sky. So they make themselves small and drop to earth where they hide in trees, under the roofs of houses and even in the clothing of unsuspecting men. Lung Wang, the dragon king, learning of their desertion from duty, sends messengers into the world to search for them. Lung may also make himself invisible, as is usually the case when man is present. These messengers are seldom seen, but when Lan Lung is found the Lung Wang, in fury, raises a great storm, killing the deserter with lightning bolts. This explains what might often seem a wanton destruction of life and property during such storms.

The convenient logic with which these stories usually ended invariably amused me and I made the mistake of smiling. Hsu Yuen Pao became indignant and proceeded to tell me more about dragons in the next hour than I truthfully cared to know.

"It is a great puzzle," he said as we finally walked the road again. "It is rare that lung allows himself to be seen by the eyes of mortal man. Such sightings are auspicious occasions and would normally be related directly to the emperor. But this is Lan Lung. It is not clear to me what this could mean."

I squinted up at the bright, cloudless sky. What did *any*thing mean in this place? My whole existence was a mystery. Alice down the rabbit hole. But as for the dragon, I had to admit the little fellow was fascinating. He had displayed an interesting degree of mutability and he *did* look strikingly like the creatures I had seen in Chinese artworks. Hardly the beast of legend but a little dragon and a lot of imagination, persistently applied, can leave behind legends larger than life. Hsu Yuen Pao *believed* this was a dragon capable of all he claimed for it.

When I looked back Yuen Pao was also contemplating the sky.

"Yes," he said, "this must be so, though I am still unsure what it means."

I pleaded ignorance.

"Lung is territorial," he said in an uncharacteristically straightforward manner, still looking into the sky. "Each is responsible for the rainfall upon his own lands." The rest was obvious enough. This time I managed not to smile.

The next two days on the road provided clear enough evidence that the tales we had heard in the hills were true. The drought deepened substantially as we entered the central plain and promised to worsen. It was said that the rice crop was already unsalvageable, it being too late to plant again even if rain came soon, and despair was growing over the other, less fragile sorts of produce. And everywhere the people shook their heads and wondered what they had done to offend such a powerful dragon, for the area of the drought was extensive.

In the villages we passed, Hsu Yuen Pao bartered geomancy and spells and prayers for roots and dried preserves and goat-bladder water bags (which were lighter to carry when full), and we amended our course to follow the streams and rivers more closely. He had seen Lan Lung and did not expect rain soon.

On the evening of the fourth day we camped on the bank of a muddy stream. Yuen Pao dug for roots. He would forage as long as possible to save our stores of dried goods for harder times. Those he found were pulpy and shriveled but we boiled them in the water I had spent over an hour straining again and again. It made a bitter, unpleasant broth and the tubers were nearly tasteless but edible, and we supplemented the meal with a small handful of dried plums.

The fire was to have been extinguished as soon as the meal was prepared. Everything around us was dry as tinder and a fire of any size was perilous in the open. Yet when I moved to do so, Yuen Pao stopped me with a silent gesture. Peering intently into the dark it was several seconds before I saw what he saw. At first I thought it was a shadow by my pack but when it moved, two iridescent orange eyes flashed in the firelight and it had my complete attention.

Yuen Pao took up his small copper bowl and his chopsticks and began to eat with the same deliberate, unhurried movements with which he had steered me from the bamboo grove. I did the same, dividing my attention between Yuen Pao and the flickering eyes. Eventually the creature moved into the light and I saw that this "dragon" too was white and roughly the same size as the other. This, Yuen Pao insisted, was because it was the same dragon.

We finished our meal and sat watching the little lizard prowl about our belongings while Yuen Pao recited poetry (ostensibly to keep the two of *us* tranquil since the dragon could not hear) till the fire went out on its own. He told me to lie down and sleep, which I eventually managed to do, but for a long time I could see his silhouette against the stars as he sat in contemplation of his dragon.

In the morning the little creature was gone, but Yuen Pao continued to conduct himself with the same care as the night before. It was his belief that lung had been with us all along. He had simply been invisible as he may well have been at that very moment.

I tried to take the matter seriously. For him this was an important event and he had been allowed to participate, if only he could understand in what way. Personally, I envisioned the little fellow either sleeping quietly beneath a rock or curled up among our foodstuffs out of the heat of the sun. The notion that he might be happily feasting on dried mushrooms and plums which we would later need bothered me a great deal, but Yuen Pao would not let me sort the contents of my pack before we set out.

In the evening as I laid our small fire, the dragon appeared again. I could not tell from where. He was simply there, sitting on my pack on the ground in the smothering, breezeless heat. Again he was white. I, too, was beginning to believe it was the same dragon.

The next morning he was nowhere to be seen. This time, however, I sorted my pack. All our belongings were in order and no food had been disturbed. Perhaps he ate bugs; or a pair of swallows would last him a week. I did not bring the subject up with Yuen Pao.

Again the night and morning were the same. We were getting used to him. Yuen Pao was no longer quite so careful in his movements and he had decided that the key to the riddle was to wait for the ending. This day, however, at our noon meal (little more than mushrooms and lotus root soaked in stale water), our companion showed himself. I caught Yuen Pao staring at me and, looking down, found Lan Lung curled up in the shadow of my left knee. When we finally stood to go, the little dragon scampered to my pack and vanished beneath the flap.

From that time on I seemed to take on a different dimension in Yuen Pao's eyes. But since I was never quite sure how he regarded my ghosthood, the new status was equally unclear.

In the following weeks the dragon established himself as a permanent member of our party and my own special companion. It was impossible to say what attracted him to me. Perhaps my smell. Perhaps it was my ghosthood. He and I were both fantasies, lung and gwai, dragons and ghosts; stories to frighten children into obedience. It seemed appropriate that the myths of our existence should keep each other company.

He developed a habit of riding upon whatever part of my body shaded him from the sun, taking to my pack less and less frequently. Sometimes he would ride in one of the pockets of my loose, sleeveless coat or slither down my chest beneath my shirt and curl up next to my belly, a small bulge above my belt. He was smooth and dry to the touch and the strange aura rippling over his body (Yuen Pao called it dragon fire) was almost like a cool breeze against my skin. When he climbed a leg or arm or scampered across my shoulders his tiny claws prickled and his whiskers tickled. He seemed to absorb the moisture of my sweat, leaving a trail of dry skin in his wake. He was virtually weightless.

From time to time he would vanish, but rarely for more than a day or two. Hsu Yuen Pao said he was simply invisible, but I believed he was hunting since he left our dwindling supply of food strictly alone. Our water was the only thing we shared with him. In proportion to his size, in fact, he received a greater share than we did and even that little was nearly enough to undo us.

The hardships of the summer were incredible. The people were ravaged as badly as the land, and during the passage of the weeks became increasingly hostile to transients, guarding their stores of food and water jealously. Gaunt water buffalo stood about in the shade of tinder-dry houses and the mortality rate among the very old and the very young grew steadily. It became impossible to barter *any*thing we possessed for the things we needed, especially water. And to find a village with a good, deep, springfed well was a great fortune. Obtaining fresh water, however, even from *these* places, became an exercise in stealth.

For the most part I was unaware of the methods of pilferage employed. I was the decoy on most occasions, playing my ghostly role to the fullest. Sometimes I was convinced Yuen Pao actually did procure our ill-gotten gains by magic. He was able to come and go in the blink of an eye, sometimes seeming to literally vanish, and his skill at sleight of hand was astounding. In another place and time he would have been a masterful pickpocket.

At such rare times as we passed other travelers or stopped at a town or village Lan Lung would disappear from sight. A bit addled by the heat, perhaps, I actually began to think of him as invisible myself.

We made progress slowly. The heat became a weighty burden requiring us to stop often for rest. The rivers were reduced to muddy sludge and many streams had vanished entirely. For a time we took to traveling by night. Not that it was noticeably cooler, but it spared us the direct assault of the sun.

I lost count of the weeks, could not make out even the slightest progress toward our goal. The mountains of the southern coast looked as far away as ever. Yet there came a time when Yuen Pao changed our course away from the last river and we struck out directly for the hazy blue and gray peaks shimmering and dancing on the horizon. We crossed few roads on the last leg of our trek and passed no more villages. Our rate of travel by then could have been little more than ten miles per day and Yuen Pao guessed we had another five or six days to go. We had been on diminishing rations for a long time and foraging had long ago become useless. Two days out from the river there was so little left that any attempt to ration it further was a useless illusion and we finished it off without further pretense. The water was in no better shape but that illusion we maintained as long as we could.

Lan Lung had settled into my right pocket and for over a week had barely stirred. When Yuen Pao and I shared our small bowl of water, a bit was always left for the little dragon who would crawl into the bowl and curl up into a ball rolling over and over in an attempt to bathe himself as best he could. On the evening our food ran out I found it was necessary to help him. I carefully lifted him from my pocket with both hands, placing him in the bowl. He moved a bit, tucking his tail feebly, but did not roll over. When Hsu Yuen Pao was not looking I wet my palm from the last goat-bladder bag and stroked his dry body. He felt brittle to my touch and it seemed days since I had seen his aura about him.

Looking up from the bowl I found Yuen Pao watching me and realized he had seen what I had done. He did not disapprove. Days before, when I had mentioned that Lan Lung seemed to be suffering from thirst even more than we, he had explained that it was not thirst. It is the *presence* of moisture which preserves his powers of motion and mutability. Without this, lung becomes powerless and dies.

The following evening there was not enough water to preserve that illusion either.

The next two days became an exercise in placing one foot before the other and the space between nights became interminable, but we no longer differentiated for the sake of travel. We moved when we could move and stopped when we could do nothing else. I believed I had begun to hallucinate when we at last reached the foothills where we at least found shade and the vaguest hint of motion in the air. The leaves on the trees were not shriveled here, and farther up the slopes the grass was almost green. We rested there, digging up a half-decent root or two and locating a few edible berries. In my pocket Lan Lung was very still.

The next morning we made our way slowly into the foothills. The heat was still oppressive and the going even slower since we now had to climb and frequently had to help each other, but the world seemed fresher around us and things were making a reasonably successful attempt to grow. There was hope of water here, if only we could find it. Yuen Pao crushed leaves and grasses and put the broken vegetation into my pocket with the little dragon in the vain hope that there might be enough moisture to preserve him.

I wondered what would preserve *us*, but Yuen Pao felt if there was any great import to this dragon it was our duty to do all that was possible. I think it kept him going far longer than even the need to save his own life. As for me, I could only reflect that dying the first time had been far easier than the second seemed destined to be.

On the afternoon of the third day, amid green grass and cool shady trees, we came upon a swiftly flowing stream, very deep and clear. Snow-fed, I realized, raising my cupped hands, aching from the frigid water. The long-prayed-for moisture was more pain than comfort in my mouth and throat and transformed my stomach into a clutch of knots.

Yuen Pao filled our two copper cooking bowls from the stream and set them on a warm rock in the sun. Then he set about filling our water bags before drinking himself. As he did these things and I tried to contain my eagerness for the water, I felt a feeble stirring in my pocket. I reached in and carefully removed Lan Lung with both hands, but Yuen Pao would not let me place him in one of the bowls. The water was still too cold for his enfeebled condition. So I put the limp little lizard back into my pocket and removed the garment, hanging it on a tree branch in the shade. When the water was warmed, Yuen Pao dribbled some of it into the pocket and he and I shared the rest, refilling the bowl before starting the next. By the time we had drunk two bowls each and given as many to my pocket, the activity within had increased and it began to swell even as the water soaked through and ran off.

"It is enough," Yuen Pao said. "The belly is better filled with food."

"If we *had* any," I agreed.

"Look in the stream," he said.

There were fish in the deep swiftness of the current. Brown and white and golden orange carp, large and sleek, flashed by too rapidly for my weary eyes to follow. There was an abundance of food within reach but how to obtain it? I had neither the strength for speed nor the courage against the bone-biting cold to seriously consider trying to catch them by hand.

Pointing out a far tree Yuen Pao sent me to hang my dripping garment there, dragon and all, which I did while he took our water bags from the stream. As I watched he raised both hands, gripping the crystal hilt above his right shoulder. Murmuring in low tones, eyes closed, he uttered an incantation I could not properly hear and slowly moved his hands up and forward. What he drew forth was not a sword. I was surprised to realize that in the time I had known him I had never actually seen this object before.

Amazingly flexible, too long to be withdrawn straight, the shaft whispered from its sheath and sprang free, whipping back and forth in supple, diminishing strokes. A yard long, it was less thick at the hilt than the stem of a flower, tapering away to nothing. It shone in the sun, lustrous and brilliantly purple. Yuen Pao's face was set and serious as he gazed up and down the length of the shaft, his voice hushed and reverent as he said, "Dragon whisker."

I thought of Lan Lung, his tiny whiskers tickling my neck or hand and was dumbfounded.

Yuen Pao stepped to the bank, the crystal hilt in his right hand, and murmured a few more barely audible words. Slipping the dragon whisker into deep water, he and I knelt upon the brink and watched.

"Come, brother Yu," he said. "Come seek your master Lung Wang."

The fish and eels came from all directions, massing about the purple wand till it was no longer visible among the bodies. Even from downstream they came, fighting the current to reach the dragon, master of all scaled things upon the earth. They crushed together from bank to bank till there was barely room to move and those closest to the surface could be picked up by hand, barely wetting the fingers.

That night we feasted on eel and fish roasted upon flat rocks about a large fire. Others were prepared for drying to be carried with us for future meals. But unexpectedly, the introduction of food and water to my deprived system was too great a shock. I was sick for two days.

I do not recall if Yuen Pao was afflicted or not but I began to feel human again as we slowly climbed the foothills, following the course of the water upstream. Then there was a road and villages again, nestled in the mountain valley. The people in this land had not suffered drought at all. The crop here was good, though it could not begin to make up for the devastation upon the plains, and the people were willing to barter for Yuen Pao's skills. There were many dialects here and they seemed to vary from valley to valley. Travelers were few, especially in the higher villages and, after an initial period of suspicion, for which my own appearance was no great help, the stories of our journey and the news of the lowlands were as much in demand as spells or medications.

It would have been nice to linger in a village here or there. Our strength returned to us slowly and we tired sooner than we would have liked—the increasing altitude was no doubt a factor—but Yuen Pao would not permit delays. Inquiring after particular roads and passes he plotted our course, explaining that it would still require many days to cross the mountains and be safely on the southern slopes before the monsoon stopped all travel; we had not much time now.

Lan Lung once again took to riding upon my shoulder or occasionally on top of my head. As we reached the highest passes, however, he once again took to my pocket or to nestling beneath my shirt. It was cold here but Hsu Yuen Pao, in his infinite wisdom, proclaimed that was not the reason. We were too close to heaven here. The clouds were thickening on the southern horizon and puffy white ships sailed close over our heads. The messengers of the Lung Wang would be watching. During the last days of our crossing, Lan Lung rarely betrayed his presence, even to me. Only when he rode in my pocket was I truly aware of him.

Then we were climbing down. Though we were still high on the slopes, I was jubilant. It was almost like coming home.

Yuen Pao was known in many of the villages we passed, a fact I had come to realize was not particularly unusual. But one pleasant, near-autumn afternoon as we passed a mile or so from the outer wall of a large town, Yuen Pao stopped short in the road, nearly causing me to run him over. In my pocket, Lan Lung squirmed unhappily for a moment. Then we abruptly changed course, away from the wall and the town. He would not tell me why. At dusk, when we stopped to lay our fire, he told me a story from his seemingly inexhaustible fund.

There was once a Taoist monk (I wondered who) traveling through the mountain passes. On this road he came upon six men bearing huge baskets of oranges on their backs. These, they said, were a gift to a high official in the court of the emperor from his younger brother, a magistrate in a minor southern province. The loads were very heavy and since the monk was alone and there were thieves known to be about, it was agreed that the monk would travel with them for protection and to help bear the loads.

He took the first basket and carried it for an hour. Then he gave it back and took the next and so on till all the loads had been shared. As each man resumed his task after an hour unencumbered, he felt that the rest had been so beneficial that he now carried his load with greater ease, as though it was lighter.

At last they came to a forking of the road where the monk returned the last basket and they parted company.

Several days later the high official, in an attempt to improve his status with the emperor, gave a great feast in his honor. It was a lavish event and only goods of the finest quality were prepared. At the end of the meal the fat oranges, a rare and expensive delicacy from the south, were brought out and laid before the emperor who dearly loved them. But when he lifted one it seemed oddly light, and when the skin was broken . . . there was nothing inside. Everyone was aghast, the official not the least of all. The emperor was not amused. Another orange was opened and another till it was discovered that all the oranges were nothing but empty skins. The steward was sent for and the larder examined only to find that the fruit in all six baskets was the same.

The bearers were then brought forward and charged upon pain of death to explain the mystery. They told of the Taoist monk and said he had surely used magic to steal the oranges and leave them only the skins.

Since the peasants who bore the fruit north were far too stupid to have conceived of such a skillful theft, the emperor was inclined to believe them. But rather than gaining his favor, as the official had hoped, he instead found his own stupidity rewarded with a reduced income and the government of a distant province in the north, far from the court and power. The magistrate in the south, having lost his older brother's good graces, had also lost all hope of further advancement and privilege and counted himself lucky to have retained what he had.

Yuen Pao claimed to have been told the story by one of the bearers only a year or two before he found me, implying that all travelers in this land were suspect and monks most especially. Sometimes I wondered exactly how gullible he thought I *was*.

It was not yet mid-morning of the next day when they caught

up with us, even though we had been prudent enough to stay off the road. There were eight armed men on horseback. Any argument would have been utter stupidity and, though we proceeded at a fast forced march, it was dusk before we reached the great gate of the town wall. Our belongings were confiscated and we spent the night in a hovel on the edge of town. By the smell and the consistency of the floor it was a structure frequently used to house swine, which was a clear statement of what the magistrate thought of us.

Lan Lung, who had been in my pocket that morning, was gone. He had vanished, as was his habit when strangers were about. But this time, Yuen Pao said, he would not return. Lung has no love for men and their communities. When I naively suggested he might join us again on the road, Yuen Pao did not reply.

In the end, even I was acute enough to realize what a man seeking status would consider proper satisfaction for the affronted dignity of his emperor, though I still did not believe the business about the oranges. The fact that I had had nothing to do with anything was unimportant. By now the magistrate had heard all he required from the nearby villages. In his mind I would be an integral part of Hsu Yuen Pao and his Taoist magic.

There was no sleep that night. This time it was I who stood in the dark watching the lightning far to the south as the monsoons gathered at the coast and wondering about omens and dragons.

At dawn we were ushered out and made to stand waiting like penned sheep in the town square throughout the dismal gray morning and on into afternoon. Awaiting Pei Tae Kwan's pleasure. Waiting to die at his leisure.

It was unclear to everyone, including myself, if a ghost could be killed, though I had a pretty good notion by now. But as there was no answer, Pei Tae Kwan had willingly accepted for himself the honor of discovering the facts.

The executioner arrived well before noon and stood like a statue among his swords. A dozen guards, stoic and heavily armed, encircled us. Beyond them, curious villagers and bold little boys eyed us carefully, pointing and talking loudly. Old women peered between the shoulders of the guards and railed at us. Yuen Pao was unmoved by the abuse. I simply did not understand the dialect.

From time to time he would send a child or old woman scurrying away with an upraised hand and a few words. It seemed to occur to none of them that if his magic was really so potent we would not have remained the captives we were.

We were permitted to say little to each other, but in truth there was little to say. I was strangely calm. What my impatient nature would normally have considered a tortuous wait was of little bother to me. I found myself thinking most about my little Lan Lung. Would he find another safe refuge now that my long fall seemed destined at last to shatter me at the foot of the wall?

Hsu Yuen Pao leaned upon the trunk of the one tree in the square and seemed as indifferent as I, though I will probably never know *his* reasons.

The murky overcast had grown dense and slate grey by early afternoon. The air was a sullen broth of humidity, and water droplets occasionally fell out of suspension, creating a fine mist. Though they threatened heavily, hanging low and pregnant overhead, the clouds did not open and drown us.

Pei Tae Kwan showed his face at last about mid-afternoon, making his way slowly down the street from the ornate monumental gate. The men in the drum towers signaled his approach and a wave of silence fell upon the villagers as he passed. He took his time quite deliberately and I had to admit it was finally beginning to get on my nerves.

Entering the armed circle he walked around slowly, looking us over with obvious contempt. When he spoke, the tone of his voice was unmistakable — insulting, berating, humiliating. Two servants who had followed him into the guarded circle now began rummaging through our belongings which had been dumped on the ground several feet away. They smashed our rice bowls under foot and broke our chopsticks, throwing the pieces in our faces. They opened the boxes and containers of Yuen Pao at the magistrate's command, spilling the dust to show his contempt for us. We could not buy him. We had hardly expected to.

The boys opened the black lacquered container and spilled out the shards of variegated bone we had collected at the Dragon Gate. They broke the lid from the carved box of red cinnabar and emptied the pale yellow dust of ground dragon bones into the dirt, shouting and picking out small round rubies (petrified dragon blood Hsu Yuen Pao had called them).

Alarmed, the magistrate left us and took the gems from the boys, sending them out among the villagers. He laughed at Yuen Pao, placing the stones in a pocket of his gown, and called out mockingly as he kicked our belongings about. He spied the black scabbard and drew out the shining purple whisker which quivered in his hand like a stiff whip. There was silence for a moment, then more loud chatter. He bellowed, holding the prize aloft for all to see, and looked at Hsu Yuen Pao, his eyes alight with greedy triumph. He brandished it like a sword and advanced upon us, kicking my pack out of his way. I saw it moved aside by his foot with an odd jerk which seemed more like a lurch to my eye, and it suddenly began to writhe and swell on the ground.

At the collective cry from the crowd, Pei Tae Kwan turned and, seeing the churning from within the cloth, beat at it with the dragon whisker, then backed away and fled beyond the line of his guards as the bag swelled again.

Weapons drawn, the soldiers formed rank around the magistrate and one man sprang forward, striking a blow to the bag with his sword. There was a muffled sound like the distant toll of a bell and the pack split to shreds as lung burst forth, growing to immense size in an instant. His serpentine body writhed, his tail lashing about, massive cowlike head high, four clawed forepaws slashing air. He was an explosion of silver and blue in the darkness of afternoon, fifty feet long. His voice was the booming of a gong. In the damp air his breath shone bright. Dragon fire played over his body. Beneath his chin was the great blue pearl of the sea, and upon his left shoulder was a long, ragged wound of red.

So rapidly did lung grow to his full, terrible size, that the soldier who had struck the blow was crushed beneath the scaled belly without even the time to scream. Then lung leapt, much as I had seen him do that first day in the bamboo grove. But now his body blotted out the sky, and when he landed amidst the terrified screams of the people, men died beneath his huge feet and thrashing tail. The living fled in panic—villagers, soldiers and dignitaries—but the magistrate Pei Tae Kwan, the dragon whisker still clutched in his hand, lay beneath the right forefoot of the great saurian, a foot-long claw imbedded in his chest.

The gong of his voice beat again and lung moved around the tree dragging the body of Pei a step or two before it dropped from his claw. I watched, numb but fascinated, only slowly becoming aware of a persistent tugging at my arm. When I looked at Yuen Pao, I was surprised to see the fear so plainly on his face, but I recognized it to be the fear of a prudent man. As the thunder began to rumble above and a hot wind came up at our backs, I looked once more at Lan Lung, my little pet, and realized the magnitude of my folly. This was no pet; had *never* been one. I, perhaps, had been his. This was Tsao Lung, a great scaled dragon, Lord of Rain, Ruler of Rivers, Commander of the Floods. The monsoons at our backs were under his control as were the clouds above our heads. He was deaf to the voice of man and paid no heed to the puniness of his life. Had I expected obedience from this creature? Affection? At that moment I would count myself lucky if he did not even notice me.

The town wall preventing retreat, the dragon between us and the street, Yuen Pao and I moved slowly about the tree, keeping it between us and the dragon as we maneuvered toward the door of the nearest house.

Lightning startled me and the dragon turned, watching us. His breath was a bright haze about his head and he favored his left leg. Out beyond the tree, the house seemed very far away. Behind the great reptilian body we could see a knot of people, the boldest of the curious, peering from the shelter of the memorial gate. The lightning and thunder came again and lung turned end to end, facing in our direction now. Body arched, head waving high, his voice boomed once more. Yuen Pao tensed beside me as my own muscles set for a bolt to the door, but there was no time to run. The dragon sprang in the air, his arc long and flat, looming even huger as he hurtled toward us.

My muscles jerked in an attempt to run, but I fell instead as the dragon dropped to the ground barely ten feet from me, twisting his head and body away to confront what I suddenly saw falling from the sky, and landing farther up the street. Another dragon, this one gold and orange. He was five-clawed and the pearl beneath his chin was the color of honey.

Sheltered behind the wall-like back of Lan Lung, we scrambled for the house, but as we moved, he moved, leaping away up the street. A moment later there was an ear-ringing crash of lightning, shattering the tree across the square barely a yard from the tip of his tail.

I thought of Yuen Pao's story. Lan Lung, the lazy dragon. For desertion of his post and duty, Lung Wang would send messengers to seek him and, when found, would destroy him with lightning bolts.

The two dragons confronted each other, rearing on their hind legs, their breath at last turning to fire as the rain came. Their voices beat upon the ear and when they leapt to each other, the ground shook beneath their bodies. They changed size rapidly and often, looking for advantage. Scales as big as a man's hand littered the street like fallen leaves as the dragons, red clawed, red fanged, rolled about in each other's embrace. Lightning struck twice more, gouging the road and shattering the wall. The rain poured down in dark streets till all that could be seen was the fiery glow of their bodies and breath. They could no longer be told apart.

Then, as Yuen Pao and I sheltered in the doorway of the house, the quaking earth stilled, the brightness diminished, and there came a great quiet beneath the beating of the rain.

Slowly, as the torrent thinned, a mountainous form could be seen lying in the street, motionless, fireless, and beyond it, burning faintly, another dragon stood, its head waving slowly in the air upturned to the clouds.

I wiped rain from my eyes, straining for a glimpse of color through the sheets of gray. I could not help but care. I had been his refuge till the end, even after I believed he had left me, and, in spite of all I had just seen, if he had scampered, mouse-sized, toward the door where I hid, I would have sheltered him again, foolish as it doubtless would have been. But in the thinning rain I could identify neither the dead dragon nor the live one.

Then the final bolt of lightning struck.

Hours later, when the rain stopped, there was not so much as a splintered bone in the muddy, cratered street. But beneath the blasted tree Yuen Pao found one large round scale of silver scalloped in blue. I wear it on a braided cord about my neck like an amulet. It marks me, though that is hardly necessary these days. Word of mouth travels swiftly in this land. The villagers saw from whence the dragon came. They knew whose pack it was. It was never established whether or not a ghost could die a second death (and I am still not sure about the oranges), but no one questioned the power of ghostly magic. It has been mainly to my advantage, I suppose; only occasionally have I resented it. I wear the reputation as I wear my "amulet" and the name the people gave me.

I am called Lung Gwai.

The Dragon Ghost.

Here is a dragon with a very different problem than Lucie Chin's Lan Lung. RICHARD L. WEXELBLAT, *author of the definitive* History of Programming Languages, *is a mathematical genius who writes delightful verse in his scant spare time.*

The Dragon Over Hackensack

BY RICHARD L. WEXELBLAT

Unexpectedly a red dragon appeared over Hackensack NJ
　One late winter afternoon.
Two F-104s of the New Jersey Air National Guard scrambled to meet it.

In a move surprising to some observers,
　Though not all,
The dragon breathed a stream of fire . . .
That completely missed the planes
　But incinerated: an empty wooden water tower on the Bijou,
　　　　　　　　　　a billboard that used to blow smoke rings,
　　　　　　　　　　and the ABC Action-Cam hot air balloon.

One F-104 attacked with 105mm cannon,
The other with Sidewinder heat-seeking missiles.

Of course, the cannon shells bounced off of the dragon's scales.
The Sidewinders missed and eventually fell to earth in the
　Great Swamp, just missing a deer on the runway of
　Morristown Airport.

The dragon, flattered or annoyed by all this attention,
Reversed course and flew off
Out of sight
In the direction of Long Island,
Pausing only to eat the top 50 feet
Off the leftmost of the two World Trade Center Towers.

The Pentagon ignored the report on the incident.

MARY SHELLEY *wrote many fantastic novels and stories, but she is best known for* Frankenstein, *written in friendly competition with Lord Byron's, John Polidori and of course, Mary's husband, the poet Percy Bysshe Shelley, a Byronic hero-demon who dominated his wife with an influence both inspiring and vampiric. When Mary wrote "The Transformation" in 1831, she was thirty-four. Percy had been dead for nearly a decade, yet his equivocal personality still possessed her, as reflected in the character of the narrator of this bizarre tale, a weak person with a great capacity to do either good or evil. The denouement seems to suggest that the author still could not abandon all hope that her late husband's soul was magnificent, at least in its potential for virtue. Though she died twenty years later in 1851, it is unlikely that Mary ever exorcised her great angel-fiend.*

The Transformation

BY MARY W. SHELLEY

"Forthwith this frame of mine was wrenched
  With a woeful agony,
Which forced me to begin my tale;
  And then it left me free.

"Since then, at an uncertain hour,
  That agony returns:
And till my ghastly tale is told,
  This heart within me burns."

—SAMUEL TAYLOR COLERIDGE
"The Ancient Mariner"

I have heard it said, that, when any strange, supernatural, and necromantic adventure has occurred to a human being, that being, however desirous he may be to conceal the same, feels at certain periods torn up as it were by an intellectual earthquake, and is forced to bare the inner depths of his spirit to another. I am a witness of the truth of this. I have dearly sworn to myself never to reveal to human ears the horrors to which I once, in excess of fiendly pride, delivered myself over. The holy man who heard my confession, and reconciled me to the Church, is dead. None knows that once—

Why should it not be thus? Why tell a tale of impious tempting of Providence, and soul-subduing humiliation? Why? answer me, ye who are wise in the secrets of human nature! I only know that so it is; and in spite of strong resolve,—of a pride that too much masters me—of shame, and even of fear, so to render myself odious to my species,—I must speak.

Genoa! my birthplace—proud city! looking upon the blue Mediterranean—dost thou remember me in my boyhood, when thy cliffs and promontories, thy bright sky and gay vineyards, were my world? Happy time? when to the young heart the narrow-bounded universe, which leaves, by its very limitation, free scope to the imagination, enchains our physical energies, and, sole period in our lives, innocence and enjoyment are united. Yet, who can look back to childhood, and not remember its sorrows and its harrowing fears? I was born with the most imperious, haughty, tameless spirit. I quailed before my father only; and he, generous and noble, but capricious and tyrannical, at once fostered and checked the wild impetuosity of my character, making obedience necessary, but inspiring no respect for the motives which guided his commands. To be a man, free, independent; or, in better words, insolent and domineering, was the hope and prayer of my rebel heart.

My father had one friend, a wealthy Genoese noble, who in a political tumult was suddenly sentenced to banishment, and his property confiscated. The Marchese Torella went into exile alone. Like my father, he was a widower: he had one child, the almost infant Juliet, who was left under my father's guardianship. I should certainly have been unkind to the lovely girl, but that I was forced by my position to become her protector. A variety of childish incidents all tended to one point,—to make Juliet see in me a rock of defence; I in her, one who must perish through the soft sensibility of her nature too rudely visited, but for my guardian care. We grew up together. The opening rose in May was not more sweet than this dear girl. An irradiation of beauty was spread over her face. Her form, her step, her voice—my heart weeps even now, to think of all of relying, gentle, loving, and pure, that she enshrined. When I was eleven and Juliet eight years of age, a cousin of mine, much older than either—he seemed to us a man— took great notice of my playmate; he called her his bride, and asked her to marry him. She refused, and he insisted, drawing her unwillingly towards him. With the countenance and emotions of a maniac I threw myself on him—I strove to draw his sword—I clung to his neck with the ferocious resolve to strangle him: he was obliged to call for assistance to disengage himself from me. On that night I led Juliet to the chapel of our house: I made her touch the sacred relics—I harrowed her child's heart, and profaned her child's lips with an oath, that she would be mine, and mine only.

Well, those days passed away. Torella returned in a few years, and became wealthier and more prosperous than ever. When I was seventeen, my father died; he had been magnificent to prodigality; Torella rejoiced that my minority would afford an opportunity for repairing my fortunes. Juliet and I had been affianced beside my father's deathbed—Torella was to be a second parent to me.

I desired to see the world, and I was indulged. I went to Florence, to Rome, to Naples; thence I passed to Toulon, and at length reached what had long been the bourne of my wishes, Paris. There was wild work in Paris then. The poor king, Charles the Sixth, now sane, now mad, now a monarch, now an abject slave, was the very mockery of humanity. The queen, the dauphin, the Duke of Burgundy, alternately friends and foes,—now meeting in prodigal feasts, now shedding blood in rivalry,—were blind to the miserable state of their country, and the dangers that impended over it, and gave themselves wholly up to dissolute enjoyment or savage strife. My character still followed me. I was arrogant and self-willed; I loved display, and above all, I threw off all control. My young friends were eager to foster passions which furnished them with pleasures. I was deemed handsome—I was master of every knightly accomplishment. I was disconnected with any political party. I grew a favourite with all: my presumption and arrogance was pardoned in one so young: I became a spoiled child. Who could control me? not the letters and advice of Torella—only strong necessity visiting me in the abhorred shape of an empty purse. But there were means to refill this void. Acre after acre, estate after estate, I sold. My dress, my jewels, my horses and their caparisons, were almost unrivalled in gorgeous Paris, while the lands of my inheritance passed into possession of others.

The Duke of Orleans was waylaid and murdered by the Duke of Burgundy. Fear and terror possessed all Paris. The dauphin and the queen shut themselves up; every pleasure was suspended. I grew weary of this state of things, and my heart yearned for my boyhood's haunts. I was nearly a beggar, yet still I would go there, claim my bride, and rebuild my fortunes. A few happy ventures as a merchant would make me rich again. Nevertheless, I would not return in humble guise. My last act was to dispose of my remaining estate near Albaro for half its worth, for ready money. Then I despatched all kinds of artificers, arras, furniture or regal splendour, to fit up the last relic of my inheritance, my palace in Genoa. I lingered a little longer yet, ashamed at the part of the prodigal returned, which I feared I should play. I sent my horses. One matchless Spanish jennet I despatched to my promised bride: its caparisons flamed with jewels and cloth of gold. In every part I caused to be entwined the initials of Juliet and her Guido. My present found favour in hers and in her father's eyes.

Still to return a proclaimed spendthrift, the mark of impertinent wonder, perhaps of scorn, and to encounter singly the reproaches or taunts of my fellow-citizens, was no alluring prospect. As a shield between me and censure, I invited some few of the most reckless of my comrades to accompany me: thus I went armed against the world, hiding a rankling feeling, half fear and half penitence, by bravado.

I arrived in Genoa. I trod the pavement of my ancestral palace. My proud step was no interpreter of my heart, for I deeply felt that, though surrounded by every luxury, I was a beggar. The first step I took in claiming Juliet must widely declare me such. I read contempt or pity in the looks of all. I fancied that rich and poor, young and old, all regarded me with derision. Torella came not near me. No wonder that my second father should expect a son's deference from me in waiting first on him. But, galled and stung by a sense of my follies and demerit, I strove to throw the blame on others. We kept nightly orgies in Palazzo Carega. To sleepless, riotous nights followed listless, supine mornings. At the Ave Maria we showed our dainty persons in the streets, scoffing at the sober citizens, casting insolent glances on the shrinking women. Juliet was not among them—no, no; if she had been there, shame would have driven me away, if love had not brought me to her feet.

I grew tired of this. Suddenly I paid the Marchese a visit. He was at his villa, one among the many which deck the suburb of San Pietro d'Arena. It was the month of May, the blossoms of the fruit-trees were fading among thick, green foliage; the vines were shooting forth; the ground strewed with the fallen olive blooms; the firefly was in the myrtle hedge; heaven and earth wore a mantle of surpassing beauty. Torella welcomed me kindly, though seriously; and even his shade of displeasure soon wore away. Some resemblance to my father—some look and tone of youthful ingenuousness, softened the good old man's heart. He sent for his daughter—he presented me to her as her betrothed. The chamber became hallowed by a holy light as she entered. Hers was that cherub look, those large, soft eyes, full dimpled cheeks, and mouth of infantine sweetness, that expresses the rare union of happiness and love. Admiration first possessed me; she is mine! was the second proud emotion, and my lips curled with haughty triumph. I had not been the *enfant gâté* of the beauties of France not to have learnt the art of pleasing the soft heart of woman. If towards men I was overbearing, the deference I paid to them was the more in contrast. I commenced my courtship by the display of a thousand gallantries to Juliet, who, vowed to me from infancy, had never admitted the devotion of others; and who, though accustomed to expressions of admiration, was uninitiated in the language of lovers.

For a few days all went well. Torella never alluded to my extravagance; he treated me as a favourite son. But the time came, as we discussed the preliminaries to my union with his daughter, when this fair face of things should be overcast. A contract had been drawn up in my father's lifetime. I had rendered this, in fact, void by having squandered the whole of the wealth which was to have been shared by Juliet and myself. Torella, in consequence, chose to consider this bond as cancelled, and proposed another, in which, though the wealth he bestowed was immeasurably increased, there were so many restrictions as to the mode of spending it, that I, who saw independence only in free career being given to my own imperious will, taunted him as taking advantage of my situation, and refused utterly to subscribe to his conditions. The old man mildly strove to recall me to reason. Roused pride became the tyrant of my thought: I listened with indignation—I repelled him with disdain.

"Juliet, thou art mine! Did we not interchange vows in our

innocent childhood? Are we not one in the sight of God? and shall thy cold-hearted, cold-blooded father divide us? Be generous, my love, be just; take not away a gift, last treasure of thy Guido—retract not thy vows—let us defy the world, and, setting at nought the calculations of age, find in our mutual affection a refuge from every ill."

Fiend I must have been with such sophistry to endeavour to poison that sanctuary of holy thought and tender love. Juliet shrank from me affrighted. Her father was the best and kindest of men, and she strove to show me how, in obeying him, every good would follow. He would receive my tardy submission with warm affection, and generous pardon would follow my repentance; profitless words for a young and gentle daughter to use to a man accustomed to make his will law, and to feel in his own heart a despot so terrible and stern that he could yield obedience to nought save his own imperious desires! My resentment grew with resistance; my wild companions were ready to add fuel to the flame. We laid a plan to carry off Juliet. At first it appeared to be crowned with success. Midway, on our return, we were overtaken by the agonized father and his attendants. A conflict ensued. Before the city guard came to decide the victory in favour of our antagonists, two of Torella's servitors were dangerously wounded.

This portion of my history weighs most heavily with me. Changed man as I am, I abhor myself in the recollection. May none who hear this tale ever have felt as I. A horse driven to fury by a rider armed with barbed spurs was not more a slave than I to the violent tyranny of my temper. A fiend possessed my soul, irritating it to madness. I felt the voice of conscience within me; but if I yielded to it for a brief interval, it was only to be a moment after torn, as by a whirlwind, away—born along on the stream of desperate rage—the plaything of the storms engendered by pride. I was imprisoned, and, at the instance of Torella, set free. Again I returned to carry off both him and his child to France, which hapless country, then preyed on by free-booters and gangs of lawless soldiery, offered a grateful refuge to a criminal like me. Our plots were discovered. I was sentenced to banishment; and, as my debts were already enormous, my remaining property was put in the hands of commissioners for their payment. Torella again offered his mediation, requiring only my promise not to renew my abortive attempts on himself and his daughter. I spurned his offers, and fancied that I triumphed when I was thrust out from

Genoa, a solitary and penniless exile. My companions were gone: they had been dismissed from the city some weeks before, and were already in France. I was alone—friendless, with neither sword at my side, nor ducat in my purse.

I wandered along the sea-shore, a whirlwind of passion possessing and tearing my soul. It was as if a live coal had been set burning in my breast. At first I meditated on what *I should do*. I would join a band of freebooters. Revenge!—the word seemed balm to me; I hugged it, caressed it, till, like a serpent, it stung me. Then again I would abjure and despise Genoa, that little corner of the world. I would return to Paris, where so many of my friends swarmed; where my services would be eagerly accepted; where I would carve out fortune with my sword, and make my paltry birthplace and the false Torella rue the day when they drove me, a new Coriolanus, from her walls. I would return to Paris— thus on foot—a beggar—and present myself in my poverty to those I had formerly entertained sumptuously? There was gall in the mere thought of it.

The reality of things began to dawn upon my mind, bringing despair in its train. For several months I had been a prisoner: the evils of my dungeon had whipped my soul to madness, but they had subdued my corporeal frame. I was weak and wan. Torella had used a thousand artifices to administer to my comfort; I had detected and scorned them all, and I reaped the harvest of my obduracy. What was to be done? Should I crouch before my foe, and sue for forgiveness?—Die rather ten thousand deaths!—Never should they obtain that victory! Hate—I swore eternal hate! Hate from whom?—to whom?—From a wandering outcast—to a mighty noble! I and my feelings were nothing to them: already had they forgotten one so unworthy. And Juliet!—her angel face and sylph-like form gleamed among the clouds of my despair with vain beauty; for I had lost her—the glory and flower of the world! Another will call her his!—that smile of paradise will bless another!

Even now my heart fails within me when I recur to this rout of grimvisaged ideas. Now subdued almost to tears, now raving in my agony, still I wandered along the rocky shore, which grew at each step wilder and more desolate. Hanging rocks and hoar precipices overlooked the tideless ocean; black caverns yawned; and for ever, among the seaworn recesses, murmured and dashed the unfruitful waters. Now my way was almost barred by an abrupt promontory, now rendered nearly impracticable by fragments fallen from the cliff. Evening was at hand, when, seaward, arose, as if on the waving of a wizard's wand, a murky web of clouds, blotting the late azure sky, and darkening and disturbing the till now placid deep. The clouds had strange, fantastic shapes, and they changed and mingled and seemed to be driven about by a mighty spell. The waves raised their white crests; the thunder first muttered, then roared from across the waste of waters, which took a deep purple dye, flecked with foam. The spot where I stood looked, on one side, to the wide-spread ocean; on the other, it was barred by a rugged promontory. Round this cape suddenly came, driven by the wind, a vessel. In vain the mariners tried to force a path for her to the open sea—the gale drove her on the rocks. It will perish!—all on board will perish! Would I were among them! And to my young heart the idea of death came for the first time blended with that of joy. It was an awful sight to behold that vessel struggling with her fate. Hardly could I discern the sailors, but I heard them. It was soon all over! A rock, just covered by the tossing waves, and so unperceived, lay in wait for its prey. A crash of thunder broke over my head at the moment that, with a frightful shock, the vessel dashed upon her unseen enemy. In a brief space of time she went to pieces. There I stood in safety; and there were my fellow-creatures battling, how hopelessly, with annihilation. Methought I saw them struggling— too truly did I hear their shrieks, conquering the barking surges in their shrill agony. The dark breakers threw hither and thither the fragments of the wreck: soon it disappeared. I had been fascinated to gaze till the end: at last I sank on my knees—I covered my face with my hands. I again looked up; something was floating on the billows towards the shore. It neared and neared. Was that a human form? It grew more and more distinct; and at last a mighty wave, lifting the whole freight, lodged it upon a rock. A human being bestriding a sea-chest!—a human being! Yet was it one? Surely never such had existed before—a misshapen dwarf, with squinting eyes, distorted features, and body deformed, till it became a horror to behold. My blood, lately warming towards a fellow-being so snatched from a watery tomb, froze in my heart. The dwarf got off his chest; he tossed his straight, struggling hair from his odious visage.

"By St. Beelzebub!" he exclaimed, "I have been well bested." He looked round and saw me. "Oh, by the fiend! here is another ally of the mighty One. To what saint did you offer prayers, friend—if not to mine? Yet I remember you not on board."

I shrank from the monster and his blasphemy. Again he questioned me, and I muttered some inaudible reply. He continued: —

"Your voice is drowned by this dissonant roar. What a noise the big ocean makes! Schoolboys bursting from their prison are not louder than these waves set free to play. They disturb me. I will no more of their ill-timed brawling. Silence, hoary One!—Winds, avaunt!—to your homes!—Clouds, fly to the antipodes, and leave our heaven clear!"

As he spoke, he stretched out his two long, lank arms, that looked like spider's claws, and seemed to embrace with them the expanse before him. Was it a miracle? The clouds became broken and fled; the azure sky first peeped out, and then was spread a calm field of blue above us; the stormy gale was exchanged to the softly breathing west; the sea grew calm; the waves dwindled to riplets.

"I like obedience even in these stupid elements," said the dwarf. "How much more in the tameless mind of man! It was a well-got-up storm, you must allow—and all of my own making."

It was tempting Providence to interchange talk with this magician. But *Power*, in all its shapes, is respected by man. Awe, curiosity, a clinging fascination, drew me towards him.

"Come, don't be frightened, friend," said the wretch: "I am good humoured when pleased; and something does please me in your well-proportioned body and handsome face, though you look a little woe-begone. You have suffered a land—I, a sea wreck. Perhaps I can allay the tempest of your fortunes as I did my own. Shall we be friends?"—And he held out his hand; I could not touch it. "Well, then, companions—that will do as well. And now, while I rest after the buffeting I underwent just now, tell me why, young and gallant as you seem, you wander thus alone and downcast on this wild sea-shore."

The voice of the wretch was screeching and horrid, and his contortions as he spoke were frightful to behold. Yet he did gain a kind of influence over me, which I could not master, and I told him my tale. When it was ended, he laughed long and loud: the rocks echoed back the sound: hell seemed yelling around me.

"Oh, thou cousin of Lucifer!" said he; "so thou too hast fallen through thy pride; and, though bright as the son of Morning, thou art ready to give up thy good looks, thy bride, and thy well-being, rather than submit thee to the tyranny of good. I honour thy choice, by my soul!—So thou hast fled, and yield the day; and mean to starve on these rocks, and to let the birds peck out thy dead eyes, while thy enemy and thy betrothed rejoice in thy ruin. Thy pride is strangely akin to humility, methinks."

As he spoke, a thousand fanged thoughts stung me to the heart.

"What would you that I should do?" I cried.

"I!—Oh, nothing, but lie down and say your prayers before you die. But, were I you, I know the deed that should be done."

I drew near him. His supernatural powers made him an oracle in my eyes; yet a strange unearthly thrill quivered through my frame as I said, "Speak!—teach me—what act do you advise?"

"Revenge thyself, man!—humble thy enemies!—set thy foot on the old man's neck, and possess thyself of his daughter!"

"To the east and west I turn," cried I, "and see no means! Had I gold, much could I achieve; but, poor and single, I am powerless."

The dwarf had been seated on his chest as he listened to my story. Now he got off; he touched a spring; it flew open! What a mine of wealth—of blazing jewels, beaming gold, and pale silver— was displayed therein. A mad desire to possess this treasure was born within me.

"Doubtless," I said, "one so powerful as you could do all things."

"Nay," said the monster humbly, "I am less omnipotent than I seem. Some things I possess which you may covet; but I would give them all for a small share, or even for a loan of what is yours."

"My possessions are at your service," I replied bitterly—"my poverty, my exile, my disgrace—I make a free gift of them all."

"Good! I thank you. Add one other thing to your gift, and my treasure is yours."

"As nothing is my sole inheritance, what besides nothing would you have?"

"Your comely face and well-made limbs."

I shivered. Would this all-powerful monster murder me? I had no dagger. I forgot to pray—but I grew pale.

"I ask for a loan, not a gift," said the frightful thing: "lend me your body for three days—you shall have mine to cage your soul the while, and, in payment, my chest. What say you to the bargain?—Three short days."

We are told that it is dangerous to hold unlawful talk; and well do I prove the same. Tamely written down, it may seem incredible that I should lend any ear to this proposition; but, in spite of his unnatural ugliness, there was something fascinating in a being whose voice could govern earth, air, and sea. I felt a keen desire to comply; for with that chest I could command the world. My only hesitation resulted from a fear that he would not be true to his bargain. Then, I thought, I shall soon die here on these lonely sands, and the limbs he covets will be mine no more:—it is worth the chance. And, besides, I knew that, by all the rules of art-magic, there were formulae and oaths which none of its practisers dared break. I hesitated to reply; and he went on, now displaying his wealth, now speaking of the petty price he demanded, till it seemed madness to refuse. Thus is it;—place our bark in the current of the stream, and down, over fall and cataract it is hurried; give up our conduct to the wild torrent of passion, and we are away, we know not whither.

He swore many an oath, and I adjured him by many a sacred name; till I saw this wonder of power, this ruler of the elements, shiver like an autumn leaf before my words; and as if the spirit spake unwillingly and perforce within him, at last, he, with broken voice, revealed the spell whereby he might be obliged, did he wish to play me false, to render up the unlawful spoil. Our warm life-blood must mingle to make and to mar the charm.

Enough of this unholy theme. I was persuaded—the thing was done. The morrow dawned upon me as I lay upon the shingles, and I knew not my own shadow as it fell from me. I felt myself changed to a shape of horror, and cursed my easy faith and blind credulity. The chest was there—there the gold and precious stones for which I had sold the frame of flesh which nature had given me. The sight a little stilled my emotions: three days would soon be gone.

They did pass. The dwarf had supplied me with a plenteous store of food. At first I could hardly walk, so strange and out of joint were all my limbs; and my voice—it was that of the fiend. But I kept silent, and turned my face to the sun, that I might not see my shadow, and counted the hours, and ruminated on my future conduct. To bring Torella to my feet—to possess my Juliet in spite of him—all this my wealth could easily achieve. During dark night I slept, and dreamt of the accomplishment of my desires. Two suns had set—the third dawned. I was agitated, fearful. Oh expectation, what a frightful thing art thou, when kindled more by fear than hope! How dost thou twist thyself round the heart, torturing its pulsations! How dost thou dart unknown pangs all through our feeble mechanism, now seeming to shiver us like broken glass, to nothingness—now giving us a fresh strength, which can *do* nothing, and so torments us by a sensation, such as the strong man must feel who cannot break his fetters, though they bend in his grasp. Slowly paced the bright, bright orb up the eastern sky; long it lingered in the zenith, and still more slowly wandered down the west: it touched the horizon's verge— it was lost! Its glories were on the summits of the cliff—they grew dun and grey. The evening star shone bright. He will soon be here.

He came not!—By the living heavens, he came not!—and night dragged out its weary length, and, in its decaying age, "day began to grizzle its dark hair"; and the sun rose again on the most miserable wretch that ever upbraided its light. Three days thus I passed. The jewels and the gold—oh, how I abhorred them!

Well, well—I will not blacken these pages with demoniac ravings. All too terrible were the thoughts, the raging tumult of ideas that filled my soul. At the end of that time I slept; I had not before since the third sunset; and I dreamt that I was at Juliet's feet, and she smiled, and then she shrieked—for she saw my transformation—and again she smiled, for still her beautiful lover knelt before her. But it was not I—it was he, the fiend, arrayed in my limbs, speaking with my voice, winning her with my looks of love. I strove to warn her, but my tongue refused its office; I strove to tear him from her, but I was rooted to the ground—I awoke with the agony. There were the solitary hoar precipices— there the plashing sea, the quiet strand, and the blue sky over all. What did it mean? was my dream but a mirror of the truth? was he wooing and winning my betrothed? I would on the instant back to Genoa—but I was banished. I laughed—the dwarf's yell burst from my lips—I banished! Oh no! they had not exiled the four limbs I wore; I might with these enter, without fear of incurring the threatened penalty of death, my own, my native city.

I began to walk towards Genoa. I was somewhat accustomed to my distorted limbs; none were ever so ill-adapted for a straight-forward movement; it was with infinite difficulty that I proceeded. Then, too, I desired to avoid all the hamlets strewed here and there on the seabeach, for I was unwilling to make a display of my hideousness. I was not quite sure that, if seen, the mere boys would not stone me to death as I passed, for a monster; some ungentle salutations I did receive from the few peasants or fishermen I chanced to meet. But it was dark night before I approached Genoa. The weather was so balmy and sweet that it struck me that the Marchese and his daughter would very probably have quitted the city for their country retreat. It was from Villa Torella that I had attempted to carry off Juliet; I had spent many an hour reconnoitering the spot, and knew each inch of ground in its vicinity. It was beautifully situated, embosomed in trees, on the margin of a stream. As I drew near, it became evident that my conjecture was right; nay, moreover, that the hours were being then devoted to feasting and merriment. For the house was lighted up; strains of soft and gay music were wafted towards me by the breeze. My heart sank within me. Such was the generous kindness of Torella's heart that I felt sure that he would not have indulged in public manifestations of rejoicing just after my unfortunate banishment, but for a cause I dared not dwell upon.

The country people were all alive and flocking about; it became necessary that I should conceal myself; and yet I longed to address some one, or to hear others discourse, or in any way to gain intelligence of what was really going on. At length, entering the walls that were in immediate vicinity to the mansion, I found one dark enough to veil my excessive frightfulness; and yet others as well as I were loitering in its shade. I soon gathered all I wanted to know—all that first made my very heart die with horror, and then boil with indignation. Tomorrow Juliet was to be given to the penitent, reformed, beloved Guido—tomorrow my bride was to pledge her vows to a fiend from hell! And I did this!—my accursed pride—my demoniac violence and wicked self-idolatry had caused this act. For if I had acted as the wretch who had stolen my form had acted—if, with a mien at once yielding and dignified, I had presented myself to Torella, saying, I have done wrong, forgive me; I am unworthy of your angel-child, but permit me to claim her hereafter, when my altered conduct shall manifest that I abjure my vices, and endeavour to become in some sort worthy of her. I go to serve against the infidels; and when my zeal for religion and my true penitence for the past shall appear to you to cancel my crimes, permit me again to call myself your son. Thus had he spoken; and the penitent was welcomed even as the prodigal son of Scripture: the fatted calf was killed for him; and he, still pursuing the same path, displayed such open-hearted regret for his follies, so humble a concession of all his rights, and so ardent a resolve to reacquire them by a life of contrition and virtue, that he quickly conquered the kind old man; and full pardon, and the gift of his lovely child, followed in swift succession.

Oh, had an angel from Paradise whispered to me to act thus! But now, what would be the innocent Juliet's fate? Would God permit the foul union—or, some prodigy destroying it, link the dishonoured name of Carega with the worst of crimes? To-morrow at dawn they were to be married: there was but one way to prevent this—to meet mine enemy, and to enforce the ratification of our agreement. I felt that this could only be done by a mortal struggle. I had no sword—if indeed my distorted arms could wield a soldier's weapon—but I had a dagger, and in that lay my hope. There was no time for pondering or balancing nicely the question: I might die in the attempt; but besides the burning jealousy and despair of my own heart, honour, mere humanity, demanded that I should fall rather than not destroy the machinations of the fiend.

The guests departed—the lights began to disappear; it was evident that the inhabitants of the villa were seeking repose. I hid myself among the trees—the garden grew desert—the gates were closed—I wandered round and came under a window—ah! well did I know the same!—a soft twilight glimmered in the room—the curtains were half withdrawn. It was the temple of innocence and beauty. Its magnificence was tempered, as it were, by the slight disarrangements occasioned by its being dwelt in, and all the objects scattered around dispayed the taste of her who hallowed it by her presence. I saw her enter with a quick light step—I saw her approach the window—she drew back the curtain yet further, and looked out into the night. Its breezy freshness played among her ringlets, and wafted them from the transparent marble of her brow. She clasped her hands, she raised her eyes to heaven. I heard her voice. Guido! she softly murmured—mine own Guido! and then, as if overcome by the fuliness of her own heart, she sank on her knees;—her upraised eyes—her graceful attitude—the beaming thankfulness that lighted up her face—oh, these are tame words! Heart of mine, thou imagest ever, though thou canst not portray, the celestial beauty of that child of light and love.

I heard a step—a quick firm step along the shady avenue. Soon I saw a cavalier, richly dressed, young and, methought, graceful to look on, advance. I hid myself yet closer. The youth approached; he paused beneath the window. She arose, and again looking out she saw him, and said—I cannot, no, at this distant time I cannot record her terms of soft silver tenderness; to me they were spoken, but they were replied to by him.

"I will not go," he cried: "here where you have been, where your memory glides like some heaven-visiting ghost, I will pass the long hours till we meet, never, my Juliet, again, day or night, to part. But do you, my love, retire; the cold morn and fitful breeze will make thy cheek pale, and fill with languor thy love-lighted eyes. Ah, sweetest! could I press one kiss upon them, I could, methinks, repose."

And then he approached still nearer, and methought he was about to clamber into her chamber. I had hesitated, not to terrify her; now I was no longer master of myself. I rushed forward—I threw myself on him—I tore him away—I cried, "O loathsome and foul-shaped wretch!"

I need not repeat epithets, all tending, as it appeared, to rail at a person I at present feel some partiality for. A shriek rose from Juliet's lips. I neither heard nor saw—I *felt* only mine enemy, whose throat I grasped, and my dagger's hilt; he struggled, but could not escape. At length hoarsely he breathed these words: "Do!—strike home! destroy this body—you will still live: may your life be long and merry!"

The descending dagger was arrested at the word, and he, feeling my hold relax, extricated himself and drew his sword, while the uproar in the house, and flying of torches from one room to the other, showed that soon we should be separated. In the midst of my frenzy there was much calculation:—fall I might, and so that he did not survive, I cared not for the death-blow I might deal against myself. While still, therefore, he thought I paused, and while I saw the villainous resolve to take advantage of my hesitation, in the sudden thrust he made at me, I threw myself on his sword, and at the same moment plunged my dagger, with a true, desperate aim, in his side. We fell together, rolling over each other, and the tide of blood that flowed from the gaping wound of each mingled on the grass. More I know not—I fainted.

Again I return to life: weak almost to death, I found myself stretched upon a bed—Juliet was kneeling beside it. Strange! my first broken request was for a mirror. I was so wan and ghastly, that my poor girl hesitated, as she told me afterwards; but, by the mass! I thought myself a right proper youth when I saw the dear reflection of my own well-known features. I confess it is a weakness, but I avow it, I do entertain a considerable affection for the countenance and limbs I behold, whenever I look at a glass; and have more mirrors in my house, and consult them oftener, than any beauty in Genoa. Before you too much condemn me, permit me to say that no one better knows than I the value of his own body; no one, probably, except myself, ever having had it stolen from him.

Incoherently I at first talked of the dwarf and his crimes, and reproached Juliet for her too easy admission of his love. She thought me raving, as well she might; and yet it was some time before I could prevail on myself to admit that the Guido whose penitence had won her back for me was myself; and while I cursed bitterly the monstrous dwarf, and blest the well-directed blow that had deprived him of life, I suddenly checked myself when I heard her say, Amen! knowing that him whom she reviled was my very self. A little reflection taught me silence—a little practice enabled me to speak of that frightful night without any very excessive blunder. The wound I had given myself was no mockery of one— it was long before I recovered—and as the benevolent and generous Torella sat beside me, talking such wisdom as might win friends to repentance, and mine own dear Juliet hovered near me, administering to my wants, and cheering me by her smiles, the work of my bodily cure and mental reform went on together. I have never, indeed, wholly recovered my strength—my cheek is paler since—my person a little bent. Juliet sometimes ventures to allude bitterly to the malice that caused this change, but I kiss her on the moment, and tell her all is for the best. I am a fonder and more faithful husband, and true is this—but for that wound, never had I called her mine.

I did not revisit the sea-shore, nor seek the fiend's treasure; yet, while I ponder on the past, I often think, and my confessor was not backward in favouring the idea, that it might be a good rather than an evil spirit, sent by my guardian angel, to show me the folly and misery of pride. So well at least did I learn this lesson, roughly taught as I was, that I am known now by all my friends and fellow-citizens by the name of Guido il Cortese.

EDWARD D. HOCH *is the enormously prolific author of literally hundreds of detective, crime and espionage short stories, including the wonderful Nick Velvet series about a thief who steals things no one else would ever think of bothering with. Ed's feverish output of fiction is only rivalled by the unqualified excellence of his writing and surpassed solely by the sunny nature of his dispositon. And yet he has penned a handful of rather nasty horror stories, most of them dating back to the early 1960s when "Doc" Lowndes' late lamented* The Magazine of Horror *was being published. "The Faceless Thing," one of these tales, is a favorite of its author. Though a great sense of menace lurks in its earlier moments, Ed is after a very different effect than the usual horrific shiver . . . and I find it far bleaker than the garden variety of grue.*

The Faceless Thing

BY EDWARD D. HOCH

Sunset: golden flaming clouds draped over distant canyons barely seen in the dusk of the dying day; farmland gone to rot; fields in the foreground given over wildly to the running of the rabbit and the woodchuck; the farmhouse gray and paint-peeled, sleeping possibly but more likely dead—needing burial.

It hadn't changed much in all those years. It hadn't changed; only died.

He parked the car and got out, taking it all in with eyes still intent and quick for all their years. Somehow he hadn't really thought it would still be standing. Farmhouses that were near collapse fifty years ago shouldn't still be standing; not when all the people, his mother and father and aunt and the rest, were all long in their graves.

He was an old man, had been an old man almost as long as he could remember. Youth to him was only memories of this farm, so many years before, romping in the hay with his little sister at his side; swinging from the barn ropes, exploring endless dark depths out beyond the last field. After that, he was old—through misty college days and marriage to a woman he hadn't loved, through a business and political career that carried him around the world. And never once in all those years had he journeyed back to this place, this farmhouse now given over to the weeds and insects. They were all dead; there was no reason to come back . . . no reason at all.

Except the memory of the ooze.

A childhood memory, a memory buried with the years, forgotten sometimes but always there, crowded into its own little space in his mind, was ready to confront him and startled him with its vividness.

The ooze was a place beyond the last field, where water always collected in the springtime and after a storm; water running over dirt and clay and rock, merging with the soil until there was nothing underfoot but a black ooze to rise above your boots. He'd followed the stream rushing with storm water, followed it to the place where it cut into the side of the hill.

It was the memory of the tunnel, really, that had brought him back—the dark tunnel leading nowhere, gurgling with rain-fed water, barely large enough for him to fit through. A tunnel floored with unseen ooze, peopled by unknown danger; that was a place for every boy.

Had he only been ten that day? Certainly he'd been no more than eleven, leading the way while his nine-year-old sister followed. "This way. Be careful of the mud." She'd been afraid of the dark, afraid of what they might find there. But he'd called encouragement to her; after all, what could there be in all this ooze to hurt them?

How many years? Fifty?

"What *is* it, Buddy?" She'd always called him Buddy. What is it, Buddy? Only darkness, and a place maybe darker than dark, with a half-formed shadow rising from the ooze. He'd brought along his father's old lantern, and he fumbled to light it.

"Buddy!" she'd screamed—just once—and in the flare of the match he'd seen the thing, great and hairy and covered with ooze; something that lived in the darkness here, something that hated the light. In that terrifying instant it had reached out for his little sister and pulled her into the ooze.

That was the memory, a memory that came to him sometimes only at night. It had pursued him down the years like a fabled hound, coming to him, reminding him, when all was well with the world. It was like a personal demon sent from Hades to torture him. He'd never told anyone about that thing in the ooze, not even his mother. They'd cried and carried on when his sister was found the next day, and they'd said she'd drowned. He was not one to say differently.

And the years had passed. For a time, during his high school days, he read the local papers—searching for some word of the thing, some veiled news that it had come out of that forgotten cavern. But it never did; it liked the dark and damp too much. And, of course, no one else ever ventured into the stream bed. That was a pursuit only for the very young and very foolish.

By the time he was twenty, the memory was fading, merging with other thoughts, other goals, until at times he thought it only a child's dream. But then at night it would come again in all its vividness, and the thing in the ooze would beckon him.

A long life, long and crowded . . . One night he'd tried to tell his wife about it, but she wouldn't listen. That was the night he'd realized how little he'd ever loved her. Perhaps he'd only married her because, in a certain light, she reminded him of that sister of his youth. But the love that sometimes comes later came not at all to the two of them. She was gone now, like his youth, like his family and friends. There was only this memory remaining. The memory of a thing in the ooze.

Now the weeds were tall, beating against his legs, stirring nameless insects to flight with every step. He pressed a handkerchief against his brow, sponging the sweat that was forming there. Would the dark place still be there, or had fifty years of rain and dirt sealed it forever?

"Hello there," a voice called out. It was an old voice, barely carrying with the breeze. He turned and saw someone on the porch of the deserted farmhouse. An old woman, ancient and wrinkled.

"Do I know you?" he asked, moving closer.

"You may," she answered. "You're Buddy, aren't you? My, how old I've gotten. I used to live at the next farm, when you were just a boy. I was young then myself. I remember you."

"Oh! Mrs . . . ?" The name escaped him, but it wasn't important.

"Why did you come back, Buddy? Why, after all these years?"

He was an old man. Was it necessary to explain his actions to this woman from the past? "I just wanted to see the place," he answered. "Memories, you know."

"Bitter memories. Your little sister died here, did she not?" The old woman should have been dead, should have been dead and in her grave long ago.

He paused in the shade of the porch roof. "She died here, yes, but that was fifty years ago."

"How old we grow, how ancient! Is that why you returned?"

"In a way. I wanted to see the spot."

"Ah! The little brook back there beyond the last field. Let me walk that way with you. These old legs need exercise."

"Do you live here?" he asked, wanting to escape her now but knowing not how.

"No, still down the road. All alone now. Are you all alone, too?"

"I suppose so." The high grass made walking difficult.

"You know what they all said at the time, don't you? They all said you were fooling around, like you always did, and pushed her into the water."

There was a pain in his chest from breathing so hard. He was an old man. "Do you believe that?"

"What does it matter?" she answered. "After all these fifty years, what does it matter?"

"Would you believe me," he began, then hesitated into silence. Of course she wouldn't believe him, but he had to tell now. "Would you believe me if I told you what happened?"

She was a very old woman and she panted to keep up even his slow pace. She was ancient even to his old eyes, even in his world where now everyone was old. "I would believe you," she said.

"There was something in the ooze. Call it a monster, a demon, if you want. I saw it in the light of a match, and I can remember it as if it were yesterday. It took her."

"Perhaps," she said.

"You don't believe me."

"I said I would. This sun is hot today, even at twilight."

"It will be gone soon. I hate to hurry you, old woman, but I must reach the stream before dark."

"The last field is in sight."

Yes, it was in sight. But how would he ever fit through that small opening, how would he face the thing, even if by some miracle it still waited there in the ooze? Fifty years was a long time.

"Wait here," he said as they reached the little stream at last. It hadn't changed much, not really.

"You won't find it." He lowered his aged body into the bed of the stream, feeling once again the familiar forgotten ooze closing over his shoes.

"No one has to know," she called after him. "Even if there was something, that was fifty years ago."

But he went on, to the place where the water vanished into the rock. He held his breath and groped for the little flashlight in his pocket. Then he ducked his head and followed the water into the black.

It was steamy here, steamy and hot with the sweat of the earth. He flipped on the flashlight with trembling hands and followed its narrow beam with his eyes. The place was almost like a room in the side of the hill, a room perhaps seven feet high, with a floor of mud and ooze that seemed almost to bubble as he watched.

"Come on," he said softly, almost to himself. "I know you're there. You've got to be there."

And then he saw it, rising slowly from the ooze. A shapeless thing without a face, a thing that moved so slowly it might have been dead. An old, very old thing. For a long time he watched it, unable to move, unable to cry out. And even as he watched, the thing settled back softly into the ooze, as if even this small exertion had tired it.

"Rest," he said, very quietly. "We are all so old now."

And then he made his way back out of the cave, along the stream, and finally pulled himself from the clinging ooze. The ancient woman was still waiting on the bank, with fireflies playing about her in the dusk.

"Did you find anything?" she asked him.

"Nothing," he answered.

"Fifty years is a long time. You shouldn't have come back."

He sighed and fell into step beside her. "It was something I had to do."

"Come up to my house, if you want. I can make you a bit of tea."

His breath was coming better now, and the distance back to the farmhouse seemed shorter than he'd remembered. "I think I'd like that," he said . . .

LOVERS
AND OTHER MONSTERS

Ever since Alfred Hitchcock juxtaposed nudity and knifework in *Psycho*, lesser filmmakers have been showing us countless unclad damsels bloodily murdered, usually just before or after the act of love—as if feminine sexuality were something deserving punishment. Bluestockings make a lot of fuss about the adolescent inoffensiveness of *Playboy* centerfolds but seem to ignore the true pornography of such repugnant fare as *Friday the 13th, Prom Night* and the like. Even Steven Spielberg employed this form of sexploitation in the needlessly graphic opening of *Jaws*.

Yet the wedding, so to speak, of sensuality and horror is a venerable institution in the literature of the occult and gruesome. Demon lovers, sexy vampires, sadistic spouses, incestuous relatives all appear in the following tales, but mostly I have tried to put the emphasis on the psychological terrors accompanying the concept of love and/or sex in its more frightening permutations.

A few of the stories, notably those by Card, Poe, Lee and Matheson, depend for their power on revenge, mostly prompted by loyalty to a mistreated loved one. These are definitely not for the squeamish.

Sample sparingly from this section. Here there be nightmares!

The late JACK SNOW *was a native of Piqua, Ohio, where he was born in 1907. A career in radio led him to New York, where he became an NBC executive. Snow wrote the two most Baumlike sequels to* The Wizard of Oz, *the eerie* Magical Mimics in Oz *and* The Shaggy Man of Oz, *the official rollcall of that wonderful land,* Who's Who in Oz, *and a fine short story,* "Murder in Oz," *which appeared in* Oziana, *the official publication of the International Wizard of Oz Society. "The Anchor," an idyllic but ultimately chilling story, comes from Snow's scarce collection of fantasy tales,* Dark Music.

The Anchor

BY JACK SNOW

How Ailil loved the beauties of the old lake! Like an ancient well into which flowed the potent spells of the deep forest about it, the hollow of silent, black-shaded water lay motionless in the cup of the woods; a cup of loveliness fit for the lips of strange, forgotten Gods to sip from. As this thought occurred to Ailil he nodded with a pleased little smile. There it lay, cool and limpid as a great glistening jewel mounted in the green filigree of drooping willows that wept their trailing branches about the shore. And behind these loomed the deep shadows of the forest pines, vague and shapeless in the faint moonlight.

Tonight Ailil had rowed to the very center of the lake, and was lying in his tiny boat intoxicating himself with the deep, mad beauty about him. A vast distance over his head, there was a slender crescent moon, and stars glimmered faintly through a thin mist that overhung the lake like a veil, protecting it from ancient eyes that might peer down through the limitless heavens. Night birds cried out their weird notes, strange half human wails that issued from bird throats and blended with the eerie monotony of the thrumming bass of the frogs.

Ailil lay for a long time, listening and watching, curiously alert. He was acutely conscious of the ancient charm of the things about him. And, as in all things that are purely of the earth, there was something faintly sinister, something that grimaced and threatened ever so gently and subtly. Here was majestic, elemental beauty armed with its primeval, overpowering appeal . . . often are the Pipes of Pan heard in salute of a new devotee.

Ailil loved the lake. He loved it as a part of his own life. The thought of ever leaving it, or of ever going very far from it, wounded him like a physical pain. Every night, he slipped away and lay on its bosom, as he was doing tonight, calm, peaceful and quietly happy as he floated amid the deep beauty. Lachrymal fronds of willows drooped about the shore, and thin wisps of spiraling mist rose slowly from the lake's night blue surface, wavering and gliding.

Occasionally a firefly darted over the water, lighting the scene with the green glow of its cold, phosphorescent fire, and like the symphonic composition of an inspired madman, the base of the frogs and the thin wailing of the swamp birds echoed among the trees.

The soft lapping of the water on the sides of the boat recalled Ailil from his dreaming, and he noticed that his little craft had slowly drifted back toward the shore. Arousing himself, he pulled at the oars which slipped noiselessly through the dark waters, and in a few minutes, he was once more in the center of the lake.

Tonight he was free to dream as long as he wished. He would spend the whole night with this beauty, it would be his first night on the lake. Alone through all the deep hours of the night, and the wan moments of the early dawn, when the sun would mingle mists of grey and gold with the blue of the lake, and the somber green of the trees, he would rest alone and content on the bosom of this wild enchantment that he loved.

Once more in the center of the lake, Ailil lifted an ancient, time-rusted anchor and dropped it over the side of the boat. Silently and quickly it plunged through the dark depths of the water. How deep this ancient well must be! Coil after coil of the rope unwound, jerking and sliding over the side of the boat as if it were being sucked into the depths of a fathomless abyss. Finally, with a slight quiver of the rope, the anchor touched bottom, and Ailil made fast the rope, looping it about a hook on the boat's side.

With a sigh, he leaned back once more in the soft cushions that padded the hard boards of the crude boat. He thought of nothing, he was content merely to lie there with the calm and peace of the beauty about him. How long he remained thus he did not know.

It might have been an hour, or merely minutes, for nothing happened to disturb the tranquillity of the scene. There was nothing to claim his attention other than the strange similarity of the lake to a dark mirror, and the curiously twisted shadows of the willows that kneeled about the shore, trailing their branches in the water.

A huge moth, rising seemingly from nowhere, fluttered past his face, its wings brushing his cheek as it passed in silent flight. The great white wings beat the air like frail shadows as the creature fluttered slowly past him in its curious rising and falling flight. These great night moths always impressed Ailil as an ephemeral part of the night; they seemed almost a bit of the night itself, given life for a few brief hours and then sinking into quick dissolution with the rising of the sun. A faint, indescribable odor of mustiness and age-old strangeness was wafted to Ailil as the creature brushed past him, fluttering toward the tiny cabin which sheltered the opposite end of the boat. The door of the cabin was opened, and drawn by the darkness, the moth fluttered through the opening, and as Ailil watched, became a grey ghost, and then was lost in the gloom of the cabin's recesses.

Ailil smiled. He would have an interesting trophy of his night on the lake. The creature must have tired its fragile wings with the long flight across the water, and sought the boat for rest. Ailil thought it strange that he should not have noticed it as it approached; he reflected that it seemed almost to have risen from the water beside the boat, so suddenly did it flutter past him.

And then the moth was forgotten as Ailil once more contemplated the shore and the grotesquely shaped trunks and branches of the willows which his fancy never tired of endowing with gnarled and twisted natures to correspond with their physical shapes of grotesquerie, emphasized in the diffused moonlight that glimmered through the mist of the lake. Again he dreamed, and again he knew not for how long. Time was nothing. For him it had ceased to be, and he existed as might a ripple on the lake's surface, or as the willows weeping on the shore.

Slowly Ailil felt himself returning. Gradually his attention was being drawn back to the captivation of his mind and body, while unaccountably the projection of his thoughts into the nothingness of this dark abyss of beauty was being terminated. With something like annoyance, he realized this, and vaguely he wondered why.

Suddenly he knew! He was not alone. His mind was bright, alert and clear, wiped free of the cobwebs of dreams. Quickly he sat up and stared incredulously toward the cabin at the farther end of the boat.

Seated before the entrance of the cabin, was a young girl. She was merely sitting and staring at him with a wan and curious smile on her pale lips. Masses of golden hair floated down her back, and away from her head, mingling and becoming one with the sheen of the moonlight. The faintest of colors tinged the ivory pallor of her cheeks, and about her lips played the wisp of a smile, as tender and appealing as a child's.

Ailil could only stare, incredulously. He was overwhelmed in an instant with the loveliness of the picture. It possessed him and filled him with a fascination that held something of awe. He could not speak, and for several minutes he simply sat there and stared at this strange beauty that blended so perfectly with the ancient loveliness of the lake. Here, pictured in the exquisite moldings of human flesh, was a mortal representation of the lake's eternal charm.

And then, a thousand thoughts began whirling in wildest confusion in Ailil's mind. How did she get here? Who was she? Why was she here? The very commonplaceness of these riddles served to bring him closer to reality, and he realized that the girl must have hidden herself in the cabin of the boat. She could easily have escaped notice, since he never used the cabin except in the daytime, and for storage. Once more, he gazed at her. What a lovely stowaway she was! She had risen from her seat at the end of the boat, and was making her way toward him. The touch of her filmy white dress, brushing him, as she seated herself beside him, was like the trailing garment of a water Goddess, an Amphitrite with all the ancient charms of the seas at her command. Her closeness was overpowering, intoxicating to Ailil's beauty-drugged senses.

"You are not angry with me," she was speaking, "for annoying you? I so love the lake, and its beauty . . . and you too love it. That, I know."

Her voice was like the soft, caressing murmur of a thousand little streams, whispering in their hidden channels through night shaded forests of cool and damp depths. Murmuring and rising and falling imperceptibly, her words blended into a monotone of soft music. Ailil could not be sure that she was speaking, except for the exquisite tones that lingered in his mind and seemed to echo from a far distance.

"You are lovely," he breathed, "you are more lovely than the lake can ever be. Never did I dream of finding such beauty, alive and on the earth in this day." Ailil's throat was strangely dry, and he spoke in a husky, low-pitched voice. He could find nothing more to say. He could only stare at her, marveling, and praying that he would not awake from this mad, beautiful dream.

Already, she seemed to have forgotten him, and to have lost herself in the beauty of the night. Smiling faintly, as if all the world's happiness were hers, and she was possessed of a deep, soft joy, she leaned back into the cushions that pillowed the seat. Ailil gasped at the loveliness of her graceful throat and neck, as the moonlight filled the tiny hollows with a bluish glow, and lighted her eyes with wells of deep, glowing light.

And then Ailil's arms were about her, drawing her close to him, and their lips met in a kiss that was pure ecstasy and such wild delight as Ailil had never before known. Throughout the night, they lay there in the small dark boat, floating on the surface of the black lake. To Ailil it might have been the lake of Paradise on which they rested. The hours were tinged with the strangeness of mystery, and the utter loveliness of the surroundings, and the cries of the wild things in the swamp.

A faint greyness was stealing into the sky; the moon shone brightly and the first hush of the dawn light was creeping over the earth. Ailil awoke with a strange feeling of desolation and utter, unbearable loneliness. With wretched apprehension, his eyes immediately sought the loveliness of the creature of the night. She was gone. No trace of her remained, only the memory of her haunting charm.

A chilling illness seized Ailil. A wave of physical suffering and nausea swept over him. All was lost; all this wild beauty that he had loved so madly. Slowly the sun was routing the nocturnal beauties of the lake, and in a short time all the strange loveliness of the night would be gone. Ailil felt that he must flee, that he must hasten and leave the lake far behind him. He would hide away in the depths of the woods where the sun could not shine, where the gloom of the trees prevailed, and the light could not penetrate.

Frenziedly he began pulling up the heavy anchor. God! Would it never end? How deep was this ancient well that dropped into the center of the woodland like a vast cavity! Coil after coil of the rope, he tugged through the resisting waters. It was soaked through and slippery to the touch after the night in the lake. It reminded Ailil of the coils of a thin, brown serpent as it writhed and twisted from the depths of the abyss.

At last he could feel the heavy iron of the anchor swaying at the end of the rope. It was nearing the surface, and with a few more tugs he would be hauling it aboard, and leaving the accursed spot until night fell once more, and he could no longer resist the mad call of the dark waters.

And then Ailil saw that which sent him forever from the lake, never to return. Caught on a fork of the anchor was a human skeleton, dripping with mud and ooze, and long divested of the clothing of flesh which Ailil knew in a terrible moment had once been white, and tinged with the pallor of finely chiseled ivory.

TANITH LEE *is a British novelist and scriptwriter whose children's books
and adult fantasies have received widespread acclaim and won the
prestigious World Fantasy Award and its companion, the British Fantasy
Award. Her numerous books include* The Birthgrave, Death's Master *and*
Red As Blood, *a remarkable short-story collection from which "When the
Clock Strikes" is taken. The tales in* Red as Blood *are principally derived
from The Brothers Grimm, but rendered in even grimmer (pun intended)
terms. The following* cauchemar *is based on a tale we all know and love,
but Lee's edition is definitely not the Disney version.*

When the Clock Strikes

BY TANITH LEE

Yes, the great ballroom is filled only with dust now. The slender
columns of white marble and the slender columns of rose-red
marble are woven together by cobwebs. The vivid frescoes, on
which the Duke's treasury spent so much, are dimmed by the dust;
the faces of the painted goddesses look grey. And the velvet
curtains—touch them, they will crumble. Two hundred years now,
since anyone danced in this place on the sea-green floor in the
candle-gleam. Two hundred years since the wonderful clock struck
for the very last time.

I thought you might care to examine the clock. It was considered
exceptional in its day. The pedestal is ebony and the face fine
porcelain. And these figures, which are of silver, would pass
slowly about the circlet of the face. Each figure represents, you
understand, an hour. And as the appropriate hours came level
with this golden bell, they would strike it the correct number of
times. All the figures are unique, as you see. Beginning at the first
hour, they are, in this order, a girl-child, a dwarf, a maiden, a
youth, a lady and a knight. And here, notice, the figures grow
older as the day declines: a queen and king for the seventh and
eighth hours, and after these, an abbess and a magician and next
to last, a hag. But the very last is strangest of all. The twelfth
figure; do you recognize him? It is Death. Yes, a most curious

clock. It was reckoned a marvellous thing then. But it has not
struck for two hundred years. Possibly you have been told the
story? No? Oh, but I am certain that you have heard it, in another
form, perhaps.

However, as you have some while to wait for your carriage, I
will recount the tale, if you wish.

I will start with what was said of the clock. In those years, this
city was prosperous, a stronghold—not as you see it today. Much
was made in the city that was ornamental and unusual. But the
clock, on which the twelfth hour was Death, caused something of
a stir. It was thought unlucky, foolhardy, to have such a clock. It
began to be murmured, jokingly by some, by others in earnest,
that one night when the clock struck the twelfth hour, Death
would truly strike with it.

Now life has always been a chancy business, and it was more so
then. The Great Plague had come but twenty years before and was
not yet forgotten. Besides, in the Duke's court there was much
intrigue, while enemies might be supposed to plot beyond the city
walls, as happens even in our present age. But there was another
thing.

It was rumoured that the Duke had obtained both his title and
the city treacherously. Rumour declared that he had systematically
destroyed those who had stood in line before him, the members
of the princely house that formerly ruled here. He had accomplished the task slyly, hiring assassins talented with poisons and
daggers. But rumour also declared that the Duke had not been
sufficiently thorough. For though he had meant to rid himself of
all that rival house, a single descendant remained, so obscure he
had not traced her—for it was a woman.

Of course, such matters were not spoken of openly. Like the
prophecy of the clock, it was a subject for the dark.

Nevertheless, I will tell you at once, there was such a descendant
he had missed in his bloody work. And she was a woman. Royal
and proud she was, and seething with bitter spite and a hunger for
vengeance, and as bloody as the Duke, had he known it, in her
own way.

For her safety and disguise, she had long ago wed a wealthy
merchant in the city, and presently bore the man a daughter. The
merchant, a dealer in silks, was respected, a good fellow but not
wise. He rejoiced in his handsome and aristocratic wife. He never
dreamed what she might be about when he was not with her. In

fact, she had sworn allegiance to Satanas. In the dead of night she would go up into an old tower adjoining the merchant's house, and there she would say portions of the Black Mass, offer sacrifice, and thereafter practise witchcraft against the Duke. This witchery took a common form, the creation of a wax image and the maiming of the image that, by sympathy, the injuries inflicted on the wax be passed on to the living body of the victim. The woman was capable in what she did. The Duke fell sick. He lost the use of his limbs and was racked by excruciating pains from which he could get no relief. Thinking himself on the brink of death, the Duke named his sixteen-year-old son his heir. This son was dear to the Duke, as everyone knew, and be sure the woman knew it too. She intended sorcerously to murder the young man in his turn, preferably in his father's sight. Thus, she let the Duke linger in his agony, and commenced planning the fate of the prince.

Now all this while she had not been toiling alone. She had one helper. It was her own daughter, a maid of fourteen, that she had recruited to her service nearly as soon as the infant could walk. At six or seven, the child had been lisping the satanic rite along with her mother. At fourteen, you may imagine, the girl was well versed in the Black Arts, though she did not have her mother's natural genius for them.

Perhaps you would like me to describe the daughter at this point. It has a bearing on the story, for the girl was astonishingly beautiful. Her hair was the rich dark red of antique burnished copper, her eyes were the hue of the reddish-golden amber that traders bring from the East. When she walked, you would say she was dancing. But when she danced, a gate seemed to open in the world, and bright fire spangled inside it, but she was the fire.

The girl and her mother were close as gloves in a box. Their games in the old tower bound them closer. No doubt the woman believed herself clever to have got such a helpmate, but it proved her undoing.

It was in this manner. The silk merchant, who had never suspected his wife for an instant of anything, began to mistrust the daughter. She was not like other girls. Despite her great beauty, she professed no interest in marriage, and none in clothes or jewels. She preferred to read in the garden at the foot of the tower. Her mother had taught the girl her letters, though the merchant himself could read but poorly. And often the father peered at the books his daughter read, unable to make head or tail of them, yet somehow not liking them. One night very late, the silk merchant came home from a guild dinner in the city, and he saw a slim pale shadow gliding up the steps of the old tower, and he knew it for his child. On impulse, he followed her, but quietly. He had not considered any evil so far, and did not want to alarm her. At an angle of the stair, the lighted room above, he paused to spy and listen. He had something of a shock when he heard his wife's voice rise up in glad welcome. But what came next drained the blood from his heart. He crept away and went to his cellar for wine to stay himself. After the third glass he ran for neighbours and for the watch.

The woman and her daughter heard the shouts below and saw the torches in the garden. It was no use dissembling. The tower was littered with evidence of vile deeds, besides what the woman kept in a chest beneath her unknowing husband's bed. She understood it was all up with her, and she understood too how witchcraft was punished hereabouts. She snatched a knife from the altar.

The girl shrieked when she realized what her mother was at. The woman caught the girl by her red hair and shook her.

"Listen to me, my daughter," she cried, "and listen carefully, for the minutes are short. If you do as I tell you, you can escape their wrath and only I need die. And if you live I am satisifed, for you can carry on my labour after me. My vengeance I shall leave you, and my witchcraft to exact it by. Indeed, I promise you stronger powers than mine. I will beg my lord Satanas for it and he will not deny me, for he is just, in his fashion, and I have served him well. Now, will you attend?"

"I will," said the girl.

So the woman advised her, and swore her to the fellowship of Hell. And then the woman forced the knife into her own heart and dropped dead on the floor of the tower.

When the men burst in with their swords and staves and their torches and their madness, the girl was ready for them.

She stood blank-faced, blank-eyed, with her arms hanging at her sides. When one touched her, she dropped down at his feet.

"Surely she is innocent," this man said. She was lovely enough that it was hard to accuse her. Then her father went to her and took her hand and lifted her. At that the girl opened her eyes and she said, as if terrified: "How did I come here? I was in my chamber and sleeping—"

"The woman has bewitched her," her father said.

He desired very much that this be so. And when the girl clung to his hand and wept, he was certain of it. They showed her the body with the knife in it. The girl screamed and seemed to lose her senses totally.

She was put to bed. In the morning, a priest came and questioned her. She answered steadfastly. She remembered nothing, not even of the great books she had been observed reading. When they told her what was in them, she screamed again and apparently would have thrown herself from the narrow window, only the priest stopped her.

Finally, they brought her the holy cross in order that she might kiss it and prove herself blameless.

Then she knelt, and whispered softly, that nobody should hear but one — "Lord Satanas, protect thy handmaid." And either that gentleman has more power than he is credited with or else the symbols of God are only as holy as the men who deal in them, for she embraced the cross and it left her unscathed.

At that, the whole household thanked God. The whole household saving, of course, the woman's daughter. She had another to thank.

The woman's body was burnt, and the ashes put into unconsecrated ground beyond the city gates. Though they had discovered her to be a witch, they had not discovered the direction her witchcraft had selected. Nor did they find the wax image with its limbs all twisted and stuck through with needles. The girl had taken that up and concealed it. The Duke continued in his distress, but he did not die. Sometimes, in the dead of night, the girl would unearth the image from under a loose brick by the hearth, and gloat over it, but she did nothing else. Not yet. She was fourteen and the cloud of her mother's acts still hovered over her. She knew what she must do next.

The period of mourning ended.

"Daughter," said the silk merchant to her, "why do you not remove your black? The woman was malign and led you into wickedness. How long will you mourn her, who deserves no mourning?"

"Oh my father," said she, "never think I regret my wretched mother. It is my own unwitting sin I mourn." And she grasped his hand and spilled her tears on it. "I would rather live in a convent,"

said she, "than mingle with proper folk. And I would seek a
convent too, if it were not that I cannot bear to be parted from
you."

Do you suppose she smiled secretly as she said this? One might
suppose it. Presently she donned a robe of sackcloth and poured
ashes over her red-copper hair. "It is my penance," she said, "I
am glad to atone for my sins."

People forgot her beauty. She was at pains to obscure it. She
slunk about like an aged woman, a rag pulled over her head, dirt
smeared on her cheeks and brow. She elected to sleep in a cold
cramped attic and sat all day by a smoky hearth in the kitchens.
When someone came to her and begged her to wash her face and
put on suitable clothes and sit in the rooms of the house, she
smiled modestly, drawing the rag or a piece of hair over her face.
"I swear," she said, "I am glad to be humble before God and
men."

They reckoned her pious and they reckoned her simple. Two
years passed. They mislaid her beauty altogether, and reckoned
her ugly. They found it hard to call to mind who she was exactly,
as she sat in the ashes, or shuffled unattended about the streets
like a crone.

At the end of the second year, the silk merchant married again.
It was inevitable, for he was not a man who liked to live alone.

On this occasion, his choice was a harmless widow. She already
had two daughters, pretty in an unremarkable style. Perhaps the
merchant hoped they would comfort him for what had gone
before, this normal cheery wife and the two sweet, rather silly
daughters, whose chief interests were clothes and weddings.
Perhaps he hoped also that his deranged daughter might be drawn
out by company. But that hope foundered. Not that the new
mother did not try to be pleasant to the girl. And the new sisters,
their hearts grieved by her condition, went to great lengths to
enlist her friendship. They begged her to come from the kitchens
or the attic. Failing in that, they sometimes ventured to join her,
their fine silk dresses trailing on the greasy floor. They combed
her hair, exclaiming, when some of the ash and dirt were removed,
on its colour. But no sooner had they turned away, than the girl
gathered up handfuls of soot and ash and rubbed them into her
hair again. Now and then, the sisters attempted to interest their
bizarre relative in a bracelet or a gown or a current song. They
spoke to her of the young men they had seen at the suppers or

the balls which were then given regularly by the rich families of the city. The girl ignored it all. If she ever said anything it was to do with penance and humility. At last, as must happen, the sisters wearied of her, and left her alone. They had no cares and did not want to share in hers. They came to resent her moping greyness, as indeed the merchant's second wife had already done.

"Can you do nothing with the girl?" she demanded of her husband. "People will say that I and my daughters are responsible for her condition and that I ill-treat the maid from jealousy of her dead mother."

"Now how could anyone say that?" protested the merchant. "When you are famous as the epitome of generosity and kindness."

Another year passed, and saw no huge difference in the household.

A difference there was, but not visible.

The girl who slouched in the corner of the hearth was seventeen. Under the filth and grime she was, impossibly, more beautiful, although no one could see it.

And there was one other invisible item—her power (which all this time she had nurtured, saying her prayers to Satanas in the black of midnight), her power was rising like a dark moon in her soul.

Three days after her seventeenth birthday, the girl straggled about the streets as she frequently did. A few noted her and muttered it was the merchant's ugly simple daughter and paid no more attention. Most did not know her at all. She had made herself appear one with the scores of impoverished flotsam which constantly roamed the city, beggars and starvelings. Just outside the city gates, these persons congregated in large numbers, slumped around fires of burning refuse or else wandering to and fro in search of edible seeds, scraps, the miracle of a dropped coin. Here the girl now came, and began to wander about as they did. Dusk gathered and the shadows thickened. The girl sank to her knees in a patch of earth as if she had found something. Two or three of the beggars sneaked over to see if it were worth snatching from her—but the girl was only scrabbling in the empty soil. The beggars, making signs to each other that she was touched by God—mad—left her alone. But, very far from mad, the girl presently dug up a stoppered clay urn. In this urn were the ashes and charred bones of her mother. She had got a clue as to the location of the urn by devious questionings here and there. Her occult power had helped her to be sure of it.

In the twilight, padding along through the narrow streets and alleys of the city, the girl brought the urn homeward. In the garden at the foot of the old tower, gloom-wrapped, unwitnessed, she unstoppered the urn and buried the ashes freshly. She muttered certain unholy magics over the grave. Then she snapped off the sprig of a young hazel tree, and planted it in the newly turned ground.

I hazard you have begun to recognize the story by now. I see you suppose I tell it wrongly. Believe me, this is the truth of the matter. But if you would rather I left off the tale . . . No doubt your carriage will soon be here—No? Very well. I shall continue.

I think I should speak of the Duke's son at this juncture. The prince was nineteen, able, intelligent, and of noble bearing. He was of that rather swarthy type of looks one finds here in the north, but tall and slim and clear-eyed. There is an ancient square where you may see a statue of him, but much eroded by two centuries, and the elements. After the city was sacked, no care was lavished on it.

The Duke treasured his son. He had constant delight in the sight of the young man and what he said and did. It was the only happiness the invalid had.

Then, one night, the Duke screamed out in his bed. Servants came running with candles. The Duke moaned that a sword was transfixing his heart, an inch at a time. The prince hurried into the chamber, but in that instant the Duke spasmed horribly and died. No mark was on his body. There had never been a mark to show what ailed him.

The prince wept. They were genuine tears. He had nothing to reproach his father with, everything to thank him for. Nevertheless, they brought the young man the seal ring of the city, and he put it on.

It was winter, a cold blue-white weather with snow in the streets and countryside and a hard wizened sun that drove thin sharp blades of light through the sky, but gave no warmth. The Duke's funeral cortege passed slowly across the snow, the broad open chariots draped with black and silver, the black-plumed horses, the chanting priests with their glittering robes, their jeweled crucifixes and golden censers. Crowds lined the roadways to watch the spectacle. Among the beggar women stood a girl. No one noticed her. They did not glimpse the expression she veiled in her ragged scarf. She gazed at the bier pitilessly. As the young prince rode by in his sables, the seal ring on his hand, the eyes of the girl burned through her ashy hair, like a red fox through grasses.

The Duke was buried in the mausoleum you can visit to this day, on the east side of the city. Several months elapsed. The prince put his grief from him, and took up the business of the city competently. Wise and courteous he was, but he rarely smiled. At nineteen his spirit seemed worn. You might think he guessed the destiny that hung over him.

The winter was a hard one, too. The snow had come, and having come was loath to withdraw. When at last the spring returned, flushing the hills with colour, it was no longer sensible to be sad.

The prince's name day fell about this time. A great banquet was planned, a ball. There had been neither in the palace for nigh on three years, not since the Duke's fatal illness first claimed him. Now the royal doors were to be thrown open to all men of influence and their families. The prince was liberal, charming and clever even in this. Aristocrat and rich trader were to mingle in the beautiful dining room, and in this very chamber, among the frescoes, the marbles and the candelabra. Even a merchant's daughter, if the merchant were notable in the city, would get to dance on the sea-green floor, under the white eye of the fearful clock.

The clock. There was some renewed controversy about the clock. They did not dare speak to the young prince. He was a skeptic, as his father had been. But had not a death already occurred? Was the clock not a flying in the jaws of fate? For those disturbed by it, there was a dim writing in their minds, in the dust of the street or the pattern of blossoms. *When the clock strikes —* But people do not positively heed these warnings. Man is afraid of his fears. He ignores the shadow of the wolf thrown on the paving before him, saying: It is only a shadow.

The silk merchant received his invitation to the palace, and to be sure, thought nothing of the clock. His house had been thrown into uproar. The most luscious silks of his workshop were carried into the house and laid before the wife and her two daughters, who chirruped and squealed with excitement. The merchant stood smugly by, above it all, yet pleased at being appreciated. "Oh, father!" cried the two sisters, "may I have this one with the gold piping?" "Oh, father, this one with the design of pineapples?"

Later, a jeweller arrived and set out his trays. The merchant was generous. He wanted his women to look their best. It might be the night of their lives. Yet all the while, at the back of his mind, a little dark spot, itching, aching. He tried to ignore the spot, not scratch at it. His true daughter, the mad one. Nobody bothered to tell her about the invitation to the palace. They knew how she would react, mumbling in her hair about her sin and her penance, paddling her hands in the greasy ash to smear her face. Even the servants avoided her, as if she were just the cat seated by the fire. Less than the cat, for the cat saw to the mice—Just a block of stone. And yet, how fair she might have looked, decked in the pick of the merchant's wares, jewels at her throat. The prince himself could not have been unaware of her. And though marriage was impossible, other less holy, though equally honorable contracts, might have been arranged to the benefit of all concerned. The merchant sighed. He had scratched the darkness after all. He attempted to comfort himself by watching the two sisters exult over their apparel. He refused to admit that the finery would somehow make them seem but more ordinary than they were by contrast.

The evening of the banquet arrived. The family set off. Most of the servants sidled after. The prince had distributed largesse in the city; oxen roasted in the squares and the wine was free by royal order.

The house grew sombre. In the deserted kitchen the fire went out.

By the hearth, a segment of gloom rose up.

The girl glanced around her, and she laughed softly and shook out her filthy hair. Of course, she knew as much as anyone, and more than most. This was to be her night, too.

A few minutes later she was in the garden beneath the old tower, standing over the young hazel tree which thrust up from the earth. It had become strong, the tree, despite the harsh winter. Now the girl nodded to it. She chanted under her breath. At length a pale light began to glow, far down near where the roots of the tree held to the ground. Out of the pale glow flew a thin black bird, which perched on the girl's shoulder. Together, the girl and the bird passed into the old tower. High up, a fire blazed that no one had lit. A tub steamed with scented water that no one had drawn. Shapes that were not real and barely seen flitted about. Rare perfumes, the rustle of garments, the glint of gems as yet invisible filled and did not fill the restless air.

Need I describe further? No. You will have seen paintings which depict the attendance upon a witch of her familiar demons. How one bathes her, another anoints her, another brings clothes and ornaments. Perhaps you do not credit such things in any case. Never mind that. I will tell you what happened in the courtyard before the palace.

Many carriages and chariots had driven through the square, avoiding the roasting oxen, the barrels of wine, the cheering drunken citizens, and so through the gates into the courtyard. Just before ten o'clock (the hour, if you recall the clock, of the magician) a solitary carriage drove through the square and into the court. The people in the square gawped at the carriage and pressed forward to see who would step out of it, this latecomer. It was a remarkable vehicle that looked to be fashioned of solid gold, all but the domed roof that was transparent flashing crystal. Six black horses drew it. The coachman and postillions were clad in crimson, and strangely masked as curious beasts and reptiles. One of these beastmen now hopped down and opened the door of the carriage. Out came a woman's figure in a cloak of white fur, and glided up the palace stair and in at the doors.

There was dancing in the ballroom. The whole chamber was bright and clamorous with music and the voices of men and women. There, between those two pillars, the prince sat in his chair, dark, courteous, seldom smiling. Here the musicians played, the deep-throated viol, the lively mandolin. And there the dancers moved up and down on the sea-green floor. But the music and the dancers had just paused. The figures on the clock were themselves in motion. The hour of the magician was about to strike.

As it struck, through the doorway came the figure in the fur coat. And, as if they must, every eye turned to her.

For an instant she stood there, all white, as though she had brought the winter snow back with her. And then she loosed the cloak from her shoulders, it slipped away, and she was all fire.

She wore a gown of apricot brocade embroidered thickly with gold. Her sleeves and the bodice of her gown were slashed over ivory satin sewn with large rosy pearls. Pearls, too, were wound in her hair that was the shade of antique burnished copper. She was so beautiful that when the clock was still, nobody spoke. She was so beautiful it was hard to look at her for very long.

The prince got up from his chair. He did not know he had. Now he started out across the floor, between the dancers, who parted silently to let him through. He went toward the girl in the doorway as if she drew him by a chain.

The prince had hardly ever acted without considering first what he did. Now he did not consider. He bowed to the girl.

"Madam," he said. "You are welcome. Madam," he said. "Tell me who you are."

She smiled.

"My rank," she said. "Would you know that, my lord? It is similar to yours, or would be were I now mistress in my dead mother's palace. But, unfortunately, an unscrupulous man caused the downfall of our house."

"Misfortune indeed," said the prince. "Tell me your name. Let me right the wrong done you."

"You shall," said the girl. "Trust me, you shall. For my name, I would rather keep it secret for the present. But you may call me, if you will, a pet name I have given myself—Ashella."

"Ashella . . . But I see no ash about you," said the prince, dazzled by her gleam, laughing a little, stiffly, for laughter was not his habit.

"Ash and cinders from a cold and bitter hearth," said she. But she smiled again. "Now everyone is staring at us, my lord, and the musicians are impatient to begin again. Out of all these ladies, can it be you will lead me in the dance?"

"As long as you will dance," he said. "You shall dance with me."

And that is how it was.

There were many dances, slow and fast, whirling measures and gentle ones. And here and there, the prince and the maiden were parted. Always then he looked eagerly after her, sparing no regard for the other girls whose hands lay in his. It was not like him, he was usually so careful. But the other young men who danced on that floor, who clasped her fingers or her narrow waist in the dance, also gazed after her when she was gone. She danced, as she appeared, like fire. Though if you had asked those young men whether they would rather tie her to themselves, as the prince did, they would have been at a loss. For it is not easy to keep pace with fire.

The hour of the hag struck on the clock.

The prince grew weary of dancing with the girl and losing her in the dance to others and refinding her and losing her again.

Behind the curtains there is a tall window in the east wall that opens on the terrace above the garden. He drew her out there, into the spring night. He gave an order, and small tables were brought with delicacies and sweets and wine. He sat by her, watching every gesture she made, as if he would paint her portrait afterward.

In the ballroom, here, under the clock, the people murmured. But it was not quite the murmur you would expect, the scandalous murmur about a woman come from nowhere that the prince had made so much of. At the periphery of the ballroom, the silk merchant sat, pale as a ghost, thinking of a ghost, the living ghost of his true daughter. No one else recognized her. Only he. Some trick of the heart had enabled him to know her. He said nothing of it. As the step-sisters and wife gossiped with other wives and sisters, an awful foreboding weighed him down, sent him cold and dumb.

And now it is almost midnight, the moment when the page of the night turns over into day. Almost midnight, the hour when the figure of Death strikes the golden bell of the clock. And what will happen when the clock strikes? Your face announces that you know. Be patient; let us see if you do.

"I am being foolish," said the prince to Ashella on the terrace. "But perhaps I am entitled to be foolish, just once in my life. What are you saying?" For the girl was speaking low beside him, and he could not catch her words.

"I am saying a spell to bind you to me," she said.

"But I am already bound."

"Be bound then. Never go free."

"I do not wish it," he said. He kissed her hands and he said, "I do not know you, but I will wed you. Is that proof your spell has worked? I will wed you, and get back for you the rights you have lost."

"If it were only so simple," said Ashella, smiling, smiling. "But the debt is too cruel. Justice requires a harsher payment."

And then, in the ballroom, Death struck the first note on the golden bell.

The girl smiled and she said,

"I curse you in my mother's name."

The second stroke.

"I curse you in my own name."

The third stroke.

"And in the name of those that your father slew."

The fourth stroke.

"And in the name of my Master, who rules the world."

As the fifth, the sixth, the seventh strokes pealed out, the prince stood nonplussed. At the eighth and the ninth strokes, the strength of the malediction seemed to curdle his blood. He shivered and his brain writhed. At the tenth stroke, he saw a change in the loveliness before him. She grew thinner, taller. At the eleventh stroke, he beheld a thing in a ragged black cowl and robe. It grinned at him. It was all grin below a triangle of sockets of nose and eyes. At the twelfth stroke, the prince saw Death and knew him.

In the ballroom, a hideous grinding noise, as the gears of the clock failed. Followed by a hollow booming, as the mechanism stopped entirely.

The conjuration of Death vanished from the terrace.

Only one thing was left behind. A woman's shoe. A shoe no woman could ever have danced in. It was made of glass.

Did you intend to protest about the shoe? Shall I finish the story, or would you rather I did not? It is the ending you are familiar with. Yes, I perceive you understand that, now.

I will go quickly, then, for your carriage must soon be here. And there is not a great deal more to relate.

The prince lost his mind. Partly from what he had seen, partly from the spells the young witch had netted him in. He could think of nothing but the girl who had named herself Ashella. He raved that Death had borne her away but he would recover her from Death. She had left the glass shoe as token of her love. He must discover her with the aid of the shoe. Whomsoever the shoe fitted would be Ashella. For there was this added complication, that Death might hide her actual appearance. None had seen the girl before. She had disappeared like smoke. The one infallible test was the shoe. That was why she had left it for him.

His ministers would have reasoned with the prince, but he was past reason. His intellect had collapsed as totally as only a profound intellect can. A lunatic, he rode about the city. He struck out at those who argued with him. On a particular occasion, drawing a dagger, he killed, not apparently noticing what he did. His demand was explicit. Every woman, young or old, maid or married, must come forth from her home, must put her foot into the shoe of glass. They came. They had no choice. Some approached in terror, some weeping. Even the aged beggar women obliged, and they cackled, enjoying the sight of royalty gone mad. One alone did not come.

Now it is not illogical that out of the hundreds of women whose feet were put into the shoe, a single woman might have been found that the shoe fitted. But this did not happen. Nor did the situation alter, despite a lurid fable that some, tickled by the idea of wedding the prince, cut off their toes that the shoe might fit them. And if they did, it was to no avail, for still the shoe did not.

Is it really surprising? The shoe was sorcerous. It constantly changed itself, its shape, its size, in order that no foot, save one, could ever be got into it.

Summer spread across the land. The city took on its golden summer glaze, its fetid summer smell.

What had been a whisper of intrigue, swelled into a steady distant thunder. Plots were being hatched.

One day, the silk merchant was brought, trembling and grey of face, to the prince. The merchant's dumbness had broken. He had unburdened himself of his fear at confession, but the priest had not proved honest. In the dawn, men had knocked on the door of the merchant's house. Now he stumbled to the chair of the prince.

Both looked twice their years, but, if anything, the prince looked the elder. He did not lift his eyes. Over and over in his hands he turned the glass shoe.

The merchant, stumbling too in his speech, told the tale of his first wife and his daughter. He told everything, leaving out no detail. He did not even omit the end: that since the night of the banquet the girl had been absent from his house, taking nothing with her—save a young hazel from the garden beneath the tower.

The prince leapt from his chair.

His clothes were filthy and unkempt. His face was smeared with sweat and dust . . . it resembled, momentarily, another face.

Without guard or attendant, the prince ran through the city toward the merchant's house, and on the road, the intriguers waylaid and slew him. As he fell, the glass shoe dropped from his hands, and shattered in a thousand fragments.

There is little else worth mentioning.

Those who usurped the city were villains and not merely that, but fools. Within a year, external enemies were at the gates. A year more, and the city had been sacked, half burnt out, ruined. The manner in which you find it now, is somewhat better than it was then. And it is not now anything for a man to be proud of. As you were quick to note, many here earn a miserable existence by conducting visitors about the streets, the palace, showing them the dregs of the city's past.

Which was not a request, in fact, for you to give me money. Throw some from your carriage window if your conscience bothers you. My own wants are few.

No, I have no further news of the girl, Ashella, the witch. A devotee of Satanas, she has doubtless worked plentiful woe in the world. And a witch is long-lived. Even so, she will die eventually. None escapes Death. Then you may pity her, if you like. Those who serve the gentleman below—who can guess what their final lot will be? But I am very sorry the story did not please you. It is not, maybe, a happy choice before a journey.

And there is your carriage at last.

What? Ah, no, I shall stay here in the ballroom where you came on me. I have often paused here through the years. It is the clock. It has a certain—what shall I call it—power, to draw me back.

I am not trying to unnerve you. Why should you suppose that? Because of my knowledge of the city, of the story? You think that I am implying that I myself am Death? Now you laugh. Yes, it is absurd. Observe the twelfth figure on the clock. Is he not as you have always heard Death described? And am I in the least like that twelfth figure?

Although, of course, the story was not as you have heard it, either.

Son of a British army surgeon, LAFCADIO HEARN *(1850–1909) lived in England, New Orleans and Paris, but the most significant trip he took was to Japan, where he so fell in love with the land, the people and the culture that he changed his name and became a Japanese citizen. A poet whose prose may properly be described as tone poems, Hearn adapted many Oriental legends into English, including quite a few "ghost stories." The Japanese paid a remarkable compliment to his memory when they filmed* Kwaidan, *a brilliant anthology of terror tales derived from Hearn rather than the native myths that he refashioned into evocative prose. "Oshidori," taken from the book,* Kwaidan, *is one of Hearn's more evanescent tales, but the ending shocked me with its sudden violence and the understated irony of its final sentence.*

Oshidori

BY LAFCADIO HEARN

There was a falconer and hunter, named Sonjō, who lived in the district called Tamura-no-Gō, of the province of Mutsu. One day he went out hunting, and could not find any game. But on his way home, at a place called Akanuma, he perceived a pair of *oshidori** (mandarin-ducks), swimming together in a river that he was about to cross. To kill *oshidori* is not good; but Sonjō happened to be very hungry, and he shot at the pair. His arrow pierced the male: the female escaped into the rushes of the further shore, and disappeared. Sonjō took the dead bird home, and cooked it.

That night he dreamed a dreary dream. It seemed to him that a beautiful woman came into his room, and stood by his pillow, and began to weep. So bitterly did she weep that Sonjō felt as if his heart were being torn out while he listened. And the woman cried to him: "Why,—oh! why did you kill him?—of what wrong was he guilty? . . . At Akanuma we were so happy together,— and you killed him! . . . What harm did he ever do you? Do you even know what you have done?—oh! do you know what a cruel

*From ancient time, in the Far East, these birds have been regarded as emblems of conjugal affection.

what a wicked thing you have done? . . . Me too you have killed, — for I will not live without my husband! . . . Only to tell you this I came." . . . Then again she wept aloud, — so bitterly that the voice of her crying pierced into the marrow of the listener's bones; — and she sobbed out the words of this poem: —

> Hi kururéba
> Sasoëshi mono wo—
> 　Akanuma no
> Makomo no kuré no
> Hitori-né zo uki!

*["At the coming of twilight I invited him to return with me—! Now to sleep alone in the shadow of the rushes of Akanuma—ah! what misery unspeakable!"]**

And after having uttered these verses she exclaimed: — "Ah, you do not know—you cannot know what you have done! But to-morrow, when you go to Akanuma, you will see, — you will see . . ." So saying, and weeping very piteously, she went away.

When Sonjō awoke in the morning, this dream remained so vivid in his mind that he was greatly troubled. He remembered the words: — "But tomorrow, when you go to Akanuma, you will see, — you will see." And he resolved to go there at once, that he might learn whether his dream was anything more than a dream.

So he went to Akanuma; and there, when he came to the river-bank, he saw the female *oshidori* swimming alone. In the same moment the bird perceived Sonjō; but, instead of trying to escape, she swam straight towards him, looking at him the while in a strange fixed way. Then, with her beak, she suddenly tore open her own body, and died before the hunter's eyes . . .

Sonjō shaved his head, and became a priest.

*There is a pathetic double meaning in the third verse; for the syllables composing the proper name *Akanuma* ("Red Marsh") may also be read as *akanu-ma*, signifying "the time of our inseparable (or delightful) relation." So the poem can also be thus rendered: — "When the day began to fail, I had invited him to accompany me . . . ! Now, after the time of that happy relation, what misery for the one who must slumber alone in the shadow of the rushes!" — The *makomo* is a sort of large rush, used for making baskets.

Bram Stoker paid an oblique compliment to SHERIDAN LEFANU *in* Dracula's Guest *(elsewhere in this volume) by setting his story in one of the same locales referred to in "Carmilla," the most important vampire tale in English prior to* Dracula. *Many critics regard LeFanu (1814–1873) as the greatest writer of the English ghost story. I would certainly place him amongst the top ten. Like Stoker, LeFanu was born in Dublin, grand-nephew of the major 18th century dramatist, Richard Brinsley Sheridan. Though he initially studied for a legal career, LeFanu soon embarked on his true career, that of journalist, editor and author. Many of his supernatural tales are acknowledged classics. "Carmilla," like several of his other tales, is surprisingly contemporary in its psychosexual undertone. Even today, the strain of lesbianism in this vampire yarn may raise a few blue stockings, if not eyebrows.*

Carmilla

BY SHERIDAN LEFANU

I
An Early Fright

In Styria, we, though by no means magnificent people, inhabit a castle, or schloss. A small income, in that part of the world, goes a great way. Eight or nine hundred a year does wonders. Scantily enough ours would have answered among wealthy people at home. My father is English, and I bear an English name, although I never saw England. But here, in this lonely and primitive place, where everything is so marvellously cheap, I really don't see how ever so much more money would at all materially add to our comforts, or even luxuries.

My father was in the Austrian service, and retired upon a pension and his patrimony, and purchased this feudal residence, and the small estate on which it stands, a bargain.

Nothing can be more picturesque or solitary. It stands on a slight eminence in a forest. The road, very old and narrow, passes in front of its drawbridge, never raised in my time, and its moat, stocked with perch, and sailed over by many swans, and floating on its surface white fleets of waterlilies.

Over all this the schloss shows its many-windowed front; its towers, and its Gothic chapel.

The forest opens in an irregular and very picturesque glade before its gate, and at the right a steep Gothic bridge carries the road over a stream that winds in deep shadow through the wood.

I have said that this is a very lonely place. Judge whether I say truth. Looking from the hall door towards the road, the forest in which our castle stands extends fifteen miles to the right, and twelve to the left. The nearest inhabited schloss of any historic associations, is that of old General Spielsdorf, nearly twenty miles away to the right.

I have said "the nearest *inhabited* village," because there is, only three miles westward, that is to say in the direction of General Spielsdorf's schloss, a ruined village, with its quaint little church, now roofless, in the aisle of which are the mouldering tombs of the proud family of Karnstein, now extinct, who once owned the equally desolate château which, in the thick of the forest, overlooks the silent ruins of the town.

Respecting the cause of the desertion of this striking and melancholy spot, there is a legend which I shall relate to you another time.

I must tell you now, how very small is the party who constitute the inhabitants of our castle. I don't include servants, or those dependants who occupy rooms in the buildings attached to the schloss. Listen, and wonder! My father, who is the kindest man on earth, but growing old; and I, at the date of my story, only nineteen. Eight years have passed since then. I and my father constituted the family at the schloss. My mother, a Styrian lady, died in my infancy, but I had a good-natured governess, who had been with me from, I might almost say, my infancy. I could not remember the time when her fat, benignant face was not a familiar picture in my memory. This was Madame Perrodon, a native of Berne, whose care and good nature in part supplied to me the loss of my mother, whom I do not even remember, so early I lost her. She made a third at our little dinner party. There was a fourth, Mademoiselle De Lafontaine, a lady such as you term, I believe, a "finishing governess." She spoke French and German, Madame Perrodon French and broken English, to which my father and I added English, which, partly to prevent its becoming a lost language among us, and partly from patriotic motives, we spoke every day. The consequence was a Babel, at which strangers used to laugh, and which I shall make no attempt to reproduce in this narrative. And there were two or three young lady friends besides, pretty nearly of my own age, who were occasional visitors, for longer or shorter terms; and these visits I sometimes returned.

These were our regular social resources; but of course there were chance visits from "neighbours" of only five or six leagues distance. My life was, notwithstanding, rather a solitary one, I can assure you.

My gouvernantes had just so much control over me as you might conjecture such sage persons would have in the case of a rather spoiled girl, whose only parent allowed her pretty nearly her own way in everything.

The first occurrence in my existence, which produced a terrible impression upon my mind, which, in fact, never has been effaced, was one of the very earliest incidents of my life which I can recollect. Some people will think it so trifling that it should not be recorded here. You will see, however, by-and-by, why I mention it. The nursery, as it was called, though I had it all to myself, was a large room in the upper storey of the castle, with a steep oak roof. I can't have been more than six years old, when one night I awoke, and looking round the room from my bed, failed to see the nursery-maid. Neither was my nurse there; and I thought myself alone. I was not frightened, for I was one of those happy children who are studiously kept in ignorance of ghost stories, of fairy tales, and of all such lore as makes us cover up our heads when the door creaks suddenly, or the flicker of an expiring candle makes the shadow of a bed-post dance upon the wall, nearer to our faces. I was vexed and insulted at finding myself, as I conceived, neglected, and I began to whimper, preparatory to a hearty bout of roaring; when to my surprise, I saw a solemn, but very pretty face looking at me from the side of the bed. It was that of a young lady who was kneeling, with her hands under the coverlet. I looked at her with a kind of pleased wonder, and ceased whimpering. She caressed me with her hands, and lay down beside me on the bed, and drew me towards her, smiling; I felt immediately delightfully soothed, and fell asleep again. I was wakened by a sensation as if two needles ran into my breast very deep at the same moment, and I cried loudly. The lady started back, with her eyes fixed on me, and then slipped down upon the floor, and, as I thought, hid herself under the bed.

I was now for the first time frightened, and I yelled with all my might and main. Nurse, nursery-maid, housekeeper, all came running in, and hearing my story, they made light of it, soothing me all they could meanwhile. But, child as I was, I could perceive that their faces were pale with an unwonted look of anxiety, and I saw them look under the bed, and about the room, and peep under tables and pluck open cupboards; and the housekeeper whispered to the nurse: "Lay your hand along that hollow in the bed; some one *did* lie there, so sure as you did not; the place is still warm."

I remember the nursery-maid petting me, and all three examining my chest, where I told them I felt the puncture, and pronouncing that there was no sign visible that any such thing had happened to me.

The housekeeper and the two other servants who were in charge of the nursery, remained sitting up all night; and from that time a servant always sat up in the nursery until I was about fourteen.

I was very nervous for a long time after this. A doctor was called in, he was pallid and elderly. How well I remember his long saturnine face, slightly pitted with smallpox, and his chestnut wig. For a good while, every second day, he came and gave me medicine, which of course I hated.

The morning after I saw this apparition I was in a state of terror, and could not bear to be left alone, daylight though it was, for a moment.

I remember my father coming up and standing at the bedside, and talking cheerfully, and asking the nurse a number of questions, and laughing very heartily at one of the answers; and patting me on the shoulder, and kissing me, and telling me not to be frightened, that it was nothing but a dream and could not hurt me.

But I was not comforted, for I knew the visit of the strange woman was *not* a dream; and I was *awfully* frightened.

I was a little consoled by the nursery-maid's assuring me that it was she who had come and looked at me, and lain down beside me in the bed, and that I must have been half-dreaming not to have known her face. But this, though supported by the nurse, did not quite satisfy me.

I remembered, in the course of that day, a venerable old man, in a black cassock, coming into the room with the nurse and housekeeper, and talking a little to them, and very kindly to me; his face was very sweet and gentle, and he told me they were going to pray, and joined my hands together, and desired me to say, softly, while they were praying, "Lord hear all good prayers for us, for Jesus' sake." I think these were the very words, for I often repeated them to myself, and my nurse used for years to make me say them in my prayers.

I remembered so well the thoughtful sweet face of that white-haired old man, in his black cassock, as he stood in that rude, lofty, brown room, with the clumsy furniture of a fashion three hundred years old, about him, and the scanty light entering its shadowy atmosphere through the small lattice. He kneeled, and the three women with him, and he prayed aloud with an earnest quavering voice for, what appeared to me, a long time. I forget all my life preceding that event, and for some time after it is all obscure also, but the scenes I have just described stand out vivid as the isolated pictures of the phantasmagoria surrounded by darkness.

II
A Guest

I am now going to tell you something so strange that it will require all your faith in my veracity to believe my story. It is not only true, nevertheless, but truth of which I have been an eye-witness.

It was a sweet summer evening, and my father asked me, as he sometimes did, to take a little ramble with him along that beautiful forest vista which I have mentioned as lying in front of the schloss.

"General Spielsdorf cannot come to us so soon as I had hoped," said my father, as we pursued our walk.

He was to have paid us a visit of some weeks, and we had expected his arrival next day. He was to have brought with him a young lady, his niece and ward, Mademoiselle Rheinfeldt, whom I had never seen, but whom I had heard described as a very charming girl, and in whose society I had promised myself many happy days. I was more disappointed than a young lady living in a town, or a bustling neighbourhood can possibly imagine. This visit, and the new acquaintance it promised, had furnished my day-dream for many weeks.

"And how soon does he come?" I asked.

"Not till autumn. Not for two months, I dare say," he answered. "And I am very glad now, dear, that you never knew Mademoiselle Rheinfeldt."

"And why?" I asked, both mortified and curious.

"Because the poor young lady is dead," he replied. "I quite forgot I had not told you, but you were not in the room when I received the General's letter this evening."

I was very much shocked. General Spielsdorf had mentioned in his first letter, six or seven weeks before, that she was not so well as he would wish her, but there was nothing to suggest the remotest suspicion of danger.

"Here is the General's letter," he said, handing it to me. "I am afraid he is in great affliction; the letter appears to me to have been written very nearly in distraction."

We sat down on a rude bench, under a group of magnificent lime-trees. The sun was setting with all its melancholy splendour behind the sylvan horizon, and the stream that flows beside our home, and passes under the steep old bridge I have mentioned, wound through many a group of noble trees, almost at our feet, reflecting in its current the fading crimson of the sky. General Spielsdorf's letter was so extraordinary, so vehement, and in some places so self-contradictory, that I read it twice over—the second time aloud to my father—and was still unable to account for it, except by supposing that grief had unsettled his mind.

It said: "I have lost my darling daughter, for as such I loved her. During the last days of dear Bertha's illness I was not able to write to you. Before then I had no idea of her danger. I have lost her, and now learn *all*, too late. She died in the peace of innocence, and in the glorious hope of a blessed futurity. The fiend who betrayed our infatuated hospitality has done it all. I thought I was receiving into my house innocence, gaiety, a charming companion for my lost Bertha. Heavens! what a fool have I been! I thank God my child died without a suspicion of the cause of her sufferings. She is gone without so much as conjecturing the nature of her illness, and the accursed passion of the agent of all this misery. I devote my remaining days to tracking and extinguishing a monster. I am told I may hope to accomplish my righteous and merciful purpose. At present there is scarcely a gleam of light to guide me. I curse my conceited incredulity, my despicable affection of superiority, my blindness, my obstinacy—all—too late. I cannot write or talk collectedly now. I am distracted. So

soon as I shall have a little recovered, I mean to devote myself for
a time to enquiry, which may possibly lead me as far as Vienna.
Some time in the autumn, two months hence, or earlier if I live,
I will see you—that is, if you permit me; I will then tell you all
that I scarce dare put upon paper now. Farewell. Pray for me,
dear friend."

In these terms ended this strange letter. Though I had never
seen Bertha Rheinfeldt my eyes filled with tears at the sudden
intelligence; I was startled, as well as profoundly disappointed.

The sun had now set, and it was twilight by the time I had
returned the General's letter to my father.

It was a soft clear evening, and we loitered, speculating upon
the possible meanings of the violent and incoherent sentences
which I had just been reading. We had nearly a mile to walk before
reaching the road that passes the schloss in front, and by that time
the moon was shining brilliantly. At the drawbridge we met
Madame Perrodon and Mademoiselle De Lafontaine, who had
come out, without their bonnets, to enjoy the exquisite moonlight.

We heard their voices gabbling in animated dialogue as we
approached. We joined them at the drawbridge, and turned about
to admire with them the beautiful scene.

The glade through which we had just walked lay before us. At
our left the narrow road wound away under clumps of lordly trees,
and was lost to sight amid the thickening forest. At the right the
same road crosses the steep and picturesque bridge, near which
stands a ruined tower which once guarded that pass; and beyond
the bridge an abrupt eminence rises, covered with trees, and
crouching in its shadows, some grey ivy-clustered rocks.

Over the sward and low grounds a thin film of mist was stealing,
like smoke, marking the distance with a transparent veil; and here
and there we could see the river faintly flashing in the moonlight.

No softer, sweeter scene could be imagined. The news I had just
heard made it melancholy; but nothing could disturb its character
of profound serenity, and the enchanted glory and vagueness of
the prospect.

My father, who enjoyed the picturesque, and I, stood looking
in silence over the expanse beneath us. The two good governesses,
standing a little way behind us, discoursed upon the scene, and
were eloquent upon the moon.

Madame Perrodon was fat, middle-aged, and romantic, and
talked and sighed poetically. Mademoiselle De Lafontaine—in

right of her father, who was a German, assumed to be psychological, metaphysical, and something of a mystic—now declared that
when the moon shone with a light so intense it was well known
that it indicated a special spiritual activity. The effect of the full
moon in such a state of brilliancy was manifold. It acted on
dreams, it acted on lunacy, it acted on nervous people; it had
marvellous physical influences connected with life. Mademoiselle
related that her cousin, who was mate of a merchant ship, having
taken a nap on deck on such a night, lying on his back, with his
face full in the light of the moon, had wakened, after a dream of
an old woman clawing him by the cheek, with his features horribly
drawn to one side; and his countenance had never quite recovered
its equilibrium.

"The moon, this night," she said, "is full of idyllic and magnetic
influence—and see, when you look behind you at the front of the
schloss how all its windows flash and twinkle with that silvery
splendour, as if unseen hands had lighted up the rooms to receive
fairy guests."

There are indolent states of the spirits in which, indisposed to
talk ourselves, the talk of others is pleasant to our listless ears;
and I gazed on, pleased with the tinkle of the ladies' conversation.

"I have got into some of my moping moods to-night," said my
father, after a silence, and quoting Shakespeare, whom, by way
of keeping up our English, he used to read aloud, he said:

>   *'In truth I know not why I am so sad:*
>   *It wearies me; you say it wearies you;*
>   *But how I got it—came by it.'*

"I forget the rest. But I feel as if some great misfortune were
hanging over us. I suppose the poor General's afflicted letter has
had something to do with it."

At this moment the unwonted sound of carriage wheels and
many hoofs upon the road, arrested our attention.

They seemed to be approaching from the high ground overlook-
ing the bridge, and very soon the equipage emerged from that
point. Two horsemen first crossed the bridge, then came a carriage
drawn by four horses, and two men rode behind.

It seemed to be the travelling carriage of a person of rank; and
we were all immediately absorbed in watching that very unusual
spectacle. It became, in a few moments, greatly more interesting,

for just as the carriage had passed the summit of the steep bridge, one of the leaders, taking fright, communicated his panic to the rest, and after a plunge or two, the whole team broke into a wild gallop together, and dashing between the horsemen who rode in front, came thundering along the road towards us with the speed of a hurricane.

The excitement of the scene was made more painful by the clear, longdrawn screams of a female voice from the carriage window.

We all advanced in curiosity and horror; my father in silence, the rest with various ejaculations of terror.

Our suspense did not last long. Just before you reach the castle drawbridge, on the route they were coming, there stands by the roadside a magnificent lime-tree, on the other stands an ancient stone cross, at sight of which the horses, now going at a pace that was perfectly frightful, swerved so as to bring the wheel over the projecting roots of the tree.

I knew what was coming. I covered my eyes, unable to see it out, and turned my head away; at the same moment I heard a cry from my ladyfriends, who had gone on a little.

Curiosity opened my eyes, and I saw a scene of utter confusion. Two of the horses were on the ground, the carriage lay upon its side with two wheels in the air; the men were busy removing the traces, and a lady, with a commanding air and figure had got out, and stood with clasped hands, raising the handkerchief that was in them every now and then to her eyes. Through the carriage door was now lifted a young lady, who appeared to be lifeless. My dear old father was already beside the elder lady, with his hat in his hand, evidently tendering his aid and the resources of his schloss. The lady did not appear to hear him, or to have eyes for anything but the slender girl who was being placed against the slope of the bank.

I approached; the young lady was apparently stunned, but she was certainly not dead. My father, who piqued himself on being something of a physician, had just had his fingers on her wrist and assured the lady, who declared herself her mother, that her pulse, though faint and irregular, was undoubtedly still distinguishable. The lady clasped her hands and looked upward, as if in a momentary transport of gratitude; but immediately she broke out again in that theatrical way which is, I believe, natural to some people.

She was what is called a fine looking woman for her time of life, and must have been handsome; she was tall, but not thin, and dressed in black velvet, and looked rather pale, but with a proud and commanding countenance, though now agitated strangely.

"Was ever being so born to calamity?" I heard her say, with clasped hands, as I came up. "Here am I, on a journey of life and death, in prosecuting which to lose an hour is possibly to lose all. My child will not have recovered sufficiently to resume her route for who can say how long. I must leave her; I cannot, dare not, delay. How far on, sir, can you tell, is the nearest village? I must leave her there; and shall not see my darling, or even hear of her till my return, three months hence."

I plucked my father by the coat, and whispered earnestly in his ear: "Oh! papa, pray ask her to let her stay with us—it would be so delightful. Do, pray."

"If Madame will entrust her child to the care of my daughter, and of her good gouvernante, Madame Perrodon, and permit her to remain as our guest, under my charge, until her return, it will confer a distinction and an obligation upon us, and we shall treat her with all the care and devotion which so sacred a trust deserves."

"I cannot do that, sir, it would be to task your kindness and chivalry too cruelly," said the lady, distractedly.

"It would, on the contrary, be to confer on us a very great kindness at the moment when we most need it. My daughter has just been disappointed by a cruel misfortune, in a visit from which she had long anticipated a great deal of happiness. If you confide this young lady to our care it will be her best consolation. The nearest village on your route is distant, and affords no such inn as you could think of placing your daughter at; you cannot allow her to continue her journey for any considerable distance without danger. If, as you say, you cannot suspend your journey, you must part with her to-night, and nowhere could you do so with more honest assurances of care and tenderness than here."

There was something in this lady's air and appearance so distinguished, and even imposing, and in her manner so engaging, as to impress one, quite apart from the dignity of her equipage, with a conviction that she was a person of consequence.

By this time the carriage was replaced in its upright position, and the horses, quite tractable, in the traces again.

The lady threw on her daughter a glance which I fancied was

not quite so affectionate as one might have anticipated from the beginning of the scene; then she beckoned slightly to my father, and withdrew two or three steps with him out of hearing; and talked to him with a fixed and stern countenance, not at all like that with which she had hitherto spoken.

I was filled with wonder that my father did not seem to perceive the change, and also unspeakably curious to learn what it could be that she was speaking, almost in his ear, with so much earnestness and rapidity.

Two or three minutes at most I think she remained thus employed, then she turned, and a few steps brought her to where her daughter lay, supported by Madame Perrodon. She kneeled beside her for a moment and whispered, as Madame supposed, a little benediction in her ear; then hastily kissing her she stepped into her carriage, the door was closed, the footmen in stately liveries jumped up behind, the outriders spurred on, the postillions cracked their whips, the horses plunged and broke suddenly into a furious canter that threatened soon again to become a gallop, and the carriage whirled away, followed at the same rapid pace by the two horsemen in the rear.

III
We Compare Notes

We followed the cortege with our eyes until it was swiftly lost to sight in the misty wood; and the very sound of the hoofs and the wheels died away in the silent night air.

Nothing remained to assure us that the adventure had not been an illusion of a moment but the young lady, who just at that moment opened her eyes. I could not see, for her face was turned from me, but she raised her head, evidently looking about her, and I heard a very sweet voice ask complainingly, "Where is mama?"

Our good Madame Perrodon answered tenderly, and added some comfortable assurances.

I then heard her ask:

"Where am I? What is this place?" and after that she said, "I don't see the carriage; and Matska, where is she?"

Madame answered all her questions in so far as she understood them; and gradually the young lady remembered how the misadventure came about, and was glad to hear that no one in, or in attendance on, the carriage was hurt; and on learning that her mama had left her here, till her return in about three months, she wept.

I was going to add my consolations to those of Madame Perrodon when Mademoiselle De Lafontaine placed her hand upon my arm, saying:

"Don't approach, one at a time is as much as she can at present converse with; a very little excitement would possibly overpower her now."

As soon as she is comfortably in bed, I thought, I will run up to her room and see her.

My father in the meantime had sent a servant on horseback for the physician, who lived about two leagues away; and a bedroom was being prepared for the young lady's reception.

The stranger now rose, and leaning on Madame's arm, walked slowly over the drawbridge and into the castle gate.

In the hall, servants waited to receive her, and she was conducted forthwith to her room.

The room we usually sat in as our drawing-room is long, having four windows, that looked over the moat and drawbridge, upon the forest scene I have just described.

It is furnished in old carved oak, with large carved cabinets, and the chairs are cushioned with crimson Utrecht velvet. The walls are covered with tapestry, and surrounded with great gold frames, the figures being as large as life, in ancient and very curious costume, and the subjects represented are hunting, hawking, and generally festive. It is not too stately to be extremely comfortable; and here we had our tea, for with his usual patriotic leanings he insisted that the national beverage should make its appearance regularly with our coffee and chocolate.

We sat here this night, and with candles lighted, were talking over the adventure of the evening.

Madame Perrodon and Mademoiselle De Lafontaine were both of our party. The young stranger had hardly lain down in her bed when she sank into a deep sleep; and those ladies had left her in the care of a servant.

"How do you like our guest?" I asked, as soon as Madame entered. "Tell me all about her?"

"I like her extremely," answered Madame, "she is, I almost think, the prettiest creature I ever saw; about your age, and so gentle and nice."

"She is absolutely beautiful," threw in Mademoiselle, who had peeped for a moment into the stranger's room.

"And such a sweet voice!" added Madame Perrodon.

"Did you remark a woman in the carriage, after it was set up again, who did not get out," inquired Mademoiselle, "but only looked from the window?"

"No, we had not seen her."

Then she described a hideous black woman, with a sort of coloured turban on her head, and who was gazing all the time from the carriage window, nodding and grinning derisively towards the ladies, with gleaming eyes and large white eye-balls, and her teeth set as if in fury.

"Did you remark what an ill-looking pack of men the servants were?" asked Madame.

"Yes," said my father, who had just come in, "ugly, hang-dog looking fellows, as ever I beheld in my life. I hope they mayn't rob the poor lady in the forest. They are clever rogues, however; they got everything to rights in a minute."

"I dare say they are worn out with too long travelling," said Madame. "Besides looking wicked, their faces were so strangely lean, and dark, and sullen. I am very curious, I own; but I dare say the young lady will tell us all about it to-morrow, if she is sufficiently recovered."

"I don't think she will," said my father, with a mysterious smile, and a little nod of his head, as if he knew more about it than he cared to tell us.

This made us all the more inquisitive as to what had passed between him and the lady in the black velvet, in the brief but earnest interview that had immediately preceded her departure.

We were scarcely alone, when I entreated him to tell me. He did not need much pressing.

"There is no particular reason why I should not tell you. She expressed a reluctance to trouble us with the care of her daughter, saying she was in delicate health, and nervous, but not subject to any kind of seizure—she volunteered that—nor to any illusion; being, in fact, perfectly sane."

"How very odd to say all that!" I interpolated. "It was so unnecessary."

"At all events it *was* said," he laughed, "and as you wish to know all that passed, which was indeed very little, I tell you. She then said, 'I am making a long journey of *vital* importance — she emphasized the word — rapid and secret; I shall return for my child in three months; in the meantime, she will be silent as to who we are, whence we come, and whither we are travelling.' That is all she said. She spoke very pure French. When she said the word 'secret', she paused for a few seconds, looking sternly, her eyes fixed on mine. I fancy she makes a great point of that. You saw how quickly she was gone. I hope I have not done a very foolish thing, in taking charge of the young lady."

For my part, I was delighted. I was longing to see and talk to her; and only waiting till the doctor should give me leave. You, who live in towns, can have no idea how great an event the introduction of a new friend is, in such a solitude as surrounded us.

The doctor did not arrive till nearly one o'clock; but I could no more have gone to my bed and slept, than I could have overtaken, on foot, the carriage in which the princess in black velvet had driven away.

When the physician came down to the drawing-room, it was to report very favourably upon his patient. She was now sitting up, her pulse quite regular, apparently perfectly well. She had sustained no injury, and the little shock to her nerves had passed away quite harmlessly. There could be no harm certainly in my seeing her, if we both wished it; and, with this permission, I sent, forthwith, to know whether she would allow me to visit her for a few minutes in her room.

The servant returned immediately to say that she desired nothing more.

You may be sure I was not long in availing myself of this permission.

Our visitor lay in one of the handsomest rooms in the schloss. It was, perhaps, a little stately. There was a sombre piece of tapestry opposite the foot of the bed, representing Cleopatra with the asps to her bosom; and other solemn classic scenes were displayed, a little faded, upon the other walls. But there was gold carving, and rich and varied colour enough in the other decorations of the room, to more than redeem the gloom of the old tapestry.

There were candles at the bed-side. She was sitting up; her slender pretty figure enveloped in the soft silk dressing-gown, embroidered with flowers, and lined with thick quilted silk, which her mother had thrown over her feet as she lay upon the ground.

What was it that, as I reached the bed-side and had just begun my little greeting, struck me dumb in a moment, and made me recoil a step or two from before her? I will tell you.

I saw the very face which had visited me in my childhood at night, which remained so fixed in my memory, and on which I had for so many years so often ruminated with horror, when no one suspected of what I was thinking.

It was pretty, even beautiful; and when I first beheld it, wore the same melancholy expression.

But this almost instantly lighted into a strange fixed smile of recognition.

There was a silence of fully a minute, and then at length *she* spoke; I could not.

"How wonderful!" she exclaimed. "Twelve years ago, I saw your face in a dream and it has haunted me ever since."

"Wonderful indeed!" I repeated, overcoming with an effort the horror that had for a time suspended my utterances. "Twelve years ago, in vision or reality, *I* certainly saw you. I could not forget your face. It has remained before my eyes ever since."

Her smile had softened. Whatever I had fancied strange in it, was gone, and it and her dimpling cheeks were now delightfully pretty and intelligent.

I felt reassured, and continued more in the vein which hospitality indicated, to bid her welcome, and to tell her how much pleasure her accidental arrival had given us all, and especially what a happiness it was to me.

I took her hand as I spoke. I was a little shy, as lonely people are, but the situation made me eloquent, and even bold. She pressed my hand, she laid hers upon it, and her eyes glowed, as, looking hastily into mine, she smiled again, and blushed.

She answered my welcome very prettily. I sat down beside her, still wondering; and she said:

"I must tell you my vision about you; it is so very strange that you and I should have had, each of the other so vivid a dream, that each should have seen, I you and you me, looking as we do now, when of course we both were mere children. I was a child, about six years old, and I awoke from a confused and troubled dream, and found myself in a room, unlike my nursery, wainscoted clumsily in some dark wood, and with cupboards and bedsteads, and chairs, and benches placed about it. The beds were, I thought, all empty, and the room itself without anyone but myself in it; and I, after looking about me for some time, and admiring especially an iron candlestick with two branches, which I should certainly know again, crept under one of the beds to reach the window; but as I got from under the bed, I heard someone crying; and looking up, while I was still upon my knees, I saw *you*—most assuredly you—as I see you now; a beautiful young lady, with golden hair and large blue eyes, and lips—your lips— you, as you are here. Your looks won me; I climbed on the bed and put my arms about you, and I think we both fell asleep. I was roused by a scream; you were sitting up screaming. I was frightened, and slipped down upon the ground, and, it seemed to me, lost consciousness for a moment; and when I came to myself, I was again in my nursery at home. Your face I have never forgotten since. I could not be misled by mere resemblance. You *are* the lady whom I saw then."

It was now my turn to relate my corresponding vision, which I did, to the undisguised wonder of my new acquaintance.

"I don't know which should be most afraid of the other," she said, again smiling—"If you were less pretty I think I should be very much afraid of you, but being as you are, and you and I both so young, I feel only that I have made your acquaintance twelve years ago, and have already a right to your intimacy; at all events it does seem as if we were destined, from our earliest childhood, to be friends. I wonder whether you feel as strangely drawn towards me as I do to you; I have never had a friend—shall I find one now?" She sighed, and her fine dark eyes gazed passionately on me.

Now the truth is, I felt rather unaccountably towards the beautiful stranger. I did feel, as she said, "drawn towards her," but there was also something of repulsion. In this ambiguous feeling, however, the sense of attraction immensely prevailed. She interested and won me; she was so beautiful and so indescribably engaging.

I perceived now something of languor and exhaustion stealing over her, and hastened to bid her good night.

"The doctor thinks," I added, "that you ought to have a maid to sit up with you to-night; one of ours is waiting, and you will find her a very useful and quiet creature."

"How kind of you, but I could not sleep, I never could with an attendant in the room. I shan't require any assistance—and, shall I confess my weakness, I am haunted with a terror of robbers. Our house was robbed once, and two servants murdered, so I always lock my door. It has become a habit—and you look so kind I know you will forgive me. I see there is a key in the lock."

She held me close in her pretty arms for a moment and whispered in my ear, "Good night, darling, it is very hard to part with you, but good night; to-morrow, but not early, I shall see you again."

She sank back on the pillow with a sigh, and her fine eyes followed me with a fond and melancholy gaze, and she murmured again "Good night, dear friend."

Young people like, and even love, on impulse. I was flattered by the evident, though as yet undeserved, fondness she showed me. I liked the confidence with which she at once received me. She was determined that we should be very near friends.

Next day came and we met again. I was delighted with my companion; that is to say, in many respects.

Her looks lost nothing in daylight—she was certainly the most beautiful creature I had ever seen, and the unpleasant remembrance of the face presented in my early dream, had lost the effect of the first unexpected recognition.

She confessed that she had experienced a similar shock on seeing me, and precisely the same faint antipathy that had mingled with my admiration of her. We now laughed together over our momentary horrors.

IV

Her Habits—A Saunter

I told you that I was charmed with her in most particulars.

There were some that did not please me so well.

She was above the middle height of women. I shall begin by describing her. She was slender, and wonderfully graceful. Except that her movements were languid—*very* languid—indeed, there was nothing in her appearance to indicate an invalid. Her complexion was rich and brilliant; her features were small and beautifully formed; her eyes large, dark, and lustrous; her hair was quite wonderful, I never saw hair so magnificently thick and long when it was down about her shoulders; I have often placed my hands under it, and laughed with wonder at its weight. It was exquisitely fine and soft, and in colour a rich very dark brown, with something of gold. I loved to let it down, tumbling with its own weight, as, in her room, she lay back in her chair talking in her sweet low voice, I used to fold and braid it, and spread it out and play with it. Heavens! If I had but known all!

. I said there were particulars which did not please me. I have told you that her confidence won me the first night I saw her; but I found that she exercised with respect to herself, her mother, her history, everything in fact connected with her life, plans, and people, an ever wakeful reserve. I dare say I was unreasonable, perhaps I was wrong; I dare say I ought to have respected the solemn injunction laid upon my father by the stately lady in black velvet. But curiosity is a restless and unscrupulous passion, and no one girl can endure, with patience, that hers should be baffled by another. What harm could it do anyone to tell me what I so ardently desired to know? Had she no trust in my good sense or honour? Why would she not believe me when I assured her, so solemnly, that I would not divulge one syllable of what she told me to any mortal breathing?

There was a coldness, it seemed to me, beyond her years, in her smiling melancholy persistent refusal to afford me the least ray of light.

I cannot say we quarrelled upon this point, for she would not quarrel upon any. It was, of course, very unfair of me to press her, very ill-bred, but I really could not help it; and I might just as well have let it alone.

What she did tell me amounted, in my unconscionable estimation—to nothing.

It was all summed up in three very vague disclosures:

First—Her name was Carmilla.

Second—Her family was very ancient and noble.

Third—Her home lay in the direction of the west.

She would not tell me the name of her family, nor their armorial bearings, nor the name of their estate, nor even that of the country they lived in.

You are not to suppose that I worried her incessantly on these subjects. I watched opportunity, and rather insinuated than urged my inquiries. Once or twice, indeed, I did attack her more directly. But no matter what my tactics, utter failure was invariably the result. Reproaches and caresses were all lost upon her. But I must add this, that her evasion was conducted with so pretty a melancholy and deprecation, with so many, and even passionate declarations of her liking for me, and trust in my honour, and with so many promises that I should at last know all, that I could not find it in my heart long to be offended with her.

She used to place her pretty arms about my neck, draw me to her, and laying her cheek to mine, murmur with her lips near my ear, "Dearest, your little heart is wounded; think me not cruel because I obey the irresistible law of my strength and weakness; if your dear heart is wounded, my wild heart bleeds with yours. In the rapture of my enormous humiliation I live in your warm life, and you shall die—die, sweetly die—into mine. I cannot help it; as I draw near to you, you, in your turn, will draw near to others, and learn the rapture of that cruelty, which yet is love; so, for a while, seek to know no more of me and mine, but trust me with all your loving spirit."

And when she had spoken such a rhapsody, she would press me more closely in her trembling embrace, and her lips in soft kisses gently glow upon my cheek.

Her agitations and her language were unintelligible to me.

From these foolish embraces, which were not of very frequent occurrence, I must allow, I used to wish to extricate myself; but my energies seemed to fail me. Her murmured words sounded like a lullaby in my ear, and soothed my resistance into a trance, from which I only seemed to recover myself when she withdrew her arms.

In these mysterious moods I did not like her. I experienced a strange tumultuous excitement that was pleasurable, ever and anon, mingled with a vague sense of fear and disgust. I had no distinct thoughts about her while such scenes lasted, but I was conscious of a love growing into adoration, and also of abhorrence. This I know is paradox, but I can make no other attempt to explain the feeling.

I now write, after an interval of more than ten years, with a trembling hand, with a confused and horrible recollection of certain occurrences and situations, in the ordeal through which I was unconsciously passing; though with a vivid and very sharp remembrance of the main current of my story. But, I suspect, in all lives there are certain emotional scenes, those in which our passions have been most wildly and terribly roused, that are of all others the most vaguely and dimly remembered.

Sometimes after an hour of apathy, my strange and beautiful companion would take my hand and hold it with a fond pressure, renewed again and again; blushing softly, gazing in my face with languid and burning eyes, and breathing so fast that her dress rose and fell with the tumultuous respiration. It was like the ardour of a lover; it embarrassed me; it was hateful and yet over-powering; and with gloating eyes she drew me to her, and her hot lips travelled along my cheek in kisses; and she would whisper, almost in sobs, "You are mine, you *shall* be mine, you and I are one for ever." Then she has thrown herself back in her chair, with her small hands over her eyes, leaving me trembling.

"Are we related," I used to ask; "what can you mean by all this? I remind you perhaps of some one whom you love; but you must not, I hate it; I don't know you—I don't know myself when you look so and talk so."

She used to sigh at my vehemence, then turn away and drop my hand.

Respecting these very extraordinary manifestations I strove in vain to form any satisfactory theory—I could not refer them to affectation or trick. It was unmistakably the momentary breaking out of suppressed instinct and emotion. Was she, notwithstanding her mother's volunteered denial, subject to brief visitations of insanity; or was there here a disguise and a romance? I had read in old story books of such things. What if a boyish lover had found his way into the house, and sought to prosecute his suit in masquerade, with the assistance of a clever old adventuress. But there were many things against this hypothesis, highly interesting as it was to my vanity.

I could boast of no little attentions such as masculine gallantry delights to offer. Between these passionate moments there were long intervals of common-place, of gaiety, of brooding melancholy, during which, except that I detected her eyes so full of melancholy fire, following me, at times I might have been as nothing to her. Except in these brief periods of mysterious excitement her ways were girlish; and there was always a languor about her, quite incompatible with a masculine system in a state of health.

In some respects her habits were odd. Perhaps not so singular in the opinion of a town lady like you, as they appeared to us rustic people. She used to come down very late, generally not till one o'clock, she would then take a cup of chocolate, but eat nothing; we then went out for a walk, which was a mere saunter, and she seemed, almost immediately, exhausted, and either returned to the schloss or sat on one of the benches that were placed, here and there, among the trees. This was a bodily languor in which her mind did not sympathise. She was always an animated talker, and very intelligent.

She sometimes alluded for a moment to her own home, or mentioned an adventure or situation, or an early recollection, which indicated a people of strange manners, and described customs of which we knew nothing. I gathered from these chance hints that her native country was much more remote than I had at first fancied.

As we sat thus one afternoon under the trees a funeral passed us by. It was that of a pretty young girl, whom I had often seen, the daughter of one of the rangers of the forest. The poor man was walking behind the coffin of his darling; she was his only child, and he looked quite heartbroken. Peasants walking two-and-two came behind, they were singing a funeral hymn.

I rose to mark my respect as they passed, and joined in the hymn they were very sweetly singing.

My companion shook me a little roughly, and I turned surprised.

She said brusquely, "Don't you perceive how discordant that is?"

"I think it very sweet, on the contrary," I answered, vexed at the interruption, and very uncomfortable, lest the people who composed the little procession should observe and resent what was passing.

I resumed, therefore, instantly, and was again interrupted. "You pierce my ears," said Carmilla, almost angrily, and stopping her ears with her tiny fingers. "Besides, how can you tell that your religion and mine are the same; your forms wound me, and I hate funerals. What a fuss! Why *you* must die—*everyone* must die; and all are happier when they do. Come home."

"My father has gone on with the clergyman to the churchyard. I thought you knew she was to be buried to-day."

"*She?* I don't trouble my head about peasants. I don't know who she is," answered Carmilla, with a flash from her fine eyes.

"She is the poor girl who fancied she saw a ghost a fortnight ago, and has been dying ever since, till yesterday, when she expired."

"Tell me nothing about ghosts. I shan't sleep to-night if you do."

"I hope there is no plague or fever coming; all this looks very like it," I continued. "The swineherd's young wife died only a week ago, and she thought something seized her by the throat as she lay in her bed, and nearly strangled her. Papa says such horrible fancies do accompany some forms of fever. She was quite well the day before. She sank afterwards, and died before a week."

"Well, *her* funeral is over, I hope, and *her* hymn sung; and our ears shan't be tortured with that discord and jargon. It has made me nervous. Sit down here, beside me; sit close; hold my hand; press it hard—hard—harder."

We had moved a little back, and had come to another seat.

She sat down. Her face underwent a change that alarmed and even terrified me for a moment. It darkened, and became horribly livid; her teeth and hands were clenched, and she frowned and compressed her lips, while she stared down upon the ground at her feet, and trembled all over with a continued shudder as irrepressible as ague. All her energies seemed strained to suppress a fit, with which she was then breathlessly tugging; and at length a low convulsive cry of suffering broke from her, and gradually the hysteria subsided. "There! That comes of strangling people with hymns!" she said at last. "Hold me, hold me still. It is passing away."

And so gradually it did; and perhaps to dissipate the sombre impression which the spectacle had left upon me, she became unusually animated and chatty; and so we got home.

This was the first time I had seen her exhibit any definable symptoms of that delicacy of health which her mother had spoken of. It was the first time, also, I had seen her exhibit anything like temper.

Both passed away like a summer cloud; and never but once afterwards did I witness on her part a momentary sign of anger. I will tell you how it happened.

She and I were looking out of one of the long drawing-room windows, when there entered the courtyard, over the drawbridge, a figure of a wanderer whom I knew very well. He used to visit the schloss generally twice a year.

It was the figure of a hunchback, with the sharp lean features that generally accompany deformity. He wore a pointed black beard, and he was smiling from ear to ear, showing his white fangs. He was dressed in buff, black, and scarlet, and crossed with more straps and belts than I could count, from which hung all manner of things. Behind, he carried a magic-lantern, and two boxes, which I well knew, in one of which was a salamander, and in the other a mandrake. These monsters used to make my father laugh. They were compounded of parts of monkeys, parrots, squirrels, fish, and hedgehogs, dried and stitched together with great neatness and startling effect. He had a fiddle, a box of conjuring apparatus, a pair of foils and masks attached to his belt, several other mysterious cases dangling about him, and a black staff with copper ferrules in his hand. His companion was a rough spare dog, that followed at his heels, but stopped short, suspiciously at the drawbridge, and in a little while began to howl dismally.

In the meantime, the mountebank, standing in the midst of the courtyard, raised his grotesque hat, and made us a very ceremonious bow, paying his compliments very volubly in execrable French, and German not much better. Then, disengaging his fiddle, he began to scrape a lively air, to which he sang with a merry discord, dancing with ludicrous airs and activity, that made me laugh, in spite of the dog's howling.

Then he advanced to the window with many smiles and salutations, and his hat in his left hand, his fiddle under his arm, and with a fluency that never took breath, he gabbled a long advertisement of all his accomplishments, and the resources of the various arts which he placed at our service, and the curiosities and entertainments which it was in his power, at our bidding, to display.

"Will your ladyships be pleased to buy an amulet against the oupire, which is going like the wolf, I hear, through these woods," he said, dropping his hat on the pavement. "They are dying of it right and left, and here is a charm that never fails; only pinned to the pillow, and you may laugh in his face."

These charms consisted of oblong slips of vellum, with cabalistic ciphers and diagrams upon them.

Carmilla instantly purchased one, and so did I.

He was looking up, and we were smiling down upon him, amused; at least, I can answer for myself. His piercing black eye, as he looked up in our faces, seemed to detect something that fixed for a moment his curiosity.

In an instant he unrolled a leather case, full of all manner of odd little steel instruments.

"See here, my lady," he said, displaying it, and addressing me, "I profess, among other things less useful, the art of dentistry. Plague take the dog!" he interpolated. "Silence, beast! He howls so that your ladyships can scarcely hear a word. Your noble friend, the young lady at your right, has the sharpest tooth,—long, thin, pointed, like an awl, like a needle; ha, ha! With my sharp and long sight, as I look up, I have seen it distinctly; now if it happens to hurt the young lady, and I think it must, here am I, here are my file, my punch, my nippers; I will make it round and blunt, if her ladyship pleases; no longer the tooth of a fish, but of a beautiful young lady as she is. Hey? Is the young lady displeased? Have I been too bold? Have I offended her?"

The young lady, indeed, looked very angry as she drew back from the window.

"How dares that mountebank insult us so? Where is your father? I shall demand redress from him. My father would have had the wretch tied up to the pump, and flogged with a cart-whip, and burnt to the bones with the castle brand!"

She retired from the window a step or two, and sat down, and had hardly lost sight of the offender, when her wrath subsided as suddenly as it had risen, and she gradually recovered her usual tone, and seemed to forget the little hunchback and his follies.

My father was out of spirits that evening. On coming in he told us that there had been another case very similar to the two fatal ones which had lately occurred. The sister of a young peasant on his estate, only a mile away, was very ill, had been, as she described it, attacked very nearly in the same way, and was now slowly but steadily sinking.

"All this," said my father, "is strictly referable to natural causes. These poor people infect one another with their superstitions, and so repeat in imagination the images of terror that have infested their neighbours."

"But that very circumstance frightens one horribly," said Carmilla.

"How so?" inquired my father.

"I am so afraid of fancying I see such things; I think it would be as bad as reality."

"We are in God's hands; nothing can happen without His permission, and all will end well for those who love him. He is our faithful creator; He has made us all, and will take care of us."

"Creator! *Nature!*" said the young lady in answer to my gentle father. "And this disease that invades the country is natural. Nature. All things proceed from Nature—don't they? All things in the heaven, in the earth, and under the earth, act and live as

Nature ordains? I think so."

"The doctor said he would come here to-day," said my father, after a silence. "I want to know what he thinks about it, and what he thinks we had better do."

"Doctors never did me any good," said Carmilla.

"Then you have been ill?" I asked.

"More ill than ever you were," she answered.

"Long ago?"

"Yes, a long time. I suffered from this very illness; but I forget all but my pain and weakness, and they were not so bad as are suffered in other diseases."

"You were very young then?"

"I dare say; let us talk no more of it. You would not wound a friend?" She looked languidly in my eyes, and passed her arm round my waist lovingly, and led me out of the room. My father was busy over some papers near the window.

"Why does your papa like to frighten us?" said the pretty girl, with a sigh and a little shudder.

"He doesn't, dear Carmilla, it is the very furthest thing from his mind."

"Are you afraid, dearest?"

"I should be very much if I fancied there was any real danger of my being attacked as those poor people were."

"You are afraid to die?"

"Yes, every one is."

"But to die as lovers may—to die together, so that they may live together. Girls are caterpillars while they live in the world, to be finally butterflies when the summer comes; but in the meantime there are grubs and larvae, don't you see—each with their peculiar propensities, necessities and structure. So says Monsieur Buffon, in his big book, in the next room."

Later in the day the doctor came, and was closeted with papa for some time. He was a skilful man, of sixty and upwards, he wore powder, and shaved his pale face as smooth as a pumpkin. He and papa emerged from the room together, and I heard papa laugh, and say as they came out:

"Well, I do wonder at a wise man like you. What do you say to hippogriffs and dragons?"

The doctor was smiling, and made answer, shaking his head—

"Nevertheless life and death are mysterious states, and we know little of the resources of either."

And so they walked on, and I heard no more. I did not then know what the doctor had been broaching, but I think I guess it now.

V

A Wonderful Likeness

This evening there arrived from Gratz the grave, dark-faced son of the picture cleaner, with a horse and cart laden with two large packing cases, having many pictures in each. It was a journey of ten leagues, and whenever a messenger arrived at the schloss from our little capital of Gratz, we used to crowd about him in the hall, to hear the news.

This arrival created in our secluded quarters quite a sensation. The cases remained in the hall, and the messenger was taken charge of by the servants till he had eaten his supper. Then with assistants, and armed with hammer, ripping-chisel, and turnscrew, he met us in the hall, where we had assembled to witness the unpacking of the cases.

Carmilla sat looking listlessly on, while one after the other the old pictures, nearly all portraits, which had undergone the process of renovation, were brought to light. My mother was of an old Hungarian family, and most of these pictures, which were about to be restored to their places, had come to us through her.

My father had a list in his hand, from which he read, as the artist rummaged out the corresponding numbers. I don't know that the pictures were very good, but they were, undoubtedly, very old, and some of them very curious also. They had, for the most part, the merit of being now seen by me, I may say, for the first time; for the smoke and dust of time had all but obliterated them.

"There is a picture that I have not seen yet," said my father. "In one corner, at the top of it, is the name, as well as I could read, 'Marcia Karnstein,' and the date '1698'; and I am curious to see how it has turned out."

I remembered it; it was a small picture, about a foot and a half high, and nearly square, without a frame; but it was so blackened by age that I could not make it out.

The artist now produced it, with evident pride. It was quite beautiful; it was startling; it seemed to live. It was the effigy of Carmilla!

"Carmilla, dear, here is an absolute miracle. Here you are, living, smiling, ready to speak, in this picture. Isn't it beautiful, papa? And see, even the little mole on her throat."

My father laughed, and said "Certainly it is a wonderful likeness," but he looked away, and to my surprise seemed but little struck by it, and went on talking to the picture cleaner, who was also something of an artist, and discoursed with intelligence about the portraits or other works, which his art had just brought into light and colour, while *I* was more and more lost in wonder the more I looked at the picture.

"Will you let me hang this picture in my room, papa?" I asked.

"Certainly, dear," said he, smiling, "I'm very glad you think it so like. It must be prettier even than I thought it, if it is."

The young lady did not acknowledge this pretty speech, did not seem to hear it. She was leaning back in her seat, her fine eyes under their long lashes gazing on me in contemplation, and she smiled in a kind of rapture.

"And now you can read quite plainly the name that is written in the corner. It is not Marcia; it looks as if it was done in gold. The name is Mircalla, Countess Karnstein, and this is a little coronet over it, and underneath A.D. 1698. I am descended from the Karnsteins; that is, mama was."

"Ah!" said the lady, languidly, "so am I, I think, a very long descent, very ancient. Are there any Karnsteins living now?"

"None who bear the name, I believe. The family were ruined, I believe, in some civil wars, long ago, but the ruins of the castle are only about three miles away."

"How interesting!" she said, languidly. "But see what beautiful moonlight!" She glanced through the hall-door, which stood a little open. "Suppose you take a little ramble round the court, and look down at the road and river."

"It is so like the night you came to us," I said.

She sighed, smiling.

She rose, and each with her arm about the other's waist, we walked out upon the pavement.

In silence, slowly we walked down to the drawbridge, where the beautiful landscape opened before us.

"And so you were thinking of the night I came here?" she almost whispered. "Are you glad I came?"

"Delighted, dear Carmilla," I answered.

"And you asked for the picture you think like me, to hang in your room," she murmured with a sigh, as she drew her arm closer about my waist, and let her pretty head sink upon my shoulder.

"How romantic you are, Carmilla," I said. "Whenever you tell me your story, it will be made up chiefly of some one great romance."

She kissed me silently.

"I am sure, Carmilla, you have been in love; that there is, at this moment, an affair of the heart going on."

"I have been in love with no one, and never shall," she whispered, "unless it should be with you."

How beautiful she looked in the moonlight!

Shy and strange was the look with which she quickly hid her face in my neck and hair, with tumultuous sighs, that seemed almost to sob, and pressed in mine a hand that trembled.

Her soft cheek was glowing against mine. "Darling, darling," she murmured, "I live in you; and you would die for me, I love you so."

I started from her.

She was gazing on me with eyes from which all fire, all meaning had flown, and a face colourless and apathetic.

"Is there a chill in the air, dear?" she said drowsily. "I almost shiver; have I been dreaming? Let us come in. Come; come; come in."

"You look ill, Carmilla; a little faint. You certainly must take some wine," I said.

"Yes, I will. I'm better now. I shall be quite well in a few minutes. Yes, do give me a little wine," answered Carmilla, as we approached the door. "Let us look again for a moment; it is the last time, perhaps, I shall see the moonlight with you."

"How do you feel now, dear Carmilla? Are you really better?" I asked.

I was beginning to take alarm, lest she should have been stricken with the strange epidemic that they said had invaded the country about us.

"Papa would be grieved beyond measure," I added, "if he thought you were ever so little ill, without immediately letting us know. We have a very skilful doctor near this, the physician who was with papa to-day."

"I'm sure he is. I know how kind you all are; but, dear child, I am quite well again. There is nothing ever wrong with me, but a little weakness. People say I am languid; I am incapable of exertion; I can scarcely walk as far as a child of three years old; and every now and then the little strength I have falters, and I become as you have just seen me. But after all I am very easily set up again; in a moment I am perfectly myself. See how I have recovered."

So, indeed, she had; and she and I talked a great deal, and very animated she was; and the remainder of that evening passed without any recurrence of what I called her infatuations. I mean her crazy talk and looks, which embarrassed, and even frightened me.

But there occurred that night an event which gave my thoughts quite a new turn, and seemed to startle even Carmilla's languid nature into momentary energy.

VI
A Very Strange Agony

When we got into the drawing-room, and had sat down to our coffee and chocolate, although Carmilla did not take any, she seemed quite herself again, and Madame, and Mademoiselle De Lafontaine, joined us, and made a little card party, in the course of which papa came in for what he called his "dish of tea."

When the game was over he sat down beside Carmilla on the sofa, and asked her, a little anxiously, whether she had heard from her mother since her arrival.

She answered "No."

He then asked whether she knew where a letter would reach her at present.

"I cannot tell," she answered ambiguously, "but I have been thinking of leaving you; you have been already too hospitable and too kind to me. I have given you an infinity of trouble, and I should wish to take a carriage to-morrow, and post in pursuit of her; I know where I shall ultimately find her, although I dare not yet tell you."

"But you must not dream of any such thing," exclaimed my father, to my great relief. "We can't afford to lose you so, and I won't consent to your leaving us, except under the care of your mother, who was so good as to consent to your remaining with us till she should herself return. I should be quite happy if I knew that you heard from her; but this evening the accounts of the

progress of the mysterious disease that has invaded our neighbourhood grow even more alarming; and my beautiful guest, I do feel
the responsibility, unaided by advice from your mother, very
much. But I shall do my best; and one thing is certain, that you
must not think of leaving us without her distinct direction to that
effect. We should suffer too much in parting from you to consent
to it easily."

"Thank you, sir, a thousand times for your hospitality," she
answered, smiling bashfully. "You have all been too kind to me;
I have seldom been so happy in all my life before, as in your
beatiful château, under your care, and in the society of your dear
daughter."

So he gallantly, in his old-fashioned way, kissed her hand,
smiling and pleased at her little speech.

I accompanied Carmilla as usual to her room, and sat and
chatted with her while she was preparing for bed.

"Do you think," I said at length, "that you will ever confide
fully in me?"

She turned round smiling, but made no answer, only continued
to smile on me.

"You won't answer that?" I said. "You can't answer pleasantly;
I ought not to have asked you."

"You were quite right to ask me that, or anything. You do not
know how dear you are to me, or you could not think any
confidence too great to look for. But I am under vows, no nun
half so awfully, and I dare not tell my story yet, even to you. The
time is very near when you shall know everything. You will think
me cruel, very selfish, but love is always selfish; the more ardent
the more selfish. How jealous I am you cannot know. You must
come with me, loving me, to death; or else hate me and still come
with me, and *hating* me through death and after. There is no such
word as indifference in my apathetic nature."

"Now, Carmilla, you are going to talk your wild nonsense
again," I said hastily.

"Not I, silly little fool as I am, and full of whims and fancies;
for your sake I'll talk like a sage. Were you ever at a ball?"

"No; how you do run on. What is it like? How charming it must
be."

"I almost forget, it is years ago."

I laughed.

"You are not so old. Your first ball can hardly be forgotten yet."

"I remember everything about it—with an effort. I see it all, as divers see what is going on above them, through a medium, dense, rippling, but transparent. There occurred that night what has confused the picture, and made its colours faint. I was all but assassinated in my bed, wounded *here*," she touched her breast, "and never was the same since."

"Were you near dying?"

"Yes, very—a cruel love—strange love, that would have taken my life. Love will have its sacrifices. No sacrifice without blood. Let us go to sleep now; I feel so lazy. How can I get up just now and lock my door?"

She was lying with her tiny hands buried in her rich wavy hair, under her cheek, her little head upon the pillow, and her glittering eyes followed me wherever I moved, with a kind of shy smile that I could not decipher.

I bid her good night, and crept from the room with an uncomfortable sensation.

I often wondered whether our pretty guest ever said her prayers. *I* certainly had never seen her upon her knees. In the morning she never came down until long after our family prayers were over, and at night she never left the drawing-room to attend our brief evening prayers in the hall.

If it had not been that it had casually come out in one of our careless talks that she had been baptised, I should have doubted her being a Christian. Religion was a subject on which I had never heard her speak a word. If I had known the world better, this particular neglect or antipathy would not have so much surprised me.

The precautions of nervous people are infectious, and persons of a like temperament are pretty sure, after a time, to imitate them. I had adopted Carmilla's habit of locking her bedroom door, having taken into my head all her whimsical alarms about midnight invaders and prowling assassins. I had also adopted her precaution of making a brief search through her room, to satisfy herself that no lurking assassin or robber was "ensconced."

These wise measures taken, I got into my bed and fell asleep. A light was burning in my room. This was an old habit, of very early date, and which nothing could have tempted me to dispense with.

Thus fortified I might take my rest in peace. But dreams come through stone walls, light up dark rooms, or darken light ones, and their persons make their exits and their entrances as they please, and laugh at locksmiths.

I had a dream that night that was the beginning of a very strange agony.

I cannot call it a nightmare, for I was quite conscious of being asleep. But I was equally conscious of being in my room, and lying in bed, precisely as I actually was. I saw, or fancied I saw, the room and its furniture just as I had seen it last, except that it was very dark, and I saw something moving round the foot of the bed, which at first I could not accurately distinguish. But I soon saw that it was a sooty-black animal that resembled a monstrous cat. It appeared to me about four or five feet long, for it measured fully the length of the hearthrug as it passed over it; and it continued to-ing and fro-ing with the lithe, sinister restlessness of a beast in a cage. I could not cry out, although as you may suppose, I was terrified. Its pace was growing faster, and the room rapidly darker and darker, and at length so dark that I could no longer see anything of it but its eyes. I felt it spring lightly on the bed. The two broad eyes approached my face, and suddenly I felt a stinging pain as if two large needles darted, an inch or two apart, deep into my breast. I waked with a scream. The room was lighted by the candle that burnt there all through the night, and I saw a female figure standing at the foot of the bed, a little at the right side. It was in a dark loose dress, and its hair was down and covered its shoulders. A block of stone could not have been more still. There was not the slightest stir of respiration. As I stared at it, the figure appeared to have changed its place, and was now nearer the door; then, close to it, the door opened, and it passed out.

I was now relieved, and able to breathe and move. My first thought was that Carmilla had been playing me a trick, and that I had forgotten to secure my door. I hastened to it, and found it locked as usual on the inside. I was afraid to open it—I was horrified. I sprang into my bed and covered my head up in the bedclothes, and lay there more dead than alive till morning.

VII
Descending

It would be vain my attempting to tell you the horror with which, even now, I recall the occurrence of that night. It was no such transitory terror as a dream leaves behind it. It seemed to deepen by time, and communicated itself to the room and the very furniture that had encompassed the apparition.

I could not bear next day to be alone for a moment. I should have told papa, but for two opposite reasons. At one time I thought he would laugh at my story, and I could not bear its being treated as a jest; and at another, I thought he might fancy that I had been attacked by the mysterious complaint which had invaded our neighbourhood. I had myself no misgivings of the kind, and as he had been rather an invalid for some time, I was afraid of alarming him.

I was comfortable enough with my good-natured companions, Madame Perrodon, and the vivacious Mademoiselle De Lafontaine. They both perceived that I was out of spirits and nervous, and at length I told them what lay so heavy at my heart.

Mademoiselle laughed, but I fancied that Madame Perrodon looked anxious.

"By-the-by," said Mademoiselle, laughing, "the long lime-tree walk, behind Carmilla's bedroom-window, is haunted!"

"Nonsense!" exclaimed Madame, who probably thought the theme rather inopportune, "and who tells that story, my dear?"

"Martin says that he came up twice, when the old yard-gate was being repaired, before sunrise, and twice saw the female figure walking down the lime-tree avenue."

"So he well might, as long as there are cows to milk in the river fields," said Madame.

"I daresay; but Martin chooses to be frightened, and never did I see fool *more* frightened."

"You must not say a word about it to Carmilla, because she can see down that walk from her room window," I interposed, "and she is, if possible, a greater coward than I."

Carmilla came down rather later than usual that day.

"I was so frightened last night," she said, so soon as were together, "and I am sure I should have seen something dreadful if it had not been for that charm I bought from the poor little hunchback whom I called such hard names. I had a dream of something black coming round my bed, and I awoke in a perfect horror, and I really thought, for some seconds, I saw a dark figure near the chimney-piece, but I felt under my pillow for my charm, and the moment my fingers touched it, the figure disappeared, and I felt quite certain, only that I had it by me, that something frightful would have made its appearance, and, perhaps, throttled me, as it did those poor people we heard of."

"Well, listen to me," I began, and recounted my adventure, at the recital of which she appeared horrified.

"And had you the charm near you?" she asked, earnestly.

"No, I had dropped it into a china vase in the drawing-room, but I shall certainly take it with me to-night, as you have so much faith in it."

At this distance of time I cannot tell you, or even understand, how I overcame my horror so effectively as to lie alone in my room that night. I remember distinctly that I pinned the charm to my pillow. I fell asleep almost immediately, and slept even more soundly than usual all night.

Next night I passed as well. My sleep was delightfully deep and dreamless. But I wakened with a sense of lassitude and melancholy, which, however, did not exceed a degree that was almost luxurious.

"Well, I told you so," said Carmilla, when I described my quiet sleep, "I had such delightful sleep myself last night; I pinned the charm to the breast of my nightdress. It was too far away the night before. I am quite sure it was all fancy, except the dreams. I used to think that evil spirits made dreams, but our doctor told me it is no such thing. Only a fever passing by, or some other malady, as they often do, he said, knocks at the door, and not being able to get in, passes on, with that alarm."

"And what do you think the charm is?" said I.

"It has been fumigated or immersed in some drug, and is an antidote against the malaria," she answered.

"Then it acts only on the body?"

"Certainly; you don't suppose that evil spirits are frightened by bits of ribbon, or the perfumes of a druggist's shop? No, these complaints, wandering in the air, begin by trying the nerves, and so infect the brain, but before they can seize upon you, the antidote repels them. That I am sure is what the charm has done for us. It is nothing magical, it is simply natural."

I should have been happier if I could have quite agreed with Carmilla, but I did my best, and the impression was a little losing its force.

For some nights I slept profoundly; but still every morning I felt the same lassitude, and a languor weighed upon me all day. I felt myself a changed girl. A strange melancholy was stealing over me, a melancholy that I would not have interrupted. Dim thoughts of death began to open, and an idea that I was slowly sinking took gentle, and, somehow, not unwelcome, possession of me. If it was sad, the tone of mind which this induced was also sweet. Whatever it might be, my soul acquiesced in it.

I would not admit that I was ill, I would not consent to tell my papa, or to have the doctor sent for.

Carmilla became more devoted to me than ever, and her strange paroxysms of languid adoration more frequent. She used to gloat on me with increasing ardour the more my strength and spirits waned. This always shocked me like a momentary glare of insanity.

Without knowing it, I was now in a pretty advanced stage of the strangest illness under which mortal ever suffered. There was an unaccountable fascination in its earlier symptoms that more than reconciled me to the incapacitating effect of that stage of the malady. This fascination increased for a time, until it reached a certain point, when gradually a sense of the horrible mingled itself with it, deepening, as you shall hear, until it discoloured and perverted the whole state of my life.

The first change I experienced was rather agreeable. It was very near the turning point from which began the descent of Avernus.

Certain vague and strange sensations visited me in my sleep. The prevailing one was of that pleasant, peculiar cold thrill which we feel in bathing, when we move against the current of a river. This was soon accompanied by dreams that seemed interminable, and were so vague that I could never recollect their scenery and persons, or any one connected portion of their action. But they left an awful impression, and a sense of exhaustion, as if I had passed through a long period of great mental exertion and danger. After all these dreams there remained on waking a remembrance of having been in a place very nearly dark, and of having spoken to people whom I could not see; and especially of one clear voice, of a female's very deep, that spoke as if at a distance, slowly, and producing always the same sensation of indescribable solemnity and fear. Sometimes there came a sensation as if a hand was drawn softly along my cheek and neck. Sometimes it was as if warm lips kissed me, and longer and more lovingly as they reached my throat, but there the caress fixed itself. My heart beat faster, my breathing rose and fell rapidly and full drawn; a sobbing, that rose into a sense of strangulation, supervened, and turned into a dreadful convulsion, in which my senses left me and I became unconscious.

It was now three weeks since the commencement of this unaccountable state. My sufferings had, during the last week, told upon my appearance. I had grown pale, my eyes were dilated and darkened underneath, and the languor which I had long felt began to display itself in my countenance.

My father asked me often whether I was ill; but, with an obstinacy which now seems to me unaccountable, I persisted in assuring him that I was quite well.

In a sense this was true. I had no pain, I could complain of no bodily derangement. My complaint seemed to be one of the imagination, or the nerves, and, horrible as my sufferings were, I kept them, with a morbid reserve, very nearly to myself.

It could not be that terrible complaint which the peasants called the oupire, for I had now been suffering for three weeks, and they were seldom ill for much more than three days, when death put an end to their miseries.

Carmilla complained of dreams and feverish sensations, but by no means of so alarming a kind as mine. I say that mine were extremely alarming. Had I been capable of comprehending my condition, I would have invoked aid and advice on my knees. The narcotic of an unsuspected influence was acting upon me, and my perceptions were benumbed.

I am going to tell you now of a dream that led immediately to an odd discovery.

One night, instead of the voice I was accustomed to hear in the dark, I heard one, sweet and tender, and at the same time terrible, which said, "Your mother warns you to beware of the assassin." At the same time a light unexpectedly sprang up, and I saw Carmilla, standing, near the foot of my bed, in her white nightdress, bathed, from her chin to her feet, in one great stain of blood.

I wakened with a shriek, possessed with the one idea that Carmilla was being murdered. I remember springing from my bed, and my next recollection is that of standing on the lobby, crying for help.

Madame and Mademoiselle came scurrying out of their rooms in alarm; a lamp burned always on the lobby, and seeing me, they soon learned the cause of my terror.

I insisted on our knocking at Carmilla's door. Our knocking was unanswered. It soon became a pounding and an uproar. We shrieked her name, but all was vain.

We all grew frightened, for the door was locked. We hurried back, in panic, to my room. There we rang the bell long and furiously. If my father's room had been at the side of the house, we would have called him up at once to our aid. But, alas! he was quite out of hearing, and to reach him involved an excursion for which we none of us had courage.

Servants, however, soon came running up the stairs; I had got on my dressing-gown and slippers meanwhile, and my companions were already similarly furnished. Recognising the voices of the servants on the lobby, we sallied out together; and having renewed, as fruitlessly, our summons at Carmilla's door, I ordered the men to force the lock. They did so, and we stood, holding our lights aloft, in the doorway, and so stared into the room.

We called her by name; but there was still no reply. We looked round the room. Everything was undisturbed. It was exactly in the state in which I had left it on bidding her good night. But Carmilla was gone.

VIII
Search

At sight of the room, perfectly undisturbed except for our violent entrance, we began to cool a little, and soon recovered our senses sufficiently to dismiss the men. It had struck Mademoiselle that possibly Carmilla had been wakened by the uproar at her door, and in her first panic had jumped from her bed, and hid herself in a press, or behind a curtain, from which she could not, of course, emerge until the majordomo and his myrmidons had withdrawn. We now recommenced our search, and began to call her by name again.

It was all to no purpose. Our perplexity and agitation increased. We examined the windows, but they were secured. I implored of Carmilla, if she had concealed herself, to play this cruel trick no longer—to come out, and to end our anxieties. It was all useless. I was by this time convinced that she was not in the room, nor in the dressing-room, the door of which was still locked on this side. She could not have passed it. I was utterly puzzled. Had Carmilla discovered one of those secret passages which the old housekeeper said were known to exist in the schloss, although the tradition of their exact situation had been lost? A little time would, no doubt, explain all—utterly perplexed as, for the present, we were.

It was past four o'clock, and I preferred passing the remaining hours of darkness in Madame's room. Daylight brought no solution of the difficulty.

The whole household, with my father at its head, was in a state of agitation next morning. Every part of the château was searched. The grounds were explored. Not a trace of the missing lady could be discovered. The stream was about to be dragged; my father was in distraction; what a tale to have to tell the poor girl's mother on her return. I, too, was almost beside myself, though my grief was quite of a different kind.

The morning was passed in alarm and excitement. It was now one o'clock, and still no tidings. I ran up to Carmilla's room, and found her standing at her dressing-table. I was astounded. I could not believe my eyes. She beckoned me to her with her pretty finger, in silence. Her face expressed extreme fear.

I ran to her in an ecstasy of joy; I kissed and embraced her again and again. I ran to the bell and rang it vehemently, to bring others to the spot, who might at once relieve my father's anxiety.

"Dear Carmilla, what has become of you all this time? We have been in agonies of anxiety about you," I exclaimed. "Where have you been? How did you come back?"

"Last night has been a night of wonders," she said.

"For mercy's sake, explain all you can."

"It was past two last night," she said, "when I went to sleep as usual in my bed, with my doors locked, that of the dressing-room, and that opening upon the gallery. My sleep was uninterrupted, and, so far as I know, dreamless; but I woke just now on the sofa in the dressing-room there, and I found the door between the rooms open, and the other door forced. How could all this have happened without my being wakened? It must have been accompanied with a great deal of noise, and I am particularly easily wakened; and how could I have been carried out of my bed without my sleep having been interrupted, I whom the slightest stir startles?"

By this time, Madame, Mademoiselle, my father, and a number of the servants were in the room. Carmilla was, of course, overwhelmed with inquiries, congratulations, and welcomes. She had but one story to tell, and seemed the least able of all the party to suggest any way of accounting for what had happened.

My father took a turn up and down the room, thinking. I saw Carmilla's eye follow him for a moment with a sly, dark glance.

When my father had sent the servants away, Mademoiselle having gone in search of a little bottle of valerian and sal volatile, and there being no one now in the room with Carmilla, except my father, Madame, and myself, he came to her thoughtfully, took her hand very kindly, led her to the sofa, and sat down beside her.

"Will you forgive me, my dear, if I risk a conjecture, and ask a question?"

"Who can have a better right?" she said. "Ask what you please, and I will tell you everything. But my story is simply one of bewilderment and darkness. I know absolutely nothing. Put any question you please. But you know, of course, the limitations mama has placed me under."

"Perfectly, my dear child. I need not approach the topics on which she desires our silence. Now, the marvel of last night consists in your having been removed from your bed and your room, without being wakened, and this removal having occurred apparently while the windows were still secured, and the two doors locked upon the inside. I will tell you my theory, and first ask you a question."

Carmilla was leaning on her hand dejectedly; Madame and I were listening breathlessly.

"Now, my question is this. Have you ever been suspected of walking in your sleep?"

"Never, since I was very young indeed."

"But you did walk in your sleep when you were young?"

"Yes; I know I did. I have been told so often by my old nurse."

My father smiled and nodded.

"Well, what has happened is this. You got up in your sleep, unlocked the door, not leaving the key, as usual, in the lock, but taking it out and locking it on the outside; you again took the key out, and carried it away with you to some one of the five-and-twenty rooms on this floor, or perhaps upstairs or downstairs. There are so many rooms and closets, so much heavy furniture, and such accumulations of lumber, that it would require a week to search this old house thoroughly. Do you see, now, what I mean?"

"I do, but not all," she answered.

"And how, papa, do you account for her finding herself on the sofa in the dressing-room, which we had searched so carefully?"

"She came there after you had searched it, still in her sleep, and at last awoke spontaneously, and was as much surprised to find herself where she was as any one else. I wish all mysteries were as easily and innocently explained as yours, Carmilla," he said, laughing. "And so we may congratulate ourselves on the certainty that the most natural explanation of the occurrence is one that involves no drugging, no tampering with locks, no burglars, or poisoners, or witches—nothing that need alarm Carmilla, or anyone else, for our safety."

Carmilla was looking charmingly. Nothing could be more beautiful than her tints. Her beauty was, I think, enhanced by that graceful languor that was peculiar to her. I think my father was silently contrasting her looks with mine, for he said:

"I wish my poor Laura was looking more like herself"; and he sighed.

So our alarms were happily ended, and Carmilla restored to her friends.

IX

The Doctor

As Carmilla would not hear of an attendant sleeping in her room, my father arranged that a servant should sleep outside her door, so that she could not attempt to make another such excursion without being arrested at her own door.

That night passed quietly; and next morning early, the doctor, whom my father had sent for without telling me a word about it, arrived to see me.

Madame accompanied me to the library; and there the grave little doctor, with white hair and spectacles, whom I mentioned before, was waiting to receive me.

I told him my story, and as I proceeded he grew graver and graver.

We were standing, he and I, in the recess of one of the windows, facing one another. When my statement was over, he leaned with his shoulders against the wall, and with his eyes fixed on me earnestly, with an interest in which was a dash of horror.

After a minute's reflection, he asked Madame if he could see my father.

He was sent for accordingly, and as he entered, smiling, he said:

"I dare say, doctor, you are going to tell me that I am an old fool for having brought you here; I hope I am."

But his smile faded into shadow as the doctor, with a very grave face, beckoned him to him.

He and the doctor talked for some time in the same recess where I had just conferred with the physician. It seemed an earnest and argumentative conversation. The room is very large, and I and Madame stood together, burning with curiosity, at the farther end. Not a word could we hear, however, for they spoke in a very low tone, and the deep recess of the window quite concealed the doctor from view, and very nearly my father, whose foot, arm, and shoulder only could we see; and the voices were, I suppose, all the less audible for the sort of closet which the thick wall and window formed.

After a time my father's face looked into the room; it was pale, thoughtful, and, I fancied, agitated.

"Laura, dear, come here for a moment. Madame, we shan't trouble you, the doctor says, at present."

Accordingly I approached, for the first time a little alarmed; for, although I felt very weak, I did not feel ill; and strength, one always fancies, is a thing that may be picked up when we please.

My father held out his hand to me, as I drew near, but he was looking at the doctor, and he said:

"It certainly *is* very odd; I don't understand it quite. Laura, come here, dear; now attend to Doctor Spielsberg, and recollect yourself."

"You mentioned a sensation like that of two needles piercing the skin, somewhere about your neck, on the night when you experienced your first horrible dream. Is there still any soreness?"

"None at all," I answered.

"Can you indicate with your finger about the point at which you think this occurred?"

"Very little below my throat—*here*," I answered.

I wore a morning dress, which covered the place I pointed to.

"Now you can satisfy yourself," said the doctor. "You won't mind your papa's lowering your dress a very little. It is necessary, to detect a symptom of the complaint under which you have been suffering."

I acquiesced. It was only an inch or two below the edge of my collar.

"God bless me!—so it is," exclaimed my father, growing pale.

"You see it now with your eyes," said the doctor, with a gloomy triumph.

"What is it?" I exclaimed, beginning to be frightened.

"Nothing, my dear young lady, but a small blue spot, about the size of the tip of your little finger; and now," he continued, turning to papa, "the question is what is best to be done?"

"Is there any danger?" I urged, in great trepidation.

"I trust not, my dear," answered the doctor. "I don't see why you should not recover. I don't see why you should not begin *immediately* to get better. That is the point at which the sense of strangulation begins?"

"Yes," I answered.

"And—recollect as well as you can—the same point was a kind of centre of that thrill which you described just now, like the current of a cold stream running against you?"

"It may have been; I think it was."

"Ay, you see?" he added, turning to my father. "Shall I say a word to Madame?"

"Certainly," said my father.

He called Madame to him, and said:

"I find my young friend here far from well. It won't be of any great consequence, I hope; but it will be necessary that some steps be taken, which I will explain by-and-by; but in the meantime, Madame, you will be so good as not to let Miss Laura be alone for one moment. That is the only direction I need give for the present. It is indispensable."

"We may rely upon your kindness, Madame, I know," added my father.

Madame satisfied him eagerly.

"And you, dear Laura, I know you will observe the doctor's direction."

"I shall have to ask your opinion upon another patient, whose symptoms slightly resemble those of my daughter, that have just been detailed to you—very much milder in degree, but I believe quite of the same sort. She is a young lady—our guest; but as you say you will be passing this way again this evening, you can't do better than take your supper here, and you can then see her. She does not come down till the afternoon."

"I thank you," said the doctor. "I shall be with you, then, at about seven this evening."

And then they repeated their directions to me and to Madame, and with this parting charge my father left us, and walked out with the doctor; and I saw them pacing together up and down between the road and the moat, on the grassy platform in front of the castle, evidently absorbed in earnest conversation.

The doctor did not return. I saw him mount his horse there, take his leave, and ride away eastward through the forest.

Nearly at the same time I saw the man arrive from Dranfield with the letters, and dismount and hand the bag to my father.

In the meantime, Madame and I were both busy, lost in conjecture as to the reasons of the singular and earnest direction which the doctor and my father had concurred in imposing. Madame, as she afterwards told me, was afraid the doctor apprehended a sudden seizure, and that, without prompt assistance, I might either lose my life in a fit, or at least be seriously hurt.

The interpretation did not strike me; and I fancied, perhaps luckily for my nerves, that the arrangement was prescribed simply to secure a companion, who would prevent my taking too much exercise, or eating unripe fruit, or doing any of the fifty foolish things to which young people are supposed to be prone.

About half an hour after my father came in—he had a letter in his hand—and said:

"This letter had been delayed; it is from General Spielsdorf. He might have been here yesterday, he may not come till to-morrow or he may be here to-day."

He put the open letter into my hand; but he did not look pleased, as he used to when a guest, especially one so much loved as the General, was coming. On the contrary, he looked as if he wished him at the bottom of the Red Sea. There was plainly something on his mind which he did not choose to divulge.

"Papa, darling, will you tell me this?" said I, suddenly laying my hand on his arm, and looking, I am sure, imploringly in his face.

"Perhaps," he answered, smoothing my hair caressingly over my eyes.

"Does the doctor think me very ill?"

"No, dear; he thinks, if right steps are taken, you will be quite well again, at least, on the high road to a complete recovery, in a day or two," he answered, a little dryly. "I wish our good friend, the General, had chosen any other time; that is, I wish you had been perfectly well to receive him."

"But do tell me, papa," I insisted, "*what* does he think is the matter with me?"

"Nothing; you must not plague me with questions," he answered, with more irritation than I ever remember him to have displayed before; and seeing that I looked wounded, I suppose, he kissed me, and added, "You shall know all about it in a day or two; that is, all that *I* know. In the meantime you are not to trouble your head about it."

He turned and left the room, but came back before I had done wondering and puzzling over the oddity of all this; it was merely to say that he was going to Karnstein, and had ordered the carriage to be ready at twelve, and that I and Madame should accompany him; he was going to see the priest who lived near those picturesque grounds, upon business, and as Carmilla had never seen them, she could follow, when she came down, with Mademoiselle, who would bring materials for what you call a picnic, which might be laid for us in the ruined castle.

At twelve o'clock, accordingly, I was ready, and not long after, my father, Madame and I set out upon our projected drive.

Passing the drawbridge we turn to the right, and follow the road over the steep Gothic bridge, westward, to reach the deserted village and ruined castle of Karnstein.

No sylvan drive can be fancied prettier. The ground breaks into gentle hills and hollows, all clothed with beautiful wood, totally destitute of the comparative formality which artificial planning and early culture and pruning impart.

The irregularities of the ground often lead the road out of its course, and cause it to wind beautifully round the sides of broken hollows and the steeper sides of the hills, among varieties of ground almost inexhaustible.

Turning one of these points, we suddenly encountered our old friend, the General, riding towards us, attended by a mounted servant. His portmanteaus were following in a hired wagon, such as we term a cart.

The General dismounted as we pulled up, and, after the usual greetings, was easily persuaded to accept the vacant seat in the carriage and send his horse on with his servant to the schloss.

X
Bereaved

It was about ten months since we had last seen him; but that time had sufficed to make an alteration of years in his appearance. He had grown thinner; something of gloom and anxiety had taken the place of that cordial serenity which used to characterise his features. His dark blue eyes, always penetrating, now gleamed with a sterner light from under his shaggy grey eyebrows. It was not such a change as grief alone usually induces, and angrier passions seemed to have had their share in bringing it about.

We had not long resumed our drive, when the General began to talk, with his usual soldierly directness, of the bereavement, as he termed it, which he had sustained in the death of his beloved niece and ward; and he then broke out in a tone of intense bitterness and fury, inveighing against the "hellish arts" to which she had fallen a victim, and expressing, with more exasperation than piety, his wonder that Heaven should tolerate so monstrous an indulgence of the lusts and malignity of hell.

My father, who saw at once that something very extraordinary had befallen, asked him, if not too painful to him, to detail the circumstances which he thought justified the strong terms in which he expressed himself.

"I should tell you all with pleasure," said the General, "but you would not believe me."

"Why should I not?" he asked.

"Because," he answered testily, "you believe in nothing but what consists with your own prejudices and illusions. I remember when I was like you, but I have learned better."

"Try me," said my father; "I am not such a dogmatist as you suppose. Besides which, I very well know that you generally require proof for what you believe, and am, therefore, very strongly predisposed to respect your conclusions."

"You are right in supposing that I have not been led lightly into a belief in the marvellous—for what I have experienced *is* marvellous—and I have been forced by extraordinary evidence to credit that which ran counter, diametrically, to all my theories. I have been made the dupe of a preternatural conspiracy."

Notwithstanding his professions of confidence in the General's penetration, I saw my father, at this point, glance at the General, with, as I thought, a marked suspicion of his sanity.

The General did not see it, luckily. He was looking gloomily and curiously into the glades and vistas of the woods that were opening before us.

"You are going to the Ruins of Karnstein?" he said. "Yes, it is a lucky coincidence; do you know I was going to ask you to bring me there to inspect them. I have a special object in exploring. There is a ruined chapel, ain't there, with a great many tombs of that extinct family?"

"So there are—highly interesting," said my father. "I hope you are thinking of claiming the title and estates?"

My father said this gaily, but the General did not recollect the laugh, or even the smile, which courtesy exacts for a friend's joke; on the contrary, he looked grave and even fierce, ruminating on a matter that stirred his anger and horror.

"Something very different," he said, gruffly. "I mean to unearth some of those fine people. I hope, by God's blessing, to accomplish a pious sacrilege here, which will relieve our earth of certain monsters, and enable honest people to sleep in their beds without being assailed by murderers. I have strange things to tell you, my dear friend, such as I myself would have scouted as incredible a few months since."

My father looked at him again, but this time not with a glance of suspicion—with an eye, rather, of keen intelligence and alarm.

"The house of Karnstein," he said, "has been long extinct: a hundred years at least. My dear wife was maternally descended from the Karnsteins. But the name and title have long ceased to exist. The castle is a ruin; the very village is deserted; it is fifty years since the smoke of a chimney was seen there; not a roof left."

"Quite true. I have heard a great deal about that since I last saw you; a great deal that will astonish you. But I had better relate everything in the order in which it occurred," said the General. "You saw my dear ward—my child, I may call her. No creature could have been more beautiful, and only three months ago none more blooming."

"Yes, poor thing! when I saw her last she certainly was quite lovely," said my father. "I was grieved and shocked more than I can tell you, my dear friend; I knew what a blow it was to you."

He took the General's hand, and they exchanged a kind pressure. Tears gathered in the old soldier's eyes. He did not seek to conceal them. He said:

"We have been very old friends; I knew you would feel for me, childless as I am. She had become an object of very near interest to me, and repaid my care by an affection that cheered my home and made my life happy. That is all gone. The years that remain to me on earth may not be very long; but by God's mercy I hope to accomplish a service to mankind before I die, and to subserve the vengeance of Heaven upon the fiends who have murdered my poor child in the spring of her hopes and beauty!"

"You said, just now, that you intended relating everything as it occurred," said my father. "Pray do; I assure you that it is not mere curiosity that prompts me."

By this time we had reached the point at which the Drunstall road, by which the General had come, diverges from the road which we were travelling to Karnstein.

"How far is it to the ruins?" inquired the General, looking anxiously forward.

"About half a league," answered my father. "Pray let us hear the story you were so good as to promise."

XI
The Story

"With all my heart," said the General, with an effort; and after a short pause in which to arrange his subject, he commenced one of the strangest narratives I ever heard.

"My dear child was looking forward with great pleasure to the visit you had been so good as to arrange for her to your charming daughter." Here he made me a gallant but melancholy bow. "In the meantime we had an invitation to my old friend the Count Carlsfeld, whose schloss is about six leagues to the other side of Karnstein. It was to attend the series of fêtes which, you remember, were given by him in honour of his illustrious visitor, the Grand Duke Charles."

"Yes; and very splendid, I believe, they were," said my father.

"Princely! But then his hospitalities are quite regal. He has Aladdin's lamp. The night from which my sorrow dates was devoted to a magnificent masquerade. The grounds were thrown open, the trees hung with coloured lamps. There was such a display of fireworks as Paris itself had never witnessed. And such music—music, you know, is my weakness—such ravishing music!

The finest instrumental band, perhaps in the world, and the finest singers who could be collected from all the great operas in Europe. As you wandered through these fantastically illuminated grounds, the moon-lighted château throwing a rosy light from its long rows of windows, you would suddenly hear these ravishing voices stealing from the silence of some grove, or rising from boats upon the lake. I felt myself, as I looked and listened, carried back into the romance and poetry of my early youth.

"When the fireworks were ended, and the ball beginning, we returned to the noble suite of rooms that were thrown open to the dancers. A masked ball, you know, is a beautiful sight; but so brilliant a spectacle of the kind I never saw before.

"It was a very aristocratic assembly. I was myself almost the only 'nobody' present.

"My dear child was looking quite beautiful. She wore no mask. Her excitement and delight added an unspeakable charm to her features, always lovely. I remarked a young lady, dressed magnificently, but wearing a mask, who appeared to me to be observing my ward with extraordinary interest. I had seen her, earlier in the evening, in the great hall, and again, for a few minutes, walking near us, on the terrace under the castle windows, similarly employed. A lady, also masked, richly and gravely dressed, and with a stately air, like a person of rank, accompanied her as a chaperon. Had the young lady not worn a mask, I could, of course, have been much more certain upon the question whether she was really watching my poor darling. I am now well assured that she was.

"We were now in one of the *salons*. My poor dear child had been dancing, and was resting a little in one of the chairs near the door; I was standing near. The two ladies I have mentioned had approached and the younger took the chair next my ward; while her companion stood beside me, and for a little time addressed herself, in a low tone, to her charge.

"Availing herself of the privilege of her mask, she turned to me, and in the tone of an old friend, and calling me by my name, opened a conversation with me, which piqued my curiosity a good deal. She referred to many scenes where she had met me—at Court, and at distinguished houses. She alluded to little incidents which I had long ceased to think of, but which, I found, had only lain in abeyance in my memory, for they instantly started into life at her touch.

"I became more and more curious to ascertain who she was, every moment. She parried my attempts to discover very adroitly and pleasantly. The knowledge she showed of many passages in my life seemed to me all but unaccountable; and she appeared to take a not unnatural pleasure in foiling my curiosity, and in seeing me flounder in my eager perplexity, from one conjecture to another.

"In the meantime the young lady, whom her mother called by the odd name of Millarca, when she once or twice addressed her, had, with the same ease and grace, got into conversation with my ward.

"She introduced herself by saying that her mother was a very old acquaintance of mine. She spoke of the agreeable audacity which a mask rendered practicable; she talked like a friend; she admired her dress, and insinuated very prettily her admiration of her beauty. She amused her with laughing criticisms upon the people who crowded the ballroom, and laughed at my poor child's fun. She was very witty and lively when she pleased, and after a time they had grown very good friends, and the young stranger lowered her mask, displaying a remarkably beautiful face. I had never seen it before, neither had my dear child. But though it was new to us, the features were so engaging, as well as lovely, that it was impossible not to feel the attraction powerfully. My poor girl did so. I never saw anyone more taken with another at first sight, unless, indeed, it was the stranger herself, who seemed quite to have lost her heart to her.

"In the meantime, availing myself of the licence of a masquerade, I put not a few questions to the elder lady.

"'You have puzzled me utterly,' I said, laughing. 'Is that not enough? Won't you, now, consent to stand on equal terms, and do me the kindness to remove your mask?'

"'Can any request be more unreasonable?' she replied. 'Ask a lady to yield an advantage! Beside, how do you know you should recognise me? Years make changes.'

"'As you see,' I said, with a bow, and, I suppose, a rather melancholy little laugh.

"'As philosophers tell us,' she said; 'and how do you know that a sight of my face would help you?'

"'I should take chance for that,' I answered. 'It is vain trying to make yourself out an old woman; your figure betrays you.'

"'Years, nevertheless, have passed since I saw you, rather since you saw me, for that is what I am considering. Millarca, there, is my daughter; I cannot then be young, even in the opinion of people whom time has taught to be indulgent, and I may not like to be compared with what you remember me. You have no mask to remove. You can offer me nothing in exchange.'

"'My petition is to your pity, to remove it.'

"'And mine to yours, to let it stay where it is,' she replied.

"'Well, then, at least you will tell me whether you are French or German; you speak both languages so perfectly.'

"'I don't think I shall tell you that, General; you intend a surprise, and are meditating the particular point of attack.'

"'At all events, you won't deny this,' I said, 'that being honoured by your permission to converse, I ought to know how to address you. Shall I say Madame la Comtesse?'

"She laughed, and she would, no doubt, have met me with another evasion—if, indeed, I can treat any occurrence in an interview every circumstance of which was pre-arranged, as I now believe, with the profoundest cunning, as liable to be modified by accident.

"'As to that,' she began; but she was interrupted, almost as she opened her lips, by a gentleman, dressed in black, who looked particularly elegant and distinguished, with this drawback, that his face was the most deadly pale I ever saw, except in death. He was in no masquerade—in the plain evening dress of a gentleman; and he said, without a smile, but with a courtly and unusually low bow:—

"'Will Madame la Comtesse permit me to say a very few words which may interest her?'

"The lady turned quickly to him, and touched her lip in token of silence; she then said to me, 'Keep my place for me, General; I shall return when I have said a few words.'

"And with this injunction, playfully given, she walked a little aside with the gentleman in black, and talked for some minutes, apparently very earnestly. They then walked away slowly together in the crowd, and I lost them for some minutes.

"I spent the interval in cudgelling my brains for a conjecture as to the identity of the lady who seemed to remember me so kindly, and I was thinking of turning about and joining in the conversation between my pretty ward and the Countess's daughter, and trying whether, by the time she returned, I might not have a surprise in store for her, by having her name, title, château, and estates at

my fingers' ends. But at this moment she returned, accompanied
by the pale man in black, who said:

"'I shall return and inform Madame la Comtesse when her
carriage is at the door.'

"He withdrew with a bow."

XII
A Petition

"'Then we are to lose Madame la Comtesse, but I hope only
for a few hours,' I said, with a low bow.

"'It may be that only, or it may be a few weeks. It was very
unlucky his speaking to me just now as he did. Do you now know
me?'

"I assured her I did not.

"'You shall know me,' she said, 'but not at present. We are
older and better friends than, perhaps, you suspect. I cannot yet
declare myself. I shall in three weeks pass your beautiful schloss,
about which I have been making enquiries. I shall then look in
upon you for an hour or two, and renew a friendship which I never
think of without a thousand pleasant recollections. This moment
a piece of news has reached me like a thunderbolt. I must set out
now, and travel by a devious route, nearly a hundred miles, with
all the dispatch I can possibly make. My perplexities multiply. I
am only deterred by the compulsory reserve I practise as to my
name from making a very singular request of you. My poor child
has not quite recovered her strength. Her horse fell with her, at a
hunt which she had ridden out to witness, her nerves have not yet
recovered the shock, and our physician says that she must on no
account exert herself for some time to come. We came here, in
consequence, by very easy stages — hardly six leagues a day. I must
now travel day and night, on a mission of life and death — a mission
the critical and momentous nature of which I shall be able to
explain to you when we meet, as I hope we shall, in a few weeks,
without the necessity of any concealment.'

"She went on to make her petition, and it was in the tone of a
person from whom such a request amounted to conferring, rather
than seeking a favour. This was only in manner, and, as it seemed,
quite unconsciously. Than the terms in which it was expressed,
nothing could be more deprecatory. It was simply that I would

consent to take charge of her daughter during her absence.

"This was, all things considered, a strange, not to say, an audacious request. She in some sort disarmed me, by stating and admitting everything that could be urged against it, and throwing herself entirely upon my chivalry. At the same moment, by a fatality that seems to have predetermined all that happened, my poor child came to my side, and, in an undertone, besought me to invite her new friend, Millarca, to pay us a visit. She had just been sounding her, and thought, if her mama would allow her, she would like it extremely.

"At another time I should have told her to wait a little, until, at least, we knew who they were. But I had not a moment to think in. The two ladies assailed me together, and I must confess the refined and beautiful face of the young lady, about which there was something extremely engaging, as well as the elegance and fire of high birth, determined me; and, quite overpowered, I submitted, and undertook, too easily, the care of the young lady, whom her mother called Millarca.

"The Countess beckoned to her daughter, who listened with grave attention while she told her, in general terms, how suddenly and peremptorily she had been summoned, and also of the arrangement she had made for her under my care, adding that I was one of her earliest and most valued friends.

"I made, of course, such speeches as the case seemed to call for, and found myself, on reflection, in a position which I did not half like.

"The gentleman in black returned, and very ceremoniously conducted the lady from the room.

"The demeanour of this gentleman was such as to impress me with the conviction that the Countess was a lady of very much more importance than her modest title alone might have led me to assume.

"Her last charge to me was that no attempt was to be made to learn more about her than I might have already guessed, until her return. Our distinguished host, whose guest she was, knew her reasons.

"'But here,' she said, 'neither I nor my daughter could safely remain for more than a day. I removed my mask imprudently for a moment, about an hour ago, and, too late, I fancied you saw me. So I resolved to seek an opportunity of talking a little to you. Had I found that you *had* seen me, I should have thrown myself on your high sense of honour to keep my secret for some weeks. As it is, I am satisfied that you did not see me; but if you now *suspect*, or, on reflection, *should* suspect, who I am, I commit myself, in like manner, entirely to your honour. My daughter will observe the same secrecy, and I well know that you will, from time to time, remind her, lest she should thoughtlessly disclose it.'

"She whispered a few words to her daughter, kissed her hurriedly twice, and went away, accompanied by the pale gentleman in black, and disappeared in the crowd.

"'In the next room,' said Millarca, 'there is a window that looks upon the hall door. I should like to see the last of mama, and to kiss my hand to her.'

"We assented, of course, and accompanied her to the window. We looked out, and saw a handsome old-fashioned carriage, with a troop of couriers and footmen. We saw the slim figure of the pale gentleman in black, as he held a thick velvet cloak, and placed it about her shoulders and threw the hood over her head. She nodded to him, and just touched his hand with hers. He bowed low repeatedly as the door closed, and the carriage began to move.

"'She is gone,' said Millarca, with a sigh.

"'She is gone,' I repeated to myself, for the first time—in the hurried moments that had elapsed since my consent—reflecting upon the folly of my act.

"'She did not look up,' said the young lady, plaintively.

"'The Countess had taken off her mask, perhaps, and did not care to show her face,' I said; 'and she could not know that you were in the window.'

"She sighed, and looked in my face. She was so beautiful that I relented. I was sorry I had for a moment repented of my hospitality, and I determined to make her amends for the unavowed churlishness of my reception.

"The young lady, replacing her mask, joined my ward in persuading me to return to the grounds, where the concert was soon to be renewed. We did so, and walked up and down the terrace that lies under the castle windows. Millarca became very intimate with us, and amused us with lively descriptions and stories of most of the great people whom we saw upon the terrace. I liked her more and more every minute. Her gossip, without being ill-natured, was extremely diverting to me, who had been so long out of the great world. I thought what life she would give to our sometimes lonely evenings at home.

"This ball was not over until the morning sun had almost reached the horizon. It pleased the Grand Duke to dance till then, so loyal people could not go away, or think of bed.

"We had just got through a crowded saloon, when my ward asked me what had become of Millarca. I thought she had been by her side, and she fancied she was by mine. The fact was, we had lost her.

"All my efforts to find her were vain. I feared that she had mistaken, in the confusion of a momentary separation from us, other people for her new friends, and had, possibly, pursued and lost them in the extensive grounds which were thrown open to us.

"Now, in its full force, I recognised a new folly in my having undertaken the charge of a young lady without so much as knowing her name; and fettered as I was by promises, of the reasons for imposing which I knew nothing, I could not even point my inquiries by saying that the missing young lady was the daughter of the Countess who had taken her departure a few hours before.

"Morning broke. It was clear daylight before I gave up my search. It was not till near two o'clock next day that we heard anything of my missing charge.

"At about that time a servant knocked at my niece's door, to say that he had been earnestly requested by a young lady, who appeared to be in great distress, to make out where she could find the General Baron Spielsdorf and the young lady his daughter, in whose charge she had been left by her mother.

"There could be no doubt, notwithstanding the slight inaccuracy, that our young friend had turned up; and so she had. Would to heaven we had lost her!

"She told my poor child a story to account for her having failed to recover us for so long. Very late, she said, she had got to the housekeeper's bedroom in despair of finding us, and had then fallen into a deep sleep which, long as it was, had hardly sufficed to recruit her strength after the fatigues of the ball.

"That day Millarca came home with us. I was only too happy, after all, to have secured so charming a companion for my dear girl."

XIII
The Woodman

"There soon, however, appeared some drawbacks. In the first place, Millarca complained of extreme languor—the weakness that remained after her late illness—and she never emerged from her room till the afternoon was pretty far advanced. In the next place, it was accidentally discovered, although she always locked the door on the inside, and never disturbed the key from its place till she admitted the maid to assist at her toilet, that she was undoubtedly sometimes absent from her room in the very early morning, and at various times later in the day, before she wished it to be understood that she was stirring. She was repeatedly seen from the windows of the schloss, in the first faint grey of the morning, walking through the trees, in an easterly direction, and looking like a person in a trance. This convinced me that she walked in her sleep. But this hypothesis did not solve the puzzle. How did she pass out from her room, leaving the door locked on the inside? How did she escape from the house without unbarring door or window?

"In the midst of my perplexities, an anxiety of a far more urgent kind presented itself.

"My dear child began to lose her looks and health, and that in a manner so mysterious, and even horrible, that I became thoroughly frightened.

"She was at first visited by appalling dreams; then, as she fancied, by a spectre, sometimes resembling Millarca, sometimes in the shape of a beast, indistinctly seen, walking round the foot of her bed, from side to side. Lastly came sensations. One, not unpleasant, but very peculiar, she said, resembled the flow of an icy stream against her breast. At a later time, she felt something like a pair of large needles pierce her, a little below the throat, with a very sharp pain. A few nights after, followed a gradual and convulsive sense of strangulation; then came unconsciousness."

I could hear distinctly every word the kind old General was saying, because by this time we were driving upon the short grass that spreads on either side of the road as you approach the roofless village which had not shown the smoke of a chimney for more than half a century.

You may guess how strangely I felt as I heard my own symptoms so exactly described in those which had been experienced by the poor girl who, but for the catastrophe which followed, would have been at that moment a visitor at my father's château. You may suppose, also, how I felt as I heard him detail habits and mysterious peculiarities which were, in fact, those of our beautiful guest, Carmilla!

A vista opened in the forest; we were on a sudden under the chimneys and gables of the ruined village, and the towers and battlements of the dismantled castle, round which gigantic trees are grouped, overhung us from a slight eminence.

In a frightened dream I got down from the carriage, and in silence, for we had each abundant matter for thinking; we soon mounted the ascent, and were among the spacious chambers, winding stairs, and dark corridors of the castle.

"And this was once the palatial residence of the Karnsteins!" said the old General at length, as from a great window he looked out across the village, and saw the wide, undulating expanse of forest. "It was a bad family, and here its blood-stained annals were written," he continued. "It is hard that they should, after death, continue to plague the human race with their atrocious lusts. That is the chapel of the Karnsteins, down there."

He pointed down to the grey walls of the Gothic building, partly visible through the foliage, a little way down the steep. "And I hear the axe of a woodman," he added, "busy among the trees that surround it; he possibly may give us the information of which I am in search, and point out the grave of Mircalla, Countess of Karnstein. These rustics preserve the local traditions of great families, whose stories die out among the rich and titled so soon as the families themselves become extinct."

"We have a portrait, at home, of Mircalla, the Countess Karnstein; should you like to see it?" asked my father.

"Time enough, dear friend," replied the General. "I believe that I have seen the original; and one motive which has led me to you earlier than I at first intended, was to explore the chapel which we are now approaching."

"What! see the Countess Mircalla," exclaimed my father; "why, she has been dead more than a century!"

"Not so dead as you fancy, I am told," answered the General.

"I confess, General, you puzzle me utterly," replied my father, looking at him, I fancied, for a moment with a return of the suspicion I detected before. But although there was anger and detestation, at times, in the old General's manner, there was nothing flighty.

"There remains to me," he said, as we passed under the heavy arch of the Gothic church—for its dimensions would have justified its being so styled—"but one object which can interest me during the few years that remain to me on earth, and that is to wreak on her the vengeance which, I thank God, may still be accomplished by a mortal arm."

"What vengeance can you mean?" asked my father, in increasing amazement.

"I mean, to decapitate the monster," he answered, with a fierce flush, and a stamp that echoed mournfully through the hollow ruin, and his clenched hand was at the same moment raised, as if it grasped the handle of an axe, while he shook it ferociously in the air.

"What?" exclaimed my father, more than ever bewildered.

"To strike her head off."

"Cut her head off!"

"Aye, with a hatchet, with a spade, or with anything that can cleave through her murderous throat. You shall hear," he answered, trembling with rage. And hurrying forward he said:

"That beam will answer for a seat; your dear child is fatigued; let her be seated, and I will, in a few sentences, close my dreadful story."

The squared block of wood, which lay on the grass-grown pavement of the chapel, formed a bench on which I was very glad to seat myself, and in the meantime the General called to the woodman, who had been removing some boughs which leaned upon the old walls; and, axe in hand, the hardy old fellow stood before us.

He could not tell us anything of these monuments; but there was an old man, he said, a ranger of this forest, at present sojourning in the house of the priest, about two miles away, who could point out every monument of the old Karnstein family; and, for a trifle, he undertook to bring him back with him, if we would lend him one of our horses, in little more than half an hour.

"Have you been long employed about this forest?" asked my father of the old man.

"I have been a woodman here," he answered in his *patois*, "under the forester, all my days; so has my father before me, and so on, as many generations as I can count up. I could show you the very house in the village here, in which my ancestors lived."

"How came the village to be deserted?" asked the General.

"It was troubled by *revenants*, sir; several were tracked to their graves, there detected by the usual tests, and extinguished in the usual way, by decapitation, by the stake, and by burning; but not until many of the villagers were killed.

"But after all these proceedings according to law," he continued—"so many graves opened, and so many vampires deprived of their horrible animation—the village was not relieved. But a Moravian nobleman, who happened to be travelling this way, heard how matters were, and being skilled—as many people are in his country—in such affairs, he offered to deliver the village from its tormentor. He did so thus: There being a bright moon that night, he ascended, shortly after sunset, the towers of the chapel here, from whence he could distinctly see the churchyard beneath him; you can see it from that window. From this point he watched until he saw the vampire come out of his grave, and place near it the linen clothes in which he had been folded, and then glide away towards the village to plague its inhabitants.

"The stranger, having seen all this, came down from the steeple, took the linen wrappings of the vampire, and carried them up to the top of the tower, which he again mounted. When the vampire returned from his prowlings and missed his clothes, he cried furiously to the Moravian, whom he saw at the summit of the tower, and who, in reply, beckoned him to ascend and take them. Whereupon the vampire, accepting his invitation, began to climb the steeple, and so soon as he had reached the battlements, the Moravian, with a stroke of his sword, clove his skull in twain, hurling him down to the churchyard, whither, descending by the winding stairs, the stranger followed and cut his head off, and next day delivered it and the body to the villagers, who duly impaled and burnt them.

"This Moravian nobleman had authority from the then head of the family to remove the tomb of Mircalla, Countess Karnstein, which he did effectually, so that in a little while its site was quite forgotten."

"Can you point out where it stood?" asked the General, eagerly.

The forester shook his head, and smiled.

"Not a soul living could tell you that now," he said; "besides, they say her body was removed; but no one is sure of that either."

Having thus spoken, as time pressed, he dropped his axe and departed, leaving us to hear the remainder of the General's strange story.

XIV
The Meeting

"My beloved child," he resumed, "was now growing rapidly worse. The physician who attended her had failed to produce the slightest impression upon her disease, for such I then supposed it to be. He saw my alarm, and suggested a consultation. I called in an abler physician, from Gratz. Several days elapsed before he arrived. He was a good and pious, as well as a learned man. Having seen my poor ward together, they withdrew to my library to confer and discuss. I, from the adjoining room, where I awaited their summons, heard these two gentlemen's voices raised in something sharper than a strictly philosophical discussion. I knocked at the door and entered. I found the old physician from Gratz maintaining his theory. His rival was combating it with undisguised ridicule, accompanied with bursts of laughter. This unseemly manifestation subsided and the altercation ended on my entrance.

"'Sir,' said my first physician, 'my learned brother seems to think that you want a conjuror, and not a doctor.'

"'Pardon me,' said the old physician from Gratz, looking displeased, 'I shall state my own view of the case in my own way another time. I grieve, Monsieur le Général, that by my skill and science I can be of no use. Before I go I shall do myself the honour to suggest something to you.'

"He seemed thoughtful, and sat down at a table and began to write. Profoundly disappointed, I made my bow, and as I turned to go, the other doctor pointed over his shoulder to his companion who was writing, and then, with a shrug, significantly touched his forehead.

"This consultation, then, left me precisely where I was. I walked out into the grounds, all but distracted. The doctor from Gratz, in ten or fifteen minutes, overtook me. He apologised for having followed me, but said that he could not conscientiously take his leave without a few words more. He told me that he could not be mistaken; no natural disease exhibited the same symptoms; and that death was already very near. There remained, however, a day, or possibly two, of life. If the fatal seizure were at once arrested, with great care and skill her strength might possibly return. But all hung now upon the confines of the irrevocable. One more assault might extinguish the last spark of vitality which is, every moment, ready to die.

"'And what is the nature of the seizure you speak of?' I entreated.

"'I have stated all fully in this note, which I place in your hands upon the distinct condition that you send for the nearest clergyman, and open my letter in his presence, and on no account read it till he is with you; you would despise it else, and it is a matter of life and death. Should the priest fail you, then, indeed, you may read it.'

"He asked me, before taking his leave finally, whether I would wish to see a man curiously learned upon the very subject, which, after I had read his letter, would probably interest me above all others, and he urged me earnestly to invite him to visit him there; and so took his leave.

"The ecclesiastic was absent, and I read the letter by myself. At another time, or in another case, it might have excited my ridicule. But into what quackeries will not people rush for a last chance, where all accustomed means have failed, and the life of a beloved object is at stake?

"Nothing, you will say, could be more absurd than the learned man's letter. It was monstrous enough to have consigned him to a madhouse. He said that the patient was suffering from the visits of a vampire! The punctures which she described as having occurred near the throat, were, he insisted, the insertion of those two long, thin, and sharp teeth which, it is well known, are peculiar to vampires; and there could be no doubt, he added, as to the well-defined presence of the small livid mark which all concurred in describing as that induced by the demon's lips, and every symptom described by the sufferer was in exact conformity with those recorded in every case of a similar visitation.

"Being myself wholly sceptical as to the existence of any such portent as the vampire, the supernatural theory of the good doctor furnished, in my opinion, but another instance of learning and intelligence oddly associated with some one hallucination. I was so miserable, however, that, rather than try nothing, I acted upon the instructions of the letter.

"I concealed myself in the dark dressing-room, that opened upon the poor patient's room, in which a candle was burning, and watched there till she was fast asleep. I stood at the door, peeping through the small crevice, my sword laid on the table beside me, as my directions prescribed, until, a little after one, I saw a large

black object, very ill-defined, crawl, as it seemed to me, over the
foot of the bed, and swiftly spread itself up to the poor girl's
throat, where it swelled, in a moment, into a great, palpitating
mass.

"For a few moments I had stood petrified. I now sprang
forward, with my sword in my hand. The black creature suddenly
contracted towards the foot of the bed, glided over it, and,
standing on the floor about a yard below the foot of the bed, with
a glare of skulking ferocity and horror fixed on me, I saw Millarca.
Speculating I know not what, I struck at her instantly with my
sword; but I saw her standing near the door, unscathed. Horrified,
I pursued, and struck again. She was gone; and my sword flew to
shivers against the door.

"I can't describe to you all that passed on that horrible night.
The whole house was up and stirring. The spectre Millarca was
gone. But her victim was sinking fast, and before the morning
dawned, she died."

The old General was agitated. We did not speak to him. My
father walked to some little distance, and began reading the
inscriptions on the tombstones; and thus occupied, he strolled into
the door of a side-chapel to prosecute his researches. The General
leaned against the wall, dried his eyes, and sighed heavily. I was
relieved on hearing the voices of Carmilla and Madame, who were
at that moment approaching. The voices died away.

In this solitude, having just listened to so strange a story,
connected, as it was, with the great and titled dead, whose
monuments were mouldering among the dust and ivy round us,
and every incident of which bore so awfully upon my own
mysterious case—in this haunted spot, darkened by the towering
foliage that rose on every side, dense and high above its noiseless
walls—a horror began to steal over me, and my heart sank as I
thought that my friends were, after all, not about to enter and
disturb this triste and ominous scene.

The old General's eyes were fixed on the ground, as he leaned
with his hand upon the basement of a shattered monument.

Under a narrow, arched doorway, surmounted by one of those
demoniacal grotesques in which the cynical and ghastly fancy of
old Gothic carving delights, I saw very gladly the beautiful face
and figure of Carmilla enter the shadowy chapel.

I was just about to rise and speak, and nodded smiling, in
answer to her peculiarly engaging smile; when with a cry, the old

man by my side caught up the woodman's hatchet, and started forward. On seeing him a brutalised change came over her features. It was an instantaneous and horrible transformation, as she made a crouching step backwards. Before I could utter a scream, he struck at her with all his force, but she dived under his blow, and unscathed, caught him in her tiny grasp by the wrist. He struggled for a moment to release his arm, but his hand opened, the axe fell to the ground, and the girl was gone.

He staggered against the wall. His grey hair stood upon his head, and a moisture shone over his face, as if he were at the point of death.

The frightful scene had passed in a moment. The first thing I recollect after, is Madame standing before me, and impatiently repeating again and again, the question, "Where is Mademoiselle Carmilla?"

I answered at length, "I don't know—I can't tell—she went there," and I pointed to the door through which Madame had just entered; "only a minute or two since."

"But I have been standing there, in the passage, ever since Mademoiselle Carmilla entered; and she did not return."

She then began to call "Carmilla," through every door and passage and from the windows, but no answer came.

"She called herself Carmilla?" asked the General, still agitated.

"Carmilla, yes," I answered.

"Aye," he said; "that is Millarca. That is the same person who long ago was called Mircalla, Countess Karnstein. Depart from this accursed ground, my poor child, as quickly as you can. Drive to the clergyman's house, and stay there till we come. Begone! May you never behold Carmilla more; you will not find her here."

XV
Ordeal and Execution

As he spoke one of the strangest looking men I ever beheld entered the chapel at the door through which Carmilla had made her entrance and her exit. He was tall, narrow-chested, stooping, with high shoulders, and dressed in black. His face was brown and dried up with deep furrows; he wore an oddly-shaped hat with a broad leaf. His hair, long and grizzled, hung on his shoulders. He wore a pair of gold spectacles, and walked slowly, with an odd shambling gait, with his face sometimes turned up to the sky, and sometimes bowed down towards the ground, and he seemed to wear a perpetual smile; his long thin arms were swinging, and his lank hands, in old black gloves ever so much too wide for them, waving and gesticulating in utter abstraction.

"The very man!" exclaimed the General, advancing with manifest delight. "My dear Baron, how happy I am to see you, I had no hope of meeting you so soon." He signed to my father, who had by this time returned, and led the fantastic old gentleman, whom he called the Baron to meet him. He introduced him formally, and they at once entered into earnest conversation. The stranger took a roll of paper from his pocket, and spread it on the worn surface of a tomb that stood by. He had a pencil case in his fingers, with which he traced imaginary lines from point to point on the paper, which from their often glancing from it, together, at certain points of the building, I concluded to be a plan of the chapel. He accompanied, what I may term, his lecture, with occasional readings from a dirty little book, whose yellow leaves were closely written over.

They sauntered together down the side aisle, opposite to the spot where I was standing, conversing as they went; then they began measuring distances by paces, and finally they all stood together, facing a piece of the side-wall, which they began to examine with great minuteness; pulling off the ivy that clung over it, and rapping the plaster with the ends of their sticks, scraping here, and knocking there. At length they ascertained the existence of a broad marble tablet, with letters carved in relief upon it.

With the assistance of the woodman, who soon returned, a monumental inscription, and carved escutcheon, were disclosed. They proved to be those of the long lost monument of Mircalla, Countess Karnstein.

The old General, though not I fear given to the praying mood, raised his hands and eyes to heaven, in mute thanksgiving for some moments.

"To-morrow," I heard him say, "the commissioner will be here, and the Inquisition will be held according to law."

Then turning to the old man with the gold spectacles, whom I have described, he shook him warmly by both hands and said:

"Baron, how can I thank you? How can we all thank you? You will have delivered this region from a plague that has scourged its inhabitants for more than a century. The horrible enemy, thank

God, is at last tracked."

My father led the stranger aside, and the General followed. I knew that he had led them out of hearing, that he might relate my case, and I saw them glance often quickly at me, as the discussion proceeded.

My father came to me, kissed me again and again, and leading me from the chapel, said:

"It is time to return, but before we go home, we must add to our party the good priest, who lives but a little way from this; and persuade him to accompany us to the schloss."

In this quest we were successful: and I was glad, being unspeakably fatigued when we reached home. But my satisfaction was changed to dismay, on discovering that there were no tidings of Carmilla. Of the scene that had occurred in the ruined chapel, no explanation was offered to me, and it was clear that it was a secret which my father for the present determined to keep from me.

The sinister absence of Carmilla made the remembrance of the scene more horrible to me. The arrangements for the night were singular. Two servants, and Madame were to sit up in my room that night; and the ecclesiastic with my father kept watch in the adjoining dressing-room.

The priest had performed certain solemn rites that night, the purport of which I did not understand any more than I comprehended the reason of this extraordinary precaution taken for my safety during sleep.

I saw all clearly a few days later.

The disappearance of Carmilla was followed by the discontinuance of my nightly sufferings.

You have heard, no doubt, of the appalling superstition that prevails in Upper and Lower Styria, in Moravia, Silesia, in Turkish Servia, in Poland, even in Russia; the superstition, so we must call it, of the Vampire.

If human testimony, taken with every care and solemnity, judicially, before commissions innumerable, each consisting of many members, all chosen for integrity and intelligence, and constituting reports more voluminous perhaps than exist upon any one other class of cases, is worth anything, it is difficult to deny, or even to doubt the existence of such a phenomenon as the Vampire.

For my part I have heard no theory by which to explain what I myself have witnessed and experienced, other than that supplied by the ancient and well-attested belief of the country.

The next day the formal proceedings took place in the Chapel of Karnstein. The grave of the Countess Mircalla was opened; and the General and my father recognised each his perfidious and beautiful guest, in the face now disclosed to view. The features, though a hundred and fifty years had passed since her funeral, were tinted with the warmth of life. Her eyes were open; no cadaverous smell exhaled from the coffin. The two medical men, one officially present, the other on the part of the promoter of the inquiry, attested the marvellous fact that there was a faint but appreciable respiration, and a corresponding action of the heart. The limbs were perfectly flexible, the flesh elastic; and the leaden coffin floated with blood, in which to a depth of seven inches, the body lay immersed. Here then, were all the admitted signs and proofs of vampirism. The body, therefore, in accordance with the ancient practice, was raised, and a sharp stake driven through the heart of the vampire, who uttered a piercing shriek at the moment, in all respects such as might escape from a living person in the last agony. Then the head was struck off, and a torrent of blood flowed from the severed neck. The body and head was next placed on a pile of wood, and reduced to ashes, which were thrown upon the river and borne away, and that territory has never since been plagued by the visits of a vampire.

My father has a copy of the report of the Imperial Commission, with the signatures of all who were present at these proceedings, attached in verification of the statement. It is from this official paper that I have summarized my account of this last shocking scene.

XVI
Conclusion

I write all this you suppose with composure. But far from it; I cannot think of it without agitation. Nothing but your earnest desire so repeatedly expressed, could have induced me to sit down to a task that has unstrung my nerves for months to come, and reinduced a shadow of the unspeakable horror which years after my deliverance continued to make my days and nights dreadful, and solitude insupportably terrific.

Let me add a word or two about that quaint Baron Vordenburg, to whose curious lore we were indebted for the discovery of the Countess Mircalla's grave.

He had taken up his abode in Gratz, where, living upon a mere pittance, which was all that remained to him of the once princely estates of his family, in Upper Styria, he devoted himself to the minute and laborious investigation of the marvellously authenticated tradition of Vampirism. He had at his fingers' ends all the great and little works upon the subject. "Magia Posthuma," "Phlegon de Mirabilibus," "Augustinus de curâ pro Mortuis," "Philosophicae et Christianae Cogitationes de Vampiris," by John Christofer Herenberg; and a thousand others, among which I remember only a few of those which he lent to my father. He had a voluminous digest of all the judicial cases, from which he had extracted a system of principles that appear to govern—some always, and others occasionally only—the condition of the vampire. I may mention, in passing, that the deadly pallor attributed to that sort of *revenants*, is a mere melodramatic fiction. They present, in the grave, and when they show themselves in human society, the appearance of healthy life. When disclosed to light in their coffins, they exhibit all the symptoms that are enumerated as those which proved the vampire-life of the long-dead Countess Karnstein.

How they escape from their graves and return to them for certain hours every day, without displacing the clay or leaving any trace of disturbance in the state of the coffin or the cerements, has always been admitted to be utterly inexplicable. The amphibious existence of the vampire is sustained by daily renewed slumber in the grave. Its horrible lust for living blood supplies the vigour of its waking existence. The vampire is prone to be fascinated with an engrossing vehemence, resembling the passion of love, by particular persons. In pursuit of these it will exercise inexhaustible patience and stratagem, for access to a particular object may be obstructed in a hundred ways. It will never desist until it has satiated its passion, and drained the very life of its coveted victim. But it will, in these cases, husband and protract its murderous enjoyment with the refinement of an epicure, and heighten it by the gradual approaches of an artful courtship. In these cases it seems to yearn for something like sympathy and consent. In ordinary ones it goes direct to its object, overpowers with violence, and strangles and exhausts often at a single feast.

The vampire is, apparently, subject, in certain situations, to special conditions. In the particular instance of which I have given you a relation, Mircalla seemed to be limited to a name which, if not her real one, should at least reproduce, without the omission or addition of a single letter, those, as we say, anagrammatically, which compose it. *Carmilla* did this; so did *Millarca*.

My father related to the Baron Vordenburg, who remained with us for two or three weeks after the expulsion of Carmilla, the story about the Moravian nobleman and the vampire at Karnstein churchyard, and then he asked the Baron how he had discovered the exact position of the long-concealed tomb of the Countess Mircalla? The Baron's grotesque features puckered up into a mysterious smile; he looked down, still smiling on his worn spectacle-case and fumbled with it. Then looking up, he said:

"I have many journals, and other papers, written by that remarkable man; the most curious among them is one treating of the visit of which you speak, to Karnstein. The tradition, of course, discolours and distorts a little. He might have been termed a Moravian nobleman, for he had changed his abode to that territory, and was, beside, a noble. But he was, in truth, a native of Upper Styria. It is enough to say that in very early youth he had been a passionate and favoured lover of the beautiful Mircalla, Countess Karnstein. Her early death plunged him into inconsolable grief. It is the nature of vampires to increase and multiply, but according to an ascertained and ghostly law.

"Assume, at starting, a territory perfectly free from that pest. How does it begin, and how does it multiply itself? I will tell you. A person, more or less wicked, puts an end to himself. A suicide, under certain circumstances, becomes a vampire. That spectre visits living people in their slumbers; *they* die, and almost invariably, in the grave, develop into vampires. This happened in the case of the beautiful Mircalla, who was haunted by one of those demons. My ancestor, Vordenburg, whose title I still bear, soon discovered this, and in the course of the studies to which he devoted himself, learned a great deal more.

"Among other things, he concluded that suspicion of vampirism would probably fall, sooner or later, upon the dead Countess, who in life had been his idol. He conceived a horror, be she what she might, of her remains being profaned by the outrage of a posthumous execution. He has left a curious paper to prove that the vampire, on its expulsion from its amphibious existence, is projected into a far more horrible life; and he resolved to save his once beloved Mircalla from this.

"He adopted the strategem of a journey here, a pretended removal of her remains, and a real obliteration of her monument. When age had stolen upon him, and from the vale of years, he looked back on the scenes he was leaving, he considered, in a different spirit, what he had done, and a horror took possession of him. He made the tracings and notes which have guided me to the very spot, and drew up a confession of the deception that he had practised. If he had intended any further action in this matter, death prevented him; and the hand of a remote descendant has, too late for many, directed the pursuit to the lair of the beast."

We talked a little more, and among other things he said was this:

"One sign of the vampire is the power of the hand. The slender hand of Mircalla closed like a vice of steel on the General's wrist when he raised the hatchet to strike. But its power is not confined to its grasp; it leaves a numbness in the limb it seizes, which is slowly, if ever, recovered from."

The following Spring my father took me on a tour through Italy. We remained away for more than a year. It was long before the terror of recent events subsided; and to this hour the image of Carmilla returns to memory with ambiguous alternations— sometimes the playful, languid, beautiful girl; sometimes the writhing fiend I saw in the ruined church; and often from a reverie I have started, fancying I heard the light step of Carmilla at the drawing-room door.

ORSON SCOTT CARD, *one of the most promising new talents in the science-fantasy genre, lives in Salt Lake City, where he teaches writing at the University of Utah. A former editor and also a playwright, Card is justly famous for the following masterpiece of horror, a tale that one editor I know has never had the stomach to finish. After reading the first few pages, you'll see why.*

Eumenides in the Fourth Floor Lavatory

BY ORSON SCOTT CARD

Living in a fourth-floor walkup was part of his revenge, as if to say to Alice, "Throw me out of the house, will you? Then I'll live in squalor in a Bronx tenement, where the toilet is shared by four apartments! My shirts will go unironed, my tie will be perpetually awry. *See what you've done to me?*"

But when he told Alice about the apartment, she only laughed bitterly and said, "Not anymore, Howard. I won't play those games with you. You win every damn time."

She pretended not to care about him anymore, but Howard knew better. He knew people, knew what they wanted, and Alice wanted *him*. It was his strongest card in their relationship—that she wanted him more than he wanted her. He thought of this often: at work in the offices of Humboldt and Breinhardt, Designers; at lunch in a cheap lunchroom (part of the punishment); on the subway home to his tenement (Alice had kept the Lincoln Continental). He thought and thought about how much she wanted him. But he kept remembering what she had said the day she threw him out: If you ever come near Rhiannon again I'll kill you.

He could not remember why she had said that. Could not remember and did not try to remember because that line of thinking made him uncomfortable and one thing Howard insisted on being was comfortable with himself. Other people could spend hours and days of their lives chasing after some accommodation with themselves, but Howard was accommodated. Well adjusted. At ease. I'm OK, I'm OK, I'm OK. Hell with you. "If you let them make you feel uncomfortable," Howard would often say, "you give them a handle on you and they can run your life." Howard could find other people's handles, but they could never find Howard's.

It was not yet winter but cold as hell at three A.M. when Howard got home from Stu's party. A must-attend party, if you wished to get ahead at Humboldt and Breinhardt. Stu's ugly wife tried to be tempting, but Howard had played innocent and made her feel so uncomfortable that she dropped the matter. Howard paid careful attention to office gossip and knew that several earlier departures from the company had got caught with, so to speak, their pants down. Not that Howard's pants were an impenetrable barrier. He got Dolores from the front office into the bedroom and accused her of making life miserable for him. "In little ways," he insisted. "I know you don't mean to, but you've got to stop."

"What ways?" Dolores asked, incredulous yet (because she honestly tried to make other people happy) uncomfortable.

"Surely you knew how attracted I am to you."

"No. That hasn't—that hasn't even crossed my mind."

Howard looked tongue-tied, embarrassed. He actually was neither. "Then—well, then, I was—I was wrong, I'm sorry, I thought you were doing it deliberately—"

"Doing what?"

"Snub—snubbing me—never mind, it sounds adolescent, just little things, hell, Dolores, I had a stupid schoolboy crush—"

"Howard, I didn't even know I was hurting you."

"God, how insensitive," Howard said, sounding even more hurt.

"Oh, Howard, do I mean that much to you?"

Howard made a little whimpering noise that meant everything she wanted it to mean. She looked uncomfortable. She'd do anything to get back to feeling right with herself again. She was so uncomfortable that they spent a rather nice half hour making each other feel comfortable again. No one else in the office had been able to get to Dolores. But Howard could get to anybody.

He walked up the stairs to his apartment feeling very, very satisfied. Don't need you, Alice, he said to himself. Don't need nobody, and nobody's who I've got. He was still mumbling the little ditty to himself as he went into the communal bathroom and turned on the light.

He heard a gurgling sound from the toilet stall, a hissing sound. Had someone been in there with the light off? Howard went into the toilet stall and saw nobody. Then looked closer and saw a baby, probably about two months old, lying in the toilet bowl. Its nose and eyes were barely above the water; it looked terrified, its legs and hips and stomach were down the drain. Someone had obviously hoped to kill it by drowning—it was inconceivable to Howard that anyone could be so moronic as to think it would fit down the drain.

For a moment he thought of leaving it there, with the big-city temptation to mind one's own business even when to do so would be an atrocity. Saving this baby would mean inconvenience: calling the police, taking care of the child in his apartment, perhaps even headlines, certainly a night of filling out reports. Howard was tired. Howard wanted to go to bed.

But he remembered Alice saying, "You aren't even human, Howard. You're a goddam selfish monster." I am not a monster, he answered silently, and reached down into the toilet bowl to pull the child out.

The baby was firmly jammed in—whoever had tried to kill it had meant to catch it tight. Howard felt a brief surge of genuine indignation that anyone could think to solve his problems by killing an innocent child. But thinking of crimes committed on children was something Howard was determined not to do, and besides, at that moment he suddenly acquired other things to think about.

As the child clutched at Howard's arm, he noticed the baby's fingers were fused together into flipperlike flaps of bone and skin at the end of the arm. Yet the flippers gripped his arms with an unusual strength as, with two hands deep in the toilet bowl, Howard tried to pull the baby free.

At last, with a gush, the child came up and the water finished its flushing action. The legs, too, were fused into a single limb that was hideously twisted at the end. The child was male; the genitals, larger than normal, were skewed off to one side. And Howard noticed that where the feet should be were two more flippers, and near the tips were red spots that looked like putrefying sores. The child cried, a savage mewling that reminded Howard of a dog he had seen in its death throes. (Howard refused to be reminded that it had been he who killed the dog by throwing it out in the street in front of a passing car, just to watch the driver swerve; the driver hadn't swerved.)

Even the hideously deformed have a right to live, Howard thought, but now, holding the child in his arms, he felt a revulsion that translated into sympathy for whoever, probably the parents, had tried to kill the creature. The child shifted its grip on him, and where the flippers had been Howard felt a sharp, stinging pain that quickly turned to agony as it was exposed to the air. Several huge, gaping sores on his arm were already running with blood and pus.

It took a moment for Howard to connect the sores with the child, and by then the leg flippers were already pressed against his stomach, and the arm flippers already gripped his chest. The sores on the child's flippers were not sores; they were powerful suction devices that gripped Howard's skin so tightly that it ripped away when the contact was broken. He tried to pry the child off, but no sooner was one flipper free than it found a new place to hold even as Howard struggled to break the grip of another.

What had begun as an act of charity had now become an intense struggle. This was not a child, Howard realized. Children could not hang on so tightly, and the creature had teeth that snapped at his hands and arms whenever they came near enough. A human face, certainly, but not a human being. Howard threw himself against the wall, hoping to stun the creature so it would drop away. It only clung tighter, and the sores where it hung on him hurt more. But at last Howard pried and scraped it off by levering it against the edge of the toilet stall. It dropped to the ground, and Howard backed quickly away, on fire with the pain of a dozen or more stinging wounds.

It had to be a nightmare. In the middle of the night, in a bathroom lighted by a single bulb, with a travesty of humanity writhing on the floor, Howard could not believe that it had any reality.

Could it be a mutation that had somehow lived? Yet the thing had far more purpose, far more control of its body than any human infant. The baby slithered across the floor as Howard, in pain from the wounds on his body, watched in a panic of indecision. The baby reached the wall and cast a flipper onto it. The suction held and the baby began to inch its way straight up the wall. As it climbed, it defecated, a thin drool of green tracing down the wall behind it. Howard looked at the slime following the infant up the wall, looked at the pus-covered sores on his arms.

What if the animal, whatever it was, did not die soon of its terrible deformity? What if it lived? What if it were found, taken to a hospital, cared for? What if it became an adult?

It reached the ceiling and made the turn, clinging tightly to the plaster, not falling off as it hung upside down and inched across toward the light bulb.

The thing was trying to get directly over Howard, and the defecation was still dripping. Loathing overcame fear, and Howard reached up, took hold of the baby from the back, and, using his full weight, was finally able to pry it off the ceiling. It writhed and twisted in his hands, trying to get the suction cups on him, but Howard resisted with all his strength and was able to get the baby, this time headfirst, into the toilet bowl. He held it there until the bubbles stopped and it was blue. Then he went back to his apartment for a knife. Whatever the creature was, it had to disappear from the face of the earth. It had to die, and there had to be no sign left that could hint that Howard had killed it.

He found the knife quickly, but paused for a few moments to put something on his wounds. They stung bitterly, but in a while they felt better. Howard took off his shirt; thought a moment and took off all his clothes, then put on his bathrobe and took a towel with him as he returned to the bathroom. He didn't want to get any blood on his clothes.

But when he got to the bathroom, the child was not in the toilet. Howard was alarmed. Had someone found it drowning? Had they, perhaps, seen him leaving the bathroom—or worse, returning with his knife? He looked around the bathroom. There was nothing. He stepped back into the hall. No one. He stood a moment in the doorway, wondering what could have happened.

Then a weight dropped onto his head and shoulders from above, and he felt the suction flippers tugging at his face, at his head. He almost screamed. But he didn't want to arouse anyone. Somehow the child had not drowned after all, had crawled out of the toilet, and had waited over the door for Howard to return.

Once again the struggle resumed, and once again Howard pried the flippers away with the help of the toilet stall, though this time he was hampered by the fact that the child was behind and above him. It was exhausting work. He had to set down the knife so he could use both hands, and another dozen wounds stung bitterly by the time he had the child on the floor. As long as the child lay on its stomach, Howard could seize it from behind. He took it by the neck with one hand and picked up the knife with the other. He carried both to the toilet.

He had to flush twice to handle the flow of blood and pus. Howard wondered if the child was infected with some disease — the white fluid was thick and at least as great in volume as the blood. Then he flushed seven more times to take the pieces of the creature down the drain. Even after death, the suction pads clung tightly to the porcelain; Howard pried them off with the knife.

Eventually, the child was completely gone. Howard was panting with the exertion, nauseated at the stench and horror of what he had done. He remembered the smell of his dog's guts after the car hit it, and he threw up everything he had eaten at the party. Got the party out of his system, felt cleaner; took a shower, felt cleaner still. When he was through, he made sure the bathroom showed no sign of his ordeal.

Then he went to bed.

It wasn't easy to sleep. He was too keyed up. He couldn't take out of his mind the thought that he had committed murder (not murder, not murder, simply the elimination of something too foul to be alive). He tried thinking of a dozen, a hundred other things. Projects at work — but the designs kept showing flippers. His children — but their faces turned to the intense face of the struggling monster he had killed. Alice — ah, but Alice was harder to think of than the creature.

At last he slept, and dreamed, and in his dream remembered his father, who had died when he was ten. Howard did not remember any of his standard reminiscences. No long walks with his father, no basketball in the driveway, no fishing trips. Those things had happened, but tonight, because of the struggle with the monster, Howard remembered darker things that he had long been able to keep hidden from himself.

"We can't afford to get you a ten-speed bike, Howie. Not until the strike is over."

"I know, Dad. You can't help it." Swallow bravely. "And I don't mind. When all the guys go riding around after school, I'll just stay home and get ahead on my homework."

"Lots of boys don't have ten-speed bikes, Howie."

Howie shrugged, and turned away to hide the tears in his eyes. "Sure, lot of them. Hey, Dad, don't you worry about me. Howie can take care of himself."

Such courage. Such strength. He had got a ten-speed within a week. In his dream, Howard finally made a connection he had never been able to admit to himself before. His father had a rather elaborate ham radio setup in the garage. But about that time he had become tired of it, he said, and he sold it off and did a lot more work in the yard and looked bored as hell until the strike was over and he went back to work and got killed in an accident in the rolling mill.

Howard's dream ended madly, with him riding piggy-back on his father's shoulders as the monster had ridden on *him*, tonight— and in his hand was a knife, and he was stabbing his father again and again in the throat.

He awoke in early morning light, before his alarm rang, sobbing weakly and whimpering, "I killed him, I killed him, I killed him."

And then he drifted upward out of sleep and saw the time. Six-thirty. "A dream," he said. And the dream had woken him early, too early, with a headache and sore eyes from crying. The pillow was soaked. "A hell of a lousy way to start the day," he mumbled. And, as was his habit, he got up and went to the window and opened the curtain.

On the glass, suction cups clinging tightly, was the child.

It was pressed close, as if by sucking very tightly it would be able to slither through the glass without breaking it. Far below were the honks of early morning traffic, the roar of passing trucks: but the child seemed oblivious to its height far above the street, with no ledge to break its fall. Indeed, there seemed little chance it would fall. The eyes looked closely, piercingly at Howard.

Howard had been prepared to pretend that the night before had been another terribly realistic nightmare.

He stepped back from the glass, watched the child in fascination. It lifted a flipper, planted it higher, pulled itself up to a new position where it could stare at Howard eye to eye. And then, slowly and methodically, it began beating on the glass with its head.

The landlord was not generous with upkeep on the building. The glass was thin, and Howard knew that the child would not give up until it had broken through the glass so it could get to Howard.

He began to shake. His throat tightened. He was terribly afraid. Last night had been no dream. The fact that the child was here today was proof of that. Yet he had cut the child into small pieces. It could not possibly be alive. The glass shook and rattled with every blow the child's head struck.

The glass slivered in a starburst from where the child had hit it. The creature was coming in. And Howard picked up the room's one chair and threw it at the child, threw it at the window. Glass shattered and the sun dazzled on the fragments as they exploded outward like a glistening halo around the child and the chair.

Howard ran to the window, looked out, looked down and watched as the child landed brutally on the top of a large truck. The body seemed to smear as it hit, and fragments of the chair and shreds of glass danced around the child and bounced down into the street and the sidewalk.

The truck didn't stop moving; it carried the broken body and the shards of glass and the pool of blood on up the street, and Howard ran to the bed, knelt beside it, buried his face in the blanket, and tried to regain control of himself. He had been seen. The people in the street had looked up and seen him in the window. Last night he had gone to great lengths to avoid discovery, but today discovery was impossible to avoid. He was ruined. And yet he could not, could never have let the child come into the room.

Footsteps on the stairs. Stamping up the corridor. Pounding on the door. "Open up! Hey in there!"

If I'm quiet long enough, they'll go away, he said to himself, knowing it was a lie. He must get up, must answer the door. But he could not bring himself to admit that he ever had to leave the safety of his bed.

"Hey, you son-of-a-bitch—" The imprecations went on but Howard could not move until, suddenly, it occurred to him that the child could be under the bed, and as he thought of it he could feel the tip of the flipper touching his thigh, stroking and ready to fasten itself—

Howard leaped to his feet and rushed to the door. He flung it wide, for even if it was the police come to arrest him, they could protect him from the monster that was haunting him.

It was not a policeman at the door. It was the man on the first floor who collected rent. "You son-of-a-bitch irresponsible pig-kisser!" the man shouted, his toupee only approximately in place. "That chair could have hit somebody! That window's expensive! Out! Get out of here, right now, I want you out of this place, I don't care how the hell drunk you are—"

"There was—there was this thing on the window, this creature—"

The man looked at him coldly, but his eyes danced with anger. No, not anger. Fear. Howard realized the man was afraid of him.

"This is a decent place," the man said softly. "You can take your creatures and your booze and your pink stinking elephants and that's a hundred bucks for the window, a hundred bucks right now, and you can get out of here in an hour, an hour, you hear? Or I'm calling the police, you hear?"

"I hear." He heard. The man left when Howard counted out five twenties. The man seemed careful to avoid touching Howard's hands, as if Howard had become, somehow, repulsive. Well, he had. To himself, if to no one else. He closed the door as soon as the man was gone. He packed the few belongings he had brought to the apartment in two suitcases and went downstairs and called a cab and rode to work. The cabby looked at him sourly, and wouldn't talk. It was fine with Howard, if only the driver hadn't kept looking at him through the mirror—nervously, as if he was afraid of what Howard might do or try. I won't try anything, Howard said to himself, I'm a decent man. Howard tipped the cabby well and then gave him twenty to take his bags to his house in Queens, where Alice could damn well keep them for a while. Howard was through with the tenement—that one or any other.

Obviously it had been a nightmare, last night and this morning. The monster was only visible to him, Howard decided. Only the chair and the glass had fallen from the fourth floor, or the manager would have noticed.

Except that the baby had landed on the truck, and might have been real, and might be discovered in New Jersey or Pennsylvania later today.

Couldn't be real. He had killed it last night and it was whole again this morning. A nightmare. I didn't really kill anybody, he insisted. (Except the dog. Except Father, said a new, ugly voice in the back of his mind.)

Work. Draw lines on paper, answer phone calls, dictate letters, keep your mind off your nightmares, off your family, off the mess your life is turning into. "Hell of a good party last night." Yeah, it was, wasn't it? "How are you today, Howard?" Feel fine, Dolores, fine—thanks to you. "Got the roughs on the IBM thing?" Nearly, nearly. Give me another twenty minutes. "Howard, you don't look well." Had a rough night. The party, you know.

He kept drawing on the blotter on his desk instead of going to
the drawing table and producing real work. He doodled out faces.
Alice's face, looking stern and terrible. The face of Stu's ugly wife.
Dolores's face, looking sweet and yielding and stupid. And
Rhiannon's face.

But with his daughter Rhiannon, he couldn't stop with the face.

His hand started to tremble when he saw what he had drawn.
He ripped the sheet off the blotter, crumpled it, and reached
under the desk to drop it in the wastebasket. The basket lurched,
and flippers snaked out to seize his hand in an iron grip.

Howard screamed, tried to pull his hand away. The child came
with it, the leg flippers grabbing Howard's right leg. The suction
pad stung, bringing back the memory of all the pain last night. He
scraped the child off against a filing cabinet, then ran for the door,
which was already opening as several of his co-workers tumbled
into his office demanding, "What is it! What's wrong! Why did you
scream like that!"

Howard led them gingerly over to where the child should be.
Nothing. Just an overturned wastebasket, Howard's chair capsized
on the floor. But Howard's window was open, and he could not
remember opening it. "Howard, what is it? Are you tired,
Howard? What's wrong?"

I don't feel well. I don't feel well at all.

Dolores put her arm around him, led him out of the room.
"Howard, I'm worried about you."

I'm worried, too.

"Can I take you home? I have my car in the garage downstairs.
Can I take you home?"

Where's home? Don't have a home, Dolores.

"My home, then. I have an apartment, you need to lie down
and rest. Let me take you home."

Dolores's apartment was decorated in early Holly Hobby, and
when she put records on the stereo it was old Carpenters and
recent Captain and Tennille. Dolores led him to the bed, gently
undressed him, and then, because he reached out to her,
undressed herself and made love to him before she went back to
work. She was naively eager. She whispered in his ear that he was
only the second man she had ever loved, the first in five years.
Her inept lovemaking was so sincere it made him want to cry.

When she was gone he did cry, because she thought she meant
something to him and she did not.

Why am I crying? he asked himself. Why should I care? It's not my fault she let me get a handle on her . . .

Sitting on the dresser in a curiously adult posture was the child, carelessly playing with itself as it watched Howard intently. "No," Howard said, pulling himself up to the head of the bed. "You don't exist," he said. "No one's ever seen you but me." The child gave no sign of understanding. It just rolled over and began to slither down the front of the dresser.

Howard reached for his clothes, took them out of the bedroom. He put them on in the living room as he watched the door. Sure enough, the child crept along the carpet to the living room; but Howard was dressed by then, and he left.

He walked the streets for three hours. He was coldly rational at first. Logical. The creature does not exist. There is no reason to believe in it.

But bit by bit his rationality was worn away by constant flickers of the creature at the edges of his vision. On a bench, peering over the back at him; in a shop window; staring from the cab of a milk truck. Howard walked faster and faster, not caring where he went, trying to keep some intelligent process going on in his mind, and failing utterly as he saw the child, saw it clearly, dangling from a traffic signal.

What made it even worse was that occasionally a passerby, violating the unwritten law that New Yorkers are forbidden to look at each other, would gaze at him, shudder, and look away. A short European-looking woman crossed herself. A group of teenagers looking for trouble weren't looking for him—they grew silent, let him pass in silence, and in silence watched him out of sight.

They may not be able to see the child, Howard, realized, but they see something.

And as he grew less and less coherent in the ramblings of his mind, memories began flashing on and off, his life passing before his eyes like a drowning man is supposed to see, only, he realized, if a drowning man saw this he would gulp at the water, breathe it deeply just to end the visions. They were memories he had been unable to find for years; memories he would never have wanted to find.

His poor, confused mother, who was so eager to be a good parent that she read everything, tried everything. Her precocious son Howard read it, too, and understood it better. Nothing she tried ever worked. And he accused her several times of being too demanding, of not demanding enough; of not giving him enough love, of drowning him in phony affection; of trying to take over with his friends, of not liking his friends enough. Until he had badgered and tortured the woman until she was timid every time she spoke to him, careful and longwinded and she phrased everything in such a way that it wouldn't offend, and while now and then he made her feel wonderful by giving her a hug and saying, "Have I got a wonderful Mom," there were far more times when he put a patient look on his face and said, "That again, Mom? I thought we went over that years ago." A failure as a parent, that's what you are, he reminded her again and again, though not in so many words, and she nodded and believed and died inside with every contact they had. He got everything he wanted from her.

And Vaughn Robles, who was just a little bit smarter than Howard and Howard wanted very badly to be valedictorian and so Vaughn and Howard became best friends and Vaughn would do anything for Howard and whenever Vaughn got a better grade than Howard he could not help but notice that Howard was hurt, that Howard wondered if he was really worth anything at all. "Am I really worth anything at all, Vaughn? No matter how well I do, there's always someone ahead of me, and I guess it's just that before my father died he told me and told me, Howie, be better than your Dad. Be the top. And I promised him I'd be the top but hell, Vaughn, I'm just not cut out for it—" and once he even cried. Vaughn was proud of himself as he sat there and listened to Howard give the valedictory address at high school graduation. What were a few grades, compared to a true friendship? Howard got a scholarship and went away to college and he and Vaughn almost never saw each other again.

And the teacher he provoked into hitting him and losing his job; and the football player who snubbed him and Howard quietly spread the rumor that the fellow was gay and he was ostracized from the team and finally quit; and the beautiful girls he stole from their boyfriends just to prove that he could do it and the friendships he destroyed just because he didn't like being excluded and the marriages he wrecked and the co-workers he undercut and he walked along the street with tears streaming down his face, wondering where all these memories had come from and why, after such a long time in hiding, they had come out now. Yet he knew the answer. The answer was slipping behind doorways, climbing lightpoles as he passed, waving obscene flippers at him from the sidewalk almost under his feet.

And slowly, inexorably, the memories wound their way from the distant past through a hundred tawdry exploitations because he could find people's weak spots without even trying until finally memory came to the one place where he knew it could not, could not ever go.

He remembered Rhiannon.

Born fourteen years ago. Smiled early, walked early, almost never cried. A loving child from the start, and therefore easy prey for Howard. Oh, Alice was a bitch in her own right—Howard wasn't the only bad parent in the family. But it was Howard who manipulated Rhiannon most. "Daddy's feelings are hurt, Sweetheart," and Rhiannon's eyes would grow wide, and she'd be sorry, and whatever Daddy wanted, Rhiannon would do. But this was normal, this was part of the pattern, this would have fit easily into all his life before, except for last month.

And even now, after a day of grief at his own life, Howard could not face it. Could not but did. He unwillingly remembered walking by Rhiannon's almost-closed door, seeing just a flash of cloth moving quickly. He opened the door on impulse, just on impulse, as Rhiannon took off her brassiere and looked at herself in the mirror. Howard had never thought of his daughter with desire, not until that moment, but once the desire formed Howard had no strategy, no pattern in his mind to stop him from trying to get what he wanted. He was *uncomfortable*, and so he stepped into the room and closed the door behind him and Rhiannon knew no way to say no to her father. When Alice opened the door Rhiannon was crying softly, and Alice looked and after a moment Alice screamed and screamed and Howard got up from the bed and tried to smooth it all over but Rhiannon was still crying and Alice was still screaming, kicking at his crotch, beating him, raking at his face, spitting at him, telling him he was a monster, a monster, until at last he was able to flee the room and the house and, until now, the memory.

He screamed now as he had not screamed then, and threw himself against a plate-glass window, weeping loudly as the blood gushed from a dozen glass cuts on his right arm, which had gone through the window. One large piece of glass stayed embedded in his forearm. He deliberately scraped his arm against the wall to drive the glass deeper. But the pain in his arm was no match for the pain in his mind, and he felt nothing.

They rushed him to the hospital, thinking to save his life, but the doctor was surprised to discover that for all the blood there were only superficial wounds, not dangerous at all. "I don't know why you didn't reach a vein or an artery," the doctor said. "I think the glass went everywhere it could possibly go without causing any important damage."

After the medical doctor, of course, there was the psychiatrist, but there were many suicidals at the hospital and Howard was not the dangerous kind. "I was insane for a moment, Doctor, that's all. I don't want to die, I didn't want to die then, I'm all right now. You can send me home." And the psychiatrist let him go home. They bandaged his arm. They did not know that his real relief was that nowhere in the hospital did he see the small, naked, child-shaped creature. He had purged himself. He was free.

Howard was taken home in an ambulance, and they wheeled him into the house and lifted him from the stretcher to the bed. Through it all Alice hardly said a word except to direct them to the bedroom. Howard lay still on the bed as she stood over him, the two of them alone for the first time since he left the house a month ago.

"It was kind of you," Howard said softly, "to let me come back."

"They said there wasn't room enough to keep you, but you needed to be watched and taken care of for a few weeks. So lucky me, I get to watch you." Her voice was a low monotone, but the acid dripped from every word. It stung.

"You were right, Alice," Howard said.

"Right about what? That marrying you was the worst mistake of my life? No, Howard. *Meeting* you was my worst mistake."

Howard began to cry. Real tears that welled up from places in him that had once been deep but that now rested painfully close to the surface. "I've been a monster, Alice. I haven't had any control over myself. What I did to Rhiannon—Alice, I wanted to die, I wanted to die!"

Alice's face was twisted and bitter. "And I wanted you to, Howard. I have never been so disappointed as when the doctor called and said you'd be all right. You'll never be all right, Howard, you'll always be—"

"Let him be, Mother."

Rhiannon stood in the doorway.

"Don't come in, Rhiannon," Alice said.

Rhiannon came in. "Daddy, it's all right."

"What she means," Alice said, "is that we've checked her and she isn't pregnant. No little monster is going to be born."

Rhiannon didn't look at her mother, just gazed with wide eyes at her father. "You didn't need to—hurt yourself, Daddy. I forgive you. People lose control sometimes. And it was as much my fault as yours, it really was, you don't need to feel bad, Father."

It was too much for Howard. He cried out, shouted his confession, how he had manipulated her all his life, how he was an utterly selfish and rotten parent, and when it was over Rhiannon came to her father and laid her head on his chest and said, softly, "Father, it's all right. We are who we are. We've done what we've done. But it's all right now. I forgive you."

When Rhiannon left, Alice said, "You don't deserve her."

I know.

"I was going to sleep on the couch, but that would be stupid. Wouldn't it, Howard?"

I deserve to be left alone, like a leper.

"You misunderstand, Howard. I need to stay here to make sure you don't do anything else. To yourself or to anyone."

Yes. Yes, please. I can't be trusted.

"Don't wallow in it, Howard. Don't enjoy it. Don't make yourself even more disgusting than you were before."

All right.

They were drifting off to sleep when Alice said, "Oh, when the doctor called he wondered if I knew what had caused those sores all over your arms and chest."

But Howard was asleep, and didn't hear her. Asleep with no dreams at all, the sleep of peace, the sleep of having been forgiven, of being clean. It hadn't taken that much, after all. Now that it was over, it was easy. He felt as if a great weight had been taken from him.

He felt as if something heavy was lying on his legs. He awoke, sweating even though the room was not hot. He heard breathing. And it was not Alice's low-pitched, slow breath, it was quick and high and hard, as if the breather had been exerting himself.

Itself.

Themselves.

One of them lay across his legs, the flippers plucking at the blanket. The other two lay on either side, their eyes wide and intent, creeping slowly toward where his face emerged from the sheets.

Howard was puzzled. "I thought you'd be gone," he said to the children. "You're supposed to be gone now."

Alice stirred at the sound of his voice, mumbled in her sleep.

He saw more of them stirring in the gloomy corners of the room, another writhing slowly along the top of the dresser, another inching up the wall toward the ceiling.

"I don't need you anymore," he said, his voice oddly high-pitched.

Alice started breathing irregularly, mumbling, "What? What?"

And Howard said nothing more, just lay there in the sheets, watching the creatures carefully but not daring to make a sound for fear Alice would wake up. He was terribly afraid she would wake up and not see the creatures, which would prove, once and for all, that he had lost his mind.

He was even more afraid, however, that when she awoke she *would* see them. That was the one unbearable thought, yet he thought it continuously as they relentlessly approached with nothing at all in their eyes, not even hate, not even anger, not even contempt. We are with you, they seemed to be saying, we will be with you from now on. We will be with you, Howard, forever.

And Alice rolled over and opened her eyes.

At the beginning of Bram Stoker's Dracula, *Jonathan Harker awaits an ominous carriage from Castle Dracula. When it arrives, one of Harker's terrified fellow travelers murmurs "Denn die Todten reiten schnell", which Stoker translates "For the dead travel fast." It is a paraphrase of the recurring refrain of the famous German supernatural ballad, "Lenore," by* GOTTFRIED AUGUST BÜRGER *(1747–1794). Several English renderings of "Lenore" have been attempted, including a disappointing one by Sir Walter Scott. The best, yet most obscure version is by the British poet* DANTE GABRIEL ROSSETTI *(1828–1882). According to the poet's brother, Rossetti completed it in June 1844 at age sixteen, but it was never published in Rossetti's lifetime, nor did it appear amongst his posthumous papers. The manuscript turned up at an auction in 1899. It is reproduced below in hopes that it will attain the recognition it deserves.*

Lenore

BY GOTTFRIED AUGUST BÜRGER
English adaptation by Dante Gabriel Rossetti

Up rose Lenore as the red morn wore,
  From weary visions starting;
"Art faithless, William, or, William, art dead?
  'Tis long since thy departing."
For he, with Frederick's men of might,
In fair Prague waged the uncertain fight;
Nor once had he writ in the hurry of war,
And sad was the true heart that sickened afar.

The Empress and the King,
  With ceaseless quarrel tired,
At length relaxed the stubborn hate
  Which rivalry inspired:
And the martial throng, with laugh and song,
Spoke of their homes as they rode along,
And clank, clank, clank! came every rank,
With the trumpet-sound that rose and sank.

And here and there and everywhere,
  Along the swarming ways,
Went old man and boy, with the music of joy,
  On the gallant bands to gaze;
And the young child shouted to spy the vaward,
And trembling and blushing the bride pressed forward:
But ah! for the sweet lips of Lenore
The kiss and the greeting are vanished and o'er.

From man to man all wildly she ran
  With a swift and searching eye;
But she felt alone in the mighty mass,
  As it crushed and crowded by:
On hurried the troop,—a gladsome group,—
And proudly the tall plumes wave and droop:
She tore her hair and she turned her round,
And madly she dashed her against the ground.

Her mother clasped her tenderly
  With soothing words and mild:
"My child, may God look down on thee,—
  God comfort thee, my child."
"Oh! mother, mother! gone is gone!
I reck no more how the world runs on:
What pity to me does God impart?
Woe, woe, woe! for my heavy heart!"

"Help, Heaven, help and favour her!
  Child, utter an Ave Marie!
Wise and great are the doings of God;
  He loves and pities thee."
"Out, mother, out, on the empty lie!
Doth he heed my despair,—doth he list to my cry?
What boots it now to hope or to pray?
The night is come,—there is no more day."

"Help, Heaven, help! who knows the Father
  Knows surely that he loves his child:
The bread and the wine from the hand divine
  Shall make thy tempered grief less wild."
"Oh! mother, dear mother! the wine and the bread

Will not soften the anguish that bows down my head;
For bread and for wine it will yet be as late
That his cold corpse creeps from the grim grave's gate."

"What if the traitor's false faith failed,
  By sweet temptation tried,—
What if in distant Hungary
  He clasp another bride?—
Despise the fickle fool, my girl,
Who hath ta'en the pebble and spurned the pearl:
While soul and body shall hold together
In his perjured heart shall be stormy weather."

"Oh! mother, mother! gone is gone,
  And lost will still be lost!
Death, death is the goal of my weary soul,
  Crushed and broken and crost.
Spark of my life! down, down to the tomb:
Die away in the night, die away in the gloom!
What pity to me does God impart?
Woe, woe, woe! for my heavy heart!"

"Help, Heaven, help, and heed her not,
  For her sorrows are strong within;
She knows not the words that her tongue repeats,—
  Oh! count them not for sin!
Cease, cease, my child, thy wretchedness,
And think on the promised happiness;
So shall thy mind's calm ecstasy
Be a hope and a home and a bridegroom to thee."

"My mother, what is happiness?
  My mother, what is Hell?
With William is my happiness,—
  Without him is my Hell!
Spark of my life! down, down to the tomb:
Die away in the night, die away in the gloom!
Earth and Heaven, and Heaven and earth,
Reft of William are nothing worth."

Thus grief racked and tore the breast of Lenore,
  And was busy at her brain;
Thus rose her cry to the Power on high,
  To question and arraign:
Wringing her hands and beating her breast,—
Tossing and rocking without any rest;—
Till from her light veil the moon shone thro',
And the stars leapt out on the darkling blue.

But hark to the clatter and the pat pat patter!
  Of a horse's heavy hoof!
How the steel clanks and rings as the rider springs!
  How the echo shouts aloof!
While slightly and lightly the gentle bell
Tingles and jingles softly and well;
And low and clear through the door plank thin
Comes the voice without to the ear within:

"Holla! holla! unlock the gate;
  Art waking, my bride, or sleeping?
Is thy heart still free and still faithful to me?
  Art laughing, my bride, or weeping?
"Oh! wearily, William, I've waited for you,—
Woefully watching the long day thro',—
With a great sorrow sorrowing
For the cruelty of your tarrying."

"Till the dead midnight we saddled not,—
  I have journeyed far and fast—
And hither I come to carry thee back
  Ere the darkness shall be past."
"Ah! rest thee within till the night's more calm;
Smooth shall thy couch be, and soft, and warm:
Hark to the winds, how they whistle and rush
Thro' the twisted twine of the hawthorn-bush."

"Thro' the hawthorn-bush let whistle and rush,—
  Let whistle, child, let whistle!
Mark the flash fierce and high of my steed's bright eye,
  And his proud crest's eager bristle.
Up, up and away! I must not stay:

Mount swiftly behind me! up, up and away!
An hundred miles must be ridden and sped
Ere we may lie down in the bridal-bed."

"What! ride an hundred miles to-night,
  By thy mad fancies driven!
Dost hear the bell with its sullen swell,
  As it rumbles out eleven?"
"Look forth! look forth! the moon shines bright:
We and the dead gallop fast thro' the night.
'Tis for a wager I bear thee away
To the nuptial couch ere break of day."

"Ah! where is the chamber, William dear,
  And William, where is the bed?"
"Far, far from here: still, narrow, and cool;
  Plank and bottom and lid."
"Hast room for me?"—"For me and thee;
Up, up to the saddle right speedily!
The wedding-guests are gathered and met,
And the door of the chamber is open set."

She busked her well, and into the selle
  She sprang with nimble haste,—
And gently smiling, with a sweet beguiling,
  Her white hands clasped his waist:—
And hurry, hurry! ring, ring, ring!
To and fro they sway and swing;
Snorting and snuffing they skim the ground,
And the sparks spurt up, and the stones run round.

Here to the right and there to the left
  Flew fields of corn and clover,
And the bridges flashed by to the dazzled eye,
  As rattling they thundered over.
"What ails my love? the moon shines bright:
Bravely the dead men ride through the night.
Is my love afraid of the quiet dead?"
"Ah! no;—let them sleep in their dusty bed!"

On the breeze cool and soft what tune floats aloft,
  While the crows wheel overhead?—
Ding dong! ding dong! 'tis the sound, 'tis the song,—
  "Room, room for the passing dead!"
Slowly the funeral-train drew near,
Bearing the coffin, bearing the bier;
And the chime of their chant was hissing and harsh,
Like the note of the bull-frog within the marsh.

"You bury your corpse at the dark midnight,
  With hymns and bells and wailing,—
But I bring home my youthful wife
  To a bride-feast's rich regaling.
Come, chorister, come with thy choral throng,
And solemnly sing me a marriage-song;
Come, friar, come,—let the blessing be spoken,
That the bride and the bridegroom's sweet rest be unbroken."

Died the dirge and vanished the bier:—
  Obedient to his call,
Hard hard behind, with a rush like the wind,
  Came the long steps' pattering fall:
And ever further! ring, ring, ring!
To and fro they sway and swing;
Snorting and snuffing they skim the ground,
And the sparks spurt up, and the stones run round.

How flew to the right, how flew to the left,
  Trees, mountains in the race!
How to the left, and the right and the left,
  Flew town and market-place!
"What ails my love? the moon shines bright:
Bravely the dead men ride thro' the night.
Is my love afraid of the quiet dead?"
"Ah! let them alone in their dusty bed!"

See, see, see! by the gallows-tree,
  As they dance on the wheel's broad hoop,
Up and down, in the gleam of the moon
  Half lost, an airy group:—
"Ho! ho! mad mob, come hither amain,

And join in the wake of my rushing train;—
Come, dance me a dance, ye dancers thin,
Ere the planks of the marriage-bed close us in."

And hush, hush, hush! the dreamy rout
  Came close with a ghastly bustle,
Like the whirlwind in the hazel-bush,
  When it makes the dry leaves rustle:
And faster, faster! ring, ring, ring!
To and fro they sway and swing;
Snorting and snuffing they skim the ground,
And the sparks spurt up, and the stones run round.

How flew the moon high overhead,
  In the wild race madly driven!
In and out, how the stars danced about,
  And reeled o'er the flashing heaven!
"What ails my love? the moon shines bright:
Bravely the dead men ride thro' the night.
Is my love afraid of the quiet dead?"
"Alas! let them sleep in their dusty bed."

"Horse, horse! meseems 'tis the cock's shrill note,
  And the sand is well night spent;
Horse, horse, away! 'tis the break of day,—
  'Tis the morning air's sweet scent.
Finished, finished is our ride:
Room, room for the bridegroom and the bride!
At last, at last, we have reached the spot,
For the speed of the dead man has slackened not!"

And swiftly up to an iron gate
  With reins relaxed they went;
At the rider's touch the bolts flew back,
  And the bars were broken and bent;
The doors were burst with a deafening knell,
And over the white graves they dashed pell mell:
The tombs around looked grassy and grim,
As they glimmered and glanced in the moonlight dim.

But see! but see! in an eyelid's beat,
*   Towhoo! a ghastly wonder!*
The horseman's jerkin, piece by piece,
*   Dropped off like brittle tinder!*
Fleshless and hairless, a naked skull,
The sight of his weird head was horrible;
The lifelike mask was there no more,
And a scythe and a sandglass the skeleton bore.

Loud snorted the horse as he plunged and reared,
*   And the sparks were scattered round:—*
What man shall say if he vanished away,
*   Or sank in the gaping ground?*
Groans from the earth and shrieks in the air!
Howling and wailing everywhere!
Half dead, half living, the soul of Lenore
Fought as it never had fought before.

The churchyard troop,—a ghostly group,—
*   Close round the dying girl;*
Out and in they hurry and spin
*   Through the dance's weary whirl:*
"Patience, patience, when the heart is breaking;
With thy God there is no question-making:
Of thy body thou art quit and free:
Heaven keep thy soul eternally!"

ISAAC BASHEVIS SINGER, *Nobel prizewinning author, was born in 1904 in Poland and grew up in Warsaw. An illustrious resident of New York's Upper West Side, Mr. Singer chooses to write in Yiddish, and his works are then translated into English. "The Black Wedding," from the collection* The Spinoza of Market Street, *is a tale that accomplishes in a few pages all the promise undelivered in Ira Levin's overpraised novel*, Rosemary's Baby. *(For further comment, see the "Afterword.")*

The Black Wedding

BY ISAAC BASHEVIS SINGER

I

Aaron Naphtali, Rabbi of Tzivkev, had lost three-fourths of his followers. There was talk in the rabbinical courts that Rabbi Aaron Naphtali alone had been responsible for driving away his Chassidim. A rabbinical court must be vigilant, more adherents must be acquired. One has to find devices so that the following will not diminish. But Rabbi Aaron Naphtali was apathetic. The study house was old and toad-stools grew unmolested on the walls. The ritual bath fell to ruin. The beadles were tottering old men, deaf and half-blind. The rabbi passed his time practicing miracle-working cabala. It was said that Rabbi Aaron Naphtali wanted to imitate the feats of the ancient ones, to tap wine from the wall and create pigeons through combinations of holy names. It was even said that he molded a golem secretly in his attic. Moreover, Rabbi Naphtali had no son to succeed him, only one daughter named Hindele. Who would be eager to follow a rabbi under these circumstances? His enemies contended that Rabbi Aaron Naphtali was sunk in melancholy, as were his wife and Hindele. The latter, at fifteen, was already reading esoteric books and periodically went into seclusion like the holy man. It was rumored that Hindele wore a fringed garment underneath her dress like that worn by her saintly grandmother after whom she had been named.

Rabbi Aaron Naphtali had strange habits. He shut himself in

his chamber for days and would not come out to welcome visitors. When he prayed, he put on two pairs of phylacteries at once. On Friday afternoons, he read the prescribed section of the Pentateuch—not from a book but from the parchment scroll itself. The rabbi had learned to form letters with the penmanship of the ancient scribes, and he used this script for writing amulets. A little bag containing one of these amulets hung from the neck of each of his followers. It was known that the rabbi warred constantly with the evil ones. His grandfather, the old Rabbi of Tzivkev, had exorcised a dybbuk from a young girl and the evil spirits had revenged themselves upon the grandson. They had not been able to bring harm to the old man because he had been blessed by the Saint of Kozhenitz. His son, Rabbi Hirsch, Rabbi Aaron Naphtali's father, died young. The grandson, Rabbi Aaron Naphtali, had to contend with the vengeful devils all his life. He lit a candle, they extinguished it. He placed a volume on the bookshelf, they knocked it off. When he undressed in the ritual bath, they hid his silk coat and his fringed garment. Often, sounds of laughter and wailing seemed to come from the rabbi's chimney. There was a rustling behind the stove. Steps were heard on the roof. Doors opened by themselves. The stairs would screech although nobody had stepped on them. Once the rabbi laid his pen on the table and it sailed out through the open window as if carried by an unseen hand. The rabbi's hair turned white at forty. His back was bent, his hands and feet trembled like those of an ancient man. Hindele often suffered attacks of yawning; red flushes spread over her face, her throat ached, there was a buzzing in her ears. At such times incantations had to be made to drive away the evil eye.

The rabbi used to say, "They will not leave me in peace, not even for a moment." And he stamped his foot and asked the beadle to give him his grandfather's cane. He rapped it against each corner of the room and cried out, "You will not work your evil tricks on me!"

But the black hosts gained ascendency just the same. One autumn day the rabbi became ill with erysipelas and it was soon apparent that he would not recover from his sickness. A doctor was sent for from a nearby town, but on the way the axle of his coach broke and he could not complete the journey. A second physician was called for, but a wheel of his carriage came loose and rolled into a ditch, and the horse sprained his leg. The rabbi's wife went to the memorial chapel of her husband's deceased grandfather to pray, but the vindictive demons tore her bonnet from her head. The rabbi lay in bed with a swollen face and a shrunken beard, and for two days he did not speak a word. Quite suddenly he opened an eye and cried out, "They have won!"

Hindele, who would not leave her father's bed, wrung her hands and began to wail in despair, "Father, what's to become of me?"

The rabbi's beard trembled. "You must keep silent if you are to be spared."

There was a great funeral. Rabbis had come from half of Poland. The women predicted that the rabbi's widow would not last much longer. She was white as a corpse. She hadn't enough strength in her feet to follow the hearse and two women had to support her. At the burial she tried to throw herself into the grave and they could barely restrain her. All through the Seven Days of Mourning, she ate nothing. They tried to force a spoon of chicken broth into her mouth, but she was unable to swallow it. When the Thirty Days of Mourning had passed, the rabbi's wife still had not left her bed. Physicians were brought to her but to no avail. She herself foresaw the day of her death and she foretold it to the minute. After her funeral, the rabbi's disciples began to look around for a young man for Hindele. They had tried to find a match for her even before her father's death, but her father had been difficult to please. The son-in-law would eventually have to take the rabbi's place and who was worthy to sit in the Tzivkev rabbinical chair? Whenever the rabbi finally gave his approval, his wife found fault with the young man. Besides, Hindele was known to be sick, to keep too many fast days and to fall into a swoon when things did not go her way. Nor was she attractive. She was short, frail, had a large head, a skinny neck, and flat breasts. Her hair was bushy. There was an insane look in her black eyes. However, since Hindele's dowry was a following of thousands of Chassidim, a candidate was found, Reb Simon, son of the Yampol Rabbi. His older brother having died, Reb Simon would become Rabbi of Yampol after his father's death. Yampol and Tzivkev had much in common. If they were to unite, the glory of former times would return. True, Reb Simon was a divorced man with five children. But as Hindele was an orphan, who would protest? The Tzivkev Chassidim had one stipulation—that after his father's death, Reb Simon should reside in Tzivkev.

Both Tzivkev and Yampol were anxious to bring the union about. Immediately after the marriage contract was written, wedding preparations were begun, because the Tzivkev rabbinical chair had to be filled. Hindele had not yet seen her husband-to-be. She was told that he was a widower, and nothing was said about the five children. The wedding was a noisy one. Chassidim came from all parts of Poland. The followers of the Yampol court and those of the Tzivkev court began to address one another by the familiar "thou." The inns were full. The innkeeper brought straw mattresses down from the attic and put them out in corridors, granaries, and tool sheds, to accommodate the large crowd. Those who opposed the match foretold that Yampol would engulf Tzivkev. The Chassidim of Yampol were known for their crudeness. When they played, they became boisterous. They drank long daughts of brandy from tin mugs and became drunk. When they danced, the floors heaved under them. When an adversary of Yampol spoke harshly of their rabbi, he was beaten. There was a custom in Yampol that when the wife of a young man gave birth to a girl, the father was placed on a table and lashed thirty-nine times with a strap.

Old women came to Hindele to warn her that it would not be easy to be a daugher-in-law in the Yampol court. Her future mother-in-law, an old woman, was known for her wickedness. Reb Simon and his younger brothers had wild ways. The mother had chosen large women for her sons and the frail Hindele would not please her. Reb Simon's mother had consented to the match only because of Yampol's ambitions regarding Tzivkev.

From the time that the marriage negotiations started until the wedding, Hindele did not stop crying. She cried at the celebration of the writing of the marriage contract, she cried when the tailors fitted her trousseau, she cried when she was led to the ritual bath. There she was ashamed to undress for the immersion before the attendants and the other women, and they had to tear off her stays and her underpants. She would not let them remove from her neck the little bag which contained an amber charm and the tooth of a wolf. She was afraid to immerse herself in the water. The two attendants who led her into the bath, held her tightly by her wrists and she trembled like the sacrificial chicken the day before Yom Kippur. When Reb Simon lifted the veil from Hindele's face after the wedding, she saw him for the first time. He was a tall man with a broad fur hat, a pitch-black disheveled beard, wild eyes, a broad nose, thick lips, and a long moustache. He gazed at her like an animal. He breathed noisily and smelled of perspiration.

Clusters of hair grew out of his nostrils and ears. His hands, too, had a growth of hair as thick as fur. The moment Hindele saw him she knew what she had suspected long before—that her bridegroom was a demon and that the wedding was nothing but black magic, a satanic hoax. She wanted to call out "Hear, O Israel" but she remembered her father's deathbed admonition to keep silent. How strange that the moment Hindele understood that her husband was an evil spirit, she could immediately discern what was true and what was false. Although she saw herself sitting in her mother's living room, she knew she was really in a forest. It appeared to be light, but she knew it was dark. She was surrounded by Chassidim with fur hats and satin gabardines, as well as by women who wore silk bonnets and velvet capes, but she knew it was all imaginary and that the fancy garments hid heads grown with elf-locks, goose-feet, unhuman navels, long snouts. The sashes of the young men were snakes in reality, their sable hats were actually hedgehogs, their beards clusters of worms. The men spoke Yiddish and sang familiar songs, but the noise they made was really the bellowing of oxen, the hissing of vipers, the howling of wolves. The musicians had tails, and horns grew from their heads. The maids who attended Hindele had canine paws, hoofs of calves, snouts of pigs. The wedding jester was all beard and tongue. The so-called relatives on the groom's side were lions, bears, boars. It was raining in the forest and a wind was blowing. It thundered and flashed lightning. Alas, this was not a human wedding, but a Black Wedding. Hindele knew, from reading holy books, that demons sometimes married human virgins whom they later carried away behind the black mountains to co-habit with them and sire their children. There was only one thing to do in such a case—not to comply with them, never willingly submit to them, to let them get everything by force as one kind word spoken to Satan is equivalent to sacrificing to the idol. Hindele remembered the story of Joseph De La Rinah and the misfortune that befell him when he felt sorry for the evil one and gave him a pinch of tobacco.

II

Hindele did not want to march to the wedding canopy, and she planted her feet stubbornly on the floor, but the bridesmaids dragged her. They half-pulled her, half-carried her. Imps in the

images of girls held the candles and formed an aisle for her. The
canopy was a braid of reptiles. The rabbi who performed the
ceremony was under contract to Samael. Hindele submitted to
nothing. She refused to hold out her finger for the ring and had
to be forced to do so. She would not drink from the goblet and
they poured some wine into her mouth. Hobgoblins performed all
the wedding rites. The evil spirit who appeared in the likeness of
Reb Simon was wearing a white robe. He stepped on the bride's
foot with his hoof so that he might rule over her. Then he smashed
the wine glass. After the ceremony, a witch danced toward the
bride carrying a braided bread. Presently the bride and groom
were served the so-called soup, but Hindele spat everything into
her handkerchief. The musicians played a Kossack, an Angry
Dance, a Scissors Dance and a Water Dance. But their webbed
roosters' feet peeped out from under their robes. The wedding
hall was nothing but a forest swamp, full of frogs, mooncalves,
monsters, each with his ticks and grimaces. The Chassidim
presented the couple with assorted gifts, but these were devices to
ensnare Hindele in the net of evil. The wedding jester recited sad
poems and funny poems, but his voice was that of a parrot.

They called Hindele to dance the Good-Luck dance, but she did
not want to get up, knowing it was actually a Bad-Luck dance.
They urged her, pushed her, pinched her. Little imps stuck pins
into her thighs. In the middle of the dance, two she-demons
grabbed her by the arms and carried her away into a bedroom
which was actually a dark cave full of thistles, scavengers, and
rubbish. While these females whispered to her the duties of a
bride, they spat in her ear. Then she was thrown upon a heap of
mud which was supposed to be linen. For a long while, Hindele
lay in that cave, surrounded by darkness, poison weeds and lice.
So great was her anxiety that she couldn't even pray. Then the
devil to whom she was espoused entered. He assailed her with
cruelty, tore off her clothes, martyred her, abused her, shamed
her. She wanted to scream for help but she restrained herself
knowing that if she uttered a sound she would be lost forever.

All night long Hindele felt herself lying in blood and pus. The
one who had raped her snored, coughed, hissed like an adder.
Before dawn a group of hags ran into the room, pulled the sheet
from under her, inspected it, sniffed it, began to dance. That night
never ended. True, the sun rose. It was not really the sun, though,
but a bloody sphere which somebody hung in the sky. Women

came to coax the bride with smooth talk and cunning but Hindele did not pay any attention to their babble. They spat at her, flattered her, said incantations, but she did not answer them. Later a doctor was brought to her, but Hindele saw that he was a horned buck. No, the black powers could not rule her, and Hindele kept on spiting them. Whatever they bade her do, she did the opposite. She threw the soup and marchpane into the slop can. She dumped the chickens and squab which they baked for her into the outhouse. She found a page of a psalter in the mossy forest and she recited psalms furtively. She also remembered a few passages of the Torah and of the prophets. She acquired more and more courage to pray to God-Almighty to save her. She mentioned the names of holy angels as well as those of her illustrious ancestors like the Baal Shem, Rabbi Leib Sarah's, Rabbi Pinchos Korzer and the like.

Strange, that although she was only one and the others were multitudes, they could not overcome her. The one who was disguised as her husband tried to bribe her with sweet-talk and gifts, but she did not satisfy him. He came to her but she turned away from him. He kissed her with his wet lips and petted her with clammy fingers, but she did not let him have her. He forced himself on her, but she tore at his beard, pulled at his sidelocks, scratched his forehead. He ran away from her bloody. It became clear to Hindele that her power was not of this world. Her father was interceding for her. He came to her in his shroud and comforted her. Her mother revealed herself to her and gave her advice. True, the earth was full of evil spirits, but up above angels were hovering. Sometimes Hindele heard the angel Gabriel fighting and fencing with Satan. Bevies of black dogs and crows came to help him, but the saints drove them away with their palm leaves and hosannahs. The barking and the crowing were drowned out by the song which Hindele's grandfather used to sing Saturday evenings and which was called "The Sons of the Mansion."

But horror of horrors, Hindele became pregnant. A devil grew inside her. She could see him through her own belly as through a cobweb: half-frog, half-ape, with eyes of a calf and scales of a fish. He ate her flesh, sucked her blood, scratched her with his claws, bit her with his pointed teeth. He was already chattering, calling her mother, cursing with vile language. She had to get rid of him, stop his gnawing at her liver. Nor was she able to bear his blasphemy and mockery. Besides, he urinated in her and defiled her with his excrement. Miscarriage was the only way out, but how to bring it on? Hindele struck her stomach with her fist. She jumped, hrew herself down, crawled, all to get rid of that devil's bastard, but to no avail. He grew quickly and showed inhuman strength, pushed and tore at her insides. His skull was of copper, his mouth of iron. He had capricious urges. He told her to eat lime from the wall, the shell of an egg, all kinds of garbage. And if she refused, he squeezed her gall bladder. He stank like a skunk and Hindele fainted from the stench. In her swoon, a giant appeared to her with one eye in his forehead. He talked to her from a hollowed tree saying, "Give yourself up, Hindele, you are one of us."

"No, never."

"We will take revenge."

He flogged her with a fiery rod and yelled abuses. Her head became as heavy as a millstone from fear. The fingers of her hands became big and hard like rolling pins. Her mouth puckered as from eating unripe fruit. Her ears felt as if they were full of water. Hindele was not free any more. The hosts rolled her in muck, mire, slime. They immersed her in baths of pitch. They flayed her skin. They pulled the nipples of her breasts with pliers. They tortured her ceaselessly but she remained mute. Since the males could not persuade her, the female devils attacked her. They laughed with abandon, they braided their hair around her, choked her, tickled her, and pinched her. One giggled, another cried, another wiggled like a whore. Hindele's belly was big and hard as a drum and Belial sat in her womb. He pushed with elbows and pressed with his skull. Hindele lay in labor. One she-devil was a midwife and the other an aide. They had hung all kinds of charms over her canopied bed and they put a knife and a Book of Creation under her pillow, the way the evil ones imitate the humans in all manners. Hindele was in her birth throes, but she remembered that she was not allowed to groan. One sigh and she would be lost. She must restrain herself in the name of her holy forbears.

Suddenly the black one inside her pushed with all his might. A piercing scream tore itself from Hindele's throat and she was swallowed in darkness. Bells were ringing as on a gentile holiday. A hellish fire flared up. It was as red as blood, as scarlet as leprosy. The earth opened like in the time of Korah, and Hindele's canopied bed began to sink into the abyss. Hindele had lost everything, this world and the world to come. In the distance she heard the crying of women, the clapping of hands, blessings and good wishes, while she flew straight into the castle of Asmodeus where Lilith, Namah, Machlath, Hurmizah rule.

In Tzivkev and in the neighbourhood the tidings spread that Hindele had given birth to a male child by Reb Simon of Yampol. The mother had died in childbirth.

Translated by Martha Glicklich

EDGAR ALLAN POE *(1809–1849) is one of those seminal writers who surely "need no introduction." "Hop-Frog" is a late tale from the Master, first published in March 1849. Poe could be concise or verbose, but "Hop-Frog" is a model of economic storytelling. In less than four thousand words, Poe concentrates enough emotion and horror for a Grand Opera!*

Hop-Frog

BY EDGAR ALLAN POE

I never knew any one so keenly alive to a joke as the king was. He seemed to live only for joking. To tell a good story of the joke kind, and to tell it well, was the surest road to his favor. Thus it happened that his seven ministers were all noted for their accomplishments as jokers. They all took after the king, too, in being large, corpulent, oily men, as well as inimitable jokers. Whether people grow fat by joking, or whether there is something in fat itself which predisposes to a joke, I have never been quite able to determine; but certain it is that a lean joker is a *rara avis in terris*.

About the refinements, or, as he called them, the "ghosts" of wit, the king troubled himself very little. He had an especial admiration for *breadth* in a jest, and would often put up with *length*, for the sake of it. Overniceties wearied him. He would have preferred Rabelais' "Gargantua" to the "Zadig" of Voltaire: and, upon the whole, practical jokes suited his taste far better than verbal ones.

At the date of my narrative, professing jesters had not altogether gone out of fashion at court. Several of the great continental "powers" still retained their "fools," who wore motley, with caps and bells, and who were expected to be always ready with sharp witticisms, at a moment's notice, in consideration of the crumbs that fell from the royal table.

Our king, as a matter of course, retained his "fool." The fact is, he *required* something in the way of folly—if only to counter-balance the heavy wisdom of the seven wise men who were his ministers—not to mention himself.

His fool, or professional jester, was not *only* a fool, however. His value was trebled in the eyes of the king, by the fact of his being also a dwarf and a cripple. Dwarfs were as common at court, in those days, as fools; and many monarchs would have found it difficult to get through their days (days are rather longer at court than elsewhere) without both a jester to laugh *with*, and a dwarf to laugh *at*. But, as I have already observed, your jesters, in ninety-nine cases out of a hundred, are fat, round, and unwieldy— so that it was no small source of self-gratulation with our king that, in Hop-Frog (this was the fool's name), he possessed a triplicate treasure in one person.

I believe the name "Hop-Frog" was *not* that given to the dwarf by his sponsors at baptism, but it was conferred upon him, by general consent of the seven ministers, on account of his inability to walk as other men do. In fact, Hop-Frog could only get along by a sort of interjectional gait—something between a leap and a wriggle,—a movement that afforded illimitable amusement, and of course consolation, to the king, for (notwithstanding the protruberance of his stomach and a constitutional swelling of the head) the king, by his whole court, was accounted a capital figure.

But although Hop-Frog, through the distortion of his legs, could move only with great pain and difficulty along a road or floor, the prodigious muscular power which nature seemed to have bestowed upon his arms, by way of compensation for deficiency in the lower limbs, enabled him to perform many feats of wonderful dexterity, where trees or ropes were in question, or anything else to climb. At such exercises he certainly much more resembled a squirrel, or a small monkey, than a frog.

I am not able to say, with precision, from what country Hop-Frog originally came. It was from some barbarous region, however, that no person ever heard of—a vast distance from the court of our king. Hop-Frog, and a young girl very little less dwarfish than himself (although of exquisite proportions, and a marvellous dancer), had been forcibly carried off from their respective homes in adjoining provinces, and sent as presents to the king, by one of his ever-victorious generals.

Under these circumstances, it is not to be wondered at that a close intimacy arose between the two little captives. Indeed, they soon became sworn friends. Hop-Frog, who, although he made a great deal of sport, was by no means popular, had it not in his power to render Trippetta many services; but *she*, on account of her grace and exquisite beauty (although a dwarf), was universally admired and petted; so she possessed much influence; and never failed to use it, whenever she could, for the benefit of Hop-Frog.

On some grand state occasion—I forget what—the king determined to have a masquerade; and whenever a masquerade, or any thing of that kind, occurred at our court, then the talents both of Hop-Frog and Trippetta were sure to be called into play. Hop-Frog, in especial, was so inventive in the way of getting up pageants, suggesting novel characters, and arranging costume, for masked balls, that nothing could be done, it seems, without his assistance.

The night appointed for the *fête* had arrived. A gorgeous hall had been fitted up, under Trippetta's eye, with every kind of device which could possibly give *éclat* to a masquerade. The whole court was in a fever of expectation. As for costumes and characters, it might well be supposed that everybody had come to a decision on such points. Many had made up their minds (as to what *rôles* they should assume) a week, or even a month, in advance; and, in fact, there was not a particle of indecision anywhere—except in the case of the king and his seven ministers. Why *they* hesitated I never could tell, unless they did it by way of a joke. More probably, they found it difficult, on account of being so fat, to make up their minds. At all events, time flew; and, as a last resort, they sent for Trippetta and Hop-Frog.

When the two little friends obeyed the summons of the king, they found him sitting at his wine with the seven members of his cabinet council; but the monarch appeared to be in a very ill humor. He knew that Hop-Frog was not fond of wine; for it excited the poor cripple almost to madness; and madness is no comfortable feeling. But the king loved his practical jokes, and took pleasure in forcing Hop-Frog to drink and (as the king called it) "to be merry."

"Come here, Hop-Frog," said he, as the jester and his friend entered the room; "swallow this bumper to the health of your absent friends [here Hop-Frog sighed] and then let us have the benefit of your invention. We want characters—*characters*, man,—something novel—out of the way. We are wearied with this everlasting sameness. Come, drink! the wine will brighten your wits."

Hop-Frog endeavored, as usual, to get up a jest in reply to these advances from the king; but the effort was too much. It happened to be the poor dwarf's birthday, and the command to drink to his "absent friends" forced the tears to his eyes. Many large, bitter drops fell into the goblet as he took it, humbly, from the hand of the tyrant.

"Ah! ha! ha! ha!" roared the latter, as the dwarf reluctantly drained the beaker. "See what a glass of good wine can do! Why, your eyes are shining already!"

Poor fellow! his large eyes *gleamed*, rather than shone; for the effect of wine on his excitable brain was not more powerful than instantaneous. He placed the goblet nervously on the table, and looked round upon the company with a half-insane stare. They all seemed highly amused at the success of the king's "*joke*".

"And now to business," said the prime minster, a *very* fat man.

"Yes," said the king. "Come, Hop-Frog, lend us your assistance. Characters, my fine fellow; we stand in need of characters — all of us — ha! ha! ha!" and as this was seriously meant for a joke, his laugh was chorused by the seven.

Hop-Frog also laughed, although feebly and somewhat vacantly.

"Come, come," said the king, impatiently, "have you nothing to suggest?"

"I am endeavouring to think of something *novel*," replied the dwarf, abstractedly, for he was quite bewildered by the wine.

"Endeavoring!" cried the tyrant, fiercely; "what do you mean by *that?* Ah, I perceive. You are sulky, and want more wine. Here, drink this!" and he poured out another gobletful and offered it to the cripple, who merely gazed at it, gasping for breath.

"Drink, I say!" shouted the monster, "or by the fiends —"

The dwarf hesitated. The king grew purple with rage. The courtiers smirked. Trippetta, pale as a corpse, advanced to the monarch's seat, and, falling on her knees before him, implored him to spare her friend.

The tyrant regarded her, for some moments, in evident wonder at her audacity. He seemed quite at a loss what to do or say — how most becomingly to express his indignation. At last, without uttering a syllable, he pushed her violently from him, and threw the contents of the brimming goblet in her face.

The poor girl got up as best she could, and, not daring even to sigh, resumed her position at the foot of the table.

There was a dead silence for about half a minute, during which

the falling of a leaf, or of a feather, might have been heard. It was
interrupted by a low, but harsh and protracted *grating* sound which
seemed to come at once from every corner of the room.

"What—what—*what* are you making that noise for?" demanded
the king, turning furiously to the dwarf.

The latter seemed to have recovered, in great measure, from
his intoxication, and looking fixedly but quietly into the tyrant's
face, merely ejaculated:

"I—I? How could it have been me?"

"The sound appeared to come from without," observed one of
the courtiers. "I fancy it was the parrot at the window, whetting
his bill upon his cage-wires."

"True," replied the monarch, as if much relieved by the
suggestion; "but on the honor of a knight, I could have sworn that
it was the gritting of this vagabond's teeth."

Hereupon the dwarf laughed (the king was too confirmed a
joker to object to any one's laughing), and displayed a set of large,
powerful, and very repulsive teeth. Moreover, he avowed his
perfect willingness to swallow as much wine as desired. The
monarch was pacified; and having drained another bumper with
no very perceptible ill effect, Hop-Frog entered at once, and with
spirit, into the plans for the masquerade.

"I cannot tell what was the association of idea," observed he,
very tranquilly, and as if he had never tasted wine in his life, "but
just after your majesty had struck the girl and thrown the wine in
her face—*just after* your majesty had done this, and while the
parrot was making that odd noise outside the window, there came
into my mind a capital diversion—one of my own country frolics—
often enacted among us, at our masquerades: but here it will be
new altogether. Unfortunately, however, it requires a company of
eight persons, and—"

"Here we *are!*" cried the king, laughing at his acute discovery
of the coincidence; "eight to a fraction—I and my seven ministers.
Come! what is the diversion?"

"We call it," replied the cripple, "the Eight Chained Ourang-
Outangs, and it really is excellent sport if well enacted."

"*We* will enact it," remarked the king, drawing himself up, and
lowering his eyelids.

"The beauty of the game," continued Hop-Frog, "lies in the
fright it occasions among the women."

"Capital!" roared in chorus the monarch and his ministry.

"I will equip you as ourang-outangs," proceeded the dwarf; "leave all that to me. The resemblance shall be so striking, that the company of masqueraders will take you for real beasts—and of course, they will be as much terrified as astonished."

"Oh, this is exquisite!" exclaimed the king. "Hop-Frog! I will make a man of you."

"The chains are for the purpose of increasing the confusion by their jangling. You are supposed to have escaped, *en masse*, from your keepers. Your majesty cannot conceive the *effect* produced, at a masquerade, by eight chained ourang-outangs, imagined to be real ones by most of the company; and rushing in with savage cries, among the crowd of delicately and gorgeously habited men and women. The *contrast* is inimitable."

"It *must* be," said the king: and the council arose hurriedly (as it was growing late), to put in execution the scheme of Hop-Frog.

His mode of equipping the party as ourang-outangs was very simple, but effective enough for his purposes. The animals in question had, at the epoch of my story, very rarely been seen in any part of the civilized world; and as the imitations made by the dwarf were sufficiently beast-like and more than sufficiently hideous, their truthfulness to nature was thus thought to be secured.

The king and his ministers were first encased in tight-fitting stockinet shirts and drawers. They were then saturated with tar. At this stage of the process, some one of the party suggested feathers; but the suggestion was at once overruled by the dwarf, who soon convinced the eight, by ocular demonstration, that the hair of such a brute as the ourang-outang was much more efficiently represented by *flax*. A thick coating of the latter was accordingly plastered upon the coating of tar. A long chain was now procured. First, it was passed about the waist of the king, *and tied*; then about another of the party, and also tied; then about all successively, in the same manner. When this chaining arrangement was complete, and the party stood as far apart from each other as possible, they formed a circle; and to make all things appear natural, Hop-Frog passed the residue of the chain, in two diameters, at right angles, across the circle, after the fashion adopted, at the present day, by those who capture chimpanzees, or other large apes, in Borneo.

The grand saloon in which the masquerade was to take place, was a circular room, very lofty, and receiving the light of the sun only through a single window at top. At night (the season for which the apartment was especially designed) it was illuminated principally by a large chandelier, depending by a chain from the centre of the sky-light, and lowered, or elevated, by means of a counterbalance as usual; but (in order not to look unsightly) this latter passed outside the cupola and over the roof.

The arrangements of the room had been left to Trippetta's superintendence; but, in some particulars, it seems, she had been guided by the calmer judgment of her friend the dwarf. At his suggestion it was that, on this occasion, the chandelier was removed. Its waxen drippings (which, in weather so warm, it was quite impossible to prevent) would have been seriously detrimental to the rich dresses of the guests, who, on account of the crowded state of the saloon, could not *all* be expected to keep from out its centre—that is to say, from under the chandelier. Additional sconces were set in various parts of the hall, out of the way; and a flambeau, emitting sweet odor, was placed in the right hand of each of the Caryatides that stood against the wall—some fifty or sixty all together.

The eight ourang-outangs, taking Hop-Frog's advice, waited patiently until midnight (when the room was thoroughly filled with masqueraders) before making their appearance. No sooner had the clock ceased striking, however, than they rushed, or rather rolled in, all together—for the impediments of their chains caused most of the party to fall, and all to stumble as they entered.

The excitement among the masqueraders was prodigous, and filled the heart of the king with glee. As had been anticipated, there were not a few of the guests who supposed the ferocious-looking creatures to be beasts of *some* kind in reality, if not precisely ourang-outangs. Many of the women swooned with affright; and had not the king taken the precaution to exclude all weapons from the saloon, his party might soon have expiated their frolic in their blood. As it was, a general rush was made for the doors; but the king had ordered them to be locked immediately upon his entrance; and, at the dwarf's suggestion, the keys had been deposited with *him*.

While the tumult was at its height, and each masquerader attentive only to his own safety (for, in fact, there was much *real* danger from the pressure of the excited crowd), the chain by which the chandelier ordinarily hung, and which had been drawn up on its removal, might have been seen very gradually to descend, until its hooked extremity came within three feet of the floor.

Soon after this, the king and his seven friends having reeled about the hall in all directions, found themselves, at length, in its centre, and, of course, in immediate contact with the chain. While they were thus situated, the dwarf, who had followed noiselessly at their heels, inciting them to keep up the commotion, took hold of their own chain at the intersection of the two portions which crossed the circle diametrically and at right angles. Here, with rapidity of thought, he inserted the hook from which the chandelier had been wont to depend; and, in an instant, by some unseen agency, the chandelier-chain was drawn so far upward as to take the hook out of reach, and, as an inevitable consequence, to drag the ourang-outangs together in close connection, and face to face.

The masqueraders, by this time, had recovered, in some measure, from their alarm; and, beginning to regard the whole matter as a well-contrived pleasantry, set up a loud shout of laughter at the predicament of the apes.

"Leave them to *me!*" now screamed Hop-Frog, his shrill voice making itself easily heard through all the din. "Leave them to *me*. I fancy *I* know them. If I can only get a good look at them. *I* can soon tell who they are."

Here, scrambling over the heads of the crowd, he managed to get to the wall; when, seizing a flambeau from one of the Caryatides, he returned, as he went, to the centre of the room— leaped, with the agility of a monkey, upon the king's head—and thence clambered a few feet up the chain—holding down the torch to examine the group of ourang-outangs, and still screaming: "*I* shall soon find out who they are!"

And now, while the whole assembly (the apes included) were convulsed with laughter, the jester suddenly uttered a shrill whistle; when the chain flew violently up for about thirty feet— dragging with it the dismayed and struggling ourang-outangs, and leaving them suspended in mid-air between the sky-light and the floor. Hop-Frog, clinging to the chain as it rose, still maintained his relative position in respect to the eight maskers, and still (as if nothing were the matter) continued to thrust his torch down toward them, as though endeavouring to discover who they were.

So thoroughly astonished was the whole company at this ascent, that a dead silence, of about a minute's duration, ensued. It was broken by just such a low, harsh, *grating* sound, as had before attracted the attention of the king and his councillors when the former threw the wine in the face of Trippetta. But, on the present occasion, there could be no question as to *whence* the sound issued. It came from the fang-like teeth of the dwarf, who ground them and gnashed them as he foamed at the mouth, and glared, with an expression of maniacal rage, into the upturned countenances of the king and his seven companions.

"Ah, ha!" said at length the infuriated jester. "Ah, ha! I begin to see who these people *are*, now!" Here, pretending to scrutinize the king more closely, he held the flambeau to the flaxen coat which enveloped him, and which instantly burst into a sheet of vivid flame. In less than half a minute the whole eight ourang-outangs were blazing fiercely, amid the shrieks of the multitude who gazed at them from below, horror-stricken, and without the power to render them the slightest assistance.

At length the flames, suddenly increasing in virulence, forced the jester to climb higher up the chain, to be out of their reach; and, as he made this movement, the crowd again sank, for a brief instant, into silence. The dwarf seized his opportunity, and once more spoke:

"I now see *distinctly*," he said, "what manner of people these maskers are. They are a great king and his seven privy-councillors,—a king who does not scruple to strike a defenceless girl, and his seven councillors who abet him in the outrage. As for myself, I am simply Hop-Frog, the jester—and *this is my last jest.*"

Owing to the high combustibility of both the flax and the tar to which it adhered, the dwarf had scarcely made an end of his brief speech before the work of vengeance was complete. The eight corpses swung in their chains, a fetid, blackened, hideous, and indistinguishable mass. The cripple hurled his torch at them, clambered leisurely to the ceiling, and disappeared through the sky-light.

It is supposed that Trippetta, stationed on the roof of the saloon, had been the accomplice of her friend in his fiery revenge, and that, together, they effected their escape to their own country; for neither was seen again.

RAY RUSSELL *is a Californian who edited* Playboy *for several years and has written some superb fantasy fiction, including a first-rate novel,* The Case Against Satan, *which told essentially the same story as Blatty's* The Exorcist—*only Russell did it first and much better. "Sardonicus" is a wonderful neo-Gothic story, polished and understated in its terrors, and all the more disturbing for that reason. It was made into an interesting film,* Mr. Sardonicus.

Sardonicus

BY RAY RUSSELL

I
An S of Vulgar Pretension

In the late summer of the year 18—, a gratifying series of professional successes had brought me to a state of such fatigue that I had begun seriously to contemplate a long rest on the Continent. I had not enjoyed a proper holiday in nearly three years, for in addition to my regular practice, I had been deeply involved in a program of research, and so rewarding had been my progress in this special work (it concerned the ligaments and muscles, and could, it was my hope, be beneficially applied to certain varieties of paralysis) that I was loth to leave the city for more than a week at a time. Being unmarried, I lacked a solicitous wife who might have expressed concern over my health; thus it was that I had overworked myself to a point that a holiday had become absolutely essential to my well-being; hence, the letter which was put in my hand one morning near the end of that summer was most welcome.

When it was first presented to me by my valet, at breakfast, I turned it over and over, feeling the weight of its fine paper which was almost of the heaviness and stiffness of parchment; pondering the large seal of scarlet wax upon which was imprinted a device of such complexity that it was difficult to decipher; examining finally the hand in which the address had been written: *Sir Robert*

Cargrave, Harley Street, London. It was a feminine hand, that much was certain, and there was a curious touch of familiarity to its delicacy as well as to its clearness (this last an admirable quality far too uncommon in the handwriting of ladies). The fresh clarity of that hand—and where had I seen it before?—bespoke a directness that seemed contrary to the well-nigh unfathomable ornamentation of the seal, which, upon closer and more concentrated perusal, I at length concluded to be no more than a single *S*, but an *S* whose writhing curls seemed almost to grin presumptuously at one, an *S* which seemed to be constructed of little else than these grins, an *S* of such vulgar pretension that I admit to having felt vexed for an instant, and then, in the next instant, foolish at my own vexation—for surely, I admonished myself, there are things a deal more vexing than a seal which you have encountered without distemper?

Smiling at my foible, I continued to weigh the letter in my hand, searching my mind for a friend or acquaintance whose name began with *S*. There was old Shipley of the College of Surgeons; there was Lord Henry Stanton, my waggish and witty friend; and that was the extent of it. Was it Harry? He was seldom in one place for very long and was a faithful and gifted letter writer. Yet Harry's bold hand was far from effeminate, and, moreover, he would not use such a seal—unless it were as a lark, as an antic jest between friends. My valet had told me, when he put the letter in my hand, that it had come not by the post but by special messenger, and although this intelligence had not struck me as remarkable at the time, it now fed my curiosity and I broke that vexing seal and unfolded the stiff, crackling paper.

The message within was written in that same clear, faintly familiar hand. My eye first travelled to the end to find the signature, but that signature—*Madam S.*—told me nothing, for I knew of no Madam S. among my circle.

I read the letter. It is before me now as I set down this account, and I shall copy it out verbatim:

"My dear Sir Robert,

"It has been close to seven years since last we met—indeed, at that time you were not yet Sir Robert at all, but plain Robert Cargrave (although some talk of imminent knighthood was in the air), and so I wonder if you will remember Maude Randall?"

Remember Maude Randall! Dear Maude of the bell-like voice, of the chestnut hair and large brown eyes, of a temperament of such sweetness and vivacity that the young men of London had eyes for no one else. She was of good family, but during a stay in Paris there had been something about injudicious speculation by her father that had diminished the family fortunes to such an extent that the wretched man had taken his own life and the Randalls had vanished from London society altogether. Maude, or so I had heard, had married a foreign gentleman and had remained in Europe. It had been sad news, for no young man of London had ever had more doting eyes for Maude than had I, and it had pleased my fancy to think that my feelings were, at least in part, reciprocated. Remember Maude Randall? Yes, yes, I almost said aloud. And now, seven years later, she was "Madam S.," writing in that same hand I had seen countless times on invitations. I continued to read:

"I often think of you, for—although it may not be seemly to say it—the company of few gentlemen used to please me so much as yours, and the London soirees given by my dear mother, at which you were present, are among my most cherished recollections now. But there! Frankness was always my failing, as Mother used to remind me. She, dear kind lady, survived less than a year after my poor father died, but I suppose you know this.

"I am quite well, and we live in great comfort here, although we receive but rarely and are content with our own company most of the time. Mr. S. is a gracious gentleman, but of quiet and retiring disposition, and throngs of people, parties, balls, &c., are retrograde to his temperament; thus it is a special joy to me that he has expressly asked me to invite you here to the castle for a fortnight—or, if I may give you his exact words: 'For a fortnight at least, but howsoever long as it please Sir Robert to stay among such drab folk as he will think us.' (You see, I told you he was gracious!)"

I must have frowned while reading, for the words of Mr. S. were not so much gracious, I thought, as egregious, and as vulgar as his absurd seal. Still, I held these feelings in check, for I knew that my emotions towards this man were not a little coloured by jealousy. He, after all, had wooed and won Maude Randall, a young lady of discernment and fine sensibilities: could she have been capable of wedding an obsequious boor? I thought it not

likely. And a castle! Such romantic grandeur! ". . . Invite you
here to the castle . . ." she had written, but where was "here"?
The letter's cover, since it had not come by the post, offered no
clue; therefore I read on:

"It was indeed, only yesterday, in the course of conversation, that I
was recalling my old life in London, and mentioned your name. Mr. S.,
I thought, was, of a sudden, interested. 'Robert Cargrave?' he said.
'There is a well-known physician of that name, but I do not imagine it is
the same gentleman.' I laughed and told him it *was* the same gentleman,
and that I had known you before you had become so illustrious. 'Did you
know him well?' Mr. S. then asked me, and you will think me silly, but
I must tell you that for a moment I assumed him to be jealous! Such was
not the case, however, as further conversation proved. I told him you had
been a friend of my family's and a frequent guest at our house. 'This is
a most happy coincidence,' he said. 'I have long desired to meet Sir
Robert Cargrave, and your past friendship with him furnishes you with
an excellent opportunity to invite him here for a holiday.'

"And so, Sir Robert, I am complying with his request—and at the same
time obeying the dictates of my own inclination—by most cordially
inviting you to visit us for as long as you choose. I entreat you to come,
for we see so few people here and it would be a great pleasure to talk
with someone from the old days and to hear the latest London gossip.
Suffer me, then, to receive a letter from you at once. Mr. S. does not
trust the post, hence I have sent this by a servant of ours who was to be
in London on special business; please relay your answer by way of him—"

I rang for my man. "Is the messenger who delivered this letter
waiting for a reply?" I asked.
"He is sitting in the vestibule, Sir Robert," he said.
"You should have told me."
"Yes, sir."
"At any rate, send him in now. I wish to see him."
My man left, and it took me but a minute to dash off a quick
note of acceptance. It was ready for the messenger when he was
ushered into the room. I addressed him: "You are in the employ
of Madam—" I realized for the first time that I did not know her
husband's name.
The servant—a taciturn fellow with Slavic features—spoke in a
thick accent: "I am in the employ of Mr. Sardonicus, sir."
Sardonicus! A name as flamboyant as the seal, I thought to

myself. "Then deliver this note, if you please, to Madam Sardonicus, immediately you return."

He bowed slightly and took the note from my hand. "I shall deliver it to my master straightway, sir," he said.

His manner nettled me. I corrected him. "To your mistress," I said coldly.

"Madam Sardonicus will receive your message, sir," he said.

I dismissed him, and only then did it strike me that I had not the faintest idea where the castle of Mr. Sardonicus was located. I referred once again to Maude's letter:

". . . Please relay your answer by way of him and pray make it affirmative, for I do hope to make your stay in_____a pleasant one."

I consulted an atlas. The locality she mentioned, I discovered, was a district in a remote and mountainous region of Bohemia.

Filled with anticipation, I finished my breakfast with renewed appetite, and that very afternoon began to make arrangements for my journey.

II
The Sight of a Giant Skull

I am not—as my friend Harry Stanton is—fond of travel for its own sake. Harry has often chided me on this account, calling me a dry-as-dust academician and "an incorrigible Londoner"—which I suppose I am. For, in point of fact, few things are more tiresome to me than ships and trains and carriages; and although I have found deep enjoyment and spiritual profit in foreign cities, having arrived, the tedium of travel itself has often made me think twice before starting out on a long voyage.

Still, in less than a month after I had answered Maude's invitation, I found myself in her adopted homeland. Sojourning from London to Paris, thence to Berlin, finally to Bohemia, I was met at_____by a coachman who spoke imperfect English but who managed, in his solemn fashion, to make known to me that he was a member of the staff at Castle Sardonicus. He placed at my disposal a coach drawn by two horses, and after taking my bags, proceeded to drive me on the last leg of my journey.

Alone in the coach, I shivered, for the air was brisk and I was very tired. The road was full of ruts and stones, and the trip was far from smooth. Neither did I derive much pleasure by bending my glance to the view afforded by the windows, for the night was dark, and the country was, at any rate, wild and raw, not made for serene contemplation. The only sounds were the clatter of hooves and wheels, the creak of the coach, and the harsh, unmusical cries of unseen birds.

"We receive but rarely," Maude had written, and now I told myself—Little wonder! in this ragged and, one might say, uninhabitable place, far from the graces of civilized society, who indeed is there to *be* received, or, for the matter of that, to receive one? I sighed, for the desolate landscape and the thought of what might prove a holiday devoid of refreshing incident had combined to cloak my already wearied spirit in a melancholic humour.

It was when I was in this condition that Castle Sardonicus met my eye—a dense, hunched outline at first, then, with an instantaneous flicker of moonlight, a great gaping death's head, the sight of which made me inhale sharply. With the exhalation, I chuckled at myself. "Come, come, Sir Robert," I inwardly chided, "it is, after all, but a castle, and you are not a green girl who starts at shadows and quails at midnight stories!"

The castle is situated at the terminus of a long and upward-winding mountain road. It presents a somewhat forbidding aspect to the world, for there is little about it to suggest gaiety or warmth or any of those qualities that might assure the wayfarer of welcome. Rather, this vast edifice of stone exudes an austerity, cold and repellent, a hint of ancient mysteries long buried, an effluvium of medieval dankness and decay. At night, and most particularly on nights when the moon is slim or cloud-enshrouded, it is a heavy blot upon the horizon, a shadow only, without feature save for its many-turreted outline; and should the moon be temporarily released from her cloudy confinement, her fugitive rays lend scant comfort, for they but serve to throw the castle into sudden, startling chiaroscuro, its windows fleetingly assuming the appearance of sightless though all-seeing orbs, its portcullis becoming for an instant a gaping mouth, its entire form striking the physical and the mental eye as would the sight of a giant skull.

But, though the castle had revealed itself to my sight, it was a full quarter of an hour before the coach had creaked its way up the steep and tortuous road to the great gate that barred the castle grounds from intruders. Of iron the gate was wrought—black it seemed in the scant illumination—and composed of intricate twists that led, every one of them, to a central, huge device, of many curves, which in the infrequent glints of moonglow appeared to smile metallically down, but which, upon gathering my reason about me, I made out to be no more than an enlarged edition of that presumptuous seal: a massive single *S*. Behind it, at the end of the rutted road, stood the castle itself—dark, save for lights in two of its many windows.

Some words in a foreign tongue passed between my coachman and a person behind the gate. The gate was unlocked from within and swung open slowly, with a long rising shriek of rusted hinges; and the coach passed through.

As we drew near, the door of the castle was flung open and cheery light spilled out upon the road. The portcullis, which I had previously marked, was evidently a remnant from older days and now inactive. The coach drew to a halt, and I was greeted with great gravity by a butler whom I saw to be he who had carried Maude's invitation to London. I proffered him a nod of recognition. He acknowledged this and said, "Sir Robert, Madam Sardonicus awaits you, and if you will be good enough to follow me, I will take you to her presence." The coachman took charge of my bags, and I followed the butler into the castle.

It dated, I thought, to the Twelfth or Thirteenth Century. Suits of armour—priceless relics, I ascertained them to be—stood about the vast halls; tapestries were in evidence throughout; strong, heavy, richly carved furniture was everywhere. The walls were of time-defying stone, great grey blocks of it. I was led into a kind of salon, with comfortable chairs, a tea table, and a spinet. Maude rose to greet me.

"Sir Robert," she said softly, without smiling. "How good to see you at last."

I took her hand. "Dear lady," said I, "we meet again."

"You are looking well and prosperous," she said.

"I am in good health, but just now rather tired from the journey."

She gave me leave to sit, and did so herself, venturing the opinion that a meal and some wine would soon restore me. "Mr. Sardonicus will join us soon," she added.

I spoke of her appearance, saying that she looked not a day older than when I last saw her in London. This was true, in regard to her physical self, for her face bore not a line, her skin was of the same freshness, and her glorious chestnut hair was still rich in colour and gleaming with health. But what I did not speak of was the change in her spirit. She who had been so gay and vivacious, the delight of soirees, was now distant and aloof, of serious mien, unsmiling. I was sorry to see this, but attributed it to the seven years that had passed since her carefree girlhood, to the loss of her loved parents, and even to the secluded life she now spent in this place.

"I am eager to meet your husband," I said.

"And he, Sir Robert, is quite eager to meet you," Maude assured me. "He will be down presently. Meanwhile, do tell me how you have fared in the world."

I spoke, with some modesty, I hope, of my successes in my chosen field, of the knighthood I had received from the Crown; I described my London apartment, laboratory, and office; I made mention of certain mutual friends, and generally gave her news of London life; speaking particularly of the theatre (for I knew Maude had loved it) and describing Mr. Macready's farewell appearance as Macbeth at the Haymarket. When Maude had last been in London, there had been rumours of making an opera house out of Covent Garden theatre, and I told her that those plans had been carried through. I spoke of the London premiere of Mr. Verdi's latest piece at Her Majesty's. At my mention of these theatres and performances, her eyes lit up, but she was not moved to comment until I spoke of the opera.

"The opera!" she sighed. "Oh, Sir Robert, if you could but know how I miss it. The excitement of a premiere, the ladies and gentlemen in their finery, the thrilling sounds of the overture, and then the curtain rising—" She broke off, as if ashamed of her momentary transport. "But I receive all the latest scores, and derive great satisfaction from playing and singing them to myself. I must order the new Verdi from Rome. It is called *Ernani*, you say?"

I nodded, adding, "With your permission, I will attempt to play some of the more distinctive airs."

"Oh, pray do, Sir Robert!" she said.

"You will find them, perhaps, excessively modern and dissonant." I sat down at the spinet and played—just passably, I fear, and with some improvisation when I could not remember the exact notes—a potpourri of melodies from the opera.

She applauded my playing. I urged her to play also, for she was an accomplished keyboard artist and possessed an agreeable voice, as well. She complied by playing the minuet from *Don Giovanni* and then singing the *"Voi che sapete"* from *Le Nozze di Figaro*. As I stood over her, watching her delicate hands move over the keys, hearing the pure, clear tones of her voice, all my old feelings washed over me in a rush, and my eyes smarted at the unalloyed sweetness and goodness of this lady. When she asked me to join her in the duet, *"Là ci darem la mano,"* I agreed to do it, although my voice is less than ordinary. On the second singing of the word *"mano"*—"hand"—I was seized by a vagrant impulse and took her left hand in my own. Her playing was hampered, of course, and the music limped for a few measures; and then, my face burning, I released her hand and we finished out the duet. Wisely, she neither rebuked me for my action nor gave me encouragement; rather, she acted as if the rash gesture had never been committed.

To mask my embarrassment, I now embarked upon some light chatter, designed to ease whatever tension existed between us; I spoke of many things, foolish things, for the most part, and even asked if Mr. Sardonicus had later demonstrated any of the jealousy she had said, in her letter, that she had erroneously thought him to have exhibited. She laughed at this—and it brightened the room, for it was the first time her face had abandoned its grave expression; indeed, I was taken by the thought that this was the first display of human merriment I had marked since stepping into the coach—and she said, "Oh, no! To the contrary, Mr. Sardonicus said that the closer we had been in the old days, the more he would be pleased."

This seemed an odd and even coarse thing for a man to say to his wife, and I jovially replied: "I hope Mr. Sardonicus was smiling when he said that."

At once, Maude's own smile vanished from her face. She looked away from me and began to talk of other things. I was dumbfounded. Had my innocent remark given offence? It seemed not possible. A moment later, however, I knew the reason for her strange action, for a tall gentleman entered the room with a gliding step, and one look at him explained many things.

III

To Smile Forever

"Sir Robert Cargrave?" he asked, but he spoke with difficulty, certain sounds—such as the *b* in Robert and the *v* in Cargrave—being almost impossible for him to utter. To shape these sounds,

the lips must be used, and the gentleman before me was the victim
of some terrible affliction that had caused his lips to be pulled
perpetually apart from each other, baring his teeth in a continuous
ghastly smile. It was the same humourless grin I had seen once
before: on the face of a person in the last throes of lockjaw. We
physicians have a name for that chilling grimace, a Latin name,
and as it entered my mind, it seemed to dispel yet another
mystery, for the term we use to describe the lockjaw smile is: *risus
sardonicus*. A pallor approaching phosphorescence completed his
astonishing appearance.

"Yes," I replied, covering my shock at the sight of his face. "Do
I have the pleasure of addressing Mr. Sardonicus?"

We shook hands. After an exchange of courtesies, he said, "I
have ordered dinner to be served in the large dining hall one hour
hence. In the meantime, my valet will show you to your rooms,
for I am sure you will wish to refresh yourself after your journey."

"You are most kind." The valet appeared—a man of grave
countenance, like the butler and the coachman—and I followed
him up a long flight of stone stairs. As I walked behind him, I
reflected on the unsmiling faces in this castle, and no longer were
they things of wonder. For who would be disposed to smile under
the same roof with him who must smile forever? The most
spontaneous of smiles would seem a mockery in the presence of
that afflicted face. I was filled with pity for Maude's husband: of
all God's creatures, man alone is blest with the ability to smile;
but for the master of Castle Sardonicus, God's great blessing had
become a terrible curse. As a physician, my pity was tempered
with professional curiosity. His smile resembled the *risus* of
lockjaw, but lockjaw is a mortal disease, and Mr. Sardonicus, his
skullish grin notwithstanding, was very much alive. I felt shame
for some of my earlier uncharitable thoughts towards this
gentleman, for surely such an unfortunate could be forgiven much.
What bitterness must fester in his breast; what sharp despair gnaw
at his innards!

My rooms were spacious and certainly as comfortable as this
dank stone housing could afford. A hot tub was prepared, for
which my tired and dusty frame was most grateful. As I lay in it,
I began to experience the pleasant pangs of appetite. I looked
forward to dinner. After my bath, I put on fresh linen and a suit
of evening clothes. Then, taking from my bag two small gifts for
my host and hostess—a bottle of scent for Maude, a box of cigars

for her husband—I left my rooms.

I was not so foolish as to expect to find my way, unaided, to the main dining hall; but since I was early, I intended to wander a bit and let the ancient magnificence of the castle impress itself upon me.

Tapestries bearing my host's *S* were frequently displayed. They were remarkably new, their colours fresh, unlike the faded grandeur of their fellow tapestries. From this—and from Mr. Sardonicus' lack of title—I deduced that the castle had not been inherited through a family line, but merely purchased by him, probably from an impoverished nobleman. Though not titled, Mr. Sardonicus evidently possessed enormous wealth. I pondered its source. My ponderings were interrupted by the sound of Maude's voice.

I looked up. The acoustical effects in old castles are often strange—I had marked them in our own English castles—and though I stood near neither room nor door of any kind, I could hear Maude speaking in a distressed tone. I was standing at an open window which overlooked a kind of courtyard. Across this court, a window was likewise open. I took this to be the window of Maude's room; her voice was in some way being amplified and transported by the circumstantial shape of the courtyard and the positions of the two windows. By listening very attentively, I could make out most of her words.

She was saying, "I shan't. You must not ask me. It is unseemly." And then the voice of her husband replied: "You shall and will, madam. In my castle, it is I who decide what is seemly or unseemly. Not you." I was embarrassed at overhearing this private discussion on what was obviously a painful subject, so I made to draw away from the window that I might hear no more, but was restrained by the sound of my own name on Maude's lips. "I have treated Sir Robert with courtesy," she said. "You must treat him with more than courtesy," Mr. Sardonicus responded. "You must treat him with warmth. You must rekindle in his breast those affections he felt for you in other days . . ."

I could listen no longer. The exchange was vile. I drew away from the window. What manner of creature was this Sardonicus who threw his wife into the arms of other men? As a practitioner of medicine, a man dedicated to healing the ills of humankind, I had brought myself to learn many things about the minds of men, as well as about their bodies. I fully believed that, in some future time, physicians would heal the body by way of the mind, for it is in that *terra incognita* that all secrets lie hidden. I knew that love has many masks; masks of submission and of oppression; and even more terrible masks that make Nature a stranger to herself and "turn the truth of God into a lie," as St. Paul wrote. There is even a kind of love, if it can be elevated by that name, that derives its keenest pleasure from the sight of the beloved in the arms of another. These are unpleasant observations, which may one day be codified and studied by healers, but which, until then, may not be thought on for too long, lest the mind grow morbid and stagger under its load of repugnance.

With a heavy heart, I sought out a servant and asked to be taken to the dining hall. It was some distance away, and by the time I arrived there, Sardonicus and his lady were already at table, awaiting me. He arose, and with that revolting smile, indicated a chair; she also arose, and took my arm, addressing me as "Dear Sir Robert" and leading me to my place. Her touch, which at any previous time would have gladdened me, I now found distinctly not to my liking.

A hollow joviality hung over the dinner table throughout the meal. Maude's laughter struck me as giddy and false; Sardonicus drank too much wine and his speech became even more indistinct. I contrived to talk on trivial subjects, repeating some anecdotes about the London theatre which I had hitherto related to Maude, and describing Mr. Macready's interpretation of Macbeth.

"Some actors," said Sardonicus, "interpret the Scottish chieftain as a creature compounded of pure evil, unmingled with good qualities of any kind. Such interpretations are often criticized by those who feel no human being can be so unremittingly evil. Do you agree, Sir Robert?"

"No," I said, evenly; then, looking Sardonicus full in the face, I added, "I believe it is entirely possible for a man to possess not a single one of the virtues, to be a demon in human flesh." Quickly, I embarked upon a discussion of the character of Iago, who took ghoulish delight in tormenting his fellow man.

The dinner was, I suppose, first rate, and the wine an honourable vintage, but I confess to tasting little of what was placed before me. At the end of the meal, Maude left us for a time and Sardonicus escorted me into the library, whither he ordered brandy to be brought. He opened the box of cigars, expressed his admiration of them and gratitude for them, and offered them to me. I took one and we both smoked. The smoking of the cigar made Sardonicus look even more grotesque: being unable to hold it in his lips, he clenched it in his constantly visible teeth, creating an unique spectacle. Brandy was served; I partook of it freely, though I am not customarily given to heavy drinking, for I now deemed it to be beneficial to my dampened spirits.

"You used the word 'ghoulish' a few moments ago, Sir Robert," said Sardonicus. "It is one of those words one uses so easily in conversation—one utters it without stopping to think of its meaning. But, in my opinion, it is not a word to be used lightly. When one uses it, one should have in one's mind a firm, unwavering picture of a ghoul."

"Perhaps I did," I said.

"Perhaps," he admitted. "And perhaps not. Let us obtain a precise definition of the word." He arose and walked to one of the bookcases that lined the room's walls. He reached for a large two-volume dictionary. "Let me see," he murmured. "We desire Volume One, from *A* to *M*, do we not? Now then: 'ghee' . . . 'gherkin' . . . 'ghetto' . . . 'ghoom' (an odd word, eh, Sir Robert? 'To search for game in the dark') . . . 'ghost' . . . ah, 'ghoul!' 'Among Eastern nations, an imaginary evil being who robs graves and feeds upon corpses.' One might say, then, that he ghooms?" Sardonicus chuckled. He returned to his chair and helped himself to more brandy. "When you described Iago's actions as 'ghoulish,'" he continued, "did you think of him as the inhabitant of an Eastern nation? Or an imaginary being as against the reality of Othello and Desdemona? And did you mean seriously to suggest that it was his custom to rob graves and then to feed upon the disgusting nourishment he found therein?"

"I used the word in a figurative sense," I replied.

"Ah," said Sardonicus. "That is because you are English and do not believe in ghouls. Were you a Middle-European, as am I, you would believe in their existence, and would not be tempted to use the word other than literally. In my country—I was born in Poland—we understood such things. I, in point of fact, have known a ghoul." He paused for a moment and looked at me, then said, "You English are so blasé. Nothing shocks you. I sit here and tell you a thing of dreadful import and you do not even blink your eyes. Can it be because you do not believe me?"

"It would be churlish to doubt the word of my host," I replied.

"And an Englishman may be many things, but never a churl,

eh, Sir Robert? Let me refill your glass, my friend, and then let me tell you about ghouls—which, by the way, are by no means imaginary, as that stupid lexicon would have us think, and which are not restricted to Eastern nations. Neither do they— necessarily—feed upon carrion flesh, although they are interested, *most* interested, in the repellent contents of graves. Let me tell you a story from my own country, Sir Robert, a story that—if I have any gift at all as a spinner of tales—will create in you a profound belief in ghouls. You will be entertained, I hope, but I also hope you will add to your learning. You will learn, for example, how low a human being can sink, how truly *monstrous* a man can become."

IV
A Graveyard Tale

"You must transport your mind," said Sardonicus, "back a few years and to a rural region of my homeland. You must become acquainted with a family of country folk—hard-working, law-abiding, God-fearing, of moderate means—the head of which was a simple, good man named Tadeusz Boleslawski. He was an even-tempered personage, kindly disposed to all men, the loving husband of a devoted wife and father of five strong boys. He was also a firm churchman, seldom even taking the Lord's name in vain. The painted women who plied their trade in certain elaborate houses of the nearest large city, Warsaw, held no attraction for him, though several of his masculine neighbours, on their visits to the metropolis, succumbed to such blandishments with tidal regularity. Neither did he drink in excess: a glass of beer with his evening meal, a toast or two in wine on special occasions. No: hard liquor, strong language, fast women—these were not the weaknesses of Tadeusz Boleslawski. His weakness was gambling.

"Every month he would make the trip to Warsaw, to sell his produce at the markets and to buy certain necessaries for his home. While his comrades visited the drinking and wenching houses, Tadeusz would attend strictly to business affairs—except for one minor deviation. He would purchase a lottery ticket, place it securely in a small, tight pocket of his best waistcoat—which he wore only on Sundays and on his trips to the city—then put it completely out of his mind until the following month, when, on reaching the city, he would remove it from his pocket and closely scan the posted list of winners. Then, after methodically tearing the ticket to shreds (for Tadeusz never lived to win a lottery), he would purchase another. This was a ritual with him; he performed it every month for twenty-three years, and the fact that he never won did not discourage him. His wife knew of this habit, but since it was the good man's only flaw, she never remarked upon it."

Outside, I could hear the wind howling dismally. I took more brandy as Sardonicus continued:

"Years passed; three of the five sons married; two (Henryk and Marek, the youngest) were still living with their parents, when Tadeusz—who had been of sturdy health—collapsed one day in the fields and died. I will spare you an account of the family's grief; how the married sons returned with their wives to attend the obsequies; of the burial in the small graveyard of that community. The good man had left few possessions, but these few were divided, according to his written wish, among his survivors, with the largest share going, of course, to the eldest son. Though this was custom, the other sons could not help feeling a trifle disgruntled, but they held their peace for the most part—especially the youngest, Marek, who was perhaps the most amiable of them and a lad who was by nature quiet and interested in improving his lot through the learning he found in books.

"Imagine, sir, the amazement of the widow when, a full three weeks after the interment of her husband, she received word by men returning from Warsaw that the lottery ticket Tadeusz had purchased had now been selected as the winner. It was a remarkable irony, of course, but conditions had grown hard for the poor woman, and would grow harder with her husband dead, so she had no time to reflect upon that irony. She set about looking through her husband's possessions for the lottery ticket. Drawers were emptied upon the floor; boxes and cupboards were ransacked; the family Bible was shaken out; years before, Tadeusz had been in the habit of temporarily hiding money under a loose floorboard in the bedroom—this cavity was thoroughly but vainly plumbed. The sons were sent for: among the few personal effects they had been bequeathed, did the ticket languish there? In the snuff box? In any article of clothing?

"And at that, Sir Robert, the eldest son leapt up. 'An article of clothing!' he cried. 'Father always wore his Sunday waistcoat to the city when he purchased the lottery tickets—the very waistcoat in which he was buried!'

" 'Yes, yes!' the other sons chorused, saving Marek, and plans began to be laid for the exhuming of the dead man. But the widow spoke firmly: 'Your father rests peacefully,' she said. 'He must not be disturbed. No amount of gold would soothe our hearts if we disturbed him.' The sons protested with vehemence, but the widow stood her ground. 'No son of mine will profane his father's grave—unless he first kills his mother!' Grumbling, the sons withdrew their plans. But that night, Marek awoke to find his mother gone from the house. He was frightened, for this was not like her. Intuition sent him to the graveyard, where he found her, keeping a lonely vigil over the grave of her husband, protecting him from the greed of grave robbers. Marek implored her to come out of the cold, to return home; she at first refused; only when Marek offered to keep vigil all night himself did she relent and return home, leaving her youngest son to guard the grave from profanation.

"Marek waited a full hour. Then he produced from under his shirt a small shovel. He was a strong boy, and the greed of a youngest son who has been deprived of inheritance lent added strength to his arms. He dug relentlessly, stopping seldom for rest, until finally the coffin was uncovered. He raised the creaking lid. An overpowering foetor filled his nostrils and nearly made him faint. Gathering courage, he searched the pockets of the mouldering waistcoat.

"The moon proved to be his undoing, Sir Robert. For suddenly its rays, hitherto hidden, struck the face of his father, and at the sight of that face, the boy recoiled and went reeling against the wall of the grave, the breath forced from his body. Now, you must know that the mere sight of his father—even in an advanced state of decomposition—he had steeled himself to withstand; but what he had *not* foreseen—"

Here, Sardonicus leaned close to me and his pallid, grinning head filled my vision. "What he had not foreseen, my dear sir, was that the face of his father, in the rigour of death, would look directly and hideously upon him." Sardonicus' voice became an ophidian hiss. "And, Sir Robert," he added, "most terrible and most unforeseen of all, the dead lips were drawn back from the teeth *in a constant and soul-shattering smile!*"

V
The Remembrance of that Night

I know not whether it was the ghastliness of his story, or the sight of his hideous face so close to mine, or the cheerless keening of the wind outside, or the brandy I had consumed, or all of these in combination; but when Sardonicus uttered those last words, my heart was clutched by a cold hand, and for a moment—a long moment ripped from the texture of time—I was convinced beyond doubt and beyond logic that the face I looked into was the face of that cadaver, reanimated by obscure arts, to walk among the living, dead though not dead.

The moment of horror passed, at length, and reason triumphed. Sardonicus, considerably affected by his own tale, sat back in his chair, trembling. Before too long, he spoke again:

"The remembrance of that night, Sir Robert, though it is now many years past, fills me still with dread. You will appreciate this when I tell you what you have perhaps already guessed—that *I* am that ghoulish son, Marek."

I had not guessed it; but since I had no wish to tell him that I had for an instant thought he was the dead father, I said nothing.

"When my senses returned," said Sardonicus, "I scrambled out of the grave and ran as swiftly as my limbs would carry me. I had reached the gate of the graveyard when I was smitten by the fact that I had not accomplished the purpose of my mission—the lottery ticket remained in my father's pocket!"

"But surely—" I started to say.

"Surely I ignored the fact and continued to run? No, Sir Robert. My terror notwithstanding, I halted, and forced myself to retrace those hasty steps. My fear notwithstanding, I descended once more into that noisome grave. My disgust notwithstanding, I reached into the pocket of my decaying father's waistcoat and extracted the ticket! I need hardly add that, this time, I averted my eyes from his face.

"But the horror was not behind me. Indeed, it had only begun. I reached my home at a late hour, and my family was asleep. For this I was grateful, since my clothes were covered with soil and I still trembled from my fearful experience. I quietly poured water into a basin and prepared to wash some of the graveyard dirt from my face and hands. In performing my ablutions, I looked up into a mirror—*and screamed so loudly as to wake the entire house!*

"My face was as you see it now, a replica of my dead father's: the lips drawn back in a perpetual, mocking grin. I tried to close my mouth. I could not. The muscles were immovable, as if held in the gelid rigour of death. I could hear my family stirring at my scream, and since I did not wish them to look upon me, I ran from the house—never, Sir Robert, to return.

"As I wandered the rural roads, my mind sought the cause of the affliction that had been visited upon me. Though but a country lad, I had read much and I had a blunt, rational mind that was not susceptible to the easy explanations of the supernatural. I would not believe that God had placed a malediction upon me to punish me for my act. I would not believe that some black force from beyond the grave had reached out to stamp my face. At length, I began to believe it was the massive shock that had forced my face to its present state, and that my great guilt had helped to shape it even as my father's dead face was shaped. Shock and guilt: strong powers not from God above or the Fiend below, but from within my own breast, my own brain, my own soul.

"Let me bring this history to a hasty close, Sir Robert. You need only know that, despite my blighted face, I redeemed the lottery ticket and thus gained an amount of money that will not seem large to you, but which was more than I had ever seen before that time. It was the fulcrum from which I plied the lever that was to make me, by dint of shrewd speculation, one of the richest men in Central Europe. Naturally, I sought out physicians and begged them to restore my face to its previous state. None succeeded, though I offered them vast sums. My face remained fixed in this damnable unceasing smile, and my heart knew the most profound despair imaginable. I could not even pronounce my own name! By a dreadful irony, the initial letters of my first and last names were impossible for my frozen lips to form. This seemed the final indignity. I will admit to you that, at this period, I was perilously near the brink of self-destruction. But the spirit of preservation prevailed, and I was saved from that course. I changed my name. I had read of the *risus sardonicus*, and its horrible aptness appealed to my bitter mind, so I became Sardonicus—a name I can pronounce with no difficulty."

Sardonicus paused and sipped his brandy. "You are wondering," he then said, "in what way my story concerns you."

I could guess, but I said: "I am."

"Sir Robert," he said, "you are known throughout the medical world. Most laymen, perhaps, have not heard of you; but a layman such as I, a layman who avidly follows the medical journals for tidings of any recent discoveries in the curing of paralyzed muscles, has heard of you again and again. Your researches into these problems have earned you high professional regard; indeed, they have earned you a knighthood. For some time, it has been in my mind to visit London and seek you out. I have consulted many physicians, renowned men—Keller in Berlin, Morignac in Paris, Buonagente in Milan—and none have been able to help me. My despair has been utter. It prevented me from making the long journey to England. But when I heard—sublime coincidence!— that my own wife had been acquainted with you, I took heart. Sir Robert, I entreat you to heal me, to lift from me this curse, to make me look once more like a man, that I may walk in the sun again, among my fellow human beings, as one of them, rather than as a fearsome gargoyle to be shunned and feared and ridiculed. Surely you cannot, *will* not deny me?"

My feelings for Sardonicus, pendulum-like, again swung towards his favour. His story, his plight, had rent my heart, and I reverted to my earlier opinion that such a man should be forgiven much. The strange overheard conversation between Maude and him was momentarily forgotten. I said, "I will examine you, Mr. Sardonicus. You were right to ask me. We must never abandon hope."

He clasped his hands together. "Ah, sir! May you be blest forever!"

I performed the examination then and there. Although I did not tell him this, never had I encountered muscles as rigid as those of his face. They could only be compared to stone, so inflexible were they. Still, I said, "Tomorrow we will begin treatment. Heat and massage."

"These have been tried," he said, hopelessly.

"Massage differs from one pair of hands to another," I replied. "I have had success with my own techniques, and therefore place faith in them. Be comforted then, sir, and share my faith."

He seized my hand in his. "I do," he said. "I must. For if you— if even *you*, Sir Robert Cargrave, fail me . . ." He did not complete the sentence, but his eyes assumed an aspect so bitter, so full of hate, so strangely cold yet flaming, that they floated in my dreams that night.

VI

An Abyss of Humiliation and Shame

I slept not well, awakening many times in a fever compounded of drink and turbulent emotions. When the first rays of morning crept onto my pillow, I arose, little refreshed. After a cold tub and a light breakfast in my room, I went below to the salon whence music issued. Maude was already there, playing a pretty little piece upon the spinet. She looked up and greeted me. "Good morning, Sir Robert. Do you know the music of Mr. Gottschalk? He is an American pianist: this is his 'Maiden's Blush.' Amiable, is it not?"

"Most amiable," I replied, dutifully, although I was in no mood for the embroideries of politesse.

Maude soon finished the piece and closed the album. She turned to me and said, in a serious tone, "I have been told what you are going to do for my poor husband, Sir Robert. I can scarce express my gratitude."

"There is no need to express it," I assured her. "As a physician—as well as your old friend—I could not do less. I hope you understand, however, that a cure is not a certainty. I will try, and I will try to the limit of my powers, but beyond that I can promise nothing."

Her eyes shone with supplication: "Oh, cure him, Sir Robert! That I beg of you!"

"I understand your feelings, madam," I said. "It is fitting that you should hope so fervently for his recovery; a devoted wife could feel no other way."

"Oh, sir," she said, and into her voice crept now a harshness, "you misunderstand. My fervent hope springs from unalloyed selfishness."

"How may that be?" I asked.

"If you do not succeed in curing him," she told me, "I will suffer."

"I understand that, but—"

"No, you do not understand," she said. "But I can tell you little more without offending. Some things are better left unspoken. Suffice it to be said that, in order to urge you towards an ultimate effort, to the 'limit of your powers' as you have just said, my husband intends to hold over your head the threat of my punishment."

"This is monstrous!" I cried. "It cannot be tolerated. But in what manner, pray, would he dare punish you? Surely he would not beat you?"

"I wish he would be content with a mere beating," she groaned, "but his cleverness knows a keener torture. No, he holds over me—and over you, through me—a punishment far greater; a punishment (believe me!) so loathsome to the sensibilities, so unequivocally vile and degraded, that my mind shrinks from contemplating it. Spare me your further questions, sir, I implore you; for to describe it would plunge me into an abyss of humiliation and shame!"

She broke into sobbing, and tears coursed down her cheeks. No longer able to restrain my tender feelings for her, I flew to her side and took her hands in mine. "Maude," I said, "may I call you that? In the past I addressed you only as Miss Randall; at present I may only call you Madam Sardonicus; but in my heart—then as now—you are, you always have been, you always will be, simply Maude, my own dear Maude!"

"Robert," she sighed; "dearest Robert, I have yearned to hear my Christian name from your lips all these long years."

"The warmth we feel," I said, "may never, with honour, reach fulfilment. But—trust me, dearest Maude!—I will in some wise deliver you from the tyranny of that creature: this I vow!"

"I have no hope," she said, "save in you. Whether I go on as I am, or am subjected to an unspeakable horror, rests with you. My fate is in your hands—these strong, healing hands, Robert." Her voice dropped to a whisper: "Fail me not! oh fail me not!"

"Govern your fears," I said. "Return to your music. Be of good spirits; or, if you cannot, make a show of it. I go now to treat your husband, and also to confront him with what you have told me."

"Do not!" she cried. "Do not, I beseech you, Robert; lest, in the event of your failure, he devise foul embellishments upon the agonies into which he will cast me!"

"Very well," I said, "I will not speak of this to him. But my heart aches to learn the nature of the torments you fear."

"Ask no more, Robert," she said, turning away. "Go to my husband. Cure him. Then I will no longer fear those torments."

I pressed her dear hand and left the salon.

Sardonicus awaited me in his chambers. Thither, quantities of hot water and stacks of towels had been brought by the servants, upon my orders. Sardonicus was stripped to the waist, displaying a trunk strong and of good musculature, but with the same near-phosphorescent pallor of his face. It was, I now understand, the pallor of one who has avoided daylight for years. "As you see, sir," he greeted me, "I am ready for your ministrations."

I bade him recline upon his couch, and began the treatment.

Never have I worked so long with so little reward. After alternating applications of heat and of massage, over a period of three and a quarter hours, I had made no progress. The muscles of his face were still as stiff as marble; they had not relaxed for an instant. I was mortally tired. He ordered our luncheon brought to us in his chambers, and after a short respite, I began again. The clock tolled six when I at last sank into a chair, shaking with exhaustion and strain. His face was exactly as before.

"What remains to be done, sir?" he asked me.

"I will not deceive you," I said. "It is beyond my skill to alleviate your condition. I can do no more."

He rose swiftly from the couch. "You *must* do more!" he shrieked. "You are my last hope!"

"Sir," I said, "new medical discoveries are ever being made. Place your trust in Him who created you—"

"Cease that detestable gibberish at once!" he snapped. "Your puling sentiments sicken me! Resume the treatment."

I refused. "I have applied all my knowledge, all my art, to your affliction," I assured him. "To resume the treatment would be idle and foolish, for—as you have divined—the condition is a product of your own mind."

"At dinner last night," countered Sardonicus, "we spoke of the character of Macbeth. Do you not remember the words he addressed to *his* doctor?—

> *Canst thou not minister to a mind diseas'd,*
> *Pluck from the memory a rooted sorrow,*
> *Raze out the written troubles of the brain,*
> *And with some sweet oblivious antidote*
> *Cleanse the stuff'd bosom of that perilous stuff*
> *Which weighs upon the heart?*

"I remember them," I said; "and I remember, as well, the doctor's reply: *'Therein the patient must minister to himself.'*" I arose and started for the door.

"One moment, Sir Robert," he said. I turned. "Forgive my precipitate outburst a moment ago. However, the mental nature of my affliction notwithstanding, and even though this mode of treatment has failed, surely there are other treatments?"

"None," I said, "that have been sufficiently tested. None I would venture to use upon a human body."

"Ah!" he cried. "Then other treatments do exist!"

I shrugged. "Think not of them, sir. They are at present unavailable to you." I pitied him, and added: "I am sorry."

"Doctor!" he said; "I implore you to use whatever treatments exist, be they ever so untried!"

"They are fraught with danger," I said.

"Danger?" He laughed. "Danger of what? Of disfigurement? Surely no man has ever been more disfigured than I! Of death? I am willing to gamble my life!"

"*I* am not willing to gamble your life," I said. "All lives are precious. Even yours."

"Sir Robert, I will pay you a thousand pounds."

"This is not a question of money."

"Five thousand pounds, Sir Robert, *ten* thousand!"

"No."

He sank onto the couch. "Very well," he said. "Then I will offer you the ultimate inducement."

"Were it a million pounds," I said, "you could not sway me."

"The inducement I speak of," he said, "is not money. Will you hear?"

I sat down. "Speak, sir," I said, "since that is your wish. But nothing will persuade me to use a treatment that might cost you your life."

"Sir Robert," he said, after a pause, "yestereve, when I came down to meet you for the first time, I heard happy sounds in the salon. You were singing a charming melody with my wife. Later, I could not help but notice the character of your glances towards her . . ."

"They were not reciprocated, sir," I told him, "and herewith I offer you a most abject apology for my unbecoming conduct."

"You obscure my point," he said. "You are a friend of hers, from the old days in London; at that period, you felt an ardent affection for her, I would guess. This is not surprising: for she is a lady whose face and form promise voluptuous delights and yet a lady whose manner is most decorous and correct. I would guess further: that your ardour has not diminished over the years; that at the sight of her, the embers have burst into a flame. No, sir,

hear me out. What would you say, Sir Robert, were I to tell you
that you may quench that flame?"

I frowned. "Your meaning, sir?—"

"Must I speak even more plainly? I am offering you a golden
opportunity to requite the love that burns in your heart. To requite
it in a single night, if that will suffice you, or over an extended
period of weeks, months; a year, if you will; as long as you
need—"

"Scoundrel!" I roared, leaping up.

He heeded me not, but went on speaking: ". . . As my guest,
Sir Robert! I offer you a veritable Oriental paradise of unlimited
raptures!" He laughed, then entered into a catalogue of his wife's
excellences. "Consider, sir," he said, "that matchless bosom, like
alabaster which has been imbued with the pink of the rose, those
creamy limbs—"

"Enough!" I cried. "I will hear no more of your foulness." I
strode to the door.

"Yes, you will, Sir Robert," he said immediately. "You will hear
a good deal more of my foulness. You will hear what I plan to do
to your beloved Maude, should you fail to relieve me of this
deformity."

Again, I stopped and turned. I said nothing, but waited for him
to speak further.

"I perceive that I have caught your interest," he said. "Hear me:
for if you think I spoke foully before, you will soon be forced to
agree that my earlier words were, by comparison, as blameless as
the Book of Common Prayer. If rewards do not tempt you, then
threats may coerce you. In fine, Maude will be punished if you
fail, Sir Robert."

"She is an innocent."

"Just so. Hence, the more exquisite and insupportable to you
should be the thought of her punishment."

My mind reeled. I could not believe such words were being
uttered.

"Deep in the bowels of this old castle," said Sardonicus, "are
dungeons. Suppose I were to tell you that my intention is to drag
my wife thither and stretch her smooth body to unendurable
length upon the rack—"

"You would not dare!" I cried.

"My daring or lack of it is not the issue here. I speak of the rack
only that I may go on to assure you that Maude would *infinitely*

prefer that dreadful machine to the punishment I have in truth designed for her. I will describe it to you. You will wish to be seated, I think."

VII
Entertainment for a Monster

"I will stand," I said.

"As you please." Sardonicus himself sat down. "Perhaps you have marvelled at the very fact of Maude's marriage to me. When the world was so full of personable men—men like yourself, who adored her—why did she choose to wed a monster, a creature abhorrent to the eyes and who did not, moreover, have any redeeming grace of spiritual beauty, or kindness, or charm?

"I first met Maude Randall in Paris. I say 'met,' but it would be truer to simply say I saw her—from my hotel window, in fact. Even in Paris society, which abounds in ladies of remarkable pulchritude, she was to be remarked upon. You perhaps would say I fell in love with her, but I dislike that word 'love,' and will merely say that the sight of her smote my senses with most agreeable emphasis. I decided to make her mine. But how? By presenting my irresistibly handsome face to her view? Hardly. I began methodically: I hired secret operatives to find out everything about her and about her mother and father—both of whom were then alive. I discovered that her father was in the habit of speculating, so I saw to it that he received some supposedly trustworthy but very bad advice. He speculated heavily and was instantly ruined. I must admit I had not planned his consequent suicide, but when that melancholy event occurred, I rejoiced, for it worked to my advantage. I presented myself to the bereaved widow and daughter, telling them the excellent qualities of Mr. Randall were widely known in the world of affairs and that I considered myself almost a close friend. I offered to help them in any possible way. By dint of excessive humility and persuasiveness, I won their trust and succeeded in diminishing their aversion to my face. This, you must understand, from first to last, occupied a period of many months. I spoke nothing of marriage, made no sign of affection towards the daughter for at least six of these months; when I did—again, with great respect and restraint—she gently refused me. I retreated gracefully, saying only that I hoped

I might remain her and her mother's friend. She replied that she sincerely shared that hope, for although she could never look upon me as an object of love, she indeed considered me a true friend. The mother, who pined excessively after the death of the father, soon expired: another incident unplanned but welcomed by me. Now the lovely child was alone in the world in a foreign city, with no money, no one to guide her, no one to fall back upon—save kindly Mr. Sardonicus. I waited many weeks, then I proposed marriage again. For several days, she continued to decline the offer, but her declinations grew weaker and weaker until, at length, on one day, she said this to me:

"'Sir, I esteem you highly as a friend and benefactor, but my other feelings towards you have not changed. If you could be satisfied with such a singular condition; if you could agree to enter into marriage with a lady and yet look upon her as no more than a companion of kindred spirit; if the prospect of a dispassionate and childless marriage does not repulse you—as well it might— then, sir, my unhappy circumstances would compel me to accept your kind offer.'

"Instantly, I told her my regard for her was of the purest and most elevated variety; that the urgings of the flesh were unknown to me; that I lived on a spiritual plane and desired only her sweet and stimulating companionship through the years. All this, of course, was a lie. The diametric opposite was true. But I hoped, by this falsehood, to lure her into marriage; after which, by slow and strategic process, I could bring about her submission and my rapture. She still was hesitant; for, as she frankly told me, she believed that love was a noble and integral part of marriage; and that marriage without it could be only a hollow thing; and that though I knew not the urgings of the flesh, she could not with honesty say the same of herself. Yet she reiterated that, so far as my own person was concerned, a platonic relationship was all that could ever exist between us. I calmed her misgivings. We were married not long after.

"And now, Sir Robert, I will tell you a surprising thing. I have confessed myself partial to earthly pleasures; as a physician and as a man of the world, you are aware that a gentleman of strong appetites may not curb them for very long without fomenting turmoil and distress in his bosom. And yet, sir, not once in the years of our marriage—not *once*, I say—have I been able to persuade or cajole my wife into relenting and breaking the stringent terms of our marriage agreement. Each time I have attempted, she has recoiled from me with horror and disgust. This is not because of an abhorrence of all fleshy things—by her own admission—but because of my monstrous face.

"Perhaps now you will better understand the vital necessity for this cure. And perhaps also you will understand the full extent of Maude's suffering should you fail to effect that cure. For, mark me well: if you fail, my wife will be made to become a true wife to me—by main force, and not for one fleeting hour, but every day and every night of her life, whensoever I say, in whatsoever manner I choose to express my conjugal privilege!" As an afterthought, he added, "I am by nature imaginative."

I had been shocked into silence. I could only look upon him with disbelief. He spoke again:

"If you deem it a light punishment, Sir Robert, then you do not know the depth of her loathing for my person, you do not know the revulsion that wells up inside her when I but place my fingers upon her arm, you do not know what mastery of her very gorge is required of her when I kiss her hand. Think, then; think of the abomination she would feel were my attentions to grow more ardent, more demanding! It would unseat her mind, sir; of that I am sure, for she would as soon embrace a reptile."

Sardonicus arose and put on his shirt. "I suggest we both begin dressing for dinner," he said. "Whilst you are dressing, reflect. Ask yourself, Sir Robert: could you ever again look upon yourself with other than shame and loathing if you were to sacrifice the beautiful and blameless Maude Randall on an altar of the grossest depravity? Consider how ill you would sleep in your London bed, night after night, knowing what she was suffering at that very moment; suffering because *you* abandoned her, because *you* allowed her to become an entertainment for a monster."

VIII
A Token of Detestation

The days that passed after that time were, in the main, tedious yet filled with anxiety. During them, certain supplies were being brought from London and other places; Sardonicus spared no expense in procuring for me everything I said was necessary to the treatment. I avoided his society as much as I could, shunning even his table, and instructing the servants to bring my meals to my rooms. On the other hand, I sought out the company of Maude, endeavouring to comfort her and allay her fears. In those hours when her husband was occupied with business affairs, we talked together in the salon, and played music. Thus, they were days spotted with small pleasures that seemed the greater for having been snatched in the shadow of wretchedness.

I grew to know Maude, in that time, better than I had ever known her in London. Adversity stripped the layers of ceremony from our congress, and we spoke directly. I came to know her warmth, but I came to know her strength, too. I spoke outright of my love, though in the next breath I assured her I was aware of the hopelessness of that love. I did not tell her of the "reward" her husband had offered me — and which I had refused — and I was gladdened to learn (as I did by indirection) that Sardonicus, though he had abjured her to be excessively cordial to me, had not revealed the ultimate and ignoble purpose of that cordiality.

"Robert," she said once, "is it likely that he will be cured?"

I did not tell her how unlikely it was. "For your sake, Maude," I said, "I will persevere more than I have ever done in my life."

At length, a day arrived when all the necessaries had been gathered: some plants from the New World, certain equipment from London, and a vital instrument from Scotland. I worked long and late, in complete solitude, distilling a needed liquor from the plants. The next day, dogs were brought to me alive, and carried out dead. Three days after that, a dog left my laboratory alive and my distilling labours came to an end.

I informed Sardonicus that I was ready to administer the treatment. He came to my laboratory, and I imagined there was almost a gloating triumph in his immobile smile. "Such are the fruits of concealed effort," he said. "Man is an indolent creature, but light the fire of fear under him, and of what miracles is he not capable!"

"Speak not of miracles," I said, "though prayers would do you no harm now, for you will soon be in peril of your life." I motioned him towards a table and bade him lie upon it. He did so, and I commenced explaining the treatment to him. "The explorer Magellan," I said, "wrote of a substance used on darts by the savage inhabitants of the South American continent. It killed instantly, dropping large animals in their tracks. The substance was derived from certain plants, and is, in essence, the same substance I have been occupied in extracting these past days."

"A poison, Sir Robert?" he asked, wryly.

"When used full strength," I said, "it kills by bringing about a *total* relaxation of the muscles—particularly the muscles of the lungs and heart. I have long thought that a dilution of that poison might beneficially slacken the rigidly tensed muscles of paralyzed patients."

"Most ingenious, sir," he said.

"I must warn you," I went on, "that this distilment has never been used on a human subject. It may kill you. I must, perforce, urge you again not to insist upon its use; to accept your lot; and to remove the threat of punishment you now hold over your wife's head."

"You seek to frighten me, Doctor," chuckled Sardonicus; "to plant distrust in my bosom. But I fear you not—an English knight and a respected physician would never do a deed so dishonourable as to wittingly kill a patient under his care. You would be hamstrung by your gentleman's code as well as by your professional oath. Your virtues are, in short, my vices' best ally."

I bristled. "I am no murderer such as you," I said. "If you force me to use this treatment, I will do everything in my power to ensure its success. But I cannot conceal from you the possibility of your death."

"See to it that I live," he said flatly, "for if I die, my men will kill both you and my wife. They will not kill you quickly. See to it, also, that I am cured—lest Maude be subjected to a fate she fears more than the slowest of tortures." I said nothing. "Then bring me this elixir straightaway," he said, "and let me drink it off and make an end of this!"

"It is not to be drunk," I told him.

He laughed. "Is it your plan to smear it on darts, like the savages?"

"Your jest is most apposite," I said. "I indeed plan to introduce it into your body by means of a sharp instrument—a new instrument not yet widely known, that was sent me from Scotland. The original suggestion was put forth in the University of Oxford some two hundred years ago by Dr. Christopher Wren, but only recently, through development by my friend, Dr. Wood of Edinburgh, has it seemed practical. It is no more than a syringe—" I showed him the instrument—"attached to a needle; but the needle is hollow, so that, when it punctures the skin, it may carry healing drugs directly into the bloodstream."

"The medical arts will never cease earning my admiration," said Sardonicus.

I filled the syringe. My patient said, "Wait."

"Are you afraid?" I asked.

"Since that memorable night in my father's grave," he replied, "I have not known fear. I had a surfeit of it then; it will last out my lifetime. No: I simply wish to give instructions to one of my men." He arose from the table, and, going to the door, told one of his helots to bring Madam Sardonicus to the laboratory.

"Why must she be here?" I asked.

"The sight of her," he said, "may serve you as a remembrancer of what awaits her in the event of my death, or of that other punishment she may expect should your treatment prove ineffectual."

Maude was brought into our presence. She looked upon my equipment—bubbling retorts and tubes, the pointed syringe—with amazement and fright. I began to explain the principle of the treatment to her, but Sardonicus interrupted: 'Madam is not one of your students, Sir Robert; it is not necessary she know these details. Delay no longer; begin at once!"

He stretched out upon the table again, fixing his eyes upon me. I proffered Maude a comforting look, and walked over to my patient. He did not wince as I drove the needle of the syringe into the left, and then the right, side of his face. "Now, sir," I said— and the tremor in my voice surprised me—"we must wait a period of ten minutes." I joined Maude, and talked to her in low tones, keeping my eyes always upon my patient. He stared at the ceiling; his face remained solidified in that unholy grin. Precisely ten minutes later, a short gasp escaped him; I rushed to his side, and Maude followed close behind me.

We watched with consuming fascination as that clenched face slowly softened, relaxed, changed; the lips drawing closer and closer to each other, gradually covering those naked teeth and gums, the graven creases unfolding and becoming smooth. Before a minute had passed, we were looking down upon the face of a serenely handsome man. His eyes flashed with pleasure, and he made as if to speak.

"No," I said, "do not attempt speech yet. The muscles of your face are so slackened that it is beyond your power, at present, to move your lips. This condition will pass." My voice rang with exultation, and for the moment our enmity was forgotten. He nodded, then leapt from the table and dashed to a mirror which hung on a wall nearby.

Though his face could not yet express his joy, his whole body seemed to unfurl in a great gesture of triumph and a muffled cry of happiness burst in his throat.

He turned and seized my hand; then he looked full into Maude's face. After a moment, she said, "I am happy for you, sir," and looked away. A rasping laugh sounded in his throat, and he walked to my work bench, tore a leaf from one of my notebooks, and scribbled upon it. This he handed to Maude, who read it and passed it over to me. The writing said:

Fear not, lady. You will not be obliged to endure my embraces. I know full well that the restored beauty of my face will weigh not a jot in the balance of your attraction and repugnance. By this document, I dissolve our pristine marriage. You who have been a wife only in name are no longer even that. I give you your freedom.

I looked up from my reading. Sardonicus had been writing again. He ripped another leaf from the notebook and handed it directly to me. It read:

This paper is your safe conduct out of the castle and into the village. Gold is yours for the asking, but I doubt if your English scruples will countenance the accepting of my money. I will expect you to have quit these premises before morning, taking her with you.

"We will be gone within the hour," I told him, and guided Maude towards the door. Before we left the room, I turned for the last time to Sardonicus.

"For your unclean threats," I said; "for the indirect but no less vicious murder of this lady's parents; for the defiling of your own father's grave; for the greed and inhumanity that moved you even before your blighted face provided you with an excuse for your conduct; for these and for what crimes unknown to me blacken your ledger—accept this token of my censure and detestation." I struck him forcibly on his face. He did not respond. He was standing there in the laboratory when I left the room with Maude.

IX
Not God Above nor the Fiend Below

This strange account should probably end here. No more can be said of its central character, for neither Maude nor I saw him or heard of him after that night. And of us two, nothing need be imparted other than the happy knowledge that we have been most contentedly married for the past twelve years and are the parents of a sturdy boy and two girls who are the lovely images of their mother.

However, I have mentioned my friend Lord Henry Stanton, the inveterate traveller and faithful letter writer, and I must copy out now a portion of a missive I received from him only a week since, and which, in point of fact, has been the agent that has prompted me to unfold this whole history of Mr. Sardonicus:

". . . But, my dear Bobbie," wrote Stanton, "in truth there is small pleasure to be found in this part of the world, and I shall be glad to see London again. The excitements and the drama have all departed (if, indeed, they ever existed) and one must content one's self with the stories told at the hearthstones of inns, with the flames crackling and the mulled wine agreeably stinging one's throat. The natives here are most fond of harrowing stories, tales of gore and grue, of ghosts and ghouls and ghastly events, and I must confess a partiality to such entertainments myself. They will show you a stain on a wall and tell you it is the blood of a murdered innocent who met her death there fifty years before: no amount of washing will ever remove the stain, they tell you in sepulchral tones, and indeed it deepens and darkens on a certain day of the year, the anniversary of her violent passing. One is expected to nod gravely, of course, and one does, if one wishes to encourage the telling of more stories. Back in the Eleventh Century, you will be apprised, a battalion of foreign invaders were vanquished by the skeletons of long-dead patriots who arose from their tombs to defend their homeland and then returned to the earth when the enemy had been driven from their borders. (And since they are able to show you the very graves of these lively bones, how can one disbelieve them, Bobbie?) Or they will point to a desolate skull of a castle (the country here abounds in such depressing piles) and tell you of the spectral tyrant who, a scant dozen years before, despaired and died alone there. Deserted by the minions who had always hated him, the frightening creature roamed the village, livid and emaciated, his mind shattered, mutely imploring the succour of even the lowliest beggars. I say *mutely*, and that is the best part of this tall tale: for, as they tell it around the fire, these inventive folk, this poor unfortunate could not speak, could not eat, and could not drink. You ask why? For the simple reason that, though he clawed most horribly at his own face, and though he enlisted the aid of strong men—he was absolutely unable to open his mouth. Cursed by Lucifer, they say, he thirsted and starved in the midst of plenty, surrounded by kegs of drink and tables full of the choicest viands, suffering the tortures of Tantalus, until he finally died. Ah, Bobbie! the efforts of our novelists are pale stuff compared to this! English littérateurs have not the shameless wild imaginations of these people! I will never again read Mrs. Radcliffe with pleasure, I assure you, and the ghost of King Hamlet will from this day hence, strike no terror to my soul, and will fill my heart with but paltry pity. Still, I have journeyed in foreign climes quite enough for one trip, and I long for England and that good English dullness which is relieved only by you and your dear lady (to whom you must commend me most warmly). Until next month, I remain,

Your wayward friend,
HARRY STANTON
Bohemia, March 18–

Now, it would not be a difficult feat for the mind to instantly assume that the unfortunate man in that last tale was Sardonicus—indeed, it is for that reason that I have not yet shewn Stanton's letter to Maude: for she, albeit she deeply loathed Sardonicus, is of such a compassionate and susceptible nature that she would grieve to hear of him suffering a death so horrible. But I am a man of science, and I do not form conclusions on such gossamer evidence. Harry did not mention the province of Bohemia that is supposed to have been the stage of that terrible drama; and his letter, though written in Bohemia, was not mailed by Harry until he reached Berlin, so the postmark tells me nothing. Castles like that of Sardonicus are not singular in Bohemia—Harry himself says the country "abounds in such depressing piles"—so I plan to suspend conclusive thoughts on the matter until I welcome Harry home and can elicit from him details of the precise locality.

For if that "desolate skull of a castle" *is* Castle Sardonicus, and if the story of the starving man is to be believed, then I will be struck by an awesome and curious thing:

Five days I occupied myself in extracting a liquor from the South American plants. During those days, dogs were carried dead from my laboratory. I had deliberately killed the poor creatures with the undiluted poison, in order to impress Sardonicus with its deadliness. I never intended to—and, in fact, never did—prepare a safe dilution of that lethal drug, for its properties were too unknown, its potentiality too dangerous. The liquid I injected into Sardonicus was pure, distilled water—nothing more. This had always been my plan. The ordering of *materia medica* from far-flung lands was but an elaborate façade designed to work not upon the physical part of Sardonicus, but upon his mind; for after Keller, Morignac, Buonagente and my own massaging techniques had failed, I was convinced that it was only through his mind that his body could be cured. It was necessary to persuade him, however, that he was receiving a powerful medicament. His mind, I had hoped, would provide the rest—as, in truth, it did.

If the tale of the "spectral tyrant" prove true, then we must look upon the human mind with wonderment and terror. For, in that case, there was nothing—nothing corporeal—to prevent the wretched creature from opening his mouth and eating his fill. Alone in that castle, food aplenty at his fingertips, he had suffered a dire punishment which came upon him—to paraphrase Sardonicus' very words—*not from God above or the Fiend below, but from within his own breast, his own brain, his own soul.*

RICHARD MATHESON, *screenwriter, author of "Twilight Zone" scripts, short-story and fantasy-novel writer, may well be America's most important author of horrific tales. Among his huge output is the dreadful story "Blood Son" and the twice-filmed novels* I Am Legend *and* The Incredible Shrinking Man, *as well as the unarguably most frightening haunted house in English literature,* Hell House. *"Graveyard Shift" delivers maximum shock in a remarkably short space.* Warning: *you are about to read one of the most hideous horror stories ever written.*

Graveyard Shift

BY RICHARD MATHESON

DEAR PA:

I am sending you this note under Rex's collar because I got to stay here. I hope the note gets to you all right.

I couldn't deliver the tax letter you sent me with because the Widow Blackwell is killed. She is upstairs. I put her on her bed. She looks awful. I wish you would get the sheriff and the coroner Wilks.

Little Jim Blackwell, I don't know where he is right now. He is so scared he goes running around the house and hiding from me. He must have got awful scared by whoever killed his ma. He don't say a word. He just runs around like a scared cat. I see his eyes sometimes in the dark and then they are gone. They got no electric power here you know.

I came out toward sundown bringing that note. I rung the bell but there wasn't no answer so I pushed open the front door and looked in.

All the shades was down. And I heard someone running light in the front room and then feet running upstairs. I called around for the Widow but she didn't answer me.

I started upstairs and saw Jim looking down through the bannister posts. When he saw me looking at him, he run down the hall and I ain't seen him since.

I looked around the upstairs rooms. Finally, I went in the

Widow Blackwell's room and there she was dead on the floor in a puddle of blood. Her throat was cut and her eyes was wide open and looking up at me. It was an awful sight.

I shut her eyes and searched around some and I found the razor. The Widow has all her clothes on so I figure it were only robbery that the killer meant.

Well, Pa, please come out quick with the sheriff and the coronor Wilks. I will stay here and watch to see that Jim don't go running out of the house and maybe get lost in the woods. But come as fast as you can because I don't like sitting here with her up there like that and Jim sneaking around in the dark house.

LUKE

DEAR GEORGE:

We just got back from your sister's house. We haven't told the papers yet so I'll have to be the one to let you know.

I sent Luke out there with a property tax note and he found your sister murdered. I don't like to be the one to tell you but somebody has to. The sheriff and his boys are scouring the countryside for the killer. They figure it was a tramp or something. She wasn't raped though and, far as we can tell, nothing was stolen.

What I mean more to tell you about is little Jim.

That boy is fixing to die soon from starvation and just plain scaredness. He won't eat nothing. Sometimes, he gulps down a piece of bread or a piece of candy but as soon as he starts to chewing his face gets all twisted and he gets violent sick and throws up. I don't understand it at all.

Luke found your sister in her room with her throat cut ear to ear. Coroner Wilks says it was a strong, steady hand that done it because the cut is deep and sure. I am terrible sorry to be the one to tell you all this but I think it is better you know. The funeral will be in a week.

Luke and I had a long time rounding up the boy. He was like lightning. He ran around in the dark and squealed like a rat. He showed his teeth at us when we'd corner him with a lantern. His skin is all white and the way he rolls his eyes back and foams at his mouth is something awful to see.

We finally caught him. He bit us and squirmed around like a eel. Then he got all stiff and it was like carrying a two-by-four, Luke said.

We took him into the kitchen and tried to give him something to eat. He wouldn't take a bite. He gulped down some milk like he felt guilty about it. Then, in a second, his face twists and he draws back his lips and the milk comes out.

He kept trying to run away from us. Never a single word out of him. He just squeaks and mutters like a monkey talking to itself.

We finally carried him upstairs to put him to bed. He froze soon as we touched him and I thought his eyes would fall out he opened them so wide. His jaw fell slack and he stared at us like we was boogie men or trying to slice open his throat like his ma's.

He wouldn't go into his room. He screamed and twisted in our hands like a fish. He braced his feet against the wall and tugged and pulled and scratched. We had to slap his face and then his eyes got big and he got like a board again and we carried him in his room.

When I took off his clothes, I got a shock like I haven't had in years, George. That boy is all scars and bruises on his back and chest like someone has strung him up and tortured him with pliers or hot iron or God knows what all. I got a downright chill seeing that. I know they said the widow wasn't the same in her head after her husband died, but I can't believe she done this. It is the work of a crazy person.

Jim was sleepy but he wouldn't shut his eyes. He kept looking around the ceiling and the window and his lips kept moving like he was trying to talk. He was moaning kind of low and shaky when Luke and I went out in the hall.

No sooner did we leave him than he's screaming at the top of his voice and thrashing in his bed like someone was strangling him. We rushed in and I held the lantern high but we couldn't see anything. I thought the boy was sick with fear and seeing things.

Then, as if it was meant to happen, the lantern ran out of oil and all of a sudden we saw white faces staring at us from the walls and ceiling and the window.

It was a shaky minute there, George, with the kid screaming out his lungs and twisting on his bed but never getting up. And Luke trying to find the door and me feeling for a match but trying to look at those horrible faces at the same time.

Finally I found a match and I got it lit and we couldn't see the faces any more, just part of one on the window.

I sent Luke down to the car for some oil and when he come back we lit the lantern again and looked at the window and saw that the face was painted on it so's to light up in the dark. Same thing for the faces on the walls and the ceiling. It was enough to scare a man out of half his wits to think of anybody doing that inside a little boy's room.

We took him to another room and put him down to bed. When we left him he was squirming in his sleep and muttering words we couldn't understand. I left Luke in the hall outside the room to watch. I went and looked around the house some more.

In the Widow's room I found a whole shelf of psychology books. They was all marked in different places. I looked in one place and it told about a thing how they can make rats go crazy by making them think there is food in a place where there isn't. And another one about how they can make a dog lose its appetite and starve to death by hitting big pieces of pipe together at the same time when the dog is trying to eat.

I guess you know what I think. But it is so terrible I can hardly believe it. I mean that Jim might have got so crazy that he cut her. He is so small I don't see how he could.

You are her only living kin, George, and I think you should do something about the boy. We don't want to put him in a orphan home. He is in no shape for it. That is why I am telling you about him so you can judge.

There was another thing. I played a record on a phonograph in the boy's room. It sounded like wild animals all making terrible noises and even louder than them was a terrible high laughing.

That is about all, George. We will let you know if the sheriff finds the one who killed your sister because no one really believes that Jim could have done it. I wish you would take the boy and try to fix him up.

Until I hear,

SAM DAVIS

DEAR SAM:

I got your letter and am more upset than I can say.

I knew for a long time that my sister was mentally unbalanced after her husband's death, but I had no idea in the world she was so far gone.

You see, when she was a girl she fell in love with Phil. There was never anyone else in her life. The sun rose and descended on her love for him. She was so jealous that, once, because he had taken another girl to a party, she crashed her hands through a window and nearly bled to death.

Finally, Phil married her. There was never a happier couple, it seemed. She did anything and everything for him. He was her whole life.

When Jim was born I went to see her at the hospital. She told me she wished it had been born dead because she knew that the boy meant so much to Phil and she hated to have Phil want anything but her.

She never was good to Jim. She always resented him. And, that day, three years ago, when Phil drowned saving Jim's life, she went out of her mind. I was with her when she heard about it. She ran into the kitchen and got a carving knife and took it running through the streets, trying to find Jim so she could kill him. She finally fainted in the road and we took her home.

She wouldn't even look at Jim for a month. Then she packed up and took him to that house in the woods. Since then I never saw her.

You saw yourself, the boy is terrified of everyone and everything. Except one person. My sister planned that. Step by step she planned it—God help me for never realizing it before. In a whole, monstrous world of horrors she built around that boy she left him trust and need for only one person—*her*. She was Jim's only shield against those horrors. She knew that, when she died, Jim would go completely mad because there wouldn't be anyone in the world he could turn to for comfort.

I think you see now why I say there isn't any murderer.

Just bury her quick and send the boy to me. I'm not coming to the funeral.

GEORGE BARNES

"Wake Not the Dead"—also known as "The Bride of the Grave"—is a tempestuous tale of unnatural love that deserves to be compared with Sheridan LeFanu's "Carmilla" (elsewhere in this volume). JOHANN LUDWIG TIECK *(1773–1853) spent much of his life in Berlin and Dresden, where he adapted many children's tales (including "Puss in Boots") into theatrical versions. A notable Germanic translator and scholar of Shakespeare, Tieck left behind a body of significant dramatic essays and pieces, but also wrote a number of nerve-wrenching tales of terror, of which the following is a prime example. Its melodramatic intensity has the emotional impact of one of the bloodier Italian grand operas.*

Wake Not the Dead

BY JOHANN LUDWIG TIECK

"Wilt thou for ever sleep? Wilt thou never more awake, my beloved, but henceforth repose for ever from thy short pilgrimage on earth? O yet once again return! and bring back with thee the vivifying dawn of hope to one whose existence hath, since thy departure, been obscured by the dunnest shades. What! dumb? for ever dumb? Thy friend lamenteth, and thou heedest him not? He sheds bitter, scalding tears, and thou reposest unregarding his affliction? He is in despair, and thou no longer openest thy arms to him as an asylum from his grief? Say then, doth the paly shroud become thee better than the bridal veil? Is the chamber of the grave a warmer bed than the couch of love? Is the spectre death more welcome to thy arms than thy enamoured consort? Oh! return, my beloved, return once again to this anxious disconsolate bosom."

Such were the lamentations which Walter poured forth for his Brunhilda, the partner of his youthful passionate love: thus did he bewail over her grave at the midnight hour, what time the spirit that presides in the troublous atmosphere, sends his legions of monsters through mid-air; so that their shadows, as they flit beneath the moon and across the earth, dart as wild, agitating thoughts that chase each other o'er the sinner's bosom:—thus did he lament under the tall linden trees by her grave, while his head reclined on the cold stone.

Walter was a powerful lord in Burgundy, who, in his earliest youth, had been smitten with the charms of the fair Brunhilda, a beauty far surpassing in loveliness all her rivals; for her tresses, dark as the raven face of night, streaming over her shoulders, set off to the utmost advantage the beaming lustre of her slender form, and the rich dye of a cheek whose tint was deep and brilliant as that of the western heaven: her eyes did not resemble those burning orbs whose pale glow gems the vault of night, and whose immeasurable distance fills the soul with deep thoughts of eternity, but rather as the sober beams which cheer this nether world, and which, while they enlighten, kindle the sons of earth to joy and love. Brunhilda became the wife of Walter, and both being equally enamoured and devoted, they abandoned themselves to the enjoyment of a passion that rendered them reckless of aught besides, while it lulled them in a fascinating dream. Their sole apprehension was lest aught should awaken them from a delirium which they prayed might continue for ever. Yet how vain is the wish that would arrest the decrees of destiny! as well might it seek to divert the circling planets from their eternal course. Short was the duration of this phrenzied passion; not that it gradually decayed and subsided into apathy, but death snatched away his blooming victim, and left Walter to a widowed couch. Impetuous, however, as was his first burst of grief, he was not inconsolable, for ere long another bride became the partner of the youthful nobleman.

Swanhilda also was beautiful; although nature had formed her charms on a very different model from those of Brunhilda. Her golden locks waved bright as the beams of morn: only when excited by some emotion of her soul did a rosy hue tinge the lily paleness of her cheek: her limbs were proportioned in the nicest symmetry, yet did they not possess that luxuriant fullness of animal life: her eye beamed eloquently, but it was with the milder radiance of a star, tranquillizing to tenderness rather than exciting to warmth. Thus formed, it was not possible that she should steep him in his former delirium, although she rendered happy his waking hours—tranquil and serious, yet cheerful, studying in all things her husband's pleasure, she restored order and comfort in his family, where her presence shed a general influence all around. Her mild benevolence tended to restrain the fiery, impetuous disposition of Walter: while at the same time her prudence recalled him in some degree from his vain, turbulent wishes, and his aspirings after unattainable enjoyments, to the duties and pleasures of actual life. Swanhilda bore her husband two children, a son and a daughter; the latter was mild and patient as her mother, well contented with her solitary sports, and even in these recreations displayed the serious turn of her character. The boy possessed his father's fiery, restless disposition, tempered, however, with the solidity of his mother. Attached by his offspring more tenderly towards their mother, Walter now lived for several years very happily: his thoughts would frequently, indeed, recur to Brunhilda, but without their former violence, merely as we dwell upon the memory of a friend of our earlier days, borne from us on the rapid current of time to a region where we know that he is happy.

But clouds dissolve into air, flowers fade, the sands of the hour-glass run imperceptibly away, and even so, do human feelings dissolve, fade, and pass away, and with them too, human happiness. Walter's inconstant breast again sighed for the ecstatic dreams of those days which he had spent with his equally romantic, enamoured Brunhilda—again did she present herself to his ardent fancy in all the glow of her bridal charms, and he began to draw a parallel between the past and the present; nor did imagination, as it is wont, fail to array the former in her brightest hues, while it proportionably obscured the latter; so that he pictured to himself, the one much more rich in enjoyment, and the other, much less so than they really were. This change in her husband did not escape Swanhilda; whereupon, redoubling her attentions towards him, and her cares towards their children, she expected, by this means, to re-unite the knot that was slackened; yet the more she endeavoured to regain his affections, the colder did he grow,—the more intolerable did her caresses seem, and the more continually did the image of Brunhilda haunt his thoughts. The children, whose endearments were now become indispensable to him, alone stood between the parents as genii eager to effect a reconciliation; and, beloved by them both, formed a uniting link between them. Yet, as evil can be plucked from the heart of man, only ere its root has yet struck deep, its fangs being afterwards too firm to be eradicated, so was Walter's diseased fancy too far affected to have its disorder stopped, for, in a short time, it completely tyrannized over him. Frequently of a night, instead of retiring to his consort's chamber, he repaired to Brunhilda's grave, where he murmured forth his discontent, saying: "Wilt thou sleep for ever?"

One night as he was reclining on the turf, indulging in his wonted sorrow, a sorcerer from the neighbouring mountains, entered into this field of death for the purpose of gathering, for his mystic spells, such herbs as grow only from the earth wherein the dead repose, and which, as if the last production of mortality, are gifted with a powerful and supernatural influence. The sorcerer perceived the mourner, and approached the spot where he was lying.

"Wherefore, fond wretch, dost thou grieve thus, for what is now a hideous mass of mortality—mere bones, and nerves, and veins? Nations have fallen unlamented; even worlds themselves, long ere this globe of ours was created, have mouldered into nothing; nor hath any one wept over them; why then should'st thou indulge this vain affliction for a child of the dust—a being as frail as thyself, and like thee the creature but of a moment?"

Walter raised himself up:—"Let yon worlds that shine in the firmament" replied he, "lament for each other as they perish. It is true, that I who am myself clay, lament for my fellow-clay: yet is this clay impregnated with fire,—with an essence, that none of the elements of creation possess—with love: and this divine passion, I felt for her who now sleepeth beneath this sod."

"Will thy complaints awaken her: or could they do so, would she not soon upbraid thee for having disturbed that repose in which she is now hushed?"

"Avaunt, cold-hearted being: thou knowest not what is love. Oh! that my tears could wash away the earthy covering that conceals her from these eyes;—that my groan of anguish could rouse her from her slumber of death!—No, she would not again seek her earthy couch."

"Insensate that thou art, and couldst thou endure to gaze without shuddering on one disgorged from the jaws of the grave? Art thou too thyself the same from whom she parted; or hath time passed o'er thy brow and left no traces there? Would not thy love rather be converted into hate and disgust?"

"Say rather that the stars would leave yon firmament, that the sun will henceforth refuse to shed his beams through the heavens. Oh! that she stood once more before me;—that once again she reposed on this bosom!—how quickly should we then forget that death or time had ever stepped between us."

"Delusion! mere delusion of the brain, from heated blood, like to that which arises from the fumes of wine. It is not my wish to tempt thee;—to restore to thee thy dead; else wouldst thou soon feel that I have spoken truth."

"How! restore her to me," exclaimed Walter casting himself at the sorcerer's feet. "Oh! if thou art indeed able to effect that, grant it to my earnest supplication; if one throb of human feeling vibrates in thy bosom, let my tears prevail with thee: restore to me my beloved; so shalt thou hereafter bless the deed, and see that it was a good work."

"A good work! a blessed deed!"—returned the sorcerer with a smile of scorn; "for me there exists nor good nor evil; since my will is always the same. Ye alone know evil, who will that which ye would not. It is indeed in my power to restore her to thee: yet, bethink thee well, whether it will prove thy weal. Consider too, how deep the abyss between life and death; across this, my power can build a bridge, but it can never fill up the frightful chasm."

Walter would have spoken, and have sought to prevail on this powerful being by fresh entreaties, but the latter prevented him, saying: "Peace! bethink thee well! and return hither to me tomorrow at midnight. Yet once more do I warn thee, 'Wake not the dead.'"

Having uttered these words, the mysterious being disappeared. Intoxicated with fresh hope, Walter found no sleep on his couch; for fancy, prodigal of her richest stores, expanded before him the glittering web of futurity; and his eye, moistened with the dew of rapture, glanced from one vision of happiness to another. During the next day he wandered through the woods, lest wonted objects by recalling the memory of later and less happier times, might disturb the blissful idea, that he should again behold her—again fold her in his arms, gaze on her beaming brow by day, repose on her bosom at night: and, as this sole idea filled his imagination, how was it possible that the least doubt should arise; or that the warning of the mysterious old man should recur to his thoughts?

No sooner did the midnight hour approach, than he hastened before the grave-field where the sorcerer was already standing by that of Brunhilda. "Hast thou maturely considered?" inquired he.

"Oh! restore to me the object of my ardent passion," exclaimed Walter with impetuous eagerness. "Delay not thy generous action, lest I die even this night, consumed with disappointed desire; and behold her face no more.'"

"Well then," answered the old man, "return hither again tomorrow at the same hour. But once more do I give thee this friendly warning, 'Wake not the dead.'"

All in the despair of impatience, Walter would have prostrated himself at his feet, and supplicated him to fulfil at once a desire now increased to agony; but the sorcerer had already disappeared. Pouring forth his lamentations more wildly and impetuously than ever, he lay upon the grave of his adored one, until the grey dawn streaked the east. During the day, which seemed to him longer than any he had ever experienced, he wandered to and fro, restless and impatient, seemingly without any object, and deeply buried in his own reflections, as the murderer who meditates his first deed of blood: and the stars of evening found him once more at the appointed spot. At midnight the sorcerer was there also.

"Hast thou yet maturely deliberated?" inquired he, "as on the preceding night?"

"Oh what should I deliberate?" returned Walter impatiently. "I need not to deliberate: what I demand of thee, is that which thou has promised me—that which will prove my bliss. Or dost thou but mock me? If so, hence from my sight, lest I be tempted to lay my hand on thee."

"Once more do I warn thee," answered the old man with undisturbed composure, "'Wake not the dead'—let her rest."

"Aye, but not in the cold grave: she shall rather rest on this bosom which burns with eagerness to clasp her."

"Reflect, thou mayst not quit her until death, even though aversion and horror should seize thy heart. There would then remain only one horrible means."

"Dotard!" cried Walter, interrupting him, "how may I hate that which I love with such intensity of passion? how should I abhor that for which my every drop of blood is boiling?"

"Then be it even as thou wishest," answered the sorcerer; "step back."

The old man now drew a circle round the grave, all the while muttering words of enchantment. Immediately the storm began to howl among the tops of the trees; owls flapped their wings, and uttered their low voice of omen; the stars hid their mild, beaming aspect, that they might not behold so unholy and impious a spectacle; the stone then rolled from the grave with a hollow sound, leaving a free passage for the inhabitant of that dreadful tenement. The sorcerer scattered into the yawning earth, roots and herbs of most magic power, and of most penetrating odour, so that the worms crawling forth from the earth congregated together, and raised themselves in a fiery column over the grave: while rushing wind burst from the earth, scattering the mould before it, until at length the coffin lay uncovered. The moonbeams fell on it, and the lid burst open with a tremendous sound. Upon this the sorcerer poured upon it some blood from out of a human skull, exclaiming at the same time: "Drink, sleeper, of this warm stream, that thy heart may again beat within thy bosom." And, after a short pause, shedding on her some other mystic liquid, he cried aloud with the voice of one inspired: "Yes, thy heart beats once more with the flood of life: thine eye is again opened to sight. Arise, therefore, from the tomb."

As an island suddenly springs forth from the dark waves of the ocean, raised upwards from the deep by the force of subterraneous fires, so did Brunhilda start from her earthy couch, borne forward by some invisible power. Taking her by the hand, the sorcerer led her towards Walter, who stood at some little distance, rooted to the ground with amazement.

"Receive again," said he, "the object of thy passionate sighs: mayest thou never more require my aid; should that, however, happen, so wilt thou find me, during the full of the moon, upon the mountains in that spot and where the three roads meet."

Instantly did Walter recognize in the form that stood before him, her whom he so ardently loved; and a sudden glow shot through his frame at finding her thus restored to him: yet the night-frost had chilled his limbs and palsied his tongue. For a while he gazed upon her without either motion or speech, and during this pause, all was again become hushed and serene; and the stars shone brightly in the clear heavens.

"Walter!" exclaimed the figure; and at once the well-known sound, thrilling to his heart, broke the spell by which he was bound.

"Is it reality? Is it truth?" cried he, "or a cheating delusion?"

"No, it is no imposture: I am really living:—conduct me quickly to thy castle in the mountains."

Walter looked around: the old man had disappeared, but he perceived close by his side, a coal-black steed of fiery eye, ready equipped to conduct him thence; and on his back lay all proper attire for Brunhilda, who lost no time in arraying herself. This being done, she cried, "Haste, let us away ere the dawn breaks, for my eye is yet too weak to endure the light of day." Fully recovered from his stupor, Walter leaped into his saddle, and catching up, with a mingled feeling of delight and awe, the beloved being thus mysteriously restored from the power of the grave, he spurred on across the wild, towards the mountains, as furiously as if pursued by the shadows of the dead, hastening to recover from him their sister.

The castle to which Walter conducted his Brunhilda, was situated on a rock between other rocks rising up above it. Here they arrived, unseen by any save one aged domestic, on whom Walter imposed secrecy by the severest threats.

"Here will we tarry," said Brunhilda, "until I can endure the light, and until thou canst look upon me without trembling as if struck with a cold chill." They accordingly continued to make that place their abode: yet no one knew that Brunhilda existed, save only that aged attendant, who provided their meals. During seven entire days they had no light except that of tapers; during the next seven, the light was admitted through the lofty casements only while the rising or setting-sun faintly illuminated the mountain-tops, the valley being still enveloped in shade.

Seldom did Walter quit Brunhilda's side: a nameless spell seemed to attach him to her; even the shudder which he felt in her presence, and which would not permit him to touch her, was not unmixed with pleasure, like that thrilling awful emotion felt when strains of sacred music float under the vault of some temple; he rather sought, therefore, than avoided this feeling. Often too as he had indulged in calling to mind the beauties of Brunhilda, she had never appeared so fair, so fascinating, so admirable when depicted by his imagination, as when now beheld in reality. Never till now had her voice sounded with such tones of sweetness; never before did her language possess such eloquence as it now did, when she conversed with him on the subject of the past. And this was the magic fairy-land towards which her words constantly conducted him. Ever did she dwell upon the days of their first love, those hours of delight in which they had participated together when the one derived all enjoyment from the other: and so rapturous, so enchanting, so full of life did she recall to his imagination that blissful season, that he even doubted whether he had ever experienced with her so much felicity, or had been so truly happy. And, while she thus vividly portrayed their hours of

past delight, she delineated in still more glowing, more enchanting
colours, those hours of approaching bliss which now awaited them,
richer in enjoyment than any preceding ones. In this manner did
she charm her attentive auditor with enrapturing hopes for the
future, and lull him into dreams of more than mortal ecstacy; so
that while he listened to her siren strain, he entirely forgot how
little blissful was the latter period of their union, when he had
often sighed at her imperiousness, and at her harshness both to
himself and all his household. Yet even had he recalled this to
mind would it have disturbed him in his present delirious trance?
Had she not now left behind in the grave all the frailty of
mortality? Was not her whole being refined and purified by that
long sleep in which neither passion nor sin had approached her
even in dreams? How different now was the subject of her
discourse! Only when speaking of her affection for him, did she
betray anything of earthly feeling: at other times, she uniformly
dwelt upon themes relating to the invisible and future world; when
in descanting and declaring the mysteries of eternity, a stream of
prophetic eloquence would burst from her lips.

In this manner had twice seven days elapsed, and, for the first
time, Walter beheld the being now dearer to him than ever, in the
full light of day. Every trace of the grave had disappeared from
her countenance; a roseate tinge like the ruddy streaks of dawn
again beamed on her pallid cheek; the faint, mouldering taint of
the grave was changed into a delightful violet scent; the only sign
of earth that never disappeared. He no longer felt either
apprehension or awe, as he gazed upon her in the sunny light of
day: it was not until now, that he seemed to have recovered her
completely; and, glowing with all his former passion towards her,
he would have pressed her to his bosom, but she gently repulsed
him, saying: — "Not yet — spare your caresses until the moon has
again filled her horn."

Spite of his impatience, Walter was obliged to await the lapse
of another period of seven days: but, on the night when the moon
was arrived at the full, he hastened to Brunhilda, whom he found
more lovely than she had ever appeared before. Fearing no
obstacles to his transports, he embraced her with all the fervour
of a deeply enamoured and successful lover. Brunhilda, however,
still refused to yield to his passion. "What!" exclaimed she, "is it
fitting that I who have been purified by death from the frailty of
mortality, should become thy concubine, while a mere daughter

of the earth bears the title of thy wife: never shall it be. No, it must be within the walls of thy palace, within that chamber where I once reigned as queen, that thou obtainest the end of thy wishes,—and of mine also," added she, imprinting a glowing kiss on the lips, and immediately disappeared.

Heated with passion, and determined to sacrifice everything to the accomplishment of his desires, Walter hastily quitted the apartment, and shortly after the castle itself. He travelled over mountain and across heath, with the rapidity of a storm, so that the turf was flung up by his horse's hoofs; nor once stopped until he arrived home.

Here, however, neither the affectionate caresses of Swanhilda, or those of his children could touch his heart, or induce him to restrain his furious desires. Alas! is the impetuous torrent to be checked in its devastating course by the beauteous flowers over which it rushes, when they exclaim:—"Destroyer, commiserate our helpless innocence and beauty, nor lay us waste?"—the stream sweeps over them unregarding, and a single moment annihilates the pride of a whole summer.

Shortly afterwards did Walter begin to hint to Swanhilda that they were ill-suited to each other; that he was anxious to taste that wild, tumultuous life, so well according with the spirit of his sex, while she, on the contrary, was satisfied with the monotonous circle of household enjoyments:—that he was eager for whatever promised novelty, while she felt most attached to what was familiarized to her by habit: and lastly, that her cold disposition, bordering upon indifference, but ill assorted with his ardent temperament: it was therefore more prudent that they should seek apart from each other that happiness which they could not find together. A sigh, and a brief acquiescence in his wishes was all the reply that Swanhilda made: and, on the following morning, upon his presenting her with a paper of separation, informing her that she was at liberty to return home to her father, she received it most submissively: yet, ere she departed, she gave him the following warning: "Too well do I conjecture to whom I am indebted for this our separation. Often have I seen thee at Brunhilda's grave, and beheld thee there even on that night when the face of the heavens was suddenly enveloped in a veil of clouds. Hast thou rashly dared to tear aside the awful veil that separates the mortality that dreams, from that which dreameth not? Oh! then woe to thee, thou wretched man, for thou hast attached to thyself that which will prove thy destruction." She ceased: nor did Walter attempt any reply, for the similar admonition uttered by the sorcerer flashed upon his mind, all obscured as it was by passion, just as the lightning glares momentarily through the gloom of night without dispersing the obscurity.

Swanhilda then departed, in order to pronounce to her children, a bitter farewell, for they, according to national custom, belonged to the father, and, having bathed them in her tears, and consecrated them with the holy water of maternal love, she quitted her husband's residence, and departed to the home of her father.

Thus was the kind and benevolent Swanhilda driven in exile from those halls where she had presided with such grace;—from halls which were now newly decorated to receive another mistress. The day at length arrived on which Walter, for the second time, conducted Brunhilda home as a newly made bride. And he caused it to be reported among his domestics that his new consort had gained his affections by her extraordinary likeness to Brunhilda, their former mistress. How ineffably happy did he deem himself as he conducted his beloved once more into the chamber which had often witnessed their former joys, and which was now newly gilded and adorned in a most costly style: among the other decorations were figures of angels scattering roses, which served to support the purple draperies whose ample folds o'ershadowed the nuptial couch. With what impatience did he await the hour that was to put him in possession of those beauties for which he had already paid so high a price, but, whose enjoyment was to cost him most dearly yet! Unfortunate Walter! revelling in bliss, thou beholdest not the abyss that yawns beneath thy feet, intoxicated with the luscious perfume of the flower thou hast plucked, thou little deemest how deadly is the venom with which it is fraught, although, for a short season, its potent fragrance bestows new energy on all thy feelings.

Happy, however, as Walter was now, his household were far from being equally so. The strange resemblance between their new lady and the deceased Brunhilda filled them with a secret dismay,—an undefinable horror; for there was not a single difference of feature, of tone of voice, or of gesture. To add too to these mysterious circumstances, her female attendants discovered a particular mark on her back, exactly like one which Brunhilda had. A report was now soon circulated, that their lady was no other than Brunhilda herself, who had been recalled to life by the power of necromancy. How truly horrible was the idea of

living under the same roof with one who had been an inhabitant
of the tomb, and of being obliged to attend upon her, and
acknowledge her as mistress! There was also in Brunhilda much
to increase this aversion, and favour their superstition: no
ornaments of gold ever decked her person; all that others were
wont to wear of this metal, she had formed of silver: no richly
coloured and sparkling jewels glittered upon her; pearls alone,
lent their pale lustre to adorn her bosom. Most carefully did she
always avoid the cheerful light of the sun, and was wont to spend
the brightest days in the most retired and gloomy apartments: only
during the twilight of the commencing or declining day did she
ever walk abroad, but her favourite hour was when the phantom
light of the moon bestowed on all objects a shadowy appearance
and a sombre hue; always too at the crowing of the cock an
involuntary shudder was observed to seize her limbs. Imperious as
before her death, she quickly imposed her iron yoke on every one
around her, while she seemed even far more terrible than ever,
since a dread of some supernatural power attached to her,
appalled all who approached her. A malignant withering glance
seemed to shoot from her eye on the unhappy object of her wrath,
as if it would annihilate its victim. In short, those halls which, in
the time of Swanhilda were the residence of cheerfulness and
mirth, now resembled an extensive desert tomb. With fear
imprinted on their pale countenances, the domestics glided
through the apartments of the castle; and in this abode of terror,
the crowing of the cock caused the living to tremble, as if they
were the spirits of the departed; for the sound always reminded
them of their mysterious mistress. There was no one but who
shuddered at meeting her in a lonely place, in the dusk of evening,
or by the light of the moon, a circumstance that was deemed to
be ominous of some evil: so great was the apprehension of her
female attendants, they pined in continual disquietude, and, by
degrees, all quitted her. In the course of time even others of the
domestics fled, for an insupportable horror had seized them.

The art of the sorcerer had indeed bestowed upon Brunhilda an
artificial life, and due nourishment had continued to support the
restored body; yet this body was not able of itself to keep up the
genial glow of vitality, and to nourish the flame whence springs all
the affections and passions, whether of love or hate; for death had
for ever destroyed and withered it: all that Brunhilda now possessed
was a chilled existence, colder than that of the snake. It was

nevertheless necessary that she should love, and return with equal ardour the warm caresses of her spell-enthralled husband, to whose passion alone she was indebted for her renewed existence. It was necessary that a magic draught should animate the dull current in her veins and awaken her to the glow of life and the flame of love—a potion of abomination—one not even to be named without a curse—human blood, imbibed whilst yet warm, from the veins of youth. This was the hellish drink for which she thirsted: possessing no sympathy with the purer feelings of humanity; deriving no enjoyment from aught that interests in life and occupies its varied hours; her existence was a mere blank, unless when in the arms of her paramour husband, and therefore was it that she craved incessantly after the horrible draught. It was with the utmost effort that she could forbear sucking even the blood of Walter himself, as he reclined beside her. Whenever she beheld some innocent child whose lovely face denoted the exuberance of infantine health and vigour, she would entice it by soothing words and fond caress into her most secret apartment, where, lulling it to sleep in her arms, she would suck from its bosom the warm, purple tide of life. Nor were youths of either sex safe from her horrid attack: having first breathed upon her unhappy victim, who never failed immediately to sink into a lengthened sleep, she would then in a similar manner drain his veins of the vital juice. Thus children, youths, and maidens quickly faded away, as flowers gnawn by the cankering worm: the fullness of their limbs disappeared; a sallow line succeeded to the rosy freshness of their cheeks, the liquid lustre of the eye was deadened, even as the sparkling stream when arrested by the touch of frost; and their locks became thin and grey, as if already ravaged by the storm of life. Parents beheld with horror this desolating pestilence devouring their offspring; nor could simple or charm, potion or amulet avail aught against it. The grave swallowed up one after the other; or did the miserable victim survive, he became cadaverous and wrinkled even in the very morn of existence. Parents observed with horror this devastating pestilence snatch away their offspring—a pestilence which, nor herb however potent, nor charm, nor holy taper, nor exorcism could avert. They either beheld their children sink one after the other into the grave, or their youthful forms, withered by the unholy, vampire embrace of Brunhilda, assume the decrepitude of sudden age.

At length strange surmises and reports began to prevail; it was whispered that Brunhilda herself was the cause of all these horrors; although no one could pretend to tell in what manner she destroyed her victims, since no marks of violence were discernible. Yet when young childen confessed that a sudden slumber had come upon them whenever she began to converse with them, suspicion became converted into certainty, and those whose offspring had hitherto escaped unharmed, quitted their hearths and home—all their little possessions—the dwellings of their fathers and the inheritance of their children, in order to rescue from so horrible a fate those who were dearer to their simple affections than aught else the world could give.

Thus daily did the castle assume a more desolate appearance; daily did its environs become more deserted; none but a few aged decrepit old women and grey-headed menials were to be seen remaining of the once numerous retinue. Such will in the latter days of the earth be the last generation of mortals, when child-bearing shall have ceased, when youth shall no more be seen, nor any arise to replace those who shall await their fate in silence.

Walter alone noticed not, or heeded not, the desolation around him; he apprehended not death, lapped as he was in a glowing elysium of love. Far more happy than formerly did he now seem in the possession of Brunhilda. All those caprices and frowns which had been wont to overcloud their former union had now entirely disappeared. She even seemed to doat on him with a warmth of passion that she had never exhibited even during the happy season of bridal love; for the flame of that youthful blood, of which she drained the veins of others, rioted in her own. At night, as soon as he closed his eyes, she would breathe on him till he sank into delicious dreams, from which he awoke only to experience more rapturous enjoyments. By day she would continually discourse with him on the bliss experienced by happy spirits beyond the grave, assuring him that, as his affection had recalled her from the tomb, they were now irrevocably united. Thus fascinated by a continual spell, it was not possible that he should perceive what was taking place around him. Brunhilda, however, foresaw with savage grief that the source of her youthful ardour was daily decreasing, for, in a short time, there remained nothing gifted with youth, save Walter and his children, and these latter she resolved should be her next victims.

On her first return to the castle, she had felt an aversion towards

the offspring of another, and therefore abandoned them entirely
to the attendants appointed by Swanhilda. Now, however, she
began to pay considerable attention to them, and caused them to
be frequently admitted into her presence. The aged nurses were
filled with dread at perceiving these marks of regard from her
towards their young charges, yet dared they not to oppose the will
of their terrible and imperious mistress. Soon did Brunhilda gain
the affection of the children, who were too unsuspecting of guile
to apprehend any danger from her; on the contrary, her caresses
won them completely to her. Instead of ever checking their
mirthful gambols, she would rather instruct them in new sports;
often too did she recite to them tales of such strange and wild
interest as to exceed all the stories of their nurses. Were they
wearied either with play or with listening to her narratives, she
would take them on her knees and lull them to slumber. Then did
visions of the most surpassing magnificence attend their dreams:
they would fancy themselves in some garden where flowers of
every hue rose in rows one above the other, from the humble
violet to the tall sunflower, forming a parti-coloured broidery of
every hue, sloping upwards towards the golden clouds were little
angels whose wings sparkled with azure and gold descended to
bring them delicious cakes or splendid jewels; or sung to them
soothing melodious hymns. So delightful did these dreams in short
time become to the children that they longed for nothing so
eagerly as to slumber on Brunhilda's lap, for never did they else
enjoy such visions of heavenly forms. Thus were they most anxious
for that which was to prove their destruction:—yet do we not all
aspire after that which conducts us to the grave—after the
enjoyment of life? These innocents stretched out their arms to
approaching death because it assumed the mask of pleasure; for,
while they were lapped in these ecstatic slumbers, Brunhilda
sucked the life-stream from their bosoms. On waking, indeed,
they felt themselves faint and exhausted, yet did no pain nor any
mark betray the cause. Shortly, however, did their strength
entirely fail, even as the summer brook is gradually dried up; their
sports became less and less noisy; their loud, frolicsome laughter
was converted into a faint smile; the full tones of their voices died
away into a mere whisper. Their attendants were filled with horror
and despair; too well did they conjecture the horrible truth, yet
dared not to impart their suspicions to Walter, who was so
devotedly attached to his horrible partner. Death had already

smote his prey: the children were but the mere shadows of their former selves, and even this shadow quickly disappeared.

The anguished father deeply bemoaned their loss, for, notwithstanding his apparent neglect, he was strongly attached to them, nor until he had experienced their loss was he aware that his love was so great. His affliction could not fail to excite the displeasure of Brunhilda: "Why dost thou lament so fondly," said she, "for these little ones? What satisfaction could such unformed beings yield to thee unless thou were still attached to their mother? Thy heart then is still hers? Or dost thou now regret her and them because thou art satiated with my fondness and weary of my endearments? Had these young ones grown up, would they not have attached thee, thy spirit and thy affections more closely to this earth of clay—to this dust, and have alienated thee from that sphere to which I, who have already passed the grave, endeavour to raise thee? Say is thy spirit so heavy, or thy love so weak, or thy faith so hollow, that the hope of being mine for ever is unable to touch thee?" Thus did Brunhilda express her indignation at her consort's grief, and forbade him her presence. The fear of offending her beyond forgiveness and his anxiety to appease her soon dried up his tears; and he again abandoned himself to his fatal passion, until approaching destruction at length awakened him from his delusion.

Neither maiden, nor youth, was any longer to be seen, either within the dreary walls of the castle, or the adjoining territory:— all had disappeared; for those whom the grave had not swallowed up had fled from the region of death. Who, therefore, now remained to quench the horrible thirst of the female vampire save Walter himself? and his death she dared to contemplate unmoved; for that divine sentiment that unites two beings in one joy and one sorrow was unknown to her bosom. Was he in his tomb, so was she free to search out other victims and glut herself with destruction, until she herself should, at the last day, be consumed with the earth itself, such is the fatal law to which the dead are subject when awoke by the arts of necromancy from the sleep of the grave.

She now began to fix her blood-thirsty lips on Walter's breast, when cast into a profound sleep by the odour of her violet breath he reclined beside her quite unconscious of his impending fate: yet soon did his vital powers begin to decay; and many a grey hair peeped through his raven locks. With his strength, his passion also declined; and he now frequently left her in order to pass the whole day in the sports of the chase, hoping thereby to regain his wonted vigour. As he was reposing one day in a wood beneath the shade of an oak, he perceived, on the summit of a tree, a bird of strange appearance, and quite unknown to him; but, before he could take aim at it with his bow, it flew away into the clouds; at the same time letting fall a rose-coloured root which dropped at Walter's feet, who immediately took it up, and, although he was well acquainted with almost every plant, he could not remember to have seen any at all resembling this. Its delightfully odoriferous scent induced him to try its flavour, but ten times more bitter than wormwood it was even as gall in his mouth; upon which, impatient of the disappointment, he flung it away with violence. Had he, however, been aware of its miraculous quality and that it acted as a counter charm against the opiate perfume of Brunhilda's breath, he would have blessed it in spite of its bitterness: thus do mortals often blindly cast away in displeasure the unsavoury remedy that would otherwise work their weal.

When Walter returned home in the evening and laid him down to repose as usual by Brunhilda's side, the magic power of her breath produced no effect upon him; and for the first time during many months did he close his eyes in a natural slumber. Yet hardly had he fallen asleep, ere a pungent smarting pain disturbed him from his dreams; and, opening his eyes, he discerned, by the gloomy rays of a lamp, that glimmered in the apartment, what for some moments transfixed him quite aghast, for it was Brunhilda, drawing with her lips, the warm blood from his bosom. The wild cry of horror which at length escaped him, terrified Brunhilda, whose mouth was besmeared with the warm blood. "Monster!" exclaimed he, springing from the couch, "is it thus that you love me?"

"Aye, even as the dead love," replied she, with a malignant coldness.

"Creature of blood!" continued Walter, "the delusion which has so long blinded me is at an end: thou art the fiend who hast destroyed my children—who hast murdered the offspring of my vassals." Raising herself upwards and, at the same time, casting on him a glance that froze him to the spot with dread, she replied. "It is not I who have murdered them;—I was obliged to pamper myself with warm youthful blood, in order that I might satisfy thy furious desires—thou art the murderer!"—These dreadful words summoned, before Walter's terrified conscience, the threatening shades of all those who had thus perished; while despair choked his voice. "Why," continued she, in a tone that increased his horror, "why dost thou make mouths at me like a puppet? Thou who hadst the courage to love the dead—to take into thy bed, one who had been sleeping in the grave, the bed-fellow of the worm— who hast clasped in thy lustful arms, the corruption of the tomb— dost thou, unhallowed as thou art, now raise this hideous cry for the sacrifice of a few lives?—They are but leaves swept from their branches by a storm.—Come, chase these idiot fancies, and taste the bliss thou hast so dearly purchased." So saying, she extended her arms towards him; but this motion served only to increase his terror, and exclaiming: "Accursed Being,"—he rushed out of the apartment.

All the horrors of a guilty, upbraiding conscience became his companions, now that he was awakened from the delirium of his unholy pleasures. Frequently did he curse his own obstinate blindness, for having given no heed to the hints and admonitions of his children's nurses, but treating them as vile calumnies. But his sorrow was now too late, for, although repentance may gain pardon for the sinner, it cannot alter the immutable decrees of fate—it cannot recall the murdered from the tomb. No sooner did the first break of dawn appear, than he set out for his lonely castle in the mountains, determined no longer to abide under the same roof with so terrific a being; yet vain was his flight, for, on waking the following morning, he perceived himself in Brunhilda's arms, and quite entangled in her long raven tresses, which seemed to involve him, and bind him in the fetters of his fate; the powerful fascination of her breath held him still more captivated, so that, forgetting all that had passed, he returned her caresses, until awakening as if from a dream he recoiled in unmixed horror from her embrace. During the day he wandered through the solitary wilds of the mountains, as a culprit seeking an asylum from his pursuers; and, at night, retired to the shelter of a cave; fearing less to couch himself within such a dreary place, than to expose himself to the horror of again meeting Brunhilda; but alas! it was in vain that he endeavoured to flee her. Again, when he awoke, he found her the partner of his miserable bed. Nay, had he sought the centre of the earth as his hiding place; had he even imbedded himself beneath rocks, or formed his chamber in the recesses of the ocean, still had he found her his constant companion; for, by

calling her again into existence, he had rendered himself insepar-
ably hers; so fatal were the links that united them.

Struggling with the madness that was beginning to seize him,
and brooding incessantly on the ghastly visions that presented
themselves to his horror-stricken mind, he lay motionless in the
gloomiest recesses of the woods, even from the rise of sun till the
shades of eve. But, no sooner was the light of day extinguished in
the west, and the woods buried in impenetrable darkness, than the
apprehension of resigning himself to sleep drove him forth among
the mountains. The storm played wildly with the fantastic clouds,
and with the rattling leaves, as they were caught up into the air,
as if some dread spirit was sporting with these images of
transitoriness and decay: it roared among the summits of the oaks
as if uttering a voice of fury, while its hollow sound rebounding
among the distant hills, seemed as the moans of a departing sinner,
or as the faint cry of some wretch expiring under the murderer's
hand: the owl too, uttered its ghastly cry as if foreboding the wreck
of nature. Walter's hair flew disorderly in the wind, like black
snakes wreathing around his temples and shoulders; while each
sense was awake to catch fresh horror. In the clouds he seemed
to behold the forms of the murdered; in the howling wind to hear
their laments and groans; in the chilling blast itself he felt the dire
kiss of Brunhilda; in the cry of the screeching bird he heard her
voice; in the mouldering leaves he scented the charnel-bed out of
which he had awakened her. "Murderer of thy own offspring,"
exclaimed he in a voice making night and the conflict of the
element still more hideous, "paramour of a blood-thirsty vampire,
reveller with the corruption of the tomb!" while in his despair he
rent the wild locks from his head. Just then the full moon darted
from beneath the bursting clouds; and the sight recalled to his
remembrance the advice of the sorcerer, when he trembled at the
first apparition of Brunhilda rising from her sleep of death; —
namely, to seek him at the season of the full moon in the
mountains, where three roads met. Scarcely had this gleam of
hope broken in on his bewildered mind than he flew to the
appointed spot.

On his arrival, Walter found the old man seated there upon a
stone as calmly as though it had been a bright sunny day and
completely regardless of the uproar around. "Art thou come
then?" exclaimed he to the breathless wretch, who, flinging
himself at his feet, cried in a tone of anguish: — "Oh save me —

succour me—rescue me from the monster that scattereth death and desolation around her."

"And wherefore a mysterious warning? why didst thou not perceivest how wholesome was the advice—'Wake not the dead.'"

"And wherefore a mysterious warning? why didst thou not rather disclose to me at once all the horrors that awaited my sacrilegious profanation of the grave?"

"Wert thou able to listen to any other voice than that of thy impetuous passions? Did not thy eager impatience shut my mouth at the very moment I would have cautioned thee?"

"True, true:—thy reproof is just: but what does it avail now;—I need the promptest aid."

"Well," replied the old man, "there remains even yet a means of rescuing thyself, but it is fraught with horror and demands all thy resolution."

"Utter it then, utter it; for what can be more appalling, more hideous than the misery I now endure?"

"Know then," continued the sorcerer, "that only on the night of the new moon does she sleep the sleep of mortals; and then all the supernatural power which she inherits from the grave totally fails her. 'Tis then that thou must murder her."

"How! murder her!" echoed Watler.

"Aye," returned the old man calmly, "pierce her bosom with a sharpened dagger, which I will furnish thee with; at the same time renounce her memory for ever, swearing never to think of her intentionally, and that, if thou dost involuntarily, thou wilt repeat the curse."

"Most horrible! yet what can be more horrible than she herself is?—I'll do it."

"Keep then this resolution until the next new moon."

"What, must I wait until then?" cried Walter, "alas ere then, either her savage thirst for blood will have forced me into the night of the tomb, or horror will have driven me into the night of madness."

"Nay," replied the sorcerer, "that I can prevent;" and, so saying, he conducted him to a cavern further among the mountains. "Abide here twice seven days," said he; "so long can I protect thee against her deadly caresses. Here wilt thou find all due provision for thy wants; but take heed that nothing tempt thee to quit this place. Farewell, when the moon renews itself, then do I repair hither again." So saying, the sorcerer drew a magic circle around the cave, and then immediately disappeared.

Twice seven days did Walter continue in this solitude, where his companions were his own terrifying thoughts, and his bitter repentance. The present was all desolation and dread; the future presented the image of a horrible deed which he must perforce commit; while the past was empoisoned by the memory of his guilt. Did he think on his former happy union with Brunhilda, her horrible image presented itself to his imagination with her lips defiled with dropping blood: or, did he call to mind the peaceful days he had passed with Swanhilda, he beheld her sorrowful spirit with the shadows of her murdered children. Such were the horrors that attended him by day: those of night were still more dreadful, for then he beheld Brunhilda herself, who, wandering round the magic circle which she could not pass, called upon his name till the cavern re-echoed the horrible sound. "Walter, my beloved," cried she, "wherefore dost thou avoid me? art thou not mine? for ever mine—mine here, and mine hereafter? And dost thou seek to murder me?—ah! commit not a deed which hurls us both to perdition—thyself as well as me." In this manner did the horrible visitant torment him each night, and, even when she departed, robbed him of all repose.

The night of the new moon at length arrived, dark as the deed it was doomed to bring forth. The sorcerer entered the cavern; "Come," said he to Walter, "let us depart hence, the hour is now arrived:" and he forthwith conducted him in silence from the cave to a coal-black steed, the sight of which recalled to Walter's remembrance the fatal night. He then related to the old man Brunhilda's nocturnal visits and anxiously inquired whether her apprehensions of eternal perdition would be fulfilled or not. "Mortal eye," exclaimed the sorcerer, "may not pierce the dark secrets of another world, or penetrate the deep abyss that separates earth from heaven." Walter hesitated to mount the steed. "Be resolute," exclaimed his companion, "but this once is it granted to thee to make the trial, and, should thou fail now, nought can rescue thee from her power."

"What can be more horrible than she herself?—I am determined:" and he leaped on the horse, the sorcerer mounting also behind him.

Carried with a rapidity equal to that of the storm that sweeps across the plain, they in brief space arrived at Walter's castle. All the doors flew open at the bidding of his companion, and they speedily reached Brunhilda's chamber, and stood beside her couch. Reclining in a tranquil slumber, she reposed in all her native loveliness, every trace of horror had disappeared from her countenance; she looked so pure, meek and innocent that all the sweet hours of their endearments rushed to Walter's memory, like interceding angels pleading in her behalf. His unnerved hand could not take the dagger which the sorcerer presented to him. "The blow must be struck even now:" said the latter, "shouldst thou delay but an hour, she will lie at day-break on thy bosom, sucking the warm life drops from thy heart."

"Horrible! most horrible!" faltered the trembling Walter, and turning away his face, he thrust the dagger into her bosom, exclaiming—"I curse thee for ever!"—and the cold blood gushed upon his hand. Opening her eyes once more, she cast a look of ghastly horror on her husband, and, in a hollow dying accent said—"Thou too art doomed to perdition."

"Lay now thy hand upon her corpse," said the sorcerer, "and swear the oath."—Walter did as commanded, saying—"Never will I think of her with love, never recall her to mind intentionally, and, should her image recur to my mind involuntarily, so will I exclaim to it: be thou accursed."

"Thou hast now done everything," returned the sorcerer,— "restore her therefore to the earth, from which thou didst so foolishly recall her; and be sure to recollect thy oath: for, shouldst thou forget it but once, she would return, and thou wouldst be inevitably lost. Adieu—we see each other no more." Having uttered these words he quitted the apartment, and Walter also fled from this abode of horror, having first given direction that the corpse should be speedily interred.

Again did the terrific Brunhilda repose within her grave; but her image continually haunted Walter's imagination, so that his existence was one continued martyrdom, in which he continually struggled to dismiss from his recollection the hideous phantoms of the past; yet, the stronger his effort to banish them, so much the more frequently and the more vividly did they return; as the night-wanderer, who is enticed by a fire-wisp into quagmire or bog, sinks the deeper into his damp grave the more he struggles to escape. His imagination seemed incapable of admitting any other image than that of Brunhilda: now he fancied he beheld her expiring, the blood streaming from her beautiful bosom: at others he saw the lovely bride of his youth, who reproached him with having disturbed the slumbers of the tomb: and to both he was compelled to utter the dreadful words, "I curse thee for ever." The terrible imprecation was constantly passing his lips; yet was he in incessant terror lest he should forget it, or dream of her without being able to repeat it, and then, on awaking, find himself in her arms. Else would he recall her expiring words, and, appalled at their terrific import, imagine that the doom of his perdition was irrecoverably passed. Whence should he fly from himself? or how erase from his brain these images and forms of horror? In the din of combat, in the tumult of war and its incessant pour of victory to defeat; from the cry of anguish to the exultation of victory—in these he hoped to find at least the relief of distraction: but here too he was disappointed. The giant fang of apprehension now seized him who had never before known fear; each drop of blood that sprayed upon him seemed the cold blood that had gushed from Brunhilda's wound; each dying wretch that fell beside him looked like her, when expiring, she exclaimed:—"Thou too art doomed to perdition"; so that the aspect of death seemed more full of dread to him than aught beside, and this unconquerable terror compelled him to abandon the battle-field. At length, after many a weary and fruitless wandering, he returned to his castle. Here all was deserted and silent, as if the sword, or a still more deadly pestilence had laid everything waste: for the few inhabitants that still remained, and even those servants who had once shewn themselves the most attached, now fled from him, as though he had been branded with the mark of Cain. With horror he perceived that, by uniting himself as he had done with the dead, he had cut himself off from the living, who refused to hold any intercourse with him. Often, when he stood on the battlements of his castle, and looked down upon desolate fields, he compared their present solitude with the lively activity they were wont to exhibit, under the strict but benevolent discipline of Swanhilda. He now felt that she alone could reconcile him to life, but durst he hope that one, whom he so deeply aggrieved, could pardon him, and receive him again? Impatience at length got the better of fear; he sought Swanhilda, and, with the deepest contrition, acknowledged his complicated guilt; embracing her knees he beseeched her to pardon him, and to return to his desolate castle, in order that it might again become the abode of contentment and peace. The pale form which she beheld at her feet, the shadow of the lately blooming youth, touched Swanhilda. "The folly," said she gently, "though it has caused me much sorrow, has never excited my resentment or my anger. But say, where are my children?" To this dreadful interrogaton the agonized father could for a while frame no reply: at length he was obliged to confess the dreadful truth. "Then we are sundered for ever," returned Swanhilda; nor could all his tears or supplications prevail upon her to revoke the sentence she had given.

Stripped of his last earthly hope, bereft of his last consolation, and thereby rendered as poor as mortal can possibly be on this side of the grave, Walter returned homewards; when, as he was riding through the forest in the neighbourhood of his castle, absorbed in his gloomy meditations, the sudden sound of a horn roused him from his reverie. Shortly after he saw appear a female figure clad in black, and mounted on a steed of the same colour: her attire was like that of a huntress, but, instead of a falcon, she bore a raven in her hand; and she was attended by a gay troop of cavaliers and dames. The first salutations being passed, he found that she was proceeding the same road as himself; and, when she found that Walter's castle was close at hand, she requested that he would lodge her for that night, the evening being far advanced. Most willingly did he comply with this request, since the appearance of the beautiful stranger had struck him greatly; so wonderfully did she resemble Swanhilda, except that her locks were brown, and her eye dark and full of fire. With a sumptuous banquet did he entertain his guests, whose mirth and songs enlivened the lately silent halls. Three days did this revelry continue, and so exhilarating did it prove to Walter that he seemed to have forgotten his sorrows and his fears; nor could he prevail upon himself to dismiss his visitors, dreading lest, on their departure, the castle would seem a hundred times more desolate than before and his grief be proportionately increased. At his earnest request, the stranger consented to stay seven days, and again another seven days. Without being requested, she took upon herself the superintendence of the household, which she regulated as discreetly and cheerfully as Swanhilda had been wont to do, so that the castle, which had so lately been the abode of melancholy and horror, became the residence of pleasure and festivity, and Walter's grief disappeared altogether in the midst of so much gaiety. Daily did his attachment to the fair unknown increase; he even made her his confidante; and, one evening as they were walking together apart from any of her train, he related to her his melancholy and frightful history. "My dear friend," returned she, as soon as he had finished his tale, "it ill beseems a man of thy discretion to afflict thyself on account of all this. Thou hast awakened the dead from the sleep of the grave and afterwards found,—what might have been anticipated, that the dead possess no sympathy with life. What then? thou wilt not commit this error a second time. Thou hast however murdered the being whom thou hadst thus recalled again to existence—but it was only in appearance, for thou couldst not deprive that of life which properly had none. Thou hast, too, lost a wife and two children: but at thy years such a loss is most easily repaired. There are beauties who will gladly share thy couch, and make thee again a father. But thou dreadst the reckoning of hereafter:—go, open the graves and ask the sleepers there whether that hereafter disturbs them." In such manner would she frequently exhort and cheer him, so that, in a short time, his melancholy entirely disappeared. He now ventured to declare to the unknown the passion with which she had inspired him, nor did she refuse him her hand. Within seven days afterwards the nuptials were celebrated, and the very foundations of the castle seemed to rock from the wild tumultuous uproar of unrestrained riot. The wine streamed in abundance; the goblets circled incessantly: intemperance reached its utmost bounds, while shouts of laughter almost resembling madness burst from the numerous train belonging to the unknown. At length Walter, heated with wine and love, conducted his bride into the nuptial chamber: but, oh! horror! scarcely had he clasped her in his arms ere she transformed herself into a monstrous serpent, which entwining him in its horrid folds, crushed him to death. Flames crackled on every side of the apartment; in a few minutes after, the whole castle was enveloped in a blaze that consumed it entirely: while, as the walls fell in with a tremendous crash, a voice exclaimed aloud—"Wake not the dead!"

MAURICE LEVEL, *an important contributor to the infamous Grand Guignol theatre of Paris, is unjustly obscure today. His fame rests on a rare collection of* contes cruelles *published in English in the 1920s, but "Night and Silence" is not part of that volume. It first appeared in the February 1932 issue of* Weird Tales *magazine and is still unequaled in its homely dreadfulness.*

Night and Silence

BY MAURICE LEVEL

They were old, crippled, horrible. The woman hobbled about on two crutches; one of the men, blind, walked with his eyes shut, his hands outstretched, his fingers spread open; the other, a deaf-mute, followed with his head lowered, rarely raising the sad, restless eyes that were the only sign of life in his impassive face.

It was said that they were two brothers and a sister, and that they were united by a savage affection. One was never seen without the others; at the church doors they shrank back into the shadows, keeping away from those professional beggars who stand boldly in the full light so that passers-by may be ashamed to ignore their importunacy. They did not ask for anything. Their appearance alone was a prayer for help. As they moved silently through the narrow, gloomy streets, a mysterious trio, they seemed to personify Age, Night, and Silence.

One evening, in their hovel near the gates of the city, the woman died peacefully in their arms, without a cry, with just one look of distress which the deaf-mute saw, and one violent shudder which the blind man felt because her hand clasped his wrist. Without a sound she passed into eternal silence.

Next day, for the first time, the two men were seen without her. They dragged about all day without even stopping at the baker's shop where they usually received doles of bread. Toward dusk, when lights began to twinkle at the dark crossroads, when the reflection of lamps gave the houses the appearance of a smile, they bought with the few half-pence they had received two poor little candles, and they returned to the desolate hovel where the old sister lay on her pallet with no one to watch or pray for her.

They kissed the dead woman. The man came to put her in her coffin. The deal boards were fastened down and the coffin was placed on two wooden trestles; then, once more alone, the two brothers laid a sprig of boxwood on a plate, lighted their candles, and sat down for the last all-too-short vigil.

Outside, the cold wind played round the joints of the ill-fitting door. Inside, the small trembling flames barely broke the darkness with their yellow light . . . Not a sound . . .

For a long time they remained like this, praying, remembering, meditating . . .

Tired out with weeping, at last they fell asleep . . .

When they woke it was still night. The lights of the candles still glimmered, but they were lower. The cold that is the precursor of dawn made them shiver. But there was something else—what was it? They leaned forward, the one trying to see, the other to hear. For some time they remained motionless; then, there being no repetition of what had roused them, they lay down again and began to pray.

Suddenly, for the second time, they sat up. Had either of them been alone, he would have thought himself the play-thing of some fugitive hallucination. When one sees without hearing, or hears without seeing, illusion is easily created. But something abnormal was taking place; there could be no doubt about it since both were affected, since it appealed both to eyes and ears at the same time; they were fully conscious of this, but were unable to understand.

Between them they had the power of complete comprehension. Singly, each had but a partial, agonizing conception.

The deaf-mute got up and walked about. Forgetting his brother's infirmity, the blind man asked in a voice choked with fear, "What is it? What's the matter? Why have you got up?"

He heard him moving, coming and going, stopping, starting off again, and again stopping; and having nothing but these sounds to guide his reason, his terror increased till his teeth began to chatter. He was on the point of speaking again, but remembered, and relapsed into a muttering, "What can he see? What is it?"

The deaf-mute took a few more steps, rubbed his eyes, and presumably, reassured, went back to his mattress and fell asleep.

The blind man heaved a sigh of relief, and silence fell once more, broken only by the prayers he mumbled in a monotonous undertone, his soul benumbed by grief as he waited till sleep should come and pour light into his darkness.

He was almost sleeping when the murmurs which had before made him tremble, wrenched him from an uneasy doze.

It sounded like a soft scratching mingled with light blows on a plank, curious rubbings, and stifled moans.

He leaped up. The deaf-mute had not moved. Feeling that the fear that culminates in panic was threatening him, he strove to reason with himself.

"Why should this noise terrify me? . . . The night is always full of sounds . . . My brother is moving uneasily in his sleep . . . yes, that's it . . . Just now I heard him walking up and down, and there was the same noise . . . It must have been the wind . . . But I know the sound of the wind, and it has never been like that . . . it was a noise I had never heard . . . What could it have been? No . . . it could not be . . ."

He bit his fists. An awful suspicion had come to him.

"Suppose . . . no, it's not possible . . . Suppose it was . . . there it is again! . . . Again . . . louder and louder . . . some one is scratching, scratching, knocking . . . My God! A voice . . . her voice! She is calling! She is crying! Help, help!"

He threw himself out of bed and roared, "François! . . . quick! . . . Help! . . . Look! . . ."

He was half mad with fear. He tore wildly at his hair shouting "Look! . . . You've got eyes, you, you can see! . . ."

The moans became louder, the raps firmer. Feeling his way, stumbling against the walls, knocking against the packing-cases which served as furniture, tripping in the hole in the floor, he staggered about trying to find his sleeping brother.

He fell and got up again, bruised, covered with blood, sobbing, "I have no eyes! I have no eyes!"

He had upset the plate on which lay the sprig of box, and the sound of the earthenware breaking on the floor gave the finishing touch to his panic.

"Help! What have I done? Help!"

The noises grew louder and more terrifying, and as an agonizing cry sounded, his last doubts left him. Behind his empty eyes, he imagined he saw the horrible thing . . .

He saw the old sister beating against the tightly-closed lid of her coffin. He saw her super-human terror, her agony, a thousand times worse than that of any other death . . . She was there, alive,

yes alive, a few steps away from him . . . but where? She heard
his steps, his voice, and he, blind, could do nothing to help her.

Where was his brother? Flinging his arms from right to left, he
knocked over the candles: the wax flowed over his fingers, hot,
like blood. The noise grew louder, more despairing; the voice was
speaking, saying words that died away in smothered groans . . .

"Courage!" he shrieked. "I'm here! I'm coming!"

He was now crawling along on his knees, and a sudden turn
flung him against a bed; he thrust out his arms, felt a body, seized
it by the shoulders, and shook it with all the strength that remained
in him.

Violently awakened, the deaf-mute sprang up uttering horrible
cries and trying to see, but now that the candles were out, he, too,
was plunged into night, the impenetrable darkness that held more
terror for him than for the blind man. Stupefied with sleep, he
groped about wildly with his hands, which closed in a vice-like grip
on his brother's throat, stifling cries of, "Look! Look!"

They rolled together on the floor, upsetting all that came in their
way, knotted together, ferociously tearing each other with tooth
and nail. In a very short time their hoarse breathing had died
away. The voice, so distant and yet so near, was cut short by a
spasm . . . there was a cracking noise . . . the imprisoned body
was raising itself in one last supreme effort for freedom . . . a
grinding noise . . . sobs . . . again the grinding noise . . .
silence . . .

Outside, the trees shuddered as they bowed in the gale; the rain
beat against the walls. The late winter's dawn was still crouching
on the edge of the horizon. Inside the walls of the hovel, not a
sound, not a breath.

Night and Silence.

ACTS OF GOD
AND OTHER HORRORS

Cosmic terrors abound in this section, whose title was suggested by Dick Baldwin, herein represented. You may find a discernible reason for the dire events of these stories—you are certainly welcome to look—but most of the calamities choronicled in the following pages would never be owned up to by any respectable deity.

The need to believe, I've often said (and written), is an almost inescapable trap of the ego. Draw your own conclusions—if you must.

Born in Russia in 1920, ISAAC ASIMOV *is one of America's most famous science-fiction and science-fact writers, an astonishingly wide-read, urbane genius who has combined both scientific and writing careers into a distinguished life. "Ike" has written well over 300 books, all of them remarkably readable. The tale which follows is less familiar than his robot stories, but Groff Conklin admired it enough to include it in* Science-Fiction Terror Tales, *noting, however, that "Flies" horrified some people and left others perfectly unmoved. You be the judge.*

Flies

BY ISAAC ASIMOV

"Flies!" said Kendell Casey, wearily. He swung his arm. The fly circled, returned and nestled on Casey's shirt-collar.

From somewhere there sounded the buzzing of a second fly.

Dr. John Polen covered the slight uneasiness of his chin by moving his cigarette quickly to his lips.

He said, "I didn't expect to meet you, Casey. Or you, Winthrop. Or ought I call you Reverend Winthrop?"

"Ought I call you Professor Polen?" said Winthrop, carefully striking the proper vein of rich-toned friendship.

They were trying to snuggle into the cast-off shell of twenty years back, each of them. Squirming and cramming and not fitting.

Damn, thought Polen fretfully, why do people attend college reunions?

Casey's hot blue eyes were still filled with the aimless anger of the college sophomore who has discovered intellect, frustration, and the tag-ends of cynical philosophy all at once.

Casey! Bitter man of the campus!

He hadn't outgrown that. Twenty years later and it was Casey, bitter ex-man of the campus! Polen could see that in the way his finger tips moved aimlessly and in the manner of his spare body.

As for Winthrop? Well, twenty years older, softer, rounder. Skin pinker, eyes milder. Yet no nearer the quiet certainty he would never find. It was all there in the quick smile he never entirely abandoned, as though he feared there would be nothing to take its place, that its absence would turn his face into a smooth and featureless flesh.

Polen was tired of reading the aimless flickering of a muscle's end; tired of usurping the place of his machines; tired of the too much they told him.

Could they read him as he read them? Could the small restlessness of his own eyes broadcast the fact that he was damp with the disgust that had bred mustily within him?

Damn, thought Polen, why didn't I stay away?

They stood there, all three, waiting for one another to say something, to flick something from across the gap and bring it, quivering, into the present.

Polen tried. He said, "Are you still working in chemistry, Casey?"

"In my own way, yes," said Casey, gruffly. "I'm not the scientist you're considered to be. I do research on insecticides for E. J. Link at Chatham."

Winthrop said, "Are you really? You said you would work on insecticides. Remember, Polen? And with all that, the flies dare still be after you, Casey?"

Casey said, "Can't get rid of them. I'm the best proving ground in the labs. No compound we've made keeps them away when I'm around. Someone once said it was my odor. I attract them."

Polen remembered the someone who had said that.

Winthrop said, "Or else—"

Polen felt it coming. He tensed.

"Or else," said Winthrop, "it's the curse, you know." His smile intensified to show that he was joking, that he forgave past grudges.

Damn, thought Polen, they haven't even changed the words. And the past came back.

"Flies," said Casey, swinging his arm, and slapping. "Ever see such a thing? Why don't they light on you two?"

Johnny Polen laughed at him. He laughed often then. "It's something in your body odor, Casey. You could be a boon to science. Find out the nature of the odorous chemical, concentrate it, mix it with DDT, and you've got the best fly-killer in the world."

"A fine situation. What do I smell like? A lady fly in heat? It's a shame they have to pick on me when the whole damned world's a dung heap."

Winthrop frowned and said with a faint flavor of rhetoric, "Beauty is not the only thing, Casey, in the eye of the beholder."

Casey did not deign a direct response. He said to Polen, "You know what Winthrop told me yesterday? He said those damned flies were the curse of Beelzebub."

"I was joking," said Winthrop.

"Why Beelzebub?" asked Polen.

"It amounts to a pun," said Winthrop. "The ancient Hebrews used it as one of their many terms of derision for alien gods. It comes from *Ba'al*, meaning *lord* and *zevuv*, meaning *fly*. The lord of flies."

Casey said, "Come on, Winthrop, don't say you don't believe in Beelzebub."

"I believe in the existence of evil," said Winthrop, stiffly.

"I mean Beelzebub. Alive. Horns. Hooves. A sort of competition deity."

"Not at all." Winthrop grew stiffer. "Evil is a short-term affair. In the end it must lose —"

Polen changed the subject with a jar. He said, "I'll be doing graduate work for Venner, by the way. I talked with him day before yesterday, and he'll take me on."

"No! That's wonderful." Winthrop glowed and leaped to the subject-change instantly. He held out a hand with which to pump Polen's. He was always conscientiously eager to rejoice in another's good fortune. Casey often pointed that out.

Casey said, "Cybernetics Venner? Well, if you can stand him, I suppose he can stand you."

Winthrop went on. "What did he think of your idea? Did you tell him your idea?"

"What idea?" demanded Casey.

Polen had avoided telling Casey so far. But now Venner had considered it and had passed it with a cool, "Interesting!" How could Casey's dry laughter hurt it now?

Polen said, "It's nothing much. Essentially, it's just a notion that emotion is the common bond of life, rather than reason or intellect. It's practically a truism, I suppose. You can't tell what a baby thinks or even *if* it thinks, but it's perfectly obvious that it can be angry, frightened or contented even when a week old. See?

"Same with animals. You can tell in a second if a dog is happy or if a cat is afraid. The point is that their emotions are the same as those we would have under the same circumstances."

"So?" said Casey. "Where does it get you?"

"I don't know yet. Right now, all I can say is that emotions are universals. Now suppose we could properly analyze all the actions of men and certain familiar animals and equate them with the visible emotion. We might find a tight relationship. Emotion A might always involve Motion B. Then we could apply it to animals whose emotions we couldn't guess at by common sense alone. Like snakes, or lobsters."

"Or flies," said Casey, as he slapped viciously at another and flicked its remains off his wrist in furious triumph.

He went on. "Go ahead, Johnny. I'll contribute the flies and you study them. We'll establish a science of flychology and labor to make them happy by removing their neuroses. After all, we want the greatest good of the greatest number, don't we? And there are more flies than men."

"Oh, well," said Polen.

Casey said, "Say, Polen, did you ever follow up that weird idea of yours? I mean, we all know you're a shining cybernetic light, but I haven't been reading your papers. With so many ways of wasting time, something has to be neglected, you know."

"What idea?" asked Polen, woodenly.

"Come on. You know. Emotions of animals and all that sort of guff. Boy, those were the days. I used to know madmen. Now I only come across idiots."

Winthrop said, "That's right, Polen. I remember it very well. Your first year in graduate school you were working on dogs and rabbits. I believe you even tried some of Casey's flies."

Polen said, "It came to nothing in itself. It gave rise to certain new principles of computing, however, so it wasn't a total loss."

Why did they talk about it?

Emotions! What right had anyone to meddle with emotions? Words were invented to conceal emotions. It was the dreadfulness of raw emotion that had made language a basic necessity.

Polen knew. His machines had by-passed the screen of verbalization and dragged the unconscious into the sunlight. The boy and the girl, the son and the mother. For that matter, the cat and the mouse or the snake and the bird. The data rattled together in its universality and it had all poured into and through Polen until he could no longer bear the touch of life.

In the last few years he had so painstakingly schooled his thoughts in other directions. Now these two came, dabbling in his mind, stirring up its mud.

Casey batted abstractedly across the tip of his nose to dislodge a fly. "Too bad," he said. "I used to think you could get some fascinating things out of, say, rats. Well, maybe not fascinating, but then not as boring as the stuff you would get out of our somewhat-human beings. I used to think—"

Polen remembered what he used to think.

Casey said, "Damn this DDT. The flies feed on it, I think. You know, I'm going to do graduate work in chemistry and then get a job on insecticides. So help me. I'll personally get something that *will* kill the vermin."

They were in Casey's room, and it had a somewhat keroseny odor from the recently applied insecticide.

Polen shrugged and said, "A folded newspaper will always kill."

Casey detected a non-existent sneer and said instantly, "How would you summarize your first year's work, Polen? I mean aside from the true summary any scientist could state if he dared, by which I mean: 'Nothing'."

"Nothing," said Polen. "There's your summary."

"Go on," said Casey. "You use more dogs than the physiologists do and I bet the dogs mind the physiological experiments less. I would."

"Oh, leave him alone," said Winthrop. "You sound like a piano with 87 keys eternally out of order. You're a bore!"

You couldn't say that to Casey.

He said, with sudden liveliness, looking carefully away from Winthrop, "I'll tell you what you'll probably find in animals, if you look closely enough. Religion."

"What the dickens!" said Winthrop, outraged. "That's a foolish remark."

Casey smiled. "Now, now, Winthrop. *Dickens* is just a euphemism for *devil* and you don't want to be swearing."

"Don't teach me morals. And don't be blasphemous."

"What's blasphemous about it? Why shouldn't a flea consider the dog as something to be worshipped? It's the source of warmth, food, and all that's good for a flea."

"I don't want to discuss it."

"Why not? Do you good. You could even say that to an ant, an anteater is a higher order of creation. He would be too big for them to comprehend, too mighty to dream of resisting. He would move among them like an unseen, inexplicable whirlwind, visiting them with destruction and death. But that wouldn't spoil things for the ants. They would reason that destruction was simply their just punishment for evil. And the anteater wouldn't even know he was a deity. Or care."

Winthrop had gone white. He said, "I know you're saying this only to annoy me and I am sorry to see you risking your soul for a moment's amusement. Let me tell you this," his voice trembled a little, "and let me say it very seriously. The flies that torment you are your punishment in this life. Beelzebub, like all the forces of evil, may think he does evil, but it's only the ultimate good after all. The curse of Beelzebub is on you for *your* good. Perhaps it will succeed in getting you to change your way of life before it's too late."

He ran from the room.

Casey watched him go. He said, laughing, "I told you Winthrop believed in Beelzebub. It's funny the respectable names you can give to superstition." His laughter died a little short of its natural end.

There were two flies in the room, buzzing through the vapors toward him.

Polen rose and left in heavy depression. One year had taught him little, but it was already too much, and his laughter was thinning. Only his machines could analyze the emotions of animals properly, but he was already guessing too deeply concerning the emotions of men.

He did not like to witness wild murder-yearnings where others could see only a few words of unimportant quarrel.

Casey said, suddenly, "Say, come to think of it, you did try some of my flies, the way Winthrop says. How about that?"

"Did I? after twenty years, I scarcely remember," murmured Polen.

Winthrop said, "You must. We were in your laboratory and you complained that Casey's flies followed him even there. He suggested you analyze them and you did. You recorded their motions and buzzings and wing-wiping for half an hour or more. You played with a dozen different flies."

Polen shrugged.

"Oh, well," said Casey. "It doesn't matter. It was good seeing you, old man." The hearty hand-shake, the thump on the shoulder, the broad grin—to Polen it all translated into sick disgust on Casey's part that Polen was a "success" after all.

Polen said, "Let me hear from you sometimes."

The words were dull thumps. They meant nothing. Casey knew that. Polen knew that. Everyone knew that. But words were meant to hide emotion and when they failed, humanity loyally maintained the pretense.

Winthrop's grasp of the hand was gentler. He said, "This brought back old times, Polen. If you're ever in Cincinnati, why don't you stop in at the meeting-house? You'll always be welcome."

To Polen, it all breathed of the man's relief at Polen's obvious depression. Science, too, it seemed, was not the answer, and Winthrop's basic and ineradicable insecurity felt pleased at the company.

"I will," said Polen. It was the usual polite way of saying, I won't.

He watched them thread separately to other groups.

Winthrop would never know. Polen was sure of that. He wondered if Casey knew. It would be the supreme joke if Casey did not.

He *had* run Casey's flies, of course, not that once alone, but many times. Always the same answer! Always the same unpublishable answer.

With a cold shiver he could not quite control, Polen was suddenly conscious of a single fly loose in the room, veering aimlessly for a moment, then beating strongly and reverently in the direction Casey had taken a moment before.

Could Casey *not* know? Could it be the essence of the primal punishment that he never learn he was Beelzebub?

Casey! Lord of the Flies!

"The Night Wire" is one of the most popular short stories that ever appeared in Weird Tales. *The magazine's publisher later said that he had no idea it would draw such reader enthusiasm. If he'd had an inkling, he would have made it a cover story and asssigned one of the WT artists the task of translating it into a picture. I don't see how. It is told at long distance, as it were, and deserves to be fleshed out by the reader's imagination.*

The Night Wire

BY H. F. ARNOLD

"New York, September 30 CP FLASH.

"Ambassador Holliwell died here today. The end came suddenly as the ambassador was alone in his study . . . "

There is something ungodly about these night wire jobs. You sit up here on the top floor of a skyscraper and listen in to the whispers of a civilization. New York, London, Calcutta, Bombay, Singapore—they're your next-door neighbors after the street lights go dim and the world has gone to sleep.

Alone in the quiet hours between two and four, the receiving operators doze over their sounders and the news comes in. Fires and disasters and suicides. Murders, crowds, catastrophes. Sometimes an earthquake with a casualty list as long as your arm. The night wire man takes it down almost in his sleep, picking it off on his typewriter with one finger.

Once in a long time you prick up your ears and listen. You've heard of some one you knew in Singapore, Halifax or Paris, long ago. Maybe they've been promoted, but more probably they've been murdered or drowned. Perhaps they just decided to quit and took some bizarre way out. Made it interesting enough to get in the news.

But that doesn't happen often. Most of the time you sit and doze and tap, tap on your typewriter and wish you were home in bed.

Sometimes, though, queer things happen. One did the other night, and I haven't got over it yet. I wish I could.

You see, I handle the night manager's desk in a western seaport town; what the name is, doesn't matter.

There is, or rather was, only one night operator on my staff, a fellow named John Morgan, about forty years of age, I should say, and a sober, hard-working sort.

He was one of the best operators I ever knew, what is known as a "double" man. That means he could handle two instruments at once and type the stories on different typewriters at the same time. He was one of the three men I ever knew who could do it consistently, hour after hour, and never make a mistake.

Generally, we used only one wire at night, but sometimes, when it was late and the news was coming fast, the Chicago and Denver stations would open a second wire, and then Morgan would do his stuff. He was a wizard, a mechanical automatic wizard which functioned marvelously but was without imagination.

On the night of the sixteenth he complained of feeling tired. It was the first and last time I had ever heard him say a word about himself, and I had known him for three years.

It was just three o'clock and we were running only one wire. I was nodding over reports at my desk and not paying much attention to him, when he spoke.

"Jim," he said, "does it feel close in here to you?"

"Why, no, John," I answered, "but I'll open a window if you like."

"Never mind," he said. "I reckon I'm just a little tired."

That was all that was said, and I went on working. Every ten minutes or so I would walk over and take a pile of copy that had stacked up neatly beside the typewriter as the messages were printed out in triplicate.

It must have been twenty minutes after he spoke that I noticed he had opened up the other wire and was using both typewriters. I thought it was a little unusual, as there was nothing very "hot" coming in. On my next trip I picked up the copy from both machines and took it back to my desk to sort out the duplicates.

The first wire was running out the usual sort of stuff and I just looked over it hurriedly. Then I turned to the second pile of copy. I remembered it particularly because the story was from a town I had never heard of: "Xebico". Here is the dispatch. I saved a duplicate of it from our files:

"Xebico, Sept. 16 CP BULLETIN.

"The heaviest mist in the history of the city settled over the town

at 4 o'clock yesterday afternoon. All traffic has stopped and the
mist hangs like a pall over everything. Lights of ordinary intensity
fail to pierce the fog, which is constantly growing heavier.

"Scientists here are unable to agree as to the cause, and the local
weather bureau states that the like has never occurred before in
the history of the city.

"At 7 P.M. last night municipal authorities . . . (more)"

That was all there was. Nothing out of the ordinary at a bureau
headquarters, but, as I say, I noticed the story because of the name
of the town.

It must have been fifteen minutes later that I went over for
another batch of copy. Morgan was slumped down in his chair and
had switched his green electric light shade so that the gleam missed
his eyes and hit only the top of the two typewriters.

Only the usual stuff was in the righthand pile, but the lefthand
batch carried another story from Xebico. All press dispatches
come in "takes" meaning that parts of many different stories are
strung along together, perhaps with but a few paragraphs of each
coming through at a time. This second story was marked "add
fog." Here is the copy:

"At 7 P.M. the fog had increased noticeably. All lights were now
invisible and the town was shrouded in pitch darkness.

"As a peculiarity of the phenomenon, the fog is accompanied
by a sickly odor, comparable to nothing yet experienced here."

Below that in customary press fashion was the hour, 3:27, and
the initials of the operator, JM.

There was only one other story in the pile from the second wire.
Here it is:

"2nd add Xebico Fog.

"Accounts as to the origin of the mist differ greatly. Among the
most unusual is that of the sexton of the local church, who groped
his way to headquarters in a hysterical condition and declared that
the fog originated in the village churchyard.

" 'It was first visible as a soft gray blanket clinging to the earth
above the graves,' he stated. 'Then it began to rise, higher and
higher. A subterranean breeze seemed to blow it in billows, which
split up and then joined together again.

" 'Fog phantoms, writhing in anguish, twisted the mist into
queer forms and figures. And then, in the very thick midst of the
mass, something moved.

" 'I turned and ran from the accursed spot. Behind me I heard screams coming from the houses bordering on the graveyard.'

"Although the sexton's story is generally discredited, a party has left to investigate. Immediately after telling his story, the sexton collapsed and is now in a local hospital, unconscious."

Queer story, wasn't it. Not that we aren't used to it, for a lot of unusual stories come in over the wire. But for some reason or other, perhaps because it was so quiet that night, the report of the fog made a great impression on me.

It was almost with dread that I went over to the waiting piles of copy. Morgan did not move, and the only sound in the room was the tap-tap of the sounders. It was ominous, nerve-racking.

There was another story from Xebico in the pile of copy. I seized on it anxiously.

"New Lead Xebico Fog CP.

"The rescue party which went out at 11 P.M. to investigate a weird story of the origin of a fog which, since late yesterday, has shrouded the city in darkness has failed to return. Another and larger party has been dispatched.

"Meanwhile, the fog has, if possible, grown heavier. It seeps through the cracks in the doors and fills the atmosphere with a depressing odor of decay. It is oppressive, terrifying, bearing with it a subtle impression of things long dead.

"Residents of the city have left their homes and gathered in the local church, where the priests are holding services of prayer. The scene is beyond description. Grown folk and children are alike terrified and many are almost beside themselves with fear.

"Amid the wisps of vapor which partly veil the church auditorium, an old priest is praying for the welfare of his flock. They alternately wail and cross themselves.

"From the outskirts of the city may be heard cries of unknown voices. They echo through the fog in queer uncadenced minor keys. The sounds resemble nothing so much as wind whistling through a gigantic tunnel. But the night is calm and there is no wind. The second rescue party . . . (more)"

I am a calm man and never in a dozen years spent with the wires, have been known to become excited, but despite myself I rose from my chair and walked to the window. Could I be mistaken, or far down in the canyons of the city beneath me did I see a faint trace of fog? Pshaw! It was all imagination.

In the pressroom the click of the sounders seemed to have raised the tempo of their tunc. Morgan alone had not stirred from his chair. His head sunk between his shoulders, he tapped the dispatches out on the typewriters with one finger of each hand.

He looked asleep, but no; endlessly, efficiently, the two machines rattled off line after line, as relentlessly and effortlessly as death itself. There was something about the monotonous movement of the typewriter keys that fascinated me. I walked over and stood behind his chair, reading over his shoulder the type as it came into being, word by word.

Ah, here was another:

"Flash Xebico CP.

"There will be no more bulletins from this office. The impossible has happened. No messages have come into this room for twenty minutes. We are cut off from the outside and even the streets below us.

"I will stay with the wire until the end.

"It is the end, indeed. Since 4 P.M. yesterday the fog has hung over the city. Following reports from the sexton of the local church, two rescue parties were sent out to investigate conditions on the outskirts of the city. Neither party has ever returned nor was any word received from them. It is quite certain now that they will never return.

"From my instrument I can gaze down on the city beneath me. From the position of this room on the thirteenth floor, nearly the entire city can be seen. Now I can see only a thick blanket of blackness where customarily are lights and life.

"I fear greatly that the wailing cries heard constantly from the outskirts of the city are the death cries of the inhabitants. They are constantly increasing in volume and are approaching the center of the city.

"The fog yet hangs over everything. If possible, it is even heavier than before, but the conditions have changed. Instead of an opaque, impenetrable wall of odorous vapor, there now swirls and writhes a shapeless mass in contortions of almost human agony. Now and again the mass parts and I catch a brief glimpse of the streets below.

"People are running to and fro, screaming in despair. A vast bedlam of sound flies up to my window, and above all is the immense whistling of unseen and unfelt winds.

"The fog has again swept over the city and the whistling is

coming closer and closer.

"It is now directly beneath me.

"God! An instant ago the mist opened and I caught a glimpse of the streets below.

"The fog is not simply vapor—it lives! By the side of each moaning and weeping human is a companion figure, an aura of strange and vari-colored hues. How the shapes cling! Each to a living thing!

"The men and women are down. Flat on their faces. The fog figures caress them lovingly. They are kneeling beside them. They are—but I dare not tell it.

"The prone and writhing bodies have been stripped of their clothing. They are being consumed—piecemeal.

"A merciful wall of hot, steamy vapor has swept over the whole scene. I can see no more.

"Beneath me the wall of vapor is changing colors. It seems to be lighted by internal fires. No, it isn't. I have made a mistake. The colors are from above, reflections from the sky.

"Look up! Look up! The whole sky is in flames. Colors as yet unseen by man or demon. The flames are moving; they have started to intermix; the colors rearrange themselves. They are so brilliant that my eyes burn, yet they are a long way off.

"Now they have begun to swirl, to circle in and out, twisting intricate designs and patterns. The lights are racing each with each, a kaleidoscope of unearthly brilliance.

"I have made a discovery. There is nothing harmful in the lights. They radiate force and friendliness, almost cheeriness. But by their very strength, they hurt.

"As I look, they are swinging closer and closer, a million miles at each jump. Millions of miles with the speed of light. Aye, it is light, the quintessence of all light. Beneath it the fog melts into a jeweled mist radiant, rainbow-colored of a thousand varied spectra.

"I can see the streets. Why, they are filled with people! The lights are coming closer. They are all around me. I am enveloped. I . . . "

The message stopped abruptly. The wire of Xebico was dead. Beneath my eyes in the narrow circle of light from under the green lamp-shade, the black printing no longer spun itself, letter by letter, across the page.

The room seemed filled with a solemn quiet, a silence vaguely impressive, powerful.

I looked down at Morgan. His hands had dropped nervelessly at his sides, while his body had hunched over peculiarly. I turned the lamp-shade back, throwing the light squarely in his face. His eyes were staring, fixed.

Filled with a sudden foreboding, I stepped beside him and called Chicago on the wire. After a second the sounder clicked its answer.

Why? But there was something wrong. Chicago was reporting that Wire Two had not been used throughout the evening.

"Morgan!" I shouted. "Morgan! Wake up, it isn't true. Some one has been hoaxing us. Why . . ." In my eagerness I grasped him by the shoulder.

His body was quite cold. Morgan had been dead for hours. Could it be that his sensitized brain and automatic fingers had continued to record impressions even after the end?

I shall never know, for I shall never again handle the night shift. Search in a world atlas discloses no town of Xebico. Whatever it was that killed John Morgan will forever remain a mystery.

DICK BALDWIN *is a resident of Mount Vernon, N.Y., and an expert on film comedy. I met him through the Sons of the Desert, the International Laurel and Hardy society, and have included several of his fantasy tales in my anthologies. One of his tales—"Money Talks"—is a delightful send-up of the vampire legend, but the following story is not a comedy. The events described actually happened to Dick, and after he read Crane's* The Upturned Face *(elsewhere in this volume), he set down "Last Respects."*

Last Respects

BY DICK BALDWIN

It was dark in the room. The window drapes were pulled, shutting out the bright mid-day sun. The only illumination came from a small wall light, masked from the rest of the drab chamber by a curtain drawn completely around the bed which stood directly under the lamp.

Two men stood outside the curtain. Their anxious silence was broken only by a distant moan from another room.

"We should begin," Berland said at last, swallowing with difficulty.

"Wait—" The other orderly responded, putting out his hand to stop his companion from opening the curtain. "Have we got everything?" He moved toward the stretcher to examine the supplies set out upon it.

Everything was there, but he checked it all again. A large green plastic sheet (folded into sixteenths), six narrow strips of black cloth, four manila tags (with information printed by the Floor Nurse), a basin of warm water mixed with germicidal soap, towels, and two pairs of rubber gloves (one size 6½, the other, 8).

McIlnoy tested the water. "It's cold," he complained. "Maybe I ought to get—"

His voice died as Berland twitched aside the bed curtain, drenching the room in ghastly yellow light. Both stared down, tense, acutely embarrassed.

The bed's occupant lay on his back. Glassy eyes stared wide at the ceiling. The toothless mouth gaped. The final convulsion had arched the neck so that the shoulders were slightly raised, curving the upper back like a keystone bridge. The gnarled fists clutched the hem of the patient's gown so tightly that the knuckles were a chalk-blue. But the rest of the skin was ashen.

McIlnoy turned away from the sight and put on the size 8 gloves. Berland gawked numbly at the corpse. After a moment, he spoke in a hushed voice.

"What do we do first?"

"Wash it, I think."

"I gave him a shower just this morning."

"Then why do you ask?" McIlnoy snapped. "We were in the same training class. You tell *me* what to do."

Berland shifted his weight uncomfortably from foot to foot, but said nothing.

"Look," the other argued, "they told us that bodies have to be washed before getting—"

"Well, I'm telling you he's already clean!"

"All right! Then where *do* we start?"

With a jerk of his hand, Berland indicated the thin gown tightly crumpled in the dead fists. "That will have to come off. One of us has to lift him so that the other can untie the strings."

Neither moved. They stared at one another.

"*You're* wearing gloves," Berland murmured.

"There is another pair!" McIlnoy took the unused gloves and started to reach across the bed to hand them to Berland. Midway he changed his mind and tossed them away instead, snapping back his arm.

Shuddering, Berland pulled on the gloves, then lifted the head. It looked so stiff, so unmovable, that he used too much force; it came up easily. As it did, the shoulders fell to the bed with a plop. Both men gasped, and Berland dropped the head. It fell back to the pillow and rolled onto its left side. The eyes fixed vacantly on Berland's face.

"*You* pick him up," he told McIlnoy, trying to avoid the empty stare. McIlnoy flexed his fingers, hesitated, then suddenly grabbed the man by the shoulders and lifted. The head bobbed, twisted to the right, and came to rest three inches away from the second orderly's face.

"Hurry!" he urged Berland, who fumbled at the strings of the gown. They were soaked with sweat and badly knotted.

Someone in another room groaned.

At last, Berland got the final knot undone. McIlnoy quickly released the body. The top of the head, a paucity of hairs, snow white, tapped the headboard, bounced, then slid back down to the pillow.

Gently, they pulled the flimsy gown away from the sunken chest until it was halted by the firm hold on the hem of the dead man's clenched fists. Berland tugged. The hands held fast. He could have sworn they tightened their grip. He cursed. He wanted to slice off the dead fingers, sever the wrists, chop up the unfeeling hands— anything to speed the task. He yanked at the material. The movement made the body jump.

"Let's cut it off!" McIlnoy nervously suggested.

"*No!*" Berland snapped, thinking for a second that the other meant the hands. "I can get it!"

Sweating, he pulled again. There was a muted cracking sound within one of the corpse's arms. McIlnoy grasped the wrists. Berland yanked once more, and at last the gown came free. As it did, the claw-like hands unclenched.

Tossing the gown aside, Berland stood still for a moment, catching his breath. Then he looked at his companion and wanly tried to manage a smile.

"It shouldn't be too hard to close the eyes," he said lightly. "I've seen it done in hundreds of films." He placed his middle and index fingers on the lids and stroked downward. The eyes remained open. Pressing harder, he tried again. The lids moved, but rolled back when he took his fingers away. He tried a third time, applying still more force. He felt the tips of his fingers sink into soft membrane. He pulled his hand back violently and trembled.

"I can't do it. You try."

McIlnoy took a deep breath, held it. He felt sick. Putting his own fingers on the eye-lids, he stroked down while pushing up on the cheeks with the other hand. The eyes closed. They looked as if they were squinting. He slowly took his hands away. The lids stayed shut.

"Now the mouth."

It was rigid. They applied a combination of pressure upon the skull and jaw and at last, the mouth snapped shut. Immediately, the eyes sprang open. A hollow gurgle sounded from within the dead man's throat.

McIlnoy sprang back, yelping. "My God! He's not dead!"

"Get the mouth open!"

McIlnoy prized the jaws apart. Berland, feeling a little dizzy, stuck his hand into the gaping cavity. He grabbed the tongue, which had slipped down into the throat, and pulled it back out. He turned to McIlnoy. "It's liable to happen again. We'll have to clamp his mouth around it."

At length, they got both mouth and eyes closed and secured the jaw with a strip of black cloth, making a bow on the top of the head. The tongue dangled grotesquely over the thin, purple lips. They used another strip to hold the arms, which they folded across the chest. A third strip at the ankles kept the legs in place.

Next they took the blanket and top sheet, which were resting at the foot of the bed, and tossed them on the floor. They placed the green plastic shroud where the bedclothes had been and tugged on its inner right corner until it began to play out in fourths. McIlnoy lifted the legs. Berland brought the shroud under them until he reached the buttocks, which still touched the bed, then let the cloth go while he picked up the torso. His companion grasped the material and yanked it further up.

They worked quickly, intently, but were not unaware of the moans that still proceeded from some distant cubicle. The small room was hot; the air thick. The single naked bulb glinted along the plastic shroud, making points of light that dazzled their eyes. The walls shimmered in the stifling heat as if they might collapse inward.

The plastic, fully opened, extended below the feet and above the head, as well as on either side of the body. Berland affixed a manila tag to the right first toe, then folded the excess plastic up to the knees as McIlnoy took the upper residue and covered the face and neck with it. They lifted the surplus on either side, folded it across and tucked it in carefully so the patient was fully enclosed in the green, shiny sheath. They tied the covering with strips of cloth at the neck, chest, and feet and fastened tags to the chest and ankle ribbons.

The wrapping complete, they stepped back and regarded the nameless, faceless bundle. McIlnoy tittered nervously.

"It's like a Christmas present," he observed, then giggled. "How'd you like to find *that* beneath your tree?"

Berland began to laugh, a trifle hysterically. McIlnoy tried to quiet him at first, but then he, too, was swept into the mirth. He remembered the head hitting the headboard, and somehow the pun stuck him as the funniest thing in the world.

At length, they subsided in a fit of coughing. After they caught their breath, they stared at one another somewhat ashamed.

"We'd better get him onto the stretcher," said Berland.

He pushed it up flush against the left side of the bed, but forgot to lock the wheels. McIlnoy cranked the bed up level to its fullest height. They hefted the corpse by the bottom bed-sheet and moved it toward the stretcher. But the dead weight, sagging against the unanchored vehicle, pushed it away. They lowered the bundle, but there was nothing solid to rest it on. It twisted from their grasp and fell to the floor. As it did, escaping air billowed the shroud from within. McIlnoy regarded the ballooning plastic and shook his head.

"Looks like he's breathing in there," he said. "Imagine if he were still alive!"

Berland glared at him. "Knock it off!" Moving the stretcher back, he ran over the legs. They set the vehicle to one side, fixed the casters in place, and struggled with the corpse until they got it on the platform. McIlnoy strapped it on and Berland spread the white bed-sheet over the body.

After the gloomy room, the hallway seemed remarkably bright. The air was much fresher. They wheeled the body down a hall past closed doors. Within, the patients were oddly silent, and the only noises in the corridor were the squeal of metal castors and the scrabbling sound of the rustling shroud.

They stopped in front of the elevator doors. McIlnoy sighed in exhaustion, pushing the button. "The worst is over," he said. "From here on, the morgue attendant takes care of the rest."

"And that *is* the worst," said the other, shuddering. "The other day, I had lunch with an inhalation therapist who went to embalming school. She said that when muscular contractions set in, it's not unusual for corpses to move around, sit up—"

McIlnoy gestured. "Please! I don't want to hear about it."

It took the decrepit elevator ten minutes to arrive. When the doors opened, they had to shove and strain to fit the stretcher into the small car. After much effort, they managed it, but McIlnoy was practically pinned against the back wall by the vehicle. Berland, nearer to the panel of buttons, had to sit on the stretcher to reach them. He pushed the basement button.

The doors closed.

The car descended slowly, jerkily. When it was halfway between the first and second floors, the elevator shivered to a halt.

The lights went out.

A. MERRITT *is one of America's most important fantasists, but he was never prolific. His handful of novels and short stories include the popular* Seven Footprints to Satan, *"Three Lines of Old French" and the novel that H. P. Lovecraft labeled a classic:* The Moon Pool. *"The Pool of the Stone God," also known as "The God in the Pool," was not included in Merritt's sole short story collection,* The Fox Woman. *It first appeared in the September 23, 1923, issue of* American Weekly *(which Merritt edited) under the byline of W. Fenimore. Sam Moskowitz anthologized it in 1971 with the opinion that Merritt probably wrote it. Now, fourteen years later, in Mr. Moskowitz's soon-to-be-published* A. Merritt: Reflections in the Moon Pool, *it has been definitely established that this grisly little tale was indeed penned by Merritt himself.*

The Pool of the Stone God

BY A. MERRITT

This is Professor James Marston's story. A score of learned bodies have courteously heard him tell it, and then among themselves have lamented that so brilliant a man should have such an obsession. Professor Marston told it to me in San Francisco, just before he started to find the island that holds his pool of the stone god and the wings that guard it. He seemed to me very sane. It is true that the equipment of his expedition was unusual, and not the least curious part of it are the suits of fine chain mail and masks and gauntlets with which each man of the party was provided.

"The five of us," said Professor Marston, "sat side by side on the beach. There was Wilkinson the first officer, Bates and Cassidy the two seamen, Waters the pearler and myself. We had all been on our way to New Guinea, I to study the fossils for the Smithsonian. The *Moranus* had struck the hidden reef the night before and had sunk swiftly. We were then, roughly, about five hundred miles northeast of the Guinea coast. The five of us had managed to drop a lifeboat and get away. The boat was well stocked with water and provisions. Whether the rest of the crew had escaped we did not know. We had sighted the island at dawn and had made for her. The lifeboat was drawn safely up to the sands.

" 'We'd better explore a bit, anyway,' said Waters. 'This may be a perfect place for us to wait rescue. At least until the typhoon season is over. We've our pistols. Let's start by following this brook to its source, look over the place and then decide what we'll do.'

"The trees began to thin out. We saw ahead an open space. We reached it and stopped in sheer amazement. The clearing was perfectly square and about five hundred feet wide. The trees stopped abruptly at its edges as though held back by something unseen.

"But it was not this singular impression that held us. At the far end of the square were a dozen stone huts clustered about one slightly larger. They reminded me powerfully of those prehistoric structures you see in parts of England and France. I approach now the most singular thing about this whole singular and sinister place. In the centre of the space was a pool walled about with huge blocks of cut stone. At the side of the pool rose a great stone figure, carved in the semblance of a man with outstretched hands. It was at least twenty feet high and was extremely well executed. At the distance the statue seemed nude and yet it had a peculiar effect of drapery about it. As we drew nearer we saw that it was covered from ankles to neck with the most extraordinary carved wings. They looked exactly like bat wings when they were folded.

"There was something extremely disquieting about this figure. The face was inexpressibly ugly and malignant. The eyes, Mongol-shaped, slanted, evil. It was not from the face, though, that this feeling seemed to emanate. It was from the body covered with the wings—and especially from the wings. They were a part of the idol and yet they gave one the idea that they were clinging to it.

"Cassidy, a big brute of a man, swaggered up to the idol and laid his hand on it. He drew it away quickly, his face white, his mouth twitching. I followed him and, conquering my unscientific repugnance, examined the stone. It, like the huts and in fact the whole place, was clearly the work of that forgotten race whose monuments are scattered over the Southern Pacific. The carving of the wings was wonderful. They were batlike, as I have said, folded and each ended in a little ring of conventionalized feathers. They ranged in size from four to ten inches. I ran my fingers over one. Never have I felt the equal of the nausea that sent me to my knees before the idol. The wing had felt like smooth, cold stone, but I had the sensation of having touched at the back of the stone some monstrous, obscene creature of a lower world. The sensation came of course, I reasoned, only from the temperature and texture of the stone—and yet this did not really satisfy me.

"Dusk was soon due. We decided to return to the beach and examine the clearing further on the morrow. I desired greatly to explore the stone huts.

"We started back through the forest. We walked some distance and then night fell. We lost the brook. After a half hour's wandering, we thought we were approaching the beach. Then Waters clutched my arm. I stopped. Directly in front of us was the open space with the stone god leering under the moon and the green water shining at his feet!

"We had made a circle. Bates and Wilkinson were exhausted. Cassidy swore that devils or no devils he was going to camp that night beside the pool.

"The moon was very bright. And it was so very quiet. My scientific curiosity got the better of me and I thought I would examine the huts. I left Bates on guard and walked over to the largest. There was only one room and the moonlight shining through chinks in the wall illuminated it clearly. At the back were two small basins set in the stone. I looked in one and saw a faint reddish gleam reflected from a number of globular objects. I drew a half dozen of them out. They were pearls, very wonderful pearls of a peculiarly rosy hue. I ran toward the door to call Bates—and stopped.

"My eyes had been drawn to the stone idol. Was it an effect of the moonlight or did it move? No, it was the wings! They stood out from the stone and waved—they waved, I say, from the ankles to the neck of that monstrous statue.

"Bates had seen them, too. He was standing with his pistol raised. Then there was a shot. And after that the air was filled with a rushing sound like that of a thousand fans. I saw the wings loose themselves from the stone god and sweep down in a cloud upon the four men. Another cloud raced up from the pool and joined them. I could not move. The wings circled swiftly around and about the four. All were now on their feet and I never saw such horror as was in their faces.

"Then the wings closed in. They clung to my companion as they had clung to the stone.

"I fell back into the hut. I lay there through the night insane with terror. Many times I heard the fanlike rushing about the enclosure, but nothing entered my hut. Dawn came, and silence, and I dragged myself to the door. There stood the stone god with the wings carved upon him as we had seen him ten hours before.

"I ran over to the four lying on the grass. I thought that perhaps I had had a nightmare. But they were dead. That was not the worst of it. Each man was shrunken to his bones! They looked like collapsed white balloons. There was not a drop of blood in them. They were nothing but bones wrapped around in white skin.

"Mastering myself I went close to the idol. There was something different about it. It seemed larger—as though, the thought went through my mind, as though it had eaten. Then I saw that it was covered with tiny drops of blood that had dropped from the ends of the wings that clothed it.

"I do not remember what happened afterward. I awoke on the pearling schooner *Luana* which had picked me up, crazed with thirst as they supposed in the boat of the *Moranus*."

ODGEN NASH *(1902–71), best known for his whacky, sort-of-semi-metrical verse, here "plays it straight" with a dark poem worthy of Damon Runyon in his more sombre moods.*

A Tale of the Thirteenth Floor

BY OGDEN NASH

The hands of the clock were reaching high
In an old Midtown hotel;
I name no name, but its sordid fame
Is table talk in Hell.
I name no name, but Hell's own flame
Illumes the lobby garish,
A gilded snare just off Times Square
For the virgins of the parish.

The revolving door swept the grimy floor
Like a crinoline grotesque,
And a lowly bum from an ancient slum
Crept furtively past the desk.
His footsteps sift into the lift
As a knife in the sheath is slipped,
Stealthy and swift into the lift
As a vampire into a crypt.

Old Maxie, the elevator boy,
Was reading an ode by Shelley,
But he dropped the ode as it were a toad
When the gun jammed into his belly.
There came a whisper as soft as mud
In the bed of an old canal:
"Take me up to the suite of Pinball Pete,
The rat who betrayed my gal."

The lift doth rise with groans and sighs
Like a duchess for the waltz,
Then in middle shaft, like a duchess daft,
It changes its mind and halts.
The bum bites lip as the landlocked ship
Doth neither fall nor rise,
But Maxie the elevator boy
Regards him with burning eyes.
"First to explore the thirteenth floor,"
Says Maxie, "would be wise."

Quoth the bum, "There is moss on your double cross,
I have been this way before,
I have cased the joint at every point,
And there is no thirteenth floor.
The architect he skipped direct
From twelve unto fourteen,
There is twelve below and fourteen above,
And nothing in between,
For the vermin who dwell in this hotel
Could never abide thirteen."

Said Max, "Thirteen, that floor obscene,
Is hidden from human sight;
But once a year it doth appear,
On this Walpurgis night.
Ere you peril your soul in murderer's role,
Heed those who sinned of yore;
The path they trod led away from God,
And onto the thirteenth floor,
Where those they slew, a grisly crew,
Reproach them forevermore.

"We are higher than twelve and below fourteen,"
Said Maxie to the bum,
"And the sickening draft that taints the shaft
Is a whiff of kingdom come.
The sickening draft that taints the shaft
Blows through the devil's door!"
And he squashed the latch like a fungus patch,
And revealed the thirteenth floor.

It was cheap cigars like lurid scars
That glowed in the rancid gloom,
The murk was a-boil with fusel oil
And the reek of stale perfume.
And round and round there dragged and wound
A loathsome conga chain,
The square and the hep in slow lock step,
The slayer and the slain.
(For the souls of the victims ascend on high,
But their bodies below remain.)

The clean souls fly to their home in the sky,
But their bodies remain below
To pursue the Cains who emptied their veins
And harry them to and fro.
When life is extinct each corpse is linked
To its gibbering murderer,
As a chicken is bound with wire around
The neck of a killer cur.

Handcuffed to Hate come Docter Waite
(*He* tastes the poison now),
And Ruth and Judd and a head of blood
With horns upon its brow.
Up sashays Nan with her feathery fan
From *Floradora* bright;
She never hung for Caesar Young,
But she's dancing with him tonight.

Here's the bulging hip and the foam-flecked lip
Of the mad dog, Vincent Coll,
And over there that ill-met pair,
Becker and Rosenthal.
Here's Legs and Dutch and a dozen such
Of braggart bullies and brutes,
And each one bends 'neath the weight of friends
Who are wearing concrete suits.

Now the damned make way for the double damned
Who emerge with shuffling pace
From the nightmare zone of persons unknown,
With neither name nor face.
And poor Dot King to one doth cling,
Joined in a ghastly jig,
While Elwell doth jape at a goblin shape
And tickle it with his wig.

See Rothstein pass like breath on a glass,
The original Black Sox kid;
He riffles the pack, riding piggyback
On the killer whose name he hid.
And smeared like brine on a slavering swine,
Starr Faithful, once so fair,
Drawn from the sea to her debauchee,
With the salt sand in her hair.

And still they come, and from the bum
The icy sweat doth spray;
His white lips scream as in a dream,
"For God's sake, let's away!
If ever I meet with Pinball Pete
I will not seek his gore,
Lest a treadmill grim I must trudge with him
On the hideous thirteenth floor."

"For you I rejoice," said Maxie's voice,
"And I bid you go in peace,
But I am late for a dancing date
That nevermore will cease.
So remember, friend, as your way you wend,
That *I* turned the heat on Pinball Pete;
You see—*I* had a daughter, too!"

The bum reached out and he tried to shout,
But the door in his face was slammed,
And silent as stone he rode down alone
From the floor of the double damned.

DYLAN THOMAS *(1914–53), the great Welsh poet, wrote a number of less familiar prose pieces, many of them rescued from obscurity by his compatriot, Emlyn Williams, who reads Thomas superbly in his one-man show and on discs. "The Tree" comes from Thomas' collection,* Adventures in the Skin Trade.

The Tree

BY DYLAN THOMAS

Rising from the house that faced the Jarvis hills in the long distance, there was a tower for the day-birds to build in and for owls to fly around at night. From the village the light of the tower window shone like a glow-worm through the panes; but the room under the sparrows' nests was rarely lit; webs were spun over its unwashed ceilings; it stared over twenty miles of the up-and-down county, and the corners kept their secrets where there were claw marks in the dust.

The child knew the house from roof to cellar; he knew the irregular lawns and the gardener's shed where flowers burst out of their jars; but he could not find the key that opened the door of the tower.

The house changed to his moods, and a lawn was the sea or the shore or the sky or whatever he wished it. When a lawn was a sad mile of water, and he was sailing on a broken flower down the waves, the gardener would come out of his shed near the island of bushes. He, too, would take a stalk, and sail. Straddling a garden broom, he would fly wherever the child wished. He knew every story from the beginning of the world.

In the beginning, he would say, there was a tree.

What kind of tree?

The tree where the blackbird's whistling.

A hawk, a hawk, cried the child.

The gardener would look up at the tree, seeing a monstrous hawk perched on a bough or an eagle swinging in the wind.

The gardener loved the Bible. When the sun sank and the

garden was full of people, he would sit with a candle in his shed, reading of the first love and the legend of apples and serpents. But the death of Christ on a tree he loved most. Trees made a fence around him, and he knew of the changing of the seasons by the hues on the bark and the rushing of sap through the covered roots. His world moved and changed as spring moved along the branches, changing their nakedness; his God grew up like a tree from the apple-shaped earth, giving bud to His children and letting His children be blown from their places by the breezes of winter; winter and death moved in one wind. He would sit in his shed and read of the crucifixion, looking over the jars of his window-shelf into the winter nights. He would think that love fails on such nights, and that many of its children are cut down.

The child transfigured the blowsy lawns with his playing. The gardener called him by his mother's name, and seated him on his knee, and talked to him of the wonders of Jerusalem and the birth in the manger.

In the beginning was the village of Bethlehem, he whispered to the child before the bell rang for tea out of the growing darkness.

Where is Bethlehem?

Far away, said the gardener, in the East.

To the east stood the Jarvis hills, hiding the sun, their trees drawing up the moon out of the grass.

The child lay in bed. He watched the rocking horse and wished that it would grow wings so that he could mount it and ride into the Arabian sky. But the winds of Wales blew at the curtains, and crickets made a noise in the untidy plot under the window. His toys were dead. He started to cry and then stopped, knowing no reason for tears. The night was windy and cold, he was warm under the sheets; the night was as big as a hill, he was a boy in bed.

Closing his eyes, he stared into a spinning cavern deeper than the darkness of the garden where the first tree on which the unreal birds had fastened stood alone and bright as fire. The tears ran back under his lids as he thought of the first tree that was planted so near him, like a friend in the garden. He crept out of bed and tiptoed to the door. The rocking horse bounded forward on its springs, startling the child into a noiseless scamper back to bed. The child looked at the horse and the horse was quiet; he tiptoed again along the carpet, and reached the door, and turned the knob around, and ran on to the landing. Feeling blindly in front of him, he made his way to the top of the stairs; he looked down the dark stairs into the hall, seeing a host of shadows curve in and out of the corners, hearing their sinuous voices, imagining the pits of their eyes and their lean arms. But they would be little and secret and bloodless, not cased in invisible armour but wound around with cloths as thin as a web; they would whisper as he walked, touch him on the shoulder, and say S in he ear. He went down the stairs; not a shadow moved in the hall, the corners were empty. He put out his hand and patted the darkness, thinking to feel some dry and velvet head creep under the fingers and edge, like a mist, into the nails. But there was nothing. He opened the front door, and the shadows swept into the garden.

Once on the path, his fears left him. The moon had lain down on the unweeded beds, and her frosts were spread on the grass. At last he came to the illuminated tree at the long gravel end, older even than the marvel of light, with the woodlice asleep under the bark, with the boughs standing out from the body like the frozen arms of a woman. The child touched the tree; it bent as to his touch. He saw a star, brighter than any in the sky, burn steadily above the first bird's tower, and shine on nowhere but on the leafless boughs and the trunk and the travelling roots.

The child had not doubted the tree. He said his prayers to it, with knees bent on the blackened twigs the night wind fetched to the ground. Then, trembling with love and cold, he ran back over the lawns towards the house.

There was an idiot to the east of the county who walked the land like a beggar. Now at a farmhouse and now at a widow's cottage he begged for his bread. A parson gave him a suit, and it lopped round his hungry ribs and shoulders and waved in the wind as he shambled over the fields. But his eyes were so wide and his neck so clear of the country dirt that no one refused him what he asked. And asking for water, he was given milk.

Where do you come from?

From the east, he said.

So they knew he was an idiot, and gave him a meal to clean the yards.

As he bent with a rake over the dung and the trodden grain, he heard a voice rise in his heart. He put his hand into the cattle's hay, caught a mouse, rubbed his hand over its muzzle, and let it go away.

*   *   *

All day the thought of the tree was with the child; all night it stood up in his dreams as the star stood above its plot. One morning towards the middle of December, when the wind from the farthest hills was rushing around the house, and the snow of the dark hours had not dissolved from lawns and roofs, he ran to the gardener's shed. The gardener was repairing a rake he had found broken. Without a word, the child sat on a seedbox at his feet, and watched him tie the teeth, and knew that the wire would not keep them together. He looked at the gardener's boots, wet with snow, at the patched knees of his trousers, at the undone buttons of his coat, and the folds of his belly under the patched flannel shirt. He looked at his hands as they busied themselves over the golden knots of wire; they were hard, brown hands, with the stains of the soil under the broken nails and the stains of tobacco on the tops of the fingers. Now the lines of the gardener's face were set in determination as time upon time he knotted the iron teeth only to feel them shake insecurely from the handle. The child was frightened of the strength and uncleanliness of the old man; but, looking at the long, thick beard, unstained and white as fleece, he soon became reassured. The beard was the beard of an apostle.

I prayed to the tree, said the child.

Always pray to a tree, said the gardener, thinking of Calvary and Eden.

I pray to the tree every night.

Pray to a tree.

The wire slid over the teeth.

I pray to that tree.

The wire snapped.

The child was pointing over the glasshouse flowers to the tree that, alone of all the trees in the garden, had no sign of snow.

An elder, said the gardener, but the child stood up from his box and shouted so loud that the unmended rake fell with a clatter on the floor.

The first tree. The first tree you told me of. In the beginning was the tree, you said. I heard you, the child shouted.

The elder is as good as another, said the gardener, lowering his voice to humour the child.

The first tree of all, said the child in a whisper.

Reassured again by the gardener's voice, he smiled through the window at the tree, and again the wire crept over the broken rake.

God grows in strange trees, said the old man. His trees come to rest in strange places.

As he unfolded the story of the twelve stages of the cross, the tree waved its boughs to the child. An apostle's voice rose out of the tarred lungs.

So they hoisted him up on a tree, and drove nails through his belly and his feet.

There was the blood of the noon sun on the trunk of the elder, staining the bark.

The idiot stood on the Jarvis hills, looking down into the immaculate valley from whose waters and grasses the mists of morning rose and were lost. He saw the dew dissolving, the cattle staring into the stream, and the dark clouds flying away at the rumour of the sun. The sun turned at the edges of the thin and watery sky like a sweet in a glass of water. He was hungry for light as the first and almost invisible rain fell on his lips; he plucked at the grass, and, tasting it, felt it lie green on his tongue. So there was light in his mouth, and light was a sound at his ears, and the whole dominion of light in the valley that had such a curious name. He had known of the Jarvis hills; their shapes rose over the slopes of the country to be seen for miles around, but no one had told him of the valley lying under the hills. Bethlehem, said the idiot to the valley, turning over the sounds of the word and giving it all the glory of the Welsh morning. He brothered the world around him, sipped at the air, as a child newly born sips and brothers the light. The life of the Jarvis valley, steaming up from the body of the grass and the trees and the long hand of the stream, lent him a new blood. Night had emptied the idiot's veins, and dawn in the valley filled them again.

Bethlehem, said the idiot to the valley.

The gardener had no present to give the child, so he took out a key from his pocket and said, This is the key to the tower. On Christmas Eve I will unlock the door for you.

Before it was dark, he and the child climbed the stairs to the tower, the key turned in the lock and the door, like the lid of a secret box, opened and let them in. The room was empty. Where are the secrets? asked the child, staring up at the matted rafters and into the spiders' corners and along the leaden panes of the window.

It is enough that I have given you the key, said the gardener, who believed the key of the universe to be hidden in his pocket along with the feathers of birds and the seeds of flowers.

The child began to cry because there were no secrets. Over and over again he explored the empty room, kicking up the dust to look for a colourless trap-door, tapping the unpanelled walls for the hollow voice of a room beyond the tower. He brushed the webs from the window, and looked out through the dust into the snowing Christmas Eve. A world of hills stretched far away into the measured sky, and the tops of the hills he had never seen climbed up to meet the falling flakes. Woods and rocks, wide seas of barren land, and a new tide of mountain sky sweeping through the black beeches, lay before him. To the east were the outlines of nameless hill creatures and a den of trees.

Who are they? Who are they?

They are the Jarvis hills, said the gardener, which have been from the beginning.

He took the child by the hand and led him away from the window. The key turned in the lock.

That night the child slept well; there was power in snow and darkness; there was unalterable music in the silence of the stars; there was a silence in the hurrying wind. And Bethlehem had been nearer than he expected.

On Christmas morning the idiot walked into the garden. His hair was wet and his flaked and ragged shoes were thick with the dirt of the fields. Tired from the long journey from the Jarvis hills, and weak for the want of food, he sat down under the elder-tree where the gardener had rolled a log. Clasping his hands in front of him, he saw the desolation of the flower-beds and the weeds that grew in profusion on the edges of the paths. The tower stood up like a tree of stone and glass over the red eaves. He pulled his coat-collar round his neck as a fresh wind sprang up and struck the tree; he looked down at his hands and saw that they were praying. Then a fear of the garden came over him, the shrubs were his enemies, and the trees that made an avenue down to the gate lifted their arms in horror. The place was too high, peering down on to the tall hills; the place was too low, shivering up at the plumed shoulders of a new mountain. Here the wind was too wild, fuming about the silence, raising a Jewish voice out of the elder boughs; here the silence beat like a human heart. And as he sat under the cruel hills, he heard a voice that was in him cry out: Why did you bring me here?

He could not tell why he had come; they had told him to come and had guided him, but he did not know who they were. The voice of a people rose out of the garden beds, and rain swooped down from heaven.

Let me be, said the idiot, and made a little gesture against the sky. There is rain on my face, there is wind on my cheeks. He brothered the rain.

So the child found him under the shelter of the tree, bearing the torture of the weather with a divine patience, letting his long hair blow where it would, with his mouth set in a sad smile.

Who was the stranger? He had fire in his eyes, the flesh of his neck under the gathered coat was bare. Yet he smiled as he sat in his rags under a tree on Christmas Day.

Where do you come from? asked the child.

From the east, answered the idiot.

The gardener had not lied, and the secret of the tower was true; this dark and shabby tree, that glistened only in the night, was the first tree of all.

But he asked again:

Where do you come from?

From the Jarvis hills.

Stand up against the tree.

The idiot, still smiling, stood up with his back to the elder.

Put out your arms like this.

The idiot put out his arms.

The child ran as fast as he could to the gardener's shed, and, returning over the sodden lawns, saw that the idiot had not moved but stood, straight and smiling, with his back to the tree and his arms stretched out.

Let me tie your hands.

The idiot felt the wire that had not mended the rake close round his wrists. It cut into the flesh, and the blood from the cuts fell shining on to the tree.

Brother, he said. He saw that the child held silver nails in the palms of his hand.

My friend and collaborator PARKE GODWIN *won the World Fantasy Award in 1982 for his brilliant ghost story "The Fire When It Comes" and has since garnered critical acclaim for his major novels of* King Arthur *and* Queen Guinevere, Firelord *and* Beloved Exile. *He has just completed the final volume of his Arthurian triptych,* The Last Rainbow, *a novel about St. Patrick. "Stroke of Mercy" is an unusual tale, unlke anything else Parke (and I suspect, anyone) has written. He describes it as a series of études. They are all in a minor key.*

Stroke of Mercy

BY PARKE GODWIN

All Paris knows that Lord Berkeley is notoriously reckless of his life. Since he is also more skilled with a pistol than I, he will doubtless kill me at the appointed hour in defense of what he is pleased to call his honor. The more honor will redound to his name if his adversary is considered sane and not a visionary lunatic.

With the heightened perception of madness, I appreciate the comedy of the situation. We are both from countries in which dueling is outlawed. Burr killed Hamilton two years ago on my native soil, but it cost him his political future. Berkeley's England has frowned on dueling for a century. Paradoxically, it is here in Paris, the most civilized city in the world, that we come to this pass.

Berkeley came to play, of course. Arrogant, idle, and rich, he has for a year and more indulged himself with the generosity of a ruling class that bequeaths moral restraint to their commons without tax by the peerage. Paris did not corrupt him; its *laissez-faire* only obviated that discretion demanded at home.

For myself, my name is Ethan Flagg. A modest patrimony has allowed me to study literature and philosophy at the Sorbonne, a living I augment in a clerical post at the American Embassy.

Berkeley and I are of an age, three and twenty, but only he is young. I am aged with a sickness of the mind. Or let me pray that

I am. At worst, to die at his hand will put a period to those nightmare visions which have tortured me since I was twelve years of age, visions that do not change but evolve, becoming clearer and more detailed until they sear now into my waking as well as sleeping hours with a sharpness of resolution consistent as it is hellish. Denise knows something of these dreams. Though I never speak of them, I sometimes wake her at night crying out in their incomprehensible patois. They are not to understand. They are horrors.

Denise—Mlle. Denise Laurenne—is the cause of my quarrel with Berkeley. As an American without class or fortune, I was devastated with happiness when she lavishly returned the attentions I commenced after seeing her perform in *l'Opéra Comique*. We are well matched, content together from the first. If she is a few years older and more experienced, if Berkeley's insolent face leers from her recent past, I care not. Most of this infected life I could discard with ease, saving those hours which she inhabits. For her sake I am committed and likely doomed.

Berkeley doesn't care a rap for Denise now. She is *déclassée*, yesterday's diversion, her name to be bandied freely about the Anglo Club to a ripple of cognizant laughter. What I could privately ignore was intolerable when he fronted me with it in the club billiard room. He chose his time carefully for the largest audience.

"But surely *la Laurenne* has mentioned me to you?"

I looked about at the ring of his faintly sneering companions who had left off their billiards to enjoy my humiliation, though I still attempted to keep my voice lowered.

"This is not a subject for discussion in a gentlemen's club."

Berkeley took snuff with an air of studied boredom. "Demme, sirrah, are you a gentleman? It seems the definition has broadened."

"Berkeley, as you were once her friend, I urge kindness—"

"Toward whom, sir? Herself—or you?"

"For her sake, if your breeding will not suffice."

He did not expect such a ready riposte. He laughed negligently—or with the appearance of negligence—careful that his friends missed none of our exchange. "Oh come, my dear . . . Flagg, is it? We are men speaking among men. I found her quite amusing."

My retort was the more scathing for its truth. As Denise put it, the well-worn shoe is a good judge of feet. She had mentioned Berkeley, and she is nothing if not candid. "That was her word, my lord: *amusant*. She catalogued you in humorous detail as a clumsy simpleton at *amour*. Clumsy or tedious, I do forget."

Berkeley's smirk faltered. His friends edged closer like a circle of hounds around two of their breed embattled. "You are a demmed liar, Master Flagg."

"Am I so?" With icy precision, then, I proceeded to a probing corroboration of this or that particular, even to the private details of his person, which left no doubt as to the veracity of my account of Berkeley's lamentable lack of finesse with women. Poor man; as I advanced from proof to proof the flush of vicious triumph that colored his inbred features darkened to murderous anger. That he had enjoyed Denise before me was to have been his coarse joke on a common clerk. That she found him hopelessly inept was my distilled revenge. The laughter of his friends was of a different timbre now.

"But why?" I sank the dagger to its hilt. "Are we not men speaking among men? It is to laugh, my lord. As she did."

In that moment before he struck me I imagined I perceived something quite alien that peered from behind Berkeley's mask of malicious ennui; as if he were an actor aware of a role, laughing not at me but at us together on a foolish stage. But it was merely my distorted judgment; he has no such sensitivity. His open hand whipped across my cheek.
my distorted judgment; he has no such sensitivity. His open hand whipped across my cheek.

"You—shop boy!"

Thus the sad comedy begins. These affairs are straitly codified in Paris. Cards of address were exchanged, the Viscount Hampton volunteered as Berkeley's second while I was advised to engage one of my own. If we could not compose our differences, the meeting would take place no later than two mornings hence when a doctor and a suitable place had been found. Someone mentioned the convenient privacy of the St. Germain district . . .

Denise considers the duel sheer folly and urges me to apologize to Berkeley, as if it were not her honor he derided. "My honor, Ethan? *Là!*"

How desirable and dear she is, her face framed in dark curls kept very short for the wigs her roles demand. She has seen most of what the world offers women and can no longer be disillusioned by any of it. Those tight *gamine* curls framing the sad warmth of her eyes is a delightful contradiction for me.

"*Mais, bien merci*, I have not such an honor. What I have is a good life with you. That is more important. For Berkeley"—her shoulders lift and fall in a gesture only the French can render eloquent—"he is a sad fool, sadder than you guess. Let it go."

"I cannot."

"By why? I do not feel dishonored. *C'est comique.*"

May you never know just how comic, Denise. "But the comedy is not ended."

"Ah, *zut!*" She throws up exasperated hands. "You men. It is not my honor but your own pride."

"He insulted you."

Denise smiles. "France herself has been used to insult since Julius Caesar. Everyone who fancied conquest has found his shortest route through Paris. She has learned to relax in the supine position, as have women. Men take what they want, women what God sends them. So we survive; it is the world."

"And am I just one more conqueror?"

"*Non, mon cher.*" Denise holds out the arms I can never deny. "When God sent you, he was feeling generous. Come: do not talk, but love me."

In her all-cleansing embrace I enjoy the only sure sanity I have ever known. Later, as Denise slumbers beside me, I stare wakefully at the moon sinking beyond our window and ponder the shape of time. There are heady new forces abroad in the world. France has built in blood what Jefferson and Paine conceived in noble experiment. The old order, Berkeley's order, is dying, but what will grow in its place? Rousseau eulogizes the perfectible human spirit with no title but Mankind, Beethoven's new symphonies are hammer strokes at the chains of tradition, but what Prometheus do we free?

And so the sickness comes over me as it spreads insensibly over the face of time. I begin to perspire profusely. Thank God Denise is asleep; perhaps this time she can sleep through it. The blood pounds in my ears; I grind my face into the pillow. The sensation of nausea engulfs me. I resist, pray with my whole being. God help me, I am here now in Paris. It is May 15, 1806. May 15. It is—

July 3, 1863. The sun's baked Gettysburg bone-dry for three days. Lieutenant Cushing's tunic is open and the front of his red underwear sticks to his chest. I'm stripped down to drawers with a bandanna around my head and tight over my ears. The sky is made of loud iron, the whistle and scream and boom of shells. Yesterday Lee had eighty guns bearing on this hill; today there's more than a hundred and twenty. He's tried our flanks for two days, and we threw him back. Old Robert E's got to fish or cut bait today. First he's got to knock out Cushing's guns.

They're trying. The Southern batteries have shelled us for two straight hours. Not the whole line, just us. We're down to three guns. The rest are junk along with their crews, and every God-damned cannon in the Army of Northern Virginia is pointed across the valley right at me.

Cushing chews a dead see-gar, staring at the trees on the opposite slope. "Why'd Lee wait? He coulda took us yesterday before we dug in."

"Down!" We flatten out as the shell screams over and explodes somewhere near number four gun. Sure enough, someone pipes up: "Number four gun. Short in the crew."

Cush leans his head against the wall, eyes shut, tuckered out. "Flagg, get that gun firing."

I round up three ammunition carriers to fill out the powder-grimy crew. It's just quarter of three. We're loading number four when it happens.

"Here they come."

Across the valley the blue Virginia flag bobs out of the covering trees, flanked by gray ranks, wave after wave of them, moving down the slope like a slow tide.

"That's Pickett."

"Prime . . . ready."

"Stand by to fire."

Pickett's Virginians are part of Dutch Longstreet's command. Old Dutch is a cautious man, but he's held off too long this time. There's all of Hancock's corps behind this wall. We've faced Pickett before: we know his brigadiers.

"There's Kemper."

"And Garnett."

"And that old dandy, Armistead."

My men stop talking. They know what's going to happen. Pickett's men must move across the valley bottom with no cover at all, every inch of it boxed and known to our guns. Nobody talks about that anymore. My mouth is full of cotton, watching them come on so slow in such straight marching order. They're leaving wounded like a leaky bucket; you can follow their path by the gray drops.

They halt once to give us a rifle burst. Off to my left, someone screams with a high, gurgly sound like a butchered hog.

"It's the lieutenant. They got Cushing."

Cush is shot through the mouth and crotch, the worst kind of wound. He won't last till night, but I can't think of that now. There's fifteen thousand Johnnys crossing the valley, more people than I ever saw at one time, and Armistead's brigade is running now, straight at me. I pick up Cush's sword—waving a sword in my dirty underwear, that's what I'll remember about Gettysburg— and run hunched over back to number four, while a fat mother-hen staff officer reins up his horse and sits there like someone was going to take one of those glass-plate pictures of him.

"You there! Who's on Mr. Cushing's guns? Who's in command?"

I jam the sword upright in the ground. "Me, Flagg. Stand by, one, two and four."

"Prime . . . ready."

"Fire!"

Another shell comes in way too close. "They got Schulz's whole crew. Number one's out."

"Fire!"

My throat is raw with smoke and screaming. We swab, load, prime, and fire. The world is all black and red and that one roar tearing out of my lungs. *Fire . . . fire . . .* There's another roar, dull and far on our left, that I realize is our other batteries as they tear into the remains of Pickett's lost division. The gray ranks are ragged and thin now, no longer anything like lines but still coming. The smoke blossoms out and blows away to show bigger and bigger holes where men ain't anymore, like a boy scooping up lead soldiers from the floor with both hands. But Armistead staggers on toward me with the pitiful remains of his brigade.

"They're too close, Flagg. We're shooting over."

"Battle range! Battle range! Run 'em down!"

The gun is flattened out to point-blank range. We work like maniacs over it, seeing nothing, knowing nothing except the gun.

"Fire!"

"Fire!"

"Fire!"

"Number two out."

"Fire!"

Armistead reaches the wall in front of us. He's wounded, but he jumps the top and gets as far as the muzzle of number four, waving his damned fool hat on his sword, yelling for his men to follow. He sees me too late as I swing Cush's sword two-handed. Die, you son of a—

He could've got me, but he was slow. And so, for me, the war goes on.

"They're goin' back. They're beat."

"Don't let 'em. Fire!"

We go on tearing up Pickett like old newspaper as he limps home over seven thousand bodies. I want to yell at George Pickett, touch him, make it personal, somehow, because it's getting damned hard to be a person anymore.

"Pickett, you—"

You what? You were a person once, too. They tell me you were one of those damned Daguerreo-type posing fools who loved war. You could still live like that in '61, but there's no way now. Seven thousand bodies in the valley down there, divided between a few cannon. How many are mine? Three, four hundred? I never broke a law in my life and I've killed more men than the busiest murderer in history. I thought about that at Bull Run the first time my gun tore up a line of Johnnys. I can't think of it now, it costs too much. You used to dream of swords and honor, Pickett. I wonder what you'll dream tonight.

We swab the gun and let it cool. The war goes on.

Denise makes our morning chocolate and discreetly absents herself on the arrival of Berkeley's second, Viscount Hampton. Son of the Earl of Albermarle, young Hampton is cap-à-pied the high-blooded dandy in fitted doeskin breeches and Gieves-tailored coat. He stands with the distance of my worn carpet between us, as if to tread on it would soil the soles of his mirror-polished shoes.

"Master Flagg: Lord Berkeley has instructed me to accept your public apology."

"*C'est dommage.* I had hoped you brought his."

"Then, as it is . . . "

"As it is."

Excellent lines for comedy. One can see Kean in my role, though I hear he loves life.

"The pistols will be Gastin Renettes loaded with the fullest allowable charge," Hampton advises. "There will be heavy recoil and less accuracy. On the other hand, in the event of a hit . . . " He elides the thought, searching me for any sign of wavering, finds none and continues. "He leaves it to you to choose a single discharge at will or exchange of shots until one party is sufficiently wounded."

"One shot at will."

Our business is concluded, yet some atom of humanity stays Hampton. "Flagg, I cannot fault you alone in this affair, but Harry Berkeley has fought before. I urge you to apologize."

"No."

"You are a helpless clerk. He has wagered his life—even foolishly—more often than I can think of. Have you ever discharged a pistol?"

"Even a cannon, my lord. Indeed, there have been days on end when I did little else."

I did not think Hampton a man for irony, but he surprises me. "You are very like him: a plain brick wall. That the two of you should duel—" Hampton shrugs. "Very well. Tomorrow morning at six. The small park beyond St. Germain." His head chops up and down once, and he withdraws.

Shortly afterward my own second arrives: Rijn van den Tronck, a friend from New York City and a fellow student at the Sorbonne. He has been to see Berkeley. Stocky, blond, and apple-cheeked, Rijn looks now like a schoolboy fresh from a stiff caning.

"He laughed at me, Ethan. He will accept an apology only if it is public. He will make none himself."

"I expected no grace from Berkeley." We sit down to the remaining chocolate and toast from breakfast. There is another important detail now, the letters I have written.

"This to my father in Washington City. In the event . . . "

"I understand."

"This to Denise."

Rijn shuffles the letters, searching for the right words. "What does she think of this?"

"I would not dwell on that. This last to yourself. It authorizes you to draw on my bank for such arrangements as may be necessary. There is a bequest for your studies. The balance to Denise."

Rijn tucks the letters in a pocket of his waistcoat. "I want no profit from this."

"Have no fear. It is not enough to embarrass your scruples."

"How do you feel, Ethan?"

"Dear Rijn, privately I am terrified for my life—as a miser fears the loss of a false penny. But I am more afraid of my sickness than of dying."

"These dreams you will not speak of: would you confide them to a physician?"

"I dare not. I should be barred up in Charenton for life."

"What are these dreams?"

"Parts of hell."

"And you will not tell even me?"

Tell Rijn? I peer into that stolid *yonker* face, its expression a testament to a sane universe and the ever-improving spirit of man.

"How could I? The mercy and justice of God, the application of humanist philosophy, these are a fixed center to the wheel of your life."

"And yours, Ethan."

"Would it help you to know there is no more God?"

"Don't say that again, Ethan."

"That someday the bare truth of this will permeate the acts, if not the sentience, of the most brutish minds; that a few will accept it, even more flee from it as they have fled down the centuries from every truth worthy of the name—"

"Stop!"

"How stop? Of the most lucid philosophy, how much has the world ever *used?* The great majority, Rijn, unable to endure the reality of God or the reality of *no* God, of personal freedom and sole responsibility, will whirl in futile circles, tearing at each other for the sake of motion. Describe this in detail? For your sanity, no."

"And you will not seek any cure?"

There is Berkeley and tomorrow.

"I seek nothing else, Rijn."

He bends across the table to grip my arm. "You can only seek while you live. Berkeley means to kill you."

"Right on, man. That mother's gonna blow me away."

The table blurs in front of me. My skin sheens with perspiration, my mind expands like a pustulant bubble. Rijn has never seen one of my attacks. He is stunned at the bastard English.

"What . . . what did you say?"

The demitasse falls from my hand, shattering on the table.

"Number one engine doesn't sound good. Skeet says there are leaves hanging off the tail assembly."

"Denise! Come quickly!"

She is at my side instantly. "It is the speech of his sickness," she says tremulously. *"Bon Dieu*, it comes day and night now. Get him to bed, Rijn. We must hold his arms."

"Hold me tight, Denise . . . "

"I will, my darling."

I feel Rijn's sturdy grip on one arm, the light, loving touch of Denise on the other. "What is today? The sixteenth of May. Say it; that sometimes staves it off. The sixteenth of May in the year of our Blessed Lord, 1806. *Say it."*

"The sixteenth of May . . . " They repeat it with me, over and over and—

"—over the target in seven minutes."

Lt. Saylors, the pilot, sounds shaky on the intercom, like we all feel. This is a bad run. Number one engine isn't turning over right. You can feel when all four engines on a B-24 are copacetic, a deep, steady drone. You get so you hear trouble quick.

"Over the target—shit, we're under it."

Gordini's right. We're coming in at treetop level to stay under the kraut radar. That's why a screwed-up engine is bad news. No room for error at fifty feet with a full bomb load.

The kraut phone-spotters must have picked us up by now.

Saylors again: "Six minutes to target. Commo check. Copilot."

"Check," says Borowski.

"Bombardier-navigator."

Sweeney in the greenhouse: "Ding-how."

"Engineer. Hey, Garson."

"Roger, you're five by." In my earphones, Garson sounds worried. "Just listening to number one."

"Sounds bad."

"What's your temp gauge reading?"

"Too high."

"Same here. Can you ease off number one, skip?"

"Negative," Saylors says. "Not now I can't."

"She's gonna go."

"She goes, you're out of a job."

"She goes, you're out of the war."

"Bird dog it, Garson. I'll feather if we have to. Left waist, talk to me."

I hear the clack-clack, clack-*clack*, as Gordini cocks the bolt on his .50. "Left waist, loud and clear."

"Roger. Right waist. Flagg?"

I try not to sound as scared as I am. I'm a short-timer. Five more missions and I rotate. After the fortieth I started praying for milk runs, but it's been Ploesti all month. "Right waist, loud and clear."

"Tail bay, sound off."

In the tail greenhouse, Skeet Mahoney does a Bugs Bunny over the 'com. "Eeeahh—what's up, Doc? You're alive and five by five. What's our altitude, skip?"

"Doesn't even read."

Skeet laughs over the 'com. "You won't believe this. We got leaves hanging off the tail assembly. Purple Heart, men! I been goosed by an oak tree."

Saylors again, sharp: "Knock off the chatter. All turrets clear your guns."

I give the .50 two short bursts. Beautiful and smooth, like a Krupa drum riff. "Right waist clear."

"Left waist clear."

"Tail clear."

"Okay, pot right. Four minutes to target. Going upstairs."

I feel it in my stomach as the Liberator pulls up steep to make altitude for the bomb run. The other ships climb with us. The German fighters will be here any time now. Forty-four missions, this is forty-five, five to go. I won't make it. I was born in this waist bay, in a greasy leather flight suit and flak vest, and I'll die in it.

We make bombing altitude, sweating number one engine all the way, but we're formed and ready for the bomb run.

"Five hundred, Sween. Take it."

"Roger."

"Everybody look out for company."

Three minutes to Ploesti, the big kraut gas station. A lot of oil they won't get to use. In the nose greenhouse Sweeney is the boss now.

"Commencing run."

"You got it. Give me a heading."

"Adjust to course . . . 030."

"030, roger."

"Bomb bay doors open."

"Bandits!" Skeet squeaks with excitement. "ME-109s, six

o'clock high!"

"Steady, steady."

"Easy, Skeet," I tell him. "Let 'em break first. Suck 'em in."

Sweeney barks at Saylors: *"Steady* on 030. Give me some trim."
What he sees now through the Norden is our whole payoff.

"Correcting to 030."

"Right . . . hold it. Hold it." Sweeney's nothing now but an eye
and cross-hairs and a thumb on the bomb-release button. "Hold
it . . . "

The MEs dive through our formation like a school of sharks.
Messerschmidts, long thin wasps, fast and hard to knock down. I
watch them wheel away, waiting, saving ammo for when we'll
really need it. And then from nowhere two more hit us.

"Going to seven o'clock, Skeet!"

"Bombs away!"

"Ding-how! Let's go home."

The ship jerks and lifts with the loss of the bomb weight. The
burning oil rigs below tilt toward me as Saylors banks her up in a
climbing turn. As we level out, the first of the flak hits us. They've
got to protect Ploesti, we've been hitting it so much. The anti-
aircraft cover has doubled in the last month, it's Flak Alley now,
the sky is full of sloppy inkblots as the bursts blossom out. There's
a flat *boof* and the screech of metal punching through metal.
Someone makes an awful sound on the 'com. I twist around to
Gordy.

"Hey, who?"

Gordini's nothing but blood under his helmet. That's it, my
personal kiss of death. Gordy and I started out together, one of
the first crews in North Africa. If he can get it . . .

"Three o'clock, Flagg!"

I swivel around, swinging the gun. Gordy got it, not me, not
yet. "I see him."

The ME turns tight and comes in with the sun behind him.
White sky and a black bird getting bigger and bigger. I used to
love the sky. Will I ever look at it again without searching, without
fear? We all of us have that tight look now, like scared hawks that
have no love for the sky but only exist in it as long as they're fast.

I give the kraut a burst and he veers off, wobbling. The waist
bay is full of smoke. "What's burning?"

"Anybody hit?"

"Gordy."

"Six o'clock!"

"I'm on it."

"Way to go, Skeet."

The ship lurches as we take another burst of flak. The drone of the engines strains higher.

"Number four's burning. Fire in number four!"

"Lead 'em, Skeet. Lead 'em!"

"Feathering number four."

We're running on three engines now, and the waist is foggy with smoke. "Waist to pilot, what's burning?"

"Two o'clock! Coming around to you, Flagg."

The ME is turning in, still broadside to me, a good shot. I lead him and get off a solid burst before the .50 jams. My lungs are full of smoke. I go on oxygen as the next blast of flak staggers the ship. Borowski is screaming over the intercom, and for an awful moment I think no one's left in the cockpit.

"Sween!"

That's all I hear before the junk of our nose greenhouse falls below and behind me, Sween twisted up in it. Then number one engine starts to miss. That's bad, that's Sweat City. Two engines gone, we'll fall behind the formation, what's left of it. Two MEs, sensing us for a loser, turn in at five o'clock. Skeet's gun *bud-dud-duts* in a short burst, and then quits. The fighters come on, eight guns wide open, tracers streaming into our tail.

"Skeet? Hey, tail! Sound off."

Skeet chokes something into the 'com.

"Pilot to waist. Get back to Mahoney when you can."

"Wilco. Where's the fire?"

"Aux wiring, no big deal."

I haul the .50 breech open, pull out the bent shell case that caused the stoppage, then yank back the bolt twice to cock it, glaring out at the white panel of sky where less than half our flight is wavering home. Lot of Maydays on the radio. We hope someone's listening, even the krauts. They crash, they ditch over Rumania, over the Adriatic, over Italy and the Mediterranean. To be captured, to be picked up by air-sea, to drown, to spend a crazy day or two drinking wine with Italians before coming home to fly again. A Purple Heart and two bucks extra on payday.

We've taken a lot of flak, but we're beyond German fighter range. "Waist to pilot. Gonna check out Skeet."

I belly along the crawlspace with the medical kit over my

shoulder. The tail greenhouse is chewed ribbons. By the time I wrestle off Skeet's flak vest and leather jacket, I'm working on a corpse. I plug into his 'com set.

"Waist to pilot. Skeet bought it. How're you doing up there?"

"Engineer, how's two and three?"

"Overheating."

"Okay, I'll try to ease her down. Flagg, get back on the waist."

Crawling back to my gun, I feel the familiar jerk and grind of the landing gear. Borowski's trying it out. This time there's more grind than jerk.

"They hit the gear. We can't lock down."

I look at the mess of Gordini behind his gun. I'm not going to make the Big Fifty, but I did this time, and so it goes on while the sky beyond the right waist bay, the curtained window, deepens to morning blue.

I am in bed, Denise sobbing against my cheek.

"The ship's junk. We had to belly in."

Over Denise's thin shoulder, Rijn holds the open Bible, praying in a low, earnest voice.

"They had to cut Skeet out of the greenhouse."

"You see?" Denise raises her tear-streaming eyes to Rijn. "You see what I live with, what I love?"

"Rijn . . . you have been praying?"

"For you, Ethan. God help you."

"I told you: God is gone. Even Satan is obsolete. There's only us."

And I stare past them to the May morning beyond our window with the self-preserving keenness of a frightened hawk. Be swift, tomorrow Berkeley, be skilled. God has abdicated, and his throne is left to the hunting birds.

There will be prisoners at Auschwitz who survive only so long as they clean, weigh, and keep accurate tally of the gold parted from the teeth of other, gassed prisoners. Like the camp officials who are more intrigued with the economy of Zyklon B than its ultimate use, they cannot afford to ponder what they do, and blot it out by concentrating on weights and the fluctuating value of gold. All true horror sheaths itself in banality.

On this early morning, the day of my death, Denise concentrates on our chocolate and poached eggs as if their correct preparation is the answer to all conflict. She speaks with studied ease about the coming evening, not about the hours in between.

She will not be here for supper; she performs in *Tartuffe*. Her eyes dart again and again to the door. She listens for Rijn's step on the stair. I must pretend with her.

"We will dine in Montmartre after the theatre. I fancy venison in wine tonight."

"But it is so expensive, Ethan."

"Oh, just this once. We will make a treat of it."

The footsteps thud on the stair. The napkin crumples in her fist. I rise to admit Rijn.

"The carriage is waiting, Ethan."

I turn to take up my cloak. Denise is holding it ready. She arranges it about my shoulders with a too-bright smile.

"*Bon chance, cheri*. Rijn, we dine in Montmartre tonight after my performance. Will you join us?"

He takes his cue from my imperative glance. "With pleasure."

"Why do you not both come to the theatre?"

"We will be there," I promise.

"*Je t'aime*, Ethan."

I start to embrace her one last time. "You have made me very—"

"No, don't!" Denise's hands carve the shape of helplessness in the air. "Go quickly."

This is our parting. Any other would be unbearable.

Our carriage rolls along the Boulevard St. Germain as the early sun splashes across doors and windows. The breeze is heavy with the scent of dew and spring flowers. It will be a warm day: good weather at Gettysburg, over Ploesti, north of Da Nang. And one day will come a wind so hot that glass melts and steel itself drips like tallow. Distant, but in three years the man will be born who orders my guns to Gettysburg. It begins.

Our driver turns the horses onto an uncobbled road. We jolt with the ruts, and I catch sight of a bare, dead tree among the greenery. Napalm does things like that.

I lean back against the upholstered seat. I know my symptoms well; it will not be a bad attack this time, more like a light doze. If I keep my eyes closed, Rijn will think I am merely at ease or praying.

We defoliated so much of Vietnam, the whole ecology is shot. Less jungle for Cong to hide in, but I know they mined this trail. Even spaced out on grass, you get a feel for mines.

August 4, 1969. S-2 said the trail is cleared of mines, but Big John steps on a toe-popper and loses half his foot. While they're dragging him off the trail, Barrio gets himself fucked up on a betty mine. The platoon freezes. Radio calls for a dust-off to pull out the wounded. Nobody wants to move. Sergeant Tuck is moving up and down the scared line, chewing ass in pure Tennessee backwoods, making one man move, then another. We go on, single file and uptight, putting our feet in the same place as the guy in front until we reach the paddy and slide into nice safe mud.

We don't need those mines, not after a week of search-and-destroy. I've been on uppers most of it and a little hash this morning. I couldn't make it any other way. Lost too many good guys. I'm going into that village flying like the rest of the platoon. All but Tuck.

Tuck's RA, bucking for thirty years. Without the army he'd be pumping gas back in Trashville. He digs this shit; he goes after Charlies for the fun of it when the rest of us would just stay cool. He gets people wasted, guys who were real short and counting days till they got back to the world.

I don't feel much, but I can still be scared. Big John and Barrio and me were the last of the old squad. My chances have run clean off the slide rule, man. Today, tomorrow I'll get it. With hash it won't hurt so much.

The navy fighters lay down napalm, but they must be smoking themselves, because most of it goes wide. The heat is unbelievable as we move in. Napalm sucks up the air; if you don't burn you can smother.

We hear incoming: Cong 82-mm. mortars. Somebody in Third Platoon starts popping smoke grenades, figuring the Cong is still in the village. The wind blows the smoke right down on us. Nobody can see anything. We're flushing old men and women and little dinks out of the huts, all of us blind with brown and yellow smoke. A white blur of movement flickers in the corner of my eye. I wheel and fire out of reflex. It's a dink, maybe ten years old. He grabs his arm and runs screaming back into the hut.

Tuck chops his arm at the few lousy huts. "Burn 'em all. This one first if they won't come out."

"It's just a dink in there."

"What're you, Flagg? the fuckin Red Cross? Burn it."

Screw it. For all I know the dink would drop a grenade in the gas tank of someone's jeep tomorrow. I put my lighter to the roof thatch and the hut goes up fast. Tuck lobs a frag grenade inside. It goes off like the end of the world. The roof lifts, then falls through, nothing but fire now.

The black sizzling thing crawls out of the hut and flops over, twisting like bacon on a skillet as the fire fries and splits its skin. Thank God for the hash. Used to be something like that would make me sick. But I'm out of it now, don't feel a thing. Not even when Tuck gets zapped.

One minute he's in front of me, then going over backwards with the stray round from shit knows where; maybe someone in our own platoon. Screw Tuck. He got a lot of guys scratched for nothing. The hash high makes it funny. Tuck falls and falls forever like trick photography, and I'm laughing as we pull out of the village. What the hell, I'm splitsville anyway, never gonna make it back to the world. Tuck got it, not me, and so it goes on . . .

"Ethan? We've arrived."

We alight from the carriage. Already the day is turning humid. A hundred paces away among the trees are Berkeley and Hampton, both in black, and two other men.

"Ethan, for the last time, I implore you—"

"Let me thank you for your friendship now, Rijn. I have loved you." I fumble for his square hand, but he embraces me fiercely.

"Then for that love and Denise's, stop this. You are ill. Give him his meaningless apology. This is insanity."

"Come. They are waiting."

We move toward the assignation over wet grass that whistles about our boots, through scarlet azaleas and yellow marigolds. The forest at morning looks new-made, virginal, the sins to come unthinkable. It is a good day to leave it.

"By God, Flagg," Berkeley yawns by way of greeting. "I did not suppose you would be so prompt."

"It is a habit of shop boys, my lord."

Hampton opens the pistol case, murmuring introductions: the bewhiskered doctor still red-eyed from too little sleep, his hastily recruited assistant, a young medical student. Hampton offers the pistols to Rijn for inspection. He does not take them.

"Lord Berkeley—doctor—my friend is genuinely ill—"

"Rijn, no more."

"He is in no condition to fight."

Hampton remarks gravely. "By coincidence, Lord Berkeley himself is not in the best of health."

Berkeley inclines his head to me. "Nevertheless, sufficient to the time."

Rijn is desperate. "Then compose, reconcile."

Berkeley removes his high, buckled hat. "That consideration is past, is it not, Flagg?"

"As are many things. Give me a pistol, Rijn."

Rijn examines each weapon and offers me one reluctantly. How solid and final it feels in my hand. Hampton draws Rijn and the others to one side. "Master Flagg has stipulated a single exchange of shots. Back to back, gentlemen. Twenty paces to my count, turn on my command. Single shot at will."

Berkeley's shoulders press against mine; he turns his head slightly to me. *"Bon chance,* shop boy."

"One, two—"

We step out; the last scene of the comedy begins, an historic performance. We are burying Man as an individual. Our farce has the absurd motives of artificial honor, but at least each of us completes and understands the whole violence as the will of an individual. The conflicts to come will employ more and more men who understand less and less of what they do until they are drugged numb by the very proliferation and banality of horrors.

"Eleven, twelve—"

To us, freedom has an elitist meaning. To that coming mass, it will be a terror. When men walk stultified through obscenities, the last thing their atrophied souls will want is to control, to assert, to understand. As the horror grows they will hurl their missiles from farther and farther away. As the crime grows, the artificial innocence must be greater until, one day, there will not be enough distance to purchase detachment at any price.

"Nineteen, twenty."

Is death so frightening that we must labor to make it meaningless? We are near extinct, Berkeley, having still shoulders to bear the burden of being individuals, of declaring ourselves, first and last, *responsible.* Neither of us deserves tomorrow.

"Turn!"

We whirl in upon each other like dancers, the last of an age. Berkeley's arm comes down in mirror movement to mine. He is slim and erect before me. We are beautiful, two Greek columns, proud but past. In the wine-sweet morning the two shots merge into one explosion.

My God . . . he missed.

The pistol bucked so hard in my hand, surely my shot would have gone wild. But Berkeley staggers and sinks to his knees. Instantly Hampton and the doctor are at him opening the black coat. Rijn runs to me, tearful with relief.

"God be praised, I need not send those letters. It is over."

But I am hurrying toward Berkeley. There is a spreading stain on his shirt just under his heart. I kneel beside him, feeling that there has been, somehow, an unimaginable mistake that must be set right. Berkeley's gaze is fixed somewhere beyond me, his lips moving silently.

"Hampton, how could he miss?"

"You fool! He meant to."

The doctor opens Berkeley's shirt to reveal the smallish wound and the larger discoloration around it. "It is very close to the heart. There is internal hemorrhaging. I am afraid . . . "

Hampton sobs over the head cradled in his arms, strangled with grief and bewilderment. "You have freed him. Harry, it is enough this time? Have you found it? Oh, Flagg, if you knew how he sought this! Let it not be on your conscience. You have shown him mercy."

"Red Fox Leader to Red Fox Four . . . "

"He pursued death as this demon pursued him—"

"Red Fox Four . . . "

"—as if there were no God left in the world."

"Be still!" I bend close to Berkeley as the pattering, fevered whisper rises to an audible voice. His head moves sharply from side to side, not in delirium but searching and alert. I have seen that look before: just before he struck me in the Anglo Club. Saylors had it after a month on the Ploesti run.

The doctor closes his bag: "A matter of moments. It will not help to move him."

"Red Fox Leader!" The voice is clear and unemotional, the accent still recognizably Oxfordian but clipped and subtly shaded with overtones Hampton will not live long enough to hear spoken in London.

"Red Fox Leader to Red Fox Four, do you read me, Richard? Take the flight. No, I can't bail out. Bloody flak got my chute . . . a piece of me too, I'm afraid. Canopy jammed. I'm burning. Romney air-sea rescue. Romney air-sea, this is Red Fox Leader. Mayday, Mayday. Can't make the coast, losing airspeed and altitude rapidly. Course 285, airspeed 220 and falling. Going to belly in if I can. Hope you people arrive first. Mayday, Mayday. Approximate position . . ."

His head swivels left and right and up. Even as his eyes close, Berkeley searches a sky I have known, empty white or full of death, with the look of a frightened hawk.

Thus Berkeley's lesson to me: the infection is spreading. Though isolated in my disease, I am not alone.

Berkeley went down over the Channel. For me the war goes on.

I hear nothing Rijn says to me. Plodding back to the coffin of my carriage, I shred the unsent letters, scattering white blossoms amid the scarlet and yellow. There is always hope. I cannot live forever. The Romantics have toyed with opium and suicide, but theirs is a self-consciously tragic muse. Mine is banality. I will dine with Denise in Montmartre and wait for good flying weather over Washington and Moscow.

LEONID ANDREYEV *(1871–1919) disapproved of the czarist regime, but was equally revolted by the communists. The darkness of his vision is most familiar in his gargoylish play* He Who Gets Slapped, *but is ably represented by the following tale, one of the most chilling works ever penned: an existential reduction of the legend of the man resurrected by Jesus.*

Lazarus

BY LEONID ANDREYEV

When Lazarus left the grave, where for three days and three nights he had been under the enigmatical sway of death, and returned alive to his dwelling, for a long time no one noticed in him those sinister things which made his name a terror as time went on. Gladdened by the sight of him who had been returned to life, those near to him made much of him, and satisfied their burning desire to serve him, in solicitude for his food and drink and garments. They dressed him gorgeously, and when, like a bridegroom in his bridal clothes, he sat again among them at the table and ate and drank, they wept with tenderness. And they summoned the neighbors to look at him who had risen miraculously from the dead. These came and shared the joy of the hosts. Strangers from far-off towns and hamlets came and adored the miracle in tempestuous words. The house of Mary and Martha was like a beehive.

Whatever was found new in Lazarus' face and gestures was thought to be some trace of a grave illness and of the shocks recently experienced. Evidently the destruction wrought by death on the corpse was only arrested by the miraculous power, but its effects were still apparent; and what death had succeeded in doing with Lazarus' face and body was like an artist's unfinished sketch seen under thin glass. On Lazarus' temples, under his eyes, and in the hollows of his cheeks, lay a deep and cadaverous blueness; cadaverously blue also were his long fingers, and around his finger-nails, grown long in the grave, the blue had become purple and dark. On his lips, swollen in the grave, the skin had burst in places, and thin reddish cracks were formed, shining as though covered with transparent mica. And he had grown stout. His body, puffed up in the grave, retained its monstrous size and showed those frightful swellings in which one sensed the presence of the rank liquid of decomposition. But the heavy corpselike odor which penetrated Lazarus' grave-clothes and, it seemed, his very body, soon entirely disappeared, the blue spots on his face and hands grew paler, and the reddish cracks closed up, although they never disappeared altogether. That is how Lazarus looked when he appeared before people, in his second life, but his face looked natural to those who had seen him in the coffin.

In addition to the changes in his appearance, Lazarus' temper seemed to have undergone a transformation, but this had attracted no attention. Before his death Lazarus had always been cheerful and carefree, fond of laughter and a merry joke. It was because of this brightness and cheerfulness, with not a touch of malice and darkness that the Master had grown so fond of him. But now Lazarus had grown grave and taciturn, he never jested, nor responded with laughter to other people's jokes; and the words which he very infrequently uttered were the plainest, most ordinary and necessary words, as deprived of depth and significance as those sounds with which animals express pain and pleasure, thirst and hunger. They were the words that one can say all one's life, and yet they give no indication of what pains and gladdens the depths of the soul.

Thus, with the face of a corpse which for three days had been under the heavy sway of death, dark and taciturn, already appallingly transformed, but still unrecognized by anyone in his new self, he was sitting at the feast-table among friends and relatives, and his gorgeous nuptial garments glittered with yellow gold and bloody scarlet. Broad waves of jubilation, now soft, now tempestuously sonorous, surged around him; warm glances of love were reaching out for his face, still cold with the coldness of the grave; and a friend's warm palm caressed his blue, heavy hand. Music played—the tympanum and the pipe, the cithara and the harp. It was as though bees hummed, grasshoppers chirped and birds warbled over the happy house of Mary and Martha.

One of the guests incautiously lifted the veil. By a thoughtless word he broke the serene charm and uncovered the truth in all its naked ugliness. Ere the thought formed itself in his mind, his lips uttered with a smile: "Why do you not tell us what happened yonder?"

All grew silent, startled by the question. It was as if it occurred to them only now that for three days Lazarus had been dead, and they looked at him, anxiously awaiting his answer. But Lazarus kept silence.

"You do not wish to tell us," wondered the man; "is it so terrible yonder?"

And again his thought came after his words. Had it been otherwise, he would not have asked this question, which at that very moment oppressed his heart with its insufferable horror. Uneasiness seized all present, and with a feeling of heavy weariness they awaited Lazarus' words, but he was sternly and coldly silent, and his eyes were lowered. As if for the first time, they noticed the frightful blueness of his face and his repulsive obesity. On the table, as if forgotten by Lazarus, rested his bluish-purple wrist, and to this all eyes turned, as if it were from it that the awaited answer was to come. The musicians were still playing, but now the silence reached them too, and even as water extinguishes scattered embers, so were their merry tunes extinguished in the silence. The pipe grew silent; the voices of the sonorous tympanum and the murmuring harp died away; and as if the strings had burst, the cithara answered with a tremulous, broken note. Silence.

"You do not wish to say?" repeated the guest, unable to check his chattering tongue. But the stillness remained unbroken, and the bluish purple hand rested motionless. And then he stirred slightly and everyone felt relieved. He lifted up his eyes, and lo! straightway embracing everything in one heavy glance, fraught with weariness and horror, he looked at them—Lazarus who had risen from the dead.

It was the third day since Lazarus had left the grave. Ever since then many had experienced the pernicious power of his eye, but neither those who were crushed by it forever, nor those who found the strength to resist in it the primordial sources of life, which is as mysterious as death, never could they explain the horror which lay motionless in the depth of his black pupils. Lazarus looked calmly and simply with no desire to conceal anything, but also with no intention to say anything: he looked coldly, as one who is infinitely indifferent to those alive. Many carefree people came close to him without noticing him, and only later did they learn with astonishment and fear who that calm stout man was that walked slowly by, almost touching them with his gorgeous and dazzling garments. The sun did not cease shining when he was looking nor did the fountain hush its murmur, and the sky overhead remained cloudless and blue. But the man under the spell of his enigmatical look heard no more the fountain and saw not the sky overhead. Sometimes he wept bitterly, sometimes he tore his hair and in a frenzy called for help; but more often it came to pass that apathetically and quietly he began to die, and so he languished many years, before everybody's eyes wasted away, colorless, flabby, dull, like a tree silently drying up in a stony soil. And of those who gazed at him, the one who wept madly sometimes felt again the stir of life; the others never.

"So you do not wish to tell us what you have seen yonder?" repeated the man. But now his voice was impassive and dull, and deadly gray weariness showed in Lazarus' eyes. And deadly gray weariness covered like dust all the faces, and with dull amazement the guests stared at each other and did not understand wherefore they had gathered here and sat at the rich table. The talk ceased. They thought it was time to go home, but could not overcome the weariness which glued their muscles, and they kept on sitting there, yet apart and torn away from each other, like pale fires scattered over a dark field.

But the musicians were paid to play, and again they took their instruments, and again tunes full of studied mirth and studied sorrow began to flow and to rise. They unfolded the customary melody, but the guests harkened in dull amazement. Already they knew not why it is necessary, and why it is well, that people should pluck strings, inflate their cheeks, blow in thin pipes, and produce a bizarre, many-voiced noise.

"What bad music!" said someone.

The musicians took offense and left. Following them, the guests left one after another, for night was already come. And when placid darkness encircled them and they began to breathe with more ease, suddenly Lazarus' image loomed up before each one in formidable radiance: the blue face of a corpse, grave clothes gorgeous and resplendent, a cold look in the depths of which lay motionless an unknown horror. As though petrified, they were standing far apart, and darkness enveloped them, but in the darkness blazed brighter and brighter the supernatural vision of him who for three days had been under the enigmatical sway of death. For three days had he been dead: thrice had the sun risen and set, but he had been dead. And now he is again among them, touches them, looks at them, and through the black disks of his pupils, as through darkened glass, stares the unknowable Yonder.

No one was taking care of Lazarus, for no friends, no relatives were left to him, and the great desert, which encircled the holy city, came near the very threshold of his dwelling. And the desert entered his house, and stretched on his couch, like a wife, and extinguished the fires. No one was taking care of Lazarus. One after the other, his sisters—Mary and Martha—forsook him. For a long while Martha was loath to abandon him, for she knew not who would feed him and pity him. She wept and prayed. But one night, when the wind was roaming in the desert and with a hissing sound the cypresses were bending over the roof, she dressed noiselessly, and secretly left the house. Lazarus probably heard the door slam; it banged against the sidepost under the gusts of the desert wind, but he did not rise to go out and look at her that was abandoning him. All the night long the cypresses hissed over his head and plaintively thumped the door, letting in the cold, greedy desert.

Like a leper he was shunned by everyone, and it was proposed to tie a bell to his neck, as is done with lepers, to warn people against sudden meetings. But someone remarked, growing frightfully pale, that it would be too horrible if by night the moaning of Lazarus' bell were suddenly heard under the pillows, and so the project was abandoned.

And since he did not take care of himself, he would probably have starved to death, had not the neighbors brought him food in fear of something that they sensed but vaguely. The food was brought to him by children; they were not afraid of Lazarus, nor did they mock him with naive cruelty, as children are wont to do with the wretched and miserable. They were indifferent to him, and Lazarus answered them with the same coldness; he had no desire to caress the black little curls, and to look into their innocent shining eyes. Given to Time and to the desert, his house was crumbling down, and long since had his famishing goats

wandered away to the neighbouring pastures. His bridal garments
became threadbare. Ever since that happy day when the musicians
played, he had worn them unaware of the difference of the new
and the worn. The bright colours grew dull and faded; vicious dogs
and the sharp thorns of the desert turned the tender fabric into
rags.

By day, when the merciless sun slew all things alive, and even
scorpions sought shelter under stones and writhed there in a mad
desire to sting, he sat motionless under the sun's rays, his blue face
and the uncouth, bushy beard lifted up, bathing in the fiery flood.

When people still talked to him, he was once asked: "Poor
Lazarus, does it please you to sit thus and to stare at the sun?"

And he had answered: "Yes, it does."

So strong, it seemed, was the cold of his three days' grave, so
deep the darkness that there was no heat on earth to warm
Lazarus, nor a splendor that could brighten the darkness of his
eyes. That is what came to the mind of those who spoke to
Lazarus, and with a sigh they left him.

And when the scarlet, flattened globe would lower, Lazarus
would set out for the desert and walk straight toward the sun, as
if striving to reach it. He always walked straight toward the sun,
and those who tried to follow him and to spy upon what he was
doing at night in the desert, retained in their memory the black
silhouette of a tall stout man against the red background of an
enormous flattened disk. Night pursued them with her horrors,
and so they did not learn of Lazarus' doings in the desert, but the
vision of the black on red was forever branded on their brains.
Just as a beast with a splinter in its eye furiously rubs its muzzle
with its paws, so they too foolishly rubbed their eyes, but what
Lazarus had given was indelible, and Death alone could efface it.

But there were people who lived far away, who never saw
Lazarus and knew of him only by report. With daring curiosity,
which is stronger than fear and feeds upon it, with hidden
mockery, they would come to Lazarus who was sitting in the sun
and enter into conversation with him. By this time Lazarus'
appearance had changed for the better and was not so terrible.
The first minute they snapped their fingers and thought of how
stupid the inhabitants of the holy city were; but when the short
talk was over and they started homeward, their looks were such
that the inhabitants of the holy city recognized them at once and

said: "Look, there is one more fool on whom Lazarus has set his eye;" and they shook their heads regretfully, and lifted up their arms.

There came brave, intrepid warriors, with tinkling weapons; happy youths came with laughter and song; busy tradesmen, jingling their money, ran in for a moment, and haughty priests leaned their crosiers against Lazarus' door, and they were all strangely changed, as they came back. The same terrible shadow swooped down upon their souls and gave a new appearance to the old familiar world.

Those who still had the desire to speak, expressed their feelings thus:

"All things tangible and visible grew hollow, light and transparent, similar to lightsome shadows in the darkness of night;

"For that great darkness, which holds the whole cosmos, was dispersed neither by the sun nor by the moon and the stars, but like an immense black shroud enveloped the earth and like a mother embraced it;

"It penetrated all the bodies, iron and stone, and the particles of the bodies, having lost their ties, grew lonely; and it penetrated into the depth of the particles, and the particles became lonely;

"For that great void, which encircles the cosmos, was not filled by things visible, neither by the sun, nor by the moon and the stars, but reigned unrestrained, penetrating everywhere, severing body from body, particle from particle;

"In the void, hollow trees spread hollow roots threatening a fantastic fall; temples, palaces, and houses loomed up and they were hollow; and in the void men moved about restlessly, but they were light and hollow like shadows;

"For time was no more, and the beginning of all things came near their end: the building was still being built, and builders were still hammering away, and its ruins were already seen and the void in its place; the man was still being born, but already funeral candles were burning at his head, and now they were extinguished, and there was the void in place of the man and of the funeral candles;

"And wrapped by void and darkness the man in despair trembled in the face of the horror of the infinite."

Thus spake the men who had still a desire to speak. But, surely, much more could those have told who wished not to speak, and died in silence.

*　　*　　*

At that time there lived in Rome a renowned sculptor. In clay, marble and bronze he wrought bodies of gods and men, and such was their beauty that people called them immortal. But he himself was discontented and asserted that there was something even more beautiful, that he could not embody either in marble or in bronze. "I have not yet gathered the glimmers of the moon, nor have I my fill of sunshine," he was wont to say, "and there is no soul in my marble, no life in my beautiful bronze." And when on moonlight nights he slowly walked along the road, crossing the black shadows of cypresses, his white tunic glittering in the moonshine, those who met him would laugh in a friendly way and say:

"Are you going to gather moonshine, Aurelius? Why then did you not fetch baskets?"

And he would answer, laughing and pointing to his eyes:

"Here are the baskets wherein I gather the sheen of the moon and the glimmer of the sun."

And so it was: the moon glimmered in his eyes and the sun sparkled therein. But he could not translate them into marble, and therein lay the serene tragedy of his life.

He was descended from an ancient patrician race, had a good wife and children, and suffered from no want.

When the obscure rumor about Lazarus reached him, he consulted his wife and friends and undertook the far journey to Judea to see him who had miraculously risen from the dead. He was somewhat weary in those days and he hoped that the road would sharpen his blunted senses. What was said of Lazarus did not frighten him: he had pondered much over Death, did not like it, but he disliked also those who confused it with life. "In this life are life and beauty," thought he; "beyond is Death, and enigmatical; and there is no better thing for a man to do than to delight in life and the beauty of all things living." He had even a vainglorious desire to convince Lazarus of the truth of his own view and restore his soul to life, as his body had been restored. This seemed so much easier because the rumors, shy and strange, did not render the whole truth about Lazarus and but vaguely warned against something frightful.

Lazarus had just risen from the stone in order to follow the sun which was setting in the desert, when a rich Roman, attended by an armed slave, approached him and addressed him in a sonorous voice: "Lazarus!"

And Lazarus beheld a superb face, lit with glory, and arrayed in fine clothes, and precious stones sparkling in the sun. The red light lent to the Roman's face and head the appearance of gleaming bronze: that also Lazarus noticed. He resumed obediently his place and lowered his weary eyes.

"Yes, you are ugly, my poor Lazarus," quietly said the Roman, playing with his golden chain; "you are even horrible, my poor friend; and Death was not lazy that day when you fell so heedlessly into his hands. But you are stout, and, as the great Caesar used to say, fat people are not ill-tempered; to tell the truth, I don't understand why men fear you. Permit me to spend the night in your house; the hour is late, and I have no shelter."

Never had anyone asked Lazarus' hospitality.

"I have no bed," said he.

"I am somewhat of a soldier and I can sleep sitting," the Roman answered. "We shall build a fire."

"I have no fire."

"Then we shall have our talk in the darkness, like two friends. I think you will find a bottle of wine."

"I have no wine."

The Roman laughed.

"Now I see why you are so somber and dislike your second life. No wine! Why, then we shall do without it: there are words that make the head go round better than the Falcrnian."

By a sign he dismissed the slave, and they remained alone. And again the sculptor started speaking, but it was as if, together with the setting sun, life had left his words; and they grew pale and hollow, as if they staggered on unsteady feet, as if they slipped and fell down, drunk with the heavy lees of weariness and despair. And black chasms grew up between the words, like far-off hints of the great void and the great darkness.

"Now I am your guest, and you will not be unkind to me, Lazarus!" said he. "Hospitality is the duty even of those who for three days were dead. Three days, I was told, you rested in the grave. There it must be cold . . . and thence comes your ill habit of going without fire and wine. As to me, I like fire; it grows dark here so rapidly . . . The lines of your eyebrows and forehead are quite, quite interesting: they are like ruins of strange palaces, buried in ashes after an earthquake. But why do you wear such ugly and queer garments? I have seen bridegrooms in your country, and they wear such clothes—are they not funny?—and terrible? . . . But are you a bridegroom?"

The sun had already disappeared, a monstrous black shadow came running from the east, it was as if gigantic bare feet began rumbling on the sand, and the wind sent a cold wave along the backbone.

"In the darkness you seem still larger, Lazarus, as if you have grown stouter in these moments. Do you feed on darkness, Lazarus? I would fain have a little fire—at least a little fire, a little fire. I feel somewhat chilly, your nights are so barbarously cold. Were it not so dark, I should say that you were looking at me, Lazarus. Yes, it seems to me you are looking . . . Why, you are looking at me, I feel it—but there you are smiling."

Night came, and filled the air with heavy blackness.

"How well it will be, when the sun will rise tomorrow, anew . . . I am a great sculptor, you know; that is how my friends call me. I create. Yes, that is the word . . . but I need daylight. I give life to the cold marble, I melt sonorous bronze in fire, in bright hot fire . . . Why did you touch me with your hand?"

"Come," said Lazarus. "You are my guest."

They went to the house. And a long night enveloped the earth.

The slave, seeing that his master did not come, went to seek him, when the sun was already high in the sky. And he beheld his master side by side with Lazarus: in profound silence they were sitting right under the dazzling and scorching rays of the sun and looking upward. The slave began to weep and cried out: "My master, what has befallen you, master?"

The very same day the sculptor left for Rome. On the way Aurelius was pensive and taciturn, staring attentively at everything—the men, the ship, the sea, as if trying to retain something. On the high sea a storm burst upon them, and all through it Aurelius stayed on the deck and eagerly scanned the seas looming near and sinking with a dull boom.

At home his friends were frightened at the change which had taken place in Aurelius, but he calmed them, saying meaningly: "I have found it."

And without changing the dusty clothes he wore on his journey, he fell to work, and the marble obediently resounded under his sonorous hammer. Long and eagerly he worked, admitting no one, until one morning he announced that the work was ready and ordered his friends to be summoned, severe critics and connoisseurs of art. And to meet them he put on bright and gorgeous garments, that glittered with yellow gold—and scarlet byssus.

"Here is my work," said he thoughtfully.

His friends glanced, and a shadow of profound sorrow covered their faces. It was something monstrous, deprived of all the lines and shapes familiar to the eye, but not without a hint at some new, strange image.

On a thin, crooked twig, or rather on an ugly likeness of a twig, rested askew a blind, ugly, shapeless, outspread mass of something utterly and inconceivably distorted, a mad heap of wild and bizarre fragments, all feebly and vainly striving to part from one another. And, as if by chance, beneath one of the wildly-rent salients a butterfly was chiseled with divine skill, all airy loveliness, delicacy, and beauty with transparent wings, which seemed to tremble with an impotent desire to take flight.

"Wherefore this wonderful butterfly, Aurelius?" said somebody falteringly.

But it was necessary to tell the truth, and one of his friends who loved him best said firmly: "This is ugly, my poor friend. It must be destroyed. Give me the hammer."

And with two strokes he broke the monstrous mass into pieces, leaving only the infinitely delicate butterfly untouched.

From that time on Aurelius created nothing. With profound indifference he looked at marble and bronze, and on his former divine works, where everlasting beauty rested. With the purpose of arousing his former fervent passion for work and awakening his deadened soul, his friends took him to see other artists' beautiful works, but he remained indifferent as before, and the smile did not warm up his tightened lips. And only after listening to lengthy talks about beauty, he would retort wearily and indolently: "But all this is a lie."

By day, when the sun was shining, he went into his magnificent, skillfully built garden, and having found a place without shadow, he exposed his bare head to the glare and heat. Red and white butterflies fluttered around; from the crooked lips of a drunken satyr, water streamed down with a splash into a marble cistern, but he sat motionless and silent, like a pallid reflection of him who, in the far-off distance, at the very gate of the stony desert, sat under the fiery sun.

*   *   *

And now it came to pass that the great, deified Augustus himself summoned Lazarus. The imperial messengers dressed him gorgeously, in solemn nuptial clothes, as if Time had legalized them, and he was to remain until his very death the bridegroom of an unknown bride. It was as if an old, rotting coffin had been gilded and furnished with new, gay tassels. And men, all in trim and bright attire, rode after him, as if in bridal procession indeed, and those foremost trumpeted loudly, bidding people to clear the way for the emperor's messengers. But Lazarus' way was deserted: his native land cursed the hateful name of him who had miraculously risen from the dead, and people scattered at the very news of his appalling approach. The solitary voice of the brass trumpets sounded in the motionless air, and the wilderness alone responded with its languid echo.

Then Lazarus went by sea. And his was the most magnificently arrayed and the most mournful ship that ever mirrored itself in the azure waves of the Mediterranean Sea. Many were the travelers aboard, but like a tomb was the ship, all silence and stillness, and the despairing water sobbed at the steep, proudly curved prow. All alone sat Lazarus exposing his head to the blaze of the sun, silently listening to the murmur and splash of the wavelets, and afar seamen and messengers were sitting, a vague group of weary shadows. Had the thunder burst and the wind attacked the red sails, the ships would probably have perished, for none of those aboard had either the will or the strength to struggle for life. With a supreme effort some mariners would reach the board and eagerly scan the blue, transparent deep, hoping to see a naiad's pink shoulder flash in the hollow of an azure wave, or a drunken gay centaur dash along and in frenzy splash the wave with his hoof. But the sea was like a wilderness, and the deep was dumb and deserted.

With utter indifference Lazarus set his feet on the street of the eternal city, as if all her wealth, all the magnificence of her palaces built by giants, all the resplendence, beauty, and music of her refined life were but the echo of the wind in the desert quicksand. Chariots were dashing, and along the streets were moving crowds of strong, fair, proud builders of the eternal city and haughty participants in her life; a song sounded; fountains and women laughed a pearly laughter; drunken philosophers harangued, and the sober listened to them with a smile; hoofs struck the stone pavements. And surrounded by cheerful noise, a stout, heavy man was moving, a cold spot of silence and despair, and on his way he sowed disgust, anger, and vague, gnawing weariness. Who dares to be sad in Rome? the citizens wondered indignantly, and frowned. In two days the entire city already knew *all* about him who had miraculously risen from the dead, and shunned him shyly.

But some daring people there were, who wanted to test their strength, and Lazarus obeyed their imprudent summons. Kept busy by state affairs, the emperor constantly delayed the reception, and seven days did he who had risen from the dead go about visiting others.

And Lazarus came to a cheerful Epicurean, and the host met him with laughter: "Drink, Lazarus, drink!" he shouted. "Would not Augustus laugh to see you drunk?"

And half-naked drunken women laughed, and rose petals fell on Lazarus' blue hands. But then the Epicurean looked into Lazarus' eyes and his gaiety ended forever. Drunkard remained he for the rest of his life; never did he drink, yet forever was he drunk. But instead of the gay reverie which wine brings with it, frightful dreams began to haunt him, the sole food of his stricken spirit. Day and night he lived the poisonous vapors of his nightmares, and Death itself was not more frightful than its raving, monstrous forerunners.

And Lazarus came to a youth and his beloved, who loved each other and were most beautiful in their passions. Proudly and strongly embracing his love, the youth said with serene regret: "Look at us Lazarus, and share our joy. Is there anything stronger than love?"

And Lazarus looked. And for the rest of their life they kept loving each other, but their passion grew gloomy and joyless, like those funeral cypresses whose roots feed on the decay of the graves and whose black summits in a still evening hour seek in vain to reach the sky. Thrown by the unknown forces of life into each other's embraces, they mingled tears with kisses, voluptuous pleasures with pain, and they felt themselves doubly slaves, obedient slaves to life, and patient servants of the silent Nothingness. Ever united, ever severed, they blazed like sparks and like sparks lost themselves in the boundless Dark.

And Lazarus came to a haughty sage, and the sage said to him: "I know all the horrors you can reveal to me. Is there anything you can frighten me with?"

But before long the sage felt that the knowledge of horror was far from being the horror itself, and that the vision of Death was not Death. And he felt that wisdom and folly are equal before the face of Infinity, for Infinity knows them not. And it vanished, the dividing-line between knowledge and ignorance, truth and falsehood, top and bottom, and the shapeless thought hung suspended in the void. Then the sage clutched his gray head and cried out frantically: "I can not think! I can not think!"

Thus under the indifferent glance for him, who miraculously had risen from the dead, perished everything that asserts life, its significance and joys. And it was suggested that it was dangerous to let him see the emperor, that it was better to kill him, and having buried him secretly, to tell the emperor that he had disappeared no one knew whither. Already swords were being whetted and youths devoted to the public welfare prepared for the murder, when Augustus ordered Lazarus to be brought before him next morning, thus destroying the cruel plans.

If there was no way of getting rid of Lazarus, at least it was possible to soften the terrible impression his face produced. With this in view, skilful painters, barbers, and artists were summoned, and all night long they were busy over Lazarus' head. They cropped his beard, curled it, and gave it a tidy, agreeable appearance. By means of paints they concealed the corpselike blueness of his hands and face. Repulsive were the wrinkles of suffering that furrowed his old face, and they were puttied, painted, and smoothed; then, over the smooth background, wrinkles of good-tempered laughter and pleasant carefree mirth were skillfully painted with fine brushes.

Lazarus submitted indifferently to everything that was done to him. Soon he was turned into a becomingly stout, venerable old man, into a quiet and kind grandfather of numerous offspring. It seemed that the smile, with which only a while ago he was spinning funny yarns, was still lingering on his lips and that in the corner of his eye serene tenderness was hiding, the companion of old age. But people did not dare change his nuptial garments, and they could not change his eyes, two dark and frightful glasses through which the unknowable Yonder looked at men.

Lazarus was not moved by the magnificence of the imperial palace. It was as if he saw no difference between the crumbling

house, closely pressed by the desert, and the stone palace, solid
and fair, and indifferently he passed into it. The hard marble of
the floors under his feet grew similar to the quicksand of the
desert, and the multitude of richly dressed and haughty men
became like void air under his glance. No one looked into his face,
as Lazarus passed by, fearing to fall under the appalling influence
of his eyes; but when the sound of his heavy footsteps had
sufficiently died down, the courtiers raised their heads and with
fearful curiosity examined the figure of a stout, tall, slightly bent
old man, who was slowly penetrating into the very heart of the
imperial palace. Were Death itself passing, it would be faced with
no greater fear: for until then the dead alone knew Death, and
those alive knew Life only—and there was no bridge between
them. But this extraordinary man, although alive, knew Death,
and enigmatical, appalling, was his cursed knowledge. "Woe!"
people thought; "he will take the life of our great, deified
Augustus;" and then sent curses after Lazarus, who meanwhile
kept on advancing into the interior of the palace.

Already did the emperor know who Lazarus was, and prepared
to meet him. But the monarch was a brave man, and felt his own
tremendous, unconquerable power, and in his fatal duel with him
who had miraculously risen from the dead he wanted not to invoke
human help. And so he met Lazarus face to face.

"Lift not your eyes upon me, Lazarus," he ordered. "I heard
your face is like that of Medusa and turns into stone whomsoever
you look at. Now, I wish to see you and talk with you, before I
turn into stone," he added in a tone of kingly jesting, not devoid
of fear.

Coming close to him, he carefully examined Lazarus' face and
his strange festal garments. And although he had a keen eye, he
was deceived by his appearance.

"So. You do not appear terrible, my venerable old man. But
the worse for us, if horror assumes such a respectable and pleasant
air. Now let us have a talk."

Augustus sat, and questioning Lazarus with his eye as much as
with words, started the conversation: "Why did you not greet me
as you entered?"

Lazarus answered indifferently: "I knew not it was necessary."

"Are you a Christian?"

"No."

Augustus approvingly shook his head.

"That is good. I do not like Christians. They shake the tree of life before it is covered with fruit, and disperse its odorous bloom to the winds. But who are you?"

With a visible effort Lazarus answered: "I was dead."

"I had heard that. But who are you now?"

Lazarus was silent, but at last repeated in a tone of weary apathy: "I was dead."

"Listen to me, stranger," said the emperor, distinctly and severely giving utterance to the thought that had come to him at the beginning, "my realm is the realm of Life, my people are of the living, not of the dead. You are here one too many. I know not who you are and what you saw there; but, if you lie, I hate lies, and if you tell the truth, I hate your truth. In my bosom I feel the throb of life; I feel strength in my arm, and my proud thoughts, like eagles, pierce the space. And yonder in the shelter of my rule, under the protection of laws created by me, people live and toil and rejoice. Do you hear the battle cry, the challenge men throw into the face of the future?"

Augustus, as if in prayer, stretched forth his arms and exclaimed solemnly: "Be blessed, O great and divine Life!"

Lazarus was silent, and with growing sternness the emperor went on: "You are not wanted here, miserable remnant, snatched from under Death's teeth, you inspire weariness and disgust with life; like a caterpillar in the fields, you gloat on the rich ear of joy and belch out the drivel of despair and sorrow. Your truth is like a rusty sword in the hands of a nightly murderer, and as a murderer you shall be executed. But before that, let me look into your eyes. Perchance only cowards are afraid of them, but in the brave they awake the thirst for strife and victory; then you shall be rewarded, not executed . . . Now, look at me, Lazarus."

At first it appeared to the deified Augustus that a friend was looking at him, so soft, so tenderly fascinating was Lazarus' glance. It promised not horror, but sweet rest, and the Infinite seemed to him a tender mistress, a compassionate sister, a mother. But stronger and stronger grew its embraces, and already the mouth, greedy of hissing kisses, interfered with the monarch's breathing, and already to the surface of the soft tissues of the body came the iron of the bones and tightened its merciless circle, and unknown fangs, blunt, and cold, touched his heart and sank into it with slow indolence.

"It pains," said the deified Augustus, growing pale. "But look at me, Lazarus, look."

It was as if some heavy gates, ever closed, were slowly moving apart, and through the growing interstice the appalling horror of the Infinite poured in slowly and steadily. Like two shadows entering the shoreless void and the unfathomable darkness; they extinguished the sun, ravished the earth from under the feet, and the roof from over the head. No more did the frozen heart ache.

Time stood still and the beginning of each thing grew frightfully near to its end. Augustus' throne, just erected, crumbled down, and the void was already in the place of the throne and of Augustus. Noiselessly did Rome crumble down, and a new city stood on its site and it too was swallowed by the void. Like fantastic giants, cities, states and countries fell down and vanished in the void darkness, and with uttermost indifference did the insatiable black womb of the Infinite swallow them.

"Halt!" ordered the emperor.

In his voice sounded already a note of indifference, his hands dropped in languor, and in the vain struggle with the onrushing darkness his fiery eyes now blazed up, and now went out.

"My life you have taken from me, Lazarus," said he in a spiritless, feeble voice.

And these words of hopelessness saved him. He remembered his people, whose shield he was destined to be, and keen salutary pain pierced his deadened heart. "They are doomed to death," he thought wearily. "Serene shadows in the darkness of the Infinite," thought he, and horror grew upon him. "Frail vessels with living, seething blood, with a heart that knows sorrow and also great joy," said he in his heart, and tenderness pervaded it.

Thus pondering and oscillating between the poles of Life and Death, he slowly came back to life, to find in its suffering and in its joys a shield against the darkness of the void and the horror of the Infinite.

"No, you have not murdered me, Lazarus," said he firmly, "but I will take your life. Begone."

That evening the deified Augustus partook of his meats and drinks with particular joy. Now and then his lifted hand remained suspended in the air, and a dull glimmer replaced the bright sheen of his fiery eye. It was the cold wave of Horror that surged at his feet. Defeated, but not undone, ever awaiting its hour, that

Horror stood at the emperor's bedside, like a black shadow all through his life, it swayed his nights but yielded the days to the sorrows and joys of life.

The following day, the hangman with a hot iron burned out Lazarus' eyes. Then he was sent home. The deified Augustus dared not kill him.

Lazarus returned to the desert, and the wilderness met him with hissing gusts of wind and the heat of the blazing sun. Again he was sitting on a stone, his rough, bushy beard lifted up; and the two black holes in place of his eyes looked at the sky with an expression of dull terror. Afar off the holy city stirred noisily and restlessly, but around him everything was deserted and dumb. No one approached the place where lived he who had miraculously risen from the dead, and long since his neighbors had forsaken their houses. Driven by the hot iron into the depth of his skull, his cursed knowledge hid there in an ambush. As if leaping out from an ambush it plunged its thousand invisible eyes into the man, and no one dared look at Lazarus.

And in the evening, when the sun, reddening and growing wider, would come nearer and nearer the western horison, the blind Lazarus would slowly follow it. He would stumble against stones and fall, stout and weak as he was; would rise heavily to his feet and walk on again; and on the red screen of the sunset his black body and outspread hands would form a monstrous likeness of a cross.

And it came to pass that once he went out and did not come back. Thus seemingly ended the second life of him who for three days had been under the enigmatical sway of death, and rose miraculously from the dead.

THE BEAST WITHIN

Several years ago, I was having drinks at the Museum Cafe in New York with D. F. "Davy" Jones, author of the popular *Colossus* trilogy of science-fiction thrillers. The subject turned to terror and the things that "really" frighten. "Davy" stared broodingly into his glass and said, "Corpses don't bother me at all. But people scare the bejesus out of me!" The stories in this section support his thesis—that the greatest enemy we have to fear is the beast within, the savage lurking in every human breast.

Two kinds of horrors may be found here: man's inhumanity to his own species and—perhaps even more dreadful—the power of the human mind to create a tailor-made Hell for its "owner."

A. M. BURRAGE, *born in Middlesex, England, is an all-but-forgotten master of fantasy fiction. "The Waxwork" is one of his finest performances, a shivery tale of ominous surroundings that prey mightily upon the nerves of the hero.*

The Waxwork

BY A. M. BURRAGE

While the uniformed attendants of Marriner's Waxworks were ushering the last stragglers through the great glass-panelled double doors, the manager sat in his office interviewing Raymond Hewson.

The manager was a youngish man, stout, blond and of medium height. He wore his clothes well and contrived to look extremely smart without appearing over-dressed. Raymond Hewson looked neither. His clothes, which had been good when new and which were still carefully brushed and pressed, were beginning to show signs of their owner's losing battle with the world. He was a small, spare, pale man, with lank, errant brown hair, and although he spoke plausibly and even forcibly he had the defensive and somewhat furtive air of a man who was used to rebuffs. He looked what he was, a man gifted somewhat above the ordinary, who was a failure through his lack of self-assertion.

The manager was speaking.

"There is nothing new in your request," he said. "In fact we refuse it to different people—mostly young bloods who have tried to make bets—about three times a week. We have nothing to gain and something to lose by letting people spend the night in our Murderers' Den. If I allowed it, and some young idiot lost his senses, what would be my position? But your being a journalist somewhat alters the case."

Hewson smiled.

"I suppose you mean that journalists have no senses to lose."

"No, no," laughed the manager, "but one imagines them to be responsible people. Besides, here we have something to gain;

publicity and advertisement."

"Exactly," said Hewson, "and there I thought we might come to terms."

The manager laughed again.

"Oh," he exclaimed, "I know what's coming. You want to be paid twice, do you? It used to be said years ago that Madame Tussaud's would give a man a hundred pounds for sleeping alone in the Chamber of Horrors. I hope you don't think that we have made any such offer. Er—what is your paper, Mr. Hewson?"

"I am freelancing at present," Hewson confessed, "working on space for several papers. However, I should find no difficulty in getting the story printed. The *Morning Echo* would use it like a shot. 'A Night with Marriner's Murderers.' No live paper could turn it down."

The manager rubbed his chin.

"Ah! And how do you propose to treat it?"

"I shall make it gruesome, of course; gruesome with just a saving touch of humour."

The other nodded and offered Hewson his cigarette-case.

"Very well, Mr. Hewson," he said. "Get your story printed in the *Morning Echo*, and there will be a five-pound note waiting for you here when you care to come and call for it. But first of all, it's no small ordeal that you're proposing to undertake. I'd like to be quite sure about you, and I'd like you to be quite sure about yourself. I own I shouldn't care to take it on. I've seen those figures dressed and undressed, I know all about the process of their manufacture, I can walk about in company downstairs as unmoved as if I were walking among so many skittles, but I should hate having to sleep down there alone among them."

"Why?" asked Hewson.

"I don't know. There isn't any reason. I don't believe in ghosts. If I did I should expect them to haunt the scene of their crimes or the spot where their bodies were laid, instead of a cellar which happens to contain their waxwork effigies. It's just that I couldn't sit alone among them all night, with their seeming to stare at me in the way they do. After all, they represent the lowest and most appalling types of humanity, and—although I would not own it publicly—the people who come to see them are not generally charged with the very highest motives. The whole atmosphere of the place is unpleasant, and if you are susceptible to atmosphere I warn you that you are in for a very uncomfortable night."

Hewson had known that from the moment when the idea had first occurred to him. His soul sickened at the prospect, even while he smiled casually upon the manager. But he had a wife and family to keep, and for the past month he had been living on paragraphs, eked out by his rapidly dwindling store of savings. Here was a chance not to be missed—the price of a special story in the *Morning Echo*, with a five-pound note to add to it. It meant comparative wealth and luxury for a week, and freedom from the worst anxieties for a fortnight. Besides, if he wrote the story well, it might lead to an offer of regular employment.

"The way of transgressors—and newspaper men—is hard," he said. "I have already promised myself an uncomfortable night because your murderer's den is obviously not fitted up as an hotel bedroom. But I don't think your waxworks will worry me much."

"You're not superstitious?"

"Not a bit," Hewson laughed.

"But you're a journalist; you must have a strong imagination."

"The news editors for whom I've worked have always complained that I haven't any. Plain facts are not considered sufficient in our trade, and the papers don't like offering their readers unbuttered bread."

The manager smiled and rose.

"Right," he said. "I think the last of the people have gone. Wait a moment. I'll give orders for the figures downstairs not to be draped, and let the night people know that you'll be here. Then I'll take you down and show you round."

He picked up the receiver of a house telephone, spoke into it and presently replaced it.

"One condition I'm afraid I must impose on you," he remarked. "I must ask you not to smoke. We had a fire scare down in the Murderers' Den this evening. I don't know who gave the alarm, but whoever it was it was a false one. Fortunately there were very few people down there at the time, or there might have been a panic. And now, if you're ready, we'll make a move."

Hewson followed the manager through half a dozen rooms where attendants were busy shrouding the kings and queens of England, the generals and prominent statesmen of this and other generations, all the mixed herd of humanity whose fame or notoriety had rendered them eligible for this kind of immortality. The manager stopped once and spoke to a man in uniform, saying something about an arm-chair in the Murderers' Den.

"It's the best we can do for you, I'm afraid," he said to Hewson. "I hope you'll be able to get some sleep."

He led the way through an open barrier and down ill-lit stone stairs which conveyed a sinister impression of giving access to a dungeon. In a passage at the bottom were a few preliminary horrors, such as relics of the Inquisition, a rack taken from a mediaeval castle, branding irons, thumb-screws, and other mementoes of man's one-time cruelty to man. Beyond the passage was the Murderers' Den.

It was a room of irregular shape with a vaulted roof, and dimly lit by electric lights burning behind inverted bowls of frosted glass. It was, by design, an eerie and uncomfortable chamber—a chamber whose atmosphere invited its visitors to speak in whispers. There was something of the air of a chapel about it, but a chapel no longer devoted to the practice of piety and given over now for base and impious worship.

The waxwork murderers stood on low pedestals with numbered tickets at their feet. Seeing them elsewhere, and without knowing whom they represented, one would have thought them a dull-looking crew, chiefly remarkable for the shabbiness of their clothes, and as evidence of the changes of fashion even among the unfashionable.

Recent notorieties rubbed dusty shoulders with the old "favourites." Thurtell, the murderer of Weer, stood as if frozen in the act of making a shop-window gesture to young Bywaters. There was Lefroy the poor half-baked little snob who killed for gain so that he might ape the gentleman. Within five yards of him sat Mrs. Thompson, the erotic romanticist, hanged to propitiate British middle-class matronhood. Charles Peace, the only member of that vile company who looked uncompromisingly and entirely evil, sneered across a gangway at Norman Thorne. Browne and Kennedy, the two most recent additions, stood between Mrs. Dyer and Patrick Mahon.

The manager, walking around with Hewson, pointed out several of the more interesting of these unholy notabilities.

"That's Crippen; I expect you recognize him. Insignificant little beast who looks as if he couldn't tread on a worm. That's Armstrong. Looks like a decent, harmless country gentleman, doesn't he? There's old Vaquier; you can't miss him because of his beard. And of course this—"

"Who's that?" Hewson interrupted in a whisper, pointing.

"Oh, I was coming to him," said the manager in a light undertone. "Come and have a good look at him. This is our star turn. He's the only one of the bunch that hasn't been hanged."

The figure which Hewson had indicated was that of a small, slight man not much more than five feet in height. It wore little waxed moustaches, large spectacles, and a caped coat. There was something so exaggeratedly French in its appearance that it reminded Hewson of a stage caricature. He could not have said precisely why the mild-looking face seemed to him so repellent, but he had already recoiled a step and, even in the manager's company, it cost him an effort to look again.

"But who is he?" he asked.

"That," said the manager, "is Dr. Bourdette."

Hewson shook his head doubtfully.

"I think I've heard the name," he said, "but I forget in connection with what."

The manager smiled.

"You'd remember better if you were a Frenchman," he said. "For some long while that man was the terror of Paris. He carried on his work of healing by day, and of throat-cutting by night, when the fit was on him. He killed for the sheer devilish pleasure it gave him to kill, and always in the same way—with a razor. After his last crime he left a clue behind him which set the police upon his track. One clue led to another, and before very long they knew that they were on the track of the Parisian equivalent of our Jack the Ripper, and had enough evidence to send him to the madhouse or the guillotine on a dozen capital charges.

"But even then our friend here was too clever for them. When he realised that the toils were closing about him he mysteriously disappeared, and ever since the police of every civilised country have been looking for him. There is no doubt that he managed to make away with himself, and by some means which has prevented his body coming to light. One or two crimes of a similar nature have taken place since his disappearance, but he is believed almost for certain to be dead, and the experts believe these recrudescences to be the work of an imitator. It's queer, isn't it, how every notorious murderer has imitators?"

Hewson shuddered and fidgeted with his feet.

"I don't like him at all," he confessed. "Ugh! What eyes he's got!"

"Yes, this figure's a little masterpiece. You find the eyes bite into you? Well, that's excellent realism, then, for Bourdette practised mesmerism, and was supposed to mesmerise his victims before dispatching them. Indeed, had he not done so, it is impossible to see how so small a man could have done his ghastly work. There were never any signs of a struggle."

"I thought I saw him move," said Hewson with a catch in his voice.

The manager smiled.

"You'll have more than one optical illusion before the night's out, I expect. You shan't be locked in. You can come upstairs when you've had enough of it. There are watchmen on the premises, so you'll find company. Don't be alarmed if you hear them moving about. I'm sorry I can't give you any more light, because all the lights are on. For obvious reasons we keep this place as gloomy as possible. And now I think you had better return with me to the office and have a tot of whisky before beginning your night's vigil."

The member of the night staff who placed the arm-chair for Hewson was inclined to be facetious.

"Where will you have it, sir?" he asked, grinning. "Just 'ere, so as you can 'ave a little talk with Crippen when you're tired of sitting still? Or there's old Mother Dyer over there, making eyes and looking as if she could do with a bit of company. Say where, sir."

Hewson smiled. The man's chaff pleased him if only because, for the moment at least, it lent the proceedings a much-desired air of the commonplace.

"I'll place it myself, thanks," he said. "I'll find out where the draughts come from first."

"You won't find any down here. Well, good night, sir. I'm upstairs if you want me. Don't let 'em sneak up behind you and touch your neck with their cold and clammy 'ands. And you look out for that old Mrs. Dyer; I b'lieve she's taken a fancy to you."

Hewson laughed and wished the man good night. It was easier than he had expected. He wheeled the arm-chair—a heavy one upholstered in plush—a little way down the central gangway, and deliberately turned it so that its back was towards the effigy of Dr. Bourdette. For some undefined reason he liked Dr. Bourdette a great deal less than his companions. Busying himself with arranging the chair he was almost light-hearted, but when the

attendant's footfalls had died away and a deep hush stole over the
chamber he realised that he had no slight ordeal before him.

The dim unwavering light fell on the rows of figures which were
so uncannily like human beings that the silence and the stillness
seemed unnatural and even ghastly. He missed the sound of
breathing, the rustling of clothes, the hundred and one minute
noises one hears when even the deepest silence has fallen upon a
crowd. But the air was as stagnant as water at the bottom of a
standing pond. There was not a breath in the chamber to stir a
curtain or rustle a hanging drapery or start a shadow. His own
shadow, moving in response to a shifted arm or leg, was all that
could be coaxed into motion. All was still to the gaze and silent
to the ear. "It must be like this at the bottom of the sea," he
thought, and wondered how to work the phrase into his story on
the morrow.

He faced the sinister figures boldly enough. They were only
waxworks. So long as he let that thought dominate all others he
promised himself that all would be well. It did not, however, save
him long from the discomfort occasioned by the waxen stare of
Dr. Bourdette, which, he knew, was directed upon him from
behind. The eyes of the little Frenchman's effigy haunted and
tormented him, and he itched with the desire to turn and look.

"Come!" he thought, "my nerves have started already. If I turn
and look at that dressed-up dummy it will be an admission of
funk."

And then another voice in his brain spoke to him.

"It's because you're afraid that you won't turn and look at him."

The two Voices quarrelled silently for a moment or two, and at
last Hewson slewed his chair round a little and looked behind him.

Among the many figures standing in stiff, unnatural poses, the
effigy of the dreadful little doctor stood out with a queer
prominence, perhaps because a steady beam of light beat straight
down upon it. Hewson flinched before the parody of mildness
which some fiendishly skilled craftsman had managed to convey
in wax, met the eyes for one agonised second, and turned again
to face the other direction.

"He's only a waxwork like the rest of you," Hewson muttered
defiantly. "You're all only waxworks."

They were only waxworks, yes, but waxworks don't move. Not
that he had seen the least movement anywhere, but it struck him
that, in the moment or two while he had looked behind him, there

had been the least subtle change in the grouping of the figures in front. Crippen, for instance, seemed to have turned at least one degree to the left. Or, thought Hewson, perhaps the illusion was due to the fact that he had not slewed his chair back into its exact original position. And there were Field and Grey, too; surely one of them had moved his hands. Hewson held his breath for a moment, and then drew his courage back to him as a man lifts a weight. He remembered the words of more than one news editor and laughed savagely to himself.

"And they tell me I've got no imagination!" he said beneath his breath.

He took a notebook from his pocket and wrote quickly.

"Mem.—Deathly silence and unearthly stillness of figures. Like being at bottom of sea. Hypnotic eyes of Dr. Bourdette. Figures seem to move when not being watched."

He closed the book suddenly over his fingers and looked round quickly and awfully over his right shoulder. He had neither seen nor heard a movement, but it was as if some sixth sense had made him aware of one. He looked straight into the vapid countenance of Lefroy which smiled vacantly back as if to say, "It wasn't I!"

Of course it wasn't he, or any of them; it was his own nerves. Or was it? Hadn't Crippen moved again during that moment when his attention was directed elsewhere? You couldn't trust that little man! Once you took your eyes off him he took advantage of it to shift his position. That was what they were all doing, if he only knew it, he told himself; and half rose out of his chair. This was not quite good enough! he was going. He wasn't going to spend the night with a lot of waxworks which moved while he wasn't looking.

. . . Hewson sat down again. This was very cowardly and very absurd. They *were* only waxworks and they *couldn't* move; let him hold that thought and all would yet be well. Then why all that silent unrest about him?—a subtle something in the air which did not quite break the silence and happened, whichever way he looked, just beyond the boundaries of his vision.

He swung round quickly to encounter the mild but baleful stare of Dr. Bourdette. Then, without warning, he jerked his head back to stare straight at Crippen. Ha! he'd nearly caught Crippen that time! "You'd better be careful, Crippen—and all the rest of you! If I do see one of you move I'll smash you to pieces! Do you hear?"

He ought to go, he told himself. Already he had experienced

enough to write his story, or ten stories, for the matter of that. Well, then, why not go? The *Morning Echo* would be none the wiser as to how long he had stayed, nor would it care so long as his story was a good one. Yes, but that night watchman upstairs would chaff him. And the manager—one never knew—perhaps the manager would quibble over that five-pound note which he needed so badly. He wondered if Rose were asleep of if she were lying awake and thinking of him. She'd laugh when he told her that he had imagined . . .

This was a little too much! It was bad enough that the waxwork effigies of murderers should move when they weren't being watched, but it was intolerable that they should *breathe*. Somebody was breathing. Or was it his own breath which sounded to him as if it came from a distance? He sat rigid, listening and straining until he exhaled with a long sigh. His own breath after all, or—if not, something had divined that he was listening and had ceased breathing simultaneously.

Hewson jerked his head swiftly around and looked all about him out of haggard and hunted eyes. Everywhere his gaze encountered the vacant waxen faces, and everywhere he felt that by just some least fraction of a second had he missed seeing a movement of hand or foot, a silent opening or compression of lips, a flicker of eyelids, a look of human intelligence now smoothed out. They were like naughty children in a class, whispering, fidgeting and laughing behind their teacher's back, but blandly innocent when his gaze was turned upon them.

This would not do! This distinctly would not do! He must clutch at something, grip with his mind upon something which belonged essentially to a workaday world, to the daylight London streets. He was Raymond Hewson, an unsuccessful journalist, a living and breathing man, and these figures grouped around him were only dummies, so they could neither move nor whisper. What did it matter if they were supposed to be lifelike effigies of murderers? They were only made of wax and sawdust, and stood there for the entertainment of morbid sightseers and orange-sucking trippers. That was better! Now what was that funny story which somebody had told him in the Falstaff yesterday? . . .

He recalled part of it, but not all, for the gaze of Dr. Bourdette, urged, challenged, and finally compelled him to turn.

Hewson half-turned, and then swung his chair so as to bring him face to face with the wearer of those dreadful hypnotic eyes. His own eyes were dilated, and his mouth, at first set in a grin of terror, lifted at the corners in a snarl. Then Hewson spoke and woke a hundred sinister echoes.

"You moved, damn you!" he cried. "Yes, you did, damn you! I saw you!"

Then he sat quite still, staring straight before him, like a man found frozen in the Arctic snows.

Dr. Bourdette's movements were leisurely. He stepped off his pedestal with the mincing care of a lady alighting from a bus. The platform stood about two feet from the ground, and above the edge of it a plush-covered rope hung in arc-like curves. Dr. Bourdette lifted up the rope until it formed an arch for him to pass under, stepped off the platform and sat down on the edge facing Hewson. Then he nodded and smiled and said "Good evening."

"I need hardly tell you," he continued, in perfect English in which was traceable only the least foreign accent, "that not until I overheard the conversation between you and the worthy manager of this establishment, did I suspect that I should have the pleasure of a companion here for the night. You cannot move or speak without my bidding, but you can hear me perfectly well. Something tells me that you are—shall I say nervous? My dear sir, have no illusions. I am not one of these contemptible effigies miraculously come to life: I am Dr. Bourdette himself."

He paused, coughed and shifted his legs.

"Pardon me," he resumed, "but I am a little stiff. And let me explain. Circumstances with which I need not fatigue you, have made it desirable that I should live in England. I was close to this building this evening when I saw a policeman regarding me a thought too curiously. I guessed that he intended to follow and perhaps ask me embarrassing questions, so I mingled with the crowd and came in here. An extra coin bought my admission to the chamber in which we now meet, and an inspiration showed me a certain means of escape.

"I raised a cry of fire, and when all the fools had rushed to the stairs I stripped my effigy of the caped coat which you behold me wearing, donned it, hid my effigy under the platform at the back, and took its place on the pedestal.

"I own that I have since spent a very fatiguing evening, but fortunately I was not always being watched and had opportunities to draw an occasional deep breath and ease the rigidity of my pose. One small boy screamed and exclaimed that he saw me moving. I understood that he was to be whipped and put straight to bed on his return home, and I can only hope that the threat has been executed to the letter.

"The manager's description of me, which I had the embarrassment of being compelled to overhear, was biased but not altogether inaccurate. Clearly I am not dead, although it is as well that the world thinks otherwise. His account of my hobby, which I have indulged for years, although, through necessity, less frequently of late, was in the main true although not intelligently expressed. The world is divided between collectors and non-collectors. With the non-collectors we are not concerned. The collectors collect anything, according to their individual tastes, from money to cigarette cards, from moths to matchboxes. I collect throats."

He paused again and regarded Hewson's throat with interest mingled with disfavour.

"I am obliged to the chance which brought us together tonight," he continued, "and perhaps it would seem ungrateful to complain. From motives of personal safety my activities have been somewhat curtailed of late years, and I am glad of this opportunity of gratifying my somewhat unusual whim. But you have a skinny neck, sir, if you will overlook a personal remark. I should never have selected you from choice. I like men with thick necks . . . thick red necks . . ."

He fumbled in an inside pocket and took out something which he tested against a wet forefinger and then proceeded to pass gently to and fro across the palm of his left hand.

"This is a little French razor," he remarked blandly. "They are not much used in England, but perhaps you know them? One strops them on wood. The blade, you will observe, is very narrow. They do not cut very deep, but deep enough. In just one little moment you shall see for yourself. I shall ask you the little civil question of all the polite barbers: Does the razor suit you, sir?"

He rose up, a diminutive but menacing figure of evil, and approached Hewson with the silent, furtive step of a hunting panther.

"You will have the goodness," he said, "to raise your chin a little. Thank you, and a little more. Just a little more. Ah, thank you! . . . *Merci, m'sieur . . . Ah, merci . . . merci. . . .*"

Over one end of the chamber was a thick skylight of frosted

glass which, by day, let in a few sickly and filtered rays from the floor above. After sunrise these began to mingle with the subdued light from the electric bulbs, and this mingled illumination added a certain ghastliness to a scene which needed no additional touch of horror.

The waxwork figures stood apathetically in their places, waiting to be admired or execrated by the crowds who would presently wander fearfully among them. In their midst, in the centre gang way, Hewson sat still, leaning far back in his arm-chair. His chin was uptilted as if he were waiting to receive attention from a barber, and although there was not a scratch upon his throat, nor anywhere upon his body, he was cold and dead. His previous employers were wrong in having credited him with no imagination.

Dr. Bourdette on his pedestal watched the dead man unemotionally. He did not move, nor was he capable of motion. But then, after all, he was only a waxwork.

"The Silent Couple," originally titled in French "The House of Silence," appeared in the Parisian newspaper Figaro, *which was first published in 1826. This obscure tale is a fine example of what we call the* conte cruelle, *though its cruelties are of the spirit, rather than the torture chamber—and therefore, all the more dreadful.*

The Silent Couple

BY PIERRE COURTOIS

Every day, weather permitting, I walk with my husband amongst the linden trees surrounding the town square. We are both rheumatic, so he leans on his cane while I, by force of habit, clasp his arm, though my hand trembles as I touch him.

Today, though autumn sun shines on the church and offices, the school and Town Hall of the square, my husband, Mr. Mezange, wears a wool overcoat, and I have on my hat with the white ribbon. We have always lived here; we have always walked here. On rare occasions, we visit the seashore and the South, but we always return and on sunny days, we always walk. My husband expects it, and I am a dutiful wife. I do not speak to him anymore, nor he to me, but still I tread in his path, still I am darkened by his shadow.

We sit down now, as we often do, upon a bench on the sunlit side of the square, an old crippled couple who watch the passersby, people and pets, but we never break the silence that separates us.

My husband is a man of means, though some call him a miserly wretch. But no matter, I am totally devoted to his needs. Daily, I move dutifully from the kitchen to the laundry readying lunch or dinner at the hours he expects his meals. I spare nothing to keep his linen clean, but still I will not speak to him.

Mr. Mezange is six years older than I. Stoop-shouldered, shrunken, crippled with gout, he leans on his cane and takes small steps as we stroll. How harmless he seems now, this quiet old man, but still I will not say a word to him, not when we walk, not at home, not through the long silent evenings of the past two years. There is nothing left to say. Habit sustains me in my automatic and punctual routines, and whether it is a nice day and we go outside or it rains and we stay within, taking our meals together, he is alone whether I am with him or not.

Our lips are sealed to one another. The only communication that ever passes between us comes from the happenstance of our eyes meeting, and this we both avoid. I have studied my own ash-gray eyes in the glass and see the resignation and melancholy and fear within their depths. They are the eyes of a sick woman, and they are ringed by the dark shadows that come from many sleepless nights.

But my husband's eyes are different. Two sharp creases between his brows pinch his face with cruelty. Underneath the reddish lids, small circles gleam in the center of his pupils, almost as if his eyes were cut from metal. They, too, are round from sleeplessness, and they seem both frightening and frightened. Except by accident, it has been two years since I have looked him in the eye. At table, I avoid sitting opposite him, and when we are walking or now while we rest upon this bench, I never turn my head toward him.

Why do we never speak? Because if I opened my mouth, his eyes would watch me, and I would remember. And so my lips are sealed, and so are his. It is a pact of silence, and though we never agreed to it aloud, it is a vow we will not dishonour.

Two years ago, we took a trip to the South. Mr. Mezange was in one of his rare generous moods. I never objected to a change of scene, so we agreed to spend two weeks on the shores of the Mediterranean.

My husband, normally penurious, was in a decidedly frivolous mood. He actually wanted to visit a gambling casino. I went along, of course, but soon saw it was a disastrous mistake. He lost a great deal of money and his temper grew ugly. I stood behind him at the table and tried what I could do in timid whispers to calm him, but to no avail. He was furious, the more so because one of his neighbors at the table was a well-to-do woman in stylish clothes and expensive jewelry who played with a vengeance and was greatly favored by luck.

My husband's steely eyes stayed fixed upon her.

When we left the casino just before daybreak, it was at the same time as the wealthy woman. Our path led us down a deserted road cloaked in wavering pale shadows. The woman walked several paces ahead of us. Suddenly, without warning or a hint to me of what was in his heart, Mr. Mezange dashed forwards and threw himself upon her. I uttered one cry of dismay and horror, but already he had his scarf in her mouth, gagging her, and his hands clutched her neck, squeezing it with all his strength.

For a second, I thought of running, but then my husband grasped me by the arm and whispered, "Quick! Help me! Her money!" I stood there, rooted to the spot, till he saw I was incapable of motion, and then, releasing me, he stooped down and with great difficulty wrenched her bag from hands clutched tight in the agony of death.

While I watched, frozen in a state of wordless, mindless complicity, he dragged his victim across the road and tumbled her body into a muddy ditch. Clasping his fingers so tight about my arm I felt his nails digging into my flesh, he tugged me away, half-pushing, half-pulling me into our hotel and up to our room, where we stayed just long enough to pack and pay our bill. We caught the first train home . . . and ever since silence weighs on us like a tombstone. Time and again, I have yearned to lift its crushing weight from my conscience, but out of fear and out of that duty which habit accustomed me to, I have never betrayed my husband.

Neither of us learned the aftermath of his dreadful crime, yet none of its details grow dim—I still see her bulging eyes, the blood spurting from her nose, crimson in the pale shadows of dawn. My nightmares never go away, and yet my lips are sealed to the world and especially to him.

The autumn air is chilly. Mr. Mezange hunches over and pulls his collar high. I spy this from the corner of my eye, for I do not turn my head toward him. I face the road, and so I see the car that slows and stops in front of our bench. The driver emerges and goes to the fountain for some water.

My God, there is a woman sitting in the car . . . she is alone . . . she reads . . . her head is down, but through the open window, light strikes her face in high relief. I know her face. A haunting resemblance? The ghostly image of remembrance?

No.

The chill I feel is more than the breath of October. This is no phantom likeness; it is *she*. I am not mistaken, for look! my husband glances up, and he, too, is startled. His hand tightens on the handle of his cane.

She stops reading as her chauffeur returns to the car, and now she sits up straight and leans towards the open window of her door. Her head is at the window. She knows! She has recognized her assailant, a man who thought he murdered her . . . and his silent accomplice.

All my strength is gone. My heart races, but I cannot bear to hear her incriminating voice; I must be the first to speak, but how? There are no words, there have been no words for two long years. And now for the first time in all that silent interval, I turn my head and look into my husband's eyes; and he knows, yes, I *will* speak, I will tell his victim, "Yes, an accomplice, but an unwilling one, robbed of volition by the horror of what my husband did." No more will I keep his secret, no more will I be the dutifully obedient wife, I am without pity—and now, *see!* His eyes, oh! the fear in them, the pleading! They are not my husband's eyes, I do not recognize them, they are the pain-filled eyes of some wounded animal.

But I have waited too long. The woman speaks first, before I have a chance to unburden my soul.

"Pardon, sir, madame . . . is it far before we reach the chateau at Civray? My chauffeur must have taken the wrong road."

Two years of silence, and all for what? At last I am able to speak, because words are not within my husband's power, and I tell her, "We don't know. We don't live around here." And that is all. The car starts up again and quickly chugs off into the distance.

My husband and I get up and retrace our way homeward, taking slow steps, in no hurry to return to the solitude of our home, where we will not look into one another's eyes nor will we talk about that ultimate betrayal, that moment of triumph and capitulation that leads us back forever and forever to our house of silence.

Translated by Faith Lancereau and adapted by Marvin Kaye

JACK LONDON, *born in San Francisco in 1876, had a life that must have been an inspiration to any member of the "beat" generation who read works other than those by Kerouac and Ferlinghetti. Rancher, pirate, vagrant, seaman, London also wrote many eminently enjoyable tales and novels of high adventure before his death in 1916.* The Sea Wolf, The Call of the Wild, *"To Build a Fire" and many, many other fine tales distinguish his fabulous career. "Moon-Face," which appeared in volume form in 1906, is a kind of rural "Cask of Amontillado." Its idea reportedly was inspired by a tale in* Black Cat *magazine one year earlier.*

Moon-Face

BY JACK LONDON

John Claverhouse was a moon-faced man. You know the kind, cheekbones wide apart, chin and forehead melting into the cheeks to complete the perfect round, and the nose, broad and pudgy, equidistant from the circumference, flattened against the very center of the face like a dough ball upon the ceiling. Perhaps that is why I hated him, for truly he had become an offense to my eyes, and I believed the earth to be cumbered with his presence. Perhaps my mother may have been superstitious of the moon and looked upon it over the wrong shoulder at the wrong time.

Be that as it may, I hated John Claverhouse. Not that he had done me what society would consider a wrong or an ill turn. Far from it. The evil was of a deeper, subtler sort, so elusive, so intangible, as to defy clear, definite analysis in words. We all experience such things at some period in our lives. For the first time we see a certain individual, one who the very instant before we did not dream existed; and yet, at the first moment of meeting, we say, "I do not like that man." Why do we not like him? Ah, we do not know why; we know only that we do not. We have taken a dislike, that is all. And so I with John Claverhouse.

What right had such a man to be happy? Yet he was an optimist. He was always gleeful and laughing. All things were always all right, curse him! Ah! How it grated on my soul that he should be so happy! Other men could laugh, and it did not bother me. I even used to laugh myself, before I met John Claverhouse.

But his laugh! It irritated me, maddened me, as nothing else under the sun could irritate or madden me. It haunted me, gripped hold of me, and would not let me go. It was a huge, Gargantuan laugh. Waking or sleeping, it was always with me, whirring and jarring across my heartstrings like an enormous rasp. At break of day it came whooping across the fields to spoil my pleasant morning reverie. Under the aching noonday glare, when the green things drooped and the birds withdrew to the depths of the forest, and all nature drowsed, his great "Ha! Ha!" and "Ho! Ho!" rose up to the sky and challenged the sun. And at black midnight, from the lonely crossroads where he turned from town into his own place, came his plaguey cachinnations to rouse me from my sleep and make me writhe and clench my nails into my palms.

I went forth privily in the nighttime and turned his cattle into his fields, and in the morning heard his whooping laugh as he drove them out again. "It is nothing," he said, "the poor dumb beasties are not to be blamed for straying into fatter pastures."

He had a dog he called Mars, a big, splendid brute, part deerhound and part bloodhound, and resembling both. Mars was a great delight to him, and they were always together. But I bided my time and one day when opportunity was ripe lured the animal away and settled for him with strychnine and beefsteak. It made positively no impression on John Claverhouse. His laugh was as hearty and frequent as ever, and his face as much like the full moon as it always had been.

Then I set fire to his haystacks and his barn. But the next morning, being Sunday, he went forth blithe and cheerful.

"Where are you going?" I asked him as he went by the crossroads.

"Trout," he said, and his face beamed like a full moon. "I just dote on trout."

Was there ever such an impossible man! His whole harvest had gone up in his haystacks and barn. It was uninsured, I knew. And yet, in the face of famine and the rigorous winter, he went out gaily in quest of a mess of trout, forsooth, because he "doted" on them! Had gloom but rested, no matter how lightly, on his brow, or had his bovine countenance grown long and serious and less like the moon, or had he removed that smile but once from off his face, I am sure I could have forgiven him for existing. But no, he grew only more cheerful under misfortune.

I insulted him. He looked at me in slow and smiling surprise.

"I fight you? Why?" he asked slowly. And then he laughed. "You are so funny! Ho! Ho! You'll be the death of me! He! He! He! Oh! Ho! Ho! Ho!"

What would you do? It was past endurance. By the blood of Judas, how I hated him. Then there was that name—Claverhouse! What a name! Wasn't it absurd? Claverhouse! Merciful heaven, *why* Claverhouse? Again and again I asked myself that question. I should not have minded Smith, or Brown, or Jones—but *Claverhouse!* I leave it to you. Repeat it to yourself—Claverhouse. Just listen to the ridiculous sound of it—Claverhouse! Should a man live with such a name? I ask you. "No," you say. And "no" said I.

But I bethought me of his mortgage. What with his crops and barn destroyed, I knew he would be unable to meet it. So I got a shrewd, close-mouthed, tightfisted money lender to get the mortage transferred to him. I did not appear, but through this agent I forced the foreclosure, and but few days (no more, believe me, than the law allowed) were given John Claverhouse to remove his goods and chattels from the premises. Then I strolled down to see how he took it, for he had lived there upward of twenty years. But he met me with his saucer-eyes twinkling and the light glowing and spreading in his face till it was as a full-risen moon.

"Ha! Ha! Ha!" he laughed. "The funniest tyke, that youngster of mine! Did you ever hear the like? Let me tell you. He was down playing by the edge of the river when a piece of the bank caved in and splashed him. 'Oh, papa!' he cried, 'a great big puddle flewed up and hit me.'"

He stopped and waited for me to join him in his infernal glee.

"I don't see any laugh in it," I said shortly, and I know my face went sour.

He regarded me with wonderment, and then came the damnable light, glowing and spreading, as I have described it, till his face shone soft and warm like the summer moon, and then the laugh—" Ha! Ha! That's funny! you don't see it, eh? He! He! Ho! Ho! Ho! He doesn't see it! Why, look here. You know a puddle—"

But I turned on my heel and left him. That was the last. I could stand it no longer. The thing must end right there, I thought, curse him. The earth should be quit of him. And as I went over the hill, I could hear his monstrous laugh reverberating against the sky.

Now, I pride myself on doing things neatly, and when I resolved to kill John Claverhouse I had it in mind to do so in such a fashion that I should not look back upon it and feel ashamed. I hate bungling, and I hate brutality. To me there is something repugnant in merely striking a man with one's naked fist—faugh! it is sickening! So, to shoot, or stab, or club John Claverhouse (oh, that name!) did not appeal to me. And not only was I impelled to do it neatly and artistically, but also in such manner that not the slightest possible suspicion could be directed against me.

To this end I bent my intellect, and after a week of profound incubation, I hatched the scheme. Then I set to work. I bought a water-spaniel bitch, five months old, and devoted my whole attention to her training. Had anyone spied upon me, they would have remarked that this training consisted entirely of one thing— retrieving. I taught the dog, which I called Bellona, to fetch sticks I threw into the water, and not only to fetch, but to fetch at once, without mouthing or playing with them. The point was that she was to stop for nothing, but to deliver the stick in all haste. I made a practice of running away and leaving her to chase me, with the stick in her mouth, till she caught me. She was a bright animal and took to the game with such eagerness that I was soon content.

After that, at the first casual opportunity, I presented Bellona to John Claverhouse. I knew what I was about, for I was aware of a little weakness of his and of a little private sinning of which he was regularly and inveterately guilty.

"No," he said when I placed the end of the rope in his hand. "No, you don't mean it." And his mouth opened wide and he grinned all over his damnable moon-face.

"I—I kind of thought, somehow, you didn't like me," he explained. "Wasn't it funny for me to make such a mistake?" And at the thought he held his sides with laughter.

"What is her name?" he managed to ask between paroxysms.

"Bellona," I said.

"He! He!" he tittered. "What a funny name!"

I gritted my teeth, for his mirth put them on edge, and snapped out between them, "She was the wife of Mars, you know."

Then the light of the full moon began to suffuse his face, until he exploded with, "That was my other dog. Well, I guess she's a widow now. Oh! Ho! Ho! E! He! He! Ho!" he whooped after me, and I turned and fled swiftly over the hill.

The week passed by, and on Saturday evening I said to him, "You go away Monday, don't you?"

He nodded his head and grinned.

"Then you won't have another chance to get a mess of those trout you just dote on."

But he did not notice the sneer. "Oh, I don't know," he chuckled. "I'm going up tomorrow to try pretty hard."

Thus was assurance made doubly sure, and I went back to my house hugging myself with rapture.

Early next morning I saw him go by with a dipnet and gunnysack, and Bellona trotting at his heels. I knew where he was bound and cut out by the back pasture and climbed through the underbrush to the top of the mountain. Keeping carefully out of sight, I followed the crest along for a couple of miles to a natural amphitheater in the hills, where the little river raced down out of a gorge and stopped for breath in a large and placid rockbound pool. That was the spot! I sat down on the croup of the mountain, where I could see all that occurred, and lighted my pipe.

Ere many minutes had passed John Claverhouse came plodding up the bed of the stream. Bellona was ambling about him, and they were in high feather, her short snappy barks mingling with his deeper chest notes. Arrived at the pool, he threw down the dipnet and sack and drew from his hip pocket what looked like a large fat candle. But I knew it to be a stick of "giant," for such was his method of catching trout. He dynamited them. He attached the fuse by wrapping the "giant" tightly in a piece of cotton. Then he ignited the fuse and tossed the explosive into the pool.

Like a flash, Bellona was into the pool after it. I could have shrieked aloud for joy. Claverhouse yelled at her, but without avail. He pelted her with clods of rocks, but she swam steadily on till she got the stick of "giant" in her mouth, when she whirled about and headed for shore. Then, for the first time, he realized his danger and started to run. As foreseen and planned by me, she made the bank and took out after him. Oh, I tell you, it was great! As I have said, the pool lay in a sort of amphitheatre. Above and below, the stream could be crossed on steppingstones. And around and around, up and down and across the stones, raced Claverhouse and Bellona. I could never have believed such an ungainly man could run so fast. But run he did, Bellona hotfooted after him, and gaining. And then, just as she caught up, he in full stride and she leaping with nose at his knee, there was a sudden flash, a burst of smoke, a terrific detonation, and where man and dog had been the instant before there was naught to be seen but a big hole in the ground.

"Death from accident while engaged in illegal fishing." That was the verdict of the coroner's jury, and that is why I pride myself on the neat and artistic way in which I finished off John Claverhouse. There was no bungling, no brutality, nothing of which to be ashamed in the whole transaction, as I am sure you will agree. No more does his infernal laugh go echoing among the hills, and no more does his fat moon-face rise up to vex me. My days are peaceful now, and my night's sleep deep.

WALT WHITMAN *(1819–1892) is generally considered America's greatest nineteenth century poet. It is a real find to bring forth this rare excursion into prose, first printed in 1841. According to Whitman, it is a true anecdote. One wonders who suffered more, the pupil or the teacher?*

Death in the School-Room (A Fact)

BY WALT WHITMAN

Ting-a-ling-ling-ling! went the little bell on the teacher's desk of a village-school one morning, when the studies of the earlier part of the day were about half completed. It was well understood that this was a command for silence and attention; and when these had been obtain'd, the master spoke. He was a low thick-set man, and his name was Lugare.

"Boys," said he, "I have had a complaint enter'd, that last night some of you were stealing fruit from Mr. Nichols's garden. I rather think I know the thief. Tim Barker, step up here, sir."

The one to whom he spoke came forward. He was a slight, fair-looking boy of about thirteen; and his face had a laughing, good-humor'd expression, which even the charge now preferr'd against him, and the stern tone and threatening look of the teacher, had not entirely dissipated. The countenance of the boy, however, was too unearthly fair for health; it had, notwithstanding its fleshy, cheerful look, a singular cast as if some inward disease, and that a fearful one, were seated within. As the stripling stood before that place of judgment—that place so often made the scene of heartless and coarse brutality, of timid innocence confused, helpless childhood outraged, and gentle feelings crush'd—Lugare looked on him with a frown which plainly told that he felt in no very pleasant mood. (Happily a worthier and more philosophical system is proving to men that schools can be better govern'd than by lashes and tears and sighs. We are waxing toward that consummation when one of the old-fashion'd school-masters, with his cowhide, his heavy birch-rod, and his many ingenious methods of child-torture, will be gazed upon as a scorn'd memento of an ignorant, cruel, and exploded doctrine. May propitious gales speed that day!)

"Were you by Mr. Nichols's garden-fence last night?" said Lugare.

"Yes, sir," answer'd the boy, "I was."

"Well, sir, I'm glad to find you so ready with your confession. And so you thought you could do a little robbing, and enjoy yourself in a manner you ought to be ashamed to own, without being punish'd, did you?"

"I have not been robbing," replied the boy quickly. His face was suffused, whether with resentment or fright, it was difficult to tell. "And I didn't do anything last night, that I am ashamed to own."

"No impudence!" exclaim'd the teacher, passionately, as he grasp'd a long and heavy ratan: "give me none of your sharp speeches, or I'll thrash you till you beg like a dog."

The youngster's face paled a little; his lip quiver'd, but he did not speak.

"And pray, sir," continued Lugare, as the outward signs of wrath disappear'd from his features; "what were you about the garden for? Perhaps you only receiv'd the plunder, and had an accomplice to do the more dangerous part of the job?"

"I went that way because it is on my road home. I was there again afterwards to meet an acquaintance; and—and—But I did not go into the garden, nor take anything away from it. I would not steal,—hardly to save myself from starving."

"You had better have stuck to that last evening. You were seen, Tim Barker, to come from under Mr. Nichols's garden-fence, a little after nine o'clock, with a bag full of something or other over your shoulders. The bag had every appearance of being filled with fruit, and this morning the melon-beds are found to have been completely clear'd. Now, sir, what was there in that bag?"

Like fire itself glow'd the face of the detected lad. He spoke not a word. All the school had their eyes directed at him. The perspiration ran down his white forehead like rain-drops.

"Speak, sir!" exclaimed Lugare, with a loud strike of his ratan on the desk.

The boy look'd as though he would faint. But the unmerciful teacher, confident of having brought to light a criminal, and exulting in the idea of the severe chastisement he should now be justified in inflicting, kept working himself up to a still greater and greater degree of passion. In the meantime, the child seem'd hardly to know what to do with himself. His tongue cleav'd to the roof of his mouth. Either he was very much frighten'd, or he was actually unwell.

"Speak, I say!" again thunder'd Lugare; and his hand, grasping his ratan, tower'd above his head in a very significant manner.

"I hardly can, sir," said the poor fellow faintly. His voice was husky and thick. "I will tell you some—some other time. Please let me go to my seat—I a'n't well."

"Oh yes; that's very likely;" and Mr. Lugare bulged out his nose and cheeks with contempt. "Do you think to make me believe your lies? I've found you out, sir, plainly enough; and I am satisfied that you are as precious a little villain as there is in the State. But I will postpone settling with you for an hour yet. I shall then call you up again; and if you don't tell the whole truth then, I will give you something that'll make you remember Mr. Nichols's melons for many a month to come:—go to your seat."

Glad enough of the ungracious permission, and answering not a sound, the child crept tremblingly to his bench. He felt very strangely, dizzily—more as if he was in a dream than in real life; and laying his arms on his desk, bow'd down his face between them. The pupils turn'd to their accustom'd studies, for during the reign of Lugare in the village-school, they had been so used to scenes of violence and severe chastisement, that such things made but little interruption in the tenor of their way.

Now, while the intervening hour is passing, we will clear up the mystery of the bag, and of young Barker being under the garden fence on the preceding night. The boy's mother was a widow, and they both had to live in the very narrowest limits. His father had died when he was six years old, and little Tim was left a sickly emaciated infant whom no one expected to live many months. To the surprise of all, however, the poor child kept alive, and seem'd to recover his health, as he certainly did his size and good looks. This was owing to the kind offices of an eminent physician who had a country-seat in the neighborhood, and who had been interested in the widow's little family. Tim, the physician said, might possibly outgrow his disease; but everything was uncertain. It was a mysterious and baffling malady; and it would not be wonderful if he should in some moment of apparent health be suddenly taken away. The poor widow was at first in a continual state of uneasiness; but several years had now pass'd, and none of the impending evils had fallen upon the boy's head. His mother seem'd to feel confident that he would live, and be a help and an honor to her old age; and the two struggled on together, mutually happy in each other, and enduring much of poverty and discomfort without repining, each for the other's sake.

Tim's pleasant disposition had made him many friends in the village, and among the rest a young farmer named Jones, who, with his elder brother, work'd a large farm in the neighborhood on shares. Jones very frequently made Tim a present of a bag of potatoes or corn, or some garden vegetables, which he took from his own stock; but as his partner was a parsimonious, high-tempered man, and had often said that Tim was an idle fellow, and ought not to be help'd because he did not work, Jones generally made his gifts in such a manner that no one knew anything about them, except himself and the grateful objects of his kindness. It might be, too, that the widow was loth to have it understood by the neighbors that she received food from anyone; for there is often an excusable pride in people of her condition which makes them shrink from being consider'd as objects of "charity" as they would from the severest pains. On the night in question, Tim had been told that Jones would send them a bag of potatoes, and the place at which they were to be waiting for him was fixed at Mr. Nichols's garden-fence. It was this bag that Tim had been seen staggering under, and which caused the unlucky boy to be accused and convicted by his teacher as a thief. That teacher was one little fitted for his important and responsible office. Hasty to decide, and inflexibly severe, he was the terror of the little world he ruled so despotically. Punishment he seemed to delight in. Knowing little of those sweet fountains which in children's breasts ever open quickly at the call of gentleness and kind words, he was fear'd by all for his sternness, and loved by none. I would that he were an isolated instance in his profession.

The hour of grace had drawn to its close, and the time approach'd at which it was usual for Lugare to give his school a joyfully-receiv'd dismission. Now and then one of the scholars would direct a furtive glance at Tim, sometimes in pity, sometimes in indifference or inquiry. They knew that he would have no mercy shown him, and though most of them loved him, whipping was too common there to exact much sympathy. Every inquiring glance, however, remain'd unsatisfied, for at the end of the hour,

Tim remain'd with his face completely hidden, and his head bow'd in his arms, precisely as he had lean'd himself when he first went to his seat. Lugare look'd at the boy occasionally with a scowl which seem'd to bode vengeance for his sullenness. At length the last class had been heard, and the last lesson recited, and Lugare seated himself behind his desk on the platform, with his longest and stoutest ratan before him.

"Now, Barker," he said, "we'll settle that little business of yours. Just step up here."

Tim did not move. The school-room was as still as the grave. Not a sound was to be heard, except occasionally a long-drawn breath.

"Mind me, sir, or it will be the worse for you. Step up here, and take off your jacket!"

The boy did not stir any more than if he had been of wood. Lugare shook with passion. He sat still a minute, as if considering the best way to wreak his vengeance. That minute, passed in death-like silence, was a fearful one to some of the children, for their faces whiten'd with fright. It seem'd, as it slowly dropp'd away, like the minute which precedes the climax of an exquisitely-performed tragedy, when some mighty master of the histrionic art is treading the stage, and you and the multitude around you are waiting, with stretch'd nerves and suspended breath, in expectation of the terrible catastrophe.

"Tim is asleep, sir," at length said one of the boys who sat near him.

Lugare, at this intelligence, allow'd his features to relax from their expression of savage anger into a smile, but that smile look'd more malignant if possible, than his former scowls. It might be that he felt amused at the horror depicted on the faces of those about him; or it might be that he was gloating in pleasure on the way in which he intended to wake the slumberer.

"Asleep! are you, my young gentleman!" said he; "let us see if we can't find something to tickle your eyes open. There's nothing like making the best of a bad case, boys. Tim, here, is determin'd not to be worried in his mind about a little flogging, for the thought of it can't even keep the little scoundrel awake."

Lugare smiled again as he made the last observation. He grasp'd his ratan firmly, and descended from his seat. With light and stealthy steps he cross'd the room, and stood by the unlucky sleeper. The boy was still as unconscious of his impending punishment as ever. He might be dreaming some golden dream of youth and pleasure; perhaps he was far away in the world of fancy, seeing scenes, and feeling delights, which cold reality never can bestow. Lugare lifted his ratan high over his head, and with the true and expert aim which he had acquired by long practice, brought it down on Tim's back with a force and whacking sound which seem'd sufficient to awake a freezing man in his last lethargy. Quick and fast, blow follow'd blow. Without waiting to see the effect of the first cut, the brutal wretch plied his instrument of torture first on one side of the boy's back, and then on the other, and only stopped at the end of two or three minutes from weariness. But still Tim show'd no signs of motion; and as Lugare, provoked at his torpidity, jerk'd away one of the child's arms, on which he had been leaning over the desk, his head dropp'd down on the board with a dull sound, and his face lay turn'd up and exposed to view. When Lugare saw it, he stood like one transfix'd by a basilisk. His countenance turn'd to a leaden whiteness; the ratan dropp'd from his grasp; and his eyes, stretch'd wide open, glared as at some monstrous spectacle of horror and death. The sweat started in great globules seemingly from every pore in his face; his skinny lips contracted, and show'd his teeth; and when he at length stretch'd forth his arm, and with the end of one of his fingers touch'd the child's cheek, each limb quiver'd like the tongue of a snake; and his strength seemed as though it would momentarily fail him. The boy was dead. He had probably been so for some time, for his eyes were turn'd up, and his body was quite cold. Death was in the school-room, and Lugare had been flogging a corpse.

The true pinnacle of man's bestial nature surely must be warfare. STEPHEN
CRANE, *born in Newark in 1871, died in Germany at the age of 29 after
writing the famous Civil War novel* The Red Badge of Courage, *and
several shorter works. "The Upturned Face" is another war piece, a vignette
which plumbs to the true depths of terror without any stagy trappings
whatever. It is over quickly, but I doubt that you will ever forget it.*

The Upturned Face

BY STEPHEN CRANE

"What will we do now?" said the adjutant, troubled and excited.

"Bury him," said Timothy Lean.

The two officers looked down close to their toes where lay the
body of their comrade. The face was chalk-blue; gleaming eyes
stared at the sky. Over the two upright figures was a windy sound
of bullets, and on the top of the hill Lean's prostrate company of
Spitzbergen infantry was firing measured volleys.

"Don't you think it would be better—" began the adjutant. "We
might leave him until to-morrow."

"No," said Lean. "I can't hold that post an hour longer. I've got
to fall back, and we've got to bury old Bill."

"Of course," said the adjutant, at once. "Your men got
intrenching tools?"

Lean shouted back to his little line, and two men came slowly,
one with a pick, one with a shovel. They started in the direction
of the Rostina sharp-shooters. Bullets cracked near their ears.
"Dig here," said Lean gruffly. The men, thus caused to lower their
glances to the turf, became hurried and frightened merely because
they could not look to see whence the bullets came. The dull beat
of the pick striking the earth sounded amid the swift snap of close
bullets. Presently the other private began to shovel.

"I suppose," said the adjutant, slowly, "we'd better search his
clothes for—things."

Lean nodded. Together in curious abstraction they looked at the
body. Then Lean stirred his shoulders suddenly, arousing himself.

"Yes," he said, "we'd better see what he's got." He dropped to his knees, and his hands approached the body of the dead officer. But his hands wavered over the buttons of the tunic. The first button was brick-red with drying blood, and he did not seem to dare touch it.

"Go on," said the adjutant, hoarsely.

Lean stretched his wooden hand, and his fingers fumbled the blood-stained buttons. At last he rose with ghastly face. He had gathered a watch, a whistle, a pipe, a tobacco pouch, a handkerchief, a little case of cards and papers. He looked at the adjutant. There was a silence. The adjutant was feeling that he had been a coward to make Lean do all the grisly business.

"Well," said Lean, "that's all, I think. You have his sword and revolver?"

"Yes," said the adjutant, his face working, and then he burst out in a sudden strange fury at the two privates. "Why don't you hurry up with that grave? What are you doing, anyhow? Hurry, do you hear? I never saw such stupid—"

Even as he cried out in his passion the two men were laboring for their lives. Ever overhead the bullets were spitting.

The grave was finished. It was not a masterpiece—a poor little shallow thing. Lean and the adjutant again looked at each other in a curious silent communication.

Suddenly the adjutant croaked out a weird laugh. It was a terrible laugh, which had its origin in that part of the mind which is first moved by the singing of the nerves. "Well," he said, humorously to Lean, "I suppose we had best tumble him in."

"Yes," said Lean. The two privates stood waiting, bent over their implements. "I suppose," said Lean, "it would be better if we laid him in ourselves."

"Yes," said the adjutant. Then apparently remembering that he had made Lean search the body, he stooped with great fortitude and took hold of the dead officer's clothing. Lean joined him. Both were particular that their fingers should not feel the corpse. They tugged away; the corpse lifted, heaved, toppled, flopped into the grave, and the two officers, straightening, looked again at each other—they were always looking at each other. They sighed with relief.

The adjutant said, "I suppose we should—we should say something. Do you know the service, Tim?"

"They don't read the service until the grave is filled in," said

Lean, pressing his lips to an academic expression.

"Don't they?" said the adjutant, shocked that he had made the mistake.

"Oh, well," he cried, suddenly, "let us—let us say something—while he can hear us."

"All right," said Lean. "Do you know the service?"

"I can't remember a line of it," said the adjutant.

Lean was extremely dubious. "I can repeat two lines, but—"

"Well, do it," said the adjutant. "Go as far as you can. That's better than nothing. And the beasts have got our range exactly."

Lean looked at his two men. "Attention," he barked. The privates came to attention with a click, looking much aggrieved. The adjutant lowered his helmet to his knee. Lean, bareheaded, he stood over the grave. The Rostina sharpshooters fired briskly.

"Oh, Father, our friend has sunk in the deep waters of death, but his spirit has leaped toward Thee as the bubble arises from the lips of the drowning. Perceive, we beseech, O Father, the little flying bubble, and—"

Lean, although husky and ashamed, had suffered no hesitation up to this point, but he stopped with a hopeless feeling and looked at the corpse.

The adjutant moved uneasily. "And from Thy superb heights—" he began, and then he too came to an end.

"And from Thy superb heights," said Lean.

The adjutant suddenly remembered a phrase in the back part of the Spitzbergen burial service, and he exploited it with the triumphant manner of a man who has recalled everything, and can go on.

"Oh, God, have mercy—"

"Oh, God, have mercy—" said Lean.

"Mercy," repeated the adjutant, in quick failure.

"Mercy," said Lean. And then he was moved by some violence of feeling, for he turned suddenly upon his two men and tigerishly said, "Throw the dirt in."

The fire of the Rostina sharpshooters was accurate and continuous.

One of the aggrieved privates came forward with his shovel. He lifted his first shovel-load of earth, and for a moment of inexplicable hesitation it was held poised above this corpse, which from its chalk-blue face looked keenly out from the grave. Then the soldier emptied his shovel on—on the feet.

Timothy Lean felt as if tons had been swiftly lifted from off his forehead. He had felt that perhaps the private might empty the shovel on—on the face. It had been emptied on the feet. There was a great point gained there—ha, ha!—the first shovelful had been emptied on the feet. How satisfactory!

The adjutant began to babble. "Well, of course—a man we've messed with all these years—impossible—you can't, you know, leave your intimate friends rotting on the field. Go on, for God's sake, and shovel, you!"

The man with the shovel suddenly ducked, grabbed his left arm with his right hand, and looked at his officer for orders. Lean picked the shovel from the ground. "Go to the rear," he said to the wounded man. He also addressed the other private. "You get under cover, too; I'll finish this business."

The wounded man scrambled hard still for the top of the ridge without devoting any glances to the direction whence the bullets came, and the other man followed at an equal pace; but he was different, in that he looked back anxiously three times.

This is merely the way—often—of the hit and unhit.

Timothy Lean filled the shovel, hesitated, and then in a movement which was like a gesture of abhorrence he flung the dirt into the grave, and as it landed it made a sound—plop! Lean suddenly stopped and mopped his brow—a tired laborer.

"Perhaps we have been wrong," said the adjutant. His glance wavered stupidly. "It might have been better if we hadn't buried him just at this time. Of course, if we advance to-morrow the body would have been—"

"Damn you," said Lean, "shut your mouth!" He was not the senior officer.

He again filled the shovel and flung the earth. Always the earth made that sound—plop! For a space Lean worked frantically, like a man digging himself out of danger.

Soon there was nothing to be seen but the chalk-blue face. Lean filled the shovel. "Good God," he cried to the adjutant. "Why didn't you turn him somehow when you put him in? This—" Then Lean began to stutter.

The adjutant understood. He was pale to the lips. "Go on, man," he cried, beseechingly, almost in a shout. Lean swung back the shovel. It went forward in a pendulum curve. When the earth landed it made a sound—plop!

Here is one of the characteristically ferocious tales of AMBROSE BIERCE, *America's great cynic who disappeared in Mexico in 1914 and was never heard from since. Born in 1842 to an impoverished Connecticut family, Bierce spent most of his career in San Francisco, first as a political writer, later as a columnist for the Hearst paper* The San Francisco Examiner. *His fiction is distinguished by mordant satire and often ghoulish comedy. There is perhaps a trace of the latter in "One Summer Night," which, nevertheless, is a brutal little miniature.*

One Summer Night

BY AMBROSE BIERCE

The fact that Henry Armstrong was buried did not seem to prove that he was dead; he had always been a hard man to convince. That he was really buried, the testimony of his senses compelled him to admit. His posture—flat upon his back, with his hands crossed on his stomach and tied with something that he easily broke without profitably altering the situation—the strict confinement of his entire person, the black darkness and profound silence, made a body of evidence impossible to controvert and he accepted it without cavil.

But dead—no; he was only very, very ill. He had, withal, the invalid's apathy and did not greatly concern himself about the uncommon fate that had been allotted to him. No philosopher was he—just a plain, common-place person gifted, for the time being, with a pathological indifference: the organ that he feared consequences with was torpid. So, with no particular apprehension for his immediate future, he fell asleep and all was peace with Henry Armstrong.

But something was going on overhead. It was a dark summer night, shot through with infrequent shimmers of lightning silently firing a cloud lying low in the west and portending a storm. There brief, stammering illuminations brought out with ghastly distinctness the monuments and headstones of the cemetery and seemed to set them dancing. It was not a night in which any credible witness was likely to be straying about a cemetery, so the three men who were there, digging into the grave of Henry Armstrong, felt reasonably secure.

Two of them were young students from a medical college a few miles away; the third was a gigantic man known as Jess. For many years Jess had been employed about the cemetery as a man-of-all-work and it was his favorite pleasantry that he knew "every soul in the place." From the nature of what he was now doing it was inferable that the place was not so populous as its register may have shown it to be.

Outside the wall, at the part of the grounds farthest from the public road, were a horse and a light wagon, waiting.

The work of excavation was not difficult: the earth with which the grave had been loosely filled a few hours before offered little resistance and was soon thrown out. Removal of the casket from its box was less easy, but it was taken out, for it was a perquisite of Jess, who carefully unscrewed the cover and laid it aside, exposing the body in black trousers and white shirt. At that instant the air sprang to flame, a crackling shock of thunder stunned the world and Henry Armstrong tranquilly sat up. With inarticulate cries, the men fled in terror, each in a different direction. For nothing on earth could two of them have been persuaded to return. But Jess was of another breed.

In the gray of the morning the two students, pallid and haggard from anxiety and with the terror of their adventure still beating tumultuously in their blood, met at the medical college.

"You saw it?" cried one.

"God! yes—what are we to do?"

They went around to the rear of the building, where they saw a horse, attached to a light wagon, hitched to a gatepost near the door of the dissecting room. Mechanically they entered the room. On a bench in the obscurity sat Jess. He rose, grinning, all eyes and teeth.

"I'm waiting for my pay," he said.

Stretched naked on a long table lay the body of Henry Armstrong, the head defiled with blood and clay from a blow with a spade.

The Easter Egg

BY H. H. MUNRO
("Saki")

It was distinctly hard lines for Lady Barbara, who came of good fighting stock, and was one of the bravest women of her generation, that her son should be so undisguisedly a coward. Whatever good qualities Lester Slaggby may have possessed, and he was in some respects charming, courage could certainly never be imputed to him. As a child he had suffered from childish timidity, as a boy from unboyish funk, and as a youth he had exchanged unreasoning fears for others which were more formidable from the fact of having a carefully-thought-out basis. He was frankly afraid of animals, nervous with firearms, and never crossed the Channel without mentally comparing the numerical proportion of life belts to passengers. On horseback he seemed to require as many hands as a Hindu god, at least four for clutching the reins, and two more for patting the horse soothingly on the neck. Lady Barbara no longer pretended not to see her son's prevailing weakness; with her usual courage she faced the knowledge of it squarely, and, mother-like, loved him none the less.

Continental travel, anywhere away from the great tourist tracks, was a favoured hobby with Lady Barbara, and Lester joined her as often as possible. Eastertide usually found her at Knobaltheim, an upland township in one of those small princedoms that make inconspicuous freckles on the map of Central Europe.

A long-standing acquaintanceship with the reigning family made her a personage of due importance in the eyes of her old friend the Burgomaster, and she was anxiously consulted by that worthy on the momentous occasion when the Prince made known his intention of coming in person to open a sanitorium outside the town. All the usual items in a programme of welcome, some of them fatuous and commonplace, others quaint and charming, had been arranged for, but the Burgomaster hoped that the resourceful English lady might have something new and tasteful to suggest in the way of loyal greeting. The Prince was known to the outside world, if at all, as an old-fashioned reactionary, combating modern progress, as it were, with a wooden sword; to his own people he was known as a kindly old gentleman with a certain endearing stateliness which had nothing of standoffishness about it. Knobaltheim was anxious to do its best. Lady Barbara discussed the matter with Lester and one or two acquaintances in her little hotel, but ideas were difficult to come by.

"Might I suggest something to the Gnädige Frau?" asked a sallow high-cheek-boned lady to whom the English-woman had spoken once or twice, and whom she had set down in her mind as probably a Southern Slav.

"Might I suggest something for the Reception Fest?" she went on, with a certain shy eagerness. "Our little child here, our baby, we will dress him in little white coat, with small wings, as an Easter angel, and he will carry a large white Easter egg, and inside shall be a basket of plover eggs, of which the Prince is so fond, and he shall give it to his Highness as Easter offering. It is so pretty an idea; we have seen it done once in Syria."

Lady Barbara looked dubiously at the proposed Easter angel, a fair, wooden-faced child of about four years old. She had noticed it the day before in the hotel, and wondered rather how such a tow-headed child could belong to such a dark-visaged couple as the woman and her husband; probably, she thought, an adopted baby, especially as the couple were not young.

"Of course Gnädige Frau will escort the little child up to the Prince," pursued the woman; "but he will be quite good, and do as he is told."

"We haf some pluffers' eggs shall come fresh from Wien," said the husband.

The small child and Lady Barbara seemed equally unenthusiastic about the pretty idea; Lester was openly discouraging, but when the Burgomaster heard of it he was enchanted. The combination of sentiment and plovers' eggs appealed strongly to his Teutonic mind.

On the eventful day the Easter angel, really quite prettily and quaintly dressed, was a centre of kindly interest to the gala crowd marshalled to receive his Highness. The mother was unobtrusive and less fussy than most parents would have been under the circumstances, merely stipulating that she should place the Easter egg herself in the arms that had been carefully schooled how to hold the precious burden. Then Lady Barbara moved forward, the child marching stolidly and with grim determination at her side. It had been promised cakes and sweets galore if it gave the egg well and truly to the kind old gentleman who was waiting to receive it. Lester had tried to convey to it privately that horrible smackings would attend any failure in its share of the proceedings, but it is doubtful if his German caused more than an immediate distress. Lady Barbara had thoughtfully provided herself with an emergency supply of chocolate sweetmeats; children may sometimes be timeservers, but they do not encourage long accounts. As they approached nearer to the princely dais Lady Barbara stood discreetly aside, and the stolid-faced infant walked forward alone, with staggering but steadfast gait, encouraged by a murmur of elderly approval. Lester, standing in the front row of the onlookers, turned to scan the crowd for the beaming faces of the happy parents. In a side-road which led to the railway station he saw a cab; entering the cab with every appearance of furtive haste were the dark-visaged couple who had been so plausibly eager for the "pretty idea." The sharpened instinct of cowardice lit up the situation to him in one swift flash. The blood roared and surged to his head as though thousands of floodgates had been opened in his veins and arteries, and his brain was the common sluice in which all the torrents met. He saw nothing but a blur around him. Then the blood ebbed away in quick waves, till his very heart seemed drained and empty, and he stood nervelessly, helplessly, dumbly watching the child, bearing its accursed burden with slow, relentless steps nearer and nearer to the group that waited sheeplike to receive him. A fascinated curiosity compelled Lester to turn his head towards the fugitives; the cab had started at hot pace in the direction of the station.

The next moment Lester was running, running faster than any

of those present had ever seen a man run, and—he was not running away. For that stray fraction of his life some unwonted impulse beset him, some hint of the stock he came from, and he ran unflinchingly towards danger. He stooped and clutched at the Easter egg as one tries to scoop up the ball in Rugby football. What he meant to do with it he had not considered, the thing was to get it. But the child had been promised cakes and sweetmeats if it safely gave the egg into the hands of the kindly old gentleman; it uttered no scream, but it held to its charge with limpet grip. Lester sank to his knees, tugging savagely at the tightly clasped burden, and angry cries rose from the scandalized onlookers. A questioning, threatening ring formed round him, then shrank back in recoil as he shrieked out one hideous word. Lady Barbara heard the word and saw the crowd race away like scattered sheep, saw the Prince forcibly hustled away by his attendants; also she saw her son lying prone in an agony of overmastering terror, his spasm of daring shattered by the child's unexpected resistance, still clutching frantically, as though for safety, at that white-satin gew-gaw, unable to crawl even from its deadly neighbourhood, able only to scream and scream and scream. In her brain she was dimly conscious of balancing, or striving to balance, the abject shame which had him now in thrall against the one compelling act of courage which had flung him grandly and madly on to the point of danger. It was only for the fraction of a minute that she stood watching the two entangled figures, the infant with its woodenly obstinate face and body tense with dogged resistance, and the boy limp and already nearly dead with a terror that almost stifled his screams; and over them the long gala streamers flapping gaily in the sunshine. She never forgot the scene; but then, it was the last she ever saw.

Lady Barbara carries her scarred face with its sightless eyes as bravely as ever in the world, but at Eastertide her friends are careful to keep from her ears any mention of the children's Easter symbol.

One of the two or three greatest American mystery novelists in the first half of this century was JOHN DICKSON CARR, *whose locked room puzzles virtually defined the genre of the impossible crime. Good as his Dr. Fell mysteries are, I have always preferred the ones he wrote under the pseudonym of Carter Dickson, which Carr mostly reserved for his fat, outrageous British detective, H.M. (Sir Henry Merrivale). Born in 1905 in Uniontown, Pa., Carr was the son of a U.S. Congressman, Wood Nicholas Carr. Much of his life was spent in England, where he wrote for the BBC. Sir Henry Merrivale appeared in approximately two dozen novels, but Carr also wrote one novella and one short story in which H.M. again played detective. "The House in Goblin Wood" is the short story, and though it has its hilarious moments, it is also heavy with menace. A second reading will show just how dark it really is.*

The House in Goblin Wood

BY JOHN DICKSON CARR

In Pall Mall, that hot July afternoon three years before the war, an open saloon car was drawn up to the curb just opposite the Senior Conservatives' Club.

And in the car sat two conspirators.

It was the drowsy post-lunch hour among the clubs, where only the sun remained brilliant. The Rag lay somnolent; the Atheneum slept outright. But these two conspirators, a dark-haired young man in his early thirties and a fair-haired girl perhaps half a dozen years younger, never moved. They stared intently at the Gothic-like front of the Senior Conservatives'.

"Look here, Eve," muttered the young man, and punched at the steering wheel. "Do you think this is going to work?"

"I don't know," the fair-haired girl confessed. "He absolutely *loathes* picnics."

"Anyway, we've probably missed him."

"Why so?"

"He can't have taken as long over lunch as that!" her companion protested, looking at a wrist watch. The young man was rather shocked. "It's a quarter to four! Even if . . ."

"Bill! There! Look there!"

Their patience was rewarded by an inspiring sight.

Out of the portals of the Senior Conservatives' Club, in awful majesty, marched a large, stout, barrel-shaped gentleman in a white linen suit.

His corporation preceded him like the figurehead of a man-of-war. His shell-rimmed spectacles were pulled down on a broad nose, all being shaded by a Panama hat. At the top of the stone steps he surveyed the street with a lordly sneer.

"Sir Henry!" called the girl.

"Hey?" said Sir Henry Merrivale.

"I'm Eve Drayton. Don't you remember me? You knew my father!"

"Oh, ah," said the great man.

"We've been waiting here a terribly long time," Eve pleaded. "Couldn't you see us for just five minutes?—The thing to do," she whispered to her companion, "is to keep him in a good humour. Just keep him in a good humour!"

As a matter of fact, H. M. was in a good humour, having just triumphed over the Home Secretary in an argument. But not even his own mother could have guessed it. Majestically, with the same lordly sneer, he began in grandeur to descend the steps of the Senior Conservatives'. He did this, in fact, until his foot encountered an unnoticed object lying some three feet from the bottom.

It was a banana skin.

"Oh, dear!" said the girl.

Now it must be stated with regret that in the old days certain urchins, of what were then called the "lower orders," had a habit of placing such objects on the steps in the hope that some eminent statesman would take a toss on his way to Whitehall. This was a venial but deplorable practice, probably accounting for what Mr. Gladstone said in 1882.

In any case, it accounted for what Sir Henry Merrivale said now.

From the pavement, where H. M. landed in a seated position, arose in H. M.'s bellowing voice such a torrent of profanity, such a flood of invective and vile obscenities, as has seldom before blasted the holy calm of Pall Mall. It brought the hall porter hurrying down the steps, and Eve Drayton flying out of the car.

Heads were now appearing at the windows of the Atheneum

across the street.

"Is it all right?" cried the girl, with concern in her blue eyes. "Are you hurt?"

H. M. merely looked at her. His hat had fallen off, disclosing a large bald head; and he merely sat on the pavement and looked at her.

"Anyway, H. M., get up! Please get up!"

"Yes, sir," begged the hall porter, "for heaven's sake get up!"

"Get up?" bellowed H.M., in a voice audible as far as St. James's Street. "Burn it all, how *can* I get up?"

"But why not?"

"My behind's out of joint," said H. M. simply. "I'm hurt awful bad. I'm probably goin' to have spinal dislocation for the rest of my life."

"But, sir, people are looking!"

H. M. explained what these people could do. He eyed Eve Drayton with a glare of indescribable malignancy over his spectacles.

"I suppose, my wench, *you're* responsible for this?"

Eve regarded him in consternation.

"You don't mean the banana skin?" she cried.

"Oh, yes, I do," said H. M., folding his arms like a prosecuting counsel.

"But we—we only wanted to invite you to a picnic!"

H. M. closed his eyes.

"That's fine," he said in a hollow voice. "All the same, don't you think it'd have been a subtler kind of hint just to pour mayonnaise over my head or shove ants down the back of my neck? Oh, lord love a duck!"

"I didn't mean that! I meant . . ."

"Let me help you up, sir," interposed the calm, reassuring voice of the dark-haired and blue-chinned young man who had been with Eve in the car.

"So you want to help too, hey? And who are *you?*"

"I'm awfully sorry!" said Eve. "I should have introduced you! This is my fiancé. Dr. William Sage."

H. M.'s face turned purple.

"I'm glad to see," he observed, "you had the uncommon decency to bring along a doctor. I appreciate that, I do. And the car's there, I suppose, to assist with the examination when I take off my pants?"

The hall porter uttered a cry of horror.

Bill Sage, either from jumpiness and nerves or from sheer inability to keep a straight face, laughed loudly.

"I keep telling Eve a dozen times a day," he said, "that I'm not to be called 'doctor.' I happen to be a surgeon—"

(Here H. M. really did look alarmed.)

"—but I don't think we need operate. Nor, in my opinion," Bill gravely addressed the hall porter, "will it be necessary to remove Sir Henry's trousers in front of the Senior Conservatives' Club."

"Thank you very much, sir."

"We had an infernal nerve to come here," the young man confessed to H. M. "But I honestly think, Sir Henry, you'd be more comfortable in the car. What about it? Let me give you a hand up?"

Yet even ten minutes later, when H. M. sat glowering in the back of the car and two heads were craned round toward him, peace was not restored.

"All right!" said Eve. Her pretty, rather stolid face was flushed; her mouth looked miserable. "If you won't come to the picnic, you won't. But I did believe you might do it to oblige me."

"Well . . . now!" muttered the great man uncomfortably.

"And I did think, too, you'd be interested in the other person who was coming with us. But Vicky's—difficult. She won't come either, if you don't."

"Oh? And who's this other guest?"

"Vicky Adams."

H. M.'s hand, which had been lifted for an oratorical gesture, dropped to his side.

"Vicky Adams? That's not the gal who . . . ?"

"Yes!" Eve nodded. "They say it was one of the great mysteries, twenty years ago, that the police failed to solve."

"It was, my wench," H. M. agreed somberly. "It was."

"And now Vicky's grown up. And we thought if you of all people went along, and spoke to her nicely, she'd tell us what really happened on that night."

H. M.'s small, sharp eyes fixed disconcertingly on Eve.

"I say, my wench. What's your interest in all this?"

"Oh, reasons." Eve glanced quickly at Bill Sage, who was again punching moodily at the steering wheel, and checked herself. "Anyway, what difference does it make now? If you won't go with us . . ."

H. M. assumed a martyred air.

"I never said I *wasn't* goin' with you, did I?" he demanded. (This was inaccurate, but no matter.) "Even after you practically made a cripple of me, I never said I *wasn't* goin'?" His manner grew flurried and hasty. "I got to get back to my office."

"We'll drive you there, H. M."

"No, no, no," said the practical cripple, getting out of the car with surprising celerity. "Walkin' is good for my stomach if it's not so good for my behind. I'm a forgivin' man. You pick me up at my house tomorrow morning. G'bye."

And he lumbered off in the direction of the Haymarket.

It needed no close observer to see that H. M. was deeply abstracted. He remained so abstracted, indeed, as to be nearly murdered by a taxi at the Admiralty Arch; and he was halfway down Whitehall before a familiar voice stopped him.

"Afternoon, Sir Henry!"

Burly, urbane, buttoned up in blue serge, with his bowler hat and his boiled blue eye, stood Chief Inspector Masters.

"Bit odd," the Chief Inspector remarked affably, "to see you taking a constitutional on a day like this, and how are you, sir?"

"Awful," said H. M. instantly. "But that's not the point. Masters, you crawlin' snake! You're the very man I wanted to see."

Few things startled the Chief Inspector. This one did.

"You," he repeated, "wanted to see *me?*"

"Uh-huh."

"And what about?"

"Masters, do you remember the Victoria Adams case about twenty years ago?"

The Chief Inspector's manner suddenly changed and grew wary.

"Victoria Adams case?" he ruminated. "No, sir, I can't say I do."

"Son, you're lyin'! You were sergeant to old Chief Inspector Rutherford in those days, and well I remember it!"

Masters stood on his dignity.

"That's as may be, sir. But twenty years ago . . ."

"A little girl of twelve or thirteen, the child of very wealthy parents, disappeared one night out of a country cottage with all the doors and windows locked on the inside. A week later, while everybody was havin' screaming hysterics, the child reappeared again: through the locks and bolts, tucked up in her bed as usual.

And to this day nobody's ever known what really happened."

There was a silence, while Masters shut his jaws hard.

"This family, the Adamses," persisted H. M., "owned the cottage, down Aylesbury way, on the edge of Goblin Wood, opposite the lake. Or was it?"

"Oh, ah," growled Masters. "It was."

H. M. looked at him curiously.

"They used the cottage as a base for bathin' in summer, and ice skatin' in winter. It was black winter when the child vanished, and the place was all locked up inside against drafts. They say her old man nearly went loopy when he found her there a week later, lying asleep under the lamp. But all she'd say, when they asked her where she'd been, was, '*I don't know.*'"

Again there was a silence, while red buses thundered through the traffic press of Whitehall.

"You've got to admit, Masters, there was a flaming public rumpus. I say: did you ever read Barrie's *Mary Rose?*"

"No."

"Well, it was a situation straight out of Barrie. Some people, y'see, said that Vicky Adams was a child of a faerie who'd been spirited away by the pixies . . ."

Whereupon Masters exploded.

He removed his bowler hat and made remarks about pixies, in detail, which could not have been bettered by H. M. himself.

"I know, son, I know." H. M. was soothing. Then his big voice sharpened. "Now tell me. Was all this talk strictly true?"

"What talk?"

"Locked windows? Bolted doors? No attic trap? No cellar? Solid walls and floor?"

"Yes, sir," answered Masters, regaining his dignity with a powerful effort, "I'm bound to admit it *was* true."

"Then there wasn't any jiggery-pokery about the cottage?"

"In your eye there wasn't," said Masters.

"How d'ye mean?"

"Listen, sir." Masters lowered his voice. "Before the Adamses took over that place, it was a hideout for Chuck Randall. At that time he was the swellest of the swell mob; we lagged him a couple of years later. Do you think Chuck wouldn't have rigged up some gadget for a getaway? Just so! Only . . ."

"Well? Hey?"

"We couldn't find it," grunted Masters.

"And I'll bet that pleased old Chief Inspector Rutherford?"

"I tell you straight; he was fair up the pole. Especially as the kid herself was a pretty kid, all big eyes and dark hair. You couldn't help trusting her story."

"Yes," said H. M. "That's what worries me."

"Worries you?"

"Oh, my son!" said H. M. dismally. "Here's Vicky Adams, the spoiled daughter of dotin' parents. She's supposed to be 'odd' and 'fey.' She's even encouraged to be. During her adolescence, the most impressionable time of her life, she gets wrapped round with the gauze of a mystery that people talk about even yet. What's that woman like now, Masters? What's that woman like now?"

"Dear Sir Henry!" murmured Miss Vicky Adams in her softest voice.

She said this just as William Sage's car, with Bill and Eve Drayton in the front seat, and Vicky and H. M. in the back seat, turned off the main road. Behind them lay the smoky-red roofs of Aylesbury, against a brightness of late afternoon. The car turned down a side road, a damp tunnel of greenery, and into another road which was little more than a lane between hedgerows.

H. M.—though cheered by three good-sized picnic hampers from Fortnum & Mason, their wickerwork lids bulging with a feast—did not seem happy. Nobody in that car was happy, with the possible exception of Miss Adams herself.

Vicky, unlike Eve, was small and dark and vivacious. Her large light-brown eyes, with very black lashes, could be arch and coy; or they could be dreamily intense. The late Sir James Barrie might have called her a sprite. Those of more sober views would have recognized a different quality: she had an inordinate sex appeal, which was as palpable as a physical touch to any male within yards. And despite her smallness, Vicky had a full voice like Eve's. All these qualities she used even in so simple a matter as giving traffic directions.

"First right," she would say, leaning forward to put her hands on Bill Sage's shoulders. "Then straight on until the next traffic light. Ah, clever boy!"

"Not at all, not at all!" Bill would disclaim, with red ears and rather an erratic style of driving.

"Oh, yes, you are!" And Vicky would twist the lobe of his ear, playfully, before sitting back again.

(Eve Drayton did not say anything. She did not even turn

round. Yet the atmosphere, even of that quiet English picnic party, had already become a trifle hysterical.)

"Dear Sir Henry!" murmured Vicky, as they turned down into the deep lane between the hedgerows. "I do wish you wouldn't be so materialistic! I do, really. Haven't you the tiniest bit of spirituality in your nature?"

"Me?" said H. M. in astonishment. "I got a very lofty spiritual nature. But what I want just now, my wench, is grub.—Oi!"

Bill Sage glanced round.

"By that speedometer," H. M. pointed, "we've now come forty-six miles and a bit. We didn't even leave town until people of decency and sanity were having their tea. Where are we *going?*"

"But didn't you know?" asked Vicky, with wide-open eyes. "We're going to the cottage where I had such a dreadful experience when I was a child."

"Was it such a dreadful experience, Vicky dear?" inquired Eve.

Vicky's eyes seemed far away.

"I don't remember, really. I was only a child, you see. I didn't understand. I hadn't developed the power for myself then."

"What power?" H. M. asked sharply.

"To dematerialize," said Vicky. "Of course."

In that warm sun-dusted lane, between the hawthorn hedges, the car jolted over a rut. Crockery rattled.

"Uh-huh. I see," observed H. M. without inflection. "And where do you go, my wench, when you dematerialize?"

"Into a strange country. Through a little door. You wouldn't understand. Oh, you *are* such Philistines!" moaned Vicky. Then, with a sudden change of mood, she leaned forward and her whole physical allurement flowed again toward Bill Sage. "*You* wouldn't like me to disappear, would you, Bill?"

(Easy! Easy!)

"Only," said Bill, with a sort of wild gallantry, "if you promised to reappear again straightaway."

"Oh, I should have to do that." Vicky sat back. She was trembling. "The power wouldn't be strong enough. But even a poor little thing like me might be able to teach you a lesson. Look there!"

And she pointed ahead.

On their left, as the lane widened, stretched the ten-acre gloom of what is fancifully known as Goblin Wood. On their right lay a small lake, on private property and therefore deserted.

The cottage—set well back into a clearing of the wood so as to face the road, screened from it by a line of beeches—was in fact a bungalow of rough-hewn stone, with a slate roof. Across the front of it ran a wooden porch. It had a seedy air, like the long yellow-green grass of its front lawn. Bill parked the car at the side of the road, since there was no driveway.

"It's a bit lonely, ain't it?" demanded H. M. His voice boomed out against that utter stillness, under the hot sun.

"Oh, yes!" breathed Vicky. She jumped out of the car in a whirl of skirts. "That's why *they* were able to come and take me. When I was a child."

"They?"

"Dear Sir Henry! Do I need to explain?"

Then Vicky looked at Bill.

"I must apologize," she said, "for the state the house is in. I haven't been out here for months and months. There's a modern bathroom, I'm glad to say. Only kerosene lamps, of course. But then," a dreamy smile flashed across her face, "you won't need lamps, will you? Unless . . ."

"You mean," said Bill, who was taking a black case out of the car, "unless you disappear again?"

"Yes, Bill. And promise me you won't be frightened when I do."

The young man uttered a ringing oath which was shushed by Sir Henry Merrivale, who austerely said he disapproved of profanity. Eve Drayton was very quiet.

"But in the meantime," Vicky said wistfully, "let's forget it all, shall we? Let's laugh and dance and sing and pretend we're children! And surely our guest must be even more hungry by this time?"

It was in this emotional state that they sat down to their picnic.

H. M., if the truth must be told, did not fare too badly. Instead of sitting on some hummock of ground, they dragged a table and chairs to the shaded porch. All spoke in strained voices. But no word of controversy was said. It was only afterward, when the cloth was cleared, the furniture and hampers pushed indoors, the empty bottles flung away, that danger tapped a warning.

From under the porch Vicky fished out two half-rotted deck chairs, which she set up in the long grass of the lawn. These were to be occupied by Eve and H. M., while Vicky took Bill Sage to inspect a plum tree of some remarkable quality she did not specify.

Eve sat down without comment. H. M., who was smoking a black cigar opposite her, waited some time before he spoke.

"Y' know," he said, taking the cigar out of his mouth, "you're behaving remarkably well."

"Yes." Eve laughed. "Aren't I?"

"Are you pretty well acquainted with this Adams gal?"

"I'm her first cousin," Eve answered simply. "Now that her parents are dead, I'm the only relative she's got. I know *all* about her."

From far across the lawn floated two voices saying something about wild strawberries. Eve, her fair hair and fair complexion vivid against the dark line of Goblin Wood, clenched her hands on her knees.

"You see, H. M.," she hesitated, "there was another reason why I invited you here. I—I don't quite know how to approach it."

"I'm the old man," said H. M., tapping himself impressively on the chest. "You tell me."

"Eve, darling!" interposed Vicky's voice, crying across the ragged lawn. "Coo-ee! Eve!"

"Yes, dear?"

"I've just remembered," cried Vicky, "that I haven't shown Bill over the cottage! You don't mind if I steal him away from you for a little while?"

"No, dear! Of course not!"

It was H. M., sitting so as to face the bungalow, who saw Vicky and Bill go in. He saw Vicky's wistful smile as she closed the door after them. Eve did not even look round. The sun was declining, making fiery chinks through the thickness of Goblin Wood behind the cottage.

"I won't let her have him," Eve suddenly cried. "I won't! I won't! I won't!"

"Does she want him, my wench? Or, which is more to the point, does he want her?"

"He never has," Eve said with emphasis. "Not really. And he never will."

H. M., motionless, puffed out cigar smoke.

"Vicky's a faker," said Eve. "Does that sound catty?"

"Not necessarily. I was just thinkin' the same thing myself."

"I'm patient," said Eve. Her blue eyes were fixed. "I'm terribly, terribly patient. I can wait years for what I want. Bill's not making much money now, and I haven't got a bean. But Bill's got great talent under that easygoing manner of his. He *must* have the right girl to help him. If only . . ."

"If only the elfin sprite would let him alone. Hey?"

"Vicky acts like that," said Eve, "toward practically every man she ever meets. That's why she never married. She says it leaves her soul free to commune with other souls. This occultism—"

Then it all poured out, the family story of the Adamses. This repressed girl spoke at length, spoke as perhaps she had never spoken before. Vicky Adams, the child who wanted to attract attention, her father Uncle Fred and her mother Aunt Margaret seemed to walk in vividness as the shadows gathered.

"I was too young to know her at the time of the 'disappearance,' of course. But, oh, I knew her afterward! And I thought . . ."

"Well?"

"If I could get *you* here," said Eve, "I thought she'd try to show off with some game. And then you'd expose her. And Bill would see what an awful faker she is. But it's hopeless! It's hopeless!"

"Looky here," observed H. M., who was smoking his third cigar. He sat up. "Doesn't it strike you those two are being a rummy-awful long time just in lookin' through a little bungalow?"

Eve, roused out of a dream, stared back at him. She sprang to her feet. She was not now, you could guess, thinking of any disappearance.

"Excuse me a moment," she said curtly.

Eve hurried across to the cottage, went up on the porch, and opened the front door. H. M. heard her heels rap down the length of the small passage inside. She marched straight back again, closed the front foor, and rejoined H. M.

"All the doors of the rooms are shut," she announced in a high voice. "I really don't think I ought to disturb them."

"Easy, my wench!"

"I have absolutely no interest," declared Eve, with the tears coming into her eyes, "in what happens to either of them now. Shall we take the car and go back to town without them?"

H. M. threw away his cigar, got up, and seized her by the shoulders.

"I'm the old man," he said, leering like an ogre. "Will you listen to me?"

"No!"

"If I'm any reader of the human dial," persisted H. M., "that young feller's no more gone on Vicky Adams than I am. He was scared, my wench. Scared." Doubt, indecision crossed H. M.'s face. "I dunno what he's scared of. Burn me, I don't! But . . ."

"Hoy!" called the voice of Bill Sage.

It did not come from the direction of the cottage.

They were surrounded on three sides by Goblin Wood, now blurred with twilight. From the north side the voice bawled at them, followed by crackling in dry undergrowth. Bill, his hair and sports coat and flannels more than a little dirty, regarded them with a face of bitterness.

"Here are her blasted wild strawberries," he announced, extending his hand. "Three of 'em. The fruitful (excuse me) result of three quarters of an hour's hard labor. I absolutely refuse to chase 'em in the dark."

For a moment Eve Drayton's mouth moved without speech.

"Then you weren't . . . in the cottage all this time?"

"In the cottage?" Bill glanced at it. "I was in that cottage," he said, "about five minutes. Vicky had a woman's whim. She wanted some wild strawberries out of what she called the 'forest.'"

"Wait a minute, son!" said H. M. very sharply. "You didn't come out that front door. Nobody did."

"No! I went out the back door! It opens straight on the wood."

"Yes. And what happened then?"

"Well, I went to look for these damned . . ."

"No, no! What did *she* do?"

"Vicky? She locked and bolted the back door on the inside. I remember her grinning at me through the glass panel. She—"

Bill stopped short. His eyes widened, and then narrowed, as though at the impact of an idea. All three of them turned to look at the rough-stone cottage.

"By the way," said Bill. He cleared his throat vigorously. "By the way, have you seen Vicky since then?"

"No."

"This couldn't be . . .?"

"It could be, son," said H. M. "We'd better go in there and have a look."

They hesitated for a moment on the porch. A warm, moist fragrance breathed up from the ground after sunset. In half an hour it would be completely dark.

Bill Sage threw open the front door and shouted Vicky's name. That sound seemed to penetrate, reverberating, through every room. The intense heat and stuffiness of the cottage, where no window had been raised in months, blew out at them. But nobody answered.

"Get inside," snapped H. M. "And stop yowlin'." The old maestro was nervous. "I'm dead sure she didn't get out by the front door; but we'll just make certain there's no slippin' out now."

Stumbling over the table and chairs they had used on the porch, he fastened the front door. They were in a narrow passage, once handsome with parquet floor and pine-paneled walls, leading to a door with a glass panel at the rear. H. M. lumbered forward to inspect this door and found it locked and bolted, as Bill had said.

Goblin Wood grew darker.

Keeping well together, they searched the cottage. It was not large, having two good-sized rooms on one side of the passage, and two small rooms on the other side, so as to make space for bathroom and kitchenette. H. M., raising fogs of dust, ransacked every inch where a person could possibly hide.

And all the windows were locked on the inside. And the chimney flues were too narrow to admit anybody.

And Vicky Adams wasn't there.

"Oh, my eye!" breathed Sir Henry Merrivale.

They had gathered, by what idiotic impulse not even H. M. could have said, just outside the open door of the bathroom. A bath tap dripped monotonously. The last light through a frosted-glass window showed three faces hung there as though disembodied.

"Bill," said Eve in an unsteady voice, "this is a trick. Oh, I've longed for her to be exposed! This is a trick!"

"Then where is she?"

"H. M. can tell us! Can't you, H. M.?"

"Well . . . now," muttered the great man.

Across H. M.'s Panama hat was a large black handprint, made there when he had pressed down the hat after investigating a chimney. He glowered under it.

"Son," he said to Bill, "there's just one question I want you to answer in all this hokey-pokey. When you went out pickin' wild strawberries, will you swear Vicky Adams didn't go with you?"

"As God is my judge, she didn't," returned Bill, with fervency and obvious truth. "Besides, how the devil could she? Look at the lock and bolt on the back door!"

H. M. made two more violent black handprints on his hat.

He lumbered forward, his head down, two or three paces in the narrow passage. His foot half-skidded on something that had been lying there unnoticed, and he picked it up. It was a large, square section of thin, waterproof oilskin, jagged at one corner.

"Have you found anything?" demanded Bill in a strained voice.

"No. Not to make any sense, that is. But just a minute!"

At the rear of the passage, on the left-hand side, was the bedroom from which Vicky Adams had vanished as a child. Though H. M. had searched this room once before, he opened the door again.

It was now almost dark in Goblin Wood.

He saw dimly a room of twenty years before: a room of flounces, of lace curtains, of once-polished mahogany, its mirrors glimmering against white-papered walls. H. M. seemed especially interested in the windows.

He ran his hands carefully round the frame of each, even climbing laboriously up on a chair to examine the tops. He borrowed a box of matches from Bill; and the little spurts of light, following the rasp of the match, rasped against nerves as well. The hope died out of his face, and his companions saw it.

"H. M.," Bill said for the dozenth time, "where is she?"

"Son," replied H. M. despondently, "I don't know."

"Let's get out of here," Eve said abruptly. Her voice was a small scream. "I kn-know it's all a trick! I know Vicky's a faker! But let's get out of here. For God's sake let's get out of here!"

"As a matter of fact," Bill cleared his throat, "I agree. Anyway, we won't hear from Vicky until tomorrow morning."

"*Oh, yes, you will,*" whispered Vicky's voice out of the darkness.

Eve screamed.

They lighted a lamp.

But there was nobody there.

Their retreat from the cottage, it must be admitted, was not very dignified.

How they stumbled down that ragged lawn in the dark, how they piled rugs and picnic hampers into the car, how they eventually found the main road again, is best left undescribed.

Sir Henry Merrivale has since sneered at this—"a bit of a goosy feeling; nothin' much"—and it is true that he has no nerves to speak of. But he can be worried, badly worried; and that he was worried on this occasion may be deduced from what happened later.

H. M., after dropping in at Claridge's for a modest late supper of lobster and *pêche Melba*, returned to his house in Brook Street and slept a hideous sleep. It was three o'clock in the morning, even before the summer dawn, when the ringing of the bedside telephone roused him.

What he heard sent his blood pressure soaring.

"Dear Sir Henry!" crooned a familiar and sprite-like voice.

H. M. was himself again, full of gall and bile. He switched on the bedside lamp and put on his spectacles with care, so as adequately to address the phone.

"Have I got the honor," he said with dangerous politeness, "of addressin' Miss Vicky Adams?"

"Oh, yes!"

"I sincerely trust," said H. M., "you've been havin' a good time? Are you materialized yet?"

"Oh, yes!"

"Where are you now?"

"I'm afraid," there was coy laughter in the voice, "that must be a little secret for a day or two. I want to teach you a really *good* lesson. Blessings, dear."

And she hung up the receiver.

H. M. did not say anything. He climbed out of bed. He stalked up and down the room, his corporation majestic under an old-fashioned nightshirt stretching to his heels. Then, since he himself had been waked up at three o'clock in the morning, the obvious course was to wake up somebody else; so he dialed the home number of Chief Inspector Masters.

"No, sir," retorted Masters grimly, after coughing the frog out of his throat, "I do *not* mind you ringing up. Not a bit of it!" He spoke with a certain pleasure. "Because I've got a bit of news for you."

H. M. eyed the phone suspiciously.

"Masters, are you trying to do me in the eye again?"

"It's what you always try to do to me, isn't it?"

"All right, all right!" growled H. M. "What's the news?"

"Do you remember mentioning the Vicky Adams case yesterday?"

"Sort of. Yes."

"Oh, ah! Well, I had a word or two round among our people. I was tipped the wink to go and see a certain solicitor. He was old Mr. Fred Adams's solicitor before Mr. Adams died about six or seven years ago."

Here Masters's voice grew triumphant.

"I always said, Sir Henry, that Chuck Randall had planted some gadget in that cottage for a quick getaway. And I was right. The gadget was . . ."

"You were quite right, Masters. The gadget was a trick window."

The telephone, so to speak, gave a start.

"What's that?"

"A trick window." H. M. spoke patiently. "You press a spring. And the whole frame of the window, two leaves locked together, slides down between the walls far enough so you can climb over. Then you push it back up again."

"*How in lum's name do you know that?*"

"Oh, my son! They used to build windows like it in country houses during the persecution of Catholic priests. It was a good enough *second* guess. Only . . . it won't work."

Masters seemed annoyed. "It won't work now," Masters agreed. "And do you know why?"

"I can guess. Tell me."

"Because, just before Mr. Adams died, he discovered how his darling daughter had flummoxed him. He never told anybody except his lawyer. He took a handful of four-inch nails, and sealed up the top of that frame so tight an orangutang couldn't move it, and painted 'em over so they wouldn't be noticed."

"Uh-huh. You can notice 'em now."

"I doubt if the young lady herself ever knew. But, by George!" Masters said savagely. "I'd like to see anybody try the same game now!"

"You would, hey? Then will it interest you to know that the same gal has just disappeared out of the same house *again?*"

H. M. began a long narrative of the facts, but he had to break off because the telephone was raving.

"Honest, Masters," H. M. said seriously, "I'm not joking. She didn't get out through that window. But she did get out. You'd better meet me," he gave directions, "tomorrow morning. In the meantime, son, sleep well."

It was, therefore, a worn-faced Masters who went into the Visitors' Room at the Senior Conservatives' Club just before lunch on the following day.

The Visitors' Room is a dark sepulchral place, opening on an air well, where the visitor is surrounded by pictures of dyspeptic-looking gentlemen with beards. It has a pervading mustiness of wood and leather. Though whisky and soda stood on the table, H. M. sat in a leather chair far away from it, ruffling his hands across his bald head.

"Now, Masters, keep your shirt on!" he warned. "This business may be rummy. But it's not a police matter—yet."

"I know it's not a police matter," Masters said grimly. "All the same, I've had a word with the Superintendent at Aylesbury."

"Fowler?"

"You know him?"

"Sure. I know everybody. Is he goin' to keep an eye out?"

"He's going to have a look at that ruddy cottage. I've asked for any telephone calls to be put through here. In the meantime, sir—"

It was at this point, as though diabolically inspired, that the telephone rang. H. M. reached it before Masters.

"It's the old man," he said, unconsciously assuming a stance of grandeur. "Yes, yes! Masters is here, but he's drunk. You tell me first. What's that?"

The telephone talked thinly.

"Sure I looked in the kitchen cupboard," bellowed H. M. "Though I didn't honestly expect to find Vicky Adams hidin' there. What's that? Say it again! Plates? Cups that had been . . ."

An almost frightening change had come over H. M.'s expression. He stood motionless. All the posturing went out of him. He was not even listening to the voice that still talked thinly, while his eyes and his brain moved to put together facts. At length (though the voice still talked) he hung up the receiver.

H. M. blundered back to the center table, where he drew out a chair and sat down.

"Masters," he said very quietly, "I've come close to makin' the silliest mistake of my life."

Here he cleared his throat.

"I shouldn't have made it, son. I really shouldn't. But don't yell at me for cuttin' off Fowler. I can tell you now how Vicky Adams disappeared. And she said one true thing when she said she was going into a strange country."

"How do you mean?"

"She's dead," answered H. M.

The word fell with heavy weight into that dingy room, where the bearded faces looked down.

"Y' see," H. M. went on blankly, "a lot of us were right when we thought Vicky Adams was a faker. She was. To attract attention to herself, she played that trick on her family with the hocused window. She's lived and traded on it ever since. That's what sent me straight in the wrong direction. I was on the alert for some *trick* Vicky Adams might play. So it never occurred to me that this elegant pair of beauties, Miss Eve Drayton and Mr. William Sage, were deliberately conspirin' to murder *her*."

Masters got slowly to his feet.

"Did you say . . . murder?"

"Oh, yes."

Again H. M. cleared his throat.

"It was all arranged beforehand for me to be a witness. They knew Vicky Adams couldn't resist a challenge to disappear, especially as Vicky always believed she could get out by the trick window. They wanted Vicky to *say* she was goin' to disappear. They never knew anything about the trick window, Masters. But they knew their own plan very well.

"Eve Drayton even told me the motive. She hated Vicky, of course. But that wasn't the main point. She was Vicky Adam's only relative; she'd inherit an awful big scoopful of money. Eve said she could be patient. (And, burn me, how her eyes meant it when she said that!) Rather than risk any slightest suspicion of murder, she was willing to wait seven years until a disappeared person can be presumed dead.

"Our Eve, I think, was the fiery drivin' force of that conspiracy. She was only scared part of the time. Sage was scared all of the time. But it was Sage who did the real dirty work. He lured Vicky Adams into that cottage, while Eve kept me in close conversation on the lawn . . ."

H. M. paused.

Intolerably vivid in the mind of Chief Inspector Masters, who had seen it years before, rose the picture of the rough-stone bungalow against the darkling wood.

"Masters," said H. M., "why should a bath tap be dripping in a house that hadn't been occupied for months?"

"Well?"

"Sage, y'see, is a surgeon. I saw him take his black case of instruments out of the car. He took Vicky Adams into that house. In the bathroom he stabbed her, he stripped her, and *he dismembered her body in the bathtub.* —Easy, son!"

"Go on," said Masters without moving.

"The head, the torso, the folded arms and legs, were wrapped up in three large square pieces of thin transparent oilskin. Each was sewed up with coarse thread so the blood wouldn't drip. Last night I found one of the oilskin pieces he'd ruined when his needle slipped at the corner. Then he walked out of the house, with the back door still standin' unlocked, to get his wild-strawberry alibi."

"Sage went out of there," shouted Masters, "leaving the body in the house?"

"Oh, yes," agreed H. M.

"But where did he leave it?"

"In the meantime, son, what about Eve Drayton? At the end of the arranged three quarters of an hour, she indicated there was hanky-panky between her fiancé and Vicky Adams. She flew into the house. But what did she do?"

"She walked to the back of the passage. I heard her. *There she simply locked and bolted the back door.* And then she marched out to join me with tears in her eyes. And these two beauties were ready for investigation."

"Investigation?" said Masters. "*With that body still in the house?*"

"Oh, yes."

Masters lifted both fists.

"It must have given young Sage a shock," said H. M., "when I found that piece of waterproof oilskin he'd washed but dropped. Anyway, these two had only two more bits of hokey-pokey. The 'vanished' gal had to speak—to show she was still alive. If you'd been there, son, you'd have noticed that Eve Drayton's got a voice just like Vicky Adams's. If somebody speaks in a dark room, carefully imitatin' a coy tone she never uses herself, the illusion's goin' to be pretty good. The same goes for a telephone.

"It was finished, Masters. All that had to be done was remove the body from the house, and get it far away from there . . ."

"But that's just what I'm asking you, sir! Where was the body all this time? And who in blazes *did* remove the body from the house?"

"All of us did," answered H. M.

"What's that?"

"Masters," said H. M., "aren't you forgettin' the picnic hampers?"

And now, the chief Inspector saw, H. M. was as white as a

ghost. His next words took Masters like a blow between the eyes.

"Three good-sized wickerwork hampers, with lids. After our big meal on the porch, those hampers were shoved inside the house where Sage could get at 'em. He had to leave most of the used crockery behind, in the kitchen cupboard. But three wickerwork hampers from a picnic, and three butcher's parcels to go inside 'em. I carried one down to the car myself. It felt a bit funny . . ."

H. M. stretched out his hand, not steadily, toward the whisky. "Y' know," he said, "I'll always wonder if I was carrying the—head."

The Vengeance of Nitocris

BY TENNESSEE WILLIAMS

Hushed were the streets of many-peopled Thebes. Those few who passed through them moved with the shadowy fleetness of bats near dawn, and bent their faces from the sky as if fearful of seeing what in their fancies might be hovering there. Weird, high-noted incantations of a wailing sound were audible through the barred doors. On corners groups of naked and bleeding priests cast themselves repeatedly and with loud cries upon the rough stones of the walks. Even dogs and cats and oxen seemed impressed by some strange menace and foreboding and cowered and slunk dejectedly. All Thebes was in dread. And indeed there was cause for their dread and for their wails of lamentation. A terrible sacrilege had been committed. In all the annals of Egypt none more monstrous was recorded.

Five days had the altar fires of the god of gods, Osiris, been left unburning. Even for one moment to allow darkness upon the altars of the god was considered by the priests to be a great offense against him. Whole years of dearth and famine had been known to result from such an offense. But now the altar fires had been deliberately extinguished, and left extinguished for five days. It was an unspeakable sacrilege.

Hourly there was expectancy of some great calamity to befall. Perhaps within the approaching night a mighty earthquake would shake the city to the ground, or a fire from heaven would sweep upon them, or some monster from the desert, where wild and terrible monsters were said to dwell, would rush upon them and Osiris himself would rise up, as he had done before, and swallow all Egypt in his wrath. Surely some such dread catastrophe would befall them ere the week had passed. Unless—unless the sacrilege were avenged.

But how might it be avenged? That was the question high lords and priests debated. Pharaoh alone had committed the sacrilege. It was he, angered because the bridge, which he had spent five years in constructing so that one day he might cross the Nile in his chariot as he had once boasted that he would do, had been swept away by the rising waters. Raging with anger, he had flogged the priests from the temple. He had barred the temple doors and with his own breath had blown out the sacred candles. He had defiled the hallowed altars with the carcasses of beasts. Even, it was said in low, shocked whispers, in a mock ceremony of worship he had burned the carrion of a hyena, most abhorrent of all beasts to Osiris, upon the holy altar of gold, which even the most high of priests forbore to lay naked hands upon!

Surely, even though he be Pharoah, ruler of all Egypt and holder of the golden eagle, he could not be permitted to commit such violent sacrileges without punishment from man. The god Osiris was waiting for them to inflict that punishment, and if they failed to do it, upon them would come a scourge from heaven.

Standing before the awed assembly of nobles, the high Kha Semblor made a gesture with his hands. A cry broke from those who watched. Sentence had been delivered. Death had been pronounced as doom for the pharaoh.

The heavy, barred doors were shoved open. The crowd came out, and within an hour a well-organized mob passed through the streets of Thebes, directed for the palace of the pharaoh. Mob justice was to be done.

Within the resplendent portals of the palace the pharaoh, ruler of all Egypt, watched with tightened brow the orderly but menacing approach of the mob. He divined their intent. But was he not their pharaoh? He could contend with gods, so why should he fear mere dogs of men?

A woman clung to his stiffened arm. She was tall and as majestically handsome as he. A garb of linen, as brilliantly golden as the sun, entwined her body closely and bands of jet were around her throat and forehead. She was the fair and well-loved Nitocris, sister of the pharaoh.

"Brother, brother!" she cried, "light the fires! Pacify the dogs! They come to kill you."

Only more stern grew the look of the pharaoh. He thrust aside his pleading sister, and beckoned to the attendants.

"Open the doors!"

Startled, trembling, the men obeyed.

The haughty lord of Egypt drew his sword from its sheath. He slashed the air with a stroke that would have severed stone. Out on the steep steps leading between tall, colored pillars to the doors of the palace he stopped. The people saw him. A howl rose from their lips.

"Light the fires!"

The figure of the pharaoh stood inflexible as rock. Superbly tall and muscular, his bare arms and limbs glittering like burnished copper in the light of the brilliant sun, his body erect and tense in his attitude of defiance, he looked indeed a mortal fit almost to challenge gods.

The mob, led by the black-robed priests and nobles who had arrived at the foot of the steps, now fell back before the stunning, magnificent defiance of their giant ruler. They felt like demons who had assailed the heavens and had been abashed and shamed by the mere sight of that which they had assailed. A hush fell over them. Their upraised arms faltered and sank down. A moment more and they would have fallen to their knees.

What happened then seemed nothing less than a miracle. In his triumph and exultation, the pharaoh had been careless of the crumbling edges of the steps. Centuries old, there were sections of these steps which were falling apart. Upon such a section had the gold-sandaled foot of the pharaoh descended, and it was not strong enough to sustain his great weight. With a scuttling sound it broke loose. A gasp came from the mob—the pharaoh was about to fall. He was palpitating, wavering in the air, fighting to retain his balance. He looked as if he were grappling with some monstrous, invisible snake, coiled about his gleaming body. A hoarse cry burst from his lips; his sword fell; and then his body thudded down the steps in a series of somersaults, and landed at the foot, sprawled out before the gasping mob. For a moment there was breathless silence. And then came the shout of a priest.

"A sign from the god!"

That vibrant cry seemed to restore the mob to all of its wolflike rage. They surged forward. The struggling body of the pharaoh was lifted up and torn to pieces by their clawing hands and weapons. Thus was the god Osiris avenged.

A week later another large assembly of persons confronted the brilliant-pillared palace. This time they were there to acknowledge a ruler, not to slay one. The week before they had rended the pharaoh and now they were proclaiming his sister empress. Priests had declared that it was the will of the gods that she should succeed her brother. She was famously beautiful, pious, and wise. The people were not reluctant to accept her.

When she was borne down the steps of the palace in her rich litter, after the elaborate ceremony of the coronation had been concluded, she responded to the cheers of the multitude with a smile which could not have appeared more amicable and gracious. None might know from that smile upon her beautiful carmined lips that within her heart she was thinking, "These are the people who slew my brother. Ah, god Issus, grant me power to avenge his death upon them!"

Not long after the beauteous Nitocris mounted the golden throne of Egypt, rumors were whispered of some vast, mysterious enterprise being conducted in secret. A large number of slaves were observed each dawn to embark upon barges and to be carried down the river to some unknown point, where they labored through the day, returning after dark. The slaves were Ethiopians, neither able to speak nor to understand the Egyptian language, and therefore no information could be gotten from them by the curious as to the object of their mysterious daily excursions. The general opinion, though, was that the pious queen was having a great temple constructed to the gods and that when it was finished, enormous public banquets would be held within it before its dedication. She meant it to be a surprise gift to the priests who were ever desirous of some new place of worship and were dissatisfied with their old altars, which they said were defiled.

Throughout the winter the slaves repeated daily their excursions. Traffic of all kinds plying down the river was restricted for several miles to within forty yards of one shore. Any craft seen to disregard that restriction was set upon by a galley of armed men and pursued back into bounds. All that could be learned was that a prodigious temple or hall of some sort was in construction.

It was late in the spring when the excursions of the workmen were finally discontinued. Restrictions upon river traffic were withdrawn. The men who went eagerly to investigate the mysterious construction returned with tales of a magnificent new temple, surrounded by rich, green, tropical verdure, situated near the bank of the river. It was a temple to the god Osiris. It had been built by the queen probably that she might partly atone for the sacrilege of her brother and deliver him from some of the torture which he undoubtedly suffered. It was to be dedicated within the month by a great banquet. All the nobles and the high priests of Osiris, of which there were a tremendous number, were to be invited.

Never had the delighted priests been more extravagant in their praises of Queen Nitrocris. When she passed through the streets in her open litter, bedazzling eyes by the glitter of her golden ornaments, the cries of the people were almost frantic in their exaltation of her.

True to the predictions of the gossipers, before the month had passed the banquet had been formally announced and to all the nobility and the priests of Osiris had been issued invitations to attend.

The day of the dedication, which was to be followed by the night of banqueting, was a gala holiday. At noon the guests of the empress formed a colorful assembly upon the bank of the river. Gayly draped barges floated at their moorings until preparations should be completed for their transportation of the guests to the temple. All anticipated a holiday of great merriment, and the lustful epicureans were warmed by visualizations of the delightful banquet of copious meats, fruits, luscious delicacies and other less innocent indulgences.

When the queen arrived, clamorous shouts rang deafeningly in her ears. She responded with charming smiles and gracious bows. The most discerning observer could not have detected anything but the greatest cordiality and kindliness reflected in her bearing toward those around her. No action, no fleeting expression upon her lovely face could have caused anyone to suspect anything except entire amicability in her feelings or her intentions. The rats, as they followed the Pied Piper of Hamlin through the streets, entranced by the notes of his magical pipe, could not have been less apprehensive of any great danger impending than were the guests of the empress as they followed her in gayly draped barges, singing and laughing down the sun-glowing waters of the Nile.

The most vivid descriptions of those who had already seen the temple did not prepare the others for the spectacle of beauty and grandeur which it presented. Gasps of delight came from the priests. What a place in which to conduct their ceremonies! They began to feel that the sacrilege of the dead pharaoh was not, after all, to be so greatly regretted, since it was responsible for the building of this glorious new temple.

The columns were massive and painted with the greatest artistry. The temple itself was proportionately large. The center of it was unroofed. Above the entrance were carved the various symbols of the god Osiris, with splendid workmanship. The building was immensely big, and against the background of green foliage it presented a picture of almost breath-taking beauty. Ethiopian attendants stood on each side of the doorway, their shining black bodies ornamented with bands of brilliant gold. On the interior the guests were inspired to even greater wonderment. The walls were hung with magnificent painted tapestries. The altars were more beautifully and elaborately carved than any seen before. Aromatic powders were burning upon them and sending up veils of scented smoke. The sacramental vessels were of the most exquisite and costly metals. Golden coffers and urns were piled high with perfect fruits of all kinds.

Ah, yes—a splendid place for the making of sacrifices, gloated the staring priests.

Ah, yes indeed, agreed the queen Nitocris, smiling with half-closed eyes, it was a splendid place for sacrifices—especially for the human sacrifice that had been planned. But all who observed that guileful smile interpreted it as gratification over the pleasure which her creation in honor of their god had brought to the priests of Osiris. Not the slightest shadow of portent was upon the hearts of the joyous guests.

The ceremony of dedication occupied the whole of the afternoon. And when it drew to its impressive conclusion, the large assembly, their nostrils quivering from the savory odor of the roasting meats, were fully ready and impatient for the banquet that awaited them. They gazed about them, observing that the whole building composed an unpartitioned amphitheater and wondering where might be the room of the banquet. However, when the concluding processional chant had been completed, the queen summoned a number of burly slaves, and by several iron rings attached to its outer edges they lifted up a large slab of the flooring, disclosing to the astonished guests the fact that the scene of the banquet was to be an immense subterranean vault.

Such vaults were decidedly uncommon among the Egyptians. The idea of feasting in one was novel and appealing. Thrilled exclamations came from the eager, excited crowd and they pressed forward to gaze into the depths, now brightly illuminated. They saw a room beneath them almost as vast in size as the amphitheater in which they were standing. It was filled with banquet tables upon which were set the most delectable foods and rich, sparkling wines in an abundance that would satiate the banqueters of Bacchus. Luxurious, thick rugs covered the floors. Among the tables passed nymphlike maidens, and at one end of the room harpists and singers stood, making sublime music.

The air was cool with the dampness of under-earth, and it was made delightfully fragrant by the perfumes of burning spices and the savory odors of the feast. If it had been heaven itself which the crowd of the queen's guests now gazed down upon they would not have considered the vision disappointing. Perhaps even if they had known the hideous menace that lurked in those gay-draped walls beneath them, they would still have found the allurement of the banquet scene difficult to resist.

Decorum and reserve were almost completely forgotten in the swiftness of the guests' descent. The stairs were not wide enough to afford room for all those who rushed upon them, and some tumbled over, landing unhurt upon the thick carpets. The priests themselves forgot their customary dignity and aloofness when they looked upon the beauty of the maiden attendants.

Immediately all of the guests gathered around the banquet tables, and the next hour was occupied in gluttonous feasting. Wine was unlimited and so was the thirst of the guests. Goblets were refilled as quickly as they were emptied by the capacious mouths of the drinkers. The singing and the laughter, the dancing and the wild frolicking grew less and less restrained until the banquet became a delirious orgy.

The queen alone, seated upon a cushioned dais from which she might overlook the whole room, remained aloof from the general hilarity. Her thick black brows twitched; her luminous black eyes shone strangely between their narrow painted lids. There was something peculiarly feline in the curl of her rich red lips. Now and again her eyes sought the section of wall to her left, where hung gorgeous braided tapestries from the East. But it seemed not the tapestries that she looked upon. Color would mount upon her brow and her slender fingers would dig still tighter into the cushions she reclined upon.

In her mind the queen Nitocris was seeing a ghastly picture. It was the picture of a room of orgy and feasting suddenly converted into a room of terror and horror; human beings one moment drunken and lustful, the next screaming in the seizure of sudden and awful death. If any of those present had been empowered to see also that picture of dire horror, they would have clambered wildly to make their escape. But none was so empowered.

With increasing wildness the banquet continued into the middle of the night. Some of the banqueters, disgustingly gluttonous, still gorged themselves at the greasy tables. Others lay in drunken stupor, or lolled amorously with the slave-girls. But most of them, formed in a great, irregular circle, skipped about the room in a barbaric, joy-mad dance, dragging and tripping each other in uncouth merriment and making the hall ring with their ceaseless shouts, laughter and hoarse song.

When the hour had approached near to midnight, the queen, who had sat like one entranced, arose from the cushioned dais. One last intent survey she gave to the crowded room of banquet. It was a scene which she wished to imprint permanently upon her mind. Much pleasure might she derive in the future by recalling that picture, and then imagining what came afterward—stark, searing terror rushing in upon barbaric joy!

She stepped down from the dais and walked swiftly to the steps. Her departure made no impression upon the revelers. When she arrived at the top of the stairs, she looked down and observed that no one had marked her exist.

Around the walls of the temple, dim-lit and fantastic-looking at night, with the cool wind from the river sweeping through and bending the flames of the tall candelabra, stalwart guardsmen were standing at their posts, and when the gold-cloaked figure of the queen arose from the aperture, they advanced toward her hurriedly. With a motion, she directed them to place the slab of rock in its tight-fitting socket. With a swift noiseless hoist and lowering, they obeyed the command. The queen bent down. There was no change in the boisterous sounds from below. Nothing was yet suspected.

Drawing the soft and shimmering folds of her cloak about her with fingers that trembled with eagerness, excitement and the intense emotion which she felt, the queen passed swiftly across the stone floor of the temple toward the open front through which the night wind swept, blowing her cloak in sheenful waves about her tall and graceful figure. The slaves followed after in silent file, well aware of the monstrous deed about to be executed and without reluctance to play their parts.

Down the steps of the palace into the moon-white night passed the weird procession. Their way led them down an obviously secreted path through thick ranks of murmuring palms which in their low voices seemed to be whispering shocked remonstrances against what was about to be done. But in her stern purpose the queen was not susceptible to any discussion from god or man. Vengeance, strongest of passions, made her obdurate as stone.

Out upon a rough and apparently new-constructed stone pier the thin path led. Beneath, the cold, dark waters of the Nile surged silently by. Here the party came to a halt. Upon this stone pier would the object of their awful midnight errand be accomplished.

With a low-spoken word, the queen commanded her followers to hold back. With her own hand she would perform the act of vengeance.

In the foreground of the pier a number of fantastic, wand-like levers extended upward. Toward these the queen advanced, slowly and stiffly as an executioner mounts the steps of the scaffold. When she had come beside them, she grasped one upthrust bar, fiercely, as if it had been the throat of a hated antagonist. Then she lifted her face with a quick intake of breath toward the moon-lightened sky. This was to her a moment of supreme estasy. Grasped in her hand was an instrument which could release awful death upon those against whom she wished vengeance. Their lives were as securely in her grasp as was this bar of iron.

Slowly, lusting upon every triumph-filled second of this time of ecstasy, she turned her face down again to the formidable bar in her hand. Deliberately she drew it back to its limit. This was the lever that opened the wall in the banquet vault. It gave entrance to death. Only the other bar now intervened between the banqueters, probably still reveling undisturbed, and the dreadful fate which she had prepared for them. Upon this bar now her jeweled fingers clutched. Savagely this time she pulled it; then with the litheness of a tiger she sprang to the edge of the pier. She leaned over it and stared down into the inky rush of the river. A new sound she heard above the steady flow. It was the sound of waters suddenly diverted into a new channel—an eager, plunging sound. Down to the hall of revelry they were rushing—these savage waters—bringing terror and sudden death.

A cry of triumph, wild and terrible enough to make even the hearts of the brutish slaves turn cold, now broke from the lips of the queen. The pharaoh was avenged.

And even he must have considered his avenging adequate had he been able to witness it.

After the retiring of the queen, the banquet had gone on without interruption of gayety. None noticed her absence. None noticed the silent replacing of the stone in its socket. No premonition of disaster was felt. The musicians, having been informed beforehand of the intended event of the evening, had made their withdrawal before the queen. The slaves, whose lives were of little value to the queen were as ignorant of what was to happen as were the guests themselves.

Not until the wall opened up, with a loud and startling crunch, did even those most inclined toward suspicion feel the slightest uneasiness. Then it was that a few noticed the slab to have been replaced, shutting them in. This discovery, communicated throughout the hall in a moment, seemed to instill a sudden fear in the hearts of all. Laughter did not cease, but the ring of dancers were distracted from their wild jubilee. They all turned toward the mysteriously opened wall and gazed into its black depths.

A hush fell over them. And then became audible the mounting sound of rushing water. A shriek rose from the throat of a woman. And then terror took possession of all within the room. Panic like the burst of flames flared into their hearts. Of one accord, they rushed upon the stair. And it, being purposely made frail, collapsed before the foremost of the wildly screaming mob had reached its summit. Turbulently they piled over the tables, filling the room with a hideous clamor. But rising above their screams was the shrill roar of the rushing water, and no sound could be more provoking of dread and terror. Somewhere in its circuitous route from the pier to the chamber of its reception it must have met with temporary blockade, for it was several minutes after the sound of it was first detected that the first spray of that death-bringing water leapt into the faces of the doomed occupants of the room.

With the ferocity of a lion springing into the arena of a Roman amphitheater to devour the gladiators set there for its delectation, the black water plunged in. Furiously it surged over the floor of the room, sweeping tables before it and sending its victims, now face to face with their harrowing doom, into a hysteria of terror. In a moment that icy, black water had risen to their knees, although the room was vast. Some fell instantly dead from the shock, or were trampled upon by the desperate rushing of the mob. Tables were clambered upon. Lamps and candles were extinguished. Brilliant light rapidly faded to twilight, and a ghastly dimness fell over the room as only the suspended lanterns remained lit. And what a scene of chaotic and hideous horror might a spectator have beheld! The gorgeous trumpery of banquet invaded by howling waters of death! Gayly dressed merrymakers caught suddenly in the grip of terror! Gasps and screams of the dying amid tumult and thickening dark!

What more horrible vengeance could Queen Nitocris have conceived than this banquet of death? Not Diablo himself could be capable of anything more fiendishly artistic. Here in the temple of Osiris those nobles and priests who had slain the pharaoh in expiation of his sacrilege against Osiris had now met their deaths. And it was in the waters of the Nile, material symbol of the god Osiris, that they had died. It was magnificent in its irony!

I would be content to end this story here if it were but a story. However, it is not merely a story, as you will have discerned before now if you have been a student of the history of Egypt. Queen Nitocris is not a fictitious personage. In the annals of ancient Egypt she is no inconspicuous figure. Principally responsible for her prominence is her monstrous revenge upon the slayers of her brother, the narration of which I have just concluded. Glad would I be to end this story here; for surely anything following must be in the nature of an anticlimax. However, being not a mere storyteller here, but having upon me also the responsibility of a historian, I feel obligated to continue the account to the point where it was left off by Herodotus, the great Greek historian. And, therefore, I add this postscript, anticlimax though it be.

The morning of the day after the massacre in the temple, the guests of the queen not having made their return, the citizens of Thebes began to glower with dark suspicions. Rumors came to them through divers channels that something of a most extraordinary and calamitous nature had occurred at the scene of the banquet during the night. Some had it that the temple had collapsed upon the revelers and all had been killed. However, this theory was speedily dispelled when a voyager from down the river reported having passed the temple in a perfectly firm condition but declared that he had seen no signs of life about the place— only the brightly canopied boats, drifting at their moorings.

Uneasiness steadily increased throughout the day. Sage persons recalled the great devotion of the queen toward her dead brother, and noted that the guests at the banquet of last night had been composed almost entirely of those who had participated in his slaying.

When in the evening the queen arrived in the city, pale, silent, and obviously nervous, threatening crowds blocked the path of her chariot, demanding roughly an explanation of the disappearance of her guests. Haughtily she ignored them and lashed forward the horses of her chariot, pushing aside the tight mass of people. Well she knew, however, that her life would be doomed as soon as they confirmed their suspicions. She resolved to meet her inevitable death in a way that befitted one of her rank, not at the filthy hands of a mob.

Therefore, upon her entrance into the palace she ordered her slaves to fill instantly her boudoir with hot and smoking ashes. When this had been done, she went to the room, entered it, closed the door and locked it securely, and then flung herself down upon a couch in the center of the room. In a short time the scorching heat and the suffocating thick fumes of the smoke overpowered her. Only her beautiful dead body remained for the hands of the mob.

"The Informal Execution of Soupbone Pew" is one of the first stories ever written by DAMON RUNYON, *author of a huge number of tales about the underworld and half-world denizens of Broadway. (With odd appropriateness, Runyon came from Manhattan, Kansas.) One of America's most distinguished newspapermen, Runyon was close friends with the columnist Walter Winchell, who founded a cancer research institute when Runyon died of that affliction. (Ironically, cancer also claimed Winchell.) The little-known horror story below is very different in tone than most of the author's more familiar tales, several of which inspired the popular musical comedy* Guys and Dolls.

The Informal Execution of Soupbone Pew

BY DAMON RUNYON

What is it the Good Book says? I read it last night—it said:
That he who sheddeth another man's blood by man shall his blood
    be shed!
That's as fair as a man could ask it, who lives by the gun and
    knife—
But the Law don't give him an even break when it's taking away
    his life
Ho, the Law's unfair when it uses a chair, and a jolt from an
    unseen Death;
Or it makes him flop to a six-foot drop and a rope shuts off his
    breath;
If he's got to die let him die by the Book, with a Death that he
    can see,
By a gun or knife, as he went through life, and both legs kicking
    free!

                              —*Songs of the "Shut-Ins"*

The condemned man in the cell next to us laughed incessantly. He had been sentenced that morning, and they told us he had started laughing as soon as the words, "May the Lord have mercy on your soul," were pronounced. He was to be taken to the penitentiary next day to await execution.

Chicago Red had manifested a lively interest in the case. The man had killed a railroad brakeman, so one of the guards told us; had killed him coldly, and without provocation. The trial had commenced since our arrival at the county jail and had lasted three days, during which time Red talked of little else.

From the barred windows of the jail corridor, when we were exercising, we could see the dingy old criminal court across the yard and Red watched the grim procession to and from the jail each day. He speculated on the progress of the trial; he knew when the case went to the jury, and when he saw the twelve men, headed by the two old bailiffs returning after lunch the third day, he announced:

"They've got the verdict, and it's first degree murder. They ain't talking and not a one has even grinned."

Then when the unfortunate was brought back, laughing that dismal laugh, Red said:

"He's nutty. He was nutty to go. It ain't exactly right to swing that guy."

Red and I were held as suspects in connection with an affair which had been committed a full forty-eight hours before we landed in town. We had no particular fear of being implicated in the matter, and the officers had no idea that we had anything to do with it, but they were holding us as evidence to the public that they were working on the case. We had been "vagged" for ten days each.

It was no new experience for us in any respect—not even the condemned man, for we had frequently been under the same roof with men sentenced to die. The only unusual feature was Red's interest in the laughing man.

"Red," I asked, as we sat playing cards, "did you ever kill a man?"

He dropped a card calmly, taking the trick, and as he contemplated his hand, considering his next lead, he answered:

"For why do you ask me that?"

"Oh, I don't know; I just wondered," I said. "You've seen and done so many things that I thought you might accidentally have met with something of the sort."

"It isn't exactly a polite question," he replied. "I've seen some murders. I've seen quite a few, in fact. I've seen some pulled off in a chief's private office, when they was sweating some poor stiff, and I've seen some, other places."

"Did you ever kill a man?" I insisted.

He studied my lead carefully.

"I never did," he finally answered. "That is to say, I never bumped no guy off personal. I never had nothing to do with no job from which come ghosts to wake me up at night and bawl me out. They say a guy what kills a man never closes his eyes again, even when he really sleeps. I go to the hay, and my eyes are shut tight, so I know I ain't to be held now or hereafter for nothing like that."

We finished the game in silence, and Red seemed very thoughtful. He laid the cards aside, rolled a cigarette, and said:

"Listen! I never killed no guy personal, like I say; I mean for nothing he done to me. I've been a gun and crook for many years, like you know, but I'm always mighty careful about hurting anyone permanent. I'm careful about them pete jobs, so's not to blow up no harmless persons, and I always tell my outside men that, when they have to do shooting, not to try to hit anyone. If they did, accidental, that ain't my fault. One reason I took to inside work was to keep from having to kill anyone. I've been so close to being taken that I could hear the gates of the Big House slam, and one little shot would have saved me a lot of trouble, but I always did my best to keep from letting that shot go. I never wanted to kill no man. I've been in jams where guys were after me good and strong, and I always tried to get by without no killings.

"I said I never killed a guy. I helped once, but it wasn't murder. It's never worried me a — bit since, and I sleep good."

He walked to the window and peered out into the yard where a bunch of sparrows were fluttering about. Finally he turned and said:

"I hadn't thought of that for quite a while, and I never do until I see some poor stiff that's been tagged to go away. Some of them make me nervous—especially this tee-hee guy next to us. I'll tell you about Soupbone Pew—some day you can write it, if you want to."

Soupbone Pew was a rat who trained years ago with Billy Coulon, the Honey Grove Kid, and a bunch of other old-timers that you've never seen. It was before my time, too, but I've heard them talk about him. He was in the Sioux City bank tear-off, when they all got grabbed and were sent to the Big House for fifteen years each. In them days Soupbone was a pretty good guy. He had nerve, and was smart, and stood well with everybody, but a little stretch in the big stir got to him. He broke bad. Honey Grove laid a plan for a big spring—a get-away—while they were up yonder. It looked like it would go through, too, but just as they were about ready, Soupbone got cold feet and gave up his insides.

For that he got a pardon, and quit the road right off. He became a railroad brakeman, and showed up as a shack running between Dodge City and La Junta. And he became the orneriest white man that God ever let live, too.

To hoboes and guns he was like a reformed soak toward a drunk. He treated them something fierce. He was a big, powerful stiff, who could kill a man with a wallop of his hands, if he hit him right, and his temper soured on the world. Most likely it was because he was afraid that every guy on the road was out to get him because of what he'd done, or maybe it was because he knew that they knew he was yellow. Anyway, they never tried to do him, that job belonging to Coulon, Honey Grove and the others.

Soupbone cracked that no 'bo could ride his division, and he made it good, too. He beat them up when they tried it, and he made it so strong that the old heads wouldn't go against a try when he was the run. Once in a while some kid took a stab at it, but if he got caught by Soupbone he regretted it the rest of his life. I've heard of that little road into Hot Springs, where they say a reward used to be offered to any 'bo that rode it, and how a guy beat it by getting in the water-tank; and I've personally met that Wyoming gent on the Union Pacific, and all them other guys they say is so tough, but them stories is only fairy-tales for children beside what could be told about Pew. He went an awful route.

I've known of him catching guys in the pilot and throwing scalding water in on them; I've heard tell of him shoveling hot cinders into empties on poor bums laying there asleep. That trick of dropping a coupling-pin on the end of a wire down alongside a moving train, so that it would swing up underneath and knock a stiff off the rods, was about the mildest thing he did.

He was simply a devil. The other railroad men on the division wouldn't hardly speak to him. They couldn't stand his gaff, but they couldn't very well roar at him keeping 'boes off his trains because that was what he was there for.

His longest suit was beating guys up. He just loved to catch some poor old broken-down bum on his train and pound the everlasting stuffing out of him. He's sent many a guy to the hospital, and maybe he killed a few before my acquaintance with him, for all I know.

Once in a while he ran against some live one—some real gun, and not a bum—who'd given him a battle, but he was there forty ways with a sap and gat, and he'd shoot as quick as he'd slug. He didn't go so strong on the real guns, if he knew who they was, and I guess he was always afraid they might be friends of Honey Grove or Coulon.

He was on the run when I first heard of him, and some of the kids of my day would try to pot him from the road, when his train went by, but they never even come close. I've heard them talking of pulling a rail on him and letting his train go into the ditch, but that would have killed the other trainmen, and they was some good guys on that same run then. The best way to do was to fight shy of Soupbone, and keep him on ice for Honey Grove and Coulon.

Training with our mob in them days was a young kid called Manchester Slim—a real kid, not over eighteen, and as nice and quiet a youngster as I ever seen. He wasn't cut out for the road. It seems he'd had some trouble at home and run away. Old man Muller, that Dutch prowler, used to have him on his staff, but he never let this kid in on any work for some reason. He was always trying to get Slim to go home.

"Der road is hell for der kits," he used to say. "Let der old stiffs vork out dere string, und don't make no new vuns."

The Slim paid no attention to him. Still he had no great love for the life, and probably would have quit long before if he hadn't been afraid some one would think he was scared off.

They was a pete job on at La Junta, which me and 'Frisco Shine and Muller had laid out. We had jungled up—camped—in a little cottonwood grove a few miles out of town, and was boiling out soup—nitro-glycerine—from dynamite, you know—and Muller sent the Slim into town to look around a bit. It was winter and pretty cold. We had all come in from the West and was headed East. We was all broke bad, too, and needed dough the worst way.

Slim come back from town much excited. He was carrying a Denver newspaper in his hand.

"I've got to go home, Mull," he said, running up to the old man and holding out the paper. "Look at this ad."

Muller read it and called to me. He showed me a little want ad reading that Gordon Keleher, who disappeared from his home in Boston two years before, was wanted at home because his mother was dying. It was signed Pelias Keleher, and I knew who he was, all right—president of the National Bankers' Association.

"Well, you go," I said, right off the reel, and I could see that was the word he was waiting for.

"For certainly he goes," said Muller. "Nail der next rattler."

"All the passengers are late, but there's a freight due out of here tonight; I asked," said Slim.

"How much dough iss dere in dis mob?" demanded Muller, frisking himself. We all shook ourselves down, but the most we could scare up was three or four dollars.

"If you could wait until after tonight," I says, thinking of the job, but Muller broke me off with:

"Ve don't vant him to vait. Somedings might happens."

"I'd wire home for money, but I want to get to Kansas City first," said Slim. "That paper is a couple of day old, and there's no telling how long it may have been running that ad. I can stop over in K.C. long enough to get plenty of dough from some people I know there. I'm going to grab that freight."

"Soupbone on dat freight," said the 'Frisco Shine, a silent, wicked black.

"Ve'll see Soub," said Muller quietly. "I guess maybe he von't inderfere mit dis case."

We decided to abandon the job for the night, and all went uptown. The Slim was apparently very much worried, and he kept telling us that if he didn't get home in time he'd never forgive himself, so we all got dead-set on seeing him started.

We looked up the conductor of the freight due out that night and explained things to him. None of us knew him, but he was a nice fellow.

"I tell you, boys," he said, "I'd let the young fellow ride, but you'd better see my head brakeman, Soupbone Pew. He's a tough customer, but in a case like this he ought to be all right. I'll speak to him myself."

Muller went after Pew. He found him in a saloon, drinking all by his lonesome, although there was a crowd of other railroad men in there at the time. Muller knew Pew in the old days, but there was no sign of recognition between them. The old Dutchman explained to Pew very briefly.

"It vould pe a gread personal favor mit me, Soub; maype somedimes I return it."

"He can't ride my train!" said Pew shortly. "That's flat. No argument goes."

The Dutchman looked at him long and earnestly, murder showing in his eyes, and Pew slunk back close to the bar, and his hand dropped to his hip.

"Soub, der poy rides!" said Muller, his voice low but shaking with anger. "He rides your rattler. Und if anyding happens by dot poy, de Honey Grove Kit von't get no chance at you! Dot's all, Soub!"

But when he returned to us, he was plainly afraid for the Slim.

"You don't bedder go to-nid," he said. "Dot Soub is a defil, und he'll do you."

"I'm not afraid," said Slim. "He can't find me, anyhow."

The old man tried to talk him out of the idea, but Slim was determined, and finally Muller, in admiration of his spirit, said:

"Vell, if you vill go, you vill. Vun man can hide besser as two, but der Shine must go mit you as far as Dodge."

That was the only arrangement he would consent to, and while the Slim didn't want the Shine, and I myself couldn't see what good he could do, Muller insisted so strong that we all gave in.

We went down to the yards that night to see them off, and the old man had a private confab with the Shine. The only time I ever saw Muller show any feeling was when he told the boy goodbye. I guess he really liked him.

The two hid back of a pile of ties, a place where the trains slowed down, and me and Muller got off a distance and watched them. We could see Soupbone standing on top of a box-car as the train went by, and he looked like a tall devil. He was trying to watch both sides of the train at the same time, but I didn't think he saw either Slim or the Shine as they shot underneath the cars, one after the other, and nailed the rods. Then the train went off into the darkness, Soupbone standing up straight and stiff.

We went back to our camp to sleep, and the next morning before we were awake, the Shine came limping in, covered with blood and one arm hanging at his side.

I didn't have to hear his story to guess what had happened. Soupbone made them at the first stop. He hadn't expected two, but he did look for the kid. Instead of warning him off, he told him to get on top where he'd be safe. That was one of his old tricks. He didn't get to the Shine, who dodged off into the darkness, as soon as he found they were grabbed, and then caught the train after it started again. He crawled up between the cars to the deck, to tip the Slim off to watch out for Soupbone. Slim didn't suspect anything, and was thanking Soupbone, and explaining about his mother.

The moment the train got under way good, Soupbone says:

"Now my pretty boy, you're such a_____good traveler, let's see you jump off this train!"

The kid thought he was joshing, but there wasn't no josh about it. Soup pulled a gun. The Shine, with his own gun in hand, crawled clear on top and lay flat on the cars, trying to steady his aim on Soupbone. The kid was pleading and almost crying, when Soupbone suddenly jumped at him, smashed him in the jaw with the gun-barrel, and knocked him off the train. The Shine shot Soupbone in the back, and he dropped on top of the train, but didn't roll off. As the Shine was going down between the cars again, Soupbone shot at him and broke his arm. He got off all right, and went back down the road to find the kid dead—his neck broke.

Old man Muller, the mildest man in the world generally, almost went bug-house when he heard that spiel. He raved and tore around like a sure enough nut. I've known him to go backing out of a town with every man in his mob down on the ground, dead or dying, and not show half as much feeling afterward. You'd 'a' thought the kid was his own. He swore he'd do nothing else as long as he lived until he'd cut Soupbone's heart out.

The Shine had to get out of sight, because Soupbone would undoubtedly have some wild-eyed story to tell about being attacked by hoboes and being shot by one. We had no hope but what the Shine had killed him.

Old man Muller went into town and found out that was just what had happened, and he was in the hospital only hurt a little. He also found they'd brought Slim's body to town, and that most people suspected the real truth, too. He told them just how it was, especially the railroad men, and said the Shine had got out of the country. He also wired Slim's people, and we heard afterward they sent a special train after the remains.

Muller was told, too, that the train conductor had notified Pew to let Slim ride, and that the rest of the train-crew had served notice on Pew that if he threw the boy off he'd settle with them for it. And that was just what made Soupbone anxious to get the kid. It ended his railroad career there, as we found out afterwards, because he disappeared as soon as he got out of the hospital.

Meanwhile me and Muller and the Shine went ahead with that job, and it failed. Muller and the nigger got grabbed, and I had a tough time getting away. Just before we broke camp the night before, however, Muller, who seemed to have a hunch that something was going to happen, called me and the Shine to him, and said, his voice solemn:

"I vant you poys to bromise me vun ting," he said. "If I don't get der chance myself, bromise me dot venefer you find Soubbone Bew, you vill kill him deat."

And we promised, because we didn't think we would ever be called on to make good.

Muller got a long jolt for the job; the Shine got a shorter one and escaped a little bit later on, while I left that part of the country.

A couple of years later, on a bitter cold night, in a certain town that I won't name, there was five of us in the sneezer, held as suspects on a house prowl job that only one of us had anything to do with—I ain't mentioning the name of the one, either. They was me, Kid Mole, the old prize-fighter, a hophead named Squirt McCue, that you don't know, Jew Friend, a dip, and that same 'Frisco Shine. We were all in the bull-pen with a mixed assortment of drunks and vags. All kinds of prisoners was put in there over night. This pokey is down-stairs under the police station, not a million miles from the Missouri River, so if you think hard you can guess the place. We were walking around kidding the drunks, when a screw shoved in a long, tall guy who acted like he was drunk or nutty, and was hardly able to stand.

I took one flash at his map, and I knew him. It was Pew.

He flopped down in a corner as soon as the screw let go his arm. The Shine rapped to him as quick as I did, and officed Mole and the rest. They all knew of him, especially the Honey Grove business, as well as about the Manchester Slim, for word had gone over the country at the time.

As soon as the screw went up-stairs I walked over to the big stiff, laying all huddled up, and poked him with my foot.

"What's the matter with you, you big cheese?" I said. He only mumbled.

"Stand-up!" I tells him, but he didn't stir. The Shine and Mole got hold of him on either side and lifted him to his feet. He was as limber as a wet bar-towel. But then we heard the screw coming down-stairs and we got away from Pew. The screw brought in a jag—a laughing jag—a guy with his snoot full of booze and who laughed like he'd just found a lot of money. He was a little, thin fellow, two pounds lighter than a straw hat. He laughed high and shrill, more like a scream than a real laugh, and the moment the screw opened the door and tossed him in, something struck me that the laugh was phoney. It didn't sound on the level.

There wasn't no glad in it. The little guy laid on the floor and kicked his feet and kept on laughing. Soupbone Pew let out a yell at the sight of him.

"Don't let him touch me!" he bawled, rolling over against the wall. "Don't let him near me!"

"Why, you big stiff, you could eat him alive!" I says.

The jag kept on tee-heeing, not looking at us, or at Pew either for that matter.

"He's nuts," said Jew Friend.

"Shut him off," I told the Shine.

He stepped over and picked the jag up with one hand, held him out at arm's length, and walloped him on the jaw with his other hand. The jag went to sleep with a laugh sticking in his throat. Soupbone still lay against the wall moaning, but he saw that business all right, and it seemed to help him. The Shine tossed the jag into a cell. Right after that the screw came down with another drunk, and I asked him about Pew.

"Who's this boob?" I said. "Is he sick?"

"Him? Oh, he's a good one," said screw. "He only killed his poor wife—beat her to death with his two fists, because she didn't have supper ready on time, or something important. That ain't his blood on him: that's hers. He's pretty weak, now, hey? Well, he wasn't so weak a couple of hours ago, that rat! It's the wickedest murder ever done in this town, and he'll hang sure, if he ain't lynched beforehand!"

He gave Soupbone a kick as he went out, and Soupbone groaned.

Said I: "It's got to be done, gents; swing or no swing, this guy has got to go. Who is it—me?"

"Me!" said the Shine, stepping forward.

"Me!" said the Jew.

"Me!" chimed in Mole.

"All of us!" said the hophead.

"Stand him up!" I ordered.

The lights had been turned down low, and it was dark and shadowy in the jail. The only sound was the soft pad-pad of people passing through the snow on the sidewalks above our heads, the low sizzling of the water-spout at the sink, and the snores of the drunks, who were all asleep.

Us five was the only ones awake. The Shine and Mole lifted Soupbone up, and this time he was not so limp. He seemed to know that something was doing. His eyes was wide open and staring at us.

"Pew," I said in a whisper, "do you remember the kid you threw off your rattler three years ago?"

"And shot me in the arm?" asked Shine.

Pew couldn't turn any whiter, but his eyes rolled back into his head.

"Don't!" he whispered. "Don't say that. It made me crazy! I'm crazy now! I was crazy when I killed that little girl tonight. It was all on account of thinking about him. He comes to see me often."

"Well, Pew," I said, "a long time back you were elected to die. I was there when the sentence was passed, and it'd been carried out a long time ago if you hadn't got away. I guess we'll have to kill you tonight."

"Don't, boys!" he whined. "I ain't fit to die! Don't hurt me!"

"Why, you'll swing anyway!" said Friend.

"No! My God, no!" he said. "I was crazy; I'm crazy now, and they don't hang crazy people!"

I was standing square in front of him. His head had raised a little as he talked and his jaw was sticking out. I suddenly made a move with my left hand, as though to slap him, and he showed that his mind was active enough by dodging, so that it brought his jaw out further, and he said, "Don't." Then I pulled my right clear from my knee and took him on the point of the jaw. The Shine and Mole jumped back. Soupbone didn't fall; he just slid down in a heap, like his body had melted into his shoes.

We all jumped for him at the same time, but an idea popped into my head, and I stopped them. Soupbone was knocked out, but he was coming back fast. You can't kill a guy like that by hitting him. The jail was lighted by a few incandescent lights, and one of them was hung on a wire that reached down from the ceiling over the sink, and had a couple of feet of it coiled up in the middle. Uncoiled, the light would reach clear to the floor. I pointed to it, but the bunch didn't get my idea right away. The switch for the lights was inside the bull-pen, and I turned them off. I had to work fast for fear the screw upstairs would notice the lights was out and come down to see what the trouble was. A big arc outside threw a little glim through the sidewalk grating, so I could see what I was doing.

I uncoiled the wire and sawed it against the edge of the sink, close to the lamp, until it came in two. Then I bared the wire back for a foot. The gang tumbled, and carried Pew over to where the wire would reach him. I unfastened his collar, looped the naked end of the wire around his neck and secured it. By this time he was about come to, but he didn't seem to realize what was going on.

All but me got into their cells and I stepped over and turned the switchbutton just as Pew was struggling to his feet. The voltage hit him when he was on all fours. He stood straight up, stiff, like a soldier at salute. There was a strange look on his face—a surprised look. Then, as though someone had hit him from behind, his feet left the floor and he swung straight out to the length of the wire and it broke against his weight, just as I snapped off the current. Pew dropped to the floor and curled up like a big singed spider, and a smell like frying bacon filled the room.

I went over and felt of his heart. It was still beating, but very light.

"They ain't enough current," whispered Mole. "We got to do it some other way."

"Hang him wid de wire," said the Shine.

"Aw-nix!" spoke up the Jew. "I tell you that makes me sick— bumping a guy off that way. Hanging and electricity, see? That's combining them too much. Let's use the boot."

"It ain't fair, kind-a, that's a fact," whispered McCue. "It's a little too legal. The boot! Give him the boot!"

The voice of the screw came singing down the stairs:

"Is that big guy awake?"

"Yes," I shouted back, "we're all awake; he won't let us sleep."

"Tell him he'd better say his prayers!" yelled the screw. "I just got word a mob is forming to come and get him!"

"Let him alone," I whispered to the gang. Mole was making a noose of the wire, and the Shine had hunted up a bucket to stand Pew on. They drew back and Soupbone lay stretched out on the floor.

I went over and felt of his heart again. I don't remember whether I felt any beat or not. I couldn't have said I did, at the moment, and I couldn't say I didn't. I didn't have time to make sure, because suddenly there run across the floor something that looked to me like a shadow, or a big rat. Then the shrill laugh of that jag rattled through the bull-pen. He slid along half-stooped, as quick as a streak of light, and before we knew what he was doing he had pounced on Soupbone and had fastened his hands tight around the neck of the big stiff. He was laughing that crazy laugh all the time.

"I'll finish him for you!" he squeaked. He fastened his hands around Soupbone's neck. I kicked the jag in the side of the head as hard as I could, but it didn't faze him. The bunch laid hold of him and pulled, but they only dragged Soupbone all over the place. Finally the jag let go and stood up, and we could see he wasn't no more drunk than we was. He let loose that laugh once more, and just as the Shine started the bucket swinging for his head, he said: "I'm her brother!" Then he went down kicking.

We went into our cells and crawled into our bunks. Soupbone lay outside. The Shine pulled the jag into a corner. I tell you true, I went to sleep right away. I thought the screw would find out when he brought the next drunk down, but it woke up by a big noise on the stairs. The door flew open with a bang, and a gang of guys came down, wild-eyed and yelling. The screw was with them and they had tight hold of him.

"Keep in, you men!" he bawled to us.

"That's your meat!" he said to the gang, pointing at what had been Soupbone. The men pounced on him like a lot of hounds on to a rabbit, and before you could bat an eye they had a rope around Soupbone's neck and was tearing up the stairs again, dragging him along.

They must have thought he was asleep; they never noticed that he didn't move a muscle himself, and they took the person of Soupbone Pew, or anyways what had been him, outside and hung it over a telegraph wire.

We saw it there when we was sprung next morning. When the

screw noticed the blood around the bull-pen, he said:

"Holy smoke, they handled him rough!" And he never knew no different.

If the mob hadn't come—but the mob did come, and so did the laughing jag. I left him that morning watching the remains of Soupbone Pew.

"She was my sister," he said to me.

I don't know for certain whether we killed Soupbone, whether the jag did it, or whether the mob finished him; but he was dead, and he ought to have died. Sometimes I wonder a bit about it, but no ghosts come to me, like I say, so I can't tell.

They's an unmarked grave in the potter's field of this town I speak of, and once in a while I go there when I'm passing through and meditate on the sins of Soupbone Pew. But I sleep well of nights. I done what had to be done, and I close my eyes and I don't never see Soupbone Pew.

He turned once more to gazing out of the window.

"Well, what is there about condemned men to make you so nervous?" I demanded.

"I said some condemned men," he replied, still gazing. "Like this guy next door."

A loud, shrill laugh rang through the corridors.

"He's that same laughing jag," said Chicago Red.

According to anthologist Alden H. Norton, w. c. morrow deserves to be ranked along with Poe, Hawthorne and Bierce as one of the greatest terror writers in American letters. Unfortunately, Morrow's few works of fiction are quite obscure, but judging from "His Unconquerable Enemy," they should be far better known. The atrocities described below are dreadful enough, but the true terror consists of that diabolic revenge that the villain plots in spite of overwhelming barriers. This is a tale of human nature perverted beyond all sane recognition.

His Unconquerable Enemy
BY W. C. MORROW

I was summoned from Calcutta to the heart of India to perform a difficult surgical operation on one of the women of a great rajah's household. I found the rajah a man of a noble character, but possessed, as I afterward discovered, of a sense of cruelty purely Oriental and in contrast to the indolence of his disposition. He was so grateful for the success that attended my mission that he urged me to remain a guest at the palace as long as it might please me to stay, and I thankfully accepted the invitation.

One of the male servants attracted my notice for his marvelous capacity of malice. His name was Neranya, and I am certain that there must have been a large proportion of Malay blood in his veins, for, unlike the Indians (from whom he differed also in complexion), he was extremely alert, active, nervous, and sensitive. A redeeming circumstance was his love for his master. Once his violent temper led him to the commission of an atrocious crime—the fatal stabbing of a dwarf. In punishment for this the rajah ordered that Neranya's right arm (the offending one) be severed from his body. The sentence was executed in a bungling fashion by a stupid fellow armed with an axe, and I, being a surgeon, was compelled, in order to save Neranya's life, to perform an amputation of the stump, leaving not a vestige of the limb remaining.

After this he developed an augmented fiendishness. His love for the rajah was changed to hate, and in his mad anger he flung discretion to the winds. Driven once to frenzy by the rajah's scornful treatment, he sprang upon the rajah with a knife but, fortunately, was seized and disarmed. To his unspeakable dismay the rajah sentenced him for this offence to suffer amputation of the remaining arm. It was done as in the former instance. This had the effect of putting a temporary curb on Neranya's spirit, or, rather, of changing the outward manifestations of his diabolism. Being armless, he was at first largely at the mercy of those who ministered to his needs—a duty which I understook to see was properly discharged, for I felt an interest in this strangely distorted nature. His sense of helplessness, combined with a damnable scheme for revenge which he had secretly formed, caused Neranya to change his fierce, impetuous, and unruly conduct into a smooth, quiet, insinuating bearing, which he carried so artfully as to deceive those with whom he was brought in contact, including the rajah himself.

Neranya, being exceedingly quick, intelligent, and dexterous, and having an unconquerable will, turned his attention to the cultivating of an enlarged usefulness of his legs, feet, and toes, with so excellent effect that in time he was able to perform wonderful feats with those members. Thus his capability, especially for destructive mischief, was considerably restored.

One morning the rajah's only son, a young man of an uncommonly amiable and noble disposition, was found dead in bed. His murder was a most atrocious one, his body being mutilated in a shocking manner, but in my eyes the most significant of all the mutilations was the entire removal and disappearance of the young prince's arms.

The death of the young man nearly brought the rajah to the grave. It was not, therefore, until I had nursed him back to health that I began a systematic inquiry into the murder. I said nothing of my own discoveries and conclusions until after the rajah and his officers had failed and my work had been done; then I submitted to him a written report, making a close analysis of all the circumstances, and closing by charging the crime to Neranya. The rajah, convinced by my proof and argument, at once ordered Neranya to be put to death, this to be accomplished slowly and with frightful tortures. The sentence was so cruel and revolting that it filled me with horror, and I implored that the wretch be shot. Finally, through a sense of gratitude to me, the rajah relaxed. When Neranya was charged with the crime he denied it, of course, but, seeing that the rajah was convinced, he threw aside all restraint, and, dancing, laughing, and shrieking in the most horrible manner, confessed his guilt, gloated over it, and reviled the rajah to his teeth—this, knowing that some fearful death awaited him.

The rajah decided upon the details of the matter that night, and in the morning he informed me of his decision. It was that Neranya's life should be spared, but that both of his legs shoud be broken with hammers, and that then I should amputate the limbs at the trunk! Appended to his horrible sentence was a provision that the maimed wretch should be kept and tortoured at regular intervals by such means as afterward might be devised.

Sickened to the heart by the awful duty set out for me, I nevertheless performed it with success, and I care to say nothing more about that part of the tragedy. Neranya escaped death very narrowly and was a long time in recovering his wonted vitality. During all these weeks the rajah neither saw him nor made inquiries concerning him, but when, as in duty bound, I made official report that the man had recovered his strength, the rajah's eyes brightened, and he emerged with deadly activity from the stupor into which he so long had been plunged.

The rajah's palace was a noble structure, but it is necessary here to describe only the grand hall. It was an immense chamber, with a floor of polished, inlaid stone and a lofty, arched ceiling. A soft light stole into it through stained glass set in the roof and in high windows on one side. In the middle of the room was a rich fountain, which threw up a tall, slender column of water, with smaller and shorter jets grouped around it. Across one end of the hall, halfway to the ceiling, was a balcony, which communicated with the upper story of a wing, and from which a flight of stone stairs descended to the floor of the hall. During the hot summers this room was delightfully cool; it was the rajah's favorite lounging place, and when the nights were hot he had his cot taken thither, and there he slept.

This hall was chosen for Neranya's permanent prison; here was he to stay so long as he might live, with never a glimpse of the shining world or the glorious heavens. To one of his nervous, discontented nature such confinement was worse than death. At the rajah's order there was constructed for him a small pen of open ironwork, circular, and about four feet in diameter, elevated on four slender iron posts, ten feet above the floor, and placed between the balcony and the fountain. Such was Neranya's prison.

The pen was about four feet in depth, and the pen top was left open for the convenience of the servants whose duty it should be to care for him. These precautions for his safe confinement were taken at my suggestion, for, although the man was now deprived of all four of his limbs, I still feared that he might develop some extraordinary, unheard-of power for mischief. It was provided that the attendants should reach his cage by means of a movable ladder.

All these arrangements having been made, and Neranya hoisted into his cage, the rajah emerged upon the balcony to see him for the first time since the last amputation. Neranya had been lying panting and helpless on the floor of his cage, but when his quick ear caught the sound of the rajah's footfall he squirmed about until he had brought the back of his head against the railing, elevating his eyes above his chest, and enabling him to peer through the openwork of the cage. Thus the two deadly enemies faced each other. The rajah's stern face paled at sight of the hideous, shapeless thing which met his gaze; but he soon recovered, and the old hard, cruel, sinister look returned. Neranya's black hair and beard had grown long, and they added to the natural ferocity of his aspect. His eyes blazed upon the rajah with a terrible light, his lips parted, and he gasped for breath; his face was ashen with rage and despair, and his thin, distended nostrils quivered.

The rajah folded his arms and gazed down from the balcony upon the frightful wreck that he had made. Oh, the dreadful pathos of that picture; the inhumanity of it; the deep and dismal tragedy of it! Who might look into the wild, despairing heart of the prisoner and see and understand the frightful turmoil there; the surging, choking passion; unbridled but impotent ferocity; frantic thirst for a vengeance that should be deeper than hell! Neranya gazed, his shapeless body heaving, his eyes aflame; and then, in a strong, clear voice, which rang throughout the great hall, with rapid speech he hurled at the rajah the most insulting defiance, the most awful curses. He cursed the womb that had conceived him, the food that should nourish him, the wealth that had brought him power; cursed him in the name of Buddha and all the wise men; cursed by the sun, the moon, and the stars; by the continents, mountains, oceans, and rivers; by all things living; cursed his head, his heart, his entrails; cursed in a whirlwind of unmentionable words; heaped unimaginable insults and contumely upon him; called him a knave, a beast, a fool, a liar, an infamous and unspeakable coward.

The rajah heard it all calmly, without the movement of a muscle, without the slighest change of countenance; and when the poor wretch had exhausted his strength and fallen helpless and silent to the floor, the rajah, with a grim, cold smile, turned and strode away.

The days passed. The rajah, not deterred by Neranya's curses often heaped upon him, spent even more time then formerly in the great hall, and slept there oftener at night; and finally Neranya wearied of cursing and defying him, and fell into a sullen silence. The man was a study for me, and I observed every change in his fleeting moods. Generally his condition was that of miserable despair, which he attempted bravely to conceal. Even the boon of suicide had been denied him, for when he would wriggle into an erect position the rail of his pen was a foot above his head, so that he could not clamber over and break his skull on the stone floor beneath; and when he had tried to starve himself the attendants forced food down his throat; so that he abandoned such attempts. At times his eyes would blaze and his breath would come in gasps, for imaginary vengeance was working within him; but steadily he became quieter and more tractable, and was pleasant and responsive when I would converse with him. Whatever might have been the tortures which the rajah had decided on, none as yet had been ordered; and although Neranya knew that they were in contemplation, he never referred to them or complained of his lot.

The awful climax of this situation was reached one night, and even after this lapse of years I cannot approach its description without a shudder.

It was a hot night, and the rajah had gone to sleep in the great hall, lying on a high cot placed on the main floor just underneath the edge of the balcony. I had been unable to sleep in my own apartment, and so I had stolen into the great hall through the heavily curtained entrance at the end farthest from the balcony. As I entered I heard a peculiar, soft sound above the patter of the fountain. Neranya's cage was partly concealed from my view by the spraying water, but I suspected that the unusual sound came from him. Stealing a little to one side, and crouching against the dark hangings of the wall, I could see him in the faint light which dimly illuminated the hall, and then I discovered that my surmise was correct—Neranya was quietly at work. Curious to learn more, and knowing that only mischief could have been inspiring him, I sank into a thick robe on the floor and watched him.

To my great astonishment Neranya was tearing off with his teeth
the bag which served as his outer garment. He did it cautiously,
casting sharp glances frequently at the rajah, who, sleeping
soundly on his cot below, breathed heavily. After starting a strip
with his teeth, Neranya, by the same means, would attach it to the
railing of his cage and then wriggle away, much after the manner
of a caterpillar's crawling, and this would cause the strip to be torn
to the full length of his garment. He repeated this operation with
incredible patience and skill until his entire garment had been torn
into strips. Two or three of these he tied end to end with his teeth,
lips, and tongue, tightening the knots by placing one end of the
strip under his body and drawing the other taut with his teeth. In
this way he made a line several feet long, one end of which he
made fast to the rail with his mouth. It then began to dawn upon
me that he was going to make an insane attempt—impossible of
achievement without hands, feet, arms or legs—to escape from his
cage! For what purpose? The rajah was asleep in the hall—ah! I
caught my breath. Oh, the desperate, insane thirst for revenge
which could have unhinged so clear and firm a mind! Even though
he should accomplish the impossible feat of climbing over the
railing of his cage that he might fall to the floor below (for how
could he slide down the rope?), he would be in all probability
killed or stunned; and even if he should escape these dangers, it
would be impossible for him to clamber upon the cot without
rousing the rajah, and impossible even though the rajah were
dead! Amazed at the man's daring, and convinced that his
sufferings and brooding had destroyed his reason, nevertheless I
watched him with breathless interest.

With other strips tied together he made a short swing across one
side of his cage. He caught the long line in his teeth at a point not
far from the rail; then, wriggling with great effort to an upright
position, his back braced against the rail, he put his chin over the
swing, and with tremendous exertion, working the lower end of
his spine against the railing, he began gradually to ascend the side
of his cage. The labor was so great that he was compelled to pause
at intervals, and his breathing was hard and painful; and even
while thus resting he was in a position of terrible strain, and his
pushing against the swing caused it to press hard against his
windpipe and nearly strangle him.

After amazing effort he had elevated the lower end of his body until it protruded above the railing, the top of which was now across the lower end of his abdomen. Gradually he worked his body over, going backward, until there was sufficient excess of weight on the outer side of the rail; and then, with a quick lurch, he raised his head and shoulders and swung into a horizontal position on top of the rail. Of course, he would have fallen to the floor below had it not been for the line which he held in his teeth. With so great nicety had he estimated the distance between his mouth and the point where the rope was fastened to the rail, that the line tightened and checked him just as he reached the horizontal position on the rail. If one had told me beforehand that such a feat as I had just seen this man accomplish was possible, I should have thought him a fool.

Neranya was now balanced on his stomach across the top of the rail, and he eased his position by bending his spine and hanging down on either side as much as possible. Having rested thus for some minutes, he began cautiously to slide off backward, slowly paying out the line through his teeth, finding almost a fatal difficulty in passing the knots. Now, it is quite possible that the line would have escaped altogether from his teeth laterally when he would slightly relax his hold to let it slip, had it not been for a very ingenious plan to which he had resorted. This consisted in his having made a turn of the line around his neck before he attacked the wing, thus securing a threefold control of the line—one by his teeth, another by friction against his neck, and a third by his ability to compress it between his cheek and shoulder. It was quite evident now that the minutest details of a most elaborate plan had been carefully worked out by him before beginning the task, and that possibly weeks of difficult theoretical study had been consumed in the mental preparation. As I observed him I was reminded of certain hitherto unaccountable things which he had been doing for some weeks past—going through certain hitherto inexplicable motions, undoubtedly for the purpose of training his muscles for the immeasurably arduous labor which he was now performing.

A stupendous and seemingly impossible part of his task had been accomplished. Could he reach the floor in safety? Gradually he worked himself backward over the rail, in imminent danger of falling; but his nerve never wavered, and I could see a wonderful light in his eyes. With something of a lurch, his body fell against the outer side of the railing, to which he was hanging by his chin, the line still held firmly in his teeth. Slowly he slipped his chin from the rail, and then hung suspended by the line in his teeth. By almost imperceptible degrees, with infinite caution, he descended the line, and, finally, his unwieldy body rolled upon the floor, safe and unhurt!

What miracle would this superhuman monster next accomplish? I was quick and strong, and was ready and able to intercept any dangerous act; but not until danger appeared would I interfere with this extraordinary scene.

I must confess to astonishment upon having observed that Neranya, instead of proceeding directly toward the sleeping rajah, took quite another direction. Then it was only escape, after all, that the wretch contemplated, and not the murder of the rajah. But how could he escape? The only possible way to reach the outer air without great risk was by ascending the stairs to the balcony and leaving by the corridor which opened upon it, and thus fall into the hands of some British soldiers quartered thereabout, who might conceive the idea of hiding him; but surely it was impossible for Neranya to ascend that long flight of stairs! Nevertheless, he made directly for them, his method of progression this: He lay upon his back, with the lower end of his body toward the stairs; then bowed his spine upward, thus drawing his head and shoulders a little forward; straightened, and then pushed the lower end of his body forward a space equal to that through which he had drawn his head; repeating this again and again, each time, while bending his spine, preventing his head from slipping by pressing it against the floor. His progress was laborious and slow, but sensible; and, finally, he arrived at the foot of the stairs.

It was manifest that his insane purpose was to ascend them. The desire for freedom must have been strong within him! Wriggling to an upright position against the newel-post, he looked up at the great height which he had to climb, and sighed; but there was no dimming of the light in his eyes. How could he accomplish the impossible task?

His solution of the problem was very simple, though daring and perilous as all the rest. While leaning against the newel-post he let himself fall diagonally upon the bottom step, where he lay partly hanging over, but safe, on his side. Turning upon his back, he wriggled forward along the step to the rail and raised himself to an upright position against it as he had against the newel-post, fell as before, and landed on the second step. In this manner, with inconceivable labor, he accomplished the ascent of the entire flight of stairs.

It being apparent to me that the rajah was not the object of Neranya's movements, the anxiety which I had felt on that account was now entirely dissipated. The things which already he had accomplished were entirely beyond the nimblest imagination. The sympathy which I had always felt for the wretched man was now greatly quickened; and as infinitesimally small as I knew his chances for escape to be, I nevertheless hoped that he would succeed. Any assistance from me, however, was out of the question; and it never should be known that I had witnessed the escape.

Neranya was now upon the balcony, and I could dimly see him wriggling along toward the door which led out upon the balcony. Finally he stopped and wriggled to an upright position against the rail, which had wide openings between the balusters. His back was towards me, but he slowly turned and faced me and the hall. At that great distance I could not distinguish his features, but the slowness with which he had worked, even before he had fully accomplished the ascent of the stairs, was evidence all too eloquent of his extreme exhaustion. Nothing but a most desperate resolution could have sustained him thus far, but he had drawn upon the last remnant of his strength. He looked around the hall with a sweeping glance, and then down upon the rajah, who was sleeping immediately beneath him, over twenty feet below. He looked long and earnestly, sinking lower, and lower, and lower upon the rail. Suddenly, to my inconceivable astonishment and dismay, he toppled through and shot downward from his lofty height! I held my breath, expecting to see him crushed upon the stone floor beneath; but instead of that he fell full upon the rajah's breast, driving him through the cot to the floor. I sprang forward with a loud cry for help, and was instantly at the scene of the catastrophe. With indescribable horror I saw that Neranya's teeth were buried in the rajah's throat! I tore the wretch away, but the blood was pouring from the rajah's arteries, his chest was crushed in, and he was gasping in the agony of death. People came running in, terrified. I turned to Neranya. He lay upon his back, his face hideously smeared with blood. Murder, and not escape, had been his intention from the beginning; and he had employed the only method by which there was ever a possibility of accomplishing it. I knelt beside him, and saw that he, too, was dying; his back had been broken by the fall. He smiled sweetly into my face, and a triumphant look of accomplished revenge sat upon his face even in death.

ALFRED, LORD TENNYSON *(1809–1892) succeeded William Wordsworth in 1850 as Poet Laureate of England. He is perhaps best known for his epic cycle of Arthurian verses,* Idylls of the King. *"Rizpah," loosely inspired by an Old Testament story, is a heartbreaking tale of the griefs of a poor mother and the son torn away from her by a justice harsher than anything a mere demon might devise.*

Rizpah
BY ALFRED, LORD TENNYSON

I

Wailing, wailing, wailing, the wind over land and sea—
And Willy's voice in the wind, 'O mother, come out to me!'
Why should he call me to-night, when he knows that I cannot go?
For the downs are as bright as day, and the full moon stares at the
 snow.

II

We should be seen, my dear; they would spy us out of the town.
The loud black nights for us, and the storm rushing over the
 down,
When I cannot see my own hand, but am led by the creak of the
 chain,
And grovel and grope for my son till I find myself drenched with
 the rain.

III

Anything fallen again? nay—what was there left to fall?
I have taken them home, I have number'd the bones, I have
 hidden them all.

What am I saying? and what are *you?* do you come as a spy?
Falls? what falls? who knows? As the tree falls so must it lie.

IV

Who let her in? how long has she been? you—what have you
    heard?
Why did you sit so quiet? you never have spoken a word.
O—to pray with me—yes—a lady—none of their spies—
But the night has crept into my heart, and begun to darken my
    eyes.

V

Ah—you, that have lived so soft, what should *you* know of the
    night,
The blast and the burning shame and the bitter frost and the
    fright?
I have done it, while you were asleep—you were only made for
    the day.
I have gather'd my baby together—and now you may go your
way.

VI

Nay—for it's kind of you, madam, to sit by an old dying wife.
But say nothing hard of my boy, I have only an hour of life.
I kiss'd my boy in the prison, before he went out to die.
'They dared me to do it,' he said, and he never has told me a lie.
I whipt him for robbing an orchard once when he was but a
    child—
'The farmer dared me do it,' he said; he was always so wild—
And idle—and couldn't be idle—my Willy—he never could rest.
The King should have made him a soldier, he would have been
    one of his best.

VII

But he lived with a lot of wild mates, and they never would let
   him be good;
They swore that he dare not rob the mail, and he swore that he
   would;
And he took no life, but he took one purse, and when all was done
He flung it among his fellows — 'I'll none of it,' said my son.

VIII

I came into court to the judge and the lawyers. I told them my
   tale,
God's own truth — but they kill'd him, they kill'd him for robbing
   the mail.
They hang'd him in chains for a show — we had always borne a
   good name —
To be hang'd for a thief — and then put away — isn't that enough
   shame?
Dust to dust — low down — let us hide! but they set him so high
That all the ships of the world could stare at him, passing by.
God 'ill parden the hell-black raven and horrible fowls of the air,
But not the black heart of the lawyer who kill'd him and hang'd
   him there.

XI

And the jailer forced me away. I had bid him my last good-bye;
They had fasten'd the door of his cell. 'O mother!' I heard him
   cry.
I couldn't get back tho' I tried, he had something further to say,
And now I never shall know it. The jailer forced me away.

X

Then since I couldn't but hear that cry of my boy that was dead,
They seized me and shut me up: they fasten'd me down on my
   bed.

'Mother, O mother!'—he call'd in the dark to me year after year—
They beat me for that, they beat me—you know that I couldn't
    but hear;
And then at the last they found I had grown so stupid and still
They let me abroad again—but the creatures had worked their
    will.

XI

Flesh of my flesh was gone, but bone of my bone was left—
I stole them all from the lawyers—and you, will you call it a
    theft?—
My baby, the bones that had suck'd me, the bones that had
    laughed and had cried—
Theirs? O, no! they are mine—not theirs—they had moved in my
    side.

XII

Do you think I was scared by the bones? I kiss'd 'em, I buried
    'em all—
I can't dig deep, I am old—in the night by the churchyard wall.
My Willy 'ill rise up whole when the trumpet of judgment 'ill
    sound,
But I charge you never to say that I laid him in holy ground.

XIII

They would scratch him up—they would hang him again on the
    cursed tree.
Sin? O, ye, we are sinners, I know—let all that be,
And read me a Bible verse of the Lord's goodwill toward men—
'Full of compassion and mercy, the Lord'—let me hear it again;
'Full of compassion and mercy—long-suffering.' Yes, O, yes!
For the lawyer is born but to murder—the Saviour lives but to
    bless.
He'll never put on the black cap except for the worst of the worst,
And the first may be last—I have heard it in church—and the last
    may be first.

Suffering—O, long-suffering—yes, as the Lord must know,
Year after year in the mist and the wind and the shower and the
   snow.

XIV

Heard, have you? what? they have told you he never repented his
   sin.
How do they know it? are *they* his mother? are *you* of his kin?
Heard! have you ever heard, when the storm on the downs began,
The wind that 'ill wail like a child and the sea that 'ill moan like
   a man?

XV

Election, Election, and Reprobation—it's all very well.
But I go to-night to my boy, and I shall not find him in hell.
For I cared so much for my boy that the Lord has look'd into my
   care.
And He means me I'm sure to be happy with Willy, I know not
   where.

XVI

And if *he* be lost—but to save my soul, that is all your desire—
Do you think that I care for *my* soul if my boy be gone to the fire?
I have been with God in the dark—go, go, you may leave me
   alone—
You never have borne a child—you are just as hard as a stone.

XVII

Madam, I beg your pardon! I think that you mean to be kind,
But I cannot hear what you say for my Willy's voice in the wind—
The snow and the sky so bright—he used but to call in the dark,
And he calls to me now from the church and not from the
   gibbet, for hark!
Nay—you can hear it yourself—it is coming—shaking the walls—
Willy—the moon's in a cloud—Goodnight. I am going. He calls.

STANLEY ELLIN *is the distinguished author of critical acclaimed suspense novels and stories and is a past president of the Mystery Writers of America. His captivating thriller,* House of Cards, *was made into a tolerably effective film, but he is better known for the quietly cannibalistic "Specialty of the House," dramatized on television. Many of his stories have won awards, but "The Question" is a winner even by Ellin's own standards. It is one of the author's favorite stories, and no wonder—in its implications, it is among the most unsettling indictments of the contemporary human spirit ever penned.*

The Question
BY STANLEY ELLIN

I am an electrocutioner . . . I prefer this word to executioner; I think words make a difference. When I was a boy, people who buried the dead were undertakers, and then somewhere along the way they became morticians and are better off for it.

Take the one who used to be the undertaker in my town. He was a decent, respectable man, very friendly if you'd let him be, but hardly anybody would let him be. Today, his son—who now runs the business—is not an undertaker but a mortician, and is welcome everywhere. As a matter of fact, he's an officer in my Lodge and is one of the most popular members we have. And all it took to do that was changing one word to another. The job's the same but the word is different, and people somehow will always go by words rather than meanings.

So, as I said, I am an electrocutioner—which is the proper professional word for it in my state where the electric chair is the means of execution.

Not that this is my profession. Actually, it's a sideline, as it is for most of us who perform executions. My real business is running an electrical supply and repair shop just as my father did before me. When he died I inherited not only the business from him, but also the position of state's electrocutioner.

We established a tradition, my father and I. He was running the shop profitably even before the turn of the century when electricity was a comparatively new thing, and he was the first man to perform a successful electrocution for the state. It was not the state's first electrocution, however. That one was an experiment and was badly bungled by the engineer who installed the chair in the state prison. My father, who had helped install the chair, was the assistant at the electrocution, and he told me that everything that could go wrong that day did go wrong. The current was eccentric, his boss froze on the switch, and the man in the chair was alive and kicking at the same time he was being burned to a crisp. The next time, my father offered to do the job himself, rewired the chair, and handled the switch so well that he was offered the job of official electrocutioner.

I followed in his footsteps, which is how a tradition is made, but I am afraid this one ends with me. I have a son, and what I said to him and what he said to me is the crux of the matter. He asked me a question—well, in my opinion, it was the kind of question that's at the bottom of most of the world's troubles today. There are some sleeping dogs that should be left to lie; there are some questions that should not be asked.

To understand all this, I think you have to understand me, and nothing could be easier. I'm sixty, just beginning to look my age, a little overweight, suffer sometimes from arthritis when the weather is damp. I'm a good citizen, complain about my taxes but pay them on schedule, vote for the right party, and run my business well enough to make a comfortable living from it.

I've been married thirty-five years and never looked at another woman in all that time. Well, looked maybe, but no more than that. I have a married daughter and a granddaughter almost a year old, and the prettiest, smilingest baby in town. I spoil her and don't apologize for it, because in my opinion that is what grandfathers were made for—to spoil their grandchildren. Let mama and papa attend to the business; grandpa is there for the fun.

And beyond all that I have a son who asks questions. The kind that shouldn't be asked.

Put the picture together, and what you get is someone like yourself. I might be your next-door neighbor, I might be your old friend, I might be the uncle you meet whenever the family gets together at a wedding or a funeral. I'm like you.

Naturally, we all look different on the outside but we can still recognize each other on sight as the same kind of people. Deep down inside where it matters we have the same feelings, and we know that without any questions being asked about them.

"But," you might say, "there is a difference between us. You're the one who performs the executions, and I'm the one who reads about them in the papers, and that's a big difference, no matter how you look at it."

Is it? Well, look at it without prejudice, look at it with absolute honesty, and you'll have to admit that you're being unfair.

Let's face the facts, we're all in this together. If an old friend of yours happens to serve on a jury that finds a murderer guilty, you don't lock the door against him, do you? More than that: if you could get an introduction to the judge who sentences that murderer to the electric chair, you'd be proud of it, wouldn't you? You'd be honored to have him sit at your table, and you'd be quick enough to let the world know about it.

And since you're so willing to be friendly with the jury that convicts and the judge that sentences, what about the man who has to pull the switch? He's finished the job you wanted done, he's made the world a better place for it. Why must he go hide away in a dark corner until the next time he's needed?

There's no use denying that nearly everybody feels he should, and there's less use denying that it's a cruel thing for anyone in my position to face. If you don't mind some strong language, it's a damned outrage to hire a man for an unpleasant job, and then despise him for it. Sometimes it's hard to abide such righteousness.

How do I get along in the face of it? The only way possible— by keeping my secret locked up tight and never being tempted to give it away. I don't like it that way, but I'm no fool about it.

The trouble is that I'm naturally easygoing and friendly. I'm the sociable kind. I like people, and I want them to like me. At Lodge meetings or in the clubhouse down at the golf course I'm always the center of the crowd. And I know what would happen if at any such time I ever opened my mouth and let that secret out. A five minute sensation, and after that the slow chill setting in. It would mean the end of my whole life then and there, the kind of life I want to live, and no man in his right mind throws away sixty years of his life for a five minute sensation.

You can see I've given the matter a lot of thought. More than that, it hasn't been idle thought. I don't pretend to be an educated man, but I'm willing to read books on any subject that interests me, and execution has been one of my main interests ever since I got into the line. I have the books sent to the shop, where nobody takes notice of another piece of mail, and I keep them locked in a bin in my office so that I can read them in private.

There's a nasty smell about having to do it this way—at my age you hate to feel like a kid hiding himself away to read a dirty magazine—but I have no choice. There isn't a soul on earth outside of the warden at state's prison and a couple of picked guards there who know I'm the one pulling the switch at an execution, and I intend it to remain that way.

Oh, yes, my son knows now. Well, he's difficult in some ways, but he's no fool. If I wasn't sure he would keep his mouth shut about what I told him, I wouldn't have told it to him in the first place.

Have I learned anything from those books? At least enough to take a pride in what I'm doing for the state and the way I do it. As far back in history as you want to go there have always been executioners. The day that men first made laws to help keep peace among themselves was the day the first executioner was born. There have always been lawbreakers; there must always be a way of punishing them. It's as simple as that.

The trouble is that nowadays there are too many people who don't want it it be as simple as that. I'm no hypocrite, I'm not one of those narrowminded fools who thinks that every time a man comes up with a generous impulse he's some kind of crackpot. But he can be mistaken. I'd put most of the people who are against capital punishment in that class. They are fine, high-minded citizens who've never in their lives been close enough to a murderer or rapist to smell the evil in him. In fact, they're so fine and high-minded that they can't imagine anyone in the world not being like themselves. In that case, they say anybody who commits murder or rape is just a plain, ordinary human being who's had a bad spell. He's no criminal, they say, he's just sick. He doesn't need the electric chair; all he needs is a kindly old doctor to examine his head and straighten out the kinks in his brain.

In fact, they say there is no such thing as a criminal at all. There are only well people and sick people, and the ones who deserve all your worry and consideration are the sick ones. If they happen to murder or rape a few of the well ones now and then, why, just run for the doctor.

This is the argument from beginning to end, and I'd be the last one to deny that it's built on honest charity and good intentions. But it's a mistaken argument. It omits the one fact that matters.

When anyone commits murder or rape he is no longer in the human race. A man has a human brain and a God-given soul to control his animal nature. When the animal in him takes control he's not a human being any more. Then he has to be exterminated the way any animal must be if it goes wild in the middle of helpless people. And my duty is to be the exterminator.

It could be that people just don't understand the meaning of the word *duty* any more. I don't want to sound old-fashioned, God forbid, but when I was a boy things were more straightforward and clear-cut. You learned to tell right from wrong, you learned to do what had to be done, and you didn't ask questions every step of the way. Or if you had to ask any questions, the ones that mattered were *how* and *when*.

Then along came psychology, along came the professors, and the main question was always *why*. Ask yourself *why, why, why* about everything you do, and you'll end up doing nothing. Let a couple of generations go along that way, and you'll finally have a breed of people who sit around in trees like monkeys, scratching their heads.

Does this sound far-fetched? Well, it isn't. Life is a complicated thing to live. All his life a man finds himself facing one situation after another, and the way to handle them is to live by the rules. Ask yourself *why* once too often, and you can find yourself so tangled up that you go under. The show must go on. Why? Women and children first. Why? My country, right or wrong. Why? Never mind your duty. Just keep asking *why* until it's too late to do anything about it.

Around the time I first started going to school my father gave me a dog, a collie pup named Rex. A few years later Rex suddenly became unfriendly, the way a dog will sometimes, and then vicious, and then one day he bit my mother when she reached down to pat him.

The day after that I saw my father leaving the house with his hunting rifle under his arm and with Rex on a leash. It wasn't the hunting season, so I knew what was going to happen to Rex and I knew why. But it's forgivable in a boy to ask things that a man should be smart enough not to ask.

"Where are you taking Rex?" I asked my father. "What are you going to do with him?"

"I'm taking him out back of town," my father said. "I'm going to shoot him."

"But why?" I said, and that was when my father let me see that there is only one answer to such a question.

"Because it has to be done," he said.

I never forgot that lesson. It came hard; for a while I hated my father for it, but as I grew up I came to see how right he was. We both knew why the dog had to be killed. Beyond that, all questions would lead nowhere. Why the dog had become vicious, why God had put a dog on earth to be killed this way—these are the questions that you can talk out to the end of time, and while you're talking about them you still have a vicious dog on your hands.

It is strange to look back and realize now that when the business of the dog happened, and long before it and long after it, my father was an electrocutioner, and I never knew it. Nobody knew it, not even my mother. A few times a year my father would pack his bag and a few tools and go away for a couple of days, but that was all any of us knew. If you asked him where he was going he would simply say he had a job to do out of town. He was not a man you'd ever suspect of philandering or going off on a solitary drunk, so nobody gave it a second thought.

It worked the same way in my case. I found out how well it worked when I finally told my son what I had been doing on those jobs out of town, and that I had gotten the warden's permission to take him on as an assistant and train him to handle the chair himself when I retired. I could tell from the way he took it that he was as thunderstruck at this as I had been thirty years before when my father had taken me into his confidence.

"Electrocutioner?" said my son. "An *electrocutioner?*"

"Well, there's no disgrace to it," I said. "And since it's got to be done, and somebody has to do it, why not keep it in the family? If you knew anything about it, you'd know it's a profession that's often passed down in a family from generation to generation. What's wrong with a good, sound tradition? If more people believed in tradition you wouldn't have so many troubles in the world today."

It was the kind of argument that would have been more than enough to convince me when I was his age. What I hadn't taken into account was that my son wasn't like me, such as I wanted him to be. He was a grown man in his own right, but a grown man who had never settled down to his responsibilities. I had always kept closing my eyes to that, I had always seen him the way I wanted to and not the way he was.

When he left college after a year, I said, all right, there are some people who aren't made for college, I never went there, so what difference does it make. When he went out with one girl after another and could never make up his mind to marrying any of them, I said, well, he's young, he's sowing his wild oats, the time will come soon enough when he's ready to take care of a home and family. When he sat daydreaming in the shop instead of tending to business I never made a fuss about it. I knew when he put his mind to it he was as good an electrician as you could ask for, and in these soft times people are allowed to do a lot more dreaming and a lot less working than they used to.

The truth was that the only thing that mattered to me was being his friend. For all his faults he was a fine-looking boy with a good mind. He wasn't much for mixing with people, but if he wanted to he could win anyone over. And in the back of my mind all the while he was growing up was the thought that he was the only one who would learn my secret some day, and would share it with me, and make it easier to bear. I'm not secretive by nature. A man like me needs a thought like that to sustain him.

So when the time came to tell him he shook his head and said no. I felt that my legs had been kicked out from under me. I argued with him and he still said no, and I lost my temper.

"Are you against capital punishment?" I asked him. "You don't have to apologize if you are. I'd think all the more of you, if that's your only reason."

"I don't know if it is," he said.

"Well, you ought to make up your mind one way or the other," I told him. "I'd hate to think you were like every other hypocrite around who says it's all right to condemn a man to the electric chair and all wrong to pull the switch."

"Do I have to be the one to pull it?" he said. "Do you?"

"Somebody has to do it. Somebody always has to do the dirty work for the rest of us. It's not like the Old Testament days when everybody did it for himself. Do you know how they executed a man in those days? They laid him on the ground tied hand and foot, and everybody around had to heave rocks on him until he was crushed to death. They didn't invite anybody to stand around and watch. You wouldn't have had much choice then, would you?"

"I don't know," he said. And then because he was as smart as they come and knew how to turn your words against you, he said, "After all, I'm not without sin."

"Don't talk like a child," I said. "You're without the sin of murder on you or any kind of sin that calls for execution. And if you're so sure the Bible has all the answers, you might remember that you're supposed to render unto Caesar the things that are Caesar's."

"Well," he said, "in this case, I'll let you do the rendering."

I knew then and there from the way he said it and the way he looked at me that it was no use trying to argue with him. The worst of it was knowing that we had somehow moved far apart from each other and would never really be close again. I should have had sense enough to let it go at that. I should have just told him to forget the whole thing and keep his mouth shut about it.

Maybe if I had ever considered the possibility of his saying no, I would have done it. But because I hadn't considered any such possibility I was caught off balance, I was too much upset to think straight. I will admit it now. It was my own fault that I made an issue of things and led him to ask the one question he should never have asked.

"I see," I told him. "It's the same old story, isn't it? Let somebody else do it. But if they pull your number out of a hat and you have to serve on a jury and send a man to the chair, that's all right with you. At least, it's all right as long as there's somebody else to do the job that you and the judge and every decent citizen wants done. Let's face the facts, boy, you don't have the guts. I'd hate to think of you even walking by the death house. The shop is where you belong. You can be nice and cozy there, wiring up fixtures and ringing the cash register. I can handle my duties without your help."

It hurt me to say it. I had never talked like that to him before, and it hurt. The strange thing was that he didn't seem angry about it; he only looked at me, puzzled.

"Is that all it is to you?" he said. "A duty?"

"Yes."

"But you get paid for it, don't you?"

"I get paid little enough for it."

He kept looking at me that way. "Only a duty?" he said, and never took his eyes off me. "But you enjoy it, don't you?"

That was the question he asked.

You enjoy it, don't you? You stand there looking through a peephole in the wall at the chair. In thirty years I have stood there more than a hundred times looking at that chair. The guards bring somebody in. Usually he is in a daze; sometimes he screams, throws himself around and fights. Sometimes it is a woman, and a woman can be as hard to handle as a man when she is led to the chair. Sooner or later, whoever it is is strapped down and the black hood is dropped over his head. Now your hand is on the switch.

The warden signals, and you pull the switch. The current hits the body like a tremendous rush of air suddenly filling it. The body leaps out of the chair with only the straps holding it back. The head jerks, and a curl of smoke comes from it. You release the switch and the body falls back again.

You do it once more, do it a third time to make sure. And whenever your hand presses the switch you can see in your mind what the current is doing to that body and what the face under the hood must look like.

Enjoy it?

That was the question my son asked me. That was what he said to me, as if I didn't have the same feelings deep down in me that we all have.

Enoy it?

But, my God, how could anyone *not* enjoy it!

GHOSTS
AND MISCELLANEOUS
NIGHTMARES

The ghosts you are about to meet are an unusual breed of individualists; only a few resemble the common run of haunts, and even this minority has its own set of distinguishing features, from O'Brien's nasty revenant to Le Braz's penitents.Also included in this section are stories that resisted easy classification. I refer to the works by Aickman, Lovecraft and Tolkien. The Tolkien piece is taken from his popular novel, *The Hobbit,* but aficionados, completists and collectors ought to note that this version of the Gollum chapter has not been reprinted in the U.S.A. for decades. For further details, see the rubric preceding the story and also the "Afterword."

A student of the French novelist, Gustave Flaubert, GUY DE MAUPASSANT *(1850–1893) wrote a huge number of short stories during his brief life. Many of them deal with the lives of upper- and lower-class French citizens, but a sizable minority dwell upon the supernatural. "The Flayed Hand" is one of the first gruesome tales I ever read, thanks to the pictorial rendering of it by the old EC comic periodical* Classic Comics, *to which I suppose many fortyish Americans owe passing grades on their high school report cards. De Maupassant wrote a second similar tale about a severed hand, but this one, I believe, is the better of the two.*

The Flayed Hand

BY GUY DE MAUPASSANT

One evening about eight months ago I met with some college comrades at the lodgings of our friend Louis R. We drank punch and smoked, talked of literature and art, and made jokes like any other company of young men. Suddenly the door flew open, and one who had been my friend since boyhood burst in like a hurricane.

"Guess where I come from?" he cried.

"I bet on the Mabille," responded one. "No," said another, "you are too gay; you come from borrowing money, from burying a rich uncle, or from pawning your watch." "You are getting sober," cried a third, "and, as you scented the punch in Louis' room, you came up here to get drunk again."

"You are all wrong," he replied. "I come from P., in Normandy, where I have spent eight days, and whence I have brought one of my friends, a great criminal, whom I ask permission to present to you."

With these words he drew from his pocket a long, black hand, from which the skin had been stripped. It had been severed at the wrist. Its dry and shriveled shape, and the narrow, yellowed nails still clinging to the fingers, made it frightful to look upon. The muscles, which showed that its first owner had been possessed of great strength, were bound in place by a strip of parchment-like skin.

"Just fancy," said my friend, "the other day they sold the effects of an old sorcerer, recently deceased, well known in all the country. Every Saturday night he used to go to witch gatherings on a broomstick; he practised the white magic and the black, gave blue milk to the cows, and made them wear tails like that of the companion of Saint Anthony. The old scoundrel always had a deep affection for this hand, which, he said, was that of a celebrated criminal, executed in 1736 for having thrown his lawful wife head first into a well—for which I do not blame him—and then hanging in the belfry the priest who had married him. After this double exploit he went away, and, during his subsequent career, which was brief but exciting, he robbed twelve travelers, smoked a score of monks in their monastery, and made a seraglio of a convent."

"But what are you going to do with this horror?" we cried.

"Eh! parbleu! I will make it the handle to my door-bell and frighten my creditors."

"My friend," said Henry Smith, a big, phlegmatic Englishman, "I believe that this hand is only a kind of Indian meat, preserved by a new process; I advise you to make bouillon of it."

"Rail not, messieurs," said, with the utmost sang froid, a medical student who was three-quarters drunk, "but if you follow my advice, Pierre, you will give this piece of human debris Christian burial, for fear lest its owner should come to demand it. Then, too, this hand has acquired some bad habits, for you know the proverb, 'Who has killed will kill.' "

"And who has drunk will drink," replied the host as he poured out a big glass of punch for the student, who emptied it at a draught and slid dead drunk under the table. His sudden dropping out of the company was greeted with a burst of laughter, and Pierre, raising his glass and saluting the hand, cried:

"I drink to the next visit of thy master."

Then the conversation turned upon other subjects, and shortly afterward each returned to his lodgings.

About two o'clock the next day, as I was passing Pierre's door, I entered and found him reading and smoking.

"Well, how goes it?" said I. "Very well," he responded. "And your hand?"

"My hand? Did you not see it on the bell-pull? I put it there when I returned home last night. But, apropos of this, what do you think? Some idiot, doubtless to play a stupid joke on me, came ringing at my door towards midnight. I demanded who was there, but as no one replied, I went back to bed again, and to sleep."

At this moment the door opened and the landlord, a fat and extremely impertinent person, entered without saluting us.

"Sir," said he, "I pray you to take away immediately that carrion which you have hung to your bell-pull. Unless you do this I shall be compelled to ask you to leave."

"Sir," responded Pierre, with much gravity, "you insult a hand which does not merit it. Know you that it belonged to a man of high breeding?"

The landlord turned on his heel and made his exit, without speaking. Pierre followed him, detached the hand and affixed it to the bell-cord hanging in his alcove.

"That is better," he said. "This hand, like the 'Brother, all must die,' of the Trappists, will give my thoughts a serious turn every night before I sleep."

At the end of an hour I left him and returned to my own apartment.

I slept badly the following night, was nervous and agitated, and several times awoke with a start. Once I imagined, even, that a man had broken into my room, and I sprang up and searched the closets and under the bed. Towards six o'clock in the morning I was commencing to doze at last, when a loud knocking at my door made me jump from my couch. It was my friend Pierre's servant, half dressed, pale and trembling.

"Ah, sir!" cried he, sobbing, "my poor master. Someone has murdered him."

I dressed myself hastily and ran to Pierre's lodgings. The house was full of people disputing together, and everything was in a commotion. Everyone was talking at the same time, recounting and commenting on the occurrence in all sorts of ways. With great difficulty I reached the bedroom, made myself known to those guarding the door and was permitted to enter. Four police officers were standing in the middle of the apartment, pencils in hand, examining every detail, conferring in low voices and writing from time to time in their note-books. Two doctors were in consultation by the bed on which lay the unconscious form of Pierre. He was not dead, but his face was fixed in an expression of the most awful terror. His eyes were open their widest, and the dilated pupils seemed to regard fixedly, with unspeakable horror, something unknown and frightful. His hands were clenched. I raised the quilt, which covered his body from the chin downward, and saw on his neck, deeply sunk in the flesh, the marks of fingers. Some drops of blood spotted his shirt. At that moment one thing struck me. I chanced to notice that the shriveled hand was no longer attached to the bell-cord. The doctors had doubtless removed it to avoid the comments of those entering the chamber where the wounded man lay, because the appearance of this hand was indeed frightful. I did not inquire what had become of it.

I now clip from a newspaper of the next day the story of the crime with all the details that the police were able to procure:

"A frightful attempt was made yesterday on the life of young M. Pierre B., student, who belongs to one of the best families in Normandy. He returned home about ten o'clock in the evening, and excused his valet, Bouvin, from further attendance upon him, saying that he felt fatigued and was going to bed. Towards midnight Bouvin was suddenly awakened by the furious ringing of his master's bell. He was afraid, and lighted a lamp and waited. The bell was silent about a minute, than rang again with such vehemence that the domestic, mad with fright, flew from his room to awaken the concierge, who ran to summon the police, and, at the end of about fifteen minutes, two policemen forced open the door. A horrible sight met their eyes. The furniture was overturned, giving evidence of a fearful struggle between the victim and his assailant. In the middle of the room, upon his back, his body rigid, with livid face and frightfully dilated eyes, lay, motionless, young Pierre B., bearing upon his neck the deep imprints of five fingers. Dr. Bourdean was called immediately, and his report says that the aggressor must have been possessed of prodigious strength and have had an extraordinarily thin and sinewy hand, because the fingers left in the flesh of the victim five holes like those from a pistol ball, and had penetrated until they almost met. There is no clue to the motive of the crime or to its perpetrator. The police are making a thorough investigation."

The following appeared in the same newspaper next day:

"M. Pierre B., the victim of the frightful assault of which we published an account yesterday, has regained consciousness after two hours of the most assiduous care by Dr. Bourdean. His life is not in danger, but it is strongly feared that he has lost his reason. No trace has been found of his assailant."

My poor friend was indeed insane. For seven months I visited him daily at the hospital where we had placed him, but he did not recover the light of reason. In his delirium strange words escaped him, and, like all madmen, he had one fixed idea: he believed himself continually pursued by a specter. One day they came for me in haste, saying he was worse, and when I arrived I found him dying. For two hours he remained very calm, then, suddenly, rising from his bed in spite of our efforts, he cried, waving his arms as if a prey to the most awful terror: "Take it away! Take it away! It strangles me! Help! Help!" Twice he made the circuit of the room, uttering horrible screams, then fell face downward, dead.

As he was an orphan I was charged to take his body to the little village of P., in Normandy, where his parents were buried. It was the place from which he had arrived the evening he found us drinking punch in Louis R.'s room, when he had presented to us the flayed hand. His body was inclosed in a leaden coffin, and four days afterwards I walked sadly beside the old curé, who had given him his first lessons, to the little cemetery where they dug his grave. It was a beautiful day, and sunshine from a cloudless sky flooded the earth. Birds sang from the blackberry bushes where many a time when we were children we had stolen to eat the fruit. Again I saw Pierre and myself creeping along behind the hedge and slipping through the gap that we knew so well, down at the end of the little plot where they bury the poor. Again we would return to the house with cheeks and lips black with the juice of the berries we had eaten. I looked at the bushes; they were covered with fruit; mechanically I picked some and bore it to my mouth. The curé had opened his breviary, and was muttering his prayers in a low voice. I heard at the end of the walk the spades of the gravediggers who were opening the tomb. Suddenly they called out, the curé closed his book, and we went to see what they wished of us. They had found a coffin; in digging a stroke of the pickaxe had started the cover, and we perceived within a skeleton of unusual stature, lying on its back, its hollow eyes seeming yet to menace and defy us. I was troubled, I know not why, and almost afraid.

"Hold!" cried one of the men, "look there! One of the rascal's hands has been severed at the wrist. Ah, here it is!" and he picked up from beside the body a huge withered hand, and held it out to us.

"See," cried the other, laughing, "see how he glares at you, as if he would spring at your throat to make you give him back his hand."

"Go," said the curé, "leave the dead in peace, and close the coffin. We will make poor Pierre's grave elsewhere."

The next day all was finished, and I returned to Paris, after having left fifty francs with the old curé for masses to be said for the repose of the soul of him whose sepulchre we had troubled.

The late British fantasist ROBERT AICKMAN *(1914–1980) wrote many wholly original terror tales and edited several numbers of the Fontana series of "great ghost stories." I considered including "The Hospice" in my earlier anthology of ghost stories but ultimately rejected it because I honestly couldn't unravel its meaning. But over the intervening years, "The Hospice" has continued to haunt me; any work of fiction that exerts such a powerful hold on the imagination must be some sort of masterpiece. Therefore I am rectifying my earlier error by including the tale here. Its power is undeniable, and some, though not all of the mystery is dispellable upon a second reading. But the terror cannot be banished that easily.*

The Hospice

BY ROBERT AICKMAN

It was somewhere at the back of beyond. Maybury would have found it difficult to be more precise.

He was one who, when motoring outside his own territory, preferred to follow a route "given" by one of the automobile organizations, and, on this very occasion, as on other previous ones, he had found reasons to deplore all deviation. This time it had been the works manager's fault. The man had not only poured ridicule on the official route, but had stood at the yard gate in order to make quite certain that Maybury set off by the short cut which, according to him, all the fellows in the firm used, and which departed in the exactly opposite direction.

The most that could be said was that Maybury was presumably at the outer edge of the immense West Midlands conurbation. The outer edge it by now surely must be, as he seemed to have been driving for hours since he left the works, going round and round in large or small circles, asking the way and being unable to understand the answers (when answers were vouchsafed), all the time seemingly more off-course than ever.

Maybury looked at his watch. He *had* been driving for hours. By rights he should have been more than halfway home — considerably more. Even the dashboard light seemed feebler than usual; but by it Maybury saw that soon he would be out of petrol. His mind had not been on that particular matter of petrol.

Dark though it was, Maybury was aware of many trees, mountainous and opaque. It was not, however, that there were no houses. Houses there must be, because on both sides of the road, there were gates; broad single gates, commonly painted white: and, even where there were no gates, there were dim entrances. Presumably it was a costly nineteenth-century housing estate. Almost identical roads seemed to curve away in all directions. The straightforward had been genteelly avoided. As often in such places, the racer-through, the taker of a short cut, was quite systematically penalized. Probably this attitude accounted also for the failure to bring the street lighting fully up-to-date.

Maybury came to a specific bifurcation. It was impossible to make any reasoned choice, and he doubted whether it mattered much in any case.

Maybury stopped the car by the side of the road, then stopped the engine in order to save the waning petrol while he thought. In the end, he opened the door and stepped out into the road. He looked upwards. The moon and stars were almost hidden by the thick trees. It was quiet. The houses were set too far back from the road for the noise of the television sets to be heard, or the blue glare thereof seen. Pedestrians are nowadays rare in such a district at any hour, but now there was no traffic either, nor sound of traffic more remote. Maybury was disturbed by the silence.

He advanced a short distance on foot, as one does at such times. In any case, he had no map, but only a route, from which he had departed quite hopelessly. None the less, even that second and locally preferred route, the one used by all the fellows, had seemed perfectly clear at the time, and as the manager had described it. He supposed that otherwise he might not have been persuaded to embark upon it; not even coerced. As things were, his wonted expedient of merely driving straight ahead until one found some definite sign or other indication, would be dubious, because the petrol might run out first.

Parallel with each side of each road was a narrow made-up footway, with a central gravelly strip. Beyond the strip to Maybury's left was a wilderness of vegetation, traversed by a ditch, beyond which was the hedge-line of the different properties. By the light of the occasional streetlamp, Maybury could see that sometimes there was an owner who had his hedge trimmed, and sometimes an owner who did not. It would be futile to walk any further along the road, though the air was pleasantly warm and aromatic. There were Angela and their son, Tony, awaiting him; and he must resume the fight to rejoin them.

Something shot out at him from the boskage on his left.

He had disturbed a cat, returned to its feral habitude. The first he knew of it was its claws, or conceivably its teeth, sunk into his left leg. There had been no question of ingratiation or cuddling up. Maybury kicked out furiously. The strange sequel was total silence. He must have kicked the cat a long way, because on the instant there was no hint of it. Nor had he seen the colour of the cat, though there was a pool of light at that point on the footway. He fancied he had seen two flaming eyes, but he was not sure even of that. There had been no mew, no scream.

Maybury faltered. His leg really hurt. It hurt so much that he could not bring himself to touch the limb, even to look at it in the lamplight.

He faltered back to the car, and, though his leg made difficulties even in starting it, set off indecisively down the road along which he had just walked. It might well have become a case of its being wise for him to seek a hospital. The deep scratch or bite of a cat might well hold venom, and it was not pleasant to think where the particular cat had been treading, or what it might have been devouring. Maybury again looked at his watch. It was fourteen minutes past eight. Only nine minutes had passed since he had looked at it last.

The road was beginning to straighten out, and the number of entrances to diminish, though the trees remained dense. Possibly, as so often happens, the money had run out before the full development had reached this region of the property. There were still occasional houses, with entries at long and irregular intervals. Lamp posts were becoming fewer also, but Maybury saw that one of them bore a hanging sign of some kind. It was most unlikely to indicate a destination, let alone a destination of use to Maybury, but he eased and stopped none the less, so urgently did he need a clue of some kind. The sign was shaped like a club in a pack of cards, and read:

THE HOSPICE

S   N

O   GOOD FARE   O

M   I

E ACCOMMODA T

The modest words relating to accommodation were curved round the downward pointing extremity of the club.

Maybury decided almost instantly. He was hungry. He was injured. He was lost. He was almost without petrol.

He would enquire for dinner and, if he could telephone home, might even stay the night, though he had neither pyjamas nor electric razor. The gate, made of iron, and more suited, Maybury would have thought, to a farmyard bullpen, was, none the less, wide open. Maybury drove through.

The drive had likewise been surfaced with rather unattractive concrete, and it appeared to have been done some time ago, since there were now many potholes, as if heavy vehicles passed frequently. Maybury's headlights bounced and lurched disconcertingly as he proceeded, but suddenly the drive, which had run quite straight, again as on a modern farm, swerved, and there, on Maybury's left, was The Hospice. He realized that the drive he had come down, if indeed it had been a drive, was not the original main entrance. There was an older, more traditional drive, winding away between rhododendron bushes. All this was visible in bright light from a fixture high above the cornice of the building: almost a floodlight, Maybury thought. He supposed that a new entry had been made for the vehicles of the various suppliers when the place had become—whatever exactly it had become, a private hotel? a guest house? a club? No doubt the management aspired to cater for the occupants of the big houses, now that there were no longer servants in the world.

Maybury locked the car and pushed at the door of the house. It was a solid Victorian door, and it did not respond to Maybury's pressure. Maybury was discouraged by the need to ring, but he rang. He noticed that there was a second bell, lower down, marked NIGHT. Surely it could not yet be night? The great thing was to get in, to feed (the works had offered only packeted sandwiches and flavourless coffee by way of luncheon), to ingratiate himself: before raising questions of petrol, whereabouts, possible accommodation for the night, a telephone call to Angela, disinfectant for his leg. He did not much care for standing alone in a strange place under the bright floodlight, uncertain what was going to happen.

But quite soon the door was opened by a lad with curly fair hair and an untroubled face. He looked like a young athlete, as Maybury at once thought. He was wearing a white jacket and smiling helpfully.

"Dinner? Yes, certainly sir. I fear we've just started, but I'm sure we can fit you in."

To Maybury, the words brought back the seaside boarding houses where he had been taken for holidays when a boy. Punctuality in those days had been almost as important as sobriety.

"If you can give me just a couple of minutes to wash . . ."

"Certainly, sir. This way, please."

Inside, it was not at all like those boarding houses of Maybury's youth. Maybury happened to know exactly what it *was* like. The effect was that produced by the efforts of an expensive and, therefore, rather old-fashioned, furniture emporium if one placed one's whole abode and most of one's cheque-book in its hands. There were hangings on all the walls, and every chair and sofa was upholstered. Colours and fabrics were harmonious but rich. The several standard lamps had immense shades. The polished tables derived from Italian originals. One could perhaps feel that a few upholstered occupants should have been designed and purveyed to harmonize also. As it was, the room was empty, except for the two of them.

The lad held open the door marked "Gentlemen" in script, but then followed Maybury in, which Maybury had not particularly expected. But the lad did not proceed to fuss tiresomely, with soap and towel, as happens somctimes in very expensive hotels, and happened formerly in clubs. All he did was stand about. Maybury reflected that doubtless he was concerned to prevent all possible delay, dinner having started.

The dining-room struck Maybury, immediately he entered, as rather too hot. The central heating must be working with full efficiency. The room was lined with hangings similar to those Maybury had seen in the hall, but apparently even heavier. Possibly noise reduction was among the objects. The ceiling of the room had been brought down in the modern manner, as if to serve the stunted; and any window or windows had disappeared behind swathes.

It is true that knives and forks make a clatter, but there appeared to be no other immediate necessity for costly noise abatement, as the diners werc all extremely quiet; which at first seemed the more unexpected in that most of them were seated, fairly closely packed, at a single long table running down the

central axis of the room. Maybury soon reflected, however, that
if he had been wedged together with a party of total strangers, he
might have found little to say to them either.

This was not put to the test. On each side of the room were four
smaller tables, set endways against the walls, every table set for a
single person, even though big enough to accommodate four, two
on either side; and at one of these, Maybury was settled by the
handsome lad in the white jacket.

Immediately, soup arrived.

The instantaneity of the service (apart from the fact that
Maybury was late) could be accounted for by the large number of
the staff. There were quite certainly four men, all, like the lad, in
white jackets; and two women, both in dark blue dresses. The six
of them were noticeably deft and well set-up, though all were past
their first youth. Maybury could not see more because he had been
placed with his back to the end wall which contained the service
door (as well as, on the other side, the door by which the guests
entered from the lounge). At every table, the single place had
been positioned in that way, so that the occupant saw neither the
service door opening and shutting, nor, in front of him, the face
of another diner.

As a matter of fact, Maybury was the only single diner on that
side of the room (he had been given the second table down, but
did not think that anyone had entered to sit behind him at the first
table); and, on the other side of the room, there was only a single
diner also, he thought, a lady, seated at the second table likewise,
and thus precisely parallel with him.

There was an enormous quantity of soup, in what Maybury
realized was an unusually deep and wide plate. The amplitude of
the plate had at first been masked by the circumstance that round
much of its wide rim was inscribed, in large black letters, THE
HOSPICE; rather in the style of a baby's plate, Maybury thought,
if both lettering and plate had not been so immense. The soup
itself was unusually weighty too; it undoubtedly contained eggs as
well as pulses, and steps had been taken to add "thickening" also.

Maybury was hungry, as has been said, but he was faintly
disconcerted to realize that one of the middle-aged women was
standing quietly behind him as he consumed the not inconsider-
able number of final spoonfuls. The spoons seemed very large
also, at least for modern usages. The woman removed his empty
plate with a reassuring smile.

The second course was there. As she set it before him, the woman spoke confidentially in his ear of the third course: "It's turkey tonight." Her tone was exactly that in which promise is conveyed to a little boy of his favourite dish. It was as if she were Maybury's nanny; even though Maybury had never had a nanny, not exactly. Meanwhile, the second course was a proliferating elaboration of pasta; plainly homemade pasta, probably fabricated that morning. Cheese, in fairly large granules, was strewn across the heap from a large porcelain bowl without Maybury being noticeably consulted.

"Can I have something to drink? A lager will do."

"We have nothing like that, sir." It was as if Maybury knew this perfectly well, but she was prepared to play with him. There might, he thought, have been some warning that the place was unlicensed.

"A pity," said Maybury.

The woman's inflections were beginning to bore him; and he was wondering how much the rich food, all palpably fresh, and homegrown, and of almost unattainable quality, was about to cost him. He doubted very much whether it would be sensible to think of staying the night at The Hospice.

"When you have finished your second course, you may have the opportunity of a word with Mr. Falkner." Maybury recollected that, after all, he had started behind all the others. He must doubtless expect to be a little hustled while he caught up with them. In any case, he was not sure whether or not the implication was that Mr. Falkner might, under certain circumstances, unlock a private liquor store.

Obviously it would help the catching-up process if Maybury ate no more than two-thirds of the pasta fantasy. But the woman in the dark blue dress did not seem to see it like that.

"Can't you eat any more?" she enquired baldly, and no longer addressing Maybury as sir.

"Not if I'm to attempt another course," replied Maybury, quite equably.

"It's turkey tonight," said the woman. "You know how turkey just slips down you?" She still had not removed his plate.

"It's very good," said Maybury firmly. "But I've had enough."

It was as if the woman were not used to such conduct, but, as this was no longer a nursery, she took the plate away.

There was even a slight pause, during which Maybury tried to look round the room without giving an appearance of doing so. The main point seemed to be that everyone was dressed rather formally: all the men in "dark suits", all the women in "long dresses". There was a wide variety of age, but, curiously again, there were more men than women. Conversation still seemed far from general. Maybury could not help wondering whether the solidity of the diet did not contribute here. Then it occurred to him that it was as if most of these people had been with one another for a long time, during which things to talk about might have run out, and possibly with little opportunity for renewal through fresh experience. He had met that in hotels. Naturally, Maybury could not, without seeming rude, examine the one-third of the assembly which was seated behind him.

His slab of turkey appeared. He had caught up, even though by cheating. It was an enormous pile, steaming slightly, and also seeping slightly with a colourless, oily fluid. With it appeared five separate varieties of vegetable in separate dishes, brought on a tray; and a sauceboat, apparently for him alone, of specially compounded fluid, dark red and turgid. A sizeable mound of stuffing completed the repast. The middle-aged woman set it all before him swiftly but, this time, silently, with unmistakable reserve.

The truth was that Maybury had little appetite left. He gazed around, less furtively, to see how the rest were managing. He had to admit that, as far as he could see, they were one and all eating as if their lives depended on it: old as well as young, female as well as male; it was as if all had spent a long, unfed day in the hunting field. "Eating as if their lives depended on it," he said again to himself; then, struck by the absurdity of the phrase when applied to eating, he picked up his knife and fork with resolution.

"Is everything to your liking, Mr. Maybury?"

Again he had been gently taken by surprise. Mr. Falkner was at his shoulder: a sleek man in the most beautiful dinner jacket, an instantly ameliorative maître d'hôtel.

"Perfect, thank you," said Maybury. "But how did you know my name?"

"We like to remember the names of our guests," said Falkner, smiling.

"Yes, but how did you find out *my* name in the first place?"

"We like to think we are proficient at that too, Mr. Maybury."

"I am much impressed," said Maybury. Really he felt irritated

(irritated, at least), but his firm had trained him never to display irritation outside the family circle.

"Not at all," said Falkner genially. "Whatever our vocation in life, we may as well do what we can to excel." He settled the matter by dropping the subject. "Is there anything I can get for you? Anything you would like?"

"No, thank you very much. I have plenty."

"Thank *you*, Mr. Maybury. If you wish to speak to me at any time, I am normally available in my office. Now I will leave you to the enjoyment of your meal. I may tell you, in confidence, that there is steamed fruit pudding to follow."

He went quietly forward on his round of the room, speaking to perhaps one person in three at the long, central table; mainly, it seemed, to the older people, as was no doubt to be expected. Falkner wore very elegant black suede shoes, which reminded Maybury of the injury to his own leg, about which he had done nothing, though it might well be septic, even endangering the limb itself, perhaps the whole system.

He was considerably enraged by Falkner's performance about his name, especially as he could find no answer to the puzzle. He felt that he had been placed, almost deliberately, at an undignified disadvantage. Falkner's patronizing conduct in this trifling matter was of a piece with the nannying attitude of the waitress. Moreover, was the unexplained discovery of his name such a trifle, after all? Maybury felt that it had made him vulnerable in other matters also, however undefined. It was the last straw in the matter of his eating any more turkey. He no longer had any appetite whatever.

He began to pass everything systematically through his mind, as he had been trained to do; and almost immediately surmised the answer. In his car was a blue-bound file which on its front bore his name: "Mr. Lucas Maybury"; and this file he supposed that he must have left, name-upwards, on the driving seat, as he commonly did. All the same, the name was merely typed on a sticky label, and would not have been easy to make out through the car window. But he then remembered the floodlight. Even so, quite an effort had been necessary on someone's part, and he wondered who had made that effort. Again he guessed the answer: it was Falkner himself who had been snooping. What would Falkner have done if Maybury had parked the car outside the floodlighted area, as would have been perfectly possible? Used a torch? Perhaps even skeleton keys?

That was absurd.

And how much did the whole thing matter? People in business often had these little vanities, and often had he encountered them. People would do almost anything to feed them. Probably he had one or two himself. The great thing when meeting any situation was to extract the essentials and to concentrate upon them.

To some of the people Falkner was speaking for quite a period of time, while, as Maybury noticed, those seated next to them, previously saying little in most cases, now said nothing at all, but confined themselves entirely to eating. Some of the people at the long table were not merely elderly, he had observed, but positively senile: drooling, watery-eyed, and almost hairless; but even they seemed to be eating away with the best. Maybury had the horrid idea about them that eating was all they did do. "They lived for eating": another nursery expression, Maybury reflected; and at last he had come upon those of whom it might be true. Some of these people might well relate to rich foods as alcoholics relate to excisable spirits. He found it more nauseating than any sottishness; of which he had seen a certain amount.

Falkner was proceeding so slowly, showing so much professional consideration, that he had not yet reached the lady who sat by herself parallel with Maybury, on the other side of the room. At her Maybury now stared more frankly. Black hair reached her shoulders, and she wore what appeared to be a silk evening dress, a real "model", Maybury thought (though he did not really know), in many colours; but her expression was of such sadness, suffering, and exhaustion that Maybury was sincerely shocked, especially as once she must, he was sure, have been beautiful, indeed, in a way, still was. Surely so unhappy, even tragic, a figure as that could not be ploughing through a big slab of turkey with five vegetables? Without caution or courtesy, Maybury half rose to his feet in order to look.

"Eat up, sir. Why you've hardly started!" His tormentor had quietly returned to him. What was more, the tragic lady *did* appear to be eating.

"I've had enough. I'm sorry, it's very good, but I've had enough."

"You said that before, sir, and, look here you are, still eating away." He knew that he had, indeed, used those exact words. Crises are met by clichés.

"I've eaten quite enough."

"That's not necessarily for each of us to say, is it?"

"I want no more to eat of any kind. Please take all this away and just bring me a black coffee. When the time comes, if you like. I don't mind waiting." Though Maybury did mind waiting, it was necessary to remain in control.

The woman did the last thing Maybury could have expected her to do. She picked up his laden plate (he had at least helped himself to everything) and, with force, dashed it on the floor. Even then the plate itself did not break, but gravy and five vegetables and rich stuffing spread across the thick, patterned, wall-to-wall carpet. Complete, in place of comparative, silence followed in the whole room; though there was still, as Maybury even then observed, the muted clashing of cutlery. Indeed, his own knife and fork were still in his hands.

Falkner returned round the bottom end of the long table.

"Mulligan," he asked, "how many more times?" His tone was as quiet as ever. Maybury had not realized that the alarming woman was Irish.

"Mr. Maybury," Falkner continued. "I entirely understand your difficulty. There is naturally no obligation to partake of anything you do not wish. I am only sorry for what has happened. It must seem very poor service on our part. Perhaps you would prefer to go into our lounge? Would you care simply for some coffee?"

"Yes," said Maybury, concentrating upon the essential. "I should, please. Indeed, I had already ordered a black coffee. Could I possibly have a pot of it?"

He had to step with care over the mess on the floor, looking downward. As he did so, he saw something more curious. A central rail ran the length of the long table a few inches above the floor. To this rail, one of the male guests was attached by a fetter round his left ankle.

Maybury, now considerably shaken, had rather expected to be alone in the lounge until the coffee arrived. But he had no sooner dropped down upon one of the massive sofas (it could easily have seated five in a row, at least two of them stout), than the handsome boy appeared from somewhere and proceeded merely to stand about, as at an earlier phase of the evening. There were no illustrated papers to be seen, nor even brochures about Beautiful Britain, and Maybury found the lad's presence irksome. All the same, he did not quite dare to say, "There's nothing I want." He could think of nothing to say or to do; nor did the boy speak, or seem to have anything particular to do either. It was obvious that his presence could hardly be required there when everyone was in the dining room. Presumably they would soon be passing on to fruit pudding. Maybury was aware that he had yet to pay his bill. There was a baffled but considerable pause.

Much to his surprise, it was Mulligan who in the end brought him the coffee. It was a single cup, not a pot; and even the cup was of such a size that Maybury, for once that evening, could have done with a bigger. At once he divined that coffee was outside the régime of the place, and that he was being specially compensated, though he might well have to pay extra for it. He had vaguely supposed that Mulligan would have been helping to mop up in the dining-room. Mulligan, in fact, seemed quite undisturbed.

"Sugar, sir?" she said.

"One lump, please," said Maybury, eyeing the size of the cup.

He did not fail to notice that, before going, she exchanged a glance with the handsome lad. He was young enough to be her son, and the glance might mean anything or nothing.

While Maybury was trying to make the most of his meagre coffee and to ignore the presence of the lad, who must surely be bored, the door from the dining-room opened, and the tragic lady from the other side of the room appeared.

"Close the door, will you?" she said to the boy. The boy closed the door, and then stood about again, watching them.

"Do you mind if I join you?" the lady asked Maybury.

"I should be delighted."

She was really rather lovely in her melancholy way, her dress was as splendid as Maybury had supposed, and there was in her demeanour an element that could only be called stately. Maybury was unaccustomed to that.

She sat, not at the other end of the sofa, but at the centre of it. It struck Maybury that the rich way she was dressed might almost have been devised to harmonize with the rich way the room was decorated. She wore complicated, oriental-looking earrings, with pink translucent stones, like rosé diamonds (perhaps they *were* diamonds); and silver shoes. Her perfume was heavy and distinctive.

"My name is Cécile Céliména,'" she said. "How do you do? I am supposed to be related to the composer, Chaminade."

"How do you do?" said Maybury. "My name is Lucas Maybury,

and my only important relation is Solway Short. In fact, he's my cousin."

They shook hands. Her hand was very soft and white, and she wore a number of rings, which Maybury thought looked real and valuable (though he could not really tell). In order to shake hands with him, she turned the whole upper part of her body towards him.

"Who is that gentleman you mention?" she asked.

"Solway Short? The racing motorist. You must have seen him on the television."

"I do not watch the television."

"Quite right. It's almost entirely a waste of time."

"If you do not wish to waste time, why are you at The Hospice?"

The lad, still observing them, shifted, noticeably, from one leg to the other.

"I am here for dinner. I am just passing through."

"Oh! You are going then?"

Maybury hesitated. She was attractive and, for the moment, he did not wish to go. "I suppose so. When I've paid my bill and found out where I can get some petrol. My tank's almost empty. As a matter of fact, I'm lost. I've lost my way."

"Most of us here are lost."

"Why here? What makes you come here?"

"We come for the food and the peace and the warmth and the rest."

"A tremendous *amount* of food, I thought."

"That's necessary. It's the restorative, you might say."

"I'm not sure that I quite fit in," said Maybury. And then he added: "I shouldn't have thought that you did either."

"Oh, but I do! Whatever makes you think not?" She seemed quite anxious about it, so that Maybury supposed he had taken the wrong line.

He made the best of it. "It's just that you seem a little different from what I have seen of the others."

"In what way, different?" she asked, really anxious, and looking at him with concentration.

"To start with, more beautiful. You are very beautiful," he said, even though the lad was there, certainly taking in every word.

"That is kind of you to say." Unexpectedly she stretched across the short distance between them and took his hand. "What did you say your name was?"

"Lucas Maybury."

"Do people call you Luke?"

"No, I dislike it. I'm not a Luke sort of person."

"But your wife can't call you Lucas?"

"I'm afraid she does." It was a fishing question he could have done without.

"Lucas? Oh no, it's such a cold name." She was still holding his hand.

"I'm very sorry about it. Would you like me to order you some coffee?"

"No, no. Coffee is not right; it is stimulating, wakeful, overexciting, unquiet." She was gazing at him again with sad eyes.

"This is a curious place," said Maybury, giving her hand a squeeze. It was surely becoming remarkable that none of the other guests had yet appeared.

"I could not live without The Hospice," she replied.

"Do you come here often?" It was a ludicrously conventional form of words.

"Of course. Life would be impossible otherwise. All those people in the world without enough food, living without love, without even proper clothes to keep the cold out."

During dinner it had become as hot in the lounge, Maybury thought, as it had been in the dining-room.

Her tragic face sought his understanding. None the less, the line she had taken up was not a favourite of his. He preferred problems to which solutions were at least possible. He had been warned against the other kind.

"Yes," he said. "I know what you mean, of course."

"There are millions and millions of people all over the world with no clothes at all," she cried, withdrawing her hand.

"Not quite," Maybury said, smiling. "Not quite that. Or not yet."

He knew the risks perfectly well, and thought as little about them as possible. One had to survive, and also to look after one's dependents.

"In any case," he continued, trying to lighten the tone, "that hardly applies to you. I have seldom seen a more gorgeous dress."

"Yes," she replied with simple gravity. "It comes from Rome. Would you like to touch it?"

Naturally, Maybury would have liked, but, equally naturally, was held back by the presence of the watchful lad.

"Touch it," she commanded in a low voice. "God, what are you waiting for? Touch it." She seized his left hand again and forced it against her warm, silky breast. The lad seemed to take no more and no less notice than of anything else.

"Forget. Let go. What is life for, for God's sake?" There was a passionate earnestness about her which might rob any such man as Maybury of all assessment, but he was still essentially outside the situation. As a matter of fact, he had never in his life lost *all* control, and he was pretty sure by now that, for better or for worse, he was incapable of it.

She twisted round until her legs were extended the length of the sofa, and her head was on his lap, or more precisely on his thighs. She had moved so deftly as not even to have disordered her skirt. Her perfume wafted upwards.

"Stop glancing at Vincent," she gurgled up at him. "I'll tell you something about Vincent. Though you may think he looks like a Greek God, the simple fact is that he hasn't got what it takes, he's impotent."

Maybury was embarrassed, of course. All the same, what he reflected was that often there were horses for courses, and often no more to be said about a certain kind of situation than that one thing.

It did not matter much what he reflected, because when she had spoken, Vincent had brusquely left the room through what Maybury supposed to be the service door.

"Thank the Lord," he could not help remarking naïvely.

"He's gone for reinforcements," she said. "We'll soon see."

Where were the other guests? Where, by now, could they be? All the same, Maybury's spirits were authentically rising and he began caressing her more intimately.

Then, suddenly, it seemed that everyone was in the room at once, and this time all talking and fussing.

She sat herself up, none too precipitately, and with her lips close to his ear, said, "Come to me later. Number 23."

It was quite impossible for Maybury to point out that he was not staying the night in The Hospice.

Falkner had appeared.

"To bed, all," he cried genially, subduing the crepitation on the instant.

Maybury, unentangled once more, looked at his watch. It seemed to be precisely ten o'clock. That, no doubt, was the point.

Still it seemed very close upon a heavy meal.

No one moved much, but no one spoke either.

"To bed, all of you," said Falkner again, this time in a tone which might almost be described as roguish. Maybury's lady rose to her feet.

All of them filtered away, Maybury's lady among them. She had spoken no further word, made no further gesture.

Maybury was alone with Falker.

"Let me remove your cup," said Falkner courteously.

"Before I ask for my bill," said Maybury, "I wonder if you could tell me where I might possibly find some petrol at this hour?"

"Are you out of petrol?" enquired Falkner.

"Almost."

"There's nothing open at night within twenty miles. Not nowadays. Something to do with our new friends, the Arabs, I believe. All I can suggest is that I syphon some petrol from the tank of our own vehicle. It is a quite large vehicle and it has a large tank."

"I couldn't possibly put you to that trouble." In any case, he, Maybury, did not know exactly how to do it. He had heard of it, but it had never arisen before in his own life.

The lad, Vincent, reappeared, still looking pink, Maybury thought, though it was difficult to be sure with such a glowing skin. Vincent began to lock up; a quite serious process, it seemed, rather as in great-grandparental days, when prowling desperadoes were to be feared.

"No trouble at all, Mr. Maybury," said Falkner. "Vincent here can do it easily, or another member of my staff."

"Well," said Maybury, "if it would be all right . . ."

"Vincent," directed Falkner, "don't bolt and padlock the front door yet. Mr. Maybury intends to leave us."

"Very good," said Vincent, gruffly.

"Now if we could go to your car, Mr. Maybury, you could then drive it round to the back. I will show you the way. I must apologise for putting you to this extra trouble, but the other vehicle takes some time to start, especially at night."

Vincent had opened the front door for them.

"After you, Mr. Maybury," said Falkner.

Where it had been excessively hot within, it duly proved to be excessively cold without. The floodlight had been turned off. The moon had "gone in", as Maybury believed the saying was; and all the stars had apparently gone in with it.

Still, the distance to the car was not great. Maybury soon found it in the thick darkness, with Falkner coming quietly step by step behind him.

"Perhaps I had better go back and get a torch?" remarked Falkner.

So there duly was a torch. If brought to Maybury's mind the matter of the office file with his name on it, and, as he unlocked the car door, there the file was, exactly as had supposed, and, assuredly, name uppermost. Maybury threw it across to the back seat.

Falkner's electric torch was a heavy service object which drenched a wide area in cold, white light.

"May I sit beside you, Mr. Maybury?" He closed the offside door behind him.

Maybury had already turned on the headlights, torch or no torch, and was pushing at the starter, which seemed obdurate.

It was not, he thought, that there was anything wrong with it, but rather that there was something wrong with him. The sensation was exactly like a nightmare. He had of course done it hundreds of times, probably thousands of times; but now, when after all it really mattered, he simply could not manage it, had, quite incredibly, somehow lost the simple knack of it. He often endured bad dreams of just this kind. He found time with part of his mind to wonder whether this was not a bad dream. But it was to be presumed not, since now he did not wake, as we soon do when once we realize that we are dreaming.

"I wish I could be of some help," remarked Falkner, who had shut off his torch, "but I am not accustomed to the make of car. I might easily do more harm than good." He spoke with his usual bland geniality.

Maybury was irritated again. The make of car was one of the commonest there is: trust the firm for that. All the same, he knew it was entirely his own fault that he could not make the car start, and not in the least Falkner's. He felt as if he were going mad. "I don't quite know what to suggest," he said; and added: "If, as you say, there's no garage."

"Perhaps Cromie could be of assistance," said Falkner. "Cromie has been with us quite a long time and is a wizard with any mechanical problem."

No one could say that Falkner was pressing Maybury to stay the night, or even hinting towards it, as one might expect. Maybury wondered whether the funny place was not, in fact, full up. It seemed the most likely answer. Not that Maybury wished to stay the night: far from it.

"I'm not sure," he said, "that I have the right to disturb anyone else."

"Cromie is on night duty," replied Falkner. "He is always on night duty. That is what we employ him for. I will fetch him."

He turned on the torch once more, stepped out of the car, and disappeared into the house, shutting the front door behind him, lest the cold air enter.

In the end, the front door reopened, and Falkner re-emerged. He still wore no coat over his dinner suit, and seemed to ignore the cold. Falkner was followed by a burly but shapeless and shambling figure, whom Maybury first saw indistinctly standing behind Falkner in the light from inside the house.

"Cromie will soon put things to rights," said Falkner, opening the door of the car. "Won't you, Cromie?" It was much as one speaks to a friendly retriever.

But there was little, Maybury felt, that was friendly about Cromie. Maybury had to admit to himself that on the instant he found Cromie alarming, even though, what with one thing and another, there was little to be seen of him.

"Now what exactly seems wrong, Mr. Maybury?" asked Falkner. "Just tell Cromie what it is."

Falkner himself had not attempted to re-enter the car, but Cromie forced himself in and was sprawling in the front seat, next to Maybury, where Angela normally sat. He really did seem a very big, bulging person, but Maybury decisively preferred not to look at him, though the glow cast backwards from the headlights provided a certain illumination.

Maybury could not acknowledge that for some degrading reason he was unable to operate the starter, and so had to claim there was something wrong with it. He was unable not to see Cromie's huge, badly misshapen, yellow hands, both of them, as he tugged with both of them at the knob, forcing it in and out with such violence that Maybury cried out: "Less force. You'll wreck it."

"Careful, Cromie," said Falkner from outside the car. "Most of Cromie's work is on a big scale," he explained to Maybury.

But violence proved effective, as so often. Within seconds, the car engine was humming away.

"Thank you very much," said Maybury.

Cromie made no detectable response, nor did he move.

"Come on out, Cromie," said Falkner. "Come on out of it."

Cromie duly extricated himself and shambled off into the darkness.

"Now," said Maybury, brisking up as the engine purred. "Where do we go for the petrol?"

There was the slightest of pauses. Then Falkner spoke from the dimness outside. "Mr. Maybury, I have remembered something. It is not petrol that we have in our tank. It is, of course, diesel oil. I must apologise for such a stupid mistake."

Maybury was not merely irritated, not merely scared: he was infuriated. With rage and confusion he found it impossible to speak at all. No one in the modern world could confuse diesel oil and petrol in that way. But what could he possibly do?

Falkner, standing outside the open door of the car, spoke again. "I am extremely sorry, Mr. Maybury. Would you permit me to make some amends by inviting you to spend the night with us free of charge, except perhaps for the dinner?"

Within the last few minutes Maybury had suspected that this moment was bound to come in one form or another.

"Thank you," he said less than graciously. "I suppose I had better accept."

"We shall try to make you comfortable," said Falkner.

Maybury turned off the headlights, climbed out of the car once more, shut and, for what it was worth, locked the door, and followed Falkner back into the house. This time Falkner completed the locking and bolting of the front door that he had instructed Vincent to omit.

"I have no luggage of any kind," remarked Maybury, still very much on the defensive.

"That may solve itself," said Falkner, straightening up from the bottom bolt and smoothing his dinner jacket. "There's something I ought to explain. But will you first excuse me a moment?" He went out through the door at the back of the lounge.

Hotels really have become far too hot, thought Maybury. It positively addled the brain.

Falkner returned. "There is something I ought to explain," he said again. "We have no single rooms, partly because many of our visitors prefer not to be alone at night. The best we can do for you in your emergency, Mr. Maybury, is to offer you the share of a room with another guest. It is a large room and there are two beds. It is a sheer stroke of good luck that at present there is only one guest in the room, Mr. Bannard. Mr. Bannard will be glad of your company, I am certain, and you will be quite safe with him. He is a very pleasant person, I can assure you. I have just sent a message up asking him if he can possibly come down, so that I can introduce you. He is always very helpful, and I think he will be here in a moment. Mr. Bannard has been with us for some time, so that I am sure he will be able to fit you up with pyjamas and so forth."

It was just about the last thing that Maybury wanted from any point of view, but he had learned that it was of a kind that is peculiarly difficult to protest against, without somehow putting oneself in the wrong with other people. Besides he supposed that he was now committed to a night in the place, and therefore to all the implications, whatever they might be, or very nearly so.

"I should like to telephone my wife, if I may," Maybury said. Angela had been steadily on his mind for some time.

"I fear that's impossible, Mr. Maybury," replied Falkner. "I'm so sorry."

"How can it be impossible?"

"In order to reduce tension and sustain the atmosphere that our guests prefer, we have no external telephone. Only an internal link between my quarters and the proprietors."

"But how can you run a hotel in the modern world without a telephone?"

"Most of our guests are regulars. Many of them come again and again, and the last thing they come for is to hear a telephone ringing the whole time with all the strain it involves."

"They must be half round the bend," snapped Maybury, before he could stop himself.

"Mr. Maybury," replied Falkner, "I have to remind you of two things. The first is that I have invited you to be our guest in the fuller sense of the word. The second is that, although you attach so much importance to efficiency, you none the less appear to have set out on a long journey at night with very little petrol in your tank. Possibly you should think yourself fortunate that you are not spending the night stranded on some motorway."

"I'm sorry," said Maybury, "but I simply must telephone my wife. Soon she'll be out of her mind with worry."

"I shouldn't think so, Mr. Maybury," said Falkner smiling.

"Concerned, we must hope; but not quite out of her mind."

Maybury could have hit him, but at that moment a stranger entered.

"Ah, Mr. Bannard," said Mr Falkner, and introduced them. They actually shook hands. "You won't mind, Mr. Bannard, if Mr. Maybury shares your room?"

Bannard was a slender, bony little man, of about Maybury's age. He was bald, with a rim of curly red hair. He had slightly glaucous grey-green eyes of the kind that often go with red hair. In the present environment, he was quite perky, but Maybury wondered how he would make out in the world beyond. Perhaps, however, this was because Bannard was too shrimp-like to look his best in pyjamas.

"I should be delighted to share my room with anyone," replied Bannard. "I'm lonely by myself."

"Splendid," said Falkner coolly. "Perhaps you'd lead Mr. Maybury upstairs and lend him some pyjamas? You must remember that he is a stranger to us and doesn't yet know all our ways."

"Delighted, delighted," exclaimed Bannard.

"Well, then," said Falkner. "Is there anything you would like, Mr. Maybury, before you go upstairs?"

"Only a telephone," rejoined Maybury, still recalcitrant. He simply did not believe Falkner. No one in the modern world could live without a telephone, let alone run a business without one. He had begun uneasily to wonder if Falkner had spoken the whole truth about the petrol and the diesel fuel either.

"Anything you would like that we are in a position to provide, Mr. Maybury?" persisted Falkner, with offensive specificity.

"There's no telephone *here*," put in Bannard, whose voice was noticeably high, even squeaky.

"In that case, nothing," said Maybury. "But I don't know what my wife will do with herself."

"None of us knows that," said Bannard superfluously, and cackled for a second.

"Good-night, Mr Maybury. Thank you, Mr. Bannard."

Maybury was almost surprised to discover, as he followed Bannard upstairs, that it seemed a perfectly normal hotel, though overheated and decorated over-heavily. On the first landing was a full-sized reproduction of a chieftain in scarlet tartan by Raeburn. Maybury knew the picture, because it had been chosen for the firm's calendar one year, though ever since they had used girls. Bannard lived on the second floor, where the picture on the landing was smaller, and depicted ladies and gentlemen in riding dress taking refreshments together.

"Not too much noise," said Bannard. "We have some very light sleepers amongst us."

The corridors were down to half-illumination for the night watches, and distinctly sinister. Maybury crept foolishly along and almost stole into Bannard's room.

"No," said Bannard in a giggling whisper. "Not Number 13, not yet Number 12 A."

As a matter of fact Maybury had not noticed the number on the door that Bannard was now cautiously closing, and he did not feel called upon to rejoin.

"Do be quiet taking your things off, old man," said Bannard softly. "When once you've woken people who've been properly asleep, you can never quite tell. It's a bad thing to do."

It was a large square room, and the two beds were in exactly opposite corners, somewhat to Maybury's relief. The light had been on when they entered. Maybury surmised that even the unnecessary clicking of switches was to be eschewed.

"That's your bed," whispered Bannard, pointing jocularly.

So far Maybury had removed only his shoes. He could have done without Bannard staring at him and without Bannard's affable grin.

"Or perhaps you'd rather we did something before settling down?" whispered Bannard.

"No thank you," replied Maybury. "It's been a long day." He was trying to keep his voice reasonably low, but he absolutely refused to whisper.

"To be sure it has," said Bannard, rising to much the volume that Maybury had employed. "Night-night then. The best thing is to get to sleep quickly." His tone was similar to that which seemed habitual with Falkner.

Bannard climbed agilely into his own bed, and lay on his back peering at Maybury over the sheets.

"Hang your suit in the cupboard," said Bannard, who had already done likewise. "There's room."

"Thank you," said Maybury. "Where do I find the pyjamas?"

"Top drawer," said Bannard. "Help yourself. They're all alike."

And, indeed, the drawer proved to be virtually filled with

apparently identical suits of pyjamas.

"It's between seasons," said Bannard. "Neither proper summer, nor proper winter."

"Many thanks for the loan," said Maybury, though the pyjamas were considerably too small for him.

"The bathroom's in there," said Bannard.

When Maybury returned, he opened the door of the cupboard. It was a big cupboard and it was almost filled by a long line of (presumably) Bannard's suits.

"There's room," said Bannard once more. "Find yourself an empty hanger. Make yourself at home."

While balancing his trousers on the hanger and suspending it from the rail, Maybury again became aware of the injury to his leg. He had hustled so rapidly into Bannard's pyjamas that, for better or for worse, he had not even looked at the scar.

"What's the matter?" asked Bannard on the instant. "Hurt yourself, have you?"

"It was a damned cat scratched me," replied Maybury, without thinking very much.

But this time he decided to look. With some difficulty and some pain, he rolled up the tight pyjama leg. It was a quite nasty gash and there was much dried blood. He realized that he had not even thought about washing the wound. In so far as he had been worrying about anything habitual, he had been worrying about Angela.

"Don't show it to me," squeaked out Bannard, forgetting not to make a noise. All the same, he was sitting up in bed and staring as if his eyes would pop. "It's bad for me to see things like that. I'm upset by them."

"Don't worry," said Maybury. "I'm sure it's not as serious as it looks." In fact, he was far from sure; and he was aware also that it had not been quite what Bannard was concerned about.

"I don't want to know anything about it," said Bannard.

Maybury made no reply but simply rolled down the pyjama leg. About his injury too there was plainly nothing to be done. Even a request for Vaseline might lead to hysterics. Maybury tried to concentrate upon the reflection that if nothing worse had followed from the gash by now, then nothing worse might ever follow.

Bannard, however, was still sitting up in bed. He was looking pale. "I come here to forget things like that," he said. "We all do."

His voice was shaking.

"Shall I turn the light out?" enquired Maybury. "As I'm the one who's still up?"

"I don't usually do that," said Bannard, reclining once more, none the less. "It can make things unnecessarily difficult. But there's you to be considered too."

"It's your room," said Maybury, hesitating.

"All right," said Bannard. "If you wish. Turn it out. Tonight anyway." Maybury did his injured leg no good when stumbling back to his bed. All the same, he managed to arrive there.

"I'm only here for one night," he said more to the darkness than to Bannard. "You'll be on your own again tomorrow."

Bannard made no reply, and, indeed, it seemed to Maybury as if he were no longer there, that Bannard was not an organism that could function in the dark. Maybury refrained from raising any question of drawing back a curtain (the curtains were as long and heavy as elsewhere), or of letting in a little night air. Things, he felt, were better left more or less as they were.

It was completely dark. It was completely silent. It was far too hot.

Maybury wondered what the time was. He had lost all touch. Unfortunately, his watch lacked a luminous dial.

He doubted whether he would ever sleep, but the night had to be endured somehow. For Angela it must be even harder—far harder. At the best, he had never seen himself as a first-class husband, able to provide a superfluity, eager to be protective. Things would become quite impossible, if he were to lose a leg. But, with modern medicine, that might be avoidable, even at the worst: he should be able to continue struggling on for some time yet.

As stealthily as possible he insinuated himself from between the burning blankets and sheets on to the surface of the bed. He lay there like a dying fish, trying not to make another movement of any kind.

He became almost cataleptic with inner exertion. It was not a promising recipe for slumber. In the end, he thought he could detect Bannard's breathing, far, far away. So Bannard was still there. Fantasy and reality are different things. No one could tell whether Bannard slept or waked, but it had in any case become a quite important aim not to resume general conversation with Bannard. Half a lifetime passed.

There could be no doubt, now, that Bannard was both still in the room and also awake. Perceptibly, he was on the move. Maybury's body contracted with speculation as to whether Bannard in the total blackness was making toward his corner. Maybury felt that he was only half his normal size.

Bannard edged and groped interminably. Of course Maybury had been unfair to him in extinguishing the light, and the present anxiety was doubtless no more than the price to be paid.

Bannard himself seemed certainly to be entering into the spirit of the situation: possibly he had not turned the light on because he could not reach the switch; but there seemed more to it than that. Bannard could be thought of as committed to a positive effort in the direction of silence, in order that Maybury, the guest for a night, should not be disturbed. Maybury could hardly hear him moving at all, though perhaps it was a gamble whether this was consideration or menace. Maybury would hardly have been surprised if the next event had been hands on his throat.

But, in fact, the next event was Bannard reaching the door and opening it, with vast delicacy and slowness. It was a considerable anticlimax, and not palpably outside the order of nature, but Maybury did not feel fully reassured as he rigidly watched the column of dim light from the passage slowly widen and then slowly narrow until it vanished with the faint click of the handle. Plainly there was little to worry about, after all, but Maybury had probably reached that level of anxiety where almost any new event merely causes new stress. Soon, moreover, there would be the stress of Bannard's return. Maybury half realized that he was in a grotesque condition to be so upset, when Bannard was, in fact, showing him all possible consideration. Once more he reflected that poor Angela's plight was far worse.

Thinking about Angela's plight, and how sweet, at the bottom of everything, she really was, Maybury felt more wakeful than ever, as he awaited Bannard's return, surely imminent, surely. Sleep was impossible until Bannard had returned.

But still Bannard did not return. Maybury began to wonder whether something had gone wrong with his own time faculty, such as it was; something, that is, of medical significance. That whole evening and night, from soon after his commitment to the recommended route, he had been in doubt about his place in the universe, about what people called the state of his nerves. Here was evidence that he had good reason for anxiety.

Then, from somewhere within the house, came a shattering, ear-piercing scream, and then another, and another. It was impossible to tell whether the din came from near or far; still less whether it was female or male. Maybury had not known that the human organism could make so loud a noise, even in the bitterest distress. It was shattering to listen to; especially in the enclosed, hot, total darkness. And this was nothing momentary: the screaming went on and on, a paroxysm, until Maybury had to clutch at himself not to scream in response.

He fell off the bed and floundered about for the heavy curtains. Some light on the scene there must be: if possible, some new air in the room. He found the curtains within a moment, and dragged back first one, and then the other.

There was no more light than before.

Shutters, perhaps? Maybury's arm stretched out gingerly. He could feel neither wood nor metal.

The light switch. It must be found.

While Maybury fell about in the darkness, the screaming stopped on a ghoulish gurgle: perhaps as if the sufferer had vomited immensely and then passed out; or perhaps as if the sufferer had in mercy passed away altogether. Maybury continued to search.

It was harder than ever to say how long it took, but in the end he found the switch, and the immediate mystery was explained. Behind the drawback curtains was, as the children say, just wall. The room apparently had no window. The curtains were mere decoration.

All was silent once more: once more extremely silent. Bannard's bed was turned back as neatly as if in the full light of day.

Maybury cast off Bannard's pyjamas and, as quickly as his state permitted, resumed his own clothes. Not that he had any very definite course of action. Simply it seemed better to be fully dressed. He looked vaguely inside his pocket-book to confirm that his money was still there.

He went to the door and made cautiously to open it and seek some hint into the best thing for him to do, the best way to make off.

The door was unopenable. There was no movement in it at all. It had been locked at the least; perhaps more. If Bannard had done it, he had been astonishingly quiet about it; conceivably experienced.

Maybury tried to apply himself to thinking calmly.

The upshot was that once more, and even more hurriedly, he removed his clothes, disposed of them suitably, and resumed Bannard's pyjamas.

It would be sensible once more to turn out the light; to withdraw to bed, between the sheets, if possible; to stand by, as before. But Maybury found that turning out the light, the resultant total blackness, were more than he could face, however expedient.

Ineptly, he sat on the side of his bed, still trying to think things out, to plan sensibly. Would Bannard, after all this time, ever, in fact, return? At least during the course of that night?

He became aware that the electric light bulb had begun to crackle and fizzle. Then, with no further sound, it simply failed. It was not, Maybury thought, some final authoritative lights-out all over the house. It was merely that the single bulb had given out, however unfortunately from his own point of view: an isolated industrial incident.

He lay there, half in and half out, for a long time. He concentrated on the thought that nothing had actually happened that was dangerous. Ever since his schooldays (and, indeed, during them) he had become increasingly aware that there were many things strange to him, most of which had proved in the end to be apparently quite harmless.

Then Bannard was creeping back into the dark room. Maybury's ears had picked up no faint sound of a step in the passage, and, more remarkable, there had been no noise, either, of a turned key, let alone, perhaps, of a drawn bolt. Maybury's view of the bulb failure was confirmed by a repetition of the widening and narrowing column of light, dim, but probably no dimmer than before. Up to a point, lights were still on elsewhere. Bannard, considerate as before, did not try to turn on the light in the room. He shut the door with extraordinary skill, and Maybury could just, though only just, hear him slithering into his bed.

Still, there was one unmistakable development: at Bannard's return, the dark room had filled with perfume; the perfume favoured, long ago, as it seemed, by the lady who had been so charming to Maybury in the lounge. Smell is, in any case, notoriously the most recollective of the senses.

Almost at once, this time, Bannard not merely fell obtrusively asleep, but was soon snoring quite loudly.

Maybury had every reason to be at least irritated by everything that was happening, but instead he soon fell asleep himself. So long as Bannard was asleep, he was at least in abeyance as an active factor in the situation; and many perfumes have their own drowsiness, as Iago remarked. Angela passed temporarily from the forefront of Maybury's mind.

Then he was awake again. The light was on once more, and Maybury supposed that he had been awakened deliberately, because Bannard was standing there by his bed. Where and how had he found a new light bulb? Perhaps he kept a supply in a drawer. This seemed so likely that Maybury thought no more of the matter.

It was very odd, however, in another way also.

When Maybury had been at school, he had sometimes found difficulty in distinguishing certain boys from certain other boys. It had been a very large school, and boys do often look alike. None the less, it was a situation that Maybury thought best to keep to himself, at the time and since. He had occasionally made responses or approaches based upon misidentifications: but had been fortunate in never being made to suffer for it bodily, even though he had suffered much in his self-regard.

And now it was the same. Was the man standing there really Bannard? One obvious thing was that Bannard had an aureole or fringe of red hair, whereas this man's fringe was quite grey. There was also a different expression and general look, but Maybury was more likely to have been mistaken about that. The pyjamas seemed to be the same, but that meant little.

"I was just wondering if you'd care to talk for a bit," said Bannard. One had to assume that Bannard it was; at least to start off with. "I didn't mean to wake you up. I was just making sure."

"That's all right, I suppose," said Maybury.

"I'm over my first beauty sleep," said Bannard. "It can be lonely during the night." Under all the circumstances it was a distinctly absurd remark, but undoubtedly it was in Bannard's idiom.

"What was all that screaming?" enquired Maybury.

"I didn't hear anything," said Bannard. "I suppose I slept through it. But I can imagine. We soon learn to take no notice. There are sleepwalkers for that matter, from time to time."

"I suppose that's why the bedroom doors are so hard to open?"

"Not a bit," said Bannard, but he then added, "Well, partly, perhaps. Yes, partly. I think so. But it's just a knack really. We're not actually locked in, you know." He giggled. "But what makes you ask? You don't need to leave the room in order to go to the loo. I showed you, old man."

So it really must be Bannard, even though his eyes seemed to be a different shape, and even a different colour, as the hard light caught them when he laughed.

"I expect I was sleepwalking myself," said Maybury warily.

"There's no need to get the wind up," said Bannard, "like a kid at a new school. All that goes on here is based on the simplest of natural principles: eating good food regularly, sleeping long hours, not taxing the overworked brain. The food is particularly important. You just wait for breakfast, old man, and see what you get. The most tremendous spread, I promise you."

"How do you manage to eat it all?" asked Maybury. "Dinner alone was too much for me."

"We simply let Nature have its way. Or rather, perhaps, *her* way. We give Nature her head."

"But it's not *natural* to eat so much."

"That's all you know," said Bannard. "What you are old man, is effete." He giggled as Bannard had giggled, but he looked somehow unlike Maybury's recollection of Bannard. Maybury was almost certain there was some decisive difference.

The room still smelt of the woman's perfume; or perhaps it was largely Bannard who smelt of it, Bannard who now stood so close to Maybury. It was embarrassing that Bannard, if he really had to rise from his bed and wake Maybury up, did not sit down; though preferably not on Maybury's blanket.

"I'm not saying there's no suffering here," continued Bannard. "But where in the world are you exempt from suffering? At least no one rots away in some attic—or wretched bed-sitter, more likely. Here there are no single rooms. We all help one another. What can you and I do for one another, old man?"

He took a step nearer and bent slightly over Maybury's face. His pyjamas really reeked of perfume.

It was essential to be rid of him; but essential to do it uncontentiously. The prospect should accept the representative's point of view as far as possible unawares.

"Perhaps we could talk for just five or ten minutes more," said Maybury, "and then I should like to go to sleep again, if you will excuse me. I ought to explain that I slept very little last night owing to my wife's illness."

"Is your wife pretty?" asked Bannard. "Really pretty? With this and that?" He made a couple of gestures, quite conventional though not aforetime seen in drawing rooms.

"Of course she is," said Maybury. "What do you think?"

"Does she really turn you on? Make you lose control of yourself?"

"Naturally," said Maybury. He tried to smile, to show he had a sense of humour which could help him to cope with tasteless questions.

Bannard now not merely sat on Maybury's bed, but pushed his frame against Maybury's legs, which there was not much room to withdraw, owing to the tightness of the blanket, as Bannard sat on it.

"Tell us about it," said Bannard. "Tell us exactly what it's like to be a married man. Has it changed your whole life? Transformed everything?"

"Not exactly. In any case, I married years ago."

"So now there is someone else. *I* understand."

"No, actually there is not."

"Love's old sweet song still sings to you?"

"If you like to put it like that, yes. I love my wife. Besides, she's ill. And we have a son. There's him to consider, too."

"How old is your son?"

"Nearly sixteen."

"What colour are his hair and eyes?"

"Really, I'm not sure. No particular colour. He's not a baby, you know."

"Are his hands still soft?"

"I shouldn't think so."

"Do you love your son, then?"

"In his own way, yes, of course."

"I should love him, were he mine, and my wife too." It seemed to Maybury that Bannard said it with real sentiment. What was more, he looked at least twice as sad as when Maybury had first seen him: twice as old, and twice as sad. It was all ludicrous, and Maybury at last felt really tired, despite the lump of Bannard looming over him, and looking different.

"Time's up for me," said Maybury. "I'm sorry. Do you mind if we go to sleep again?"

Bannard rose at once to his feet, turned his back on Maybury's corner, and went to his bed without a word, thus causing further embarrassment.

It was again left to Maybury to turn out the light, and to shove his way back to bed through the blackness.

Bannard had left more than a waft of the perfume behind him; which perhaps helped Maybury to sleep once more almost immediately, despite all things.

Could the absurd conversation with Bannard have been a dream? Certainly what happened next was a dream: for there was Angela in her nightdress with her hands on her poor head, crying out "Wake up! Wake up! Wake up!" Maybury could not but comply, and in Angela's place, there was the boy, Vincent, with early morning tea for him. Perforce the light was on once more: but that was not a matter to be gone into.

"Good morning, Mr. Maybury."

"Good morning, Vincent."

Bannard already had his tea.

Each of them had a pot, a cup, jugs of milk and hot water, and a plate of bread and butter, all set on a tray. There were eight large triangular slices each.

"No sugar," cried out Bannard genially. "Sugar kills appetite."

Perfect rubbish, Maybury reflected; and squinted across at Bannard, recollecting his last rubbishy conversation. By the light of morning, even if it were but the same electric light, Bannard looked much more himself, fluffy red aureole and all. He looked quite rested. He munched away at his bread and butter. Maybury thought it best to go through the motions of following suit. From over there Bannard could hardly see the details.

"Race you to the bathroom, old man," Bannard cried out.

"Please go first," responded Maybury soberly. As he had no means of conveying the bread and butter off the premises, he hoped, with the aid of the towel, to conceal it in his skimpy pyjamas jacket, and push it down the water closet. Even Bannard would probably not attempt to throw his arms round him and so uncover the offence.

Down in the lounge, there they all were, with Falkner presiding indefinably but genially. Wan though authentic sunlight trickled in from the outer world, but Maybury observed that the front door was still bolted and chained. It was the first thing he looked for. Universal expectation was detectable: of breakfast, Maybury assumed. Bannard, at all times shrimpish, was simply lost in the throng. Cécile he could not see, but he made a point of not looking very hard. In any case, several of the people looked new, or at least different. Possibly it was a further example of the phenomenon Maybury had encountered with Bannard.

Falkner crossed to him at once: the recalcitrant but still privileged outsider. "I can promise you a good breakfast, Mr. Maybury," he said confidentially. "Lentils. Fresh fish. Rump steak. Apple pie made by ourselves, with lots and lots of cream."

"I mustn't stay for it," said Maybury. "I simply mustn't. I have my living to earn. I must go at once."

He was quite prepared to walk a couple of miles; indeed, all set for it. The automobile organisation, which had given him the route from which he should never have diverged, could recover his car. They had done it for him before, several times.

A faint shadow passed over Falkner's face, but he merely said in a low voice, "If you really insist, Mr. Maybury —— "

"I'm afraid I have to," said Maybury.

"Then I'll have a word with you in a moment."

None of the others seemed to concern themselves. Soon they all filed off, talking quietly among themselves, or, in many cases, saying nothing.

"Mr. Maybury," said Falkner, "you can respect a confidence?"

"Yes," said Maybury steadily.

"There was an incident here last night. A death. We do not talk about such things. Our guests do not expect it."

"I am sorry," said Maybury.

"Such things still upset me," said Falkner. "None the less I must not think about that. My immediate task is to dispose of the body. While the guests are preoccupied. To spare them all knowledge, all pain."

"How is that to be done?" enquired Maybury.

"In the usual manner, Mr. Maybury. The hearse is drawing up outside the door even as we speak. Where you are concerned, the point is this. If you wish for what in other circumstances I could call a lift, I could arrange for you to join the vehicle. It is travelling quite a distance. We find that best." Falkner was progressively unfastening the front door. "It seems the best solution, don't you think, Mr. Maybury? At least it is the best I can offer. Though you will not be able to thank Mr. Bannard, of course."

A coffin was already coming down the stairs, borne on the shoulders of four men in black, with Vincent, in his white jacket, coming first, in order to leave no doubt of the way and to prevent any loss of time.

"I agree," said Maybury. "I accept. Perhaps you would let me know my bill for dinner?"

"I shall waive that too, Mr. Maybury," replied Falkner, "in the present circumstances. We have a duty to hasten. We have others to think of. I shall simply say how glad we have all been to have you with us." He held out his hand. "Good-bye, Mr. Maybury."

Maybury was compelled to travel with the coffin itself, because there simply was not room for him on the front seat, where a director of the firm, a corpulent man, had to be accommodated with the driver. The nearness of death compelled a respectful silence among the company in the rear compartment, especially when a living stranger was in the midst; and Maybury alighted unobtrusively when a bus stop was reached. One of the under-taker's men said that he should not have to wait long.

The writings of NATHANIEL HAWTHORNE *(1804–64) might well be described as still-life studies of morality and corruption. His plots develop with glacial slowness, yet in spite of their static quality, they manage to cast a curiously compelling spell upon the patient reader. Allegory is often employed by Hawthorne, but his ethical polemic never interferes with the story; both interweave masterfully to produce climaxes of towering potency, such as the death of the judge in* The House of the Seven Gables. *I considered including the latter piece in this anthology, but it is an episode that must be read in context to be fully appreciated. Instead, I have chosen the less familiar "The Christmas Banquet," which has a similar "feel."*

The Christmas Banquet

BY NATHANIEL HAWTHORNE

"I have here attempted," said Roderick, unfolding a few sheets of manuscript, as he sat with Rosina and the sculptor in the summer-house — "I have attempted to seize hold of a personage who glides past me, occasionally, in my walk through life. My former sad experience, as you know, has gifted me with some degree of insight into the gloomy mysteries of the human heart, through which I have wandered like one astray in a dark cavern, with his torch fast flickering to extinction. But this man, this class of men, is a hopeless puzzle."

"Well, but propound him," said the sculptor. "Let us have an idea of him, to begin with."

"Why, indeed," replied Roderick, "he is such a being as I could conceive you to carve out of marble, and some yet unrealized perfection of human science to endow with an exquisite mockery of intellect; but still there lacks the last inestimable touch of a divine Creator. He looks like a man; and, perchance, like a better specimen of man than you ordinarily meet. You might esteem him wise; he is capable of cultivation and refinement, and has at least an external conscience; but the demands that spirit makes upon spirit are precisely those to which he cannot respond. When at last you come close to him you find him chill and unsubstantial — a mere vapour."

"I believe," said Rosina, "I have a glimmering idea of what you mean."

"Then be thankful," answered her husband, smiling; "but do not anticipate any further illumination from what I am about to read. I have here imagined such a man to be—what, probably, he never is—conscious of the deficiency in his spiritual organization. Methinks the result would be a sense of cold unreality wherewith he would go shivering through the world, longing to exchange his load of ice for any burden of real grief that fate could fling upon a human being."

Contenting himself with this preface, Roderick began to read.

In a certain old gentleman's last will and testament there appeared a bequest, which, as his final thought and deed, was singularly in keeping with a long life of melancholy eccentricity. He devised a considerable sum for establishing a fund, the interest of which was to be expended, annually, forever, in preparing a Christmas Banquet for ten of the most miserable persons that could be found. It seemed not to be the testator's purpose to make these half a score of sad hearts merry, but to provide that the stern or fierce expression of human discontent should not be drowned, even for that one holy and joyful day, amid the acclamations of festal gratitude which all Christendom sends up. And he desired, likewise, to perpetuate his own remonstrance against the earthly course of Providence, and his sad and sour dissent from those systems of religion or philosophy which either find sunshine in the world or draw it down from heaven.

The task of inviting the guests, or of selecting among such as might advance their claims to partake of this dismal hospitality, was confided to the two trustees or stewards of the fund. These gentlemen, like their deceased friend, were sombre humorists, who made it their principal occupation to number the sable threads in the web of human life, and drop all the golden ones out of the reckoning. They performed their present office with integrity and judgement. The aspect of the assembled company, on the day of the first festival, might not, it is true, have satisfied every beholder that these were especially the individuals, chosen forth from all the world, whose griefs were worthy to stand as indicators of the mass of human suffering. Yet, after due consideration, it could not be disputed that here was a variety of hopeless discomfort, which, if it sometimes arose from causes apparently inadequate, was thereby only the shrewder imputation against the nature and mechanism of life.

The arrangements and decorations of the banquet were probably intended to signify that death in life which had been the testator's definition of existence. The hall, illuminated by torches, was hung round with curtains of deep and dusky purple, and adorned with branches of cypress and wreaths of artificial flowers, imitative of such as used to be strewn over the dead. A sprig of parsley was laid by every plate. The main reservoir of wine was a sepulchral urn of silver, whence the liquor was distributed around the table in small vases, accurately copied from those that held the tears of ancient mourners. Neither had the stewards—if it were their taste that arranged these details—forgotten the fantasy of the old Egyptians, who seated a skeleton at every festive board, and mocked their own merriment with the imperturbable grin of a death's head. Such a fearful guest, shrouded in a black mantle, sat now at the head of the table. It was whispered, I know not with what truth, that the testator himself had once walked the visible world with the machinery of that same skeleton, and that it was one of the stipulations of his will, that he should thus be permitted to sit, from year to year, at the banquet which he had instituted. If so, it was perhaps covertly implied that he had cherished no hopes of bliss beyond the grave to compensate for the evils which he felt or imagined here. And if, in their bewildered conjectures as to the purpose of earthly existence, the banqueters should throw aside the veil, and cast an inquiring glance at this figure of death, as seeking thence the solution otherwise unattainable, the only reply would be a stare of the vacant eye caverns and a grin of the skeleton jaws. Such was the response that the dead man had fancied himself to receive when he asked of Death to solve the riddle of his life; and it was his desire to repeat it when the guests of his dismal hospitality should find themselves perplexed with the same question.

"What means that wreath?" asked several of the company, while viewing the decorations of the table.

They alluded to a wreath of cypress, which was held on high by a skeleton arm, protruding from within the black mantle.

"It is a crown," said one of the stewards, "not for the worthiest, but for the woefullest, when he shall prove his claim to it."

The guest earliest bidden to the festival was a man of soft and gentle character, who had not energy to struggle against the heavy despondency to which his temperament rendered him liable; and therefore with nothing outwardly to excuse him from happiness, he had spent a life of quiet misery that made his blood torpid, and weighed upon his breath, and sat like a ponderous night fiend upon every throb of his unresisting heart. His wretchedness seemed as deep as his original nature, if not identical with it. It was the misfortune of a second guest to cherish within his bosom a diseased heart, which had become so wretchedly sore that the continual and unavoidable rubs of the world, the blow of an enemy, the careless jostle of a stranger, and even the faithful and loving touch of a friend, alike made ulcers in it. As is the habit of people thus afflicted, he found his chief employment in exhibiting these miserable sores to any who would give themselves the pain of viewing them. A third guest was a hypochondriac, whose imagination wrought necromancy in his outward and inward world, and caused him to see monstrous faces in the household fire, and dragons in the clouds of sunset, and fiends in the guise of beautiful women, and something ugly or wicked beneath all the pleasant surfaces of nature. His neighbor at table was one who, in his early youth, had trusted mankind too much, and hoped too highly in their behalf, and, in meeting with many disappointments, had become desperately soured. For several years back this misanthrope had employed himself in accumulating motives for hating and despising his race—such as murder, lust, treachery, ingratitude, faithlessness of trusted friends, instinctive vices of children, impurity of women, hidden guilt in men of saintlike aspect—and, in short, all manner of black realities that sought to decorate themselves with outward grace or glory. But at every atrocious fact that was added to his catalogue, at every increase of the sad knowledge which he spent his life to collect, the native impulses of the poor man's loving and confiding heart made him groan with anguish. Next, with his heavy brow bent downward, there stole into the hall a man naturally earnest and impassioned, who, from his immemorial infancy, had felt the consciousness of a high message to the world; but essaying to deliver it, had found either no voice or form of speech, or else no ears to listen. Therefore his whole life was a bitter questioning of himself—"Why have not men acknowledged my mission? Am I not a self-deluding fool? What business have I on earth? Where is my grave?" Throughout the festival, he quaffed frequent draughts from the sepulchral urn of wine, hoping thus to quench the celestial fire that tortured his own breast and could not benefit his race.

Then there entered, having flung away a ticket for a ball, a gay gallant of yesterday, who had found four or five wrinkles in his brow, and more grey hairs than he could well number on his head. Endowed with sense and feeling, he had nevertheless spent his youth in folly, but had reached at last that dreary point in life where Folly quits us of her own accord, leaving us to make friends of Wisdom if we can. Thus, cold and desolate, he had come to seek Wisdom at the banquet, and wondered if the skeleton were she. To eke out the company, the stewards had invited a distressed poet from his home in the almshouse, and a melancholy idiot from the street corner. The latter had just the glimmering of sense that was sufficient to make him conscious of a vacancy, which the poor fellow, all his life long, had mistily sought to fill up with intelligence, wandering up and down the streets, and groaning miserably because his attempts were ineffectual. The only lady in the hall was one who had fallen short of absolute and perfect beauty, merely by the trifling defect of a slight cast in her left eye. But this blemish, minute as it was, so shocked the pure ideal of her soul, rather than her vanity, that she passed her life in solitude, and veiled her countenance even from her own gaze. So the skeleton sat shrouded at one end of the table and this poor lady at the other.

One other guest remains to be described. He was a young man of smooth brow, fair cheek, and fashionable mien. So far as his exterior developed him, he might much more suitably have found a place at some merry Christmas table, than have been numbered among the blighted, fate-stricken, fancy-tortured set of ill-starred banqueters. Murmurs arose among the guests as they noted the glance of general scrutiny which the intruder threw over his companions. What had he to do among them? Why did not the skeleton of the dead founder of the feast unbend its rattling joints, arise, and motion the unwelcome stranger from the board?

"Shameful!" said the morbid man, while a new ulcer broke out in his heart. "He comes to mock us!—we shall be the jest of his tavern friends!—he will make a farce of our miseries, and bring it out upon the stage!"

"O, never mind him!" said the hypochondriac, smiling sourly. "He shall feast from yonder tureen of viper soup; and there is a fricassee of scorpions on the table, pray let him have his share of it. For the dessert, he shall taste the apples of Sodom. Then, if he likes our Christmas fare, let him return again next year!"

"Trouble him not," murmured the melancholy man, with gentleness. "What matters it whether the consciousness of misery comes a few years sooner or later? If this youth deem himself happy now, yet let him sit with us for the sake of the wretchedness to come."

The poor idiot approached the young man with that mournful aspect of vacant inquiry which his face continually wore, and which caused people to say that he was always in search of his missing wits. After no little examination he touched the stranger's hand, but immediately drew back his own, shaking his head and shivering.

"Cold, cold, cold!" muttered the idiot.

The young man shivered too, and smiled.

"Gentlemen—and you, madam,"—said one of the stewards of the festival, "do not conceive so ill either of our caution or judgement, as to imagine that we have admitted this young stranger—Gervayse Hastings by name—without a full investigation and thoughtful balance of his claims. Trust me, not a guest at the table is better entitled to his seat."

The steward's guarantee was perforce satisfactory. The company, therefore, took their places, and addressed themselves to the serious business of the feast, but were soon disturbed by the hypochondriac, who thrust back his chair, complaining that a dish of stewed toads and vipers was set before him, and that there was green ditch water in his cup of wine. This mistake being amended, he quietly resumed his seat. The wine, as it flowed freely from the sepulchral urn, seemed to come imbued with all gloomy inspirations; so that its influence was not to cheer, but either to sink the revellers into a deeper melancholy, or elevate their spirits to an enthusiasm of wretchedness. The conversation was various. They told sad stories about people who might have been worthy guests at such a festival as the present. They talked of grisly incidents in human history; of strange crimes, which if truly considered, were but convulsions of agony; of some lives that had been altogether wretched, and of others, which, wearing a general semblance of happiness, had yet been deformed, sooner or later, by misfortune, as by the intrusion of a grim face at a banquet; of death-bed scenes, and what dark intimations might be gathered from the words of dying men; of suicide, and whether the more eligible

modes were by halter, knife, poison, drowning, gradual starvation, or the fumes of charcoal. The majority of the guests, as is
the custom with people thoroughly and profoundly sick at heart,
were anxious to make their own woes the theme of discussion, and
prove themselves most excellent in anguish. The misanthropist
went deep into the philosophy of evil, and wandered about in the
darkness, with now and then a gleam of discoloured light hovering
on ghastly shapes and horrid scenery. Many a miserable thought,
such as men have stumbled upon from age to age, did he now rake
up again, and gloat over it as an inestimable gem, a diamond, a
treasure far preferable to those bright, spiritual revelations of a
better world, which are like precious stones from heaven's
pavement. And then, amid his lore of wretchedness, he hid his
face and wept.

It was a festival at which the woeful man of Uz might suitably
have been a guest, together with all, in each succeeding age, who
have tasted deepest of the bitterness of life. And be it said, too,
that every son or daughter of woman, however favoured with
happy fortune, might, at one sad moment or another, have
claimed the privilege of a stricken heart, to sit down at this table.
But, throughout the feast, it was remarked that the young
stranger, Gervayse Hastings, was unsuccessful in his attempts to
catch its pervading spirit. At any deep, strong thought that found
utterance, and which was torn out, as it were, from the saddest
recesses of human consciousness, he looked mystified and bewildered; even more than the poor idiot, who seemed to grasp at such
things with his earnest heart, and thus occasionally to comprehend
them. The young man's conversation was of a colder and lighter
kind, often brilliant, but lacking the powerful characteristics of a
nature that had been developed by suffering.

"Sir," said the misanthropist bluntly, in reply to some observation by Gervayse Hastings, "pray do not address me again. We
have no right to talk together. Our minds have nothing in
common. By what claim you appear at this banquet I cannot guess;
but methinks, to a man who could say what you have just now
said, my companions and myself must seem no more than shadows
flickering on the wall. And precisely such a shadow are you to us."

The young man smiled and bowed, but drawing himself back in
his chair, he buttoned his coat over his breast, as if the banqueting
hall were growing chill. Again the idiot fixed his melancholy stare
upon the youth, and murmured, "Cold! cold! cold!"

The banquet drew to its conclusion and the guests departed. Scarcely had they stepped across the threshold of the hall when the scene that had there passed seemed like the vision of a sick fancy, or an exhalation from a stagnant heart. Now and then, however, during the year that ensued, these melancholy people caught glimpses of one another, transient, indeed, but enough to prove that they walked the earth with the ordinary allotment of reality. Sometimes a pair of them came face to face while stealing through the evening twilight, enveloped in their sable cloaks. Sometimes they casually met in churchyards. Once, also, it happened that two of the dismal banqueters mutually started at recognizing each other in the noonday sunshine of a crowded street, stalking their like ghosts astray. Doubtless they wondered why the skeleton did not come abroad at noonday too.

But whenever the necessity of their affairs compelled these Christmas guests into the bustling world, they were sure to encounter the young man who had so unaccountably been admitted to the festival. They saw him among the gay and fortunate; they caught the sunny sparkle of his eye; they heard the light and careless tones of his voice, and muttered to themselves with such indignation as only the aristocracy of wretchedness could kindle—"The traitor! The vile imposter! Providence, in its own good time, may give him a right to feast among us!" But the young man's unabashed eye dwelt upon their gloomy figures as they passed him, seeming to say, perchance with somewhat of a sneer, "First, know my secret!—then measure your claims with mine!"

The step of Time stole onward, and soon brought merry Christmas round again, with glad and solemn worship in the churches, and sports, games, festivals, and everywhere the bright face of Joy beside the household fire. Again, likewise, the hall, with its curtains of dusky purple, was illuminated by the death torches gleaming on the sepulchral decorations of the banquet. The veiled skeleton sat in state, lifting the cypress wreath above its head, as the guerdon of some guest illustrious in the qualifications which there claimed precedence. As the stewards deemed the world inexhaustible in misery, and were desirous of recognizing it in all its forms, they had not seen fit to reassemble the company of the former year. New faces now threw their gloom across the table.

There was a man of nice conscience, who bore a blood stain in his heart—the death of a fellow-creature—which, for his more

exquisite torture, had chanced with such a peculiarity of circumstances, that he could not absolutely determine whether his will
had entered into the deed or not. Therefore, his whole life was
spent in the agony of an inward trial for murder, with a continual
sifting of the details of his terrible calamity, until his mind had no
longer any thought, nor his soul any emotion, disconnected with
it. There was a mother, too—a mother once, but a desolation
now—who, many years before, had gone out on a pleasure party,
and returning, found her infant smothered in its little bed. And
ever since she has been torturted with the fantasy that her buried
baby lay smothering in its coffin. Then there was an aged lady,
who had lived from time immemorial with a constant tremor
quivering through her frame. It was terrible to discern her dark
shadow tremulous upon the wall; her lips, likewise, were tremulous; and the expression of her eye seemed to indicate that her
soul was trembling, too. Owing to the bewilderment and confusion
which made almost a chaos of her intellect, it was impossible to
discover what dire misfortune had thus shaken her nature to its
depths; so that the stewards had admitted her to the table, not
from any acquaintance with her history, but on the safe testimony
of her miserable aspect. Some surprise was expressed at the
presence of a bluff, red-faced gentleman, a certain Mr. Smith, who
had evidently the fat of many a rich feast within him, and the
habitual twinkle of whose eye betrayed a disposition to break forth
into uproarious laughter for little cause or none. It turned out,
however, that with the best possible flow of spirits, our poor friend
was afflicted with a physical disease of the heart, which threatened
instant death on the slightest cachinnatory indulgence, or even
that titillation of the bodily frame produced by merry thoughts. In
this dilemma he had sought admittance to the banquet, on the
ostensible plea of his irksome and miserable state, but, in reality,
with the hope of imbibing a life-preserving melancholy.

A married couple had been invited from a motive of bitter
humour, it being well understood that they rendered each other
unutterably miserable whenever they chanced to meet, and
therefore must necessarily be fit associates at the festival. In
contrast with these was another couple still unmarried, who had
interchanged their hearts in early life, but had been divided by
circumstances as unpalpable as morning mist, and kept apart so
long that their spirits now found it impossible to meet. Therefore,
yearning for communion, yet shrinking from one another and

choosing none beside, they felt themselves companionless in life, and looked upon eternity as a boundless desert. Next to the skeleton sat a mere son of earth—a hunter of the Exchange—a gatherer of shining dust—a man whose life's record was in his ledger, and whose soul's prison-house the vaults of the bank where he kept his deposits. This person had been greatly perplexed at his invitation, deeming himself one of the most fortunate men in the city; but the stewards persisted in demanding his presence, assuring him that he had no conception how miserable he was.

And now appeared a figure which we must acknowledge as our acquaintance of the former festival. It was Gervayse Hastings, whose presence had then caused so much question and criticism, and who now took his place with the composure of one whose claims were satisfactory to himself, and must needs be allowed by others. Yet his easy and unruffled face betrayed no sorrow. The well-skilled beholders gazed a moment into his eyes and shook their heads, to miss the unuttered sympathy—the countersign, never to be falsified—of those whose hearts are cavern mouths, through which they descend into a region of illimitable woe, and recognize other wanderers there.

"Who is this youth?" asked the man with a blood stain on his conscience. "Surely he has never gone down into the depths! I know all the aspects of those who have passed through the dark valley. By what right is he among us?"

"Ah, it is a sinful thing to come hither without a sorrow," murmured the aged lady, in accents that partook of the eternal tremor which pervaded her whole being. "Depart, young man! Your soul has never been shaken; and, therefore, I tremble so much the more to look at you."

"His soul shaken! No; I'll answer for it," said bluff Mr. Smith, pressing his hand upon his heart, and making himself as melancholy as he could, for fear of a fatal explosion of laughter. "I know the lad well; he has as fair prospects as any young man about town, and has no more right among us miserable creatures than the child unborn. He never was miserable, and probably never will be!"

"Our honoured guests," interposed the stewards, "pray have patience with us, and believe, at least, that our deep veneration for the sacredness of this solemnity would preclude any wilful violation of it. Receive this young man to your table. It may not be too much to say that no guest here would exchange his own heart for the one that beats within that youthful bosom!"

"I'd call it a bargain, and gladly, too," muttered Mr. Smith, with a perplexing mixture of sadness and mirthful conceit. "A plague upon their nonsense! My own heart is the only really miserable one in the company; it will certainly be the death of me at last!"

Nevertheless, as on the former occasion, the judgement of the stewards being without appeal, the company sat down. The obnoxious guest made no more attempt to obtrude his conversation on those about him, but appeared to listen to the table-talk with peculiar assiduity, as if some inestimable secret, otherwise beyond his reach, might be conveyed in a casual word. And in truth, to those who could understand and value it, there was rich matter in the upgushings and outpourings of these initiated souls to whom sorrow had been a talisman, admitting them into spiritual depths which no other spell can open. Sometimes out of the midst of densest gloom there flashed a momentary radiance, pure as crystal, bright as the flame of stars, and shedding such a glow upon the mysteries of life that the guests were ready to exclaim, "Surely the riddle is on the point of being solved!" At such illuminated intervals the saddest mourners felt it to be revealed that mortal griefs are but shadowy and external; no more than the sable robes voluminously shrouding a certain divine reality, and thus indicating what might otherwise be altogether invisible to mortal eye.

"Just now," remarked the trembling old woman, "I seemed to see beyond the outside. And then my everlasting tremor passed away!"

"Would that I could dwell always in these momentary gleams of light!" said the man of stricken conscience. "Then the blood stain in my heart would be washed clean away."

This strain of conversation appeared so unintelligibly absurd to good Mr. Smith, that he burst into precisely the fit of laughter which his physicians had warned him against, as likely to prove instantaneously fatal. In effect, he fell back in his chair a corpse, with a broad grin upon his face, while his ghost, perchance, remained beside it bewildered at its unpremeditated exit. This catastrophe, of course, broke up the festival.

"How is this? You do not tremble?" observed the tremulous old woman to Gervayse Hastings, who was gazing at the dead man with singular intentness. "Is it not awful to see him so suddenly vanish out of the midst of life—this man of flesh and blood, whose earthly nature was so warm and strong? There is a never-ending tremor in my soul, but it trembles afresh at this! And you are calm!"

"Would that he could teach me somewhat!" said Gervayse Hastings, drawing a long breath. "Men pass before me like shadows on the wall; their actions, passions, feelings, are flickerings of the light, and then they vanish! Neither the corpse, nor yonder skeleton, nor this old woman's everlasting tremor, can give me what I seek."

And then the company departed.

We cannot linger to narrate, in such detail, more circumstances of these singular festivals, which, in accordance with the founder's will, continued to be kept with the regularity of an established institution. In process of time the stewards adopted the custom of inviting, from far and near, those individuals whose misfortunes were prominent above other men's, and whose mental and moral development might, therefore, be supposed to possess a corresponding interest. The exiled noble of the French Revolution, and the broken soldier of the Empire, were alike represented at the table. Fallen monarchs, wandering about the earth, have found places at that forlorn and miserable feast. The statesman, when his party flung him off, might, if he chose it, be once more a great man for the space of a single banquet. Aaron Burr's name appears on the record at a period when his ruin—the profoundest and most striking, with more of moral circumstance in it than that of almost any other man—was complete in his lonely age. Stephen Girard, when his wealth weighed upon him like a mountain, once sought admittance of his own accord. It is not probable, however, that these men had any lesson to teach in the lore of discontent and misery which might not equally well have been studied in the common walks of life. Illustrious unfortunates attract a wide sympathy, not because their griefs are more intense, but because, being set on lofty pedestals, they the better serve mankind as instances and bywords of calamity.

It concerns our present purpose to say that, at each successive festival, Gervayse Hastings showed his face, gradually changing from the smooth beauty of his youth to the thoughtful comeliness of manhood, and thence to the bald, impressive dignity of age. He was the only individual invariably present. Yet on every occasion there were murmurs, both from those who knew his character and position, and from them whose hearts shrank back as denying his companionship in their mystic fraternity.

"Who is this impassive man?" had been asked a hundred times. "Has he suffered? Has he sinned? There are no traces of either. Then wherefore is he here?"

"You must inquire of the stewards or of himself," was the constant reply. "We seem to know him well here in our city, and know nothing of him but what is creditable and fortunate. Yet hither he comes, year after year, to this gloomy banquet, and sits among the guests like a marble statue. Ask yonder skeleton, perhaps that may solve the riddle!"

It was in truth a wonder. The life of Gervayse Hastings was not merely a prosperous, but a brilliant one. Everything had gone well with him. He was wealthy, far beyond the expenditure that was required by habits of magnificence, a taste of rare purity and cultivation, a love of travel, a scholar's instinct to collect a splendid library, and moreover, what seemed a magnificent liberality to the distressed. He had sought happiness, and not vainly, if a lovely and tender wife, and children of fair promise, could insure it. He had, besides, ascended above the limit which separates the obscure from the distinguished, and had won a stainless reputation in affairs of the widest public importance. Not that he was a popular character, or had within him the mysterious attributes which are essential to that species of success. To the public he was a cold abstraction, wholly destitute of those rich hues of personality, that living warmth, and the peculiar faculty of stamping his own heart's impression on a multitude of hearts by which the people recognize their favourites. And it must be owned that after his most intimate associates had done their best to know him thoroughly and love him warmly, they were startled to find how little hold he had upon their affections. They approved, they admired, but still in those moments when the human spirit most craves reality, they shrank back from Gervayse Hastings, as powerless to give them what they sought. It was the feeling of distrustful regret with which we should draw back the hand after extending it, in an illusive twilight, to grasp the hand of a shadow upon the wall.

As the superficial fervency of youth decayed, this peculiar effect of Gervayse Hastings' character grew more perceptible. His children, when he extended his arms, came coldly to his knees, but never climbed them of their own accord. His wife wept secretly, and almost adjudged herself a criminal because she shivered in the chill of his bosom. He, too, occasionally appeared not unconscious of the chillness of his moral atmosphere, and willing, if it might be so, to warm himself at a kindly fire. But age stole onward and benumbed him more and more. As the hoarfrost began to gather on him, his wife went to her grave, and was doubtless warmer there; his children either died or were scattered to different homes of their own; and old Gervayse Hastings, unscathed by grief—alone, but needing no companionship—continued his steady walk through life, and still on every Christmas day attended at the dismal banquet. His privilege as a guest had become prescriptive now. Had he claimed the head of the table, even the skeleton would have been ejected from its seat.

Finally, at the merry Christmas tide, when he had numbered fourscore years complete, this pale, high-browed, marble-featured old man once more entered the long-frequented hall, with the same impassive aspect that had called forth so much dissatisfied remark at his first attendance. Time, except in matters merely external, had done nothing for him, either of good or evil. As he took his place, he threw a calm, inquiring glance around the table, as if to ascertain whether any guest had yet appeared, after so many unsuccessful banquets, who might impart to him the mystery—the deep, warm secret—the life within the life—which, whether manifested in joy or sorrow, is what gives substance to a world of shadows.

"My friends," said Gervayse Hastings, assuming a position which his long conversance with the festival caused to appear natural, "you are welcome! I drink to you all in this cup of sepulchral wine."

The guests replied courteously, but still in a manner that proved them unable to receive the old man as a member of their sad fraternity. It may be well to give the reader an idea of the present company at the banquet.

One was formerly a clergyman, enthusiastic in his profession, and apparently of the genuine dynasty of those old puritan divines whose faith in their calling, and stern exercise of it, had placed them among the mighty of the earth. But yielding to the speculative tendency of the age, he had gone astray from the firm foundation of an ancient faith, and wandered into a cloud region, where everything was misty and deceptive, ever mocking him with a semblance of reality, but still dissolving when he flung himself upon it for support and rest. His instinct and early training demanded something steadfast; but, looking forward, he beheld vapours piled on vapours, and behind him an impassable gulf between the man of yesterday and today, on the borders of which he paced to and fro, sometimes wringing his hands in agony, and often making his own woe a theme of scornful merriment. This surely was a miserable man. Next, there was a theorist—one of a numerous tribe, although he deemed himself unique since the creation—a theorist who had conceived a plan by which all the wretchedness of earth, moral and physical, might be done away, and the bliss of the millennium at once accomplished. But the incredulity of mankind debarring him from action, he was smitten with as much grief as if the whole mass of woe which he was denied the opportunity to remedy were crowded into his own bosom. A plain old man in black attracted much of the company's notice, on the supposition that he was no other than Father Miller, who, it seemed, had given himself up to despair at the tedious delay of the final conflagration. Then there was a man distinguished for native pride and obstinacy, who, a little while before, had possessed immense wealth, and held the control of a vast moneyed interest which he had wielded in the same spirit as a despotic monarch would wield the power of his empire, carrying on a tremendous moral warfare, the roar and tremor of which was felt at every fireside in the land. At length came a crushing ruin—a total overthrow of fortune, power, and character—the effect of which on his imperious and, in many respects, noble and lofty nature, might have entitled him to a place, not merely at our festival, but among the peers of Pandemonium.

There was a modern philanthropist, who had become so deeply sensible of the calamities of thousands and millions of his fellow-creatures, and of the impracticableness of any general measures for their relief, that he had no heart to do what little good lay immediately within his power, but contented himself with being miserable for sympathy. Near him sat a gentleman in a predicament hitherto unprecedented, but of which the present epoch probably affords numerous examples. Ever since he was of capacity to read a newspaper, this person had prided himself on his consistent adherence to one political party, but, in the confusion of these latter days, had got bewildered and knew not whereabouts his party was. This wretched condition, so morally desolate and disheartening to a man who has long accustomed himself to merge his individuality in the mass of a great body, can only be conceived by such as have experienced it. His next companion was a popular orator who had lost his voice, and—as it was pretty much all that he had to lose—had fallen into a state of hopeless melancholy. The table was likewise graced by two of the gentler sex—one, a half-starved, consumptive seamstress, the representative of thousands just as wretched; the other, a woman of unemployed energy, who found herself in the world with nothing to achieve, nothing to enjoy, and nothing even to suffer. She had, therefore, driven herself to the verge of madness by dark broodings over the wrongs of her sex and its exclusion from a proper field of action. The roll of guests being thus complete, a side table had been set for three or four disappointed office seekers, with hearts as sick as death, whom the stewards had admitted partly because their calamities really entitled them to entrance here, and partly that they were in especial need of a good dinner. There was likewise a homeless dog, with his tail between his legs, licking up the crumbs and gnawing the fragments of the feast; such a melancholy air as one sometimes sees about the streets without a master, and willing to follow the first that will accept his service.

In their own way, these were as wretched a set of people as ever had assembled at the festival. There they sat, with the veiled skeleton of the founder holding aloft the cypress wreath, at one end of the table, and at the other, wrapped in furs, the withered figure of Gervayse Hastings, stately, calm, and cold, impressing the company with awe, yet so little interesting their sympathy that he might have vanished into thin air without their once exclaiming, "Whither is he gone?"

"Sir," said the philanthropist, addressing the old man, "you have been so long a guest at this annual festival, and have thus been conversant with so many varieties of human affliction, that, not improbably, you have thence derived some great and important lessons. How blessed were your lot could you reveal a secret by which all this mass of woe might be removed!"

"I know of but one misfortune," answered Gervayse Hastings, quietly, "and that is my own."

"Your own!" enjoined the philanthropist. "And, looking back on your serene and prosperous life, how can you claim to be the sole unfortunate of the human race?"

"You will not understand it," replied Gervayse Hastings, feebly, and with a singular inefficiency of pronunciation, and sometimes putting one word for another. "None have understood it—not even those who experience the like. It is a chillness—a want of earnestness—a feeling as if what should be my heart were a thing of vapour—a haunting perception of unreality! Thus seeming to possess all that other men have—all that men aim at—I have really possessed nothing, neither joy nor griefs. All things, all persons— as was truly said to me at this table long and long ago—have been like shadows flickering on the wall. It was so with my wife and children—with those who seemed my friends: it is so with yourselves, whom I see now before me. Neither have I myself any real existence, but am a shadow like the rest."

"And how is it with your views of a future life?" inquired the speculative clergyman.

"Worse than with you," said the old man, in a hollow and feeble tone; "for I cannot conceive it earnestly enough to feel either hope or fear. Mine—mine is the wretchedness! This cold heart—this unreal life! Ah! it grows colder still."

It so chanced that at this juncture the decayed ligaments of the skeleton gave way, and the dry bones fell together in a heap, thus causing the dusty wreath of cypress to drop upon the table. The attention of the company being thus diverted for a single instant from Gervayse Hastings, they perceived on turning again towards him that the old man had undergone a change. His shadow had ceased to flicker on the wall.

"Well, Rosina, what is your criticism?" asked Roderick, as he rolled up the manuscript.

"Frankly, your success is by no means complete," replied she. "It is true, I have an idea of the character you endeavour to describe; but it is rather by dint of my own thought than your expression."

"That is unavoidable," observed the sculptor, "because the characteristics are all negative. If Gervayse Hastings imbibed one human grief at the gloomy banquet, the task of describing him would have been infinitely easier. Of such persons—and we do meet with these moral monsters now and then—it is difficult to conceive how they came to exist here, or what there is in them capable of existence hereafter. They seem to be on the outside of everything; and nothing wearies the soul more than an attempt to comprehend them within its grasp."

Most people only know ROBERT BLOCH *as the author of* Psycho *and its recently released (and unexpectedly effective) sequel, but Mr. Bloch has been writing shockers for many, many years, including such unforgettable stories as "Enoch" and "Yours Truly, Jack the Ripper." He also is well known for his galumphing sense of humor, and tales such as "The Strange Island of Doctor Nork" are wonderful send-ups of the very genre Bloch so ably works within. There is nothing in the least risible, however, about "The Hungry House." It's not a nice place to visit, and you definitely wouldn't want to live there.*

The Hungry House

BY ROBERT BLOCH

At first there were just the two of them—he and she, together. That's the way it was when they bought the house.

Then *it* came. Perhaps it was there all the time; waiting for them in the house. At any rate, it was there now. And there was nothing they could do.

Moving was out of the question. They'd taken a five-year lease, secretly congratulating themselves on the low rental. It would be absurd to complain to the agent about it, and impossible to explain to their friends. For that matter, they had nowhere else to go; they had searched for months to find a home.

Besides, at first neither he nor she cared to admit that they were aware of its presence. But both of them knew it was there.

She felt it the very first evening, in the bedroom. She was sitting in front of the high, old-fashioned boudoir mirror, combing her hair. They hadn't settled all their things yet, and she didn't trouble to dust the place very thoroughly. In consequence the mirror was cloudy. And the light above it flickered.

So at first she thought it was just a trick of shadows. Some flaw in the glass perhaps. The wavering outline behind her seemed to blur the reflection oddly, and she frowned in distaste. Then she began to experience what she often called her "married feeling"—the peculiar awareness which usually denoted her husband's entrance to a room she occupied.

He must be standing behind her now. He must have come in quietly, without saying anything. Perhaps he was going to put his arms around her, surprise her, startle her. Hence the shadow on the mirror.

She turned, ready to greet him.

The room was empty. And still the odd reflection persisted, together with the sensation of a presence at her back.

She shrugged, moved her head, and made a little face at herself, in the mirror. As a smile it was a failure, because the warped glass and the poor light seemed to distort her grin into something alien—into a smile that was not altogether a composition of her own face and features.

Well, it had been a fatiguing ordeal, this moving business. She flicked a brush through her hair and tried to dismiss the problem.

Nevertheless she felt a surge of relief when he suddenly entered the bedroom. For a moment she thought of telling him, then decided not to worry him over her "nerves."

He was more outspoken. It was the following morning that the incident occurred. He came rushing out of the bathroom, his face bleeding from a razor-cut on the left cheek.

"Is that your idea of being funny?" he demanded, in the petulant, little-boy fashion she found so engaging. "Sneaking in behind me and making faces in the mirror? Gave me an awful start—look at this nick I sliced on myself."

She sat up in bed.

"But darling, I haven't been making faces at you. I didn't stir from this bed since you got up."

"Oh." He shook his head, his frown fading into a second set of wrinkles expressing bewilderment. "Oh, I see."

"What is it?" She suddenly threw off the covers and sat on the edge of the bed, wriggling her toes and peering at him earnestly.

"Nothing," he murmured. "Nothing at all. Just thought I saw you, or somebody, looking over my shoulder in the mirror. All of a sudden, you know. It must be those damned lights. Got to get some bulbs in town today."

He patted his cheek with a towel and turned away. She took a deep breath.

"I had the same feeling last night," she confessed, then bit her lip.

"You did?"

"It's probably just the lights, as you said, darling."

"Uh huh." He was suddenly preoccupied. "That must be it. I'll make sure and bring those new bulbs."

"You'd better. Don't forget, the gang is coming down for the housewarming on Saturday."

Saturday proved to be a long time in coming. In the interim both of them had several experiences which served to upset their minds much more than they cared to admit.

The second morning, after he had left for work, she went out in back and looked at the garden. The place was a mess—half an acre of land, all those trees, the weeds everywhere, and the dead leaves of autumn dancing slowly around the old house. She stood off on a little knoll and contemplated the grave gray gables of another century. Suddenly she felt lonely here. It wasn't only the isolation, the feeling of being half a mile from the nearest neighbor, down a deserted dirt road. It was more as though she were an intruder here—an intruder upon the past. The cold breeze, the dying trees, the sullen sky were welcome; they belonged to the house. She was the outsider, because she was young, because she was alive.

She felt it all, but did not think it. To acknowledge her sensations would be to acknowledge fear. Fear of being alone. Or, worse still, fear of *not* being alone.

Because, as she stood there, the back door closed.

Oh, it was the autumn wind, all right. Even though the door didn't bang, or slam shut. It merely closed. But that was the wind's work, it had to be. There was nobody in the house, nobody to close the door.

She felt in her housedress pocket for the door key, then shrugged as she remembered leaving it on the kitchen sink. Well, she hadn't planned to go inside yet anyway. She wanted to look over the yard, look over the spot where the garden had been and where she fully intended a garden to bloom next spring. She had measurements to make, and estimates to take, and a hundred things to do here outside.

And yet, when the door closed, she knew she had to go in. Something was trying to shut her out, shut her out of her own house, and that would never do. Something was fighting against her, fighting against all idea of change. She had to fight back.

So she marched up to the door, rattled the knob, found herself locked out as she expected. The first round was lost. But there was always the window.

The kitchen window was eye-level in height, and a small crate served to bring it within easy reach. The window was open a good four inches and she had no trouble inserting her hands to raise it further.

She tugged.

Nothing happened. The window must be stuck. But it wasn't stuck; she'd just opening it before going outside and it opened quite easily; besides, they'd tried all the windows and found them in good operating condition.

She tugged again. This time the window raised a good six inches and then—something slipped. The window came down like the blade of a guillotine, and she got her hands out just in time. She bit her lip, sent strength through her shoulders, raised the window once more.

And this time she stared into the pane. The glass was transparent, ordinary window glass. She'd washed it just yesterday and she knew it was clean. There had been no blur, no shadow, and certainly no movement.

But there was movement now. Something cloudy, something obscenely opaque, peered out of the window, peered out of itself and pressed the window down against her. Something matched her strength to shut her out.

Suddenly, hysterically, she realized that she was staring at her own reflection through the shadows of the trees. Of course, it had to be her own reflection. And there was no reason for her to close her eyes and sob as she tugged the window up and half-tumbled her way into the kitchen.

She was inside, and alone. Quite alone. Nothing to worry about. Nothing to worry him about. She wouldn't tell him.

He wouldn't tell her, either. Friday afternoon, when she took the car and went into town for groceries and liquor in preparation for tomorrow's party, he stayed home from the office and arranged the final details of settling down.

That's why he carried up all the garment bags to the attic—to store the summer clothes, get them out of the way. And that's how he happened to open the little cubicle under the front gable. He was looking for the attic closet; he'd put down the bags and started to work along the wall with a flashlight. Then he noticed the door and the padlock.

*   *   *

Dust and rust told their own story; nobody had come this way for a long, long time. He thought again of Hacker, the glib real-estate agent who'd handled the rental of the place. "Been vacant several years and needs a little fixing up," Hacker had said. From the looks of it, nobody had lived here for a coon's age. All the better; he could force the lock with a common file.

He went downstairs for the file and returned quickly, noting as he did so the heavy attic dust. Apparently the former occupants had left in something of a hurry—debris was scattered everywhere, and swaths and swirls scored the dust to indicate that belongings had been dragged and hauled and swept along in a haphazard fashion.

Well, he had all winter to straighten things out, and right now he'd settle for storing the garment bags. Clipping the flashlight to his belt, he bent over the lock, file in hand, and tried his skill at breaking and entering.

The lock sprung. He tugged at the door, opened it, inhaled a gust of mouldy dampness, then raised the flash and directed the beam into the long, narrow closet.

A thousand silver slivers stabbed at his eyeballs. Golden, gleaming fire seared his pupils. He jerked the flashlight back, sent the beam upwards. Again, lances of light entered his eyes.

Suddenly he adjusted his vision and comprehension. He stood peering into a room full of mirrors. They hung from cords, lay in corners, stood along the walls in rows.

There was a tall, stately full-length mirror, set in a door; a pair of plateglass ovals, inset in old-fashioned dresser-tops; a panel glass, and even a complete, dismantled bathroom medicine cabinet similar to the one they had just installed. And the floor was lined with hand-mirrors of all sizes and shapes. He noted an ornate silver-handled mirror straight from a woman's dressing table; behind it stood the vanity-mirror removed from the table itself. And there were pocket mirrors, mirrors from purse-compacts, mirrors of every size and shape. Against the far wall stood a whole series of looking-glass slabs that appeared to have been mounted at one time in a bedroom wall.

He gazed at half a hundred silvered surfaces, gazed at a half a hundred reflections of his own bewildered face.

*   *   *

And he thought again of Hacker, of their inspection of the house. He had noted the absence of a medicine cabinet at the time, but Hacker had glossed over it. Somehow he hadn't realized that there were no mirrors of any sort in the house—of course, there was no furniture, but still one might expect a door panel in a place this old.

No mirrors? Why? And why were they all stacked away up here, under lock and key?

It was interesting. His wife might like some of these—that silver-handled beauty mirror, for example. He'd have to tell her about this.

He stepped cautiously into the closet, dragging the garment bags after him. There didn't seem to be any clothes-pole here, or any hooks. He could put some up in a jiffy, though. He piled the bags in a heap, stooping, and the flashlight glittered on a thousand surfaces, sent facets of fire into his face.

Then the fire faded. The silver surfaces darkened oddly. Of course, his reflection covered them now. His reflection, and something darker. Something smoky and swirling, something that was a part of the mouldy dampness, something that choked the closet with its presence. It was behind him—no, at one side—no, in front of him—all around him—it was growing and growing and blotting him out—it was making him sweat and tremble and now it was making him gasp and scuttle out of the closet and slam the door and press against it with all his waning strength, and its name was—

Claustrophobia. That was it. Just claustrophobia, a fancy name for nerves. A man gets nervous when he's cooped up in a small place. For that matter, a man gets nervous when he looks at himself too long in a mirror. Let alone fifty mirrors!

He stood there, shaking, and to keep his mind occupied, keep his mind off what he had just half-seen, half-felt, half-known, he thought about mirrors for a moment. About looking into mirrors. Women did it all the time. Men were different.

Men, himself included, seemed to be self-conscious about mirrors. He could remember going into a clothing-store and seeing himself in one of the complicated arrangements that afforded a side and rear view. What a shock that had been, the first time—and every time, for that matter! A man looks different in a mirror. Not the way he imagines himself to be, knows himself to be. A mirror distorts. That's why men hum and sing and whistle while they shave. To keep their minds off their reflections. Otherwise they'd go crazy. What was the name of that Greek mythological character who was in love with his own image? Narcissus, that was it. Staring into a pool for hours.

Women could do it, though. Because women never saw themselves, actually. They saw an idealization, a vision. Powder, rouge, lipstick, mascara, eye-shadow, brilliantine, or merely an emptiness to which these elements must be applied. Women were a little crazy to begin with, anyway. Hadn't she said something the other night about seeing him in her mirror when he wasn't there?

Perhaps he'd better not tell her, after all. At least, not until he checked with the real-estate agent, Hacker. He wanted to find out about that business, anyway. Something was wrong, somewhere. Why had the previous owners stored all the mirrors up here?

He began to walk back through the attic, forcing himself to go slowly, forcing himself to think of something, anything, except the fright he'd had in the room of reflections.

Reflect on something. Reflections. Who's afraid of the big bad reflection? Another myth, wasn't it?

Vampires. They had no reflections. "Tell me the truth now, Hacker. The people who built this house—were they vampires?"

That was a pleasant thought. That was a pleasant thought to carry downstairs in the afternoon twilight, to hug to your bosom in the gloom while the floors creaked and the shutters banged and the night came down in the house of shadows where something peered around the corners and grinned at you in the mirrors on the walls.

He sat there waiting for her to come home, and he switched on all the lights, and he put the radio on too and thanked God he didn't have a television set because there was a screen and the screen had a reflection and the reflection might be something he didn't want to see.

But there was no more trouble that evening, and by the time she came home with her packages he had himself under control. So they ate and talked quite normally—oh, quite naturally, and if it was listening it wouldn't know they were both afraid.

They made their preparations for the party, and called up a few people on the phone, and just on the spur of the moment he suggested inviting Hacker, too. So that was done and they went to bed. The lights were all out and that meant the mirrors were dark, and he could sleep.

Only in the morning it was difficult to shave. And he caught her, yes he caught her, putting on her makeup in the kitchen, using the little compact from her purse and carefully cupping her hands against reflections.

But he didn't tell her and she didn't tell him, and if it guessed their secrets, it kept silent.

He drove off to work and she made canapes, and if at times during the long, dark, dreary Saturday the house groaned and creaked and whispered, that was only to be expected.

The house was quiet enough by the time he came home again, and somehow, that was worse. It was as though something were waiting for night to fall. That's why she dressed early, humming all the while she powdered and primped, swirling around in front of the mirror (you couldn't see too clearly if you swirled). That's why he mixed drinks before their hasty meal and saw to it that they both had several stiff ones (you couldn't see too clearly if you drank).

And then the guests tumbled in. The Teters, complaining about the winding back road through the hills. The Valliants, exclaiming over the antique paneling and the high ceilings. The Ehrs, whooping and laughing, with Vic remarking that the place looked like something designed by Charles Addams. That was a signal for a drink, and by the time Hacker and his wife arrived the blaring radio found ample competition from the voices of the guests.

He drank, and she drank, but they couldn't shut it out altogether. That remark about Charles Addams was bad, and there were other things. Little things. The Talmadges had brought flowers, and she went out to the kitchen to arrange them in a cut-glass vase. There were facets in the glass, and as she stood in the kitchen, momentarily alone, and filled the vase with water from the tap, the crystal darkened beneath her fingers, and something peered, reflected from the facets. She turned quickly, and she was all alone. All alone, holding a hundred naked eyes in her hands.

So she dropped the vase, and the Ehrs and Talmadges and Hackers and Valliants trooped out to the kitchen, and he came too. Talmadge accused her of drinking and that was reason enough for another round. He said nothing, but got another vase for the flowers. And yet he must have known, because when somebody suggested a tour of the house, he put them off:

"We haven't straightened things out upstairs yet," he said. "It's a mess, and you'd be knocking into crates and stuff."

"Who's up there now?" asked Mrs. Teters, coming into the kitchen with her husband. "We just heard an awful crash."

"Something must have fallen over," the host suggested. But he didn't look at his wife as he spoke, and she didn't look at him.

"How about another drink?" she asked. She mixed and poured hurriedly, and before the glasses were half empty, he took over and fixed another round. Liquor helped to keep people talking and if they talked it would drown out other sounds.

The stratagem worked. Gradually the group trickled back into the living room in twos and threes, and the radio blared and the laughter rose and the voices babbled to blot out the noises of the night.

He poured and she served, and both of them drank, but the alcohol had no effect. They moved carefully, as though their bodies were brittle glasses—glasses without bottom—waiting to be shattered by some sudden strident sound. Glasses hold liquor, but they never get drunk.

Their guests were not glasses, they drank and feared nothing, and the drinks took hold. People moved about, and in and out, and pretty soon Mr. Valliant and Mrs. Talmadge embarked on their own private tour of the house upstairs. It was irregular and unescorted, but fortunately nobody noticed either their departure or their absence. At least, not until Mrs. Talmadge came running downstairs and locked herself in the bathroom.

Her hostess saw her pass the doorway and followed her. She rapped on the bathroom door, gained admittance, and prepared to make discreet inquiries. None was necessary. Mrs. Talmadge, weeping and wringing her hands, fell upon her.

"That was a filthy trick!" she sobbed. "Coming up and sneaking in on us. The dirty louse—I admit we were doing a little smooching, but that's all there was to it. And it isn't as though he didn't make enough passes at Gwen Hacker himself. What I want to know is, where did he get the beard? It frightened me out of my wits."

"What's all this?" she asked—knowing all the while what it was, and dreading the words to come.

"Jeff and I were in the bedroom, just standing there in the dark, I swear it, and all at once I looked up over my shoulder at the mirror because light began streaming in from the hall. Somebody had opened the door, and I could see the glass and this face. Oh, it was my husband all right, but he had a beard on and the way he came slinking in, glaring at us—"

Sobs choked off the rest. Mrs. Talmadge trembled so that she wasn't aware of the tremors which racked the frame of her hostess. She, for her part, strained to hear the rest. "—sneaked right out again before we could do anything, but wait till I get him home— scaring the life out of me and all because he's so crazy jealous— the look on his face in the mirror—"

She soothed Mrs. Talmadge. She comforted Mrs. Talmadge. She placated Mrs. Talmadge. And all the while there was nothing to soothe or calm or placate her own agitation.

Still, both of them had restored a semblance of sanity by the time they ventured out into the hall to join the party—just in time to hear Mr. Talmadge's agitated voice booming out over the excited responses of the rest.

"So I'm standing there in the bathroom and this old witch comes up and starts making faces over my shoulder in the mirror. What gives here, anyway? What kind of a house you running here?"

He thought it was funny. So did the others. Most of the others. The host and hostess stood there, not daring to look at each other. Their smiles were cracking. Glass is brittle.

"I don't believe you." Gwen Hacker's voice. She's had one, or perhaps three, too many. "I'm going up right now and see for myself." She winked at her host and moved towards the stairs.

"Hey, hold on!" He was too late. She swept, or wobbled, past him.

"Halloween pranks," said Talmadge, nudging him. "Old babe in a fancy hairdo. Saw her plain as day. What you cook up for us here, anyhow?"

He began to stammer something, anything, to halt the flood of foolish babbling. She moved close to him, wanting to listen, wanting to believe, wanting to do anything but think of Gwen Hacker upstairs, all alone upstairs looking into a mirror and waiting to see—

The screams came then. Not sobs, not laughter, but screams. He took the stairs two at a time. Fat Mr. Hacker was right behind him, and the others straggled along, suddenly silent. There was the sound of feet clubbing the staircase, the sound of heavy breathing, and over everything the continuing high-pitched shriek of a woman confronted with terror too great to contain.

It oozed out of Gwen Hacker's voice, oozed out of her body as she staggered and half-fell into her husband's arms in the hall. The light was streaming out of the bathroom, and it fell upon the mirror that was empty of all reflection, fell upon her face that was empty of all expression.

They crowded around the Hackers—he and she were on either side and the others clustered in front—and they moved along the hall to her bedroom and helped Mr. Hacker stretch his wife out on the bed. She had passed out, and somebody mumbled something about a doctor, and somebody else said no, never mind, she'll be all right in a minute, and somebody else said well, I think we'd better be getting along.

For the first time everybody seemed to be aware of the old house and the darkness, and the way the floors creaked and the windows rattled and the shutters banged. Everyone was suddenly sober, solicitous, and extremely anxious to leave.

Hacker bent over his wife, chafing her wrists, forcing her to swallow water, watching her whimper her way out of emptiness. The host and hostess silently procured hats and coats and listened to expressions of polite regret, hasty farewells, and poorly formulated pretenses of, "Had a marvelous time, darling."

Teters, Valliants, Talmadges were swallowed up in the night. He and she went back upstairs, back to the bedroom and the Hackers. It was too dark in the hall, and too light in the bedroom. But there they were, waiting. And they didn't wait long.

Mrs. Hacker sat up suddenly and began to talk. To her husband, to them.

"I saw her," she said. "Don't tell me I'm crazy, I saw her! Standing on tiptoe behind me, looking right into the mirror. With the same blue ribbon in her hair, the one she wore the day she—"

"Please, dear," said Mr. Hacker.

She didn't please. "But I saw her. Mary Lou! She made a face at me in the mirror, and she's dead, you know she's dead, she disappeared three years ago and they never did find the body—"

"Mary Lou Dempster." Hacker was a fat man. He had two chins. Both of them wobbled.

"She played around here, you know she did, and Wilma Dempster told her to stay away, she knew all about this house, but she wouldn't and now—oh, her face!"

*   *   *

More sobs. Hacker patted her on the shoulder. He looked as though he could stand a little shoulder-patting himself. But nobody obliged. He stood there, she stood there, still waiting. Waiting for the rest.

"Tell them," said Mrs. Hacker. "Tell them the truth."

"All right, but I'd better get you home."

"I'll wait. I want you to tell them. You must, now."

Hacker sat down heavily. His wife leaned against his shoulder. The two waited another moment. Then it came.

"I don't know how to begin, how to explain," said fat Mr. Hacker. "It's probably my fault, of course, but I didn't know. All this foolishness about haunted houses—nobody believes that stuff any more, and all it does is push property values down, so I didn't say anything. Can you blame me?"

"I saw her face," whispered Mrs. Hacker.

"I know. And I should have told you. About the house, I mean. Why it hasn't rented for twenty years. Old story in the neighborhood, and you'd have heard it sooner or later anyway, I guess."

"Get on with it," said Mrs. Hacker. She was suddenly strong again and he, with his wobbling chins, was weak.

Host and hostess stood before them, brittle as glass, as the words poured out; poured out and filled them to overflowing. He and she, watching and listening, filling up with the realization, with the knowledge, with that for which they had waited.

It was the Bellman house they were living in, the house Job Bellman built for his bride back in the sixties; the house where his bride had given birth to Laura and taken death in exchange. And Job Bellman had toiled through the seventies as his daughter grew to girlhood, rested in complacent retirement during the eighties as Laura Bellman blossomed into the reigning beauty of the country—some said the state, but then flattery came quickly to men's lips in those days.

There were men aplenty; coming and going through that decade; passing through the hall in polished boots, bowing and stroking brilliantined mustachios, smirking at old Job, grinning at the servants, and gazing in moonstruck adoration at Laura.

Laura took it all as her rightful due, but land's sakes, she'd never think of it, no, not while Papa was still alive, and no, she couldn't, she was much too young to marry, and why, she'd never heard of such a thing, she'd always thought it was so much nicer just being friends—

Moonlight, dances, parties, hayrides, sleighrides, candy, flow-ers, gifts, tokens, cotillion balls, punch, fans, beauty spots, dressmakers, curlers, mandolins, cycling, and the years that whirled away. And then, one day, old Job dead in the four-poster bed upstairs, and the Doctor came and the Minister, and then the Lawyer, hack-hack-hacking away with his dry, precise little cough, and his talk of inheritance and estate and annual income.

Then she was all alone, just she and the servants and the mirrors. Laura and her mirrors. Mirrors in the morning, and the careful inspection, the scrutiny that began the day. Mirrors at night before the caller arrived, before the carriage came, before she whirled away to another triumphal entry, another fan-fluttering, pirouetting descent of the staircase. Mirrors at dawn, absorbing the smiles, listening to the secrets, the tale of the evening's triumph.

"Mirror, mirror on the wall, who is the fairest of them all?"

Mirrors told her the truth, mirrors did not lie, mirrors did not paw or clutch or whisper or demand in return for acknowledge-ment of beauty.

Years passed, but mirrors did not age, did not change. And Laura did not age. The callers were fewer and some of them were oddly altered. They seemed older, somehow. And yet how could that be? For Laura Bellman was still young. The mirrors said so, and they always told the truth. Laura spent more and more time with the mirrors. Powdering, searching for wrinkles, tinting and curling her long hair. Smiling, fluttering eyelashes, making deliciously delicate little *moues*. Swirling daintily, posturing before her own perfection.

Sometimes, when the callers came, she sent word that she was not at home. It seemed silly, somehow, to leave the mirrors. And after a while, there weren't many callers to worry about. Servants came and went, some of them died, but there were always new ones. Laura and the mirrors remained. The nineties were truly gay, but in a way other people wouldn't understand. How Laura laughed, rocking back and forth on the bed, sharing her giddy secrets with the glass!

The years fairly flew by, but Laura merely laughed. She giggled and tittered when the servants spoke to her, and it was easier now to take her meals on a tray in her room. Because there was something wrong with the servants, and with Doctor Turner who came to visit her and who was always being tiresome about going away for a rest to a lovely home.

They thought she was getting old, but she wasn't—the mirrors didn't lie. She wore the false teeth and the wig to please the others, the outsiders, but she didn't really need them. The mirrors told her she was unchanged. They talked to her now, the mirrors did, and she never said a word. Just sat nodding and swaying before them in the room reeking of powder and *patchouli*, stroking her throat and listening to the mirrors telling her how beautiful she was and what a belle she would be if she would only waste her beauty on the world. But she'd never leave here, never; she and the mirrors would always be together.

And then came the day they tried to take her away, and they actually laid hands upon her—upon her, Laura Bellman, the most exquisitely beautiful woman in the world! Was it any wonder that she fought, clawed and kicked and whined, and struck out so that one of the servants crashed headlong into the beautiful glass and struck his foolish head and died, his nasty blood staining the image of her perfection?

Of course it was all a stupid mistake and it wasn't her fault, and Doctor Turner told the magistrate so when he came to call. Laura didn't have to see him, and she didn't have to leave the house. But they always locked the door to her room now, and they took away all her mirrors.

They *took away* all her mirrors.

They left her alone, caged up, a scrawny, wizened, wrinkled old woman with no reflection. They took the mirrors away and made her old; old, and ugly, and afraid.

The night they did it, she cried. She cried and hobbled around the room, stumbling blindly in a tearsome tour of nothingness.

That's when she realized she was old, and nothing could save her. Because she came up against the window and leaned her wrinkled forehead against the cold, cold glass. The light came from behind her and as she drew away she could see her reflection in the window.

The window—it was a mirror, too! She gazed into it, gazed long and lovingly at the tear-streaked face of the fantastically rouged and painted old harridan, gazed at the corpse-countenance readied for the grave by a mad embalmer.

Everything whirled. It was her house, she knew every inch of it, from the day of her birth onwards the house was part of her. It was her room, she had lived here for ever and ever. But *this*— this obscenity—was not her face. Only a mirror could show her that, and there would never be a mirror for her again. For an instant she gazed at the truth and then, mercifully, the gleaming glass of the window-pane altered and once again she gazed at Laura Bellman, the proudest beauty of them all. She drew herself erect, stepped back, and whirled into a dance. She danced forward, a prim self-conscious smile on her lips. Danced into the window-pane, half-through it, until razored splinters of glass tore her scrawny throat.

That's how she died and that's how they found her. The Doctor came, and the servants and the lawyer did what must be done. The house was sold, then sold again. It fell into the hands of a rental agency. There were tenants, but not for long. They had trouble with mirrors.

A man died—of a heart attack, they said—while adjusting his necktie before the bureau one evening. Grotesque enough, but he had complained to people in the town about strange happenings, and his wife babbled to everyone.

A school-teacher who rented the place in the twenties "passed away" in circumstances which Doctor Turner had never seen fit to relate. He had gone to the rental agency and begged them to take the place off the market; that was almost unnecessary, for the Bellman home had its reputation firmly established by now.

Whether or not Mary Lou Dempster had disappeared here would never be known. But the little girl had last been seen a year ago on the road leading to the house and although a search had been made and nothing discovered, there was talk aplenty.

Then the new heirs had stepped in, briskly, with their pooh-poohs and their harsh dismissals of advice, and the house had been cleaned and put up for rental.

So he and she had come to live here—with it. And that was the story, all of the story.

Mr. Hacker put his arm around Gwen, harrumphed, and helped her rise. He was apologetic, he was shame-faced, he was deferential. His eyes never met those of his tenant.

He barred the doorway. "We're getting out of here, right now," he said. "Lease or no lease."

"That can be arranged. But—I can't find you another place

tonight, and tomorrow's Sunday—"

"We'll pack and get out of her tomorrow," she spoke up. "Go to a hotel, anywhere. But we're leaving."

"I'll call you tomorrow," said Hacker. "I'm sure everything will be all right. After all, you've stayed here through the week and nothing, I mean nobody has—"

His words trailed off. There was no point in saying any more. The Hackers left and they were all alone. Just the two of them.

Just the *three* of them, that is.

But now they—he and she—were too tired to care. The inevitable let-down, product of overindulgence and over-excitement was at hand.

They said nothing, for there was nothing to say. They heard nothing, for the house—and it—maintained a sombre silence.

She went to her room and undressed. He began to walk around the house. First he went to the kitchen and opened a drawer next to the sink. He took a hammer and smashed the kitchen mirror.

Tinkle-tinkle! And then a crash! That was the mirror in the hall. Then upstairs, to the bathroom. Crash and clink of broken glass in the medicine cabinet. Then a smash as he shattered the panel in his room. And now he came to her bedroom and swung the hammer against the huge oval of the vanity, shattering it to bits.

He wasn't cut, wasn't excited, wasn't upset. And the mirrors were gone. Every last one of them was gone.

They looked at each other for a moment. Then he switched off the lights, tumbled into bed beside her, and sought sleep.

The night wore on.

It was all a little silly in the daylight. But she looked at him again in the morning, and he went into his room and hauled out the suitcases. By the time she had breakfast ready he was already laying his clothes out on the bed. She got up after eating and took her own clothing from the drawers and hangers and racks and hooks. Soon he'd go up to the attic and get the garment bags. The movers could be called tomorrow, or as soon as they had a destination in mind.

The house was quiet. If it knew their plans, it wasn't acting. The day was gloomy and they kept the lights off without speaking— although both of them knew it was because of the window-panes and the story of the reflection. He could have smashed the window glass of course, but it was all a little silly. And they'd be out of here shortly.

Then they heard the noise. Trickling, burbling. A splashing sound. It came from beneath their feet. She gasped.

"Water-pipe — in the basement," he said, smiling and taking her by the shoulders.

"Better take a look." She moved towards the stairs.

"Why should you go down there? I'll tend to it."

But she shook her head and pulled away. It was her penance for gasping. She had to show she wasn't afraid. She had to show him — and it, too.

"Wait a minute," he said. "I'll get the pipe-wrench. It's in the trunk in the car." He went out the back door. She stood irresolute, then headed for the cellar stairs. The splashing was getting louder. The burst pipe was flooding the basement. It made a funny noise, like laughter.

He could hear it even when he walked up the driveway and opened the trunk of the car. These old houses always had something wrong with them; he might have known it. Burst pipes and —

Yes. He found the wrench. He walked back to the door, listening to the water gurgle, listening to his wife scream.

She *was* screaming! Screaming down in the basement, screaming down in the dark.

He ran, swinging the heavy wrench. He clumped down the stairs, down into the darkness, the screams tearing up at him. She was caught, it had her, she was struggling with it but it was strong, too strong, and the light came streaming in on the pool of water beside the shattered pipe and in the reflection he saw her face and the blackness of other faces swirling around her and holding her.

He brought the wrench up, brought it down on the black blur, hammering and hammering and hammering until the screaming died away. And then he stopped and looked down at her. The dark blur had faded away into the reflection of the water — the reflection that had evoked it. But she was still there, and she was still, and she would be still forever now. Only the water was getting red, where her head rested in it. And the end of the wrench was red, too.

For a moment he started to tell her about it, and then he realized she was gone. Now there were only the two of them left. He and it.

And he was going upstairs. He was walking upstairs, still

carrying the bloody wrench, and he was going over to the phone to call the police and explain.

He sat down in a chair before the phone, thinking about what he'd tell them, how he'd explain. It wouldn't be easy. There was this madwoman, see, and she looked into mirrors until there was more of her alive in her reflection than there was in her own body. So when she committed suicide she lived on, somehow, and came alive in mirrors or glass or anything that reflected. And she killed others or drove them to death and their reflections were somehow joined with hers so that this thing kept getting stronger and stronger, sucking away at life with that awful core of pride that could live beyond death. Woman, thy name is vanity! And that, gentlemen, is why I killed my wife . . .

Yes, it was a fine explanation, but it wouldn't hold water. Water—the pool in the basement had evoked it. He might have known it if only he'd stopped to think, to reflect. Reflect. That was the wrong word, now. Reflect. The way the window pane before him was reflecting.

He stared into the glass now, saw it behind him, surging up from the shadows. He saw the bearded man's face, the peering, pathetic, empty eyes of a little girl, the goggling grimacing stare of an old woman. It wasn't there, behind him, but it was alive in the reflection, and as he rose he gripped the wrench tightly. It wasn't there, but he'd strike at it, fight at it, come to grips with it somehow.

He turned, moving back, the ring of shadow-faces pressing. He swung the wrench. Then he saw *her* face coming up through the rest. Her face, with shining splinters where the eyes should be. He couldn't smash it down, he couldn't hit her again.

It moved forward. He moved back. His arm went out to one side. He heard the tinkle of window-glass behind him and vaguely remembered that this was how the old woman had died. The way he was dying now—falling through the window, and cutting his throat, and the pain lanced up and in, tearing at his brain and he hung there on the jagged spikes of glass, bleeding his life away.

Then he was gone.

His body hung there, but he was gone.

There was a little puddle on the floor, moving and growing. The light from outside shone on it, and there was a reflection.

Something emerged fully from the shadows now, emerged and

capered demurely in the darkness.

It had the face of an old woman and the face of a child, the face of a bearded man, and *his* face, and *her* face, changing and blending.

It capered and postured, and then it squatted, babbling. Finally, all alone in the empty house, it just sat there and waited. There was nothing to do now but wait for the next to come. And meanwhile, it could always admire itself in that growing, growing red reflection on the floor . . .

FITZ-JAMES O'BRIEN *(1828–1862) was born in Ireland and spent his youth writing for Irish, English and Scottish magazines. He came to America in 1852 and continued to write in this country. O'Brien lost his life ten years later fighting in the Civil War on the Union side. He is best remembered for the fantasy tale "What Was It?" and the following verse, a "riding" poem that is structurally reminiscent of Goethe's "The Erl-King" (elsewhere this volume).*

The Demon of the Gibbet

BY FITZ-JAMES O'BRIEN

There was no west, there was no east,
  No star abroad for eyes to see;
And Norman spurred his jaded beast
  Hard by the terrible gallows-tree.

"Oh Norman, haste across this waste,—
  For something seems to follow me!"
"Cheer up, dear Maud, for, thanked be God,
  We nigh have passed the gallows-tree!"

He kissed her lip: then—spur and ship!
  And fast they fled across the lea
But vain the heel, and rowel steel,—
  For something leaped from the gallows-tree!

*"Give me your cloak, your knightly cloak,
  That wrapped you oft beyond the sea!
The wind is bold, my bones are old,
  And I am cold on the gallows-tree!"*

"O holy God! O dearest Maud,
  Quick, quick, some prayers—the best that be!
A bony hand my neck has spanned,
  And tears my knightly cloak from me!"

"Give me your wine,—the red, red wine,
   That in the flask hangs by your knee!
Ten summers burst on me accurst,
   And I'm athirst on the gallows-tree!"

"O Maud, my life, my loving wife!
   Have you no prayer to set us free?
My belt unclasps,—a demon grasps,
   And drags my wine-flask from my knee!"

"Give me your bride, your bonnie bride,
   That left her nest with you to flee!
O she hath flown to be my own,
   For I'm alone on the gallows-tree!"

"Cling closer, Maud, and trust in God!
   Cling close!—Ah, heaven, she slips from me!"
A prayer, a groan, and he alone
   Rode on that night from the gallows-tree.

ANATOLE LE BRAZ *was born in 1859 in Saint-Servais, Brittany, and devoted his life to teaching philosophy and writing books and tales dealing with the legends of his native province. There are several peculiar folk myths attached to Christmas Eve, and Le Braz chronicled one in "The Fisherman's Story," which appeared in* Ghosts: A Treasury of Chilling Tales Old and New *(Doubleday, 1981). Here is another odd Yuletide tale, one that depends on the belief that animals briefly gain the power of speech on Christmas Eve.*

The Owl

BY ANATOLE LE BRAZ

In those days—I mean, during the era of King Louis Philippe—I made wooden shoes for a living. Our work team camped in the Gurunhuël mountain range, on a slope leading into town. Surrounding us was a magnificent forest of beech trees which have since been turned into shoes. Between all of us "cousins" (as we were accustomed to call ourselves), we comprised a sort of village of five or six huts. Mine stood next to the ruins of an old chapel, and here I lived with my wife, God bless her, and our four children, who now are scattered about the world.

The only sections of the chapel still standing are a portion of wall, a dilapidated altar overrun with brambles and here and there the bases of columns buried beneath a thick layer of moss, weeds and dead leaves, but towards the eastern side and behind the altar was one great window through which light fell on the choir, standing nearly intact at the end of a passageway, a frame for the old stones and ancient glass. Here, in the evenings after work, I loved to come and sit peacefully on the edge of this stone sculpture and smoke my pipe and think, remote from the women's chatter and the gleeful noise of the children.

There were nests of owls amongst the ruins, and late one afternoon, I don't remember how, as I was hoisting myself up to my usual seat, I startled one of these nocturnal creatures. As it fled its hole, it made such a strange sound that one might have mistaken it for someone moaning. The setting sun cast a sharp glare of winter light upon the ruins. Shocked and blinded by the dying crimson glow, the owl landed in my lap. I'd never seen one so close, only on barn doors where fearful peasants sometimes crucified them.

Totally bewildered by its predicament, the owl tottered on the edge of my lap and would have pitched downwards from our lofty perch, but I grasped its wings gently. I don't believe I've ever held anything in my hands so soft and silky, so warm and trembling. I turned the bird away from the light to spare him the bright, stabbing glare of the setting sun.

I looked into the owl's eyes and they transfixed me. Have you ever studied the eyes of an owl? They are dim, and yet like huge mirrors, you think you can see, vaguely, all sorts of mysterious things deep within. They are like the twin openings of a bottomless abyss and seemingly many miles down into their depths, one imagines one perceives great stirrings of shadows and light— undiscovered continents and oceans, processions of crowds and people who come and go like the speechless, melancholy phantoms who people our dreams.

Deeply, deeply I gazed into the owl's eyes, but it studied me as well, trembling even though its sad, compelling stare never wavered from my face. Who knows what thoughts troubled the frail creature? Did it fear that I, too, in fear, would nail it to the side of one of the surrounding beeches?

In an effort to reassure the owl and perhaps myself, as well, I smoothed its feathers and said, "Peace, peace, you poor beast. I am not a bad person. I do not wish to harm you." And it was true. We shoemakers live in the woods in quiet solitude amidst the sacred silence of Nature. Though we wield axes and fell trees, we are serene souls who love birds that keep us company as we work, singing to us as if we were their guests and they, our hosts, were anxious to soothe and entertain us in our toil. The owl does not sing and does not show itself, but still I know the sound of its mournful melody in the depths of the night, and I sense it perching on the roof of my hut, moving me towards solemn thoughts . . . remembering, sometimes, my long-dead ancestors who, according to legend, occasionally take the form of an owl in order to remind the living to respect those who are long past. For me, such thoughts are often in mind. The life hereafter preoccupies me more than life itself.

I stroked the owl's russet gray-tinged feathers and spoke my thoughts to it in a low soothing tone, imagining that it might be as old as the beech trees along the path, that once the owl saw the chapel standing where now only stones cover the ground, that once it heard the bells summoning the people to "Saints' pardon."* All the while that I spoke to it, the owl looked at me with its great eyes with their immobile pupils flecked with gold, pupils that seemed like stars against the blue velvet of the dark universe.

"Come," I said to myself, aloud, "let us return this poor blind creature to his rightful home."

I pulled back the veil of hanging ivy which hid the nest from which the owl had tumbled forth, and as I did I realized that the bird's home was not some chance cavity in the wall, but one of the compartments of an old cupboard, the kind one sees in churches to the right of the choir and generally used for storing sacred vials.

Two such vials were still there, one for wine, one for water, both covered with dirt and shrouded in layer upon layer of spiderwebs, which probably preserved them from the erosion of Time.

Next to the sacred vials lay a book. It was an enormous missal, very old and bound with metal clasps, stained with mold and corroded by humidity, but some of the gold edging still shone through.

The sight of the book made me forget the frightened owl who by then had taken refuge in a secluded corner of the cupboard. I was tempted by the missal. I knew a rather eccentric English gentleman in Belle-Isle who collected books of this type, paying their weight in gold, and even more when they were very old.

Surely the missal no longer belonged to anyone—and yet as I hid it underneath my jacket, I felt curiously evil, or at least greedy. I left my customary perch like a robber sneaking away from the scene of his crime, and as I did, the owl hooted mournfully, like a soul wailing the loss of Salvation.

---

* *Pardon du saint-*In Brittany, religious ceremonies called "pardons" occur frequently. People wearing picturesque costumes travel long distances to parade and worship at shrines dedicated to certain saints.—F.L.

II

Christmas was near. The night before the holiday, our camp leader asked me, "Would you like to go to Belle-Isle tonight? There's a shipment of shoes requested at Roll Even, the store on the Grand' Rue. You'd be in time to attend midnight mass at the village church."

I have always been a good Christian, but to my shame I accepted enthusiastically, not because of the midnight mass, but because I would have the opportunity to seek out my English friend and sell him the missal.

Alone in my hut, I took the book from its hiding place, wrapped it in a piece of cloth and slid it into the inside pocket of my jacket.

After supper, with the cart loaded and my horse harnessed, I snapped the whip and began my journey. I was in high spirits. I have heard tales of travelers who set forth on Christmas Eve and met with ill luck, but nothing of the sort occurred to me, for there was the alluring promise of great profit at the end of my ride.

The cold was biting. I wrapped myself in my coarse wool mantle, clamping the reins between my knees, my hands buried in my coat pockets. My horse was the most gentle and intelligent animal one could imagine. He understood the language of Brittany as well as I or any of my "cousins." All it took was one word for him to speed up his pace or slow down. He took the descending slope of the Gurenhuël at a trot.

It was a clear night. A layer of hoarfrost powdered the countryside. The swaying of the cart rocked me gently, and I was lost in thought, speculating on the price the missal would bring, wondering what gifts I should buy for my wife and children. I pictured in my mind's eye my loved ones' surprise and joy when I brought them such presents as only rich children receive . . . and yet the closer I got to Belle-Isle, the less the prospect pleased me. An inarticulate anxiety began to nag at me, the kind of odd uneasiness one feels when seriously contemplating an action that one knows in one's heart to be wrong.

A sudden sound startled me. Behind me, out of the chilly darkness of the night, I heard a prolonged moan, a plaintive murmur sad enough to melt the soul. I heard it again, and yet again, and each time it was longer and more heavily laden with grief.

I jerked erect, pushed my cover aside, grabbed the reins and lashed out at my horse, who took off at full speed and plunged into the heart of the forest. Gigantic trees lined the path, their entangled, barren branches woven into a ceiling shutting out the sky. On either side of the road black tree trunks hemmed us in; behind them were more trunks, thousands of bare trunks. I, who had always considered myself a child of the forest—born in its shadow, lulled in its ancient arms, nourished at its soft scented breast—I who had always lived in the woods and drew my sustenance from her noble body and blood, I, for the first time was afraid. The large familiar beeches leaned over in a menacing manner I never knew before. Their branches seemed to reach out to pluck at me and stop my horse. The trees were a horde of mute ghosts glowering down with merciless intensity, and yes, they had eyes, every one of them. Look! on each shaft, at the top of the tallest branch, two pupils gleaming large and round, immobile, glaring with a pale colorless light.

My horse was just as frightened as I. He stopped abruptly in his tracks, his legs stiff, the hairs of his mane standing on end. Did I hear his heart beating wildly against his ribs, or was it mine thundering as if it would burst?

I shook so hard that I dropped the reins and was too terrified to think of setting foot outside the cart to pick them up. I sat in agonized expectation, icy drops of sweat trickling over me, my throat clutched tight with fear. God spare me from ever having to live through such unspeakable moments of dreadful anticipation again!

And then a large shape wheeled away from one of the trees and hung in space a moment above the road before landing softly on the side of the cart; a snowflake could not have made less noise. I gazed into two bright eyes I had mistaken for the eyes of the tree and an old formula came to mind, a charm a sorcerer once taught me to ward off the Evil Eye.

"White or black?" I asked faintly. "Good or evil? From God or the devil?"

"Mathias, do you not recognize me?" a weak, doleful voice asked. "I am the owl from the ruins of Saint-Melar. You helped me then, and now I shall save you. You think you are on the road to Belle-Isle, but I tell you that you are on the road to Hell."

There is an old legend which says that on the eve of our Saviour's birth, dumb beasts are given the power of speech. Was this why the owl spoke to me, calling me by name, or was he some

long-dead forebear guiding me away from sin? . . . and yet, I told
the bird, "I did no wrong, none that I know of."

"You have a weight beneath your arm."

I blushed with shame. "I robbed no one. An old book found in
the ruins of a wall. Is that such a great sin?"

"Listen, Mathias," said the bird. "Once there was a parish at
Saint-Melar. A hundred years ago today, a priest celebrated the
midnight mass. When he was done and the congregation dispersed
to their homes, the priest was just taking off his ornaments, happy
at the thought of a warm fire awaiting him in the presbytery, when
a beggar woman appeared in the vestry asking him to give her
confession and communion. But the priest irritably replied,
'Return tomorrow morning, Brigada, for I will be here from nine
on for confession and you may take communion at the high mass.'
The old woman's eyes brimmed with tears, but not daring to insist,
she bowed humbly and left. The next day at dawn, a road laborer
found her wrapped in a shroud of snow, lying dead in a ditch."

"A terrible thing," I muttered, "but what has it to do with me?"

"Listen, Mathias, and you shall know. It was the priest's fault
that she did not die in a state of grace. In time, it came his turn
to appear before the throne of God, and God said, 'For the sin
that you committed, as long as there are two stones remaining of
the chapel at Saint-Melar, you shall provide communion on
Christmas Eve to all lost souls.' " The wind soughed sadly through
the beeches, like a choir of spectres seeking the words of some
long-forgotten hymn, and still the owl spoke to me in his low,
quavering murmur. "Here is Christmas Eve, Mathias. Soon the
midnight bells will ring. That priest is at his post, the company of
the damned assembled, the sacred vials soon to be filled, but the
great missal, *the book,* Mathias, is missing. The priest will not be
able to perform the service and who knows? perhaps he will have
to begin his hundred years of penance all over again. But you, who
stole the missal, you, Mathias Kervenno, are in far greater danger.
That which belongs to the dead becomes an instrument of hellfire
in the hands of the living."

With trembling fingers, I took the book from my pocket. "Here
it is," I muttered. "I return it to you."

"I am only an owl and cannot carry so heavy a burden. You
must take it back to where you found it."

I hope it is to my everlasting credit that I did not hesitate even
for a moment. I immediately got out of the cart, retrieved the

reins, clambered back in and invited my horse to retrace our steps.

No longer were the trees terrifying spectres, for now I knew them again—the friendly assortment of elms and beeches, chestnuts and oaks whose majesty protected and nurtured me all my life. Once more, the night had the divine calm of the holy time to come, and in my heart, too, there was gentle peace abiding.

When we reached the neighborhood of our camp, I tethered my horse to a gatepost and entered the ruins. As I did, I heard a great fluttering behind me and, turning saw that there was a huge flock of owls perched on the surrounding branches, staring down at me with eyes so filled with misery that I felt no fear, but only an immeasurable pity.

I returned the missal to its old home, made the sign of the cross as I passed in front of the altar and returned to my cart. I got back in and took the reins, ready to begin my journey anew, but just then I heard voices arising from the depths of the destroyed chapel, wan voices singing praises to the Son of God. I looked back, but no longer saw the owls. Kneeling in the ruins of the sanctuary was a crowd of people intoning a Nativity hymn while a priest with white hair extended his arms and an acolyte brought him a great, gilt-edged open missal.

I flicked the reins and my horse took off in a gallop in the direction of Belle-Isle. The bells of the Gurenhuël district, of Plongonver, of Loguenel and twenty more parishes pealed forth in the milky brightness of the night beneath the sparkling stars.

I arrived at Belle-Isle just in time to enter the church that was lit with as many lights as a cathedral, and there I attended mass.

Translated by Faith Lancereau

RALPH ADAMS CRAM *was one of America's outstanding architects and art historians. He labored to revive interest in gothic architecture and served as art critic for the* Boston Transcript. *In 1895, a Chicago publisher released a rare volume,* Black Spirits and White, *a half-dozen terror tales by Cram, the only ones he is believed to have written. One of them, "The Dead Valley," was lavishly praised by no less an authority than H. P. Lovecraft in his study,* Supernatural Horror in Literature, *and the following haunted house tale is also highly regarded. "No. 252 Rue M. Le Prince" is one of those evil places where you'd better not spend the night.*

No. 252 Rue M. Le Prince

BY RALPH ADAMS CRAM

When in May, 1886, I found myself at last in Paris, I naturally determined to throw myself on the charity of an old chum of mine, Eugène Marie d'Ardéche, who had forsaken Boston a year or more ago on receiving word of the death of an aunt who had left him such property as she possessed. I fancy this windfall surprised him not a little, for the relations between the aunt and nephew had never been cordial, judging from Eugène's remarks touching the lady, who was, it seems, a more or less wicked and witch-like old person, with a penchant for black magic, at least such was the common report.

Why she should leave all her property to d'Ardéche, no one could tell, unless it was that she felt his rather hobbledehoy tendencies toward Buddhism and occultism might some day lead him to her own unhallowed height of questionable illumination. To be sure, d'Ardéche reviled her as a bad old woman, being himself in that state of enthusiastic exactation which sometimes accompanies a boyish fancy for occultism; but in spite of his distant and repellent attitude, Mlle. Blaye de Tartas made him her sole heir, to the violent wrath of a questionable old party known to infamy as the Sar Torrevieja, the "King of the Sorcerers." The malevolent old portent, whose gray and crafty face was often seen in the Rue M. le Prince during the life of Mlle. de Tartas had, it seems, fully expected to enjoy her small wealth after her death; and when it appeared that she had left him only the contents of the gloomy old house in the Quartier Latin, giving the house itself and all else of which she died possessed to her nephew in America, the Sar proceeded to remove everything from the place, and then to curse it elaborately and comprehensively, together with all those who should ever dwell therein.

Whereupon he disappeared.

This final episode was the last word I received from Eugène, but I knew the number of the house, 252 Rue M. le Prince. So, after a day or two given to a first cursory survey of Paris, I started across the Seine to find Eugène and compel him to do the honours of the city.

Every one who knows the Latin Quarter knows the Rue M. le Prince, running up the hill towards the Garden of Luxembourg. It is full of queer houses and odd corners—or was in '86—and certainly No. 252 was, when I found it, quite as queer as any. It was nothing but a doorway, a black arch of old stone between and under two new houses painted yellow. The effect of this bit of seventeenth century masonry, with its dirty old doors, and rusty broken lantern sticking gaunt and grim out over the narrow sidewalk, was, in its frame of fresh plaster, sinister in the extreme.

I wondered if I had made a mistake in the number; it was quite evident that no one lived behind those cobwebs. I went into the doorway of one of the new hôtels and interviewed the concierge.

No, M. d'Ardéche did not live there, though to be sure he owned the mansion; he himself resided in Meudon, in the country house of the late Mlle. de Tartas. Would Monsieur like the number and the street?

Monsieur would like them extremely, so I took the card that the concierge wrote for me, and forthwith started for the river, in order that I might take a steamboat for Meudon. By one of those coincidences which happen so often, being quite inexplicable, I had not gone twenty paces down the street before I ran directly into the arms of Eugène d'Ardéche. In three minutes we were sitting in the queer little garden of the Chien Bleu, drinking vermouth and absinthe, and talking it all over.

"You do not live in your aunt's house?" I said at last, interrogatively.

"No, but if this sort of thing keeps on I shall have to. I like Meudon much better, and the house is perfect, all furnished, and nothing in it newer than the last century. You must come out with me tonight and see it. I have got a jolly room fixed up for my Buddha. But there is something wrong with this house opposite. I can't keep a tenant in it—not four days. I have had three, all within six months, but the stories have gone around and a man would as soon think of hiring the Cour des Comptes to live in as No. 252. It is notorious. The fact is, it is haunted the worst way."

I laughed and ordered more vermouth.

"That is all right. It is haunted all the same, or enough to keep it empty, and the funny part is that no one knows *how* it is haunted. Nothing is ever seen, nothing heard. As far as I can find out, people just have the horrors there, and have them so bad they have to go to the hospital afterwards. I have one ex-tenant in the Bicêtre now. So the house stands empty, and as it covers considerable ground and is taxed for a lot, I don't know what to do about it. I think I'll either give it to that child of sin, Torrevieja, or else go and live in it myself. I shouldn't mind the ghosts, I am sure."

"Did you ever stay there?"

"No, but I have always intended to, and in fact I came up here today to see a couple of rake-hell fellows I know, Fargeau and Duchesne, doctors in the Clinical Hospital beyond here, up by the Parc Mont Souris. They promised that they would spend the night with me some time in my aunt's house,—which is called around here, you must know, 'la Bouche d'Enfer'—and I thought perhaps they would make it this week, if they can get off duty. Come up with me while I see them, and then we can go across the river to Véfour's and have some luncheon, and you can get your things at the Chatham, and we will go out to Meudon, where of course you will spend the night with me."

The plan suited me perfectly, so we went up to the hospital, found Fargeau, who declared that he and Duchesne were ready for anything, the nearer the real "Bouche d'Enfer" the better; that the following Thursday they would both be off duty for the night, and that on that day they would join in an attempt to outwit the devil and clear up the mystery of No. 252.

"Does M. l'Américain go with us?" asked Fargeau.

"Why, of course," I replied, "I intend to go, and you must not refuse me, d'Ardéche; I decline to be put off. Here is a chance for you to do the honours of your city in a manner which is faultless. Show me a real live ghost, and I will forgive Paris for having lost the Jardin Mabille."

So it was settled.

Later we went down to Meudon and ate dinner in the terrace room of the villa, which was all that d'Ardéche had said, and more, so utterly was its atmosphere that of the seventeenth century. At dinner Eugène told me more about his late aunt, and the queer goings on in the old house.

Mlle. Blaye lived, it seems, all alone, except for one female servant of her own age; a severe, taciturn creature, with massive Breton features and a Breton tongue, whenever she vouchsafed to use it. No one was ever seen to enter the door of No. 252 except Jeanne the servant and the Sar Torrevieja, the latter coming constantly from none knew whither, and always entering, *never leaving*. Indeed, the neighbors, who for eleven years had watched the old sorcerer sidle crab-wise up to the bell almost every day, declared vociferously that *never* had he been seen to leave the house. Once, when they decided to keep absolute guard, the watcher, none other than Maître Garceau of the Chien Bleu, after keeping his eyes fixed on the door from ten o'clock one morning when the Sar arrived until four in the afternoon, during which time the door was unopened (he knew this, for had he not gummed a ten-centime stamp over the joint and was not the stamp unbroken?) nearly fell down when the sinister figure of Torrevieja slid wickedly by him with a dry "Pardon, Monsieur!" and disappeared again through the black doorway.

This was curious, for No. 252 was entirely surrounded by houses, its only windows opening on a courtyard into which no eye could look from the hôtels of the Rue M. le Prince and the Rue de l'Ecole, and the mystery was one of the choice possessions of the Latin Quarter.

Once a year the austerity of the place was broken, and the denizens of the whole quarter stood open-mouthed watching many carriages drive up to No. 252, many of them private, not a few with crests on the door panels, from all of them descending veiled female figures and men with coat collars turned up. Then followed curious sounds of music from within, and those whose houses joined the blank walls of No. 252 became for the moment popular, for by placing the ear against the wall strange music could distinctly be heard, and the sound of monotonous chanting voices now and then. By dawn the last guest would have departed, and for another years the hôtel of Mlle. de Tartas was ominously silent.

Eugene declared that he believed it was a celebration of "Walpurgisnacht," and certainly appearances favored such a fancy.

"A queer thing about the whole affair is," he said, "the fact that every one in the street swears that about a month ago, while I was out in Concarneau for a visit, the music and voices were heard again, just as when my revered aunt was in the flesh. The house was perfectly empty, as I tell you, so it is quite possible that the good people were enjoying an hallucination."

I must acknowledge that these stories did not reassure me; in fact, as Thursday came near, I began to regret a little my determination to spend the night in the house. I was too vain to back down, however, and the perfect coolness of the two doctors, who ran down Tuesday to Meudon to make a few arrangements, caused me to swear that I would die of fright before I would flinch. I suppose I believed more or less in ghosts, I am sure now that I am older I believe in them, there are in fact few things I can *not* believe. Two or three inexplicable things had happened to me, and, although this was before my adventure with Rendel in Paestum, I had a strong predisposition to believe some things that I could not explain, wherein I was out of sympathy with the age.

Well, to come to the memorable night of the twelfth of June, we had made our preparations, and after depositing a big bag inside the doors of No. 252, went across to the Chien Bleu, where Fargeau and Duchesne turned up promptly, and we sat down to the best dinner Père Garceau could create.

I remember I hardly felt that the conversation was in good taste. It began with various stories of Indian fakirs and Oriental jugglery, matters in which Eugène was curiously well read, swerved to the horrors of the great Sepoy mutiny, and thus to reminiscences of the dissecting-room. By this time we had drunk more or less, and Duchesne launched into a photographic and Zolaesque account of the only time (as he said) when he was possessed of the panic of fear: namely, one night many years ago, when he was locked by accident into the dissecting-room of the Loucine, together with several cadavers of a rather unpleasant nature. I ventured to protest mildly against the choice of subjects, the result being a perfect carnival of horrors, so that when we finally drank our last *crème de cacao* and started for "la Bouche d'Enfer," my nerves were in a somewhat rocky condition.

It was just ten o'clock when we came into the street. A hot dead wind drifted in great puffs through the city, and ragged masses of vapor swept the purple sky; an unsavory night altogether, one of those nights of hopeless lassitude when one feels, if one is at home, like doing nothing but drink mint juleps and smoke cigarettes.

Eugène opened the creaking door, and tried to light one of the lanterns; but the gusty wind blew out every match, and we finally had to close the outer doors before we could get a light. At last we had all the lanterns going, and I began to look around curiously. We were in a long, vaulted passage, partly carriageway, partly footpath, perfectly bare but for the street refuse which had drifted in with eddying winds. Beyond lay the courtyard, a curious place rendered more curious still by the fitful moonlight and the flashing of four dark lanterns. The place had evidently been once a most noble palace. Opposite rose the oldest portion, a three-story wall of the time of Francis I, with a great wisteria vine covering half. The wings on either side were more modern, seventeenth century, and ugly, while towards the street was nothing but a flat unbroken wall.

The great bare court, littered with bits of paper blown in by the wind, fragments of packing cases, and straw, mysterious with flashing lights and flaunting shadows, while low masses of torn vapor drifted overhead, hiding, then revealing the stars, and all in absolute silence, not even the sounds of the streets entering this prison-like place, was weird and uncanny in the extreme. I must confess that already I began to feel a slight disposition towards the horrors, but with that curious inconsequence which so often happens in the case of those who are deliberately growing scared, I could think of nothing more reassuring than those delicious verses of Lewis Carroll's:

> *Just the place for a Snark! I have said it twice,*
> *That alone should encourage the crew,*
> *Just the place for a Snark! I have said it thrice,*
> *What I tell you three times is true,* —

which kept repeating themselves over and over in my brain with feverish insistence.

Even the medical students had stopped their chaffing, and were studying the surroundings gravely.

"There is one thing certain," said Fargeau, "*anything* might have happened here without the slightest chance of discovery. Did ever you see such a perfect place for lawlessness?"

"And *anything* might happen here now, with the same certainty of impunity," continued Duchesne, lighting his pipe, the snap of the match making us all start. "D'Ardéche, your lamented relative was certainly well fixed; she had full scope here for her traditional experiments in demonology."

"Curse me if I don't believe that those same traditions were more or less founded on fact," said Eugène. "I never saw this court under these conditions before, but I could believe anything now. What's that!"

"Nothing but a door slamming," said Duchesne loudly.

"Well, I wish doors wouldn't slam in houses that have been empty eleven months."

"It is irritating," said Duchesne slipped his arm through mine; "but we must take things as they come. Remember we have to deal not only with the spectral lumber left here by your scarlet aunt, but as well with the supererogatory curse of that hell-cat Torrevieja. Come on! Let's get inside before the hour arrives for the sheeted dead to squeak and gibber in these lonely halls. Light your pipes, your tobacco is a sure protection against 'your whoreson dead bodies'; light up and move on."

We opened the hall door and entered a vaulted stone vestibule, full of dust, and cobwebby.

"There is nothing on this floor," said Eugène, "except servants' rooms and offices, and I don't believe there is anything wrong with them. I never heard that there was, anyway. Let's go upstairs."

So far as we could see, the house was apparently perfectly uninteresting inside, all eighteenth century work, the façade of the main building being, with the vestibule, the only portion of the Francis I work.

"The place was burned during the Terror," said Eugène, "for my great-uncle, from whom Mlle. de Tartas inherited it, was a good and true Royalist; he went to Spain after the Revolution, and did not come back until the accession of Charles X, when he restored the house, and then died, enormously old. This explains why it is all so new."

The old Spanish sorcerer to whom Mlle. de Tartas had left her personal property had done his work thoroughly. The house was absolutely empty, even the wardrobes and bookcases built in had been carried away; we went through room after room, finding all absolutely dismantled, only the windows and doors with their casings, the parquet floors, and the florid Renaissance mantels remaining.

"I feel better," remarked Fargeau. "The house may be haunted, but it doesn't look it, certainly; it is the most respectable place imaginable."

"Just you wait," replied Eugène. "These are only the state apartments, which my aunt seldom used, except, perhaps, on her annual 'Walpurgisnacht.' Come upstairs and I will show you a better *mise en scène*."

On this floor, the rooms fronting the court, the sleeping-rooms, were quite small—("They are the bad rooms all the same," said Eugène)—four of them, all just as ordinary in appearance as those below. A corridor ran behind them connecting with the wing corridor, and from this opened a door, unlike any of the other doors in that it was covered with green baize, somewhat moth-eaten. Eugène selected a key from the bunch he carried, unlocked the door, and with some difficulty forced it to swing inward; it was as heavy as the door of a safe.

"We are now," he said, "on the very threshold of hell itself; these rooms in here were my scarlet aunt's unholy of unholies. I never let them with the rest of the house, but keep them as a curiosity. I only wish Torrevieja had kept out; as it was, he looted them, as he did the rest of the house, and nothing is left but the walls and ceiling and floor. They are something, however, and may suggest what the former condition must have been. Tremble and enter."

The first apartment was a kind of anteroom, a cube of perhaps twenty feet each way, without windows, and with no doors except that by which we entered and another to the right. Walls, floor, and ceiling were covered with a black lacquer, brilliantly polished, that flashed the light of our lanterns in a thousand intricate reflections. It was like the inside of an enormous Japanese box, and about as empty. From this we passed to another room, and here we nearly dropped our lanterns. The room was circular, thirty feet or so in diameter, covered by a hemispherical dome; walls and ceiling were dark blue, spotted with gold stars; and reaching from floor to floor across the dome stretched a colossal figure in red lacquer of a nude woman kneeling, her legs reaching out along the floor on either side, her head touching the lintel of the door through which we had entered, her arms forming its sides, with the forearms extended and stretching along the walls until they met the long feet. The most astounding, misshapen, absolutely terrifying thing, I think, I ever saw. From the navel hung a great white object, like the traditional roc's egg of the Arabian Nights. The floor was of red lacquer, and in it was inlaid a pentagram the size of the room, made of wide strips of brass. In the centre of this pentagram was a circular disk of black stone, slightly saucer-shaped, with a small outlet in the middle.

The effect of the room was simply crushing, with this gigantic red figure crouched over it all, the staring eyes fixed on one, no matter what his position. None of us spoke, so oppressive was the whole thing.

The third room was like the first in dimensions, but instead of being black it was entirely sheathed with plates of brass—walls, ceiling, and floor—tarnished now, and turning green, but still brilliant under the lantern light. In the middle stood an oblong altar of porphyry, its longer dimensions on the axis of the suite of rooms, and at one end, opposite the range of doors, a pedestal of black basalt.

This was all. Three rooms, stranger than these, even in their emptiness, it would be hard to imagine. In Egypt, in India, they would not be entirely out of place, but here in Paris, in a commonplace *hôtel*, in the Rue M. le Prince, they were incredible.

We retraced our steps, Eugène closed the iron door with its baize covering, and we went into one of the front chambers and sat down, looking at each other.

"Nice party, your aunt," said Fargeau. "Nice old party, with amiable tastes; I am glad we are not to spend the night in *those* rooms."

"What do you suppose she did there?" inquired Duchesne. "I know more or less about black art, but that series of rooms is too much for me."

"My impression is," said d'Ardéche, "that the brazen room was a kind of sanctuary containing some image or other on the basalt base, while the stone in front was really an altar—what the nature of the sacrifice might be I don't even guess. The round room may have been used for invocations and incantations. The pentagram looks like it. Anyway, it is all just about as queer and *fin de siècle* as I can well imagine. Look here, it is nearly twelve. Let's dispose of ourselves, if we are going to hunt this thing down."

The four chambers on this floor of the old house were those said to be haunted, the wings being quite innocent, and, so far as we knew, the floors below. It was arranged that we should each occupy a room, leaving the doors open with the lights burning, and at the slightest cry or knock we were all to rush at once to the room from which the warning sound might come. There was no communication between the rooms to be sure, but, as the doors all opened into the corridor, every sound was plainly audible.

The last room fell to me, and I looked it over carefully.

It seemed innocent enough, a commonplace, square, rather lofty Parisian sleeping-room, finished in wood painted white, with a small marble mantel, a dusty floor of inlaid maple and cherry, walls hung with an ordinary French paper, apparently quite new, and two deeply embrasured windows looking out on the court.

I opened the swinging sash with some trouble, and sat down in the window seat with my lantern beside me trained on the only door, which gave on the corridor.

The wind had gone down, and it was very still without—still and hot. The masses of luminous vapor were gathering thickly overhead, no longer urged by the gusty wind. The great masses of rank wisteria leaves, with here and there a second blossoming of purple flowers, hung dead over the window in the sluggish air. Across the roofs I could hear the sound of a belated *fiacre* in the streets below. I filled my pipe again and waited.

For a time the voices of the men in the other rooms were a companionship, and at first I shouted to them now and then, but my voice echoed rather unpleasantly through the long corridors, and had a suggestive way of reverberating around the left wing beside me, and coming out at a broken window at its extremity like the voice of another man. I soon gave up my attempts at conversation, and devoted myself to the task of keeping awake.

It was not easy; why did I eat that lettuce salad at Père Garceau's? I should have known better. It was making me irresistibly sleepy, and wakefulness was absolutely necessary. It was certainly gratifying to know that I could sleep, that my courage was by me to that extent, but in the interests of science I must keep awake. But almost never, it seemed, had sleep looked so desirable. Half a hundred times, nearly, I would doze for an instant, only to awake with a start, and find my pipe gone out. Nor did the exertion of relighting it pull me together. I struck my match mechanically, and with the first puff dropped off again. It was most vexing. I got up and walked around the room. It was most annoying. My cramped position had almost put both my legs to sleep. I could hardly stand. I felt numb, as though with cold. There was no longer any sound from the other rooms, nor from without. I sank down in my window seat. How dark it was growing! I turned up the lantern. That pipe again, how obstinately it kept going out! and my last match was gone. The lantern, too, was *that* going out? I lifted my hand to turn it up again. It felt like lead, and fell beside me.

Then I awoke—absolutely. I remembered the story of "The Haunters and the Haunted." *This* was the Horror. I tried to rise, to cry out. My body was like lead, my tongue was paralyzed. I could hardly move my eyes. And the light was going out. There was no question about that. Darker and darker yet; little by little the pattern of the paper was swallowed up in the advancing night. A prickling numbness gathered in every nerve, my right arm slipped without feeling from my lap to my side, and I could not raise it—it swung helpless. A thin, keen humming began in my head, like the cicadas on a hillside in September. The darkness was coming fast.

Yes, this was it. Something was subjecting me, body and mind, to a slow paralysis. Physically I was already dead. If I could only hold my mind, my consciousness, I might still be safe, but could I? Could I resist the mad horror of this silence, the deepening dark, the creeping numbness? I knew that, like the man in the ghost story, my only safety lay here.

It had come at last. My body was dead, I could no longer move my eyes. They were fixed in that last look on the place where the door had been, now only a deepening of the dark.

Utter night: the last flicker of the lantern was gone. I sat and waited; my mind was still keen, but how long would it last? There was a limit even to the endurance of the utter panic of fear.

Then the end began. In the velvet blackness came two white eyes, milky, opalescent, small, far away—awful eyes, like a dead dream. More beautiful than I can describe, the flakes of white flame moving from the perimeter inward, disappearing in the center, like a never-ending flow of opal water into a circular tunnel. I could not have moved my eyes had I possessed the power: they devoured the fearful, beautiful things that grew slowly, slowly larger, fixed on me, advancing, growing more beautiful, the white flakes of light sweeping more swiftly into the blazing vortices, the awful fascination deepening in its insane intensity as the white, vibrating eyes grew nearer, larger.

Like a hideous and implacable engine of death the eyes of the unknown Horror swelled and expanded until they were close before me, enormous, terrible, and I felt a slow, cold, wet breath propelled with mechanical regularity against my face, enveloping me in its fetid mist, in its charnel-house deadliness.

With ordinary fear goes always a physical terror, but with me in the presence of this unspeakable Thing was only the utter and awful terror of the mind, the mad fear of a prolonged and ghostly nightmare. Again and again I tried to shriek, to make some noise, but physically I was utterly dead. I could only feel myself go mad with the terror of hideous death. The eyes were close on me— their movement so swift that they seemed to be but palpitating flames, the dead breath was around me like the depths of the deepest sea.

Suddenly a wet, icy mouth, like that of a dead cuttle-fish, shapeless, jelly-like, fell over mine. The horror began slowly to draw my life from me, but, as enormous and shuddering folds of palpitating jelly swept sinuously around me, my will came back, my body awoke with the reaction of final fear, and I closed with the nameless death that enfolded me.

What was it that I was fighting? My arms sunk through the unresisting mass that was turning me to ice. Moment by moment new folds of cold jelly swept round me, crushing me with the force of Titans. I fought to wrest my mouth from this awful Thing that sealed it, but, if ever I succeeded and caught a single breath, the wet, sucking mass closed over my face again before I could cry out. I think I fought for hours, desperately, insanely, in a silence that was more hideous than any sound—fought until I felt final death at hand, until the memory of all my life rushed over me like a flood, until I no longer had strength to wrench my face from that hellish succubus, until with a last mechanical struggle I fell and yielded to death.

Then I heard a voice say, "If he is dead, I can never forgive myself; I was to blame."

Another replied, "He is not dead, I know we can save him if only we reach the hospital in time. Drive like hell, *cocher!* Twenty francs for you, if you get there in three minutes."

Then there was night again, and nothingness until I suddenly awoke and stared around. I lay in a hospital ward, very white and sunny, some yellow *fleurs-de-lis* stood beside the head of the pallet, and a tall sister of mercy sat by my side.

To tell the story in a few words, I was in the Hôtel Dieu, where the men had taken me that fearful night of the twelfth of June. I asked for Fargeau or Duchesne, and by and by the latter came, and sitting beside the bed told me all that I did not know.

It seemed that they had sat, each in his room, hour after hour, hearing nothing, very much bored, and disappointed. Soon after two o'clock Fargeau, who was in the next room, called to me to ask if I was awake. I gave no reply, and, after shouting once or twice, he took his lantern and came to investigate. The door was locked on the inside! He instantly called d'Ardéche and Duchesne, and together they hurled themselves against the door. It resisted. Within they could hear irregular footsteps dashing here and there, with heavy breathing. Although frozen with terror, they fought to destroy the door and finally succeeded by using a great slab of marble that formed the shelf of the mantel in Fargeau's room. As the door crashed in, they were suddenly hurled back against the walls of the corridor, as though by an explosion, the lanterns were extinguished, and they found themselves in utter silence and darkness.

As soon as they recovered from the shock, they leaped into the room and fell over my body in the middle of the floor. They lighted one of the lanterns, and saw the strangest sight that can be imagined. The floor and walls to the height of about six feet were running with something that seemed like stagnant water, thick, glutinous, sickening. As for me, I was drenched with the same cursed liquid. The odor of musk was nauseating. They dragged me away, stripped off my clothing, wrapped me in their coats, and hurried to the hospital, thinking me perhaps dead. Soon after sunrise d'Ardéche left the hospital, being assured that I was in a fair way to recovery, with time, and with Fargeau went up to examine by daylight the traces of the adventure that was so nearly fatal. They were too late. Fire engines were coming down the street as they passed the Acadèmie. A neighbor rushed up to d'Ardéche: "O Monsieur! what misfortune, yet what fortune! it is true *la Bouche d'Enfer*—I beg pardon, the residence of the lamented Mlle. de Tartas—was burned, but not wholly, only the ancient building. The wings were saved, and for that great credit is due to the brave firemen, Monsieur will remember them, no doubt."

It was quite true. Whether a forgotten lantern, overturned in

the excitement, had done the work, or whether the origin of the
fire was more supernatural, it was certain that the "Mouth of Hell"
was no more. A last engine was pumping slowly as d'Ardéche
came up; half a dozen limp, and one distended, hose stretched
through the *porte cochere*, and within only the façade of Francis I
remained, draped still with the black stems of the wisteria. Beyond
lay a great vacancy, where thin smoke was rising slowly. Every
floor was gone, and the strange halls of Mlle. Blaye de Tartas were
only a memory.

With d'Ardéche I visited the place last year, but in the stead of
the ancient walls was then only a new and ordinary building, fresh
and respectable; yet the wonderful stories of the old "Bouche
d'Enfer" still lingered in the quarter, and will hold there, I do not
doubt, until the Day of Judgment.

The impact of H. P. LOVECRAFT *(1890–1937) on modern weird fiction is enormous. One may trace his influence in the work of many popular occult authors including Robert Bloch, August Derleth, Ray Bradbury, Robert E. Howard and even Stephen King (see his novella, "Jerusalem's Lot," a kind of "Dracula's Guest"-ish prologue to King's vampire novel,* Salem's Lot*). "The Rats in the Walls" is probably Lovecraft's best tale of terror, but there are vocal adherents for "The Dunwich Horror," "The Colour Out of Space" and "The Outsider." The latter, according to some critics, could pass for a newly discovered Poe manuscript. Perhaps. My personal favorite is "The Music of Erich Zann," a remakably Poe-like crescendo of undefinable menace.*

The Music of Erich Zann

BY H. P. LOVECRAFT

I have examined maps of the city with the greatest care, yet have never again found the Rue d'Auseil. These maps have not been modern maps alone, for I know that names change. I have, on the contrary, delved deeply into all the antiquities of the place, and have personally explored every region, of whatever name, which could possibly answer to the street I knew as the Rue d'Auseil. But despite all I have done, it remains an humiliating fact that I cannot find the house, the street, or even the locality, where, during the last months of my impoverished life as a student of metaphysics at the university, I heard the music of Erich Zann.

That my memory is broken, I do not wonder, for my health, physical and mental, was gravely disturbed throughout the period of my residence in the Rue d'Auseil, and I recall that I took none of my few acquaintances there. But that I cannot find the place again is both singular and perplexing; for it was within a half-hour's walk of the university and was distinguished by peculiarities which could hardly be forgotten by any one who had been there. I have never met a person who has seen the Rue d'Auseil.

The Rue d'Auseil lay across a dark river bordered by precipitous brick blear-windowed warehouses and spanned by a ponderous bridge of dark stone. It was always shadowy along that river, as if the smoke of neighboring factories shut out the sun perpetually. The river was also odorous with evil stenches which I have never smelled elsewhere, and which may some day help me to find it, since I should recognize them at once. Beyond that bridge were narrow cobbled streets with rails; and then came the ascent, at first gradual, but incredibly steep as the Rue d'Auseil was reached.

I have never seen another street as narrow and steep as the Rue d'Auseil. It was almost a cliff, closed to vehicles, consisting in several places of flights of steps, and ending at the top in a lofty ivied wall. Its paving was irregular, sometimes stone slabs, sometimes cobblestones, and sometimes bare earth with struggling greenish-grey vegetation. The houses were tall, peaked-roofed, incredibly old, and crazily leaning backward, forward, and sidewise. Occasionally an opposite pair, both leaning forward, almost met across the street like an arch; and certainly they kept most of the light from the ground below. There were a few overhead bridges from house to house across the street.

The inhabitants of that street impressed me peculiarly. At first I thought it was because they were all silent and reticent; but later decided it was because they were all very old. I do not know how I came to live on such a street, but I was not myself when I moved there. I had been living in many poor places, always evicted for want of money; until at last I came upon that tottering house in the Rue d'Auseil kept by the paralytic Blandot. It was the third house from the top of the street, and by far the tallest of them all.

My room was on the fifth story; the only inhabited room there, since the house was almost empty. On the night I arrived I heard strange music from the peaked garret overhead, and the next day asked old Blandot about it. He told me it was an old German viol-player, a strange dumb man who signed his name as Erich Zann, and who played evenings in a cheap theatre orchestra; adding that Zann's desire to play in the night after his return from the theatre was the reason he had chosen this lofty and isolated garret room, whose single gable window was the only point on the street from which one could look over the terminating wall at the declivity and panorama beyond.

Thereafter I heard Zann every night and although he kept me awake, I was haunted by the weirdness of his music. Knowing little of the art myself, I was yet certain that none of his harmonies had any relation to music I had heard before; and concluded that he was a composer of highly original genius. The longer I listened, the more I was fascinated, until after a week I resolved to make the old man's acquaintance.

One night as he was returning from his work, I intercepted Zann in the hallway and told him that I would like to know him and be with him when he played. He was a small, lean, bent person with shabby clothes, blue eyes, grotesque, satyrlike face, and nearly bald head; and at my first words seemed both frightened and angered. My obvious friendliness, however, finally melted him; and he grudgingly motioned me to follow him up the dark, creaking and rickety attic stairs. His room, one of only two in the steeply pitched garret, was on the west side, toward the high wall that formed the upper end of the street. Its size was very great, and seemed the greater because of its extraordinary barrenness and neglect. Of furniture there was only a narrow iron bedstead, a dingy washstand, a small table, a large bookcase, an iron music rack, and three old-fashioned chairs. Sheets of music were piled up in disorder about the floor. The walls were of bare boards, and had probably never known plaster; whilst the abundance of dust and cobwebs made the place seem more deserted than inhabited. Evidently Erich Zann's world of beauty lay in some far cosmos of imagination.

Motioning me to sit down, the dumb man closed the door, turned the large wooden bolt, and lighted a candle to augment the one he had brought with him. He now removed his viol from its moth-eaten covering and taking it, seated himself in the least uncomfortable of the three chairs. He did not employ the music rack, but, offering no choice and playing from memory, enchanted me for over an hour with strains I had never heard before; strains which must have been of his own devising. To describe their exact nature is impossible for one unversed in music. They were a kind of fugue, with recurrent passages of the most captivating quality, but to me they were notable for the absence of any of the weird notes I had overheard from my room below on other occasions.

These haunting notes I had remembered and had often hummed and whistled inaccurately to myself, so when the player at length laid down his bow I asked him if he would render some of them. As I began my request the wrinkled satyrlike face lost the bored placidity it had possessed during the playing, and seemed to show some curious mixture of anger and fright which I had noticed

when first I accosted the old man. For a moment I was inclined
to use persuasion, regarding rather lightly the whims of senility;
and even tried to awaken my host's weirder mood by whistling a
few of the strains to which I had listened the night before. But I
did not pursue this course for more than a moment; when the
dumb musician recognized the whistled air his face grew suddenly
distorted with an expression wholly beyond analysis, and his long,
cold, bony right hand reached out to stop my mouth and silence
the crude imitation. As he did this he further demonstrated his
eccentricity by casting a startled glance toward the lone curtained
window, as if fearful of some intruder—a glance doubly absurd
since the garret stood high and inaccessible above the adjacent
roofs, this window being the only point on the steep street, as the
concierge had told me, from which one could see over the wall at
the summit.

The old man's glance brought Blandot's remark to my mind,
and with a certain capriciousness I felt a wish to look out over the
wide and dizzying panorama of moonlit roofs and city lights
beyond the hilltop, which of all the dwellings in the Rue d'Auseil
only this crabbed musician could see. I moved toward the window
and would have drawn aside the nondescript curtains, when with
a frightened rage even greater than before, the dumb lodger was
upon me again; this time motioning with his head toward the door
as he nervously strove to drag me thither with both hands. Now
thoroughly disgusted with my host, I ordered him to release me,
and told him I would go at once. His clutch relaxed, and as he saw
my disgust and offense, his own anger seemed to subside. He
tightened his relaxing grip, but this time in a friendly manner,
forcing me into a chair; then with an appearance of wistfulness
crossed to the littered table, where he wrote many words with a
pencil, in the labored French of a foreigner.

The note which he finally handed me was an appeal for
tolerance and forgiveness. Zann said that he was old, lonely, and
afflicted with strange fears and nervous disorders connected with
his music and other things. He had enjoyed my listening to his
music, and wished I would come again and not mind his
eccentricities. But he could not play to another his weird
harmonies, and could not bear hearing them from another; nor
could he bear having anything in his room touched by another.
He had not known until our hallway conversation that I could
overhear his playing in my room, and now asked me if I would

arrange with Blandot to take a lower floor where I could not hear him in the night. He could, he wrote, defray the difference in rent.

As I sat deciphering the execrable French, I felt more lenient toward the old man. He was a victim of physical and nervous suffering, as was I; and my metaphysical studies had taught me kindness. In the silence there came a slight sound from the window—the shutter must have rattled in the night wind, and for some reason I started almost as violently as did Erich Zann. So when I had finished reading, I shook my host by the hand, and departed as a friend.

The next day Blandot gave me a more expensive room on the third floor, between the apartments of an aged money-lender and the room of a respectable upholsterer. There was no one on the fourth floor.

It was not long before I found that Zann's eagerness for my company was not as great as it had seemed while he was persuading me to move down from the fifth story. He did not ask me to call on him, and when I did call he appeared uneasy and played listlessly. This was always at night—in the day he slept and would admit no one. My liking for him did not grow though the attic room and the weird music seemed to hold an odd fascination for me. I had a curious desire to look out that window, over the wall and down the unseen slope at the glittering roofs and spires which must lie outspread there. Once I went up to the garret during theatre hours, when Zann was away, but the door was locked.

What I did succeed in doing was to overhear the nocturnal playing of the dumb old man. At first I would tiptoe to my old fifth floor, then I grew bold enough to climb the last creaking staircase to the peaked garret. There in the narrow hall outside the bolted door with the covered keyhole, I often heard sounds which filled me with an indefinable dread—the dread of vague wonder and brooding mystery. It was not that the sounds were hideous, for they were not; but that they held vibrations suggesting nothing on this globe or earth, and that at certain intervals they assumed a symphonic quality which I could hardly conceive as produced by one player. Certainly, Erich Zann was a genius of wild power. As the weeks passed, the playing grew wilder, whilst the old musician acquired an increasing haggardness and furtiveness pitiful to behold. He now refused to admit me at any time, and shunned me whenever we met on the stairs.

Then one night as I listened at the door, I heard the shrieking viol swell into a chaotic babel of sound; a pandemonium which would have led me to doubt my own sanity had there not come from behind that barred portal a piteous proof that the horror was real—the awful, inarticulate cry which only a mute can utter, and which rises only in moments of the most terrible fear or anguish. I knocked repeatedly at the door, but received no response. Afterwards I waited in the black hallway, shivering with cold and fear, till I heard the poor musician's feeble effort to rise from the floor by the aid of a chair. Believing him just conscious after a fainting fit, I renewed my rapping, at the same time calling out my name reassuringly. I heard Zann stumble to the window and close both shutter and sash, then stumble to the door, which he falteringly unfastened to admit me. This time his delight at having me present was real; for his distorted face gleamed with relief while he clutched at my coat as a child clutches at its mother's skirts.

Shaking pathetically, the old man forced me into a chair whilst he sank into another, beside which his viol and bow lay carelessly on the floor. He sat for some time inactive, nodding oddly, but having a paradoxical suggestion of intense and frightened listening. Subsequently he seemed to be satisfied, and crossing to a chair by the table he wrote me a brief note, handed it to me, and returned to the table where he began to write rapidly and incessantly. The note implored me in the name of mercy and for the sake of my own curiosity, to wait where I was until he prepared a full account in German of all the marvels and terrors which beset him. I waited and the dumb man's pencil flew.

It was perhaps an hour later, while I still waited and while the old musician's feverishly written sheets still continued to pile up, that I saw Zann start from the hint of a horrible shock. Unmistakably he was looking at the curtained window and listening shudderingly. Then I half fancied I heard a sound myself; though it was not a horrible sound, but rather an exquisitely low and infinitely distant musical note, suggesting a player in one of the neighbouring houses, or in some abode beyond the lofty wall over which I had never been able to look. Upon Zann the effect was terrible, for, dropping his pencil, suddenly he rose, seized his viol, and commenced to rend the night with the wildest playing I had ever heard from his bow save when listening at the barred door.

It would be useless to describe the playing of Erich Zann on that dreadful night. It was more horrible than anything I had ever overheard, because I could now see the expression of his face and could realize that this time the motive was stark fear. He was trying to make a noise; to ward off something or drown something out—what, I could not imagine, awesome though I felt it must be. The playing grew fantastic, delirious, and hysterical, yet kept to the last the qualities of supreme genius which I knew this strange old man possessed. I recognized the air—it was a wild Hungarian dance popular in the theatres, and I reflected for a moment that this was the first time I had ever heard Zann play the work of another composer.

Louder and louder, wilder and wilder, mounted the shrieking and whining of that desperate viol. The player was dripping with an uncanny perspiration and twisted like a monkey, always looking frantically at the curtained window. In his frienzied strains I could almost see shadowy satyrs and bacchanals dancing and whirling insanely through seething abysses of clouds and smoke and lightning. And then I thought I heard a shriller, steadier note that was not from the viol; a calm deliberate, purposeful, mocking note from far away in the West.

At this juncture the shutter began to rattle in a howling night wind which had sprung up outside as if in answer to the mad playing within. Zann's screaming viol now outdid itself, emitting sounds I never thought a viol could emit. The shutter rattled more loudly, unfastened, and commenced slamming against the window. Then the glass broke shiveringly under the persistent impacts, and the chill wind rushed in, making the candles sputter and rustling the sheets of paper on the table where Zann had begun to write out his horrible secret. I looked at Zann, and saw that he was past conscious observation. His blue eyes were bulging, glassy, and sightless, and the frantic playing had become a blind, mechanical, unrecognizable orgy that no pen could even suggest.

A sudden gust, stronger than the others, caught up the manuscript and bore it toward the window. I followed the flying sheets in desperation, but they were gone before I reached the demolished panes. Then I remembered my old wish to gaze from this window, the only window in the Rue d'Auseil from which one might see the slope beyond the wall, and the city outspread beneath. It was very dark, but the city's lights always burned, and I expected to see them there amidst the rain and wind. Yet, when

I looked from that highest of all gable windows, looked while the candles sputtered and the insane viol howled with the night-wind, I saw no city spread below, and no friendly lights gleamed from remembered streets, but only blackness of space illimitable; unimagined space much alive with motion and music, and having no semblance of anything on earth. And as I stood there looking in terror, the wind blew out both the candles in the ancient peaked garret, leaving us in savage and impenetrable darkness with chaos and pandemonium before me, and the demon madness of that night-baying viol behind me.

I staggered back in the dark, without the means of striking a light, crashing against the table, overturning a chair, and finally groped my way to the place where the blackness screamed with shocking music. To save myself and Erich Zann I could at least try, whatever the powers opposed to me. Once I thought some chill thing brushed me, and I screamed, but my scream could not be heard above that hideous viol. Suddenly out of the blackness the madly sawing bow struck me, and I knew I was close to the player. I felt ahead, touched the back of Zann's chair, and then found and shook his shoulders in an effort to bring him to his senses.

He did not respond, and still the viol shrieked on without slackening. I moved my hand to his head, whose mechanical nodding I was able to stop, and shouted in his ear that we both flee from the unknown thing of the night. But he neither answered me nor abated the frenzy of his unutterable music, while all through the garret strange currents of wind seemed to dance in the darkness and babel. When my hand touched his ear I shuddered, though I knew not why—knew not why till I felt of the still face; the ice-cold, stiffened, unbreathing face whose glossy eyes bulged uselessly into the void. And then, by some miracle, finding the door and the large, wooden bolt, I plunged wildly away from that glassy-eyed thing in the dark, and from the ghoulish howling of that accursed viol whose fury increased even as I plunged.

Leaping, floating, flying down those endless stairs through the dark house, racing mindlessly out into the narrow, steep, and ancient street of steps and tottering houses; clattering down steps and over cobbles to the lower streets and the putrid canyon-walled river; panting across the great dark bridge to the broader, healthier streets and boulevards we know; all these are terrible impressions that linger with me. And I recall that there was no wind and that the moon was out and that the lights of the city twinkled.

Despite my most careful searches and investigations, I have never since been able to find the Rue d'Auseil. But I am not wholly sorry; either for this or for the loss in undreamable abysses of the closely-written sheets which alone could have explained the music of Erich Zann.

It is a little-known fact that when J. R. R. TOLKIEN *(1892–1973) wrote his masterpiece,* Lord of the Rings, *he rewrote part of his earlier book,* The Hobbit, *so it would conform with the plot of the "ring" epic. The major change was in the fifth chapter, "Riddles in the Dark," in which the titular hero, Bilbo Baggins, meets a nasty critter named Gollum in a goblin cave. Few readers recall the first U.S. version of* The Hobbit, *published by Houghton Mifflin in 1938, yet Tolkien mentions the rewritten chapter in a prefatory note appearing in the later editions. Bilbo, he explained, was normally honest, but the evil ring made him lie about what happened in the cave and Bilbo even set down the false version in his own diary, the alleged source of* The Hobbit. *Completist that I am, I have long sought the 1938 variant of the Gollum chapter. Thanks to my friend, Faith Lancereau (who translated the Courtois and Le Braz tales elsewhere in this volume), I finally obtained a copy. With the permission of the publishers and the Tolkien Estate, I am proud to present this obscure footnote to hobbit-lore in its first reprinting in many decades. For further details, see* AFTERWORD.

NOTE: The following piece may be enjoyed even if you haven't read *The Hobbit*. Bilbo, a miniature Pickwickian, joins a group of adventurous dwarves. They are captured by goblins, but during a scuffle in a tunnel, Bilbo hits his head and passes out, unnoticed by goblin and dwarf alike. He wakes up lost, alone, armed only with an elfin dagger, Sting.

Riddles in the Dark

(Original version, 1938)

BY J. R. R. TOLKIEN

When Bilbo opened his eyes, he wondered if he had; for it was just as dark as with them shut. No one was anywhere near him. Just imagine his fright! He could hear nothing, see nothing, and he could feel nothing except the stone of the floor.

Very slowly he got up and groped about on all fours, till he touched the wall of the tunnel; but neither up nor down it could he find anything: nothing at all, no sign of goblins, no sign of dwarves. His head was swimming, and he was far from certain even of the direction they had been going in when he had his fall. He guessed as well as he could, and crawled along for a good way, till suddenly his hand met what felt like a tiny ring of cold metal lying on the floor of the tunnel. It was a turning point in his career, but he did not know it. He put the ring in his pocket almost without thinking; certainly it did not seem of any particular use at the moment. He did not go much further, but sat down on the cold floor and gave himself up to complete miserableness, for a long while. He thought of himself frying bacon and eggs in his own kitchen at home — for he could feel inside that it was high time for some meal or other; but that only made him miserabler.

He could not think what to do; nor could he think what had happened; or why he had been left behind; or why, if he had been left behind, the goblins had not caught him; or even why his head was so sore. The truth was he had been lying quiet, out of sight and out of mind, in a very dark corner for a long while.

After some time he felt for his pipe. It was not broken, and that was something. Then he felt for his pouch, and there was some tobacco in it, and that was something more. Then he felt for matches and he could not find any at all, and that shattered his hopes completely. Just as well for him, as he agreed when he came to his senses. Goodness knows what the striking of matches and the smell of tobacco would have brought on him out of dark holes in that horrible place. Still at the moment he felt very crushed. But in slapping all his pockets and feeling all round himself for matches his hand came on the hilt of his little sword — the little dagger that he got from the trolls, and that he had quite forgotten; nor do the goblins seem to have noticed it, as he wore it inside his breeches.

Now he drew it out. It shone pale and dim before his eyes. "So it is an elvish blade, too," he thought; "and goblins are not very near, and yet not far enough."

But somehow he was comforted. It was rather splendid to be wearing a blade made in Gondolin for the goblin-wars of which so many songs had sung; and also he had noticed that such weapons made a great impression on goblins that came upon them suddenly.

"Go back?" he thought. "No good at all! Go sideways? Impossible! Go forward? Only thing to do! On we go!" So up he got, and trotted along with his little sword held in front of him and one hand feeling the wall, and his heart all of a patter and a pitter.

Now certainly Bilbo was in what is called a tight place. But you must remember it was not quite so tight for him as it would have been for me or for you. Hobbits are not quite like ordinary people; and after all if their holes are nice cheery places and properly aired, quite different from the tunnels of the goblins, still they are more used to tunneling than we are, and they do not easily lose their sense of direction underground—not when their heads have recovered from being bumped. Also they can move very quietly, and hide easily, and recover wonderfully from falls and bruises, and they have a fund of wisdom and wise sayings that men have mostly never heard or have forgotten long ago.

I should not have like to have been in Mr. Baggins' place, all the same. The tunnel seemed to have no end. All he knew was that it was still going down pretty steadily and keeping in the same direction in spite of a twist and a turn or two. There were passages leading off to the side every now and then, as he knew by the glimmer of his sword, or could feel with his hand on the wall. Of these he took no notice, except to hurry past for fear of goblins or half-imagined dark things coming out of them. On and on he went, and down and down; and still he heard no sound of anything except the occasional whirr of a bat by his ears, which startled him at first, till it became too frequent to bother about. I do not know how long he kept on like this, hating to go on, not daring to stop, on, on, until he was tireder than tired. It seemed like all the way to tomorrow and over it to the days beyond.

Suddenly without any warning he trotted splash into water! Ugh! it was icy cold. That pulled him up sharp and short. He did not know whether it was just a pool in the path, or the edge of an underground stream that crossed the passage, or the brink of a deep dark subterranean lake. The sword was hardly shining at all. He stopped, and he could hear, when he listened hard, drops drip-drip-dripping from an unseen roof into the water below; but there seemed no other sort of sound.

"So it is a pool or a lake, and not an underground river," he thought. Still he did not dare to wade out into the darkness. He could not swim; and he thought, too, of nasty slimy things, with big bulging blind eyes, wriggling in the water. There are strange things living in the pools and lakes in the hearts of mountains: fish whose fathers swam in, goodness only knows how many years ago, and never swam out again, while their eyes grew bigger and bigger and bigger from trying to see in the blackness; also there are other things more slimy than fish. Even in the tunnels and caves the goblins have made for themselves there are other things living unbeknown to them that have sneaked in from outside to lie up in the dark. Some of these caves, too, go back in their beginnings to ages before the goblins, who only widened them and joined them up with passages, and the original owners are still there in odd corners, slinking and nosing about.

Deep down here by the dark water lived old Gollum. I don't know where he came from, nor who or what he was. He was Gollum—as dark as darkness, except for two big round pale eyes. He had a boat, and he rowed about quite quietly on the lake; for lake it was, wide and deep and deadly cold. He paddled it with large feet dangling over the side, but never a ripple did he make. Not he. He was looking out of his pale lamp-like eyes for blind fish, which he grabbed with his long fingers as quick as thinking. He liked meat too. Goblin he thought good, when he could get it; but he took care they never found him out. He just throttled them from behind, if they ever came down alone anywhere near the edge of the water, while he was prowling about. They very seldom did, for they had a feeling that something unpleasant was lurking down there, down at the very roots of the mountain. They had come on the lake, when they were tunneling down long ago, and they found they could go no further; so there their road ended in that direction, and there was no reason to go that way—unless the Great Goblin sent them. Sometimes he took a fancy for fish from the lake, and sometimes neither goblin nor fish came back.

Actually Gollum lived on a slimy island of rock in the middle of the lake. He was watching Bilbo now from the distance with his pale eyes like telescopes. Bilbo could not see him, but he was wondering a lot about Bilbo, for he could see that he was no goblin at all.

Gollum got into his boat and shot off from the island, while Bilbo was sitting on the brink altogether flummoxed and at the end of his way and his wits. Suddenly up came Gollum and whispered and hissed:

"Bless us and splash us, my precioussss! I guess it's a choice feast; at least a tasty morsel it'd make us, gollum!" And when he said *gollum* he made a horrible swallowing noise in his throat. That is how he got his name, though he always called himself 'my precious.'

The hobbit jumped nearly out of his skin when the hiss came in his ears, and he suddenly saw the pale eyes sticking out at him.

"Who are you?" he said, thrusting his dagger in front of him.

"What iss he, my preciouss?" whispered Gollum (who always spoke to himself through never having anyone else to speak to). This is what he had come to find out, for he was not really very hungry at the moment, only curious; otherwise he would have grabbed first and whispered afterwards.

"I am Mr. Bilbo Baggins. I have lost the dwarves and I have lost the wizard, and I don't know where I am; and I don't want to know, if only I can get away."

"What's he got in his handses?" said Gollum, looking at the sword, which he did not quite like.

"A sword, a blade which came out of Gondolin!"

"Sssss" said Gollum, and became quite polite. "Praps ye sits here and chats with it a bitsy, my preciousss. It likes riddles, praps it does, does, it?" He was anxious to appear friendly, at any rate for the moment, and until he found out more about the sword and the hobbit, whether he was quite alone really, whether he was good to eat, and whether Gollum was really hungry. Riddles were all he could think of. Asking them, and sometimes guessing them, had been the only game he had ever played with other funny creatures sitting in their holes in the long, long ago, before the goblins came, and he was cut off from his friends far under the mountains.

"Very well," said Bilbo, who was anxious to agree, until he found out more about the creature, whether he was quite alone, whether he was fierce or hungry, and whether he was a friend of the goblins.

"You ask first," he said, because he had not had time to think of a riddle.

So Gollum hissed:

> What has roots as nobody sees,
> Is taller than trees,
>   Up, up it goes,
>   And yet never grows?

"Easy!" said Bilbo. "Mountain, I suppose."

"Does it guess easy? It must have a competition with us, my preciouss! If precious asks, and it doesn't answer, we eats it, my preciousss. If it asks us, and we doesn't answer, we gives it a present, gollum!"

"All right!" said Bilbo, not daring to disagree, and nearly bursting his brain to think of riddles that could save him from being eaten.

> Thirty white horses on a red hill,
> First they champ,
> Then they stamp,
> Then they stand still.

That was all he could think of to ask—the idea of eating was rather on his mind. It was rather an old one, too, and Gollum knew the answer as well as you do.

"Chestnuts, chestnuts," he hissed. "Teeth! teeth! my preciousss; but we has only six!" Then he asked his second:

> Voiceless it cries,
> Wingless flutters,
> Toothless bites,
> Mouthless mutters.

"Half a moment!" cried Bilbo, who was still thinking uncomfortably about eating. Fortunately he had once heard something rather like this before, and getting his wits back he thought of the answer. "Wind, wind of course," he said, and he was so pleased that he made up one on the spot. "This'll puzzle the nasty little underground creature," he thought:

> An eye in a blue face
> Saw an eye in a green face.
> "That eye is like to this eye"
> Said the first eye,
> "But in low place,
> Not in high place."

"Ss, ss, ss," said Gollum. He had been underground a long long time, and was forgetting this sort of thing. But just as Bilbo was beginning to wonder what Gollum's present would be like, Gollum brought up memories of ages and ages and ages before, when he lived with his grandmother in a hole in a bank by a river, "Sss, sss, my preciouss," he said, "Sun on the daisies it means, it does."

But these ordinary above ground everyday sort of riddles were tiring for him. Also they reminded him of days when he had been less lonely and sneaky and nasty, and that put him out of temper. What is more they made him hungry; so this time he tried something a bit more difficult and more unpleasant:

> It cannot be seen, cannot be felt,
> Cannot be heard, cannot be smelt.
> It lies behind stars and under hills,
> And empty holes it fills.
> It comes first and follows after,
> Ends life, kills laughter.

Unfortunately for Gollum Bilbo had heard that sort of thing before; and the answer was all round him anyway. "Dark!" he said without even scratching his head or putting on his thinking cap.

> A box without hinges, key, or lid,
> Yet golden treasure inside is hid,

he asked to gain time, until he could think of a really hard one. This he thought a dreadfully easy chestnut, though he had not asked it in the usual words. But it proved a nasty poser for Gollum. He hissed to himself, and still he did not answer; he whispered and sputtered.

After some while Bilbo became impatient. "Well, what is it?" he said. "The answer's not a kettle boiling over, as you seem to think from the noise you are making."

"Give us a chance; let it give us a chance, my preciouss—ss—ss."

"Well," said Bilbo, after giving him a long chance, "what about your present?"

But suddenly Gollum remembered thieving from nests long ago, and sitting under the river bank teaching his grandmother, teaching his grandmother to suck—"Eggses!" he hissed. "Eggses it is!" Then he asked:

> Alive without breath,
> As cold as death;
> Never thirsty, ever drinking,
> All in mail never clinking.

He also in his turn thought this was a dreadfully easy one, because he was always thinking of the answer. But he could not remember anything better at the moment, he was so flustered by the egg-question. All the same it was a poser for poor Bilbo, who never had anything to do with the water if he could help it. I imagine you know the answer, of course, or can guess it as easy as winking, since you are sitting comfortably at home and have not the danger of being eaten to disturb your thinking. Bilbo sat and cleared his throat once or twice, but no answer came.

After a while Gollum began to hiss with pleasure to himself: "Is it nice, my preciousss? Is it juicy? Is it scrumptiously crunchable?" He began to peer at Bilbo out of the darkness.

"Half a moment," said the hobbit shivering. "I gave you a good long chance just now."

"It must make haste, haste!" said Gollum, beginning to climb out of his boat on to the shore to get at Bilbo. But when he put his long webby foot in the water, a fish jumped out in fright and fell on Bilbo's toes.

"Ugh!" he said, "it is cold and clammy!"—and so he guessed. "Fish! fish!" he cried. "It is fish!"

Gollum was dreadfully disappointed; but Bilbo asked another riddle as quick as ever he could, so that Gollum had to get back to his boat and think.

No-legs lay on one-leg, two-legs sat near on three-legs, four-legs got some.

It was not really the right time for this riddle, but Bilbo was in a hurry. Gollum might have had some trouble guessing it, if he had asked it at another time. As it was, talking of fish, "no-legs" was not so very difficult, and after that the rest was easy. "Fish on a little table, man at table sitting on a stool, the cat has the bones" that of course is the answer, and Gollum soon gave it. Then he thought the time had come to ask something hard and horrible. This is what he said:

> This thing all things devours:
> Birds, beasts, trees, flowers;

Gnaws iron, bites steel;
Grinds hard stones to meal;
Slays king, ruins town,
And beats high mountain down.

Poor Bilbo sat in the dark thinking of all the horrible names of all the giants and ogres he had ever heard told of in tales, but not one of them had done all these things. He had a feeling that the answer was quite different and that he ought to know it, but he could not think of it. He began to get frightened, and that is bad for thinking. Gollum began to get out of his boat. He flapped into the water and paddled to the bank; Bilbo could see his eyes coming towards him. His tongue seemed to stick in his mouth; he wanted to shout out: "Give me more time! Give me time!" But all that came out with a sudden squeal was:

"Time! Time!"

Bilbo was saved by pure luck. For that of course was the answer.

Gollum was disappointed once more; and now he was getting angry, and also tired of the game. It had made him very hungry indeed. This time he did not go back to the boat. He sat down in the dark by Bilbo. That made the hobbit most dreadfully uncomfortable and scattered his wits.

"It's got to ask uss a question, my preciouss, yes, yess, yesss. Jusst one more quesstion to guess, yes, yess," said Gollum.

But Bilbo simply could not think of any question with that nasty wet cold thing sitting next to him, and pawing and poking him. He scratched himself, he pinched himself; still he could not think of anything.

"Ask us! ask us!" said Gollum.

Bilbo pinched himself and slapped himself; he gripped on his little sword; he even felt in his pocket with his other hand. There he found the ring he had picked up in the passage and forgotten about.

"What have I got in my pocket?" he said aloud. He was talking to himself, but Gollum thought it was a riddle, and he was frightfully upset.

"Not fair! not fair!" he hissed. "It isn't fair, my precious, is it, to ask us what it's got in its nassty little pocketses?"

Bilbo seeing what had happened and having nothing better to

ask stuck to his question, "What have I got in my pocket?" he said louder.

"S-s-s-s-s," hissed Gollum. "It must give us three guesses, my preciouss, three guesseses."

"Very well!! Guess away!" said Bilbo.

"Handses!" said Gollum.

"Wrong," said Bilbo, who had luckily just taken his hand out again. "Guess again!"

"S-s-s-s-s," said Gollum more upset than ever. He thought of all the things he kept in his own pockets: fish-bones, goblins' teeth, wet shells, a bit of bat-wing, a sharp stone to sharpen his fangs on, and other nasty things. He tried to think what other people kept in their pockets.

"Knife!" he said at last.

"Wrong!" said Bilbo, who had lost his some time ago. "Last guess!"

Now Gollum was in a much worse state than when Bilbo had asked him the egg-question. He hissed and spluttered and rocked himself backwards and forwards, and slapped his feet on the floor, and wriggled and squirmed; but still he did not dare to waste his last guess.

"Come on!" said Bilbo. "I am waiting!" He tried to sound bold and cheerful, but he did not feel at all sure how the game was going to end, whether Gollum guessed right or not.

"Time's up!" he said.

"String, or nothing!" shrieked Gollum, which was not quite fair—working in two guesses at once.

"Both wrong," cried Bilbo very much relieved; and he jumped at once to his feet, put his back to the nearest wall, and held out his little sword. But funnily enough he need not have been alarmed. For one thing Gollum had learned long long ago was never, never, to cheat at the riddle-game, which is a sacred one and of immense antiquity. Also there was the sword. He simply sat and whispered.

"What about the present?" asked Bilbo, not that he cared very much, still he felt that he had won it, pretty fairly, and in very difficult circumstances, too.

"Must we give it the thing, preciouss? Yess, we must! We must fetch it, preciouss, and give it the present we promised." So Gollum paddled back to his boat, and Bilbo thought he had heard the last of him. But he had not. The hobbit was just thinking of going back up the passage—having had quite enough of Gollum and the dark water's edge—when he heard him wailing and squeaking away in the gloom. He was on his island (of which, of course, Bilbo knew nothing), scrabbling here and there, searching and seeking in vain, and turning out his pockets.

"Where iss it? Where iss it?" Bilbo heard him squeaking. "Lost, lost, my preciouss, lost, lost! Bless us and splash us! We haven't the present we promised, and we haven't even got it for ourselves."

Bilbo turned round and waited, wondering what it could be that the creature was making such a fuss about. This proved very fortunate afterwards. For Gollum came back and made a tremendous spluttering and whispering and croaking; and in the end Bilbo gathered that Gollum had had a ring—a wonderful, beautiful ring, a ring that he had been given for a birthday present, ages and ages before in old days when such rings were less uncommon. Sometimes he had it in his pocket; usually he kept it in a little hole in the rock on his island; sometimes he wore it— when he was very, very hungry, and tired of fish, and crept along dark passages looking for stray goblins. Then he might venture even into places where the torches were lit and made his eyes blink and smart; but he would be safe. O yes! very nearly safe; for if you slipped that ring on your finger, you were invisible; only in the sunlight could you be seen, and then only by your shadow, and that was a faint and shaky sort of shadow.

I don't know how many times Gollum begged Bilbo's pardon. He kept on saying: "We are ssorry; we didn't mean to cheat, we meant to give it our only pressent, if it won the competition." He even offered to catch Bilbo some nice juicy fish to eat as a consolation.

Bilbo shuddered at the thought of it. "No thank you!" he said as politely as he could.

He was thinking hard, and the idea came to him that Gollum must have dropped that ring sometime and that he must have found it, and that he had that very ring in his pocket. But he had the wits not to tell Gollum.

"Finding's keeping!" he said to himself; and being in a very tight place, I daresay, he was right. Anyway the ring belonged to him now.

"Never mind!" he said. "The ring would have been mine now, if you had found it; so you would have lost it anyway. And I will let you off on one condition."

"Yes, what iss it? What does it wish us to do, my precious?"

"Help me to get out of these places," said Bilbo.

Now Gollum had to agree to this, if he was not to cheat. He still very much wanted just to try what the stranger tasted like; but now he had to give up all idea of it. Still there was the little sword; and the stranger was wide awake and on the look out, not unsuspecting as Gollum liked to have the things which he attacked. So perhaps it was best after all.

That is how Bilbo got to know that the tunnel ended at the water and went no further on the other side where the mountain wall was dark and solid. He also learned that he ought to have turned down one of the side passages to the right before he came to the bottom; but he could not follow Gollum's directions for finding it again on the way up, and he made the wretched creature come and show him the way.

As they went along up the tunnel together, Gollum flip-flapping at his side, Bilbo going very softly, he thought he would try the ring. He slipped it on his finger.

"Where iss it? Where iss it gone to?" said Gollum at once, peering about with his long eyes.

"Here I am, following behind!" said Bilbo slipping off the ring again, and feeling very pleased to have it and to find that it really did what Gollum said.

Now on they went again, while Gollum counted the passages to left and right: "One left, one right, two right, three right, two left," and so on. He began to get very shaky and afraid as they left the water further and further behind; but at last he stopped by a low opening on their left (going up)—"six right, four left."

"Here'ss the passage," he whispered. "It musst squeeze in and sneak down. We durstn't go with it, my preciouss, no we durstn't, gollum!"

So Bilbo slipped under the arch, and said good-bye to the nasty miserable creature; and very glad he was. He did not feel comfortable until he felt quite sure it was gone, and he kept his head out in the main tunnel listening until the flip-flap of Gollum going back to his boat died away in the darkness. Then he went down the new passage.

It was a low narrow one roughly made. It was all right for the hobbit, except when he stubbed his toes in the dark on nasty jags in the floor; but it must have been a bit low for goblins. Perhaps it was not knowing that goblins are used to this sort of thing, and go along quite fast stooping low with their hands almost on the floor, that made Bilbo forget the danger of meeting them and hurry forward recklessly.

Soon the passage began to go up again, and after a while it climbed steeply. That slowed him down. But at last after some time the slope stopped, the passage turned a corner and dipped down again, and at the bottom of a short incline he saw filtering round another corner—a glimmer of light. Not red light as of fire or lantern, but pale ordinary out-of-doors sort of light. Then he began to run. Scuttling along as fast as his little legs would carry him he turned the corner and came suddenly right into an open place where the light, after all that time in the dark, seemed dazzlingly bright. Really it was only a leak of sunshine in through a doorway, where a great door, a stone door, was left a little open.

Bilbo blinked, and then he suddenly saw the goblins: goblins in full armour with drawn swords sitting just inside the door, and watching it with wide eyes, and the passage that led to it! They saw him sooner than he saw them, and with yells of delight they rushed upon him.

Whether it was accident or presence of mind, I don't know. Accident, I think, because the hobbit was not used yet to his new treasure. Anyway he slipped the ring on his left hand—and the goblins stopped short. They could not see a sign of him. Then they yelled twice as loud as before, but not so delightedly.

"Where is it?" they cried.

"Go back up the passage!" some shouted.

"This way!" some yelled. "That way!" others yelled.

"Look out for the door," bellowed the captain.

Whistles blew, armour clashed, swords rattled, goblins cursed and swore and ran hither and thither, falling over one another and geting very angry. There was a terrible outcry, to-do, and disturbance.

Bilbo was dreadfully frightened, but he had the sense to understand what had happened and to sneak behind a big barrel which held drink for the goblin-guards, and so get out of the way and avoid being bumped into, trampled to death, or caught by feel.

"I must get to the door, I must get to the door!" he kept on saying to himself, but it was a long time before he ventured to try. Then it was like a horrible game of blind-man's-buff. The place was full of goblins running about, and the poor little hobbit dodged this way and that, was knocked over by a goblin who could not make out what he had bumped into, scrambled away on all fours, slipped between the legs of the captain just in time, got up, and ran for the door.

It was still ajar, but a goblin had pushed it nearly to. Bilbo struggled but he could not move it. He tried to squeeze through the crack. He squeezed and squeezed, and he stuck! It was awful. His buttons had got wedged on the edge of the door and the door-post. He could see outside into the open air: there were a few steps running down into a narrow valley between tall mountains: the sun came out from behind a cloud and shone bright on the outside of the door—but he could not get through.

Suddenly one of the goblins inside shouted: "There is a shadow by the door. Something is outside!"

Bilbo's heart jumped into his mouth. He gave a terrific squirm. Buttons burst off in all directions. He was through, with a torn coat and waistcoat, leaping down the steps like a goat, while bewildered goblins were still picking up his nice brass buttons on the doorstep.

Of course they soon came down after him, hooting and hallooing, and hunting among the trees. But they don't like the sun: it makes their legs wobble and their heads giddy. They could not find Bilbo with the ring on, slipping in and out of the shadow of the trees, running quick and quiet, and keeping out of the sun; so soon they went back grumbling and cursing to guard the door. Bilbo had escaped.

AFTERWORD

Is Terror a Dying Art?

Although horror and terror commonly are employed synonymously, the dictionary unmistakably links the former term with that revulsion experienced upon witnessing something ugly, disgusting, shocking, etc. Terror carries no such connotation. Its meaning is cleaner, more profound, deriving as it does from the Latin *terrere*, to frighten.

For the past decade or more, I have been disappointed with most of the sophomoric horror tales, novels and films recommended to me, mostly by younger friends. It is not solely because my tastes are jaded (they are) that I am resoundingly unimpressed with such fare as *Rosemary's Baby, The Exorcist, The Howling, The Shining, Ghost Story, The Omen, The Thing, Creepshow, Twilight Zone the Movie,* and so on and on ad—literally—nauseam. To borrow an image from the Episcopalian priest-philosopher, Robert Farrar Capon, the public has heard so many tin fiddles squealing that it's hard to recall what a Stradivarius sounds like.

You disagree? Wade through the purple prose and puerile theology of Blatty's *The Exorcist,* then flip back and read Andreyev's bleakly existential "Lazarus" or find a copy, if you can, of Russell's first novel, *The Case Against Satan,* and read the identical story but without Blatty's artsy straining-for-effect pretentiousness. Look at *Rosemary's Baby.* Try to find anything the least bit ambiguous about its sweet-young-thing-brutalized-by-the-bogeyman plot. Some critics tried to make a case for Rosemary's predicament existing solely in her mind, but nothing Ira Levin wrote substantiates that claim, whereas Isaac Bashevis Singer accomplishes precisely that in a fraction of the verbiage in "The Black Wedding." Films? None of the above can seriously be considered in the same company as Ingmar Bergman's *The Silence* or Jack Clayton's 1961 classic, *The Innocents*. They can't even compare favorably with Val Lewton's low-budget thrillers, or the unnerving mixture of horror and poignancy in Franju's *Les Yeux Sans Visage*. And the ventriloquist episode of Cavalcanti's *Dead of Night* holds more genuine terror than all those pitifully inept Roger Corman-Poe clinkers or the Hammer Draculas with their bottomless buckets of blood.

I'm not suggesting that horror should be divorced from terror and exiled from the kingdom of night. That would be both foolish and impractical. When you romp through graveyards or play Peeping Tom to a sociopath, you must expect to feel the impact in the pit of your stomach at the same time those icy glissandos xylophone their way along your spine.

What I *am* proposing is a rebirth of artistic balance and taste by relegating horror to its rightful subsidiary position as a mere contributory device towards achieving terror. Naked horror is a meretricious effect, easy to employ, liable to pall if used too liberally or often. The true impact of Damon Runyon's "The Informal Execution of Soupbone Pew," for instance, is not the nasty hugger-mugger in the jail cell, but the unexpected revelation in the last line of the story. Here the true note of terror is sounded, rooted as it is in the awesome enigma of the human mind.

Even at its crudest, most melodramatic level, terror has the ability to stir up the secret dreads embedded in our individual and collective imaginations. By recognizing our worst nightmares, we are capable of exorcising them, at least temporarily. When a great artist turns to the terror genre, he or she elevates the exorcism process to the level of catharsis: that working-out of pity commingled with terror that the Greeks experienced at the close of a Sophoclean trilogy—a massive cultural/spiritual purging that permitted the participants to leave the sacred theatre uplifted and better equipped to deal with the everyday fears of life itself. Thus terror in its most noble incarnation is a vital component of the art of tragedy.

It therefore follows that great works of terror depend largely for their power upon characterization. By their very nature, the related genres of fantasy, the supernatural, mystery, science fiction and suspense—all of them capable of producing tales of terror—tend to stress concept, i.e., the plot gimmick, the vampire, the animated flayed hand, the sadist with the eternal smile on his face. Because concept is so striking, too many writers and film directors become enamored of the device to the detriment of character.

Imagine, for example, a film that shows a white-haired old woman feebly scrabbling in the dark among the rotting pieces of corpses that have dropped from a gallows. She finds certain bones, peers uncertainly at them, separates them from the sinews and eyeballs of more recent cadavers. She hides them in a burlap sack and scuttles away muttering, "My son . . . my son."

Well, it might work, but any shock it produced would be slight. Why? Because we know nothing about her, less about her son. But turn to Tennyson's "Rizpah" and hear the dying woman's heart-rending secret. The poet sets the son's harmlessly rakehell character swiftly, deftly, and paints his mother's anguish with such agonizing force that we weep for her and shake with rage at the towering inhumanity of that system of "justice" that destroyed both lives.

Character is more important than plot every time. Without it, a writer might just as well hide in a closet and yell "Boo!" at passersby. That, in essence, is what most modern horror literature and cinema amounts to. But when the reader begins to believe in and care about a fictional protagonist, he or she becomes susceptible to those calculated manipulations that a masterful fabulist must devise in order to invoke a sense of wonder and terror (the two often go hand in hand).

Proper manipulation of the reader's emotions requires a sense of structure and an appreciation of the greatest special effect of them all: economy. Not showing the wicked something that this way comes too soon, too clearly or too often. Watch some of those old scare movies on late-night television. Even the hack "B" film directors usually knew enough to delay the first appearance of the monster. One of the most effective oldies is *Night of the Demon*, based on M. R. James' eerie tale, "Casting the Runes." A great sense of menace is developed in the early sequences because the demon lurks just beyond view. When he finally makes his on-screen appearance, His Satanic Nibs is a decided letdown. He looks a little like Ernest Borgnine. The director (Jacques Tourneur, who usually knew better) passed the "too soon" test but displayed his critter too clearly. As for employing an effect too often, note the overused images of decay in the film *Ghost Story*. We see the rotting corpse so many times that her appearance is familiar and not in the least shocking by the end of the film. If the director had only given us the reactions of her victims and held off on what she looks like till the climax, it might have been harrowing rather than predictable.

Terror, though rooted in character and artfully orchestrated, still needs one more thing to be truly effective: an understanding of psychology, of what frightens us. This is the distinguishing requisite. What works for one person may leave another totally unmoved. Example: Ike Asimov's "Flies." Some readers understand the analogy being drawn between Casey and the flies that worship him and the possible relationship between mankind and godhead; others miss it entirely. One friend of mine who understood it perfectly merely laughed—and over the years, I've also come around to seeing "Flies" both as a tale of terror and a bit of black comedy.*

H. P. Lovecraft once stressed the importance of the fears of darkness, cold and dampness. Many of his stories begin with a night scene near the seaside, sometimes during winter—thus consciously employing all three fears to (hopefully) unsettle the reader at the very outset.

The catalog of things that really frighten us is endless. It would include odd phobias that only affect a few. Roger Price once enumerated several in his hilarious book *In One Head and Out the Other*. His "capper" was the fear of being covered with gold paint, which Price called a "gilt complex." Then Ian Fleming wrote *Goldfinger*, in which a woman is asphyxiated by being totally immersed in gold paint and the idea no longer seemed quite so funny.

Robert Bloch employs a few common terrors in "The Hungry House": fear of the unknown as the nature of the malign entity puzzles and terrifies the hapless protagonists; fear of madness when it appears that the house is haunted by a violently insane spirit; fear of pain, death and possession as bloody deaths await the heroes who become the latest in a growing population of captive ghosts.

A variation of the fear of pain (and suffering) is the use of

---

* Asimov's original title for the piece displayed his inspiration: "King Lear IV 1 36–37." This is the passage he cites—"As flies to wanton boys, are we to th' gods;/They kill us for their sport."

dismemberment in tales of terror. Sometimes the bodily parts just lic there, as in Carr's "The House in Goblin Wood," while on other occasions, they become animate with ghastly purpose (de Maupassant's "The Flayed Hand"). But I maintain that the mere existence of a severed head or hand only makes for horror. It is the calculating inhumanity of the murders in the Carr tale that makes us quake with the notion that the most innocent-looking milquetoast "may smile and smile and be a villain." As for the active extremity in the de Maupassant story, I suspect it is the inexplicable cosmic mystery it implies that is responsible for any morsel of fear we feel upon reading the tale.

This brings me to my peroration. In my estimation, the true springs of terror flow from within. Fear of aging and the loss of love, isolation in a cosmos where we do not know the questions, let alone the answers, the fear that all effort may be ultimately useless in the face of what Camus calls the terrible dark wind of the future. When the swan-woman tears her heart out rather than live without her dead lover in Hearn's "Oshidori," we tremble at a force stronger than the love of life itself. When Maurice Level's horrible trio die surrounded by cosmic indifference—by "Night and Silence"—we shiver at the thought it conjures of every irrelevant death occurring throughout the globe while we brush our teeth, make love, listen to music, laugh, or—worst of all— yawn with boredom. Most of all, the cold breath of something beyond terror blows over us when Ed Hoch's mudcreature feebly sinks back into the ooze in "The Faceless Thing." The kingdom and the power and the glory are surrounded by a world of night.

Those readers familiar with Boris Karloff's introduction to *Tales of Terror* (World Publishing Co., 1943) realize that this Afterword is essentially a sermon based on the Gospel According to the Original Frankenstein Monster. In his introduction, Karloff credited Joseph Conrad with writing the greatest description of pure terror—in all its implications—in the English language. Since I agree, I close this essay with that passage from Conrad's little-known novel *The Shadow Line:*

" . . . as I emerge on deck the ordered arrangement of the stars meets my eye, unclouded, infinitely wearisome. There they are: stars, sun, sea, light, darkness, space, great waters; the formidable Work of the Seven Days, into which mankind seems to have blundered unbidden. Or else decoyed."

MISCELLANEOUS NOTES

Bürger's "Lenore" (pp. 245–252)

It is a common theme of folk balladry that excessive mourning disturbs the rest of the dead. Variations of this message may be traced in such popular traditional songs as "The Unquiet Grave," "Lost Jimmy Whelan," "The Wife of Usher's Well" and its rural American counterpart, "The Lady Gay" and "A Suffolk Miracle," my own variant of which may be found in *Ghosts: A Treasury of Chilling Tales Old and New*. "Lenore" expands on the idea by making the behavior of its titular heroine an act of hubris offensive to her god, who abandons her to her demon-transformed lover, who at first appears to be the revenant of the man she loved, but ultimately stands for Death incarnate.

Gardner's "A Malady of Magicks" (pp. 76–90)

In spite of the success of Vonnegut and the "hitchhiker's guide" trilogy, genre publishers still shy away from what they call whimsy. A. A. Milne is whimsical (and occasionally treacly). The Ebenezum stories are not. They are devastating send-ups of the whole overwritten school of heroic literature, which my friend and collaborator Parke Godwin aptly terms "Swords and Sausage." For those who thoroughly enjoy Craig's brand of slapstick, as I do, you will want to read the other Ebenezum tales that follow "A Malady of Magicks." They are "A Drama of Dragons" in Orson Scott Card's *Dragons of Light*; "A Dealing with Demons" in Lin Carter's *Flashing Swords # 5*; "A Gathering of Ghosts" in the companion volume to this anthology, *Ghosts: A Treasury of Chilling Tales Old and New*. A fifth story, "A Whooping of Witches" and an Ebenezum novel have not yet been published.

Lee's "When the Clock Strikes"   (pp. 143–158)

Tanith Lee's chilling rendering of "Cinderella" is one of many bizarre reworkings of Grimm's fairy tales in her collection *Red As Blood*, which in both hardcover and paperback boasts a strikingly effective cover by artist Victoria Poyser. Both the book and the artist were nominated among the best in their respective categories at the prestigious World Fantasy Convention of 1984.

Stoker's "Dracula's Guest"   (pp. 3–14)

It took me years to track this tale—in fact, I first read it at the Library of Congress. (Now it is available in several editions.) While I was on its trail back in the 1950s, one of my friends told me it was a bit disappointing because Dracula didn't appear in it. This is untrue. The tall man that Harker sees at the crossroads surely is the Count himself making sure no harm comes to his guest. The hand that yanks Harker back from the tomb and its vampiric occupant recalls the similar gesture of Dracula when, in the novel, he waves away his undead mistresses with the warning that Harker is the Count's personal property. In the "guest" episode, when the wolf licks Harker's throat, it is to protect him from exposure. Dracula is usually thought of as changing to a bat, but in the novel, he takes the form of a wolf on more than one occasion. Finally, if any doubt remains, the letter that arrives at the conclusion of "Dracula's Guest" shows that the vampire-noble knew just what sort of dangers the headstrong young Englishman just escaped from. The message possesses that grim irony that Dracula more than once displays later on, but then Bela Lugosi always played him with panache!

Tolkien's "Riddles in the Dark"   (pp. 632–645)

The 1938 text is identical to later printings of *The Hobbit* until page 91 of the Houghton Mifflin edition. The last common sentence till the end of the chapter is " 'Both wrong,' cried Bilbo very much relieved; and he jumped at once to his feet, put his back to the nearest wall, and held out his little sword." Immediately following, the texts diverge, concluding on page 96 of the 1938 version and page 101 of the revised state. Tolkien rewrote this chapter so that it would conform with the plot of *Lord of the Rings*, yet he apparently overlooked the passage on page 83 (the same in both Houghton Mifflin editions) in which he says, "Deep down here by the dark water lived old Gollum. I don't know where he came from, nor who or what he was." Gollum's real name and early history are revealed in *Lord of the Rings*, so we can only assume that when Professor Tolkien fashioned his "Hobbit" rewrite, he skimmed the early part of the fifth chapter a bit too rapidly. Similarly, on page 84 of both hardcover editions, we are told that Gollum refers to himself as "my precious," whereas it is clearly stated in LOTR that he is actually addressing One Ring which Bilbo Baggins finds at the beginning of "Riddles in the Dark."

SELECTED BIBLIOGRAPHY

A comprehensive checklist of important terror and/or supernatural novels and short stories would fill a sizeable volume. Below I have merely recommended some personal favorites. Some are characteristically idiosyncratic instances of my taste, so caveat emptor.

AICKMAN, ROBERT, *Cold Hand in Mind, Painted Devils*. Two accessible collections of some of Aickman's eeriest tales.

BRADBURY, RAY, *The October Country*. For those unfortunates who don't possess a copy of *Dark Carnival*, Bradbury's first collection of weird fiction, this is a satisfactory substitute. Herein are some of the earliest efforts of one of America's greatest fantasists.

CLARK, MARY HIGGINS, *Where Are the Children?* is the book I use at NYU to demonstrate the well-constructed suspense novel. The plot swiftly grips and the terror mounts inexorably. This is what they mean by the term "page-turner."

COLLIER, JOHN, *Fancies and Goodnights*. A generous assortment of fifty short stories by an important fantasy writer. Some tales are humorous, but many are shocking. The most dreadful, in my estimation, is "The Touch of Nutmeg Makes It," an unforgettable horror story.

COZZENS, JAMES COULD, *Castaway*. The author of the bestseller *By Love Possessed* also wrote this little-known but masterful suspense fantasy which in presumably allegoric terms tells the gripping tale of a man alone in a deserted department store tracked by a strange pursuer. For heart-stopping suspense, I have never seen its equal.

DÜRRENMATT, FRIEDRICH, *Traps, The Judge and His Hangman, The Pledge, The Quarry.* Duerrenmatt, one of the world's major playwrights, created a series of four (very) short novels, each with its own noxious atmosphere. In *Traps* (basis of the play *The Deadly Game),* a salesman spending the night with four retired gentlemen—a judge, a prosecutor, a defense attorney and a hangman—is tried for murder. *The Pledge,* filmed as *It Happened in Broad Daylight,* chronicles a policeman's attempt to apprehend a rape murderer by employing methods nearly as repugnant as the crime itself. *The Quarry,* which is a sequel to *The Judge and His Hangman,* is the most terrifying of all: the story of a dying policeman who discovers that the head of his rest home is a sadistic ex-Nazi bent on turning the policeman's final days into a bout of unremitting torture.

ENDORE, GUY, *The Werewolf of Paris.* This is the lycanthropic equivalent of *Frankenstein* and *Dracula,* an unforgettable excursion into gruesome, yet oddly poignant psychosexuality and violent death.

FLEMING, IAN, *Doctor No.* If you only know James Bond's exploits from the movies, then you don't really know 007. This sixth novel in the series is laden with brooding menace and near the end of the book there is a torture sequence that makes "The Pit and the Pendulum" look like a kiddies' picnic.

GARNER, ALAN, *The Weirdstone of Brisingamen.* Redolent of Tolkien, this beautifully written fantasy adventure has more than its share of witches, night-creatures and gigantic monsters. One sequence in which the heroes must crawl through narrow tunnels in order to escape death is harrowingly claustrophobic. Ostensibly, *Weirdstone* is a children's book, but don't be fooled. It is a remarkably effective thriller for fantasy readers of all ages.

GARDNER, JOHN, *Grendel*. The story of *Beowulf* as seen through the monster's eyes is a brilliantly Beckettian fantasy novel.

GODWIN, PARKE, *Darker Places*. Parke's first novel takes one to the lower depths of murder, aberrant sex and revenge. One of the darkest novels you're ever likely to read.

GRAVES, RICHARD L., *Cobalt-60*. A political thriller in which an Arab chieftain nearly succeeds in assassinating every member of the U.S. judicial, executive and legislative branches of the government.

HIGHSMITH, PATRICIA, *Strangers on a Train*. Hitchcock's film was excellent, but the book is better. In the movie, Guy (Farley Granger) chickens out of his reciprocal murder, but not so in the novel.

HINDE, THOMAS, *The Day the Call Came*. Anthony Boucher picked this quasi-espionage thriller as one of the best books of 1964—deservedly. An English country gentleman may or may not be a spy. The author explores the thin line between being under cover and insanity.

JONES, D. F., *Implosion*. Author of many "doomsday" novels, including the justly popular "Colossus" trilogy, "Davy" Jones here concocts a hideously plausible novel of scientific genocide.

KRESSING, HARRY, *The Cook*. This wickedly urbane morality tale chronicles genteel murder and personality domination effected through the medium of fine food. Though the grue is mostly softpedaled, one confrontation between the titular cook and a rival is quite bloody enough, thanks. Ghoulish comedy, *highly* recommended!

MACHEN, ARTHUR, *The Three Imposters*. A thin plotline binds together a collection of classic terror tales. One of the best, *The Novel of the White Powder,* is so nauseatingly vivid I'm surprised it hasn't been filmed by John Carpenter.

PERUTZ, LEO, *The Master of the Day of Judgment.* Unjustly obscure today, Perutz was an important European novelist who created several wholly original fictions that mix oddly disparate elements with great effectiveness. *The Master,* for instance, is a detective story, a fantasy and a significant precursor of the psychological suspense thriller. I have no qualms whatever in proclaiming this a masterpiece.

RUSSELL, ERIC FRANK, *Sinister Barrier.* A science-fiction terror tale, a novel of invisible aliens preying upon the whole human race. It deserves to be reprinted.

SIODMAK, CURT, *Donovan's Brain.* Indifferently filmed twice, this science-fiction horror story shows little sign of aging. A ruthless industrialist is killed in a plane crash, but his brain lives on and takes possession of the scientist whose experiment is keeping it alive. The author's excellent narrative style, coupled with first-rate scientific extrapolation, makes this an enduringly readable thriller.

SLEATOR, WILLIAM, *House of Stairs.* Some of the finest writing in contemporary American letters is in the field of the YA (young adult) novel, which is virtually ignored by our "serious" critics. Sleator is one of the most interesting YA writers on hand. *House of Stairs,* a grippingly original concept, deals with several teenagers trapped in a huge enclosed area filled with stairs branching off, up and down and sideways, in all directions. They cannot see any floor or ceiling and the harsh white light makes it impossible to discern where the walls might be. They are caught in a constructivist nightmare that gradually worsens. If the climax is not as awful as it might have been had the book been aimed for an adult market, it is still quite effective on its own terms, and the epilogue, in which all mysteries are explained, is not a letdown. Highly recommended.

WALL, MERVYN, *The Unfortunate Fursey* and *The Return of Fursey.* The publisher who packages these two slim novels in one binding and finally releases them to the American public will be thrice blessed by the thanks and shekels of those who read and love great fantasy. Wonderfully funny, touching, eerie, the Fursey books tell of a poor monk beset by annoyingly friendly vampires, ghosts, witches and assorted demons. Satan himself is fond of Fursey because the diffident man's stammer makes it impossible for him to mumble exorcism prayers properly! If you can find a copy of these scarce British books, pawn your watch but *buy them*.

WELLS, H. G., *The Island of Doctor Moreau.* Less familiar than *The War of the Worlds, The Time Machine* or *The Invisible Man, Moreau* is, in my opinion, Wells' masterpiece, a well-sustained nightmare of hubris, the beastly springs of religion and the lurking savagery within every human breast.

WILDE, OSCAR, *The Picture of Dorian Gray.* This remarkable study of epigrammatic corruption is told with such suavity that the reader imagines more than is actually stated. This clearly was the author's intention and is what makes "Dorian Gray" such a compellingly loathesome experience. Once read, it is never wholly done with you.

WOOLRICH, CORNELL, *The Bride Wore Black.* Some consider this *conte cruelle* to be the best of Woolrich's many superb novels and short stories of suspense and terror (among them "Rear Window," "The Night Has a Thousand Eyes" and the classic "Three O'Clock"). If you have seen the Truffaut film of the same name, there is an enormous shock in store for you when you read the infinitely superior original. The film collapses into a sick Gallic joke, a *guignol* but not at all *grand*. That's because Truffaut debased the Woolrich story by totally ignoring a twist ending that both horrifies and lends a kind of Old Testament dignity to the otherwise lurid plot.